EAST OF THE
HAGUE LINE

❧

Gordon Holmes

ISBN: 978-1-4669-4184-7 (sc)
ISBN: 978-1-4669-4186-1 (hc)
ISBN: 978-1-4669-4185-4 (e)

Library of Congress Control Number: 2012910070

Trafford rev. 03/26/2014

 www.trafford.com

North America & international
toll-free: 1 888 232 4444 (USA & Canada)
fax: 812 355 4082

Dedication

I hereby dedicate *East of the Hague Line* to the Portland Seamen's Friend Society and to all the men who have spent their lives working and living at sea. Portland Seamen's friend Society had it's beginnings over a hundred and ninety years ago. In 1820 a group of men established a place of worship and fellowship for the men of the sea which frequented the Port of Portland Maine. This small group gradually became more organized and ultimately became the Portland Seamen's friend society which was founded in 1865 and incorporated in 1870. Through its history this organization has dedicated itself to providing financial aid to hurt, sick or indigent seamen up and down the coast of Maine. It has been my honor and privilege to serve on the board of this organization for more than 25 years.

Gordon T. Holmes Jr.

~~STEVE Kramer~~

1-800 944 9044

M FRT 18 H56DW.9

S BA706D8318

FRIDGE

SHELF & DRAWER

EA561	4	Owl tray
FPG31	2	Feather tray
EA533	4	flying piglet hook
EA527	3	vintage hook jewelry
DNB10	1 doz	ceramic flower knob
DNB26	6	ceramic flower knob
DNB27	6	ceramic flower knob
DNB30	6	ceramic flower knob
KMG3	3	glass butterfly magnets
EA523	6	little bird frame blue

INTRODUCTION

It was the morning of January 21, 1982. By 10:00 a.m. the wind had been howling out of the northwest at thirty-five miles an hour since midnight. Portland, Maine, and the entire New England coast had been battered by a northeaster for the last four days, but today the sun was out, and a clear blue sky engulfed the city. It was bitter cold and hard to breathe. No one was out. Commercial Street was extremely quiet. The snow that had fallen on the rooftops, and the sidewalks was blowing its way down the cobblestone avenues. The snow looked like a million tiny diamonds flashing in the bright sunlight. This gale was the back side of the storm.

On the harbor side of the street, the fishing boats *Jubilee* and *Gloria Walker* were tied snuggly to the wharf on the west side of docks. The entire commercial fishing fleet was home as well. No one was out at sea in this weather, none of the Portland boats anyway.

This was the year that Ronald Regan was president and George Herbert Walker Bush was vice president. The beautiful and greatly loved Princess Grace Kelly would lose control of her car and plummet to her death from a mountain road. She was fifty-two at the time. Jimmy Connors would defeat John McEnroe at Wimbledon in one of the greatest tennis matches of all time; and John Belushi, the great comedic actor, would be found dead in his hotel room off Sunset Boulevard in Los Angeles, California, from a drug overdose at the age of thirty-three.

Portland's working waterfront was the home port to over fifty commercial boats. The fishing fleet of the North Atlantic was doing pretty well. The fish landings were strong, and for the most part the boats were making money. The fishing business is a tough racket though, and all the boats had their good and their bad times.

The United States government had recently placed an embargo on Canadian swordfish that prevented them from being sold in

US markets. The reason for the ban was that Canadian swordfish were found to have elevated mercury content and were labeled by researchers and scientists as unsafe for consumption. The swordfish that were caught on the same Grand Banks by other foreign vessels, however, were sold in markets all over the world.

In 1978, in Hague, Netherlands, during a treaty negotiation between the United States and Canada, an ocean boundary was established between American and Canadian waters. It became known as the Hague Line. During those times it wasn't unusual for a few Maine boats that might be having financial problems, or simply motivated by greed, to cross the Hague Line, rendezvous with a Canadian swordfish boat, and take on their catch. They would then transport the fish back into Maine waters. They could sell the smuggled fish for a handsome profit, never even having to set a hook in the water. Even though being caught meant the man faced the consequences of a federal crime, the swordfish-smuggling business had times when it boomed in Maine—but not on this cold winter day. It would be six more months before the swordfish season and the great fish would return to the Grand Banks. For now the commercial fleet was winter fishing in the Gulf of Maine for groundfish with all hands hoping for an early spring and a break in the freezing weather.

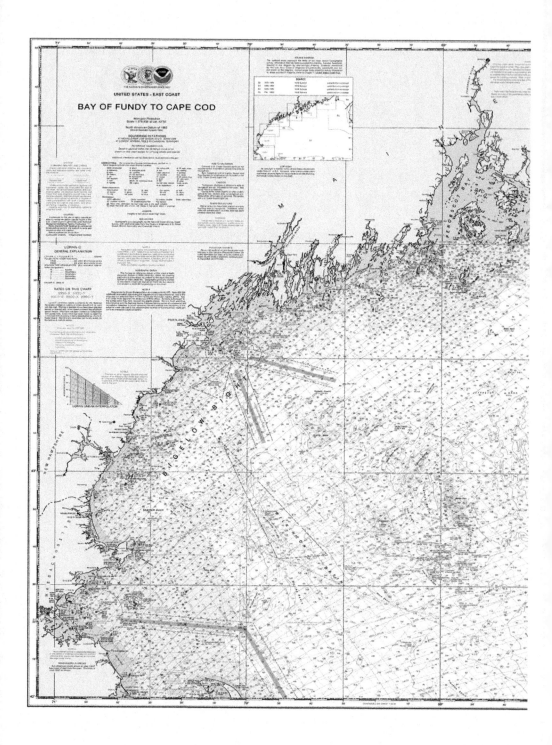

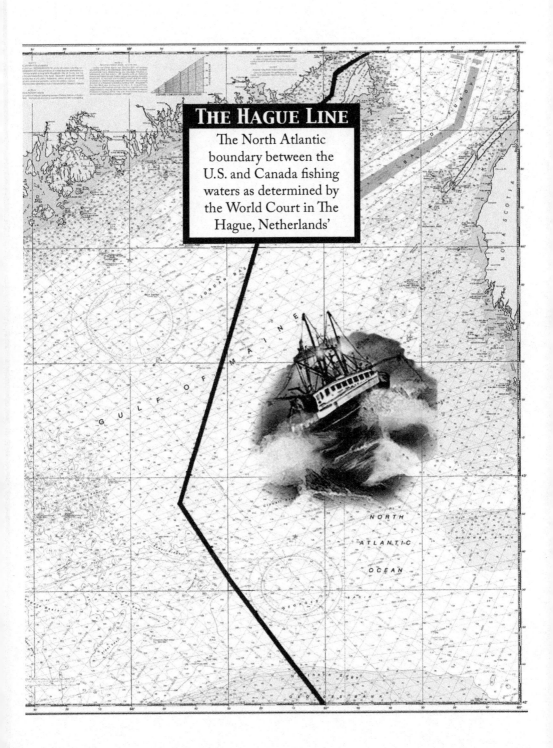

THE HAGUE LINE

The North Atlantic boundary between the U.S. and Canada fishing waters as determined by the World Court in The Hague, Netherlands'

THE MAGISTRATE

I t was just after two o'clock when the guards removed the three prisoners from their cells, placed them in chains, and escorted them down the long hallway to an exit at the back of the jail. They trudged slowly through the security lockdown chambers and out into the light of the fall afternoon. There was a white van parked and ready to transport them to the federal courthouse. No one spoke a word during the ten-minute trip from the Cumberland County Jail at the lower end of Congress Street in Portland. Three armed officers were waiting for the van when it pulled up to the rear entrance to the old granite building. The guards walked the men into a small waiting room, removed their chains, and ordered them to be seated. They were dressed in ugly orange jumpsuits with "Cumberland County Jail" stamped across their backs. They talked in low voices to each other. The guards watched them closely, never taking their eyes off the men. No smoking was allowed and they were all on edge. You could see the look of fear in their eyes. A bailiff entered the room and said, "It's time, gentlemen. Let's go." They walked slowly into the huge federal courtroom. It was an old and beautiful building. The men looked up at the intimidating grandeur of the room, and it emphasized the seriousness of their situation. One of the prisoners looked over and spotted his dad sitting there in the crowd with his back straight and his jaw tight as he watched his son start to cross the room. Then he saw his fiancée sitting beside his father; he was holding her hand. The tears were streaming down her face. He had never been so ashamed in his entire life. He hung his head, staring at the shackles on his feet as he was escorted slowly across the room.

One of the other prisoners spotted his wife. She was crying too. Her head was bent slightly forward as she took short breaths and tried not to sob. She looked tired, he thought. He knew she hadn't slept since this whole thing happened. She tried desperately to hide her face. She didn't want anyone there looking at her.

Two rows back, the third prisoner's parents sat and watched. The father was stoic. The mother was not. There was no way that her mind could accept the reality of what her eyes were witnessing.

The bailiff marched the three men over to a large flat table where two men stood waiting. One of the men said, "Okay, fellas, just take a seat and try to relax." His name was James Kelly, and he was a lawyer there to represent two of the prisoners. He had a friendly but authoritative look about him. The second man was an attorney named Peter Green. He was there as legal counsel for the third prisoner. He shook hands with him, leaned toward him, and whispered, "Things are about to begin."

The bailiff, in a loud voice, addressed the courtroom. "O'yeh, o'yeh . . . all rise for His Honor, Judge Carl Branton, United States Federal Magistrate." A small heavyset balding man in his early sixties entered the room. He moved with certain quickness, ascended three steps, and sat down behind the bench. He cracked his gavel. "Ladies and gentlemen of the court, let these proceedings begin." He peered down at the stenographer and said, "Are you all set, Mary?" She looked up and said, "Yes, thank you, Your Honor." In a clear voice Judge Branton said, "I'll begin with the government. Please go ahead."

A man sitting on the opposite side of the room stood up. "Thank you, Your Honor. I'm William Howerton, the assistant United States district attorney. I'll be representing the federal government in this matter." Judge Branton said, "Thank you, Mr. Howerton, and for the defense?" Attorney Kelley stood, introduced himself, and declared his representation of his two clients. Attorney Green was the next to speak. "My name is Peter Green, Your Honor." He stated his business before the court. The judge said, "Very well, gentlemen, let's begin." The three prisoners looked at each other and shared one single thought—*how in God's name did we get here?*

CHAPTER 1

It was early August, one of those hot Maine summer nights
without a breath of air. Even living that close to the water, it was
still sticky. Reed had just finished supper and was stretched out on
the living room couch, watching TV, when the phone rang. "I'll get
it, Ma," he said as he grabbed the phone. When he heard her voice
he couldn't believe she was calling him.

He said, "Hi, what's going on with you?"

She said, "Oh, I'm all right. I want you to come in town tonight."

Reed sat up immediately. "Are you sure it's okay? You want me
to come in tonight?"

"That's what I said, didn't I? If you don't want to come you
don't have to."

"Are you crazy? Of course I'll come."

"Come late," she whispered. "The back door will be open. So I'll
see you later then." She hung up.

Reed lit up a Marlboro and hollered, "Ma, I'm going to take a
run into town. I won't be back until late or maybe even tomorrow
morning." He ran out the front door, letting the screen bang itself
shut as he ran down off the porch of the old cottage. He hurried
down the steep path toward the water, across the pier, down the
gangway, and out onto the float. His seventeen-foot flat-bottomed
skiff was tied there. The sun was just starting to set. He fired up
the forty-horse Johnson that powered the boat. He let the lines go
and opened the skiff up and took off to the west. He was headed
for Portland Harbor. It only took him about twenty minutes to get
there. He slowed the skiff and ghosted up to one of the floats beyond
where the *Jubilee* was tied. He got out, secured the skiff, and climbed
the ladder up onto the wharf. He walked up Commercial Street and
headed for the bar. It was early, but he wanted to have a few drinks
before his old pal Tom showed up.

It was after ten when Tom Anderson pulled into one of the parking spots on Clark Street.

He was meeting Reed at Popeye's Ice House. The place was a fishermen's bar that had a reputation for getting a little wild at times. The roof of the place had the back half of an old airplane sticking out of it. On the inside there was a dummy dressed as a pilot hanging in the rafters like he had fallen out of the plane after the crash. Anderson crossed the street and walked up the sidewalk toward the bar. He wasn't really a big fan of these places. He had certainly done his share of drinking in them though because he'd always enjoyed being with the guys that hung out here.

Anderson had grown up in Falmouth with Reed. They had become friends as young boys and had stayed that way all their lives. Their common love of the ocean is what had bound them together. As kids they had both fished lobster traps in the bay and spent as many nights sleeping on the uninhabited islands of Casco Bay as they could get away with. Anderson was of Norwegian decent. He had fishing boats deep in his family history. His grandfather had been a fisherman in the old country. He and his wife had come through Ellis Island back in the early 1900s. There were uncles and great uncles that had sailed on all kinds of vessels, including one that had hunted for whales on the coast of Africa.

Anderson was a little over six feet tall and weighed just over two hundred pounds. He was what Maine people referred to as rugged. He had thick blond hair that wasn't combed very often, which gave him that "wild boy" look that the girls really liked. His eyes were such a crystal-clear blue that they startled some people when they looked at him.

Growing up, Reed and Anderson sold their lobsters to a guy named Harlan Barnes. He was the biggest dealer in Portland. Anderson liked to haul his traps as quickly as he could so he could get in town early enough to watch the big guns unload their catch. He had seen, firsthand, men unload over a thousand pounds of lobsters from one day's hauling. These guys had big beautiful boats with huge diesel engines. They were outfitted with the best radars and automatic haulers. They drove brand-new oversized pickup trucks and walked around the waterfront like they owned the world. That's what he wanted—to own the world and be like one of those guys.

As much as the lobstering interested him, he was always watching the big boats that tied up at some of the other wharfs in town, the seventy—and ninety-foot draggers that went out for long trips a hundred miles offshore. They brought home tens of thousands of pounds of fish. When he could, he used to like to hang out around the wharfs and watch the guys getting ready to leave for their trips. He loved the activity late at night. The activity of the men loading the supplies on board their boats was fascinating to him. The huge boats fully illuminated with their deck lights on, guys hollering orders to each other—it was great. From an early age he knew that if he ever got the chance to go, that was what he really wanted to do, fish the North Atlantic in the Gulf of Maine and Georges Bank.

As a kid Anderson had worked hard for what he wanted. It had to be something on and around the water though. He hung out, as much as his mother would let him, down at the boatyard in Falmouth. He painted sailboat bottoms and worked the old barge setting and hauling moorings in the fall. The winters were long, but spring would come, and it would be time for him and Reed to set their lobster traps. That was his favorite time of year. There was plenty of work to do to get ready to go lobstering, but they loved all of it. Anderson started out just like a lot of kids from the coast. You got a dozen or so traps and then built them up to around a hundred or more by the time you were in high school. The old-timers always say that once fishing is in your blood, it's there for the rest of your life. The freedom, the money, the risk—it's all part of what attracts a man to the fishing industry.

Now for the last few years Anderson had been going to college in Portland. He felt like he was there more to please his parents than he was going to school for himself.

Reed had worked really hard for what he had too. Higher education definitely wasn't for him, but fishing was. Over the years he had built up a gang of over four hundred traps and owned a great little twenty-six foot Novi boat he named the *Ruffian*. He had a job as deckhand on an offshore dragger and worked the traps as much as he could between his fishing trips. He liked the lifestyle and the money, but at twenty-eight he was looking for more than being just a deckhand on a dragger and a small time lobster catcher. He wanted to change things as soon as he could.

As Anderson made his way up to the front door of the bar, he could hear the loud noise coming from the crowd inside. The place was a full house when he walked in. The jukebox was blasting a Willie Nelson tune, and most of the patrons were pretty drunk. He recognized a lot of the guys that were there from down around the waterfront. There was an assortment of pretty tough-looking women hanging off the men, looking for free drinks and a little companionship. There were very few wives at Popeye's Ice House. He spotted Reed at a table across the bar, sitting with a guy he recognized, Stefan Bonczak.

Anderson had heard a lot of stories about Bonczak, but he had never met the man in person. According to what he had heard, Bonczak had been a deckhand on a Polish fishing boat that had been driven inshore near the New York Harbor by a late October storm. When Bonczak saw the lights on the shore, it meant only one thing to him, a chance at freedom. The story was that he had grabbed a lifejacket and jumped overboard into the cold waters and swam his way in. He managed to obtain political asylum and had been here in the States ever since. That was over ten years ago now. Anderson knew him by reputation as being one of the toughest and best captains to ever fish out of Portland. He and Reed were talking and laughing as Anderson approached the table.

"Hey, Tom, where the fuck have you been? Meet my buddy Stefan here. He's just gotten in with a huge trip of fish he caught off Georges Bank." Anderson stuck out his hand. "Good to meet you. I'm Tom Anderson." Bonczak shook his hand with a grip like a vice. "Sit the fuck down, Tom Anderson, and drink with us, boy!" Reed and Bonczak were loaded to the hilt. The waitress knew Anderson from seeing him here a few times before. She smiled at him and said, "What's it going to be, Tom?"

"Whatever is on tap, Mary. Thanks." When his beer came he reached in his pocket to get some money out to pay for it. Bonczak grabbed his arm, looked him in the eye, and said, "Not tonight, my friend. All the drinks are on me!" He threw a wad of bills on the table, which Anderson knew had to be at least two thousand dollars.

Anderson said, "Thanks, Stefan."

Bonczak said, "So, Thomas, are you a fisherman? You better be a fisherman if you're going to sit here and drink my beer! Your friend Skip here is a fisherman, and I am a fisherman. What are you?" Anderson could feel his face start to flush, as he was now the center of not only Bonczak's attention but also everyone around him. Anderson said, "I grew up on the bay lobstering, but I'm planning to go fishing with Skip and Joey Scanton on the *Jubilee*."

Bonczak started to laugh. "Lobstering ain't fishing!" Bonczak had a thoughtful look on his face. He said, "Joey Scanton . . . Joey Scanton, I know this Joey guy. He's a friend of mine. But you ain't never been fishin' though? Joey's going to hire him a green man? Is this right, Skip? Joey is hiring green men now. Is things that bad on your boat, Reed?"

Reed said, "No, Stef, we've been looking for a guy, and Anderson here needs a chance. The other guy with us, Pat Chase, and I will take care of him."

Bonczak said, "Pat Chase? I know him . . . sure he goes with Joey two, maybe three, years now. He's a good man on that boat. I would take Chase with me and make some real money. The bad weather don't bother Chase none. He would like it fishing with me."

A rough-looking woman of about forty or so snuck up behind Anderson and wrapped her arms around his neck. She was drunk and smelled of liquor and cigarettes.

She said, "Tommy Anderson, what's going on, honey? You're such a good-looking boy. I want you to come over to my place and have some fun with me tonight. What do you say, handsome?" Anderson said, "Not tonight, Janice. Why don't you go try one of these other guys? I'm sure they'd be happy to spend some time with you." Anderson was so uncomfortable he squirmed in his chair.

"But I want you though, Tommy. Come on, baby. I'll do whatever you want."

Anderson said, "I'm asking you nice, Janice. Please take you arms off me and go talk to someone else."

Janice said, "All right, tight ass. You don't know what you're missing!" *Oh yes, I do,* Anderson thought. She finally staggered off and left him alone.

Reed was laughing, "Are you going to be ready to go fishing tomorrow? Why don't you plan to come over to my place around two or so in the afternoon? I've got to help Joey get the grub, and we're setting sail around five. We can take my skiff in town and leave it there. I'll get somebody to take it back to Falmouth for me later."

Anderson said, "That sounds good to me. I've got to get my dive gear off Sewall's boat to take with us. I'll be there."

Reed said, "Who's hauling your traps while we're gone?"

"Teddy Atherton's getting them for me. Ben Sewall's getting the bait for him. Teddy loves that shit, and he'll have plenty of lobsters for his trouble. Somebody told me you got Andy Brown hauling you stuff. Is that right?"

Reed said, "Yeah, he is. I think he can do it. It's a good split for me."

Anderson didn't say anything more. He knew Andy Brown. He was a big pot smoker and wasn't much good to himself or anyone else. Anderson didn't say a word. That was Reed's business and he was staying out of it. Another beer arrived. Anderson took a drink, and someone spun his chair around hard and almost set him on the floor.

Anderson said, "What the fuck?"

A big man in a T-shirt and old ripped-up jeans was standing over him. "What? You think you're too good for my girl Janice?"

Anderson was stunned. He said, "What are you talking about?"

"You heard me, asshole! You think you're too good for her?"

Bonczak was out of his chair in two seconds and had the guy by the throat. He lifted him up so quickly he appeared to fly through the air. He slammed him against a wall. The man was so terrified he made no attempt to fight back.

Bonczak screamed in the man's face, "Now I tell you something one time! You get that whore of yours, and you leave this place before I break your head. You understand what I am telling to you?" Anderson and Reed started to laugh when they saw that the guy had pissed his pants. When Bonczak put the man back down, he ran for the door. Janice stayed behind.

When things settled down, Anderson lit up a Winston and finished his beer. Reed was getting Bonczak to tell some great stories about rough winter days offshore and two sinkings that he had survived fishing out of Poland. Anderson was getting ready to head out though. He finally got up and said, "All right, Skip, I'll see you tomorrow. Thanks for the drinks, Stefan. I'm going to take off."

Bonczak said, "Okay, boy! You go become a good fisherman with Joey Scanton, and maybe someday you'll come fish with me. You want to make some big money fishing, you go fishing with me." They shook hands. Anderson thanked him again, left the bar, and drove home to Falmouth.

Reed stayed until the last call and left the bar on foot and headed back toward the waterfront. When he got to her house, he opened the back door and stepped in. He climbed the stairs quickly and walked into her bedroom. It was so quiet he wasn't sure she was awake. The room was hot and smelled of her. He leaned over the bed and kissed her on the cheek. She stirred and smiled at him and pulled back the sheet that was covering her. She was naked, and the sight of her was almost more than he could handle. He hurriedly stripped his clothes off and got in the bed. The sex was incredible. It always was with her. He couldn't believe that he was here doing this.

After their lovemaking they laid back against the pillows.

She said, "This is really going to work for us. I know it is. It's all so close now."

Reed looked over at her. "It is, baby. It's going to be great. Just you wait and see." As much as he wanted to stay longer, he said, "I've got to go now. I'll call you tomorrow afternoon before we leave." She rolled over onto her stomach and looked at him.

He kissed her good-bye and slipped out of the house and walked down the hill and crossed Commercial Street to his skiff. It was tied there just like he had left it. The wharf and the float were in total darkness. He started the outboard and headed back out into the harbor. He motored slowly past the *Jubilee*. There were a couple of deck lights on, but the rest of the boat was dark. After he passed the no-wake zone in the inner harbor, he opened his boat to full throttle and headed back for Falmouth. He flew past the green-lighted buoy just off the eastern promenade. He couldn't get his mind off her. It was almost 3:00 a.m.

CHAPTER 2

The next day turned out to be another hot one. The heat bugs were buzzing in the trees, and you could see those waves rolling off the blacktop of the street. It was early afternoon when Anderson walked down the hill at the Falmouth town landing. The sand left over from the winter plowing was grinding under his sneakers. He was anxious to get going. He'd been looking forward to this day for a long time. It wasn't very much farther to Reed's house, but he had an important stop to make first.

He was carrying his fishing boots and a duffel bag. He had brought everything he thought he would need to be at sea for a month. He had his shaving gear, a towel, a few changes of clothes, and three cartons of Winstons. He had stuffed a couple hundred bucks of cash in a sock, just to have some spending money for the layovers when they sold their fish. He wasn't sure if Reed would be home, but he was headed down to his house anyway. There was a lot of planning to do to get ready to go fishing. Reed had been living this life for a while now, and he had it down to a science. He had his life at home with his lobster boat and traps and his life at sea on the big boat. Anderson was surprised that Reed had been around as much as he had this past summer. He'd have to remember to ask him about that.

Anderson thought it was strange that Reed had decided to have Andy Brown haul his traps for him while he was gone. He bet Andy Brown was probably pretty excited about that plan. Reed's traps fished like hell, and Brown's gang was old junk and not worth the bait he put in them. Anyone who knew Brown also knew that Reed would get screwed with that deal before it was over.

Before Anderson made it to Reed's house, he was stopping to say good-bye to his girlfriend, Kathy. She lived a few doors from up the road from the Reeds' place. He walked across the landing road and into her driveway. He and Kathy Blackwell had been a pretty hot item since she returned to Maine eight months ago.

He had been crazy about her since they were in the eighth grade, but they hadn't been dating each other seriously until just recently. After high school she left Maine for college out West. That was seven years ago. After she graduated, she stayed out there and worked for a company in Denver. What had gone on during that time was still pretty sketchy. She told Anderson that she had come home because she missed her family and friends. Now she was back, living with her mother who had recently gotten a divorce from Kathy's father. The simple fact that she was here was all that mattered to him. When they talked seriously about her being home, she simply said that she had come back for a while to try and figure out what she wanted to do with her life. They were getting really close, but he had a funny feeling that she was holding something back.

He walked toward the front of her house, but it didn't look like anybody was home. His heart sank a little. He told her he'd be coming by before he left, and he really wanted to see her. He peeked out in the backyard, and there she was, lying on a chaise lounge, getting some sun on her back. She was wearing cutoff dungaree shorts and no top. She lay there on her stomach on a beach towel. The sight of her took his breath away. Her skin was such a beautiful brown from the summer sun. She had lots of wavy blonde hair and gorgeous hazel eyes. Her pretty face had wonderful high cheekbones and a very sensual mouth. Her full shapely curves made boys and men stop and stare when they saw her.

She had always had a friendly and sweet personality, a characteristic that gave her mother fits sometimes. She was so outgoing that her mother was always scared that she would wind up in trouble from being too easy to talk to. The pure sensuality of her looks drove Anderson crazy. And the way she carried herself with such confidence was very attractive to him. Kathy was a "take charge" kind of girl, and he really liked that about her.

He smacked his hand on the back of the garage and walked into the backyard. He threw his duffel bag and boots on the ground. He did that somewhat to let her know he was there and somewhat to startle her. He wouldn't be at all disappointed if she jumped up and turned toward him so he could get a good look at her naked breasts. With a light tone to his voice, he said, "Hey, girl! What cha doin'?" As he walked toward her, she turned slowly and looked up at him and smiled. He could tell by the expression on her face that she really had been expecting him to show up.

"Hey, Tommy, come over here and sit with me a minute. Put some of that Johnson's Baby Oil on my back, will you?"

That brought a big smile to his face. *No problem there,* he thought. He stepped over to a lawn chair next to her and grabbed the clear plastic bottle. He hadn't touched her skin yet, but he could feel himself getting excited just from rubbing the oil on his hands.

Kathy loved the feel of his strong hands rubbing the warm oil on her back. After he finished, she hesitated a little. She was reluctant to say anything, but she really wanted to tell him something. She pulled her towel up around herself and sat up on her lounge chair.

She cocked her head to the side slightly and, with a big smile, said, "I'm glad you stopped by to see me, Tom."

"Kathy, I wouldn't leave without coming to see you."

She closed her eyes briefly and said, "I know you wouldn't. You know, Tom, it's all over town about you going fishing with Skip Reed and his gang. Everybody's talking about it. I know you've wanted to go fishing for a long time, and I'm glad you're getting your chance."

He smiled and said, "Good, because I'm really excited about it."

"Tom, I'm kind of worried about it too though. Those big boats are dangerous. That *Jubilee* you're going on is known for fishing in the worst weather."

Anderson raised his eyebrows, smiled, and tugged down on Kath's towel. She smiled at him. "Cut it out. I'm trying to be serious here." He made a face. "Me too . . . me too . . . here's my serious look." He leaned in and kissed her neck. She wasn't distracted.

"Tom, come on, I'm worried."

"It's summer, honey. The bad weather is months away. I'll be fine."

She said, "It still makes me nervous. They all say that Joey Scanton's a good captain though. I heard he started fishing with his father full time when he was just out of high school. Somebody said he went captain the first time when he was only eighteen because his dad was laid up."

Anderson pulled back slightly. "You sure have been doing a lot of research on my new job, haven't you? I think you seem pretty interested in what I'm doing."

"I have a mild interest. There's about a million other guys out there just like you, but I thought I'd give you a break and let you try to win my heart."

"Oh, I see. Is there anything else I should know about my new job before I set out to sea?"

"Yes, there is, and you're not going to like it."

He raised his eyebrows. "And what is that?"

"I wish you weren't going with Skip Reed. I can't stand him and I don't trust him. He creeps me out. He's such a pain when he's drinking. I know we all grew up together, but there's just something about him that I've never liked."

Anderson smiled. "Wow! Skip's all right, you know. I haven't seen him all that much over the past few years, but he used to be my best friend. I never would have got this chance to go if he hadn't set it up. I'll be fine, I promise."

"Okay, I know you're not going to change your mind anyway. I won't bring it up again."

"Is that pretty much it for now or is there more?"

"I guess that's pretty much it, smart ass. Now kiss me and hug me before I change my mind and tell you to get out of here and leave me alone forever."

Kathy dropped her towel. He could feel her naked body against his chest. She kissed him deeply on his mouth. The smell and feel of her made his heart race. She hugged him tight like she never wanted to let him go. When she pulled back a little he was inches from her beautiful breasts. She saw his handsome suntanned face looking at her. She knew exactly what he was thinking. "Go ahead, Tom, taste me." He leaned forward and, ever so gently, took Kathy's erect nipple in his mouth. There were tiny beads of sweat on her skin. She tasted salty from the hot August sun, and there was that little hint of baby oil. Kathy was still like a girl in some ways and so much of a woman in others. She felt so soft and so good. He was in another world. Kathy murmured a sweet little moaning sound that only made him more excited. He barely heard the car door slam. Kathy's mother pulled in and hollered from their driveway.

"Hey, Kathy, come help me get these groceries in."

Anderson whispered, "Holy shit!"

The mad scramble that ensued was perfectly timed. Kathy had her top on in one second, and Anderson was sitting beside her in a lawn chair the next. They made their respective moves an instant before Mrs. Blackwell rounded the corner.

"Hey, nice to see you, Mrs. Blackwell," he said with a slightly nervous pitch to his voice. "Nice to see you too, Tom." She smiled a little and looked at the pair of them. There was little doubt that Mary Blackwell knew exactly what her entrance had interrupted. Even though she had said so, Anderson wasn't convinced that Kathy's mom was any too happy to see him there. He was pretty sure that she wasn't pleased at all, in fact. He knew she didn't like seeing him get so close to her daughter. She had expectations for her that were far and beyond the Tom Andersons of the world.

He jumped up and said, "I've got to get going, Kathy. We're supposed to be in town to fuel up, get ice, and load all the food aboard the boat. Skip said we are supposed to set sail at five o'clock this afternoon. I've still got to get my dive gear off Ben Sewall's boat to take with me."

Kathy said, "You're going to take your dive gear? Now I have to worry about you out there diving with sharks all over the place."

He laughed. "No, you don't. Everyone knows that sharks don't like Norwegians. They're too tough and chewy."

"That's not funny, Tom."

"I'll be fine, you'll see. I'm sorry, but I've really got to go."

When he was set to leave, Kathy got up and hugged him tight. She whispered in his ear, "Be careful and safe, my sweet Tommy. Come home and find me as soon as you're ashore. I'll be here waiting for you . . . I love you."

She had never told him she loved him before, and the sound of it was perfect. "I love you too," came flying right out of his mouth before he knew what had happened. He knew it was true though and had been for a long time.

This was big. He had just learned that she loved him, and he had been in love with her forever. He just didn't want to admit it to himself or anyone else for fear it wouldn't work out. Suddenly, leaving for a month at sea seemed a lot less appealing. Goddamn it! Women, they did it every time. *Wow* . . . He was looking at her, thinking she's so gorgeous, so wonderful. Man, he hated to leave her, but he had to go, and that's all there was to it. Who knows, maybe the reunion would be even better than the farewell.

CHAPTER 3

Anderson grabbed his boots and duffel bag and walked back out to the street. He stopped for just a second and looked back at Kathy's house. He reached into his pocket and pulled out a fresh Winston, lit it up, and kept walking down the street. It was just past noon, and there was the sound of kids laughing and screaming down by the town landing dock and floats. He could hear their splashes as they jumped off the heavy oak frame at the end of the pier. It was a great sound that reminded him of all the summers he had spent diving and jumping off that same dock. It was only a few years ago now, but it seemed like a lifetime had passed since those days.

He was ready for a new adventure. Going offshore fishing would be a real test for him as a man, the way he saw it. There was no doubt that he was excited about going. The chance to go with these guys was a big deal. It was serious business, and he wanted to become part of it all and be respected by the other guys. Sure, Reed had been a close friend for as long as he could remember. Having him take a risk on him and getting him the site was great. This job wasn't about Skip Reed and their friendship though. This was about Tom Anderson. He wanted to prove himself and be accepted for who he was and what he could do. He was absolutely determined that he wouldn't let anyone down on that boat.

He came to Reed's house at the bottom of the hill. The place was typical of most of the old houses near the shore. It was a renovated cottage. Over the years it had been winterized and gradually improved. Reed had grown up there with his sister and his mother. His dad had left them when he was only three years old. Growing up without a father had influenced what Reed was like as a man.

The place had a wraparound front porch, weather-beaten shingles, and an old stone foundation cellar with a big wooden door that opened to the back. The rear yard was a very steep hill that led down to the water. As Anderson approached the house, he could hear a hammer banging away down in the cellar. He dropped his duffel bag and boots on the lawn beside the driveway and jogged down the path around toward the back of the house.

He charged the doorway and grabbed the top of the doorframe just like he had done a thousand times before. He swung his way through and let go at the right second. He landed right in front of Reed's trap-repairing table.

Reed was pounding a few trap nails into an oak bow from a lobster trap that he had half torn apart on his workbench. He looked up and laughed when he saw Anderson come flying through the air and land in front of him.

He said, "Hey, goofball! What's up? You ready to go?"

"I'm ready as rain!"

"We gotta get our asses in town. Scanton wants me to go with him to buy grub. You got everything you need for the trip?"

"I'm pretty set, I guess." Reed pulled out a butt and lit up.

Anderson said, "Hey, I'm hoping you'll let me know what to do when we get going on this boat so I don't look like a jerk in front of these guys."

Reed exhaled a lungful of smoke and said, "Tommy, you looking like a jerk is nothing I can fix. But I will give you some advice right off the bat here. Number one, don't stand around ever. Pay attention and jump in and help when you see what's going on."

Anderson said, "Jesus, Skip, you know I'm not going to just stand around."

"I know, I know, I'm just telling you, don't wait around to be asked. When it comes to the technical stuff you haven't seen before, don't gamble and try to do something you don't know about."

Anderson said, "I'm hoping you'll teach me what I'm expected to do."

"I'll tell you some stuff, but Pat Chase runs the deck, and he'll break you in. He's going to bust your balls some. It happens to everybody when they're starting out. If you do what he tells you, you'll be all right."

"You know I'm ready to give it a try."

"When any one of us gives you an order, do exactly what we tell you to do, nothing less and nothing more."

"What's Chase's job on the boat again?"

"He's the boat engineer and runs the deck. He's a big fuckin' pain in my balls sometimes, but he's a real good fisherman. He's put a lot of time in on these boats."

"How does Pat get along with Joey?"

"Joey really respects him. Pat's gone captain a couple of times for other boat owners. He could take the *Jubilee* if Joey wanted a trip off. Really he could step up to the wheelhouse on any boat he wants."

"How long has he been at it?"

"Jesus . . . all his life. I think he went lobstering with his old man as a kid and then went on a gillnetter at first. He's just like all the rest of us, lobstering as a kid and moving on to fishing winters to try and keep the bills paid. Pat's around thirty, I think."

Anderson said, "I've heard a lot about the mending stuff. How in hell will I learn about that?"

"You'll see when we rip up a net. In the beginning you'll be filling needles and holding twine for the rest of us while we mend. I'm no expert like Chase. He and Joey are the twine men.

They'll probably show you some of the basics."

"How come you and Pat don't get along?"

"I don't know really. He doesn't trust anybody, and he's wicked critical of people behind their backs. In spite of all that shit there's nobody Joey would rather have on that boat than Pat, including me. You'll see how it is. Just stay away from his bullshit and you'll be fine."

"Okay, tell me again about Joey."

"Joey is a great guy. He's older than us by about five years. His family moved here from Gloucester when he was just a kid. His parents still live up on the hill, in the same house they moved to back then. He's been around fishing all his life. He's third generation. You know who his old man is, right? He owns the *Gloria Walker*. Joey grew up sleeping on fishing nets for Christ sake. His old man's the best twine man I've ever seen. Peter Scanton . . . I've watched him come in with nothing but rags left for a net and rebuild it in eight hours. There's nothing Joey doesn't know about this racket. He doesn't rattle in rough weather or tough situations."

Anderson said, "Is there anything that really pisses him off?"

"Don't ever be late getting to the boat. He kicked a guy off, up in Rockland. The jerk was a half an hour late to leave the wharf. The prick was shacked up with some broad he'd met in a bar up there. He was still half drunk when he lugged his sorry ass down to the boat. Joey's all about a good time, but when that boat's ready to let the lines go, that's it. He threw all the guy's shit up on the wharf and told him he was all done and to go get a bus ticket home. He really doesn't give a shit. We went three-handed that trip."

Anderson said, "I'm never late for stuff anyway."

Reed said, "This is a big money-making boat. He doesn't have to put up with any crap from anybody, and he doesn't. Speaking of being late we gotta get out of here."

Anderson said, "I really appreciate you getting me the chance to go. I'll try real hard to do my job."

"I know you will. I've got to run in and say good-bye to my mother before we head out. She's going to put a deposit down on an apartment for me in on State Street while we're gone. She hates me coming and going at all hours of the night and day. You'd think she'd get used to it after all this time. Between you and me, I think she's got a guy hanging around she doesn't want me to see. She says I make her a nervous wreck." Reed hesitated a minute. "I'll tell you what though. If things work out right, the money worries are coming to a screeching halt and soon." He didn't elaborate on what that meant. He headed out of the cellar for the front porch.

Reed said, "Hey, have you been up to say bye-bye to that broad of yours up the street? I don't know how you got in with her, with your tiny dick and all. The bitch wouldn't give me the time of day if I was standing at a bus station trying to leave town."

Anderson bristled at that remark and said, "She's no bitch!" Reed just laughed and said, "Touchy, touchy," and ran in the house and let the screen door slam behind him. Anderson picked up his duffel bag and boots and was standing in the driveway. A few seconds later Reed came out the door with his mother, Sally. She said, "Hi, Tom. Well, you're off to sea with Skip and the boys, are you? You guys be careful and look out for each other." Then she gave Tom a motherly look. "Tom, you know the number here. If he winds up in jail again, you call me. I may decide to let him stay there, I may not."

Then she turned to her son and said, "Skip, please don't act the fool your whole life. All you've ever wanted to do is what you're doing. Most people don't get that chance. Don't screw it up." Reed just rolled his eyes.

Anderson said good-bye to Sally, and they headed down the street toward the dock where Reed's skiff was tied. He was lugging a dark-blue canvas bag. They made their way down to the float.

CHAPTER 4

Anderson decided to mention the trap-hauling arrangement with Brown. "So you're going to have Andy Brown tend your gear while we're gone, huh? Has he been hauling it right along when you're on these trips?"

"No, I had Terry Woodcock hauling them for me, but he was screwing me over on the weight. Anderson and Reed were down on the float where Reed tied his skiff off. They threw their bags and Anderson's boots up in the bow and jumped aboard. Skip yanked the starter cord, and the outboard came to life on the first pull.

"I've got to stop by the *Ruffian* on the way out. I've got to grab something." Anderson admired Reed's boat. She was big enough to carry a good load of traps and small enough to fish the rocks.

Anderson asked Reed if he was going to let Andy Brown haul out of her while they were gone. "No way in hell am I letting him touch this boat while I'm not around. Drew Taylor knows where the keys are hidden. I told him to only use them if he needed to move her in an emergency. Drew's a good guy. He won't touch her unless he needs to."

They pulled up behind the *Ruffian* and Reed jumped on board. He wasn't gone two minutes. Anderson saw him grab a small notebook from down forward. He stuffed it in his pants pocket and jumped back in the skiff. Reed looked up and said, "Hey, look who's aboard his boat. It's your buddy Ben." You could see a rowing skiff hanging off the end of Sewall's lobster boat. They pulled up to him and tied off.

Sewall said, "Hey, Tom, about the twenty I owe you for cutting the rope out of me there the other day. I haven't sold my lobsters yet. As soon as I do, I'll catch up with you and give you the money."

Anderson said, "Ya, I'm sure you will. Don't sweat it, Benny boy. I know you'd rather owe it to me than cheat me out of it." While

Anderson was talking to Ben, Skip went up into the pilothouse of the boat for a minute and then came back out.

Reed said, "We've got to get the hell out of here. We can't hang around all afternoon shootin' the shit with you, Ben."

"So who's stopping you? Get the fuck off my boat and don't hurry back."

Anderson said, "Don't forget, Ben, you're going to let Teddy Atherton have what bait he wants to haul my gear while I'm gone. Just have Barnsey put it on a separate slip for me. He knows all about it. Don't you steal any off it either, you prick."

"Maybe I will, maybe I won't. See you assholes later." Reed gave Anderson a hand getting his tank and dive belt into the skiff. The rest of the equipment was packed into a canvas bag.

Reed cranked up the Johnson while Anderson untied the bowline. Reed got the stern line and turned the throttle wide open. He brought the skiff up to a quick plane and circled back right at Ben's bow. That skiff was really quick. They skimmed across the water about two inches off Ben's starboard side, spraying water on him and his deck. Ben just looked up with a smile and an extended middle finger. He thought to himself some people just never grow up.

They were off to Portland Harbor flat out. Five minutes later Reed reached in his pocket and pulled out a can of Bud and offered one to Anderson.

"Ben's going to be pissed when he figures out you stole two of his beers."

"Ya, well, fuck him and the horse he road in on. Have a beer and enjoy the trip."

"No, I'll pass."

Reed looked annoyed. "What? Are you too good to have a beer with me now?"

"No, it's just that I'd like to not show up for a new job stinking of beer. You know what I mean?"

"Well, aren't you something special?"

With that Reed stuck his thumb over his beer can, shook it up and sprayed Anderson with warm beer and foam.

"You really are an asshole, Reed."

"You have no idea how big an asshole though, do ya?"

Fifteen minutes later Reed rounded the corner at Deek's wharf and slid in beside the *Jubilee*. She was laying tied to the pilings pulled in tight, against a camel fender. There was no wind in the harbor. The *Jubilee* was motionless. Anderson thought she was magnificent looking, all sixty-five feet of her. The hull was painted a dark green, and there was a white whaleback extending from the stem toward the stern above the top bow rail. The pilothouse was forward. You could see the brand-new paravanes painted jet-black. There was exhaust coming out of a small pipe extending from the roof of the pilothouse.

A small steady stream of water was pouring from one of the port scuppers. A deck hose was running. Anderson immediately noticed the two massive tandem net reels, each with two different nets wrapped tightly around them. He couldn't wait to get aboard and look around her.

Reed ran his skiff up beyond the *Jubilee* up to a float further up the wharf. They tied it off to a couple of open cleats. It was high tide so they could throw everything up on the wharf. Chase was standing on deck, straightening up some pen boards beside the main hatch. Anderson could see right away that Pat Chase was a big man. He had the look of a hardened fisherman. Right away you noticed his big hands. He weighed about 230 pounds, but there wasn't an ounce of fat on him. When you first saw him you thought, *If I'm in a bar and a fight breaks out, I want this guy on my side.* Reed hollered, "Hey, Pat! How's it going?"

In a less than friendly tone, Chase said, "Oh, it's going."

"This is Tom Anderson. He's the guy I was telling you and Joey about. He's hoping to talk Joey into giving him a job and go fishing with us this trip."

Anderson was stunned. He could feel his face flush with embarrassment. It was supposed to be all set for him to have this job. He thought, *Jesus Christ, Skip* . . . He should have known better than to trust his bullshit . . . goddamn it all to hell. What a fuckin' idiot he'd been to let himself get set up like this. Chase could see the look on Anderson's face. Of course he immediately felt bad for him. He knew damn well that Reed had been blowing smoke up this kid's ass. Playing the big shot and now the jig was up. This kid was sure he had a job on the boat, and it was all bullshit. He knew how Reed was.

Chase said, "Anything like that's Joey's call. I had coffee with him at Becky's about four this morning. He's had so much work to do aboard here to get ready to go I think he slept on the boat last night. He's over to Bowen's, picking up a new hanging bollard for the starboard side. That thing has been on its last legs for few months now anyway. Hey look, here he comes up the wharf. I guess you'll get your answer soon enough, kid."

Scanton jumped out of a little green Subaru station wagon. He went around back and started pulling a heavy cardboard box out on to the tailgate. Reed ran over and helped him with it. They carried the box over toward the rail of the boat. Chase came over, took the box, and lugged it down the deck toward the stern. Anderson thought it had to be the new bollard Chase was talking about.

Reed turned to Scanton and said, "This is my friend Tom Anderson, Joe. He's looking to get a job with us. He's never been before, but he's been around boats all his life. He's a diver too. Pat and I can teach him what to do."

Chase said, "Speak for yourself, Reed. I don't know this guy from a piss hole in a snow bank, Joey."

Anderson was watching Scanton's face. He was a small man, but he had a look of absolute authority about him. He carried himself with the confidence that exuded from people that were always in charge. He had dark features and weather-worn skin. His hair was a dirty blond, and he was wearing a ball cap that had "Ice and Fuel Services" printed on it.

Scanton was furious. "Goddamn it, Skip, you know how I feel about green guys on the boat. I don't take them. They're dangerous as hell, and we're going to put in some hard back-to-back trips. I can't afford to screw around with this guy. No offense to you, kid.

I'm sure you're a nice guy, but Jesus Christ, Skip." Scanton climbed down the ladder a couple of rungs, stepped on the rail, and jumped down on deck. He crossed over to the main companionway and disappeared inside.

Anderson said, "You goddamn prick, Skip. I can't believe you'd set me up like this."

Reed said, "Set you up like what? I never told you for sure that you had a site on this boat. People have to get their own jobs in this racket."

"Fuck you, Skip. What am I doing here if you didn't tell me I had a job, for Christ's sake? I'll take your skiff and head back home, you asshole." Anderson's face was bright red. He looked like he was about to take a swing at Reed.

Reed said, "Just hold your horses a minute. I'm going up to talk with Joey, and we'll see what happens."

Reed went aboard the boat and headed for the pilothouse. Anderson just stood there in a confused state of anger and disappointment. He felt completely betrayed.

Chase was on deck pulling the new bollard from the cardboard box. It weighed about a hundred pounds. He looked up at Anderson and said, "Come on down here and give me a hand with this thing. You haven't got anything else to do for a minute or two." Chase had already rigged a short piece of rope to the top of the gallous frame. It would support the weight of the bollard while he hung it in place.

Anderson said, "Sure, what the hell." Chase told him to lift the bollard while he took up on the rope. Once the huge cast iron pulley was raised, he inserted the heavy shackle that would hold it in place. After they were through with the job, Chase said, "I saw what your friend Reed just pulled on you. Just relax a minute or two. If Joey calls you up to the pilothouse to talk to him, you may get a chance to have a job. We've all been talking about going four-handed. If he doesn't decide to have you with us, take that asshole's skiff home like you said and leave it at the dock with a hole in the bottom of it."

Up in the pilothouse Scanton was sitting in the captain's chair, smoking a cigarette with his feet resting up on the wheel. Reed came up the stairs and walked in. Scanton said, "Jesus Christ, Skip, what did you have in your head bringing that guy aboard here like that? Have you lost your fuckin' mind? You've fished with me long enough to know I don't take green guys. We got some serious shit goin' on on this boat. I know we've been talking about going four handed, but I don't know if I can trust this guy not to screw everything up. Why the hell didn't you talk to me about this first? Just showing up here with him the day we're going to sail is bullshit, and you know it." Reed hung his head a little and said, "Okay, okay. I should have talked it over with you. I've known this guy all my life, and he's smart as hell. He really wants to go fishing. Look at all the experienced guys we've had on here. After the first paycheck, they go ashore, get loaded, and we never see them again. This guy will never pull that shit. We've been fishing traps in the bay since we were twelve years old. He'll learn. He's been working the mooring barge out of the boatyard for quite a few years." Scanton gave Reed a skeptical look and said, "The yard barge?" He laughed. "You ignorant jerk. You think that will help him on here? What makes you think Chase will give this guy a break? You know he's driven some pretty good men off this boat if they don't meet his standards. He won't put up with anybody's bullshit. This guy, just looking at him, feels like a college boy. He starts trying to show off his brains and talking down to Chase . . . it's over. You know I'm fuckin' right about that." Reed looked out the aft pilothouse window and saw Anderson and Chase down on deck hanging the new bollard. He said, "Look right here." Scanton looked out the window and said, "Yes, I see him."

Reed continued, "Tom's a clean guy, he's practically a nondrinker, and he's got money needs just like the rest of us. He's a certified diver, and he brought all his gear with him. I figured if we got into a situation like last time, it might be cheap insurance to have a diver with us. You never know if we'll need a man overboard. I told him he'd be on a half a share. He'll work into our deal on this boat, just trust me."

Scanton stared at Reed and didn't say anything for a while. Finally, he said, "You listen to me Skip, I can't believe you'd have the balls to talk share with anybody. I'm telling you right now if this guy screws up, it's on you, and I mean it. He pukes, you're cleaning it up. If he shits, you're wiping his ass. By the way, if he's so goddamn sober, why does he stink of stale beer?"

"That's my fault, Joe. He didn't drink that beer. I sprayed him with it as a joke."

"You're a real funny guy, aren't you, Skip? Get the hell out of here and send him up. What's his name again?"

"It's Tom, Tom Anderson. Thanks, Joe, you won't be sorry." Scanton swung around and looked Reed straight in the eye. "We'll see. Let's hope you're the one who's not going to be sorry, Skip."

Reed came out on deck and hollered to Anderson, "Joey wants to see you a minute. I've got things all set now, don't blow it." Chase was standing there furious, thinking to himself, *You've got things all set. You've got to be shitting me.* Chase turned to Anderson, "Good luck, kid. Thanks for the help with the bollard." Anderson smiled and said, "No sweat."

After Anderson had gone through the companionway, Chase turned on Reed and said, "This kid's supposed to be a friend of yours? How can you be such an asshole?"

"Fuck you, Chase. When I give a sweet shit what you think, I'll let you know."

As Anderson climbed the stairway to the pilothouse, he had no idea what to expect. Scanton was sitting in the captain's chair, looking out the forward window.

He said, "I didn't like all that bullshit a few minutes ago. I could tell by the look on your face that Reed had made some big promises to you about this site. You have to understand we've really got to make some money here, right away. I just don't have time to train a new deckhand. Shit, I don't know if you get seasick or not and could wind up in the bunk the whole trip. I don't know if you know your way around a boat at all. Lobstering and barge work . . . it ain't fishing. I also figured if you're a great friend of Reed's that Chase would want nothing to do with you."

Anderson said, "He told me two weeks ago I had a job on this boat. I've known him all my life and I believed him. What I couldn't believe was that he'd let me walk into a situation like that. I'm embarrassed as hell. I would have come in here myself and met you and talked about the job, if I had known what he was doing."

Scanton said, "Skip talks a big game. The thing is, I probably would have turned you down a week ago. Now you're here ready to go, you might as well come along, and we'll see how you do."

"Thanks, I appreciate the chance. I've always wanted to go give this a try."

Scanton said, "Pat is the guy that has to train you. Skip don't know enough to do it. It was real ballsy of him to pull this shit. I gotta tell you if Pat doesn't like you, you're screwed. So just remember that he's your boss on deck. I run everything else, okay?"

"I got it, Joey."

Scanton said, "When we settle up the boat takes 40 percent off the top after fuel and grub. I take a captain's per of 5 percent. We all split the rest. You're getting half a share."

Anderson said, "That's fine with me."

Scanton said, "Pat and Skip have been going at it pretty hard for the last few trips, and between you and me, I'm tired of it. This thing can go one of two ways. Pat wants nothing to do with you, and you're screwed, or he takes you under his wing, just to piss Skip off, and you learn how to become a fisherman over time. I have no idea which way this will go. I'm going to let you have a shot, but it's against my better judgment."

Anderson said, "I don't think you'll be sorry."

"We'll see, but if these guys can't work this out, I may have to let you go. I can't afford to let two experienced guys split this boat up for a green man."

"I understand."

"I am going to have a come-to-Jesus meeting with them in a couple of minutes. It'll help some." Scanton got out of his chair and looked out on deck. "You see what I'm talking about. Chase is about ready to wring Skip's neck right now. Get down there and put your gear away. Make sure you secure that scuba tank. I don't want it rolling around deck."

Anderson was relieved that the conversation was over. Scanton said, "Tell those two to come up here a minute."

Anderson headed back down on deck. As he came out of the companionway, he probably saved Reed from having his face smashed in. They stopped their argument and looked over at Anderson.

He said, "Well, he decided to give me a chance. I'm going with you guys. Joey says he wants to see you two upstairs." As Chase walked by Anderson, he said, "By the way, shithead, it's not upstairs, it's topside."

Anderson said, "Hang on a minute, Skip."

Reed said, "Ya, what?"

"I'll tell you what. I got a chance on this boat, no thanks to you. What you pulled on me was real crap, and I'm not going to forget it. Joey says my job depends on you getting along with Pat. We've been friends a long time. If you have any interest in that continuing, you need to knock off the bullshit."

Reed said, "Yeah, we'll see."

As Chase and Reed made their way up to the pilothouse they both knew this wasn't going to be any fun. Scanton was livid. Life on a small boat was never easy. There is no privacy whatsoever. A small group of men, 24-7, in each other's space always leads to trouble. Chase and Reed had advanced normal crew animosity to a new level.

When Scanton turned around to look at these two guys, they knew the shit was going to hit the fan. "Goddamn it, you two bastards have taken this crap far enough. I'm not going to take any more of it. You're at each other's throats constantly, and I'm real tired of it. We are here for one reason, that's to make money, nothing else. I don't give a sweet shit in hell if you want to kill each other off this boat. In fact, I'd buy tickets, but if you don't knock it off I'll get rid of both of you. Don't think I won't. I've got to come up with twenty grand that I don't have in the next thirty days, or we'll all be ashore. I don't have time for any more of your petty bullshit. Do you get it? Do your job and shut the fuck up. You guys got anything to say?" Simultaneously, Reed and Chase said, "Nope."

"Right answer . . . Now, Skip, you and I are going to buy the grub. Pat, I want you to take the cherry princess down there and set up the fish hole. Then take the boat over, fuel her up, and put the ice aboard. She'll take about two thousand gallons of fuel, and we should probably take fifteen tons of ice. Don't you think?"

Chase said, "Sounds right to me, Joey. Are you guys coming over to the fuel dock when you get done?"

Scanton said, "Yes, I'll leave my car in the lot here, and Karen can come and pick it up later."

Scanton got out of his chair. "Okay, Skip! Let's you and me head over to the store and get what we need for food."

"Yeah, give me a minute. I'll be right with you. I've got to get something." Scanton hollered after him, "It better be your wallet. I'm not buying your butts for you again this trip." He headed down to the deck and saw Anderson handing pen boards down to Chase in the fish hole. He walked over and hollered down, "Hey, Pat, when you get done building the fish hole, take this guy around the boat and show him through it. A couple of days ago I checked the water in the starting batteries for the gensets, they're down. We got any distilled water on board?"

"No, I used the last jug two trips ago on the main batteries. I'll get some over at the fuel dock and top them off."

"Okay, Skip and I are headed over to Desanto's store. Anything you want?"

"No, I'm all set. Don't forget the grub list in the galley. It's on the clipboard. There are some odds and ends we need."

Scanton yelled, "Skip, get the grub list off the clipboard!"

He crossed the deck and climbed the ladder up onto the wharf. Reed was right behind him. They jumped into Scanton's Subaru. Reed said, "Jesus, Joey, have you been living in this fuckin' thing?"

The floor of the car was covered in old cigarette packs, empty coffee cups, and Italian sandwich wrappers. Scanton said, "Hey, is this your car or mine?" He rolled the window down and lit up a cigarette. As he exhaled the smoke, he said, "What a mess of shit we're in here. I'm serious you know when I tell you guys we've got to get in some good trips. That reverse gear really screwed things up. I knew when we had the net in the wheel I was in big trouble."

Reed said, "You can't beat yourself for that Joey. The full moon tide was running so hard it could have happened to anyone."

Scanton said, "The old man has had that happen plenty, and he never took out a gear. But I'm not him."

Reed said, "None of that was your fault for Christ's sake."

"You can't blame this one on Pat. If he hadn't acted as quick as he did we never would have gotten the bag of fish on board."

"Ya, I know. He did a good job."

"Christ, I scrambled as fast as I could to get her out of gear. When I got to the wheel and felt that rumble I knew I'd blown the reverse gear. It made me sick to my stomach. The last thing I wanted to do was call the Coast Guard and get our asses towed into Portland. Dumping that five hundred pounds of lobsters overboard just added the frosting to the cake."

Reed said, "Jesus, Joey, shit like that happens on everybody's boats."

"The timing was so lousy. I was just about to bank some decent money." Scanton took a long drag on his cigarette. "That last trip we weighed out just shy of thirty thousand pounds. We stocked almost $38,000 gross after everything was said and done. After paying you guys and all the other bills, I could only come up with $7,000 cash toward the new gear. Then I had to go to Uncle Sal for the rest of the money. With my credit, Maine Marine Gear Supply wouldn't let me take an empty packing crate out of there without a check in their hands." He took another drag. "I don't know why I'm telling you all this shit. Ten minutes ago I was ready to fire you."

Reed said, "It's all right, man, we're friends too, you know."

Scanton said, "Even though Sal's my father's own brother, he's nobody to screw with. Salvatore Scantini doesn't give a shit about anything but money. If I don't pay him in thirty days, I'm screwed."

Reed said, "I've heard some pretty bad things."

"The old man told me point blank not to ask Sal for the money, but what the hell was I going to do? Sal's old-fashioned Italian. That's why he refused to change from the old family name the way everybody else did. He's proud to be part of the old ways. He lives the life. You know what that means to people who do business with him."

Reed said, "Knowing that, I'm surprised that you had the balls to get the money from him."

"Well, I did it, so that's all there is to it. I know I can catch the fish, but nothing's guaranteed. You know that as well as I do. Does that Anderson guy know how screwed up everything is on this boat, or did you bullshit him about that too?" Skip moved around in his seat, clearly uncomfortable about that question. He said, "Look, Tom Anderson's been begging me for years to try to get him hooked up with a site. He's going to have to take his chances just like the rest of us. Shit, you know he can make some good money on this boat, even with the bills you got. It's not our problem to worry about him."

"I know it isn't my problem. I hope we can make money with this guy. All new men slow you down at first."

Reed cleared his throat and, in a slightly nervous tone, said, "There's something else I want to talk to you about though that could solve a lot of problems for you."

"Yeah, what's that?"

"I got a contact that's been asking me if we want to take on some swordfish offshore and bring them in."

Scanton pulled his head back slightly. "Smuggle swords on my boat? I don't think so."

Reed said, "Hear me out before you jump to any conclusions. You know about the embargo going on with Canadian swordfish so those guys can't sell in Maine . . . they're blaming it on mercury content. This political crap that's keeping Canadian swordfish from the market in the States is bullshit. You know as well as I do those swordfish are traveling up the Gulf Stream. You can't tell me that they suddenly pick up this mercury contamination on the Grand Banks."

Joey said, "That may be but it's still against the fuckin' law."

"These Canadian boats, fishing the banks, are getting stuck up there with no way to get rid of their fish if their trips ran long, and they aren't getting shit for price. All we do is leave the slaughterhouse free and take on around thirty thousand pounds. We ice them down and run them in. We can make some real money. I'm talking a one-time thing here. We pull this off, pay some bills, bank some dough, and things are back to normal. Nobody's the wiser. The Canadian fishermen make out better than they could anywhere else. We're helping those guys out."

Scanton turned to Reed and gave him an angry look. "Are you shitting me? You want to use my fuckin' boat to smuggle these fish? Holy shit, man. That's big stuff you're talking now. Who the hell have you been talking to about this anyway? How many people on the goddamn coast of Maine know about you planning to come to me with this scheme?"

Reed quickly responded, "Nobody but the buyer. I swear, Joe, nobody."

Scanton hesitated a second. "Jesus Christ, Skip. I could lose the boat over this. When you say Canadian boats, who makes these deals?"

"The people I'm talking about are from Nova Scotia. All we have to do is run offshore, somewhere east of the Hague Line, and pick up the fish."

Scanton said sarcastically, "At least we don't have to run far offshore for these fish."

"We don't want to try this in US waters with the friggin' Coast Guard over flying us all the time."

"I don't know, I don't know, this is a big deal to me. How much money do you think we're talking about?" Reed smiled a little, knowing that Scanton had risen to the bait. "We're talking $50,000 here anyway." Reed let that settle in and said, "I know what you're thinking. Chase is going to be the fly in the ointment here. But I'm telling you if we put ten grand in his pocket he'll keep his mouth shut. You know that he's trying to raise the money to get his own boat, right? He's no goddamn saint. You know him as well as I do. I got a plan to get this fish aboard before he even knows what's happened."

Scanton pulled his hat off and ran his hand through his hair. "You just don't get Chase, do you? He's one of the best men I've ever had on any boat with me, and I'm not having you fuck with him. He'll quit at the drop of a hat, and anybody will take him fishing with them. If we try this bullshit, and I'm not saying we are, you better kiss his ass daily. You really don't get it. Pat's nobody to screw around with. You go ahead, keep it up. He's planning to break your neck for you anyway. Just you remember what I told you."

Reed was unfazed. "I'll worry about Pat Chase."

"Hey, and what are you going to do with your other buddy, Anderson? Are you planning to throw him overboard?"

"I'll deal with him from my share of the money. He won't dare say a word to anybody. I'll convince him he's just as guilty as the rest of us, just for being on board. He doesn't know his ass from his elbow. I'll take care of him, don't you worry." Scanton shook his head, thinking, *Boy, he's got it all figured out.*

He looked right at Skip. "You know, Skip, ever since I met you, that's all I've ever done is worry about what you were going to pull next."

Reed said, "I know, I know, I love you too."

He shook his head and said, "Let's go get the grub. I'll think about this swordfish deal and let you know. I don't like the sound of it. Karen is real worried about the money too. She can bust my balls pretty bad when she wants to."

Reed got real quiet. "I'm sorry you and Karen are having a hard time. You know how women are. She'll get over it just as soon as you show up with a pocketful of money."

"Yes, I know, you're probably right," Scanton replied.

CHAPTER 5

S canton and Reed drove the few minutes to Desanto's Market. The Desanto family had always catered to the fishing boats. They stocked the kind of groceries and cuts of meats that the fishing crowd wanted. Most of the boats in the Portland fleet had charge accounts at their store. They would pay off their food bills after they got their settlements from each trip. A four-man crew would typically consume about seven to eight hundred dollars worth of food each trip.

Scanton and Reed walked into the store and were greeted by Teresa Desanto, the owner's daughter. She was a pretty little blonde with great big blue eyes and a beautiful smile. Teresa was a single mom with a six-year-old daughter named Olivia. The little girl was as cute as a button and full of energy. She was always running around the store and getting into trouble. Scanton was crazy about Teresa and her daughter.

Peter Scanton, Joey's dad, and Jimmy Desanto had always been close friends. Picnics and beach cookouts in the summers were a regular thing for their families. Even though Joey had been nothing more than a kid himself at the time, he had held Teresa on his lap when she was just a little girl. Five years age difference is a big deal when you're a kid. Scanton smiled a big smile when he saw her. "Hey, gorgeous, what's going on with you?"

Teresa was standing there with her hands on her hips. "Don't you 'hey gorgeous' me! My dad is mad as hell at you. We haven't seen you in over a month. You owe us for your last two trips, and he told me not to give you any more credit in here until your bills are paid off in full." Scanton's face turned bright red. He shifted from one foot to the other. He looked at Teresa and spoke very softly. "I know, kiddo. This is all my fault. I blew the reverse gear in the boat and had to be towed home. I've been tied up for a month and a half trying to get the boat ready to go fishing. I'm so sorry for not coming in. You and your dad have always been so great to me. I didn't want to come in because I was embarrassed to show my face in here. I wanted to apologize and explain myself, but I felt like such a jerk. I'll tell you the truth, Teresa, I'm flat broke. I had to use all the money I had to buy new parts for the boat. I even had to borrow money from my uncle Sal to get the new reverse gear."

Teresa shook her head. "I knew there was something wrong. I told my dad that there had to be something going on for you to not show up."

Scanton said, "We're finally ready to go fishing. We're supposed to leave in an hour, but I've got to have groceries for the trip. I don't know what more I can say. I don't have anyone else to ask. I'd really appreciate it if you and your dad would trust me just one more time. I won't let you down, I promise."

Teresa couldn't help but feel for his situation. Her boyfriend, Olivia's father, was a fisherman. He had been lost at sea on a winter trip two years ago, and her heart still ached for him. All fishermen have this kind of stuff going on constantly. There were always broken-down boats, unpaid bills, and sometimes much worse. Teresa knew firsthand what it was like. She had lived the whole fishing nightmare, and it had ended in tragedy for her. She looked at Scanton and shook her head. Damn it, she thought, she had known him since she was just a little girl. It didn't help any that he was now standing there with Olivia in his arms. She was kissing him with what Olivia called her great big smackers. Teresa just shook her head. "Stay here a minute. I'll call my dad and talk to him." She covered her eyes. "Jesus, Joey . . . Sal Scantini?"

"I didn't have any choice at the time, Teresa."

She said, "I know you're somehow family with that guy, but everybody knows he's dangerous. If you can't pay back the money he lent you, he could really hurt you. That's serious shit, Joey."

"I know it is," Scanton said.

"You should have talked to my dad. I know he would have helped you." Scanton thought about what she was saying and couldn't help but feel he had made a stupid mistake. He regretted not talking Jimmy Desanto about what had happened. You don't know who your real friends are if you let your pride get in the way. Well, there wasn't shit he could do about all that now. What was done was done. He had to go fishing, put in a good trip or two, and pay everybody back their money.

Teresa walked away and was back a few minutes later. She came up to Scanton with a big smile on her face. "Who's your best friend, Captain Joey? That would be me, that's who. I explained everything to my dad and he was so pissed off he was screaming. He told me to tell you don't you ever let yourself get in a bad way like that again and not come talk to him about it. Jesus, Joey, he was mad on the phone."

Scanton did have to laugh at her. "I'm sorry you had to go through that."

"You know my old man. When he isn't hollering is when you want to get nervous. He said to let you have whatever you needed for your trip. He wants to see you when you get in." Teresa did her deep voice imitation of her father. "Tell that stupid bastard to go catch some fish, for Christ sake." They both laughed.

Reed couldn't believe what he had just heard. No one would ever back him like that, and he knew it. He looked at Scanton and said, "Wow! Great people, Joey. These are really great people." Then Reed couldn't resist saying, "Captain Joey? Do I have to salute you now?"

Scanton raised his eyebrows and said, "No, you don't have to salute me now, but you can kiss my ass, jerk off! You got that galley list? Let's get our shit and get out of here. We need batteries for the small handheld spotlight. The last time I used it the thing was barely working."

They needed at least six suppers and a lot of breakfast stuff. Everybody made their own sandwiches during the day depending on when their wheel watches and deck times were.

The chicken, hamburger, steak, and sausages were all a standard purchase. Jimmy Desanto's had the best premade meatballs of anyplace around. These were real Italian homemade. They were ready to throw in tomato sauce for a spaghetti dinner, fast and easy.

They bought sandwich meats, including ham, salami, turkey, and roast beef in one-pound packages. They picked up a block of sliced American cheese, five bags of potato chips, lots of chocolate chip cookies, a huge bag of Snickers candy bars, eight gallons of milk, coffee, three cases of Coke, oranges, and root beer. They grabbed six pounds of bacon, five dozen eggs, sponges, and dish detergent, Brillo pads, two eight packs of toilet paper, six rolls of paper towels, four pounds of hot dogs, four large cans of B&M baked beans, three packages of salt pork, two quarts of half-and-half, three heads of lettuce, a dozen tomatoes, celery, radishes and a fifty-pound bag of potatoes, assorted boxes of cereal, doughnuts, a five-gallon tub of Deering chocolate ice cream, and a ten-pack of Bic lighters.

One rule on the *Jubilee:* no onions, absolutely no onions under any circumstances, captain's orders. Scanton hated them. He always said they smelled like garbage to him. The galley list consisted of olive oil, three large cans of coffee, vegetable oil, butter, jelly, peanut butter, sugar, matches, canned hash, pickles, and mustard. They bought them all. They added two six packs of Bud. Scanton didn't allow drinking when they were out at sea, but when they were in, a beer on deck was okay. The *Jubilee* had a fairly large stock of canned vegetables, canned tuna, and soups left over from previous trips.

Teresa helped the checkout girl box all of the supplies, and everyone joined in to carry the provisions out to Scanton's car. After a few loads, Reed said, "Joey, I've got to run and make a quick call. I'll only be a minute and then I'll help lug the rest of this stuff out."

"Ya, go ahead, Skip."

CHAPTER 6

Reed walked over to a phone booth located just outside the entrance of the store. He looked around to see if anybody was watching him. No one was. He stepped inside. He reached into his back pocket and pulled out a small notebook. He laid it down open on the shelf inside the phone booth and lit a Marlboro. He took a long deep drag and exhaled the smoke as he prepared himself mentally to make his call.

He inserted a quarter into the slot and dialed one of the numbers written on the second page of his notebook. The operator came on the line. "Please deposit one dollar for the first three minutes." He put the change in the phone and heard the line begin to ring.

A man's voice answered. "Yup." Reed began to talk, knowing that the person on the other end of the line would recognize him. He was feeling a little shaky when he started talking.

"Hey, I've been talking to him. He has to think it all over. I'm pretty sure in a trip or so he'll be all ours. We're going to set sail in about an hour. It sounds like Gloucester this time. I may see the fat man when I'm down there. My guy's under big money pressure right now."

The man said, "Yes . . . the more pressure the better. You need to understand somethin' though. This chance I'm giving you ain't going to be out there forever. Them swordfish are moving up the Gulf Stream right now, and there's plenty other guys as hungry as you out there. Don't fuck around with me, asshole!"

Reed replied quickly, "Okay, okay, I'll call you when we get into Gloucester." The man responded with no hesitation. "Yes . . . you do that." *Click!* The line went dead. Reed could feel the sweat dripping from his face. His heart was pounding. He threw his cigarette on the floor and grabbed another quarter out of his pocket. He stuffed it in the slot and ran his right hand through his hair. He quickly punched the numbers for his next call on the keypad. The phone rang twice and a woman answered.

"Hey, babe, I just wanted to give you a quick call before we take off. We're at Desanto's getting the food together."

She whispered, "Hang on a minute." He could hear her talking in the background, "Go watch TV for a little while. Mommy needs to talk on the phone for a minute." A second later she was back on the line. "I miss you already. You know where you're going?"

"He's talking about working toward the southwest. We could make Gloucester in about six days. Probably we won't be in there until three or four in the morning of the last day."

There was a pause and she said, "I don't think I can come down there this time, Skip. But I really wish I could. I'm horny as hell. I guess I can tell you that, can't I?" He thought about that for a minute and said, "You know you can tell me anything. I've really got to get going though. I sure do love you, babe."

She said softly, "Me too. Don't worry, sweetie. It won't be long now for us."

Reed hung up and slipped his notebook back in his back pocket. He lit another cigarette and stepped out of the phone booth.

He hurried back into the store just in time to grab the last box of groceries. He walked out and carefully wedged the last of the food into the back of Scanton's station wagon. Scanton was standing beside the car and said, "Don't forget your butts. You run out again this trip, and I'm not letting you bum mine."

"Okay, I'll go get some." He ran into the store. "Hey, Teresa, give me two cartons of Marlboros, will you?" Teresa went into the case and grabbed the cigarettes. She tossed them to Reed. "Put these on the *Jubilee*, okay?" Teresa frowned a little and, with a slight shake of her head, said, "Yes, sure, Skip. Is that all right with Joey?" Reed didn't answer. He ran out to the car and jumped in on the passenger side. He put the cigarettes down on the seat beside him. Scanton said, "I hope you didn't charge those to the boat."

"No way, Joey. Jesus Christ, who do you think I am?" Scanton didn't say a word. He just started the car and swung out onto Commercial Street.

Even with the backseat folded down to optimize the room, the little car was packed to the roof. The fuel dock was only a short distance away.

CHAPTER 7

C hase was explaining the fishhold operation on the *Jubilee* to
Anderson. "This boat holds ninety thousand pounds of fish
loaded. The hold is divided up into six pens. There are three pens on
the starboard and three on the port side." Chase walked over to the
edge of the main fish hatch. "See the center area between the pens?
That's called the slaughterhouse."

Anderson said, "Okay."

"The fishhold is real important to the success of the boat.
The way the fish get layered in there and are packed in the ice will
determine the quality of the catch." He explained to Anderson how
the fish had to be separated and cared for.

"The different species of fish have to be separated. If they're
not, they put out bacteria that will rot them while we're bringing
them in."

He explained that mixing the wrong species can contaminate
an entire ten-thousand-pound pen of fish. The boat had to take on
fifteen tons of ice for a six-day trip during the summer months. Chase
took the responsibility of managing the fishhold very seriously.

He climbed down the ladder into the fishhold. He told Anderson
to start handing down pen boards. Anderson was thinking it felt good
to be doing something to help out right away. They were building the
fishhold.

As he passed down the pen boards and watched as Chase wedged
them in between the bulkhead slots. The middle pen on the starboard
side was built up almost all the way to the overhead deck. The port
number one and number three side sections were built up about
seven pen boards each.

The hold had a ladder that was hung from the top edge of the
main fish hatch. It was movable. Tom knew that the ladder would

be taken out of the way when the fish were unloaded. He'd watched these big boats take their fish out before.

The job took over fifty pen boards before Chase was done. Anderson was paying attention to what he was doing. *That's good, kid,* Chase thought. He had had plenty of green guys aboard the boat that would mindlessly hand the pen boards down to him and never even think that something might be going on that's worth learning. You never knew if a green man would catch on or not. He'd see if this guy would last past the first trip.

Chase yelled up to Anderson, "Get your ass down here a minute." Anderson threw his leg over the top of the fish hatch and descended the ladder.

Chase said, "What's going to happen here is this. See this middle pen on the starboard side? It gets filled with ice up to the top. The port side pens get filled to the top of each of these three board sections."

Anderson said, "Do we shovel the ice in?"

"No, the ice gets blown in. Each pen is done in such a way so it doesn't affect the trim of the boat. If she isn't trim, it drives Joey nuts for the whole trip, and it isn't safe if it comes off rough. You'll see what I mean when we start to blow the ice aboard."

Anderson said, "Okay."

"See those hatches right there? That deck area of the boat is called what?"

"That's the slaughterhouse," Anderson said with a smile.

"Right, now open that third hatch over there." Anderson reached down and grabbed the hatch and pulled on it. Nothing happened. "Put some ass in it, pussy." Anderson gave a really hard yank and the hatch popped free. He laid the hatch cover upside down on the deck, and Chase practically went straight up through the roof.

"Don't you ever, ever lay a hatch upside down on this or any other boat again. Now you pick that fuckin' thing up and turn it right side up *now*, goddamn it! You really are green."

Anderson said, "Jesus, I didn't know."

Chase said, "Some skippers wouldn't sail the same day after a hatch cover gets flipped." He lit up a smoke. "You may think that's a stupid ignorant dumb ass superstition, but a lot of spooky shit goes on on these boats. No one can explain luck, and you don't want to start out on this boat bringing us shit luck. You get what I'm saying?" Anderson felt embarrassed and humiliated. He had no idea about the upside-down hatch covers. He had been around waterfront long enough to know that these beliefs were serious to these guys though. He'd heard that some captains will fire a man for whistling on a wheel watch. That superstition was that the man whistling was calling up a gale force wind.

Anderson had heard about never sailing on a Friday. He knew that fishing boots left upside down to dry were bad luck. Everybody knew that most fishermen believed that the mere mention of a certain breed of animal with curly tails could sink a boat. The majority of fishermen take their superstitions very seriously and never joke about them. Anderson said, "It'll never happen again, Pat." Chase had calmed down some and seemed to accept Tom's answer. He took a deep breath, lit up another cigarette, and continued on.

He pointed to the space below revealed by the open hatch. "That's the shaft alley. See the main shaft stuffing box down there? That's that big nut around the shaft. See how there's a little water dripping out at the bottom of it? There has to be some water coming out of that stuffing box or it could burn it up. Those fuckin' things can literally burst into flames if they're wound down too tight."

Anderson could see where the shaft of the boat exited through the shaft log and through the outside of the hull.

Chase said, "See that small line?" He pointed to one on the port side and one on the starboard hanging in the bilge water. "Pull them up, one at a time." Anderson grabbed one of the lines. "That hose with that thing that looks like a can on the end, that's a strainer." He pulled up the other line. Chase said, "One is from the regular electric bilge pump for the shaft alley, the other one is the Mersa pump. The Mersa is run in emergency situations only, from a separate electric motor." Chase explained, "It gets its power from either of the generators that, in turn, power a 110-amp electric pump. That pump feeds out to a three-inch hose. It will pump a ton of water out of this thing. I hope you never see it run. We always check those two strainers for junk before we take on ice. If the strainer gets blocked we could be in big trouble."

"Why do you need two pumps?"

"The fishhold bilge takes on more water than any other compartment in the whole boat. Between the water coming in from the stuffing box and the ice melting, these pumps have got to work. It could save us from sinking if some shithead of a green man named Anderson turned a hatch cover upside down and brought us bad luck!"

Anderson didn't say anything. Chase said, "A lot of crap gets down in this bilge from fish scales and other shit that finds its way down there. The important thing is this. When we blow the ice on, we never cover these eight and nine sections of the slaughterhouse. There's always a chance we might need emergency access to the bilge."

Anderson said, "How often do we check it out down here?"

"Always between trips when we unload. The bilge alarms are set low in the shaft alley so we know if anything's going on down here. Now reach down there and get those strainers again and make sure they're clean. I'm going up on deck for a minute. Hurry up and get those done. We got to get off this friggin' wharf sometime today. And don't put that hatch back in place before I check those strainers to see if you did it right. Got it?"

"Yes, where do I put the crap that I get out of those things?"

Chase was already up the ladder. "In this five-gallon bucket." He tossed one down.

Anderson loved this stuff. He didn't like being yelled at, but he was glad Chase was taking the time to show him everything he'd need to know. Whatever job he got told to do on this boat, he'd do it, and he'd do it with a smile on his face. He cleaned those strainers perfectly and yelled up to Chase when they were done.

He came back down and checked them out and dropped them back into the bilge. Anderson placed the number six hatch cover back, and they climbed out of the hold.

Chase said, "All right, now we go through the engine room." He entered the main companionway and flipped off a switch marked "FH" for fishhold and turned on another marked "ER" for the engine room.

"See this red light? When it's on, the fishhold's lit. This one is the engine room, same thing. Don't leave those on unless you or someone else is down there. Be careful though that you know what you're doing when you switch these off. Don't guess. You turn that switch off when someone's down there unexpectedly and they could be really hurt."

Anderson said, "Okay, know where everybody is before I turn one of these switches off."

"You remember what I'm telling you. I was fishing on a boat with a guy that was in the engine room checking a dipstick with the engine running. Another crew member flipped off the light switch on the guy. The boat rolled, and the guy reached out to keep from falling. He jammed three fingers in a turning belt. We were 110 miles offshore at the time, and he had to be flown in by the Coast Guard. He was in ungodly pain. The captain had to cauterize the hand with a hot iron to stop the bleeding while we waited for the chopper."

As they climbed the ladder down into the engine room, Anderson let the story about the light switch sink in. There was a hell of a lot to learn. Running this boat was a team effort. He was beginning to understand the reluctance to having a green man on board. He realized it was nothing personal. He knew he had to do his part to protect the other men on board.

Anderson couldn't believe how clean and organized everything was down in the engine room. He knew that was a direct reflection on Chase. He had been through a few big boats before, but he had never seen an engine room as immaculate as this one. Everything was freshly painted white and gray. There was no grease or oil on the decks and no open buckets or rags kicking around like he had seen on other boats. The *Jubilee* was spotless below decks.

"This is the main engine. It's a 1271 GM. She's got plenty of power for this boat. You see that brand-new reverse gear? I bet your buddy Skippy didn't tell you about that, did he?" Anderson had never heard Reed called Skippy before. The resentment and disdain in Chase's voice made him feel extremely uncomfortable.

He said, "No, I didn't hear anything about a new gear."

"I'll bet he didn't tell you that we sucked a groundfish net into the wheel last trip and blew the old gear. Then we got a free ride home to Portland Harbor, courtesy of the US Coast Guard Group, South Portland."

"No, I didn't know anything about that."

"I'll bet he never mentioned that we've been tied up for a month and a half with no pay to get ready to go fishing again." Chase took a drag on his cigarette. "My bet is that it was all big stories about big trips, big money, good times on the old *Jubilee*, right?"

"He did paint a pretty rosy picture for me. I'll admit that."

"I hate to break it to you, kid, but your pal Skip is a lying little jerk. But that's not my problem, is it? I go on this boat for two reasons: number one, to make money, number two is Joey. He's the finest kind of a skipper. Joey can always catch a lot of fish. The big thing though is when things get fucked up on here, and they will, he doesn't scream like a lot of these other guys do. I trust him. In the summer, fishing is no big deal, but when the winter gets here, it's a whole different ball game."

Anderson was having a hard time digesting all this new information. He couldn't help but remember that Reed had warned him about Chase. Who do you believe? Your lifelong friend or this guy? He really didn't believe what Chase was saying about Reed. Maybe he didn't want to. Only time would tell. He had decided to try and keep an open mind.

Chase went over the different parts of the engine, explaining as he went what dipsticks needed to be pulled to check the various oil and fluid levels. He showed Anderson the sight glasses, the clear tubes that showed the level for the water and fuel. He explained the pump manifolds and the grease fittings mounted on the rear bulkhead that required an injection every twenty-four hours.

"Those fittings there lubricate the Babbet bearings that support the four-and-a-half-inch stainless steel main shaft."

He explained the pumping system that pumped water from the fo'c'sle, the engine room, the fishhold, and on to the lazarette. Anderson wished he had a notebook with him.

They checked out the port and starboard Northern Light gensets that supplied the 110 power to the boat. Chase showed him the power takeoff mounted on the front of the 1271 and explained that it supplied the power for the hydraulic motors that ran the winches and capstans that were used to haul the nets. The PTO powered the net reels and the jillsons used for heisting bags of fish up through the stern ramp. It was a lot of information, and Anderson was fascinated by everything he had seen and heard.

They climbed the stairs out of the engine room and entered the main companionway. Chase turned the corner with Anderson on his heels and climbed the stairs to the wheelhouse. He stopped and looked back. "Now what did I just tell you about the engine room light switch? Now go back down there and turn the fuckin' thing off and start paying attention to what tell you to do." Anderson felt his face flush but didn't say a word. He ran down the stairs and flipped the switch off. The red light went out. He sprinted back up the stairs and made his way into the pilothouse. Chase was sitting in the captain's chair and had lit himself a cigarette. Anderson decided to have one himself. Just as he lit up a voice came in over the radio.

"*Jubilee, Jubilee,* this is the *Teresa Lynn.* You on here, Joey?" Pat reached for the mic and answered.

"*Jubilee* back . . . Switch and answer on 88."

"*Teresa Lynn,* on 88."

"Joey's over getting the grub. Is that you, Marshall? Over."

"Yes . . . Who's this?"

"It's Pat Chase. How you doin', Marshall? Over."

"Yes, Pat. I'm good, old dog. What's shakin' besides that old girl you're fishin' on? Over."

"Oh nothing . . . same old shit, Marshall. We got a green guy on with us this trip. I'm taking him on a tour of the boat. Over."

"Glad it's you and not me, brother. Has he started pukin' yet? Over."

"Christ, no. We haven't left the dock yet. We're going to get fuel and ice in a little bit. If he pukes between here and the fuel dock, we're leaving him right there. Over."

Marshall said, "I got you there. If there's one thing I can't stand, it's a puker. I was just talkin' to Vern. I guess he stove up his groundfish net pretty good over to the westard. I told him it was about time to fix up that old rag he's been draggin' all over hell's kitchen for the last nine months. He responded with a rather impolite remark about somethin' I should do to myself. I couldn't quite make it out. He kinda broke up on me, Pat. Over."

A new voice came over the air. "I'm right here, goddamn it, Marshall Grimes, and you heard me plenty good, you old piece of dogfish! Over."

Marshall laughed. "Is that you, darlin'? I thought you'd be in the bunk takin' a little snooze while them deckhands of yours laced that old rag back together for you. Over."

Vern said, "I ain't got a man on this boat that knows the difference between a mendin' needle and a darnin' needle and that's the truth! Over."

"Christ, Vern, you and the truth have been strangers since you gave up your momma's nipple nearly a hundred years ago. Over."

Vern yelled, "That's it. I can't spend no more time talkin' to a mean-spirited old crackpot like you, Marshall. I got to mend up my net. The Alexander T. Over and out!"

"See ya in the funny papers, Vern. Hey, Patrick, tell Joey to give me a call when you boys get underway, will you? Over."

"Will do, Marshall . . . Hey, it's been a real thrill talkin' with you and Vern this fine afternoon.

The *Jubilee*, clear with *Teresa Lynn*."

"Finest kind, Patrick. Go easy. This is the *Teresa Lynn*, clear with the *Jubilee*." Chase looked over and smiled at Anderson and laughed a little.

Chase said, "Vern Eldridge and Marshall Grimes have been best friends since grade school. Those guys are related for Christ's sake. They're married to sisters from down on Vinalhaven. They harass each other on the radio all the time." Anderson grinned and said, "You'd never guess it, listening to them go at it."

Chase said, "Enough of that shit. We gotta get going here. We can't just stand around shootin' the shit all afternoon." He flipped a battery switch onto the "both" position, turned a key marked "ignition," and pressed a black rubber-covered button. The *Jubilee*'s diesel engine rolled over a couple of times and came to life. Anderson looked toward the stern and could see the jet-black smoke roll out from the exhaust pipe and drift back off into the clear blue summer sky.

Chase raced the engine a couple of times to clear her throat and then settled her back down to an idle.

"I'm going to explain what I want you to do with the dock lines as we let her warm up a little. You've really got to pay attention. This ain't no skiff. Once we get free of those pylons, I can't run around and help you out. You got to get this right the first time. Here's what I want you to do."

Anderson said, "Okay, I'm ready, Pat."

"There's a bowline and a stern line, a bow spring line and stern spring line. We're going to do what's called a stern spring off. All four lines are going to come aboard the boat. Don't throw any lines overboard no matter what you do. You need to flip the lines off the pylons. First you take the strain of the lines by untying them from the deck cleats. Give yourself enough slack so you can snap the lines like a whip." Pat made a low to high gesture with his hand and arm. "Start with the bowline. Next you get the stern line and then the bow springer. You leave the stern springer tied off. When you've got the other lines free and aboard the boat, I'm going to drop her into reverse to take a strain on the stern springer. I'm going to leave her in reverse. You'll see that as the strain builds the bow of the boat will be forced away from the wharf and will swing out. When the bow is far enough off the wharf, I'll take her out of gear, and the strain on the stern springer will ease off. You'll have about three seconds to flip that line off the pylon, and we'll be free and can get underway. You got it?"

Anderson thought, *I'm going to pull this off if it kills me.*

Chase said, "All right, bub, let's give this a try."

Anderson went out on deck and freed the lines in the prescribed order, bowline to stern line and next to the bow springer. He snapped everyone off like he was an old pro. With the stern spring line still cleated off, Chase dropped the *Jubilee* into reverse. The boat's bow, ever so slowly, began to swing out away from the wharf just like he said it would. The *Jubilee* never moved one inch closer to either of the two draggers tied in tight on her bow and stern. When the boat was sufficiently swung away from the wharf, Chase hollered, "Okay, let her go." Anderson released the strain on the final line by untying it from the cleat and giving it a sharp snap. The line popped aboard and they were all set. The *Jubilee* was out of her berth. Anderson walked back into the pilothouse proud as punch.

Chase said, "Well, lah dee fuckin' dah! Aren't you somethin special?"

Anderson laughed. "Yes, I am!"

The *Jubilee* slowly nudged her way out around the end of the wharf and slid out into Portland Harbor. Chase sounded the boat's horn as she left her berth. The fuel dock was about five wharves away to the westard. Chase jogged her along the shore past the old rickety buildings that made up the working waterfront. It was a beautiful summer afternoon. The sky was clear and there was practically no wind.

They passed by Antonio's floating restaurant. It had been created by converting an old passenger ferry that had been towed into Portland and permanently moored at the end of an old wharf. It was a great-looking boat. A lot of Portland people thought it wouldn't last too long. They didn't think anyone would want to sit on a stationary boat and eat seafood.

The *Jubilee* rounded the end of the pier and slid up into the docking space at Fuel and Ice Services. Chase told Anderson to tie off the bow and stern with no spring lines. Anderson had already thrown the big orange poly balls over the side, which acted as fenders when the boat was tied directly to a wharf.

As soon as the boat was secured Chase came out on deck. He walked out on the forward deck and unscrewed a cap cover on a two-inch pipe extending from the deck. The pipe was the fill port for the water tank. Chase hollered to Anderson to hand down the red water hose coiled up on the pier. He inserted it into the filler port, turned it on, and let it run.

"Go get me the fuel hose." The fuel fill ports were larger than the water port but of similar design. There were separate filler pipes for the starboard and port tanks. Chase said, "Pull out the red button. It'll call the office. The guy that answers is Ronny Colby." Tom found the red button and pulled it. The intercom crackled to life. "Vessel name please." Anderson answered, "The *Jubilee*." There was a long pause. Chase stepped over toward the starboard side of the boat closer to the fueling station intercom. He said to Anderson, "What's the holdup? All the guy's got to do is turn on a friggin' switch." A few seconds later Colby came back on the air. "Is Joey on board?"

"He's getting food for the trip. He should be here any minute."

"Tell him to come up to the office when he gets here." Chase hollered, "Hey, Ronny, what about the fuel?"

"Sorry, you'll have to stand by on that, Pat." Chase looked at Anderson. "Oh shit, what now?"

CHAPTER 8

A few minutes later Scanton pulled up to the wharf and backed down the side ramp beside the *Jubilee*. He and Reed got out and started to take the food boxes out of the car.

Chase hollered, "Hey, Joey, they won't pump our fuel. They want you to come up to the office." An angry look came across Scanton's face. He handed the box of groceries in his arms to Anderson and pointed toward the boat. Without saying a word, he turned and headed up the dock toward the office. Chase came over and took the box from Anderson. "Go on up there and get us a couple of gallon jugs of distilled water."

"Okay, I'll be right back." Anderson followed Scanton at a distance.

Reed said, "Pat, let's put this stuff aboard. The boxes are all separated out like always. If you'll hand them to me, I'll put them down. You've been bustin' your ass on the fishhold, so I'll take care of this shit."

Chase was thinking, *Where the hell is Skippy? Joey must have ripped him a new one while they were gone.* He couldn't believe all the sweetness. Nice Skippy was scarier than mean Skippy. Chase shrugged his shoulders and started grabbing food boxes.

Anderson walked into the chandlery and asked where he might find the distilled water. The clerk pointed at an isle over by the back of the store. As he walked around the end display shelf, he could hear shouting from the office area behind the cash register. Scanton's voice was loud and angry. Anderson really didn't want to eavesdrop, but the volume was such that he would have had to leave the building not to. He reached in his back pocket, pulled out three bucks, and paid for the water. He grabbed the jugs and headed back down to the boat. When he went back on board, there were groceries all over the place. There were unpacked boxes over by the fish hatch and some near the main companionway. He could see Reed lugging stuff up into the pilothouse.

"While I wait on the fuel, why don't you help Reed get some of the grub boxes down in the galley?"

Anderson said, "Okay, I'll put the distilled water over by the engine room ladder."

"Yes . . . Hey, what went on up there? They only hold up fuel here for one reason . . . no money. I know Joey took fuel and ice out of my last two checks."

"I don't know what was said. I got the water, like you told me, and left."

"Okay, kid. Go help Skip with the food, and then you and I'll ice the fishhold." Anderson climbed the ladder to the pilothouse, and Reed turned toward him. "Hey, Tom, how's it going? Is Chase treating you okay? He's all right when you get to know him, and he gets to know you. Later on we'll kick his and Joey's asses in a game of crib. That'll lighten things up a little bit."

Anderson felt a little better. There was a lot of tension on board the boat, and he hoped it would stop. "Take those three boxes down into the galley and just set them on the table."

He said, "Okay, Skip, will do." He picked up a box and started down the stairs. When he got down to the galley he put the box on the table. Out of the corner of his eye, he saw a large black cat jump down from the galley seat and glare right at him. It let out a vicious hiss. Anderson was so startled that he screamed, "Jesus H. Christ!"

Chase and Reed were above him in the pilothouse. They both burst out laughing. Reed hollered down, "I guess you just met Uncle Charley." Reed leaped down the stairs and scooped up the twenty-pound jet-black cat.

He held the cat in his arms. "This is Uncle Charley. If she doesn't like you, she'll bite. She's been living on this boat since Joey bought it. She's one tough cat, aren't you, Uncle Charley?"

Reed pointed out a small square house under the galley table. It had an opening just large enough for her to squeeze in. There was a small brass plate screwed into the wood above the opening that said "Uncle Charley, First Mate."

"Now that you've made Tom here piss his panties, you need to hit your bunk." Reed tossed the cat toward her house, and she slipped in. After he got past the shock, Anderson decided he liked the cat. He and Reed packed away the rest of the groceries.

Scanton was still up in the office. The manager, Wally Dodge, was claiming that the boat's old fuel and ice bill hadn't been paid and was refusing him any more credit. Scanton had told his wife, Karen, to pay Fuel and Ice Services three weeks before. He made out the check and signed it for her himself. He kept telling Wally Dodge that the bills were paid. He wouldn't listen. Dodge had been manager of this place for fifteen years. He'd heard all the stories. He said, "Joey, just calm down a second . . . I'm sorry but she didn't pay us. I wouldn't lie to you, for Christ sakes. What do you want me to say? I can't let you have any more credit until your last two trips are paid up."

"Goddamn it, Wally, the bill's paid . . . I told you."

"Joey, this is none of my business, and I hate to say it, but sometimes when you and other guys have written out checks, they just don't get sent. If your old lady didn't mail the check, the money is still in the account. I'm not saying she did that, but if she's got signing authority on that account, then bingo. She's got an extra three grand to spend on something else. I've been kicking around this wharf a long time, and I've seen it all. I'm sorry, man, there's just no way the bill's been paid."

Scanton asked if he could use the phone to call the house. There was no answer. Little Joey was in bed for an afternoon nap. Karen heard it but let the phone ring. She didn't feel like answering it.

Scanton hung up. "All right, Wally, what the hell are we going to do? I haven't left the wharf in a month and a half. I gotta go fishin'!"

"Okay, okay. You sell over to Portland Seafood Products, right? I know the fish buyer, Kenny Browman, pretty good. If you'll sign a note with me, authorizing Kenny to cut us a check off the top of the stock from this next trip, I'll take it over there after you leave and give it to him. I'll pump your fuel and ice for you now."

Scanton was frustrated as hell, but he knew that Wally was giving him a fair shake. What was he going to do otherwise, he thought. "Okay, Wally, I don't like it, but I have no choice. Write it up so I can get my ass out of here, will ya?" Dodge had his secretary, Maggie, write up the brief statement, and Scanton scribbled his signature on the bottom. As he walked out of the office, he heard Ronny Colby speak over the intercom. "Okay, Pat, fuel's commin'."

Scanton went over and got in his car. All the food was unloaded and on the boat. He wanted a minute to himself to think things over before they took off. He knew the boys would keep working without him. He drove out to the parking lot to where he was going to leave his car for the next few weeks and sat there a minute. He wished he could talk to his old man about Reed's swordfish deal.

Scanton's dad was completely old school. He knew what his reaction would be if he even brought it up. There was a phone booth near the exit of the parking lot. He dialed his mother's house and she picked up.

"Hi, Ma, is Dad there?"

"Yes, he is. You okay, Joey? You sound worried." Only five words but she always knew.

"No, I'm fine. Let me talk to Dad a minute." Peter Scanton picked up the phone. "Hey, Joe, how's it goin'?"

"I'm okay, Dad." He hesitated a second. "I think Karen didn't send my fuel and ice check into Wally Dodge. I had to sign a note with them to get fuel. They get to take their money off the top of this next trip from Portland Seafood. I don't really care about that so much, but I feel like I'm losing control of things. Karen's pissed at me all the time, and so I'm pissed at her. It's always about the goddamn money." Peter paused a minute before saying anything. When he did answer he said, "A fisherman's life is not easy for them or the women who are part of his life. They don't have it so good, I promise you. Sometimes it takes years for things to settle out. You got that beautiful little boy. You do what you need to take care of him . . . okay, Joey? You got your boat ready to go now, so go."

"I know I have to do that, Dad."

"You leave the shore shit that's going on here on the shore, and go catch fish. The others will take care of itself. You trust me now, Joey. You go catch the fish. That's what we do, son."

Scanton knew his father was right. He talked to his dad a while longer. He said that they were taking a green man, a friend of Reed's. He told him the new guy was a diver, so if he fucked up again and got a net in the wheel, maybe this guy could cut it out.

They talked fishing. His dad told him where he thought the fish would be now and where they might show up next.

Peter Scanton had fished the Gulf of Maine and Georges Bank his whole life and knew the migratory path of the fish like he knew his own name. He was going to sail himself again in a couple of days. He had been in a week. He was getting too old now to go like he had only a few years ago. He'd really slowed down.

The weather, the work, and the losses took their toll on all the men in the fishing business. The days of the "turnaround trips" were over for Pete Scanton. He said he'd call Joey when he got offshore in a couple of days.

Scanton always felt better after he talked to his dad. They fought like hell when they fished together on the *Gloria Walker*, but they were much closer now that he had his own boat.

"Tell Ma good-bye for me. I'll call her when we get in. Bye, Dad." Scanton hung up the phone and headed back down to the *Jubilee*.

Five minutes later he was in the pilothouse, and things still weren't ready to go yet. "Will you fuckin' assholes stop screwin' around and get this boat ready to go fishin'? Come on, let's go now. How are we doin' on the fuel, Pat?"

"Port side's full, and I'm partway through the starboard."

"Skip, finish fueling up. Pat, why don't you and the kid take on the ice now?"

"Okay, I think we got everything out of the car on board. We'll stow the fishhold grub after we get our ice aboard. Hey, Joey, Marshall called for you earlier. He's on eighty-eight."

"Okay, Pat, I'll call him on the way out." Chase looked at Anderson. "Let's go get oiled up and get the ice aboard."

The oil pants and jackets were hanging on pegs just inside the entryway. Anderson and Chase grabbed their boots and pulled on protective gear. Anderson had to scrounge up a pair of pants and a jacket. His old fowl weather gear from lobstering was nothing but rags. He hadn't had time to buy another set. These boats always had extras on board. The stuff was usually pretty tired, but he found a set that were in good shape and fit him pretty well. When Chase put on his oilskins Tom noticed they were marked "Pat Chase F/V *Jubilee*" across the back. He knew that the markings weren't just to identify the oil clothes but also to identify the fisherman's body if he was lost at sea.

Anderson followed Chase over to the fishhold. Before he started down he told Anderson to go over and tell Ronny to turn on the ice. He yelled into the intercom, "We're ready for the ice now."

Ronny came on. "How much?"

"Fifteen tons," Anderson answered.

"Okay, here it comes." Ten seconds later there was a loud rattle, and the aluminum flex pipe the ice was blown through began to shake and bang.

He jumped back aboard the boat, sprinted across the deck, and climbed down in the fishhold. He saw that Chase had tied a piece of six-thread rope around the ice hose and had cleated the other end down to the top combing of the fish hatch. He could see that tying off of the ice supply pipe helped control the hose when they sprayed the thousands of pounds of chopped ice into the appropriate pens.

Since Chase had fueled the starboard fuel tank first, he sprayed ice into the port pens. This kept the boat as trim and balanced as possible. He showed Anderson how to handle the hose and where to spray. In about a half hour the fishhold was iced. The two men both looked like snowmen. The blower shut off when all fifteen tons of ice was aboard. Chase told him to pass down the remaining food boxes that were on deck, and he packed them away in the ice. There were several gallons of milk, extra soda, packages of meat, and other items that required cooling. There was very limited space in the boat's refrigerator.

With everything stowed, they climbed out of the hold and lifted the fish hatch cover in place. Chase took a length of six-thread rope and tied the cover down tight. There were four side cleats around the perimeter of the hatch cover so it could be fastened to withstand the seas that would come crashing down on *Jubilee's* decks.

Anderson followed Chase into the main companionway. They peeled off their oilskins and hung them on the hooks. They headed up to the pilothouse.

Chase yelled down into the galley, "We should be ready to sail, Joe, whenever you are." Scanton climbed the stairs back up to the pilothouse and swung himself up into the captain's chair. He had left a pack of cigarettes up ahead of the wheel next to the fathometer. He grabbed it and took one out. "Okay, boys, let's rock and roll."

Scanton started the main engine. Chase and Anderson went down on deck to let the lines go. Anderson got the bowline and Chase got the stern. He showed him how he wanted the dock lines coiled and stowed in their locker.

Scanton throttled up the engine in reverse, and the *Jubilee* backed away from the fuel dock and into the harbor. He hit one sharp blast on the boat's horn as he backed her away. After they were a sufficient distance back, he put the boat in forward and gradually increased the rpm of the 1271 to 1,100.

They cleared the no-wake zone of Portland Harbor and jogged their way slowly toward Bug Light Point and the number five buoy. It was 5:00 p.m., August 5, 1982.

Anderson stayed down on deck and lit up a Winston. He was excited about the trip ahead. He was thinking, *So far so good . . . we're underway.* Fifteen minutes later, the boat had made her way out of the harbor. Scanton brought the engine's rpm up to 1,800.

Chase went up to the pilothouse and yelled down to Reed in the fo'c'sle that it was time to lower the paravanes.

The main mast on the *Jubilee* was a tall square frame made up of two large steel posts running from the deck skyward on the port and starboard sides of the boat. They looked a little like a small football goal post. She had an A-frame fixed boom that ran from the main mast attached at the same level as the pilothouse roof on the port and starboard sides. The A-frame configuration was wider at the base and gradually narrowed toward the top end. The fixed boom ran skyward at about a forty-five-degree angle and extended aft to the stern rising over the twin net reels and the gallous frames. The A-frame boom was held permanently in place by connecting steel pipes that extended from the top of the mast superstructure back to the rear and were attached on the sides at the end of the boom. There were four huge permanently affixed floodlights that illuminated the *Jubilee's* decks for twenty-four hour operations.

There was a pair of gallous frames mounted on the rear port and starboard decks. Gallous frames are steel and a B-frame design. They served two functions. They held the dragger's doors and the bollards that directed the towing wire off the stern of the *Jubilee* while the boat was fishing. They also had top-mounted loud speakers that connected to a loud hailer that enabled Scanton to communicate with his deckhands from the pilothouse.

The main jillson was attached about three quarters of the way up the boom. A cable ran up the boom to a block and was used as a heist to raise the bags of fish aboard the boat.

Chase, Reed, and Anderson came out on deck. The *Jubilee* had a slight but constant starboard list. The main bank of batteries was on the starboard side of the engine room. Chase made every effort to balance the boat out through weight distribution of the ice.

The boat was outfitted with giant stabilizers that extended upward from the base of the square-framed superstructure beginning at rail height. The stabilizers, called paravanes, were about thirty feet long and constructed of steel. The design and configuration of paravanes is an engineering marvel. They were built for strength and durability while at the same time made as light as possible. The core of these huge arms was a sizable round steel beam surrounded by steel strips. The strips were welded into a tapered triangular framework that narrowed at the base, became wider in the middle, and tapered down again at their highest tip. Rope lines extended to a pulley at the high end of the arm that allowed a chain to pass through it. The chain attached to an aluminum dart-shaped weight that came in at just slightly over 175 pounds.

The dart weights are called birds. With the paravanes lowered and the birds in the water, the boat gained tremendous stability in the roughest of seas. As she rolled to starboard, the bird dove on its extended chain toward the ocean floor; as the boat began its comeback roll to port, the bird resisted the upward pull via its winged-shaped design. The principle behind a paravane is the same as a diver's flipper—using surface area to create resistance.

After the paravanes are lowered and the seas became rough enough to warrant it, the captain orders the birds launched overboard. The boat was a comfortable, safer, and more efficient fishing machine with paravanes.

Chase called Anderson to his side and began to explain the process of lowering the paravanes. "This can be a dangerous job. It's a calm summer afternoon, so it's pretty easy to do right now, but trust me, when it's screechin' easterly at thirty-five it's a different story. See that ladder over there that runs up to the roof of the pilothouse? Your first job is to go up there and very carefully release that come-along that holds the paravanes in place. It keeps them tied together like handcuffs. You ever work a come-along before?"

Anderson said, "I used one all the time working the mooring barge at the boatyard. The damn thing was always rusty and frozen up. They'd have wicked strain on them, and you'd have to hit it with a hammer to free it up. The big trick was to keep the teeth from ripping a finger off, when you finally got it free." Chase laughed. "Well, kid, this one's going to be exactly the same. It's been sitting there for a month and a half in the salt air and rain, so it should be rusted solid. There's a short section of pipe lying in that gutter you can use to pound on it. Get up there and give it hell and be careful you don't get your dink stuck in it." Anderson smiled and said, "Does it hurt when you do that, Pat?" Chase grinned just a little. "Listen to that, Skip. He hasn't been on this friggin' boat one day and he's a wiseass already."

Anderson said, "Who? Me?"

Chase growled, "Kid, just get your ass movin', and get that thing unhooked, will you? I'm getting old waiting."

Anderson went over and climbed the ladder attached to the rear bulkhead adjacent to the main companionway. Where the ladder reached the roof of the pilothouse there was no hatch, just a square opening. He was able to climb through and walk over to the come-along. The end of the come-long handle was covered with a red plastic coating. You had to pull the handle toward you to take the strain off the trip dogs that held the come-along teeth from free spinning away and releasing the cable. A come-along is nothing more than a tiny winch system. As he pulled the handle forward, he had to reach into the side with his thumb and forefinger and release the trip dog by pulling it back.

Just as Chase had predicted, the unit was frozen solid. He grabbed the short section of pipe and started pounding on the side of it. By working the handle back and forth and pounding as hard as he could, the thing finally released. Now came the tricky part. Like he had done hundreds of times before on the mooring barge, click by click by click, he backed the come-along off until all the strain was released and the stay line could be undone.

He hollered down, "All set, Pat . . . and I know you'll be pleased to learn that my dink's just fine too."

Chase said, "Well, thanks for sharing that with me."

Chase pointed toward the square-framed superstructure that supported the paravanes and the fixed A-frame boom. "See those rungs made from short pieces of rebar welded on the side of the superstructure frame right there? Use those to climb on the port side. When you get three quarters of the way up, put your boot against the paravane and kick it outboard as hard as you can. Once you free it up past its fulcrum, Skip will lower it away. He'll release the block-and-tackle line and the paravanes will lower."

Chase stepped back toward the stern to get a better angle on Anderson as he sailed up the rungs. When he reached the right height, he put his boot into a notch and kicked hard against the paravanes. The stabilizer arm released from its Y-shaped berth and rolled outboard.

Chase motioned to Reed, and he slowly lowered away on the block and tackle until the paravane lay horizontally at a ninety-degree angle from the superstructure out over the water. The arm was supported by the fully extended forward, stern, and top stays. They created two perfect triangles, locking the paravane into position. The starboard side was easy. The slight list already placed outboard pressure on that side's arm. Reed simply flipped off a couple of turns on the starboard side cleat and lowered away until that paravane arm was down and in place. The block-and-tackle lines were then fully cleated off and the job was done.

The three men headed up to the pilothouse. It was about five thirty. The skies were clear with light southerly winds and the seas were calm. It was a beautiful Maine summer evening. Reed lit up a cigarette and took a deep drag. "So where are we goin', Joe?"

"We're heading down just northeast of the Outer Falls to the ninety fathom grounds and have a look around. I'd like to scare up a few flats. The price is decent right now."

The steam at eight knots would take the *Jubilee* about ten hours. That would put them on the bottom, just before daylight. Scanton turned to Anderson. "Skip tells me you're a decent cook. Why don't you show us what you can do and scrape something together for supper?"

Anderson said, "Anything in mind?"

"Nope, cook's choice, just have at it. You should find everything you need down there. Pat run down and turn the gas on for the stove. I shut it down while we were tied up. You know how I am about gas with no one on board."

Chase went down to the galley and opened the gas line shut off. He showed Anderson how to light the pilot so the top burners and the oven would light by just turning the burners on.

Anderson started looking through the refrigerator and all the cabinets to try and figure out what he had to work with. He found the big skillets, the pots, the saucepans, and bowls. The knives, spatulas, and other cooking utensils were all stowed away so they wouldn't fly all over the galley in rough weather.

The stove was outfitted with brackets that held the pots and fry pans firmly in place while you're underway in rough seas. That would be no problem on this gorgeous summer night, however.

Chase said, "Whatever you plan to make, make plenty of it."

"Okay, will do." Curiosity got the best of Chase. "What are we having?"

Anderson laughed. "Norwegian spaghetti."

"What the fuck is Norwegian spaghetti?"

"Instead of meatballs we put in pickled herring. You'll love it."

"Yummm. I can't wait."

Anderson pulled out a three-gallon pot and filled it half full of water, lit the burner under it, and put the lid on top. He hauled out a big skillet and threw a large pat of butter in and turned the burner to medium heat. He chopped up some fresh garlic and let it simmer in the fry pan. He poured two jumbo cans of tomato sauce over the garlic and stirred the mixture together. The water had come to a boil, and he put two large fistfuls of spaghetti into the boiling water while the tomato sauce simmered on low heat. He found some chopped basil, some Italian spice blend, threw in some salt and pepper, and he was ready for the famous Desanto meatballs. Even his mother had been known to make her husband, Martin, drive into Portland to pick up an order of these spicy delicacies.

What made Desanto's meatballs unique was not only the flavor but their size—twelve ounces each. One meatball per man was more than enough. He made a quick salad of lettuce, fresh tomato, celery, radishes, cukes, and green pepper. He found a can of black olives and threw in a handful. There were four different bottled dressings near the galley table so everybody could choose their own.

Anderson sat down and had a smoke while he waited for the spaghetti to finish cooking. Uncle Charley wandered out of her bunk and rubbed against his leg. "Well, hello, Uncle Charley . . . you want to be friends?" He rubbed the big cat's chin and got a loud purr from her as a reward. The cat flopped down on her side and stretched out full length and yawned. "You got it tough old girl . . . don't you?"

The plates and eating utensils were stored in a cabinet just to the right of the refrigerator. Everything was made of a heavy red plastic. He put them out on the table and turned down the spaghetti to low heat.

Chase was stretched out on his bunk. Scanton and Reed were up in the pilothouse. Anderson climbed the stairs and poked his head through the companionway. Reed was reading a nudey magazine and Scanton was still at the wheel.

Scanton reached up and grabbed the mic to the VHF radio and switched the channel to eighty-eight.

"*Teresa Lynn, Teresa Lynn,* you on here, Marshall? The *Jubilee* callin'."

"This is the *Teresa Lynn,* back to the *Jubilee.* Hey, Joey! How's it feel to be out again? Over."

"Oh good, Marshall, good. It's been a pain in the ass to lose a month and a half of fishing. You've been through it though, haven't you? Over."

"God yes, way back when your Uncle Charley and your old man and I went together, we were broke down more than we were broke up. Over."

"Ya, ya, I know it, Marshall, the old man told me that you boys would work on the engine for one day and get drunk for two. Over."

"Joey, Joey, Joey, we would work on the engine for half a day and be drunk for three. Over." Scanton laughed at the same old joke he'd heard a thousand times before.

"The old man's comin' out in a couple of days. Give him a call. My mother dragged his sorry ass down to Boston to a play. He said he felt like a whore in church, but I think he really had a good time. Over."

"Jesus, how's Gloria doin? My Grace is planning on calling her to go get lunch or something next week. Over."

"I'm sure she'll like that, Marshall. They can talk about how bad you and the old man were back in the day and how great the grandkids are now. Over."

"Where are you anyway? Over."

"I'm towin' down on the roller coaster. I've got another hour and a half and we'll haul back. Over."

"Well, I guess we're goin' to the eastard and see what's on down there. Over."

"Finest kind, boy. Pat told me you got a green guy with you this time. Has he quit pukin' yet? Over."

"Geez, Marshall, I don't think he's puked yet, but we've still got plenty of time for that. Over"

"That old wharf rat Vern's not speakin' to me no more. I guess we broke up. He got his undies in a bunch because I said he gone and forgot how to mend twine. I think he can remember how to tie the knots. He just can't remember the counts. That shit happens when you're over a hundred, ya know. Over."

"I'm sure it does. Vern always told me that *you* graduated from high school two years before him."

"That's right, I did, but he was the first island man to graduate high school, at the age of thirty-seven."

"Well, Marshall, I'm going to let you go on that one. The green man's made us supper and it smells pretty good. I'll catch you later. Over."

"Finest kind, Joey, give me a shout in a day or so. I'm going to fish a couple more days anyway or until my ice runs out. This is the *Teresa Lynn*, clear with the *Jubilee*. Over and out."

"Will do, Marshall. *Jubilee*, clear with the *Teresa Lynn*."

Scanton smiled and hung up the mic. "Skip, take the wheel. I'm goin' down and try some of your boy's cooking."

Anderson said, "You want a plate up here, Skip?"

"Yes . . . that would be great. Give me Italian and blue cheese on my salad. Did Pat put on coffee?"

Anderson said, "Yes, he did. Want some?"

"Yes, black . . . Thanks, Tom."

Anderson and Scanton made their way down to the galley. Anderson grabbed a plate and a salad bowl and served up a portion for Reed. He took two pieces of Italian bread and slathered them with butter and ran the meal up to him.

"Thank you, sir, I appreciate it." Reed took his plate and settled back in the big chair to have his supper. By the time Anderson made it back down to the galley the other men were already eating. He grabbed a plate and served himself a big helping of the spaghetti topped off with a meatball and lots of sauce. No matter how many times he had them, they were the best.

Right out of nowhere, Chase said, "I'm pretty disappointed in this meal."

Anderson thought, *Oh shit, here it comes.*

Then Chase said, "I was really looking forward to the Norwegian spaghetti."

He laughed. "I told Joey what was in it and he said he'd pass."

Anderson said, "Cooking this meal I found everything I wanted but the onions. They must have gotten left at the store."

Scanton said, "You're fuckin' A right they got left at the store and that's where they're staying."

When supper was over, everyone dumped their dishes in the galley sink. Anderson ran up and got Reed's plates and brought them back down. Scanton was holding Uncle Charley in his lap, stroking her ears. The big old cat was upside down.

Scanton told Anderson that fresh water is fairly precious on the boat and explained that there was a big nylon bag under the sink.

"We throw everything into that bag and run it up on deck and blast the dishes with the wash-down hose. You boil up a pot of fresh water to rinse them off and that's it." Anderson started loading up the bag and Chase stopped him. "You cooked. We'll get this part."

Scanton pitched in and took the dishes up on deck. Anderson followed him up. When they got out on deck, he switched a large plastic toggle-style switch, and the deck hose started pumping seawater. He laid the nylon dish bag down, poured some Dawn over them, and started spraying the dishes. "This is the *Jubilee's* power dishwasher. It works great!"

Tom walked around the outside of the pilothouse and climbed the side stairs up to the forward deck and walked up to the bow. He sat down with his back against the whaleback just ahead of the forward post. He took out a cigarette and lit it up. The *Jubilee* was slowly lunging her way toward the east-southeast at a steady eight knots. You could feel the solidness of this great old wooden boat under you. As she moved through the water, you sensed the power and weight of her mass. She was constantly shifting even though the seas were calm. There was a gentle ground swell coming out of the south.

Anderson loved the gradual roll and settle of the boat as she dipped downward in a gradual soft falling off from the crest of each swell. To him it felt like running your hand down a woman's shoulders and bare back and up to the smooth rise of the cheeks of her naked bottom. The *Jubilee* embraced you and allowed you to settle down into the trough of a sea and then gently raise you up again over the top and down the other side. The motion was hypnotic.

The sun was setting off the stern and the colors were magnificent. The Portland skyline had almost completely disappeared, but you could see the distant twinkle of the city's lights.

Anderson looked into the pilothouse and Reed was still on the wheel. He was looking right at him, and when their eyes made contact Reed smiled and gave him a short wave. In this brief instant he felt that there was a chance that he was where he really belonged. He knew he wanted to be here with his friend aboard this fishing boat and ready to face the challenges of the North Atlantic.

Anderson sat for a while out on deck, enjoying his smoke, watching as the sun disappeared from the western sky. They were underway and headed for the fishing grounds. All was well with the world.

A few minutes later, Scanton appeared at the wheel and motioned for Anderson to come into the pilothouse. When he topped the stairs, Scanton said, "Come over here a minute. Everyone takes wheel watches aboard here, and I've got to show you how all this works."

Scanton started with the radar. "This unit here is a Raytheon twenty-five-mile. Take a look in there so you can see what I'm talking about." Anderson put his face up to the Radar cone and peered in. He could see an electronic line sweeping around the surface of the screen.

Scanton said, "Those lighted up spots on there are everything from steel sea buoys to boats. Land shows up as it would if you saw it on a chart. The signal only reflects off the highest point though. You're only seeing the leading edge of the land, not the whole thing."

Anderson was still looking at the screen. Scanton said, "That big dot in the middle of the screen is us. See how that screen is divided up into rings? That tells me how far away we are from land or another boat."

Scanton adjusted the sensitivity knobs to clear up the picture a little.

"That straight red line you see coming from the middle of the screen is the EBL. That stands for electronic bearing line." Anderson watched Scanton turn the knob like he was adjusting the hour hand on a clock. "The EBL is really important when you're running this boat at night. What you really need to know is that when you're on watch, you're constantly adjusting it. You twist this dial until the red line intersects with those targets."

Scanton spun the dial to one of the bright dots on the screen. "See how I made the line go through that target? That's either a boat or a buoy. If that mark follows the line to the center of the screen that means that they're going to hit us or we're going to hit them."

Anderson said, "Okay, I think I understand. It works like a mechanical tracking device."

Scanton said, "Right. If you see that happening you need to come get one of us. Everybody's life depends on how good a job you do using that EBL, including yours, 'cause if you fuck it up, I'll kill you."

He emphasized his point further, "A lot of fishing boats have disappeared out here without any call for help and no goddamn report being filed. These foreign tankers and freighters won't report running somebody down. They know that they'll have to face a big bullshit international maritime trial. Those guys will just steam right on through, like nothing ever happened."

Anderson was already nervous about taking his first watch because what was expected of him was starting to sink in.

Scanton moved on to another piece of equipment. "This machine is a North Star LORAN-C. It's for navigation. The receiver picks up signals that get fired from LORAN stations up and down the coast. The signals come through one of the antennas mounted up on the mast. That unit converts the signals into two sets of bearing numbers that show up on that screen there."

Scanton grabbed a notepad he kept near the wheel. "I write down the numbers and use them to plot a course on the chart." He pointed toward the chart table. "The charts are all divided up into a bunch of numbers and lines called TDs. If you follow those lines to the point where they cross, you can see the exactly where we are."

Scanton reset the LORAN. "This boat works off combinations of bearings from the 1 9960W chain to the 2 9960X chain.

He stepped away from the controls and showed Anderson how the numbers could be found on the chart and where they intersected. "See this spot right there? That's where we are . . . exactly."

Scanton grabbed a Snickers bar and tore it open. "We got two pieces of electronics on board that show the depth. One of them is this Kalvin Hughes combination flasher and paper machine. Give me one of those Cokes over there will you?" Anderson reached in a cooler on the deck and passed him one.

"A guy that knows what he's doing can read the depth of the water and tell the difference between the hard and soft bottom."

Anderson said, "What are we on now?"

"We're going over real soft mud. See how thin that line is?"

"Ya, I do."

"If that marking on there was real dark black it would mean we are up on the hard bottom."

Scanton took a drag on his cigarette. "That Hughes is a really good machine. You can pick up schools of fish on it too. It takes some practice to know what you're looking at. I've been watching one these bastards a long time. The old man's got one on his boat just like it." Scanton showed him some of the markings he was talking about. Anderson looked completely confused. "Don't worry about these fine reads. All you have to know is the depth so we don't run aground while you're running the boat."

The next piece of electronics was a square-faced screen with two sets of flashing lights set up in a circle. Scanton said, "This Raytheon flasher is more of a backup. The good thing about it is you can glance at it quickly and read the depth and see when the bottom was beginning to shoal up. The top flasher is the surface. The second one is the bottom."

There was a scanner on board, but he told Anderson there would be more time spent on that when they started fishing.

The *Jubilee* had a Wood Freeman autopilot. There was a jog lever that looked like a small handle mounted on a box. With the autopilot engaged, the hydraulic steering system of the boat could be run by that little lever instead of turning the wheel.

Scanton said, "This autopilot works from a gyro compass. It's right there on the dashboard. That thing hooks up to the hydraulic steering and turns the rudder. That autopilot steers this thing on a straight magnetic course. It does it better than a man can."

Anderson said, "Really?"

"See . . . right now we're steering 120 degrees."

There was a dial on top of the gyro control that could be set on a course bearing. "If that dial is on 120 degrees, that's what we steer,

120 degrees. The boat will follow the exact course set." He turned the dial back and forth and you could feel the boat respond. "That jog lever overrides the autopilot, so you can change course a steer away from a problem quickly."

Scanton took a drink from his soda. "Some captains refuse to let the crew use the autopilot on night watches. With the autopilot doing all the steering it's a lot easier to not pay attention and fall asleep."

Scanton told Anderson to keep an eye on the compass bearing and never completely trust the electronics. He explained that all this stuff is to help navigate and not there to run the boat.

He showed Anderson the switches used to light the boat, the running lights, and the masthead light. He demonstrated and explained the towing light located on the top of the mast. He explained that it would be lit when they had nets in the water at night so that other vessels could see that they were in the act of fishing. With nets off, the boat is attached to the bottom, limiting their ability to turn away from their course.

The gauges were next—oil pressure, water temp, reverse gear pressure and temp, alternator, genset gauges, the tachometer, and the various bilge alarm indicator lights. He explained what to look for on each of them.

Anderson hoped to hell he could remember all this shit. He kept thinking about all the people he knew who said stuff like, "That guy's just a dumb ass fisherman" or "It doesn't take any brains to go fishing for a living." That kind of thing always came out of the mouth of some jerk that had never set foot on a boat in his entire life. Anderson was beginning to see that fishermen make life and death decisions every day they're out. The guys on board depend on each other to survive.

Scanton snapped off the autopilot and swung out of the captain's chair. He told Anderson to take the wheel and steer 120 degrees. Anderson stepped up and took hold of the three-foot-wide spoked wheel. Scanton said, "I'm going to let you use the autopilot on your watches, but I want you to feel her in your hands for a while."

Anderson was surprised at how little you turned the wheel before the boat would start meandering all over the place. A gentle pressure to port or starboard was all it took, just a touch really. Scanton started laughing at him when he got started. The boat was zigzagging all over the place. Scanton said, "Where the fuck you goin', kid? Greenland or Florida?"

"Fucked if I know." Anderson laughed at himself. A minute later Reed came up into the pilothouse with two big bowls of ice cream. He handed one to each of the men. "I thought there was a no-drinking rule on this boat. You can't bullshit me. I know when there's a drunk at the wheel. Now where's the fuckin' beer?"

Scanton said, "Christ, Reed, we ain't tellin' you. You'd drink it all up before we made the fishing bottom."

"Okay, you cheap pricks. Now I see how it is. Who's up next? Joe, me, or Pat?"

"I'll send sweetheart here down to get you. Go turn in for a couple hours." Reed went down to the fo'c'sle. Anderson was finally really feeling the *Jubilee*. He had straightened his course out and was steaming along in a pretty straight line. Scanton told him to snap out the pull toggle that said "autopilot" on the small engraved plastic plaque mounted just under the switch.

As soon as Anderson pulled the switch, he could feel the autopilot take over. The boat made some short quick adjustments and fell back into its steady rhythm, moving to the east-southeast at 120 degrees.

Scanton said, "Check out the radar screen now."

"That mark you're seeing is another dragger headed back toward Portland."

"How can you tell that's another boat and not a can or offshore buoy of some kind?"

"Here's why. I know where we are and there aren't any buoys down here. Second, I can tell that the target's moving and, third, by the shape of it. It takes time to learn what you're looking at. In the beginning don't be afraid to ask somebody. Don't try to play the fuckin' hero."

They ate their ice cream and continued their steam east. The sun had set, and the pilothouse was aglow with the soft green light given off from all the electronics and gauge lights.

After they set their bowls aside, Scanton said, "Look right there." He pointed to a fairly bright mark on the radar screen. He reached up and spun the EBL until it intersected the target.

"Remember I showed you the electronic bearing line? Just spin this until it hits the target. If it follows the EBL line toward the boat, we collide. If it doesn't, we can't hit it and it can't hit us."

In a few minutes, you could see the target separate from the EBL line. Tom understood how it worked now.

"Take the jog lever a little to starboard." Anderson did as ordered. He reached for the small lever in front of him and pushed it to the right. You could feel the boat start to turn in that direction.

In just a few minutes they were comin' down on the mark. "Look, there's another mark about a mile ahead of this one. Now I know it isn't a can because, again, I know where we are. It isn't a boat for two reasons. One, it's not moving, and two, it's not a large enough target to be a boat. See that's the trouble with being a new guy—you can't tell what those marks mean, and you won't be able to for quite a while." Scanton took a drag on his cigarette. "Sometimes even after all these years we fuck up too, in the rough weather. Anyway, these look like highfliers to me. That's those tall buoys the gillnet boats use to mark their gear. They make such a bright target because they have radar reflectors on them. Now if I was a prick, which I'm not, and I had the birds overboard, I'd go run right over them buoys just to fuck those guys up. But I ain't and we don't and I won't."

Anderson laughed at Scanton's joke. "Just jog away from that target. Remember, with the paravanes down, we're eighty feet wide from tip to tip." Anderson worked the jog lever until they were clear of the highfliers.

Scanton told him to switch the jog lever back to the center spot. He did, and the *Jubilee* immediately corrected course and picked up her heading at 120 degrees, east by southeast.

They steamed for another hour or so, not saying much. They just smoked and made idle conversation. Scanton finally said, "I hear Uncle Charley greeted you sharply when you startled her today."

"Yes, she did. I had no fuckin' idea in hell what was up when she spit and jumped across the galley deck in front of me. I nearly shit myself. I'll admit it."

"Well, you're not the first man to be scared of a little black pussy."

Scanton took a drag from his smoke. "Uncle Charley's a wicked hot shit. She's been on this boat since she was a kitten. I suppose Skip told you I named her for my uncle Charley."

"Yes, he did."

"He was a wicked good shit too. When I was younger, I started fishing with my old man on the *Gloria Walker*. I was constantly getting fired. Show up on the boat drunk—fired. Show up late—fired. Talk back to the old man—fired. Fuck up on the boat—fired. I was one fired motherfucker when I was younger. Every time I got fired, my mother would call my uncle Charley and talk him into taking me with him. He'd tell me he wouldn't put up with any of my bullshit. I knew he meant it, so I didn't give him any."

Anderson said, "That sounds real familiar."

Scanton continued, "He taught me most of what I know about fishing. The old man and Uncle Charley fished together for years. My old man is just as good as Charley was, but he never had the patience to teach me. He expected me to know everything he did just because I was his kid. You know what I mean?" Anderson was quiet but nodded his head.

"Uncle Charley taught me to mend twine, to splice wire, and to fix practically anything on the boat. Fishing, he showed me his hot spots and swore me to secrecy. He used to tell me that if I ever told my old man about them he'd come chop my balls off, and he meant it too. I'll never tell anyone about them unless my boy goes fishing. You probably don't know this, but my uncle was lost at sea four and a half years ago."

Scanton lit up again and took a deep drag. "When we all found out he was gone, it was the worst time in our family's life. My mother couldn't stop crying. She would scream at the old man and me and say that the same thing was going to happen to us.

"Dad was off fishing that night about twenty miles to the westard of where Uncle Charley was. They were on Cashes Ledge. It was ten below zero and a friggin' nor'west wind ripping at about twenty-five knots, and all the boats were making heavy ice on their decks and rigging. Hard call, not so shitty you had to come home, and shitty enough so you should. Uncle Charley decided to tough it out. They were all on some decent fish, according to the old man. He had talked to him on the VHF twenty minutes before he disappeared. Dad said he was his same old self. He didn't sound nervous or shook up at all. I was on one of my fired deals then, so I was supposed to be fishing with my uncle that trip, but I was home in bed sick as a bastard with the flu. I'd have been on board with Charley if not for that. Marshall Grimes was only thirty minutes south of him when all this shit happened. He and the old man went nuts when they couldn't raise him on the radio. Marshall had just hauled back so he got there first. He told me his guys were breaking ice off the *Teresa Lynn* the whole steam over there. The old man hauled back quick as he could and ran for where Charley had been fishing. He never found anything."

Scanton was silent for a minute or so. "They called it in to the Coast Guard, but they didn't have any luck either by the time they got down there. The old man kept jogging back and forth over the area where they thought Uncle Charley had been. He wouldn't give up. When the Coast Guard did show up in the 41, they put a light on him, and he was so iced up they ordered him in. He tried to get them to take his men aboard so he could stay down there alone, and keep hunting. The skipper told him to get his ass ashore. He gave in and jogged home with the *Teresa Lynn* on his stern. I guess he and Marshall never spoke a word on the trip home."

Anderson could see the pain in Scanton's eyes as he was telling him his story. He pressed on. "Uncle Charley, Sammy Towns, and a green guy named Terry Hoftman, all gone. That Terry guy . . . it was his first trip offshore, and I'm home puking my ass off."

Anderson was quiet because there was nothing to say. After a long pause he said, "I'm sorry, Joe. That really sucks."

"Worse than that, kid, worse than that."

They rode silently for about half an hour more. "I stayed pretty much drunk for a month or so after that. The *Gloria Walker* and the *Teresa Lynn* both lay at the wharf all that time. We'd had a funeral service and all that shit, but it didn't change how we felt about things. Christ, I thought my mother was going to die herself."

Anderson said, "Jesus, Joey, it must have been awful."

Scanton said, "Then one night about five o'clock this guy named Chase Bowkman showed up at my apartment door. He asked for Mr. Joseph Scanton. I told him that was me and asked him what the fuck he wanted. That son of bitch handed me a check for $83,000. He told me it was an insurance check for the lost boat *Blue Star* owned by Charles Walker. You see, Uncle Charley had gotten divorced from his wife twenty years before. The insurance guy told me my uncle had made me the beneficiary of his estate. I didn't know what to do. Karen was blown away. Later on that night I went over to my mother's house. My parents were sitting in the kitchen when I told them what had happened. The old man was shitfaced. He had been most of the time since my uncle died. I showed him the check.

"Dad started to cry a little. 'Your Uncle Charley loved you like you were his own boy, and in some ways you were.' He wiped his eyes quickly. 'What are you going to do with the money?' I told him I'd already decided I was going to buy a boat. When my mother heard that, she said, 'Of course you are!' She ran out of the kitchen and started sobbing again."

There was a long pause as the two men reflected on what had just been said. Scanton stirred in his chair and lit up another smoke. He tossed the Bic lighter up on the dashboard and exhaled. In the soft glow of the lights from the electronics and gauges, the pilothouse had an eerie look.

They steamed along in silence for quite a while, Scanton not wanting to talk and Anderson not knowing what to say. Finally, Scanton took a deep breath and said, "Go down, wake up Skip, and then turn in."

Anderson said, "Okay, we'll see you tomorrow." There was no reply. Scanton just stared out at the ocean through the forward windows.

"*Jubilee, Jubilee,* This is the Portland Marine Operator on channel 16. Please switch and answer on channel 24 for traffic."

Scanton switched the VHF to 24.

"This is the *Jubilee* standing by Portland Marine."

The operator said, "Go ahead with your call, ma'am."

"Hi, Joey. It's me." It was Karen calling from home.

"Hey, what's up?"

"Nothing really, I just called to say good night. I wish you had come home before you left. Over."

"I got so busy and we're trying to make the bottom by daylight. You know how it is. Over."

"I know but Little Joey likes to say good-bye when you take off after having been home so long. He gets used to seeing you. Over."

"I tried calling you. The fuel and ice bill didn't get paid, and I had to sign a note to get off the wharf." He was trying hard to keep the anger out of his voice.

"I thought I mailed it. You're just going to have to start taking care of some of this stuff yourself."

"Jesus, Karen, I'm working my ass off to keep us going. I think you can mail a check for me. Over."

"I'll look for it tomorrow. I'm sure it's here somewhere. I didn't call to fight with you. Have a safe trip and call me when you get in. I love you."

"Okay, thanks for the call. I love you too. The *Jubilee,* clear with Portland Marine Operator. Back to 16 and standing by."

Scanton was glad she called.

CHAPTER 9

Anderson went down into the galley and walked forward toward the bunks. He peeked under the galley table, and he could just see Uncle Charley's right front paw hanging out of her bunk. He said, "Good night, Uncle Charley."

The *Jubilee* had a door that divided the forward fo'c'sle from the galley. He opened it and entered the bunk area. He saw that Reed was asleep in the top port bunk. He stepped over and shook his shoulder. He came to immediately. Chase was asleep in the lower starboard bunk with a book lying across his chest. His reading light was still on. He had been reading a Stephen King horror novel. He never budged when Reed got up. The steady loud thrum of the 1271 helped the men sleep undisturbed. Reed pointed to an empty bunk. Reed went out to the galley and poured himself a coffee. After he had a smoke he'd head up to stand his wheel watch.

Anderson grabbed the sea bag that he had left on the galley deck earlier and tossed it up on his bunk. He climbed up into it, making sure he didn't wake Chase. As he lifted himself up, Chase groaned and rolled up on his side. His book fell off his chest and onto the deck, but he remained asleep.

Anderson flipped on his bunk light. He slipped out of his dungarees and pulled his shirt and socks off. He opened his sea bag and pulled out his nylon sleeping bag and spread it out. There was a pillow left on one end of the bunk; he grabbed it and put it under his sleeping bag up at the open end. The pillow was filthy and smelled like sweat and grease. He'd have to do something about that later. As long as he didn't actually have to put his head on the thing he thought he could stand it. He stretched out and closed his eyes. Sleep came almost immediately.

CHAPTER 10

Scanton was looking out at the black of night as they worked their way toward the Outer Falls. Something caught his eye off the port bow. He saw a yacht with powerful deck lights illuminating a boat in the distance. He grabbed his binoculars to check it out. It was almost like he was spotted by the boat the second he got a good visual on it. The lights went out and the boat disappeared. He did see that a small lobster boat that was tied off the yacht was suddenly released. It separated from the larger vessel and vanished into the darkness. That was strange, but he had seen a lot of strange things at sea. He never gave it another thought.

Scanton felt good to be back out on the water. The tie-up had taken a toll on him not only financially but also emotionally as well. The frustration of facing the endless mechanicals and watching the days fly by without any source of income was a lot to take. It was over now, and they were on their way back down to the fishing grounds. He was thinking about Karen.

He reached for a fresh cigarette when all the lights and gauges on the *Jubilee* flashed and went out. The engine was still running, but he couldn't see a thing. He slowed the boat down to an idle but left her in gear. The autopilot and all the electronics on the boat were shut down. He reached for the handheld spotlight and turned it on. There was a weak yellow light coming from its lens. He thought, *Goddamn it, Skip, I told you to get batteries for this thing at the store.* He felt his way over to the companionway leading down to the galley and made his way down below. He could smell the powerful odor of burning plastic and rubber. He knew that there was an electrical fire somewhere aboard the boat.

He moved slowly toward the fo'c'sle. Reed was sitting at the galley table. Chase was up in a second and pulling his pants on. "Jesus, Joey, what's that smell?"

"I think there's an electrical fire aboard and I gotta find it!"

"Fire aboard the boat" are the most dreaded words a fisherman can hear. A boat the size of the *Jubilee* with all the oil, fuel, and propane gas aboard can burn to the water line in less than thirty minutes. Reed said, "What do you want us to do?"

"Well, for starters . . . get the batteries for the flashlight I told you to get at the store."

"You never said anything to me about getting batteries." He knew damn well that Scanton had told him to get the batteries.

Scanton said to Anderson, "Kid, go up on the shelter deck and turn off the propane tanks."

He turned to Reed. "It doesn't matter now, Skip. Come on, Pat, let's check things out in the engine room. Skip, you stand watch up at the wheel and keep jogging southeast. Whatever you do, don't kill the engine."

"Okay, Joe." Reed led the sprint up the stairs.

Scanton grabbed the flashlight and crossed over to the stairs leading down to the engine room with Chase on his heels. Halfway down, the light went out completely. The smoke and fumes were so thick they couldn't see anything. Chase was first to spot the sparks and smoke coming from the main circuit breaker located just to the right of the fuel tanks. All the electrical for the entire boat went through that wall-mounted panel.

Scanton hollered to Chase to tell Reed to shut down the Genset so that no raw power would flow through the breaker box. Chase sprinted up the stairs and gave Reed the order, and he immediately shut down the generator. By the time Chase made it back down into the engine room, Scanton had sprayed the circuit breaker box with the fire extinguisher. The box was still smoking, and the plastic inside was still burning. Chase brought a handheld spotlight that ran from a cigarette lighter with him. He took his pocket knife out, cut the wires off the end that plugged into the cigarette lighter receptacle, and stripped the wires back to expose the copper ends underneath. In the dark he felt around to find his toolbox. When he located it he reached in and found two wire clips that he remembered were in his top tray. He attached the clips to the wires and slowly made his way over to the bank of batteries, being very careful to not become entangled in the running engine. He got on his hands and knees and felt around the battery terminals. In the darkness and smoke he had to remember which was positive and which was negative. He clipped the leads to the battery and the spotlight burst to life.

Scanton went over to the toolbox and got a big screwdriver and started removing the cover from the circuit breaker box. It was red hot! Chase handed him a clean rag that he'd dipped in bilge water to keep Scanton from burning his hands. When he got the plate off, all the breakers were burned to a crisp. There was a 100-amp breaker and eight 20-amp breakers in the box, all of them ruined. Joey yelled over the load engine noise, "We got any replacements for these breakers on board?"

"I got one of the 100 amp and two of the 20 amp!"

Scanton hollered, "We got to wire everything into the 100-amp breaker. It ain't up to code, but it will run the electronics and the lights . . . Let's get at it!"

Up in the pilothouse, Reed sent Anderson back down to the galley to open the forward hatch to get some of the smoke out of the boat. Even though Tom recognized the seriousness of the situation, there was no feeling of panic on board. Joey clearly had things under control, and he felt totally confident that they would come through this okay.

Reed was jogging slowly ahead when a giant spotlight lit up the *Jubilee*. A loud voice came blasting over a speaker.

"United States Coast Guard Group, South Portland . . . Light your vessel immediately! I repeat light your vessel immediately!"

Reed ran out on deck and hollered back that they were broken down with no electrical power.

The Coast Guard boat responded, "Prepare for boarding, *Jubilee*!"

The 41 settled up alongside them and tied off. Armed Coast Guard men boarded the boat. The young officer leading the crew was named Groves. He had a nasty attitude, and it showed in his walk as he approached the pilothouse with his service revolver drawn. The 41 had the *Jubilee's* decks completely lit by her floodlights. Lt. Groves climbed up into the pilothouse and asked Reed if he was the captain of the boat.

"No . . . I'm a deckhand and so is he," he said, pointing to Anderson.

Lt. Groves said, "Where's the captain?"

"He's down in the engine room with the engineer working on the circuit breaker box. We had a fire down there, and it shorted out the electrical system throughout the boat."

Lt. Groves turned toward one of his men and ordered him to get a light and head down into the engine room. The officer returned his service revolver to its holster.

A guy named Ricky Simms made his way below to the engine room. It was no shock to Scanton to see the young coastguardsman standing in his engine room. He was actually really glad to see the kid.

Simms said, "Can we be of assistance, Captain?"

Scanton replied, "We got things under control here. We got a replacement breaker, and we should be good to go pretty soon."

Simms could see that everything was in order as the dragger captain had stated and went back topside. Scanton was relieved. He didn't want anyone looking too closely at the way he and Chase were jury-rigging the wiring so they could get underway. Scanton motioned to Chase that he was heading up to the pilothouse to meet with the Coast Guard people. He knew that Chase had everything under control with the wiring job. When he got back up above, he sent Anderson down below to give Chase a hand finishing up.

The young officer shook Scanton's hand. "I'm Lt. Groves, Captain Scanton. I need to review your documentation certificate to verify that you are in compliance with Coast Guard regulations."

Scanton got his briefcase from a shelf and retrieved his documents for review. Lt. Groves looked the papers over very carefully and passed them back to him. The life raft and survival suits had already been inspected. A few minutes later Anderson came up into the pilothouse and said, "Pat's ready to have you start the generator." As soon as it was running, Chase flipped the breaker switch, and all the lighting and electronics aboard the boat came back to life. They were ready to go again . . . disaster averted.

Lt. Groves said, "A word to the wise captain . . . a thorough inspection of all systems is recommended after a long tie-up. Remember that in the future." Scanton nodded his head but he was thinking something else.

After the Coast Guard men were back aboard the 41 and had released the lines, Scanton hollered, "Asshole!" No one could hear him.

The *Jubilee* resumed speed and got back on course for the Outer Falls. Chase, Anderson, and Scanton went back down forward to hit the bunks. Anderson snapped off his light and lay back in his bunk and within seconds was fast asleep.

CHAPTER 11

It had been five hours, but to Anderson it felt like five minutes. Reed was shaking his shoulder. "Wake up, honey, it's time to set out."

Anderson jumped down from his bunk and threw on his clothes. He sat down on Chase's bunk and put on his sneakers. Chase was already at the galley table having coffee and a morning smoke. It was 4:00 a.m. and still dark out. Anderson said, "Mornin', Pat." Chase didn't look up but said, "Mornin'." There was a big pot of coffee going on the stove. Anderson grabbed a mug and poured a cup. Reed took his and one for Scanton and headed up to the pilothouse. Anderson sat down at the galley table with his coffee.

Uncle Charley was eating some dry cat food from her bowl under the table. Her tail was swinging back and forth in wide sweeps.

After a few minutes, Chase said, "You play any cribbage?"

Anderson said, "Ya, I do, but I'm no good at it."

Chase thought, *Now here's some bullshit. Anybody who's good at cards never admits it, and someone who is no good at it always brags about how great they are. What's this fucker up to anyway?*

Chase said, "We'll just see a little later then, won't we?"

"Okay, but I don't want you takin' advantage of my inexperience."

Chase rolled his eyes. "Okay, here we go. The shit's getting pretty deep in here." He stood up from the table. "Let's get this party goin'." He climbed the pilothouse stairs with Anderson right on his heels. Scanton was at the wheel and ready to get the gear overboard.

Scanton said to Anderson, "Hang on a minute."

Reed and Chase headed down on deck. Scanton wanted to have a word with his green man.

"You pay attention to everything those guys tell you down there and do whatever they say.

85

Don't try anything on your own. Do stuff slowly and deliberately and you'll be fine. I'll be watching everything from up here. I got my loud hailer, and I'll let you know if you get fucked up. Okay, kid? Go ahead down now."

CHAPTER 12

C hase had lit up a Marlboro as soon as they were out on deck. He looked over at Reed and said, "Here we go again. It's been kinda nice not having to listen to Captain Joey and his loud—and I emphasize loud—hailer giving orders from the bridge."

Reed said, "I haven't missed it myself, but if we fuck with that hailer again, he's going to kill us. You know that, right?"

"We . . . don't have to fuck with it. Just follow my lead."

When Anderson got down on deck, Chase said, "First thing we've got to do is to flip off the emergency bypass switch to the net reel before we can set off."

Reed's eyes narrowed a little, and a puzzled look came across his face. After a second he said, "Oh yeah, Christ, yes, I almost forgot about that."

Chase said, "Kid, inside there on the companionway bulkhead there's a switch. It's the one furthest to the stern. Go flip that up."

Anderson went in, found the switch, and flipped it. The shelter deck lights went on. He could see Chase and Reed from where he was, and they appeared to be studying something. Reed said, "Flip it up and down again." The lights flipped on and off.

Anderson walked back out on deck and Chase said, "Shit, that emergency bypass switch is fucked up again, goddamn it. Go down in the engine room and get the wire cutters off my bench down there."

Anderson turned and headed back through the companionway. He flipped on the engine room lights and went down below. He got the wire cutters and bounded back up the stairs. He flipped off the engine room lights. He wasn't about to forget about that switch again. Chase stopped him at the companionway just as he was about to step on deck.

"See that brown wire there with the black tape on it? Cut that off at the tape and run them wire cutters back down below and put them back where you got 'em."

Anderson did as ordered. He cut the taped area with one quick snip and headed down below again. He had no idea that he just snipped off the lead wires to the loud hailer speakers. There would be no orders coming from the bridge this morning.

As soon as Anderson was out of earshot, Chase looked at Reed and laughed. "This ought to be goooood." Anderson was back in a flash with the engine room lights off. Chase said, "Flip that switch now." The lights flashed on and off. Chase said, "Okay, kid, you got it. Great job! We can set off now."

It was just first light and the wind was south-southwest, light and variable. The sun was rising off the horizon and the sight was beautiful! Chase was thinking, *No matter how many times I've seen a sunrise at sea it always startles me.* To all the guys that go, no matter how young or how old, the sunrise is like the sight of a naked woman. It's impossible to take your eyes off it.

Reed stepped back toward the stern and lit up a smoke. Chase turned to Anderson. "Now listen up, kid. This is important. You pay attention. Don't touch a fuckin' thing unless Skip or I tell you to. All the shit on this boat is dangerous, and I don't want you trying to help me out by doin' something you don't know how to do and get somebody hurt. You're going to be in the stern with me most of the time. While I'm doin' shit, you've got to be the nod man. When me or Skip says to you 'now,' you look back at Joey so he can see you, and you nod your head up and down. Go ahead, try it."

Anderson started nodding his head up and down. Reed was standing where Anderson couldn't see him and was laughing so hard he thought he was going to piss himself. He had to turn his back and pretend he was coughing.

"Then if we say 'okay' you give Joey the okay sign. It's as simple as that. You got it? I know you want to get up to being a full-share man on this boat, and that's the way you do it. See, Joey can't run this boat and get these nets off without signals from the deck. If you're on the ball and give him the right signals, he'll be happy as hell. Trust me, kid, just pay attention to me and Skip. Now give me your okay sign." When Reed saw Anderson make the okay sign, he ran for the rail laughing.

Anderson said, "I'm ready."

Chase looked over to Reed, who was now standing at mid deck. He looked up at Scanton and snapped his head back in one quick motion. The *Jubilee* immediately slowed to an idle and Scanton engaged the PTO.

Reed said, "Okay, Pat, let's get the doors outboard and hung." He went over to the main winches and engaged the lever that would raise the starboard door off the deck.

The main wire ran back toward the stern and through a hanging bollard and was shackled to the door. He engaged the winch and raised the starboard door to the two blocked positions, jammed tight against the bollard.

With the door up, Chase said to Anderson, "Help me push this door out from the boat." When Reed saw it was clear, he backed off on the winch and let it settle down outboard of the rail. Chase grabbed the chain used to hang the door attached to the gallous frame and inserted it into the door bracket. As it was lowered, the weight of the door came off the main wire, and it was hung. They repeated the process on the port door.

Chase said to Anderson, "Here's how this is going to go. We're setting the flatfish net first. That's the one on the port net reel. You can see that there are twin net reels on this boat. We're going with the flatfish net for these first few tows." He walked back to the stern. "We gotta get these back straps overboard first. See that big pile of chains on deck? They attach the doors to the net." Anderson watched as Chase sorted through the chains. He was making sure there were no twists or kinks in them. Chase showed Anderson where he should be standing during the set off. "Nobody should ever get between the net and the ocean. Stay inboard of the gear all the time we're setting off and hauling back." Then Chase positioned himself in the alleyway between the two net reels.

"This clip on the end of the back strap is called a lobster claw. Your job is to pass that clip to me when I ask for it. That's what hooks the net to the doors while we're towing."

Anderson was looking at the doors and how they were rigged. Chase said, "These doors are what make the net fish. They hold it on the bottom and keep it spread open so it can suck up whatever is in its path. What they do is pull slightly away from each other and spread the opening of the net to its widest possible position."

Anderson said, "What do those things weigh anyway?"

Chase said, "They're close to a thousand pounds each."

Anderson was told to stand in the corner of the starboard stern rail with the lobster claw in hand. When Chase motioned to him, he reached past the end of the net reel and handed it to him. Chase secured it to a hook located just under the stern rail. Then he broke the chain over the rail to lessen the strain and ordered Anderson to start feeding the back straps overboard.

Reed was doing the exact same thing on the port stern corner.

Chase said, "Skip, Joey wants us to pull the net off the reel and look it over before we set off."

The net had been lying on the reel for over a month and a half and the inspection was standard operating procedure. The net reel control levers are located on the frame that supports the reels. Scanton had already engaged the hydraulics from controls he had in the pilothouse.

Reed pressed the port net reel lever forward, and the reel began to turn slowly.

Chase said, "Hey, kid, give Joey a wave and a nod." Anderson immediately did as ordered. He could see that Joey had the radio mic in his hand and was talking to somebody. Chase kept chuckling to himself.

Chase said, "This first part of the net coming off the reel is called the cod end. See that brass clip on the end of it? That's what keeps the net closed up so this fish don't fall out. The cod end is where all the fish wind up when we haul back at the end of the tow."

Anderson helped Reed and Chase pull the net out on deck. Reed told him they needed to pull apart and spread it as wide as they could. "What we're looking for is any holes or rips."

They worked through the chaffing gear, the extra heavy poly twine that's attached to the cod end mesh. It protects the net from being torn to shreds while it gets dragged over the bottom.

Anderson stopped and said, "How about this? Does this matter?" Chase came over and took a look. "Of course it matters. Is that big enough for fish to fall out? We call that a bullet hole. Run up forward and get me a needle full of twine. It's in a milk crate right on deck beside the companionway. It's the double green twine . . . Oh, hey . . . and give Joey an okay sign on the way up." Anderson ran up forward and found the needle of twine and gave Joey the sign. He hustled back.

"Stick your fingers in the twine meshes and pull it open and away from me. Then just hold it." Chase whipped out a sharp knife and started cutting the net in every direction. Anderson was watching and thought, *He's making a little tear into a big one.*

He said, "What are you doing now?"

"I'm sorry, kid, but I haven't got time to teach you now. Basically we call this a three legger, to a sider, back to a three legger." Chase flashed through the mending in a few minutes and cut the finish knot. He slipped the needle and twine in a plastic pocket taped to the net reel frame.

After Chase fixed the hole, Reed kept slowly backing the net off the reel. They kept spreading it out on deck. Chase explained that after the cod end came the lengthening piece and then the bosom of the net. Now Anderson could see the foot rope, the head rope, and the cans; but they would leave all that part where it was. Reed stopped the reel and changed direction so he could wind the net back on again.

He wanted to keep the net as smooth and flat as he could. Reed kept it going until the cod end was picked up off the deck and back up on the top of the reel. Then he reversed the reel again and the cod end fell overboard and began to pay off the stern.

Reed said, "Hey, Tom, you better give Joey an okay sign so he doesn't fuck things up down here." Anderson thought it was strange that Joey was still talking on the radio. It must be something important.

After he gave Joey the sign, Reed and Chase started laughing again.

He couldn't figure out what was so goddamn funny. Anderson said, "He's been on the radio a hell of a long time. He must be talking to somebody important." Chase smiled and said, "Ya, he is! He's talking to some very fucking important people."

Scanton could see the net going overboard, so he increased the boat's speed a little. Reed continued to let the net go. The cod end, the lengthening piece, the belly, the bosom, and the wings were all paid out and set overboard in a matter of a few minutes. Anderson watched intently when the cans that floated the top of the net went over and then the large roller sections. He couldn't believe that all this stuff didn't get snarled into a big ball.

They ran off seventy-five fathoms of ground cable. Chase said, "Once the ground cable's overboard I've got to attach this hammerlock to the eye in the end of the ground cable. One side has four links of chain that connect to another hammer lock and a flat link." Anderson was now completely lost. Connecting and unconnecting all these lengths of cable and chain must be how they transferred the net from the reels to the doors. He could see the sections of chain slowly peeling off the reel. Then Chase connected one of the ground cables to that lobster claw at the end of the back straps. Now he could see how they made the switch. This was complicated stuff. He hoped he would be able to figure it out in time.

Reed kept backing the reel off and the chain began to slacken. At the end of the chain was another flat link and lobster claw. Chase passed it to Anderson, and he attached it to the flat link on the door like he had been told to do. Chase yelled, "That chain section is called the idler. Once we hook that up, the doors can be released and we can set off the main wires."

With Reed on the port winch and Chase on the starboard, they started releasing the big cable. Chase said, "That wire is marked in twenty-five-fathom and fifty-fathom sections with that heavy white poly twine. We can watch the marks and keep the wire even as it rolls off the winches. We are going to set off over 325 fathoms of wire." The final job was to set the brakes on the winches. When Reed and Chase set those brakes, Anderson could feel the tremendous strain run through the whole boat as the gear began to be towed over the bottom. The cables snapped and popped; the bollards rattled and shifted. Anderson stared at the wire cables where they entered the water. He realized now that it was finally happening. The *Jubilee* was fishing.

Anderson had a great rush of anticipation. He couldn't explain it, but there was this powerful feeling of confidence that they were going to catch a lot of fish.

The boys stood on deck, watching the cables. They hauled out cigarettes and lit up.

The boat was rigged with a set of speakers, separate from the hailer that Scanton had hooked into a tape deck. He gave them a full blast of James Brown . . . "Whoa-oa-oa . . . I feel good . . . da da da da da da da . . . I knew that I would now . . . da da da da da da da . . . I feeel good . . . like i knew that I would now . . . so good . . . so good . . . I got you!"

Chase stepped back and could see Scanton dancing around the pilothouse and motioning for them to come up.

When they were all up in the pilothouse, Scanton, with a half smile on his face, said, "You fuckers think you're pretty funny, don't you?"

Chase said, "Whaaat?"

"You know whaaat. You bastards cut the speaker wires off to my loud hailer again, didn't you?"

"No, Joey, we didn't do it. He did it." He started pointing to Anderson.

"Just because you fuckin' smart asses didn't want to listen to me tell you what to do, you cut my speakers off again."

"No really, Joe, we didn't do it. It was your green guy, I'm telling you. I saw him do it!"

Scanton said, "Yeah, and you two assholes tricked him into it."

Anderson now understood that he had been the butt end of a big practical joke.

Chase started laughing. "How'd you figure it out, Joey?"

"I have to admit that the kid here was doin' pretty good fooling me with all the okay signs and all that bullshit, but when I finally caught on, I yelled over the hailer, 'Why don't you three guys come up here and suck my dick?' Then the kid gives me the okay sign and nods his head yes. I knew what was up. I know you two are queer, but the kid don't look that way to me."

They all laughed. "You did so good on supper last night, let's see how you do on breakfast. You two assholes can go rewire my fuckin' speakers."

Chase and Reed headed down on deck, and Anderson went back to the galley. When they stepped out of the companionway, Chase said, "That was pretty funny. Look, it doesn't take two of us to rewire those speakers. Why don't you do it, and I'll start getting the deck ready for haul back?"

Reed said, "Yeah, makes sense to me. I'll give you a hand as soon as I get this thing fixed."

Reed finished up his rewiring job on the hailer speakers in a just a few minutes. "How you doing with your list, Pat?"

"I've got to do my engine room rounds, but if you'd hit the fishhold and smooth out the ice and start a bed in number five, that would be good."

Reed nodded his head. "Done."

Anderson had a great breakfast underway. He'd fried up a pound of bacon and a dozen sausage links, made batter for pancakes, and prepared a big bowl of scrambled eggs with cheese. He had a large stack of pancakes going when the boys came in off the deck. There was a fresh pot of coffee on the stove, and both men went for their mugs immediately. Chase went up to the pilothouse with his coffee. A few minutes later Scanton was seated at the galley table. Anderson grabbed a plate, filled it up for Chase, and ran it up to him. "Looks good, kid, but I'm still going to kick your sorry ass on the cribbage board."

"I'm sure you will. I told you I was no good at it."

When Anderson went back down to the galley, Scanton and Reed were talking seriously. They stopped the minute he came down the galley stairs. He didn't think much of it though.

Scanton restarted the conversation. "So you and Skip grew up together?"

"Yes, right in Falmouth. We met as kids and have hung out with each other ever since. I taught him everything he knows about lobstering."

"Shit," Reed said, "I had to teach you how to fill a bait bag, for Christ sake."

Anderson smiled. "Did you grow up in Portland, Joey?"

"No. I grew up in Gloucester, but we moved here when I was about fifteen. I wanted to quit school and go fishing, but my mother put her foot down. I graduated from high school by the skin of my teeth. I was what they call magna cum lucky. I started fishin' right after I got out though on the old man's boat, like I was telling you last night. I was a kid with a pocketful of money living in a man's world long before my time. Don't get me wrong. I've got no regrets. I think that this is the life I was cut out for. I'll keep doin' it too, unless I go to jail for killing two asshole crew members for fuckin' with my loud hailer." They laughed. Scanton got up and put his dishes in the sink.

"I'm going to change Uncle Charley's litter box. If you want, bring the dishes up on deck. I'll blast them off."

"Okay," Anderson said, "I'll run them up to you." Before Scanton headed up the stairs, he said, "I guess you guys have got the deck ready, Skip. Why don't you take the tow and let Pat take a break? He had last watch."

"Sure thing, Joe." Reed lit up a cigarette and dumped his dishes in the sink. He went up to the pilothouse to take the helm. When Anderson came back up to the pilothouse Reed was sitting in the captain's chair with his feet up on the dash, reading one of his X-rated paperbacks. He asked him how he knew where he was supposed to be going.

Reed said, "Take a look at this." He stepped over to the chart table where Uncle Charley was spread out full length, soaking up the sunshine. He picked her up and threw her over his shoulder. He showed Anderson where they were. The Outer Falls was marked on the chart. He moved his finger a couple of inches to the left and explained that Joey had taken bearings as they were approaching the bottom to pinpoint their location. "Joey has a book of tows with the bearings for all of the Gulf of Maine and Georges Bank listed out."

He explained that this tow was set up from a point to the northeast of the Outer Falls on the ninety-fathom grounds. Reed put Uncle Charley back on the chart.

"We went to the top of the tow and set off. We'll tow toward the south, southwest at 210 degrees for about four hours, and then we'll haul back. We're just about two hours into the tow now."

Anderson asked, "Do we set right back off again as soon as we get the fish aboard?"

"Yes, as soon as the bag is dumped, we'll set it off again. We're fishing steady while we put the fish down in the hold. We'll be going twenty-four hours a day from now on, until we get a trip aboard. If I were you, I'd go hit the bunk for a nap while you've got a chance."

"Thanks, Skip, I'll see you in a bit."

"Yup." He went back to reading his skin book.

Scanton came back up through the pilothouse with the bag of dishes in tow. He asked Reed how he was doing. He said, "Catching fish, Joe, I'm just trying to catch some fish."

"Wake me in an hour." Scanton headed down to his bunk.

"I'm turning in for an hour or so before we're ready to start to haul back."

"Okay, Joey, I'll see you when you get up."

After Anderson finished up he climbed up into his berth and couldn't believe that he was going to take a nap at eight o'clock in the morning.

The *Jubilee* rose and fell in her usual smooth steady motion. He could feel the drag of her nets holding her back as they swept the ocean floor. All the captain and crew had to do now was wait and see what they would have in the nets.

Reed, up at the wheel, was thinking about his life in general. One thing he was absolutely sure of was that he was not going to wind up doing this shit for the rest of his life. He'd seen plenty of old guys running their old boats long past their prime. He'd been around enough of that to know that wasn't for him. Year after year these guys scraped together just enough money to get by. They worked twenty-four hours a day while they were at sea. Bullshit. No fucking way was he going to be burned up and tired like Joey's old man. These bastards always got their hands and legs all screwed up with arthritis in the end. Fuck that. Life was too short. He was smarter than that and he knew it. Screw those asshole teachers over at the high school, always trying to make him look dumb. He'd show them all where the bear shit in the buckwheat before this was over. Everyone needed a big break in life, and his was all planned.

He kept an eye on the trawl clock. He'd wake Joey in about forty-five minutes. All he had to do was keep his mouth shut, do his job, and see how things played out. That's exactly what he was going to do too. It wouldn't hurt to make some money off this boat while he went through the motions either.

After forty-five minutes had passed Reed went to wake Scanton. There was another hour left on the tow before they'd haul back. Scanton came up and hopped up into the captain's chair. He asked Reed if he'd seen anything showing on the Kalvin Hughes. Reed reached over and picked up a length of paper coming out of the bottom of the sounder and tore it off and handed it to him.

Reed said, "It looked like some decent schools a couple of times like here and through this section here." Scanton looked at the dark clouded scratches over a fair amount of the paper.

He didn't comment.

Reed went down below and poured himself a fresh cup. "You want coffee, Joe?"

"Yeah, give me one, and get those guys up, will ya?" Reed woke the other two men. "We're about ready to haul back. Let go of your dicks and get your asses up on deck."

Scanton was set to go. "Let's see how they look, boys." The threesome headed down to the deck to haul back. Scanton gave the deck a loud blast of "Shake it up, baby."

Reed and Chase started the haulback. Reed was on the port winch and Chase was on the starboard. There was a feeling of excitement on board. Everyone was anticipating a good set. Chase had a wise-guy look on his face and said to Anderson, "Hauling back is just like setting off, only in reverse."

Anderson smiled and said, "Thanks for that."

Anderson stood by and watched the powerful winches wind up the 325 fathoms of wire. He could see the wire marks as the cable wound past him onto the giant drums.

The main winches ran steadily for about twenty-five minutes, but that time flew by. He felt like a ten-year-old on Christmas morning. The three door marks appeared on the wire, and he knew that the doors and net were close behind.

Scanton ordered, "Get ready to hang the doors."

He slowed down the engine so the men could stop the winches with the doors tight against the hanging bollards. Chase motioned to Anderson to follow him to the stern.

They had to unhook the hanging chain from the gallous frame and insert it into the eye on the door. When Reed saw that the chain was in place, he backed off on the starboard winch and lowered the door until it was hanging from its chain.

They crossed over to the port side, and Anderson hooked up that door. Chase positioned himself between the reels, and Anderson unhooked the idler chain from the top section of the door and passed it over.

Scanton told Skip to run the net reel up a bit and then he gave the order. "All right, boys, haul her back!" He took the *Jubilee* back up to 1,600 rpm, and Reed engaged the net reel to full haul back.

The seventy-five fathoms of ground cables came on board quickly. Suddenly there was a wake breaking the surface a few boat lengths behind the stern. Reed hollered, "How about that!"

"It looks good to me!" Chase yelled back.

A massive swarm of seagulls suddenly appeared from nowhere. They were hovering over the full cod end being towed behind the boat. There were hundreds of birds swooping and diving. The screeching noise was deafening.

The reel continued to haul in the net. Scanton yelled over the hailer, "Skip, show the kid how to strap the bag . . . I want him doing it!" Reed told Anderson to run up and get his hooded oil jacket on. While he was gone Reed grabbed a piece of one-inch rope with an eye splice in each end. It was about twelve feet long. Reed, pointing at the net, said, "Look, when the cod end shows at the start of the ramp, you're going to wrap this strap around it. You crawl in under the reel to do it. Pass this rope around it three times. I'm going to back off on the jillson, and Pat will hand you a hook. You make sure that the hook is cleanly placed into the eye splices, and I'll start putting a strain on the bag. Put your hood up. You're going to get soaked."

Slowly the net began to wind onto the reel until the cod end was in plain sight. Chase hollered, "Go ahead, kid. Strap it up." Anderson went in under the reel and passed the strap around the net. He could see the huge bag of fish being towed off the stern. He made a second pass and a third and brought the two eye splices together. Chase passed him the jillson hook and he inserted it into the eye splices. Reed started the jillson, and it gradually began pulling the bag of fish up to the stern.

Chase reversed the net reel so the cod end could be pulled on board up the ramp. The seawater was pouring off the net as it was hauled higher and higher. Anderson thought the sight was glorious! The net inched forward on the deck under the reel and at the same time was being lifted skyward. This was a big bag of fish. Chase looked up at it and said to Anderson, "That makes my dick harder than Chinese arithmetic, right there."

Even though it was a calm sea there was always a slow roll going on this far from shore. Chase said, "Watch this, kid." When the net was raised high enough so that the bottom of the cod end cleared the checkerboards, he grabbed the length of rope hanging from the brass clip on the cod end. The net started to swing forward. He held onto the rope until the last possible second and then ran up and took a couple of turns around a cleat on a checkerboard bracket. The slack in the rope suddenly came too. The weight of the fish combined with the forward momentum of the bag snapped the pin out of the clip. Five thousand pounds of fish spilled out of the net and overflowed the decks.

Scanton boomed over the hailer, "Any you guys want to come up here and kiss my ass?"

All three turned around and gave him the finger. "Just checking to see if my hailer was working. Now you boys can set off again and then put our fish away."

They gave him the finger again.

"I know you love me, don't you, boys? Don't forget to count the baskets when you put the fish down. I feel another song comin' on."

Chase said, "It's a good thing them hailer speakers only work one way. I'll try to remember the count, unless I'm brain dead."

CHAPTER 13

Scanton steamed the *Jubilee* into position for setoff and slowed the engine. Reed lowered the jillson hook while Anderson removed the strap. Chase drew up the cod end clip and hammered the shiv back into place with a wooden mallet made for the job. It took about ten minutes to get the net back on the reel. They set off immediately. The net, the ground cables, the idler chain, the back straps, the doors, and the wire were set out without a hitch; and the boat was fishing again.

Anderson unhooked the doors alone this time and unhooked the lobster claws for the transfer. The setoff was smooth. Chase was thinking to himself, *The kid's going to think this is easy duty. Wait till a shackle lets go, or we get a twist in something. He'll see.* Chase lit up another Marlboro. "Let's get the fish put away."

He opened the fish hatch cover and climbed down into the fishhold. Suddenly, orange scale baskets came flying out from down below. Scanton yelled, "Catch those things. I don't want them all stove up. They aren't free, you know." Within minutes thirty scale baskets were on deck and the picking and cleaning process began.

Reed turned on the deck hose and positioned it so that seawater was pouring over the fish. Every fish had to be thoroughly washed and loaded into scale baskets. Each basket held about eighty pounds. Chase kept a careful count so he could report back the numbers that were dumped into the pens so they could track the weight. Scanton had a logbook and recorded the yield of each tow with date and time. Chase took great pride in producing an accurate count so he and Scanton could estimate the fish on board within a couple of thousand pounds.

This first haulback was almost exclusively flatfish. When the baskets were filled Chase told Anderson to follow him down into the hold. Reed started passing baskets down. The fish had been loaded brown side up. Chase showed Anderson how to grab a scale basket and, in one forward motion, flip the basket so the fish landed in the pens white side up. He explained that stored that way, they lasted longer. "Some fish always flip over during the dumping, and we have to turn them over by hand. We are going to pack in two layers of fish and then cover them with a layer of ice."

After the flatfish were stowed they started cutting and gutting the groundfish. It took about an hour and a half to get all the fish below and iced. They had one chicken halibut and fifty pounds of lobsters. The lobsters got thrown into a big plastic barrel that had seawater running through it 24-7.

Chase's basket count was fifty dabs, twelve gray sole, and five mixed groundfish, bringing the tally to about 5360 pounds. He was pretty happy with that kind of weight from the first tow.

Anderson asked Chase to fillet a couple of haddock for him while they were washing down the deck and the empty scale baskets. With the decks cleaned up, they hosed off their oil clothes and headed up to the pilothouse.

Chase gave Joey the count. It was 11:30 a.m., August 6, 1982. Scanton made his first entry in the daily log.

When Scanton took back the helm, he showed Anderson where they were working. The second tow was underway, and Scanton decided to go through the gauges with Anderson another time so he was sure that he knew what to watch for. It was a clear sunny afternoon. There was a ten-knot wind coming from the southwest, and they were doing an end-for-end tow. The bottom was a consistent 90-95 fathoms. The autopilot was on and steering 210 degrees. They were working toward the west southwest. He gave him a rough idea of how the marks on the paper indicated the hardness of the bottom and places where you could see schools of fish. He said, "This is a fairly simple tow. Just keep her steady on where she's going. You really shouldn't have to touch anything. She's towing at 1,600 rpm and she'll be fine. If the net hangs up, we'll feel it. Don't panic and start grabbin' stuff. Somebody will come right up. Pay attention to these gauges. Keep your eyes open for other boats."

Anderson was nervous as hell, and he couldn't believe he was going to be standing his first watch while they were towing. He looked at Joey and said, "Okay."

"This time of year there's a ton of idiots out here running around that don't know their ass from a hole in the ground." Scanton said, "They think they own the ocean. Especially the sailboat jerks. I've had the stupid bastards try to wave me off course while we were towing for Christ's sake. They didn't want to lay off a tack. I'm not shittin' you. I swear they tell them in sailboat school that when they're sailing they have the right of way over the whole ocean. One of them starts coming down on you, get on channel 16 and scream at them if you want to. Then run them the fuck over. I had one son of a bitch report me to the goddamn Coast Guard once. The lieutenant that runs the 41 out of Boothbay Harbor knows me pretty good, and he read the guy the friggin' riot act. We've gotten drunk with him a few times up at the Thistle. Just remember this: when we're towing we got the right of way over the fuckin' pope."

Scanton got up and stepped toward the galley stairs. "We got about two and a half more hours on this tow. I'm going to get a quick nap. Keep your eye on the trawl clock and wake me up a half hour before haulback."

After Scanton left the wheelhouse, Anderson calmed down a little. He really liked this. Scanton seemed to trust him enough to let him stand a towing watch. He loved the feel of the boat. There was all this power and weight. Sometimes it felt like the *Jubilee* was alive and part of the hunt. He had already heard the other guys talk to the boat. They'd say shit like, "Come on, old girl . . . swing up into it." Or "All right, back off just a whisker now." The boat seemed to have a soul, and he was getting to know her a little now.

Just as he was settling in, the radio cracked to life. "*Jubilee, Jubilee,* this is the *Margret A. Wilson* . . . whiskey, tango, foxtrot 3999. Come in, *Jubilee.*" Anderson keyed the mic. "This is the *Jubilee.* Go ahead, please."

"*Margret A. Wilson* back. Switch up to 65."

"*Jubilee* up to 65." He switched the VHF.

A voice came over the air, "You on here, Joey?"

Anderson said, "Joey's down forward. Can I get him for you? Over."

"Oh Christ, no. I'm David Wilson. I'm running a tug a few miles inside you. I'm towing a barge up into Bath. Joey and I are old friends. He's probably getting his beauty sleep and Christ knows he needs it. Over."

"I'll let him know you called."

"Finest find. Where you guys going this time? I haven't seen him out here for quite a while. Somebody told me he was broken down. Over."

"We're going to work our way west. We're fishing now. I'm new on the boat, so I really don't know much about what's going on. Over."

Wilson said, "No shit . . . you're a green man? Are Skip and Pat bustin' your balls pretty good for you?"

"No, they're all right. So far I'm doing all the cooking on here. They're screwing with me a little, I guess, but as soon as they stop it, I'm going to stop pissing in their chowder. Over."

You could hear Wilson laughing. "All right then. Make 'em some good grub. The *Jubilee* has never been known for her upscale dining cuisine. The few times I've stayed aboard her on a drunk, all they had was peanut butter sandwiches. Over."

"I'll do better than that. Over."

"Finest kind then. Tell that little prick Joey to call me when he gets up. I'm going to let him buy me a couple of beers if we can hook up ashore somewhere. Over."

"Okay, I will. Over."

"This is the *Margaret A. Wilson* WTF 3999, clear with the *Jubilee* and standing by on 16. Over and out."

"*Jubilee*, clear with the *Margret A. Wilson*. Out."

Anderson settled back in the chair and gave the gauges the once-over. Everything was stable. He walked over and took a look at the paper coming out of the sounder. He didn't know what the hell he was looking at, but he looked at it anyway. He figured he might as well go through the motions. He started hunting around the pilothouse for something to read. No classics available. Skip had a large collection of *Hustler* and *Penthouse* magazines. Anderson thought they may be too sophisticated for his taste. He had to remember that "none of his book learning" was going to do him any good out here. He did find an old beat-up copy of a Western called *The Wilderness of the Rockies*. He thought why not? Next time he'd bring a book or two. Maybe Chase will be finished with his King soon.

The afternoon couldn't have been more beautiful. There was a slight southwest chop. The windows in the pilothouse were open, and the steady heartbeat of the 1271 was comforting. Anderson was relieved that his tow was going along well and was uneventful.

The Western was pretty good. Man finds horse. Man finds woman. Man shoots horse. Man finds another horse and shoots woman. Ahh . . . life in the Wild West.

Anderson kept an eye on the trawl clock, and before long it was time to wake Scanton and the boys. As he went through the galley, he gave a quick look at the chowder. It was doing fine. He walked back to the fo'c'sle and found Scanton in his bunk. He shook him awake and said, "Half hour to haulback, Joey."

Scanton sat right up and said, "How did it go? Everything okay?"

"Yes, it seems to be fine."

"Okay, good . . . good . . . I'll be right up."

Anderson sprinted back up to the pilothouse, not wanting to let the helm go unattended for any longer than necessary. He quickly scanned the gauges and all was in order. Scanton was up in just a few minutes and back in charge.

Reed and Chase came up and Scanton said, "All right, guys, let's see what we've got. The boys went down, got oiled up, and stepped out on deck. This time they got hit with a loud blast of "There ain't no cure for the summertime blues!"

Chase said, "Well, at least he's original, and thank Christ he's not singin' it." They had to admit they all got a kick out of it.

Reed said, "Let's get going." He gave Scanton the thumbs up, and the *Jubilee* slowed for the PTO to be engaged. Scanton took her back up to towing speed. Chase and Reed got on the winches and started the haulback. Anderson could feel the power of the winches under his feet and the tremendous resistance of the doors and net.

The tide had shifted, and you could feel the struggle between the manmade gear and the forces of nature. The tide was running hard against the starboard side, making it a little tricky for Scanton to hold the boat on a straight course.

The wire rattled and strained its way onto the drums. In roughly the same time as the last haulback, probably twenty-five minutes or so, the main wire was on board. Scanton saw the door markers appear and slowed the boat down to an idle.

Reed raised the port door and Anderson ran back and hooked it up. Chase did the same on the starboard side, and Scanton nudged the engine speed up again. Reed started the reel, and the idlers were unhooked from the tops of the two doors and hooked back into the reel. The back straps were unhooked from the ground cables' flat links and started to roll up onto the reel. A few minutes later, the net broke the surface.

Once more a beautiful wake appeared behind the *Jubilee*. Anderson was ready to strap the bag as soon as the net was up the ramp. Chase passed him the jillson hook, and the bag of fish was on its way forward under the reel. Reed stayed on the jillson as Chase backed off on the reel until the bag was set to come up off the deck. The wind had picked up enough, so the forward swing of the bag was stopped dead by the cod end line tied off on the checker board bracket. The fish spilled out on deck like a giant piñata that had been perfectly struck.

Scanton came on his hailer. "That bag looks about the same as last time, but I think I see more gray sole. I'm going to move over a berth and try it my way." He started singing in a loud voice, "Regrets, I've had a few."

Reed said, "Jesus Christ, boys, listen to that, and it's only the second tow." Scanton finished with a strong "I did it myyyy waaayyy!" He swung the boat around to the north-northeast bearing thirty degrees.

The deck gang had the net back in the water, fishing again in about forty minutes. They started putting the fish down. Scanton came over the hailer. "I want you boys to pull that groundfish net off the reel and check her over. When you're done, let me know."

Anderson was already starting to get into the rhythm of things and didn't have to be told his every move. This bag had thirty baskets of large gray sole, twenty baskets of dabs, ten baskets of hake, and a few haddock and cod. There were about sixty pounds of lobsters.

When they were done cleaning up, they tried to get Scanton's attention. Chase sent Anderson up to the pilothouse to get Scanton to slow the engine down to engage the PTO.

Chase said, "Frank Sinatra must have gone back to his dressing room." No one could see him from down on deck.

Scanton was actually bent over his charts, and Uncle Charley was helping him sort things out with broad strokes of her tail. Anderson said, "They sent me up to get you to engage the PTO." Scanton didn't move from the chart table. "Here's what we're going to do tonight. I'm going to finish this tow just south of the Daffy bottom. We're going to steam to the westard for about an hour. Then we're going to take that groundfish net and go up into the fifty-five-fathom bunches to the nor'ed of Cashes. Tell those guys I want them to go through that groundfish net real good."

Scanton took a quick glance at the LORAN. He slowed the *Jubilee* back to an idle and engaged the PTO and then took her back up to 1,600. Anderson went back down on deck and told the boys what Joey had said about checking the net.

Chase and Reed knew the net was in good condition. During the long tie-up, both nets had been off the boat and thoroughly reworked. They knew though that after a long time sitting on the reel at the wharf, it made sense to rewind it. Chase stepped back to the starboard reel and started paying the net off. Anderson and Reed were positioned up forward and began flaking it out on to the deck. They checked it over carefully and didn't find any holes or tears.

They rewound the net and were done on deck for a while. They headed up to the pilothouse and gave Scanton the tally for the second tow. It was five thirty in the afternoon. Scanton made his entry. They had approximately ten thousand pounds of fish on board in two tows.

Anderson said, "Guys, there's a big pot of fish chowder down on the stove."

Scanton said, "Yes? Sounds good. Get me a bowl with plenty of crackers, will ya?" Anderson went down to the galley and saw Uncle Charley sprawled across the galley table. He shooed her off and she gave him a very ugly look. He ladled up a large bowl of chowder, grabbed a handful of crackers and a spoon, and ran them up topside.

Anderson told Scanton that David Wilson had called while he was sleeping. The rest of the crew ate down at the galley table. Reed explained to Anderson that ground fishing up on the hard bottom, in the shoal water, was going to be very different from flat fishing the deep water, on the mud bottom. The roller sections are a hell of a lot bigger in diameter. That lets the net drag over much rougher bottom.

Reed said, "You'll see when we get going."

After supper they all just hung out and talked. It was going to be a long night, but no one felt like sleeping.

Scanton finished his chowder and sat back in his captain's chair. He had a lot on in his mind. He'd been thinking about home. He understood what his dad said about leaving the shore stuff onshore, but to him that was just avoiding his problems. It was nothing more than just hiding from them out at sea. There was no doubt that Karen had a lot to deal with taking care of Little Joey while he was gone. Lots of women had done it though. Most wives of offshore fishermen had closer relationships with their children than traditional mothers. It was sure as hell true for Joey and his mother. He could never describe to anybody how deep their relationship was or how he felt about her. The hard thing for fishermen's wives seemed to be that they were always waiting. They waited for the boat to come home. They waited for the settlement check. They waited for the call to come from offshore, and they waited for the weather report. Most women of fishing families would tell you they just waited their lives away.

It seemed to him that Karen was changing. Whenever he came home, she was always on edge. Their sex life had really suffered in the past eight months. She would let him have sex with her, but that's what it was, just an accommodation. He felt like she could have cared less about him. She was just going through the motions. It didn't help any that he was so tired when he got home. She used to come meet him between trips when they landed fish away from home, but not anymore. She always used their son for an excuse. He knew that was bullshit because she had a sister that wanted Little Joey anytime Karen wanted to leave him there. Elizabeth was single and loved her nephew to death. His mother would always take him too at the drop of a hat. He knew they were all just lame excuses. Lately, it had become worse. She seemed so nervous all the time. It was like she was drinking too much coffee or something. He couldn't believe the money thing. Karen was a trained bookkeeper. He'd met her when she did the books for Portland Harbor Seafood Products. She worked in the office and gave him his settlement checks back when the family sold their fish there.

It was crazy that somehow she had lost the fuel check. The envelope probably fell down between the seats in her car, but it wasn't like her at all. She would never let that go intentionally. They had to have the fuel bill paid to make a living, and she knew it. She wasn't stupid.

The whole thing was driving him nuts. He wished he could have talked to her before he had to go. He hated leaving on a fight. It made him worried and distracted. They always had such a great time together, but that was before his uncle Charley had died and he bought the boat.

Karen really wanted him to keep fishing on the *Gloria Walker* or someone else's boat and buy her a house. She kept saying if he didn't want to work with his old man, he could sign on as a captain for an owner. She even wanted him to think about going to Alaska and make some real money. Karen wanted more from life than he was providing for her. After this latest mess with the reverse gear, he'd thought about that, plenty. Sometimes he felt like he was in quicksand. Christ, he just wanted to get things under control. At least she had called him on the way out. He guessed that was something anyway.

This trip was going good so far, and maybe things would work out. Thank God the crew seemed to have settled down. At least Chase and Reed weren't ragging at each other constantly.

This goddamn swordfish thing with Skip . . . Christ, he didn't like the sounds of it. Charley Lambert on the *Katherine and Amy* had been doing it. He'd said it was easy money once you had the fish aboard. There was plenty of market for them. Everybody kept their mouths shut because if you knew about it then you were part of it. He'd ten times rather just catch a bunch of fish and tell Skip to shove his swordfish deal up his ass. He didn't know who Reed was lined up with. It made him nervous. He had to put his mind back on his fishing. He thought they should have a pretty good set this time too.

Going up on The Bunches in the fifty-five-fathom grounds was always risky business, but this was one of his uncle's hot spots. He'd been on board when he had taken some seven-thousand-pound bags out of there. Of course, he had been on board when he had ripped the whole bosom and belly out of the net too. Fuck it, he was going to try it anyway. If he ripped up the net they could always go back over to these flatfish tows anyway. He guessed he'd call David Wilson; he could always get him out of a funk.

Scanton picked up the mic. "*Margaret A. Wilson, Margaret A. Wilson,* the *Jubilee* callin'.""

"*Margaret A Wilson,* WTF 3999 back on 16. Where to, Joey?"

"Let's try 70."

"Seventy."

"How you doing, Joey?"

"Good. How you doin', old dog? Over."

"I'm okay, Joey. Things all right?"

"Yeah, David. No fish around, but that's par for the course. Over."

"Hey, I talked to your new kid this afternoon. He said he was pissin' in the chowder over there. I hope you didn't eat any. Over."

"That bastard better not have pissed in my chowder, I'll shit down his throat. Over."

"Oh Christ, Joe, I'm sure he was just screwing around with me. I hope. Over."

Scanton said, "It tasted like pretty good chowder, so I guess it was okay. Over."

Wilson said, "So when are we going to get together and get drunk again? Over."

"Jesus, Dave, I don't know. Since this breakdown I gotta catch up on fish, and playing with you is always bad news. Over."

"Aww, come on, Joey, a couple of nights in jail will do you good. Over."

"That's what you think. My old lady is ready to throw me out now as it is, and she don't like you worth a shit either. Over."

"Now you're breaking my heart. When my old lady threw me out it was best thing she ever did for me. I had the snip snip done before we broke up, and I'm king of the bar scene now. Just like high school, only no homework. Over."

"It sounds great, but I'll have to get back to you later on that one. Over."

"You don't know what you're missing. Over."

Scanton thought to himself, *Oh yes, I do.*

Scanton said, "Finest kind, Dave. I've got to wake the gang up for haulback. Catch you later. This is the *Jubilee*, clear with *Margaret A. Wilson*, standing by on 16."

"Okay, Joey. Hope the trip improves. *Margaret A. Wilson*, WTF 3999, clear with the *Jubilee*, back on 16 and standing by."

Scanton thought, *That's some way to live. Dragging barges up and down the coast of Maine days and dragging whores in and out of your house at night . . . greeeeat.* He checked the sounding papers over and saw fish in a couple of spots. It was time to get the boys up. He headed down to the bunks. Uncle Charley was laying on her back with her feet flopped back like she was under arrest. He grabbed her bowl and dished her out some chowder. "I hope he didn't piss in this, old girl. If he did, you got my permission to bite him in the balls." He went forward and got the boys off their bunks.

"It's haulback time, ladies. Let's go."

Scanton grabbed a coffee on the way through the galley and climbed topside. They all came up quickly.

"It's going to be a long night for everybody, so let's make it a good one, okay?" Scanton said.

Chase said, "Aye Aye, Captain Stuebing."

Scanton said to Anderson, "What's this shit about you pissing in the chowder anyway, kid?"

"Oh, I only did that in Pat and Skip's chowder, not in yours."

"Oh, that's okay then. Get the fuck out of here and go haul back."

On the way down, Reed said, "What's this pissing in the chowder shit about anyway?"

"Oh nothing," Anderson said. "I was just screwin' around with that friend of Joey's, Dave Wilson."

"Oh Christ, he's a riot, that guy. He got us all locked up in Boothbay a few months ago. He started a brawl and threw a chair at a window, and it smashed right through the frame. It hit a tourist's Mercedes outside. The cops came, and we were all drunk as hell, so we all got locked up. It cost him a couple of grand, but he makes big money with that tug of his."

They could hear the crackling in the speakers as Scanton was keying the mic. "Good evening, ladies and gentlemen. I'm broadcasting live from high above the decks of the fishing vessel *Jubilee,* located on the 12850 line east of Cashes Ledge, in the heart of downtown Gulf of Maine. It's the Captain Joey Show bringing you the great sounds of . . . *Mick Jagger* . . .

I can't get no . . . satisfaction, I can't get no . . . good reaction, I try, and I try . . . I can't get no, no no no . . . no satisfaction!

Pat said, "We gotta get that boy to a shrink. Now he thinks he's Casey Kasem. He needs a little rest in the loony bin."

A look came across Reed's face, and you knew he had come up with a brainstorm. He said, "Come on, you guys." All three stepped out where Scanton had a clear view from the pilothouse window. They simultaneously dropped their oil pants and dungarees. They presented Scanton a triple moon. He said, "Oh good, boys, you guys are finally showing me your intelligent side. Now I'm not gonna say which one, but one of you needs to do a better job wiping next time. Now haul back my net!" All four were laughing as the boys pulled their oil pants back on.

Reed and Chase stepped up to the winches, and Anderson gave Scanton a wave. The boat slowed to engage the PTO and came right back up to towing speed. The haulback went smooth, but there was one tense moment when the idler chain got inboard of the starboard door. Chase got hold of it, flipped it outside, and everything was fine. The net was heavily mudded up, but Scanton towed it around for a while, and it came on board pretty clean. Reed and Chase swapped off this time, and Chase ran the jillson. Anderson strapped the bag, and Reed tied off the cod end line on the checkerboard bracket and released the bag of fish perfectly.

The boys started to put the fish down. Chase and Anderson were down in the fishhold shoveling ice. They had to open another pen, so they dropped back to number six. They shoveled a bed in number seven, at the forward part of the slaughterhouse, for the groundfish. They put what hake they had on the bottom and worked up. Anderson tossed the empty fish totes out on deck to hose them out.

They had thirty baskets of gray sole, twenty-four dabs, and ten mixed groundfish totaling 5120 pounds. There were about ninety pounds of lobsters. It was 7:00 p.m. August 6.

CHAPTER 14

It was just before dawn on August 6 when Andy Brown rowed out across the anchorage in his dinghy to get aboard his leaky old skiff to go out and haul traps. The *Jubilee* and Skip Reed had been gone a couple of days now, and it was time to go. His skiff was twenty feet long and about six feet wide. It had been built in the 1940s. She was a flat bottom with chine-built sides. His hauler engine was an old rusted-out Briggs and Stratton engine that was hooked up to a chain-driven shaft and steel winch head for hauling traps. The hauling davit was constructed from an inch-and-a-half piece of galvanized water pipe. It had a snatch block bolted through the end so Brown could raise his traps high enough to pull them across the rail and into the skiff. It looked like an upside-down *L* with a pulley hanging off the short end.

Describing Brown's outfit as a filthy mess would hardly do it justice. It was worse than that. The boat had a severe leak on its port side just under the chine. He kept a load of bricks on the starboard side of the boat to try and keep the leak out of water so the skiff didn't sink overnight on its mooring. Brown was always relieved when he rowed out and found the boat still afloat. The rig was powered by an old beat-up forty-horse Johnson. The engine rings were pretty nearly burnt out, and it smoked like it was on fire until it had run about a half hour, and they swelled up from the engine's heat. There was a rickety trap table running along the starboard side.

Brown had four full bushels of bait on board. Today he was going to haul his traps and Reed's for the first time. He had three old wooden lobster crates aboard in anticipation of a big catch.

He pulled hard on the old Johnson, and after about six tries it sputtered to life. The outboard steered from an extended throttle handle that allowed him to stand up and see where he was going. He hadn't painted the bottom of his boat in two years, and it was pretty grassed up. The best he had done was to scrape it down some in the spring. Nothing supported grass and barnacles better than bare pine. Quite an outfit all and all, but it was Andy's, and he never had anything much better than this old skiff in his entire life.

He was twenty-five years old and lived in a trailer park near the water with his mother. He figured that they did all right together. She had a job over at the shopping center at a Zayre's retail department store, where she was a checker.

While the outboard warmed up, Andy put his filthy old oil pants on. He kept them stuffed up under his hauling table. They were covered in mud and dried-on bait juice.

Before he let go of the mooring line, he reached in his pocket and hauled out a joint. He found his trusty Bic lighter and fired up. He took a big drag, held the smoke in, and waited for the wonderful feel of the dope washing through his body. He loved his pot. There were no two ways about it. The stuff made him feel good, and Andy could never figure out what the harm was anyway. His mother was a big pothead back in her day. Every once in a while she still liked to split a bong with him. She used to smoke a ton of the shit, and nothing ever happened to her. She had a trailer, a job, a used Ford Fairlane. Andy was proud of his mother, and she was doing pretty well really.

He took another deep hit. His plan was to start hauling down toward Clapboard Island. The sun was just coming up, and it was time to go get started.

He tied his leaky old dinghy on the mooring line and let it go. He headed down toward the spindle on the northeast end of Clapboard Island. He had a dozen old wrecked traps in a row down there along the shore of the island.

He managed to get his hauler engine started, engaged the winch, and he was ready to go. He grabbed his first buoy and pulled the trap up to the snatch block on the davit and yanked the trap aboard. There was nothing in it. That might have been because there was a big hole in the back head of the trap. Andy was either too lazy or too stoned to even notice it. He rebaited the trap and set it over again.

The lobsters must hold a guy like Andy Brown in rather high regard. He supplied them with a twenty-four-hour sunken lunch wagon, and the price was free!

He hauled the other eleven traps. He caught three lobsters out of them and one was a one-claw. After the twelve traps were hauled, he got out his joint and went for another hit.

Andy loved hauling traps. The way he did it, things went along pretty quickly. He wasn't slowed down by all that measuring and banding stuff. He didn't put too much bait in his traps because he hated to waste it. He hauled through all his one hundred traps in about four hours. He had twenty-two lobsters. *Not bad,* he thought to himself, *a quarter pound to a trap.* Pretty good really . . . he bet there were a lot of guys doing a lot worse than that. He took another long drag on his joint. It was almost gone, but he knew he could roll another one later on.

Now he was going to go try some of Reed's gear. He'd get to see firsthand how well "Mr. Big Deal," Skip Reed, actually did. The traps he was fishing were out away from the island, in about eight fathoms of water.

Andy grabbed Reed's first buoy and hauled the end line. The trap broke the rail, and he pulled it on board. There were five beautiful select lobsters in the first trap. Andy was pissed. He thought that goddamn Skip Reed was just showing off. He was trying to make him look stupid. Who the fuck did he think he was catching all these lobsters?

Reed had his traps set up in five-trap trawls, a buoy on each end and ten fathoms of rope between each of the traps that were tied together in a line. He hauled the string for a total of fifteen counters. He was even more pissed . . . then it dawned on him. He was hauling these traps, not Big Time Reed. He was catching these lobsters, and he was the big deal now. It took a while for the information to work its way through Andy's cannabis-muddled brain, but when it did, he was firing on all three cylinders.

He figured that Mr. Arnold Reed was a million miles from here. That always gave Andy a laugh. Not many people knew that Skip's real name was Arnold. He thought the name fit him like a glove. He kept hauling, baiting, and setting. Out of the first sixty traps he had filled a crate with lobsters and started on the next one.

Andy was a little more generous with the bait on Skip's traps. Maybe that was his problem—that he didn't put enough bait in his traps. Even in his muddled state of mind, he did notice that Skip's gear did look in a little better shape than his. He kept working his way to the east. He managed to haul another sixty and had a second crate full and part of another. His skiff was leaking like a sieve from all the weight on board. He was almost over to Basket Island.

He ran up to another end buoy and hauled the string. He had twenty lobsters out of it. He thought, *I bet these traps have been sitting here for a month. That's why they're fishing so good.*

He didn't think it was funny that they still had bait in them if they had been setting over that length of time.

After he set that string back, right where he hauled it, he tied two crates of lobsters together and threw them overboard tied to the end line. They would stay alive back in the ocean. They would die in his skiff in the blistering summer heat. Andy hated to leave all those lobsters there like that, but if somebody screwed around with them, they'd have Andy Brown to reckon with.

From zero to hero in one short day . . . He ran off toward the power plant on Cousin's Island and hauled all the traps around the spindle down there and filled the third crate. He hauled some of his own gear near the red can off the southern side of Basket and had ten out of twenty-five from those traps.

Reed had three more strings further to the south but only got twenty more lobsters out of those. Andy mumbled, *What's going on, Mr. Reed? You losing your touch?* He ran over to the first two crates that he had left overboard and had all he could do to get them out of the water. With 360 pounds aboard, he thought his old skiff was going to sink right there. Water was pouring in like a wide open faucet.

He figured that once he got going, the water would run by and not leak in. It takes a lot of pot to come up with an interesting theory like that. He opened the Johnson up and headed for Portland. It was about four in the afternoon.

It felt like it took forever to get the boat up on a plane. The water ran in worse than it had before. He had to keep bailing while he was running along to keep the skiff from sinking. He had made it all the way down to Cow Island when he ran across a group of girls from the Yacht Club taking sailing lessons. With all this weight aboard, Andy's skiff was kicking up one hell of a wake. He had seen some of these girls before. There was a blonde girl with huge tits that he remembered from school. She seemed to be in charge of things. He used to see her sometimes at the Landing Market. She always looked at him like he was a piece of dog shit. He really didn't care. He loved the way she smelled. He ran his skiff straight through the whole crowd. He nearly rolled a few of the little sailboats over. The broad with the big tits gave him the finger as he went by. He thought, *Yes, you wish, bitch . . . you wish.*

Andy had to do some serious thinking now. He had to figure out how to divide up these lobsters. It was all a little foggy already as to who had caught what. He wanted to be fair with Skip after all. He had to tell Mr. Barnes whose was what. He thought and thought. Finally, he decided that the first 170 pounds were his and the other 200 or so were Skip's. As he kept on going he had second thoughts. That's not really fair. After all, Skip was giving him a chance and everything. Two hundred for him and a 160 for Skip was much better. He was doing all the work for Christ sake.

He kept motoring along and bailing. He thought maybe he'd take some of his money and get it fixed. Then he thought maybe he would just run up to the Harris Company and pick up a pump and a battery. Then he wouldn't have to fix the leak. He might even get some running lights for nights when he went down to Green Island to visit his cousin Danny.

Andy was thinking that he hadn't seen Danny in quite a while. He'd have to get down there to the island pretty soon and check things out. He kept looking at those three crates of lobsters he had. He knew things were going to be different from now on. Those pricks in at the lobster place won't be calling him names anymore after he showed up with this haul.

Probably he would get the bottom painted on this old boat too. He could always take the paint money out of Skip's share. Why the hell not? He was out here bustin' his balls to help Reed out!

He got far enough ahead on his bailing so he could light up and take a couple of hits on a new joint. He ran up past Fort Gorges and on into the head of Portland Harbor. He slowed down at the no-wake zone. He didn't want to screw around with any of these fake marine cops riding around in little speedboats with blue lights on their roofs.

Portland Lobster Company was on the Brown Street wharf. Harlan Barnes had a pretty good setup in there. He had three long floats linked together. You could come in and tie up, sell your lobsters, get your fuel and bait, and be on your way. Everybody that sold their lobsters there liked the fact that there was enough room so you didn't get driven out of there in a big rush. The real full-time guys, like Andy, hated to be rushed at the end of a long hard day.

He swung into the unloading float, tied up the skiff, and killed his engine. The guy that ran the unloading winch for Harlan was named Steve Warner. He was a major asshole and he started right in on Andy.

"Well, if it ain't Quarter Pound Brown. Somebody better let Barnsey know he's here, so he can call for an extra truck to lug his lobsters. I imagine he'll probably fill all the tanks we got in this place."

The regular wharf rats who always hung around the dock thought this was the funniest line they'd ever heard.

Andy said, "Why don't you shut the fuck up, Warner, and get a man down here with a basket for my lobsters?"

"Yes, sir, Captain Quarter Pound, but I don't think we got any bushel baskets left up here."

Andy said, "Quit fuckin' around. These lobsters are going to get weak in this heat."

"Big fuckin' deal. We can cook up your haul and make us up a lobster roll." After a few more belly laughs from Warner's audience, a kid slowly made his way down the ladder to Andy's skiff.

He and Andy filled the first one-hundred-pound basket and signaled for Warner to haul it up. Warner started to wander off. He was suffering from an apparent shock after seeing Andy with a hundred pounds of lobsters. He came back and rather reluctantly lowered the basket again.

Andy and the kid filled it. When Steve Warner had that basket hauled up, he yelled down, "Hey, Quarter Pound, who you luggin' lobsters for anyway?"

Brown said, "Just weigh my lobsters, fuckface, and keep your mouth shut." When the third basket came up filled and he needed it again, Warner finally stopped talking.

Harland Barnes came out on the wharf and looked down at Andy. "Pretty good day today for you, Andy. Come on up to the office when you get done. Steve here will put bait and gas aboard for you while you and I settle up. You want a Coke, Andy?"

"Yes, sir, Mr. Barnes."

Andy walked into Harlan Barnes's office and sat down in a chair in front of his desk.

"So, Andy, how does your slip read today?" Andy handed Harlan the slip. It had 374 pounds written on it. "Quite a catch today, Andy. How many of these lobsters belong to Skip?"

"Yes . . . they crawled pretty good where I've been fishing up around the Clapboard spindle." Harlan smiled and said, "Uh huh."

"Skip's share is a 120 pounds. His stuff has been setting a good long time. He didn't do as good as I thought he would." Harlan just looked at Andy. He had been buying lobsters all his life. He knew Andy was completely full of shit. "Does Skip get all of that 120 or just half of it?"

Andy missed the sarcasm in Harlan's voice. "No, all of the 120 pounds is his."

"Your total pay is $561. We have to take out $60 for your bait and $15 for your gas and oil. You need any gloves or bands?"

"I need a bag of bands."

"Now, Andy, you've owed me $500 bucks since last winter. I'm going to take out $250 from this haul."

Harland handed Andy $234 cash. Andy took the money but, by the look on his face, was pretty disappointed. Harland said, "Andy, you got a big chance here. Skip's letting you haul his gear for him. It gives you an opportunity to make some good money. You can replace some of that old junk you're fishing and make something of yourself. Just go to work . . . and Andy . . . don't blow it."

Andy dropped his head. "I know it, Mr. Barnes. I'll try. Thanks a lot. I'll see you tomorrow."

He left the office, wandered down the street to his favorite diner, and walked in. He stepped up to the lunch bar and ordered a cheeseburger, some fries, and a beer. He was sitting there enjoying his lunch when Drew Taylor walked in. He sat down next to Andy. "Hi, Andy, how's it going?"

"Good, Drew. How are you doing?"

Drew said, "I'm okay. You go haul today?"

"Yes, I hauled my stuff and Skip Reed's. I'll tell you one thing, for all Reed's big talk, he sure left me a big mess out there to try and sort through."

"No kidding. It's good of you to help Skip out like this."

"Christ, I can't take care of my own stuff. I'm so busy with all his junk."

"I'm sure Skip appreciates all you're doing for him."

"I sure hope so. This turned out to be a royal pain in the ass." Andy got done with his meal and pulled out a big wad of cash. He wanted Drew to get a good look at it. He peeled off a few bills and threw them on the lunch bar like this was par for the course for him. He said good-bye to Drew and left the diner.

He walked back over to Barnsey's and went out on the wharf. He looked down at his skiff. There it was, bait aboard and ready to go. There was a bag of lobster bands on top of his crates. He went over to the soda machine and bought himself a Coke. He was looking down at the water when he noticed a boat that he didn't recognize tied up at the end of the float. It was a nice looking twenty-eight-foot Jones Porter. It had the name *Frayed Knot, Green Island* on the stern.

That's just what we need—another new guy. Another beginner who would be chasing me all over the goddamn bay trying to figure out where I'm catching all my lobsters, Andy thought.

He sure was acclimating into the role of a big shot very quickly.

Then he saw something that really pissed him off. This new jerk had the same buoy colors as his cousin Danny. He thought, *What an asshole.* Danny was going to hit the roof when he heard about this little deal. He was just about to go down the ladder and give this guy a piece of his mind when he spotted this Oriental-looking guy taking pictures all over the place. He was a Joe Tourist all right. He had a stupid-looking baseball cap on with a flat brim, a sweatshirt that said "I Love Maine," and dark sunglasses. He was taking a bunch of pictures of this strange boat. "What kind of a name was *Frayed Knot* anyway?" Andy didn't get it.

This Chinese asshole was probably taking pictures for one of those Maine calendars that were in all the gift shops. This guy should take some pictures of Andy's boat if he wanted to show a real Maine lobster catcher.

He went down the ladder and turned to walk up and speak to the guy on the boat.

When he looked up and saw who it was, he almost dropped his Coke. It was Andy's cousin, Danny, standing aboard the lobster boat. He walked over. "Nice boat, cousin!" Danny looked up a little uneasy. "Hey, Andy, I been meaning to get a hold of you."

"Where the fuck did this come from?" Danny told Andy to come aboard. The boat wasn't brand new, but it was a beauty. It had one of those Hydroslave haulers, an eight-cylinder Chevy Crusader engine, and a Raytheon flasher. There was a string of brand-new four-foot lobster traps stacked across her stern. The boat had a blue plastic barrel with a deck hose pumping saltwater through it to keep lobsters alive without having to put them overboard.

"Okay, Danny, where did you come up with this rig?"

"I've been saving for it for quite a while. My old Hampton was getting pretty tired. The lobsters have been crawling pretty good for me, so I bought it."

"Okay, you lying fuck, now you tell me how you really bought it. Your traps are worse shit than mine. That Hampton is so rotten the rats moved off it two years ago! You're either stealing lobsters, hauling other people's gear, or somebody died and left you money. I know fucking A well that didn't happen because we're related, and if somebody died, I'd know about it!"

"Jesus, Andy, keep your voice down. Take a run down to the island and come up to the house tonight. I'll tell you about it."

Andy backed away. "Okay, cousin, but this better be good. I'll see you later on tonight then."

Danny started his engine and pulled away from the float. Those little V8s were as quiet as a mouse in church. Andy watched Danny pull out and slip through the water as smooth as hot lead through warm butter. For the first time in their lives Andy looked at his cousin with pure hatred. He was overcome with jealousy.

He wandered back down to his skiff and climbed aboard. He looked up and saw the tourist taking a picture of his boat. He waved at the guy and thought to himself, *Well, Chink boy, you're smartening up after all*. He started up his Johnson outboard and headed off back east, toward Green Island.

Once he got out of the inner harbor, he slowed down to an idle and rolled himself a fresh joint. After a few hits, he opened the outboard up and was on his way. It was a flat, calm late afternoon, and he was skimming across the bay at a good clip. His curiosity was at an all-time high. He couldn't wait to get down to the island to hear this story.

It took him about a half hour to make it down to the town float at Green Island. He took his bait tubs off the boat and put them on the dock. He found a piece of old canvas and some junk bricks and covered the bait up so the goddamn seagulls wouldn't get at it. He walked up the hill to Danny's house.

CHAPTER 15

The house was on a side street halfway across the island. It was a ramshackle winterized cottage that had belonged to Danny's aunt on his mother's side. He inherited the house because no one in the rest of the family, or in the rest of the world for that matter, wanted it. The place was practically falling into the ground.

Danny lived there with his girlfriend. Her name was Tammy. She had more tattoos than the woman in the tent at the Cumberland Fair. She never really left the house much other than to take her daily walks down to South Beach. She loved her pot and so did he. They were a perfect match on that score. Danny didn't really even like her very much anymore. He figured she was about as good as he was going to do though. The selection of females willing to live with a guy like him, in a hovel like his place year-round, was very limited.

When they first met, the sex was pretty good, but after the years went by, the interest diminished to the point of no return. Danny didn't give a shit. According to him there were plenty of broads in town who he hooked up with whenever he felt the urge. Since Tammy never left the island, that was no problem.

Andy trudged up the hill and down the side street to Danny's place. When he walked through the door, Tammy was coming out of the bathroom. She had taken a shower and had nothing on. Andy was totally unimpressed, and his standards were not very high to begin with. Sometimes having some clothes on created at least the possibility of something good. This completely eliminated any hope of that.

Andy said, "Hi there, Tammy. How are you doin', dear?"

"I'm fine, Andy. I'll be out in a minute. Danny's down to the store picking up some beer. If you want something to eat, help yourself."

The house was a total filthy mess. It reminded him of the trailer he and his mother lived in. He felt right at home. He moved some magazines and smelly old blankets off the couch and flopped down on it. About twenty minutes passed before Danny rattled into the driveway in his island beater. It was a rusted-out Toyota pickup truck. He slammed his way into the house with a twelve-pack under his arm. Without saying hello, he asked Andy if he wanted a beer.

"Sure, I'll have one."

They sat there in the quiet for a few minutes. Andy finally broke the silence. "Okay, asshole, where did you come up with the money for that new boat of yours?"

"All right, all right, the truth of the matter is this. I ran into some people who showed me how to make some quick money." He paused and took a long drag on his cigarette. "There's a lot of different people doing it. I got my chance, I did it, and I'm done with it now. I got what I wanted and got out while the getting was good."

Andy was losing his patience with Danny. "What the fuck was it, for Christ's sake?"

"I was transporting grass for some guy that I never heard of or ever met." Andy couldn't believe his ears. "You've been smuggling pot?"

Danny said, "I guess you could call it that."

"Holy shit, man. I can't fuckin' believe it. My pussy cousin Danny, a drug smuggler. How did you do it?"

"I told you. I met some people who set this up. I took the old Hampton and met this boat offshore a ways. They put the bales of pot aboard me, and I ran it up into the harbor in the middle of the night. There was a truck waiting for the stuff. They unloaded me in about ten minutes. I got $5,000 every time I did it, and I did it three times. That's it."

Andy was quiet. He had to process all this, and he wasn't exactly quick-witted anyway. This was a lot to comprehend for him.

Finally he said, "Somebody paid you $5,000 to run a boatload of pot up into the harbor, and you have no idea who this is for or where it goes. Is that it?"

Danny said, "That's it, nothing more, nothing less."

"How did you get out? No one's hassled you since you stopped?"

"No one gives a shit who does this, Andy. There are plenty of people who want to do this job. I've seen some guys out there lugging pot that you wouldn't believe. There's some lawyers and businesspeople doin' this shit. Big deals, I'm not shitting you, Andy, big-deal assholes, right from good old Portland, Maine."

It took Andy all of about three seconds to make his decision. "Goddamn it, I want in. I'm sick of fishing old ratty traps. I'm sick of being called names and being broke all the time. I want in, and you're going to tell me how to get in."

"No fuckin' way. You can't run off where you need to go in that piece of shit skiff of yours for one thing. Plus, you'd get caught playing the role with a big wad of cash, running your mouth off, and we'll all be screwed. I just don't trust you for something like this, no way."

"Well, guess what, motherfucker. You either let me in or I'll do some talkin' right now. If you think you're going to get a new boat and traps and leave me suckin' hind tit, you're stupider than you look."

Tammy came running out of the bedroom. "What's all the screaming about out here?"

Danny said, "It's none of your business, bitch. Get the fuck back in that room and keep your mouth shut." Tammy turned back and slammed the door.

Danny said, "Jesus, man. If I help you with this, you've got to change your ways. You have to do like I did. You've got to keep your mouth shut. You can't go strutting around acting like a big deal. There are some real hard-core guys in this racket. You have to mind your own business and not make a big show. I didn't spend a dime of this money for three weeks after I did the run. They told me to wait six months, but the lobsters were coming up soon. I figured, where I'm down to the island here, that nobody would give a damn what I did. No one pays that much attention to the shit that goes on down here anyway."

Andy said, "What makes you think I can't play it cool? I'm just as cool as you are. I've never had a break in my whole life. I'm going to pull this off."

Danny said, "What are you going to do for a boat to lug this stuff in?"

"Why don't we go get it in your boat?"

"There is no 'we' in this deal. I'm done and nobody's luggin' any pot in my new boat. I don't give a shit. I'll burn it first."

"Settle down, cousin. I've got another idea. I can figure out how to get that *Ruffian* of Skip Reed's. He's gone for at least another two weeks. How often can you make a trip anyway?"

"You can go every two days," Danny said. "That's what I did. You'll get ten bales. They're all wrapped up in plastic. Anybody wants to know what it is . . . its seaweed for packing lobsters when they ship them. You're going to piss your pants when you see the boat that brings the fuckin' pot. It's a goddamn yacht called *Invincible*. The thing is like one of those beautiful boats like you see at that floating restaurant place."

Andy said, "How do you know how to meet them?"

Danny lit up again. "I'm getting to that. I'll let you know when you got to go. It'll be after midnight. You steam down to the dumping grounds. You know that small buoy with the yellow light on it? You remember when we were kids and my old man took us fishing off near the cod ledges?"

"Sure, I do. I don't remember how to go though. Christ, we were just little kids."

"That's where you go anyway. I'll give you a compass course to steer. You got to have a radio that works, and you leave it on channel 8. You don't say anything."

"How do they know I'm down there?"

Danny said, "They'll be watching you. They've got all the best navigation equipment money can buy on that boat. You don't have to be right on the mark. They'll come find you. The first time I did it, it scared the shit out of me. I was going along and they just appeared. I was in total darkness in that old Hampton and *pow.* They lit me up like a Christmas tree."

Andy said, "No shit?"

"That's why you listen to the radio. They give you a compass bearing one time. That's serious now. You'll only get it just the once. You don't respond. You just steer that bearing, and they'll find you."

"How long are you running around down there?"

"The time changes every time. Once I steamed twenty minutes, the next time it was almost an hour. The last time they picked me up in fifteen minutes. When they do get to you, just pull into them. They put the pot on board you in about ten minutes. You steam back into Bug Light Point or wherever they tell you to go."

Andy said, "Bug Light, that's over by South Portland. That little light house rig, right?"

"That's it. There's a truck waiting for you right there. They'll get the shit off you. They'll give you your cash, and you just get out of there. That's it in a nutshell."

Andy was sitting there on the couch, reeling from what he'd just learned. He always talked a big game, but the thought of steaming way offshore in the middle of the night to get a boatload of pot scared the shit out of him. Running around after dark in the bay was one thing, steaming out into Hussey Sound in Reed's lobster boat was another. He and Danny sat there for a while, not saying much of anything.

Danny pulled out a Ziploc bag full of pot. He called Tammy out from the bedroom.

"Where are your papers?" Tammy went into the kitchen and brought some Zig-Zags into the living room and handed them to Danny. He rolled himself a joint and tossed the bag of dope to Andy.

"Is this some of the shit you lugged in?"

"No, I forgot to mention that. Whatever you do, don't touch the bales. If you want some pot for yourself, take these guys a dozen lobsters. They'll give you a big bag of shit for your personal use."

The three of them sat there on the couch and got totally wrecked. Before long they were all laughing and having a grand old time without a care in the world. Tammy had forgotten all about being screamed at. The night wore on. Tammy and Danny finally went to bed, and Andy curled up on the couch and passed out.

Andy came to just before dawn. Tammy came out of the bedroom, staggered into the kitchen, and put a box of Cheerios out on the table with a jug of milk.

Andy walked over and found a dirty bowl in the sink and rinsed it out. The dish towel was so filthy he decided he'd be better off not drying the bowl at all. He poured some of the cereal in it with a little of the milk. He found some sugar on the counter. It was so melted together he had to chop it up with a knife before he put it on. Danny came out of the bedroom a few minutes later. None of them spoke. After Andy was finished eating, he got up and walked out. Before he left he said he'd see them later. There was no reply.

CHAPTER 16

Scanton was up in the pilothouse waiting for the tally. He had reset his course to start the steam up into the fifty-five fathom grounds. A call came in on 16.

"*Jubilee, Jubilee,* this is the *Jessica.* You on this one, Joey?"

"*Jubilee* back. Right here, Rusty."

Rusty Martin was one of Scanton's closest friends. They had hung out together off and on all their lives. Rusty had been the best man when he and Karen got married. The boat he was running now was an eighty-five-foot autoliner out of Rockland. It was owned by a large Massachusetts fish company that ran under the trade name Betty's Sea Food. The inside joke was that the corporate name was Betty's Always Ready Fish Inc. The checks came under that name. Rusty always said he worked for Barf Inc.

Built in East Boothbay, the *Jessica* was beautiful. She had a massive shelter deck, and all operations ran under cover. Rusty fished her in brutal weather. The boat was only three years old and was state of the art. They ran twenty-four hours a day, usually for ten-day trips when they were inside and longer when they went to the Grand Banks. She carried an eleven-man deck crew and held three hundred thousand pounds of fish. The boat had a flash freezer on board, allowing for the long trips.

"Let's go up to channel 88"

"Yup, 88." Scanton flipped the radio. "You on here, Rusty?"

"Hey, Joe, where are you guys? Over."

"I'm down on the bucket bottom."

That was code for the spot where the *Jubilee* was fishing. A year or so ago he had given Rusty two buckets of lobsters in that general vicinity. The crew had tossed the covered five-gallon buckets overboard with a three-fathom line and a buoy attached. The *Jessica* gaffed it up, and there were lobsters for dinner that night. Boats never gave out their positions over the airways unless they were in trouble.

Rusty said, "Yes, I got ya. We're about three hours to the south-southeast of you, up on the hard bottom. Scanton said, "You doin' anything down there?"

Scanton knew immediately that would put Rusty and the *Jessica* down on Davis Swell.

Rusty said, "We should scrape a trip together."

Scanton said, "I'm getting ready to try up in the rock pile and rip up a net here in an hour or so."

"Yeah, I see. How the boys behaving? Over."

Scanton said, "The bastards just mooned me from the deck. I don't know why they do that shit. I always treat them with respect. Over."

"Yes, yes, Jesus, Joe, I know you do. Christ, half the guys on this boat are out on a work release program I negotiated with the state prison in Thomaston. One huge guy on here killed somebody. I nicknamed him Hacksaw. He's as big as a house and dumber than a hake. Over."

"Jesus, Rusty, you better be careful he don't get pissed off and kill you. Over."

"I know. I keep a billy club in my stateroom just in case. Over."

Joey smiled. "I forget you got a stateroom. I don't know if I should be talkin' to you. Over."

"What the hell you talkin' about? Uncle Charley's got a stateroom. You can crawl in there with her, for Christ's sake. Over."

"Thanks for that, Rusty. We got a green guy on with us this time, a friend of Skip's. He's trying his ass off. He's a decent cook though. Over."

Martin said, "Well, that counts for something. I don't remember the grub on that tub of yours ever being too good. What's the guy's name?"

"It's Tom Anderson. He's from Falmouth, like your buddy Skip. Over."

"Jesus, I know that kid. I used to see him skiing at that Hurricane rope tow place in West Falmouth, when we were growing up. He's a pretty good shit. We used to have a blast up at that friggin' hill. The Nortons ran that place for years. No shit . . . he'll be all right. Old Pat will shape him up or throw him overboard. Over."

"We'll see. School's still out. We haven't had any fuckups yet, and it's been flat ass calm. My mother could work on deck in weather like this. Over."

"Your mother could probably catch more fish than you too, so you'd better leave her home, before someone finds that out. Over."

"I know that, and she'd put in harder weather than me too. Over."

"All right, Joe, finest kind., I got Skip Cathcart with me, and he's going to take over so I can get some sleep. Over."

"Yeah, all right, Rusty, say hi to Skipper C. for me. I've had some times with that bird. Over."

"Yeah, Joe, haven't we all? Okay, I'll give you a shout later on then. This is the *Jessica*, clear with the *Jubilee*. Back to 16 and standing by."

"Okay, Rusty, watch out for old Hacksaw, and sleep tight in your stateroom, you big pussy. This is the *Jubilee*, clear with the *Jessica*, back on 16."

Scanton thought, that's a great site Rusty's got, but he had to catch a huge volume of fish to keep her going. If anybody could do it though, it was Martin. He was one of the best fixed-gear fishermen on the East Coast.

When the boys came up from being on deck they walked right through and headed down below, not wanting to disturb Scanton while he was talking with Rusty. Chase had written down the basket count on a piece of paper and slipped it to Scanton. It was nine o'clock.

They were down below at the galley table, and, by the sounds of things, having a game of cutthroat on the cribbage board. They had already cut for the deal and Chase was up. He reshuffled the deck and pushed the cards in front of Anderson. "Want to cut 'em?"

Anderson cut the cards. Chase said, "Thank you very much!" and pegged two holes for himself.

Anderson said, "See, I told you I wasn't any good at this."

Any experienced cribbage player would never cut the cards for a dealer. Chase dealt five cards to each player and one for the crib. The game was underway. The exchange was typical of the millions of cribbage games that had been played at sea for almost four hundred years. The game of cribbage was invented in the 1800s by an Englishman.

The pegging portion of the game, played on a board with two rows of 120 holes drilled in it, was always lively with personally insulting verbal assaults going back and forth from player to player.

A three-handed game usually had two players that were neck and neck and one that was lagging behind. There was no particular reason for this to happen. It just seems like that's how it goes.

You would hear things like, "I can't get a goddamn cut." That phrase always comes out as a plea to the cribbage gods. "Who dealt this fuckin' mess anyways?" is another line that gets used as the players studied their cards for discard, even though all the players, including the guy that said it, knew perfectly well who dealt the cards.

Luck at cribbage is a funny thing. It seems to come and go like the weather. When you were hot, you were hot, and with that went the bragging rights.

This is a game that should always be played sober. Many a famous barroom brawl has started over a superheated game of cribbage with a dollar-a-game bet on the table.

Scanton's rule on the boat was simple. Play all the cribbage you want but no money bets, period.

He had seen enough animosity, living in such close quarters under difficult conditions, to know.

What people did off the boat was their business. What happened on the *Jubilee* was his business.

The game progressed quickly, and they were on fourth street, very near the end. Reed and Chase were almost even, with seven holes to go for Reed to take the game. Both Reed and Chase had counted. Anderson was up. He was way behind. He flipped his hand over. He had eight points (no threat), and then he picked up his crib. That's the extra hand that goes to the dealer. He said, "Something is wrong here. I'm not sure about this." Chase said, "Oh . . . here we go."

Anderson shrugged and said, "You boys should check my count, but I think I've got a dozen here, and that would put me out!" Reed hollered, "Well, you fuckin' douche bag, asshole." Anderson said, "I know, I know, playin' against guys with your talent? It had to be a mistake. It probably won't happen again in a million years." Chase said, "Yeah, well, fuck you too, bub." They all laughed and got up from the table. Reed said, "Well, after that I feel like taking a big dump." He marched over to the head. Anderson said, "Great! Thanks for that report."

Chase said, "Don't plug that thing up in there and leave it."

Anderson headed topside. Scanton said, "Take her for a minute. I'm goin' get a sandwich or something. Anderson looked out at the ocean as the *Jubilee* made her way west. He knew from the atmosphere on the boat that things were going to be different on this new piece of bottom. Scanton had turned the VHF over to the NOAA channel to listen for a weather report. The National Oceanic Atmospheric Agency forecasts broadcasts on a special frequency that runs twenty-four hours a day. Fishermen's lives depend on the accuracy and the reliability of those forecasts. The automated message sounded like a talking robot. Anderson listened to the report intently. There was a severe thundershower moving toward Cumberland County from the west over Sebago Lake at a rapid pace. They were giving winds of twenty-five to thirty, with gusts up to forty. Small craft warnings were posted to all marine vessels within thirty-five nautical miles of Catfish rock.

Scanton brought his sandwich up with him. The *Jubilee* was steaming 270 degrees to the west. Their destination was a piece of bottom the fisherman called The Bunches just northeast of Sigsbee

Ridge. They had about a half hour's steam left before they made the bottom.

They were now over a hundred miles offshore. There was a great deal of moisture in the air, off the horizon, and it was refracting the moonlight into a multiple of spectacular colors. If you tried to paint it and got it right, no one would believe you.

Anderson asked Scanton what the differences would be in the groundfish net compared to the flatfish net. He told him that the length and size of the nets are similar, but that the mesh size is larger on the groundfish net. The major noticeable difference is in the size and weight of the roller sections. The groundfish net is designed to go up over the hard broken bottom.

"There's risk to going up on to this bottom, and lots of guys don't do it, but if we sneak in and out without a lot of damage, we could do okay."

"Pat was telling me that we'll see a lot more cod and haddock on this type of bottom."

"That's right, we should. The thing is when you're off on the mud and you get screwed up, you load up with mud. On this bottom, you can tear the belly out of the net in two minutes."

"Well, I hope that doesn't happen."

"You and me both, kiddo."

Anderson went back down forward, made a quick sandwich, and sat down at the galley table. Uncle Charley came out of her bunk and swarmed around his feet. He reached down and picked her up. "Well, Uncle Charley, how did I do for my first day on your boat?"

CHAPTER 17

Scanton yelled down, "Ten minutes to set off." They all headed up. Chase took a quick look at the paper machine. The lines were coal black, indicating the hardness of the bottom. There were clouds of what looked like dust above the lines. There were ridges and humps and drop-offs. The depth was fifty-six fathoms. Chase said, "This ought to be fun."

Scanton said, "There's a lot of tide running up in here. Let's get a net in the water."

Reed said, "How much wire, Joe?"

"Let's go 150 fathoms, Skip."

"Okay."

Reed followed Anderson and Chase down to the deck. There would be no music blasting, no moons would be flashed, and there would be no hailers unhooked. This piece of bottom was serious.

Everybody was oiled up and ready to go. Reed gave Scanton the wave and the boat slowed down. The wind had picked up to about eighteen knots and was coming out of the west. Scanton would be towing about 170 degrees across this bottom. The wind would be coming down on the *Jubilee's* starboard side. The tide was running from the east and was making up a fairly good chop. Joey saw that the action was getting heavy enough that he wanted the birds to the paravanes overboard.

"Hey, boys, before we set off I want you to launch the birds."

Chase and Reed picked up the heavy aluminum darts connected to the paravane arms by chain. The starboard bird was first. They heaved it overboard, making very sure they were both clear of the chain when it hit the water. They switched over to the port and let that one fly. Once birds were overboard, it took practically all the roll out of the boat. It was time to set off.

Chase was on the starboard winch and Reed on the port. The doors were raised from the gallous frames and unchained. The back straps were in position, hooked under the stern rail. Chase was operating the net reel. The cod end went off, and the rest of the net went overboard smoothly. The huge roller sections peeled off the net reel and into the water. The legs were next. They're only fifteen fathoms in length. The reel was holding back on the idler chains. The back straps were reattached when the idlers were hooked back to the top of the doors and ready for set-off. Everything was working right. The doors were released and the main wire began to pay out.

Reed said, "One hundred fifty fathoms." Chase nodded his head, and the set-off was nearly complete. The main wire took about fifteen minutes to pay out and the gear was in the water.

Anderson could immediately feel the difference in the way the boat felt fishing up on the hard bottom. She strained and shook as the net and doors bounced along. You'd feel her start to hang up and then free up again as she struggled. The wires bounced, snapped, and groaned. The hanging bollards on the gallous frames jerked and shook as the boat forged ahead.

The boys headed up to the pilothouse but remained completely silent. They didn't want to break Scanton's concentration. His hands were very soft and steady on the throttle. He had to maintain an even speed. A sudden slowdown could turn disastrous for the net on the bottom. A burst of speed could turn the boat and tear the wings and belly out of the net.

Looking at the rudder indicator you could see that the boat was turned about ten degrees off course to the port. Scanton was steering to offset the hard running tide and keep the boat headed in the perfect direction. Scanton would not relinquish the helm for even a minute during this tow. It would last about two hours, and he would be spent when it was over.

The boys went down forward. Chase started back in on his King novel, and Reed grabbed the cards and started playing solitaire. Anderson stretched out on his bunk, just listening to the sounds of the boat. No one slept.

The wind had picked up another three knots, and it had started to rain. A couple of calls came in on the radio, but Scanton didn't answer them. The time crawled by. You could hear the scanner working as it made its sonar sweep around in half circles. *Tick . . . tick . . . tick . . . tick . . . crack . . . tick . . . tick.* The scanner acted like a large electronic flashlight sweeping back and forth as the boat made its way forward. Scanton could steer by its sound.

Another hour went by, and Scanton called the boys up for the haulback. The *Jubilee* was pounding hard into the chop. The spray and rain were pummeling the boat. When the crew went out on deck, the anticipation was great.

There was lightning cracking all around them, and the men were ready for whatever was to come. Anderson was so excited he was beside himself. When the haulback began, the wire seemed to fly on board. Once the wings, rollers, and belly came up the ramp, the wake that they were looking for broke off the stern.

Anderson's eyes almost popped out of his head. It looked like a whale's broach. The gulls were on them again, in the hundreds. They got the lengthening piece in as quick as possible. Anderson scrambled to get the strap around the net. Pat screamed over the wind and rain, "We're going to need to double jillson these! You'll have to hook up alone!" Reed lowered the port side jillson, and Anderson tracked it down. The wind was off the boat's stern, so the sea spray at that point was minimal. The deck lights were on and the sea around them was jet-black. Anderson had never felt more centered in his life. It was all about being right here, right now. He hooked the strap into the port jillson hook. Chase lowered the starboard jillson, and Anderson hooked that one into the strap too.

Pat and Skip slowly hauled the huge bag of fish up under the reel. Pat hollered, "Tom . . . you're going to have to back off the reel! Push the handle forward, slowly!" The bag was inching its way up the ramp. Anderson slowly rolled the net reel backward, allowing the net to climb toward the top of the boom. Chase and Reed stopped. Chase screamed, "Get up here and take over my jillson . . . Now, Tom, now!"

When Anderson got forward to Chase, he said, "You did good, kid. Now you've got to keep running this up so I can release the cod end."

You could see the fish in the bag now, and Anderson couldn't believe his own eyes. The sight was unreal. Chase went back to the reel. Anderson and Reed continued to raise the net high into the rigging. The cod end cleared the deck and started to swing forward. Chase ran and grabbed the clip end. He sprinted to the checker bracket with the tie-down cleat. Two quick turns and the bag swung forward with such force Anderson was sure it was going to tear the cleat right off the deck, but it held and the bag released.

It would turn out to be 7,200 pounds of perfect large codfish. Anderson had no idea that codfish grew that big. Scanton closed his eyes a second and whispered, "Thanks, Uncle Charley."

He grabbed his hailer mic and screamed, "A little Otis Redding for you boys! Wellllllllll . . . you know you make me wanta shout . . . kick my heels up and shout . . . throw my hands up and shout . . . hey hey hey!

This time he was right. That's how everybody felt on that boat. It was time to shout. It was huge, and that's all there was to it. Scanton turned down the music.

He said, "Well, gentlemen, let's do that again."

He brought the boat 180 degrees around. The net got rewound onto the reel. The wedge was pounded into the cod end clip, and they were ready to get the net back in the water. They flew through the set-off. It probably took just as long as it had before, but that's not how it felt.

When the brakes were set, you could feel the *Jubilee* start to take hold of the bottom again. All was well; they were fishing. Reed got out the knives, and Chase removed the main hatch cover. He told Anderson they would throw the cod down into the slaughterhouse for now and pitch them into iced pens later. Anderson's job would be to gut and gill the fish and then throw them into a flooded deck checker near the hatch to wash them.

Over the rain and wind, Chase screamed, "You see why it's the slaughterhouse now, kid?" Anderson shook his head yes.

The three men started working the deck hard. They dressed the fish as an efficient team. Chase had a half a pen full in about forty-five minutes. Then it happened.

The *Jubilee* fetched up and stopped dead in the water. She started to twist to the starboard side. The chop was now breaking over her broad stern. The net and doors were hung down.

Scanton immediately took the boat out of gear and hollered over the hailer, "Take her back slow." Chase and Reed ran to the winches.

Scanton said to himself, "Get up here, kid."

With *Jubilee* out of gear, the winches were hauling the boat backward over the ground tackle. The seas were breaking over her stern now, and the wind had elevated to twenty-five knots. The driving rain was making it hard to see. Scanton came over the hailer.

"Tom, get up here!" Anderson ran up to the pilothouse. As he did he was thinking, *This tow is the first time I've been called by my name.* As soon as he was beside Scanton, he said, "You've got to take over for me up here. You don't need to touch anything unless I motion to you from the deck. If I wave you ahead, I want you to knock her in gear. Don't give her any throttle though, unless I make this motion." Scanton spun his finger around in a circle. "If I do that, only take her up to 1,200 rpm, okay? Try to stay calm. We've been through this a hundred times before. That net will come up, you'll see."

Scanton left. He put on boots and oilskins and ran out on deck. Anderson watched out the pilothouse window. He saw him come out of the companionway.

Chase reached down and pulled up Scanton's pant leg.

"Oh good, Joey, your boots are on. You forget your slippers?"

"No, I still got 'em on inside my boots, shithead."

Scanton told Chase to come off the starboard winch. He sent him back to the starboard gallous frames to watch for the seventy-five fathom markers. He knew by the way the *Jubilee* was lying that the starboard door was the one that was hung down. They had to be careful that the doors were hauled back as evenly as possible. A free door that wasn't carefully controlled and hauled too quickly could be pulled up hard against the bottom of the hull. It could easily smash right through the planks and sink the boat. Even though it didn't feel like it, the free door was much more of a problem than the one that was hung down.

Scanton told Reed to keep pace with him on the port winch. Anderson could see from the pilothouse that the wires were beginning to be pulled, almost straight up and down.

Chase went back to the stern rail. Anderson's heart was in his throat, watching the seas come up over the stern and break over Chase. The powerful man just hung on and let it come as he watched for the marks. The *Jubilee* drifted further and further back; the strain on the starboard wire was intensifying. Chase raised his left arm with a clenched fist, letting Scanton know that the seventy-five fathom marker had broken the surface.

Scanton quickly motioned to Chase and ordered Reed to stop the port winch. After he called Chase back to the starboard winch and ran back up to the pilothouse. Scanton yelled at Anderson, "Get out of the way now and get back down on deck. Go pull open the scuppers and let the water off the deck!"

He stepped to the controls and snapped the *Jubilee* into reverse. He slowly increased the rpm. The boat responded and began to back down.

When he got down on deck, Anderson scrambled to open the quarter-inch steel gates that were closing the scupper ports from the open sea. The angle of the wires shifted toward the bow of the boat. You could feel the strain as the wires took up and heeled the *Jubilee* to starboard.

Scanton gave her more throttle and the starboard rail rolled under. Anderson was opening the third scupper on the starboard side when a sea broke over his head. He'd never felt anything like that before. It took him a second to realize that he was okay. The deck was awash, and the scuppers were draining water overboard at full capacity. Scanton eased off the throttle to allow the decks to clear. As soon as the boat was stable, he grabbed the loud hailer and ordered Anderson back from the rail. Anderson was not quick enough. Scanton opened the throttle on 1271, and her great power could be felt through the entire hull of the sixty-five-foot boat. The starboard rail rolled deeper than it had before. When the next sea broke, it caught Anderson sideways and drove him to the deck. He crashed forward over the starboard checker and found himself slammed into the middle of five thousand pounds of codfish.

Scanton grabbed his mic and yelled, "Welcome aboard, kid!"

At that critical moment, the starboard door released. The boat was free from the fierce grip of the ocean floor. You could almost hear her sigh of relief. The winches were reengaged, and another twenty-five fathoms of wire were hauled aboard. Scanton pressed the *Jubilee* into forward to keep the doors and net away from the wheel.

The haulback could now resume. With the doors hung and the legs hauled, the net was coming into view. All eyes were on the ramp to see what damage had been done to the net. Gradually, it showed. The starboard wing end was ripped from front to back and the belly was in tatters. Gradually, the lengthening piece and the cod end were up. To everyone's amazement there were fish in the bag, and Anderson scrambled to strap off the cod end. Chase handed him the jillson hook, and the net was raised within minutes.

Chase said, "All right, boy wonder, since you did such a good job doing the codfish breaststroke, I think you should try your luck at dumping this bag."

Reed raised the jillson hook, lifting the net. Chase stood by with a grin on his face, waiting for a screwup. Anderson grabbed the clip line and followed the swinging cod end forward. He flipped the two turns around the checkerboard cleat one under, one over. The bag slammed to a stop, and the fish poured out of the cod end, just like he knew what he was doing.

Chase couldn't mask the look of surprise on his face. Over the howl of the wind, Anderson screamed, "By the way, a pair of fours is worth two points, the way I count 'em." Chase gave him the finger.

Scanton headed back to the eastard toward the flatfish tows. By Chase's estimation, there was about 7,500 pounds of fish on deck. The crew jumped right into the job at hand. These were beautiful twenty-, thirty-, and forty-pound cod. The knives were flying. The fish guts were everywhere, and the flooded wash checker was soon filled. Anderson was doing his best to keep up, but he was falling behind. Chase and Reed switched off, giving him a hand getting the fish down into the slaughterhouse. They cleaned, steamed, rocked, and rolled their way east.

It took a little over an hour to get the fish below. Chase had sent Anderson down into the hold several times to shovel ice and shelve off pens. Each pen had to be divided halfway between the deck and the top of the hold. The weight of the fish on top would crush the ones on the bottom if you didn't.

When the boys finally trudged their way up to the pilothouse to turn in the tally, Chase had estimated those two tows at 15,100 pounds.

It was 1:00 a.m., August 7.

CHAPTER 18

Andy wandered down the island road toward the landing. When he got down to the skiff it was still afloat, much to his relief. He put his bait back aboard and bailed out the skiff. Everything was pretty well set up from the day before. He started the outboard and filled a couple of bait irons while he waited for it to warm up. Last night while Danny and Tammy had been so stoned they weren't paying attention to him, so he helped himself to some of their pot. He had grabbed some papers too and rolled himself a fresh joint. He started to panic a little when he couldn't find his trusty Bic. After searching through all his pockets though, he finally came up with it. The damn thing was stuck in his watch pocket. He was relieved to find it. He lit up his joint and took a deep hit.

Andy never really considered himself a pothead. He could quit doing this shit any time he wanted. He just couldn't figure out why he should stop doing something he enjoyed so much. It didn't hurt anybody after all, and it made him feel really good.

He took a few more hits and then untied his dock lines. His plan was to head back over toward the power plant, and then work back toward Cow Island and the sound. He left the wharf and opened up his old outboard. It was another beautiful morning. The sun was rising. He was staring at it and almost ran into a red nun buoy just a short way from the float. He pushed his tiller handle hard to the right. The starboard side of the skiff skimmed the buoy, and the davit smacked it with a hard ring.

He said out loud, "Well, I guess that'll wake you up!" There was just a little bit of a wind whip on the surface of the bay and not a cloud in the sky. It was going to be a great day.

By the time Andy got over to the first group of traps, it was full daylight. He slowed up his outboard and started his hauler. It took a few yanks before the old engine took hold and ran.

The first string had six counters in it. Andy was disappointed.

"Jeez, Skip, you're kind of slacking off on that set, aren't you?"

Andy had very high expectations when it came to the performance of other people.

He kept hauling along. Before he knew it, he had a crate full and it was only nine thirty in the morning. While he was working, all he could really think about was about making that pot run—$5,000 for three hours' work. Christ, that was more than $500 an hour. Holy shit! That was more than $800 an hour! He didn't want to figure out all that complicated math stuff right now anyway. He just knew he was going to do it. He had to figure out a way to get Reed's boat. That little Novi was perfect in a lot of ways. He had never run a boat bigger than his skiff by himself before, but he was sure he could do it. He had gone stern man with Reed plenty of times. It wasn't like he didn't know the boat. He wasn't stupid after all.

He kept on hauling and setting the traps. He had one more string to get before he went down to Cow Island and the sound. He was pretty nervous about what was coming up. All the big boys fished down that way.

The first time Andy had ever hauled a trawl string by himself was yesterday. He kept hauling. He had a twelve count in the last string.

He was all set now. He started to feel a little better. He had a short run over to Cow to get that gear. He hauled out what was left of his joint and took another couple of hits. He didn't really like what he saw ahead of him down that way—lots of boats running back and forth. Everybody and his brother were out hauling that morning. He'd bet there were a dozen boats right down where he was headed.

Oh well, he'd see how it went. There were several strings on the north, northeast side of the island. He found the first end line and started. Things were in good shape. The first six trawls had forty-five counters in them. There was another six trawls, end for end, to the west. He hauled through those traps and came up with thirty more lobsters. His second crate was full.

He had just set off the last trap when a thirty-five-foot lobster boat pulled up alongside him. Andy looked up and thought the guy was going to roll him over. That boat came flying toward him at full speed. The guy threw his huge V8 diesel into reverse just before he was about to run him down. The eight-inch exhaust pipe rolled a billow of black smoke into the morning sky. Andy knew the guy's name. It was Alan Watson; the boat was the *Lydia Marie*.

Watson was thirty-five years old and a third-generation lobsterman. People around said he fished over two thousand traps. He had two sternmen on board with him and they fished year-round. This was a tough guy and he was afraid of nothing and nobody. He had on a black baseball cap that he wore backward with dark sunglasses and a nasty look on his face.

Andy was scared to death. Watson pulled Andy's skiff over to him and tied a line around his davit and then to a cleat mounted beside his hauling station.

"So what's going on, Quarter Pound Brown? I see you're hauling traps for that fuckin' little prick Skip Reed," Watson said with a nasty tone.

Andy didn't know if he should answer or him or cry. "Yes, Skip asked me to help him out while he's out dragging."

Watson had nothing but contempt in his voice. "Did it ever enter that fuckin' ignorant head of yours that some guys out here don't want you hauling Reed's gear? That little bastard needs to figure out whether he's a goddamn dragger man or a lobster catcher. You aren't doing yourself any favors hauling his shit for him."

Andy was practically shaking. "I don't want any trouble, Mr. Watson."

"It's bad enough that we have to put up with moron skiff fisherman like you, fucking everything up out here. We don't need you helping out the Reeds of the world. Are you going to try and haul the rest of his gang outside here in that piece of shit skiff of yours?"

"I was planning to try."

"Let me tell you something, you potted-up little prick of misery. You drag any of Reed's gear into one fuckin' trap of mine, and I'll make you sorry you were ever born. You get that, Quarter Pound?"

"Yes, sir, Mr. Watson. I'll be real careful."

Watson untied Andy's skiff. "You, better be."

He backed his boat off, spun his wheel hard to starboard, and nailed it. Andy could see the guys standing behind him laughing their asses off as they roared out of there.

Andy closed his eyes and dropped his head. He was glad that Watson's boat was so fast because it meant he was gone away from him that much quicker. He wished people would just leave him alone. That prayer had been said by a lot more lobstermen than just Andy Brown.

He really needed to forget about Alan Watson and get the gear hauled. He ran up between Cow Island and Great Diamond and crossed the sound over toward Green. Reed's first string only had one end line showing. Andy spun around six times and couldn't find the other end. He grabbed the buoy and started hauling. His old Briggs and Stratton almost stalled out. When the traps made it to the surface, they were in a huge ball. He could see the first trap and it looked like it was full of lobsters. The side of his skiff was almost hauled underwater to where he was nearly swamped. The ground swells were rolling up the Hussey from the south. He was getting more and more nervous by the second. He pulled as hard as he could and managed to get three of the traps up on his trap table. The strain was unreal. The next two traps were off the bottom and hanging straight down from his davit. He grabbed his old rusty knife and cut the first trap on his table free. He threw it into the bottom of the skiff. The second trap was full of seaweed, and the door was wide open. He cut it away and threw it on top of the first trap. The line was twisted in a ball. He was dealing with the third trap when the *Lydia Marie* steamed by kicking up a major wake. The starboard rail went under and the skiff damn near sunk. He moved quickly to the port side to keep his boat upright.

He started bailing as fast as he could. He used his five-gallon bucket and got enough water out of the skiff to keep her up. For the first time ever, Andy really wanted to put on his grease-covered old life jacket. He knew that he could sink if this happened again, and he couldn't swim a stroke. He kept hauling and got the other two traps aboard. The end line was a ball of knots and the buoy was gone. He sorted his way through the mess and tried to retie the traps and untangle the ground line. By the time the string was back overboard, he had spent an hour on it. He had caught four lobsters, and they were all in one trap.

He moved on down toward School Rock. There was another string down there he could see. Both buoys were showing and were stretched out perfectly. Thank God, he thought.

He grabbed the buoy on the high end and started hauling. He had about three fathoms aboard and the hauler had slowed down to a crawl. The rope kept coming and coming. The line was building on the bottom of the skiff. He had never hauled an end line over ten fathoms before. He kept hauling. He guessed that the end line was over twenty fathoms. The first trap broke the surface, and it was so tightly wound into itself that he had to cut it out to get it into the boat. The tide was running hard, and he was dragging the gear all over the place. He couldn't help it. There were other buoys all around him. He saw one of Alan Watson's highfliers and almost pissed his pants.

He didn't even open any of the doors when he got the traps aboard, and he still couldn't hold the skiff up over the gear in the running tide. It was a friggin' outboard, for Christ's sake. He couldn't haul and run the boat at the same time. The last two traps came up tangled in somebody else's gear. The worst part was that the traps in the ball belonged to two different guys.

After he got the string on board, he got away from that spot as fast as he could. If he had set that string back on that piece of bottom, there would have been three guys ready to kill him, not just one.

He had twenty-one counters in the string. It didn't matter. He'd had enough. He was bailing his skiff out again when Danny pulled up in the *Frayed Knot* and grabbed the port rail on Andy's skiff. He shouted at him to shut off his Briggs and Stratton so he could hear.

"You're really struggling out here in this tide, aren't you?" Danny said.

"I am. I've had enough of this shit. Christ, look at that chine leak. It's doubled in the last two days. This piece of shit is going to get me killed."

"I was watching you. You towed into two other strings just now. Even though you shifted away from them, they'll know who did it. Everybody's watching you."

Andy said, "I'm in way over my head down here. The first time I ever hauled a stringer by myself was yesterday."

"What did Watson want? I saw him come running up on you."

"He just wanted to bust my balls, the prick. He said that nobody wanted me hauling Reed's traps. He said Reed needed to figure out if he was a lobsterman or a dragger man.

Danny said, "What an asshole. His grandfather and father set him up with that huge gang of traps and new boat. He runs around like he owns the fuckin' bay. He didn't have to earn his shit like you and I did."

That one even gave brain-dead Andy pause. He thought, *Lugging* pot *is earning shit?* He didn't say anything.

Andy said, "Whatever . . . he scared the crap out of me. I'm going in town and sell these lobsters. Then I'm going to figure out how to get the keys to Reed's boat. I'm doing that for two reasons. I'm going to haul this goddamn gear if it kills me, and I'm going to go get a load of that pot too."

Danny said, "I'll need to talk to my contact, but I bet you can make a run tonight. Andy. If you can't get that boat, you gotta let me know."

"Don't you worry about it, cousin. I'll have that boat if I have to hotwire it."

Danny looked kind of funny at Andy. "Jesus Christ! When did you grow a set of balls anyway? Last night?"

Andy said, "Yeah, well, fuck you too. I'll see you down at your place in a few hours. I gotta get going."

CHAPTER 19

Andy spun his skiff around and headed toward Portland. The chine leak was really going full tilt. He had to bail while he was underway to keep the boat afloat. The stain of hauling in the deep water had stressed his old skiff to the max and opened up his chine leak even more. He thought he might have to have somebody who knew what they were doing help him fix it. He was thankful that he made his way up into Portland harbor quickly.

There was nobody around the float when he pulled in. On a beautiful day like this everybody was out hauling. Even Steve Warner wasn't out on the dock running his mouth. Andy was grateful for that at least. He tied off his skiff, climbed the ladder, and went into the building where Harlan's office was located.

Warner was sitting behind Harlan's desk, looking like a big deal when Andy walked in. "Where's Mr. Barnes today, Warner?"

Warner, with a snotty tone, said, "Well, well, if isn't Quarter Pound Brown. What the fuck business is it of yours where Mr. Barnes is?"

Andy took a deep breath. "I'd like to sell some lobsters and buy some bait, ass face."

Warner said, "I think you should show me a little more respect, Quarter Pound. Mr. Barnes left me in charge here while he's gone to have some lunch. I don't think he gives a flying fuck about you or your lobsters."

Andy said, "Knock it off, will ya? I just want to sell my lobsters and get out of this shithole."

Just then, Harlan Barnes opened the door to his office. "What do you think you're doing behind my desk, Warner?" he shouted. "Get your ass out of there before I call the Cumberland County Jail and get your work release permit revoked. I ever catch you in here again, I'll drop you off over there myself." Steve Warner was white in the face. "Yes, sir, Mr. Barnes. Sorry, Mr. Barnes, it won't happen again."

Barnes walked over to his desk. His back was turned on Andy.

Brown made a face at Warner and gave him the finger. He was out the door in three seconds.

Barnes said, "Don't let that asshole get to you, Andy. What can I do for you today?"

Andy explained to him that his skiff was leaking real bad and about trying to haul in the Hussey out in the big tide. Andy looked like a beaten man. Not just discouraged either—beaten. Andy told Harlan he was going to try to get a hold of Skip Reed to see if he could use his boat so he could finish hauling his traps.

Harlan said, "All right, let's see if we can do that." Andy wasn't expecting this. He thought he'd just steal the boat and beg for forgiveness later. He hadn't figured out that there might be another approach to solving his problem.

Harlan turned around and took his VHF mic and keyed the button.

"*Jubilee, Jubilee,* this is Portland Lobster Company on 16. Over."

A few seconds passed. "This is the *Jubilee* back to Portland Lobster. Go ahead."

Harlan said to switch up to 65. When they were on the same channel, Harlan said, "*Jubilee,* this is Harlan Barnes from Portland Lobster. Who's this, please?"

"Pat Chase. Over."

"Hi, Pat, thanks for getting back to us. Is Skip Reed aboard? Over."

"Yes, he is, Harlan. I'll get him up here. You hang on a second. Over."

"Thanks, Pat. We'll stand by. Over."

Chase hollered down to the galley and told Reed there was a call for him. He came up still eating a sandwich and took the mic.

"This is Skip. Who's this? Over."

"Hey, Skip, Harlan Barnes here. How's it going out there on the high seas, kid? Over."

"I'm all right. I was just getting a sandwich. What's up, Harlan?"

"I've just had a chat with your buddy Andy Brown. He's got a problem. He's having a hard time trying to haul your deepwater gear in that rickety old skiff of his. It sounds to me like she's opened up on him pretty bad. He wants to know if he can use your boat to haul out of until you get back? Over."

"Oh Jesus Christ, Harlan, I don't know if I want that idiot running my boat. I suppose he's sitting right there with you, isn't he? Over."

"Yes, as a matter of fact, he's here with me. Over."

"Damn it, Harlan, I don't know."

"Well, Skip, it's your call. He's been doing pretty good." Harlan gave Andy a direct stare and continued on, "He said your share out of the first haul was about 275 pounds. He's willing to change the split to sixty-forty your way since he'd be using your boat. He'll still pay for all the fuel. Over." Andy closed his eyes, frowned, and nodded his head yes.

"All right, Harlan, put that friggin' yahoo on the line. Over"

Andy took the mic away from Harlan. He'd never used a VHF radio before. He looked at the mic and said, "Hello?" He was so nervous he put the mic up to his ear so he could hear the response. Harlan just said, "Oh god," and shook his head.

Reed said, "All right, dipshit, the keys are up under the fire extinguisher down forward. You just unsnap the thing and they're right there. You've got to check the oil and water before you start her up. There's extra oil right there and a freshwater jug if either of them is low. Whatever you do, don't you put any saltwater in that engine. Now pay attention. You *have* to open the raw water seacock before you run her, or you'll seize her up solid. You've seen me open that seacock before. It's on the starboard side just ahead of the engine. Open is when you've got the handle straight up and down. You also have to open the valve for the raw water pump for the live tank, or you'll blow that line off that. When you put her on the hook at night, you have to close those valves. You getting this, Andy? Over."

"Yes, Skip. I'm getting it, I think."

"You'd better do more than think. You wreck that engine or screw up my boat and I'll break your goddamn ass. Put Harlan back on."

Harlan took the mic. "Yeah, Skip, I'm right here. Over"

"Harlan, try to keep an eye on him, will ya? I know you're not out there, but everybody talks to you. Just give me a call if you hear anything weird going on, okay? Hey, Quarter Pound. I'll give you a call in about four hours from now. Leave the radio on. Get a hold of Drew Taylor and tell him that I let you take the boat. Thanks for the call, Harlan. This is the *Jubilee*, clear with Portland Lobster."

"Portland Lobster . . . clear with the *Jubilee*. Back to 16 and standing by."

Harlan said, "There you go, Andy. Now you can go haul. Try to use your head, will ya? What have you got for lobsters today?"

"I don't know. I've got to get them weighed." Harlan laughed. "Oh, I got a feeling that they're all weighed. All right, look now, Andy. I know I changed the weight on you that you tallied yesterday, but you and I both know you were screwing Skip. He's going to give you a chance, letting you use his boat. Don't mess it up. Go haul the traps, bait 'em up good, and see where it goes. Pay Skip his honest share, and you'll still make more money than you ever have in your whole life."

Andy said, "I know what you guys expect of me, and I won't let you down."

"Here's what I'm going to do with you. I assume those lobsters you had today are all Skip's, right?"

"Yes," Andy said reluctantly. This honesty stuff was going to take a little getting used to.

"I'll take out the 152 pounds for Skip and split the rest fifty-fifty. We'll catch up your debt to me next time. I'm going to take out tomorrow's bait of course. Do you need any gloves or bands?"

"No, I'm all set." Andy figured he'd find some on the *Ruffian* and use those. He didn't want this new no-cheating policy to get completely out of hand after all. Andy went back out onto the dock.

The lobsters were weighed; the new bait was on board. His gas tank was full, and the skiff was bailed. Steve Warner handed him his slip and kept his eyes down when he did it. Andy thought he was going to lose it when Warner said, "Thanks, Andy."

Andy thought, *Wow, that Cumberland County Jail must be some horrible place to see an attitude change like that at just the prospect of being sent back there.*

Andy's slip read 234 pounds. After deducting Skip's share, the bait, and fuel Harlan gave him $160.

He walked back over to his favorite diner. When he sat down, he ordered his cheeseburger and some fries again. He had a beer with it. Why not? He'd had quite a day so far, and there was still a lot ahead for him yet. The burger tasted great. He was looking around the restaurant, checking out the girls, when Drew Taylor walked through the door. He came over and grabbed the stool next to Andy. He was surprised to see Drew there two days in a row.

"How's it going, Drew? You come in here every day?"

"Almost every day. See, I have to come into Portland to get parts for the chandlery, at Handy's. It's my lunch hour, and besides I've got the hots for that waitress Sharon over there. You know her . . . she's from Falmouth."

"Yes, I guess so. A lot of those snobby bitches from Falmouth didn't like me much, so fuck them."

Drew thought, *Now there's a shock.*

Drew said, "So how's it going with the traps now?"

Andy said, "Good, really. Hey, I'm supposed to let you know that Skip called me over at Portland Lobster there. He wants me to start using the *Ruffian* to haul our gear. Harlan Barnes, that owns the lobster-buying place, and I are pretty tight. Not to brag or nothing, but he's always saying I'm one of his top guys. Anyway he recommended me for the job where I was already tending Skip's traps and all."

Drew said, "Okay. I guess they told you where the keys were then."

Andy said, "Yes, they did. I'm all set there. My only problem right now is that haulin' in that nasty tide down in the Hussey. I've got a leak started in my skiff that's pretty bad. I'm so busy bailing Skip's ass out of trouble that I can't tend to my own stuff."

Drew said, "Why don't you just leave it tied up down at the float in front of Handy's? I'll get it and put it on a trailer. I'll stick it up back in the boatyard. No one will notice it's there for a while, and then you can fix it later on."

Andy said, "Boy, that sounds wicked good. I really thank you for that, Drew."

"Sure, you're doing a lot for Skip so I can pitch in too." Drew lowered his voice. "Andy, do you think you could score a little weed for me? I think if I could get Sharon there a little smoked up, I could probably have a good time for myself."

Andy said, "Sure, I can, but that shit ain't free, you know."

Drew felt like saying, "Boatyard services aren't free either, asshole!" but he held his tongue. Drew said, "Okay, Andy, do what you can, and let me know."

Andy looked over across the diner, and that same Oriental-looking guy that was taking all the pictures down at Barnsey's was at it again. Now he's snapping away in this friggin' diner. These tourists are weird.

Andy said good-bye to Drew and walked back to the dock. When he got there, the skiff was bailed out again, dry, and ready to go.

"Now they're starting to get the idea down here finally. Maybe they'll be calling me Two-Pound Brown pretty soon." He thought about that, and it didn't really sound that much better.

He jumped aboard his skiff and headed for Falmouth. He skimmed along, thinking things were going to be really good for him in the immediate future. It felt good to have some cool shit happening in his life for once. He thought about that broad Sharon that Drew was talking about back at the diner. If she liked a little weed, maybe he'd get her to split a bone with him. Then he could have a little of that "rich girl pussy." There had to be something better than his friend, crazy Mary, from the trailer park out there.

Andy didn't think about much else on the way back to Falmouth. He did fire up another joint though. Riding across the bay in his skiff and smoking a joint was his idea of a great afternoon.

By the time he pulled up alongside of the *Ruffian*, he was pretty stoned. He went aboard and tried to remember where the keys were. He sat there for half an hour with a blank stare on his face. Then he remembered that they were hanging on a seacock forward of the engine. He hunted high and low and couldn't find them anywhere. He was trashing around down forward, and he banged his head on the fire extinguisher. That pissed him off, but then he remembered where the keys really were. He yanked the fire extinguisher out of the holder, found the keys, and threw the extinguisher unit up on some life jackets and rain gear Reed had on the V-berth. Goddamn piece of shit. Andy's head really hurt.

He managed to muster the presence of mind to open the seacock and check the oil and water. It was a little low, so he topped it off with the oil jug he found sitting on the floorboards. He went back out to the wheel, put the key in the ignition, and hit the starter button. The *Ruffian* started up like she'd been run yesterday. He played around with the throttle a little and pulled her in and out of gear quickly, both forward and reverse. He tried the hauler handle and the shivs turned perfectly.

Man, was he going to love hauling in this boat. Just for the hell of it he fired up the live tank. Nothing came out. Then he remembered to open the second seacock that supplied the raw water for that pump. Slick as a bastard, he thought. The water came pouring out of the hose and started filling the big blue barrel that Reed used as a lobster tank. No more crates overboard. What a relief. It really must have been for a guy who had never had a full crate of lobsters in his life before yesterday.

Andy loaded the bait over from his skiff to the *Ruffian*. He took the painter from his skiff and tied it to a ring bolt on the *Ruffian's* stern. He went up on the bow and let the mooring line go and went back to the wheel and put the boat in gear. The little Novi moved forward.

Andy had no idea how close he had come to running over the *Ruffian's* mooring line and getting it in the wheel. He motored his way over to the Handy's dock with his skiff in tow. When he got there, he tried landing the *Ruffian* for the first time. He smashed it into the float. He panicked and threw it into reverse, and his skiff smashed square into her stern. The skiff's bow stem made a nice big dent in the *Ruffian's* stern. Andy was embarrassed and took a quick look up the dock to see if anyone was watching him; thankfully, no one was.

When he finally got straightened out, Drew was on his way down to help him. Andy said, "Thanks a lot for getting your ass down here to help me." Drew tied up the skiff, and Andy went aboard it to get his oil pants. He had no idea that this would be the last time that he would ever step aboard that skiff. He got back aboard the *Ruffian* and started her up again. He waved good-bye to Drew and thanked him for his help. He passed him a small bag of pot.

It was about two o'clock, so there was plenty of time to go haul some gear. He untied the dock lines and headed down the fairway leading out of Handy's and into the bay. As soon as he passed the last fairway marker by York Ledge, he sped up the engine and steered back toward the south and Hussey Sound. He turned the VHF radio on. He was too scared to make a call, but he knew Reed would be trying to get him soon. He left the radio on channel 16. He could hear the other calls being made. He wanted to learn the lingo so he wouldn't sound like an idiot when he talked on it.

The little boat ran like a watch. She was smooth and quiet. He was thinking, *So this is how the other half lives.* Then it dawned on him . . . now he was the other half. The other half of what? Now he was confused. He'd better have a joint and get things into perspective. It was 2:40 p.m., August 8.

CHAPTER 20

The *Jubilee* was now carrying approximately twenty-nine thousand pounds of fish and a little over two hundred pounds of lobsters. There was about twenty minutes to go to the flatfish bottom. Scanton said, "Skip, I need you and Pat to go pull that flatfish net off and take the roller sections off. Put the fourteen-foot bosom cookie sweep on the net in its place. I'm going to come down and adjust the back straps before we set out."

The deck gang was starting to show the first signs of fatigue. It wasn't unusual on a trip for a dragger crew to stay up for twenty-four hours, working the deck with no sleep. Scanton told Anderson to go get a big pot of coffee going before he went out to help the boys with the roller sections.

When they got back on deck, Reed started the reel and slowly backed the net off. Anderson was down in just a few minutes. He and Chase started flaking the net onto the deck. They moved fairly quickly. Chase headed for the engine room to get the tools they'd need to take the roller sections off. The shackles could be a real battle, but fortunately they had been maintained when the net was up on the wharf in Portland. The cookie section went on smoothly, and the flatfish roller section was jillsoned off the deck and coiled in an empty checkerboard on the port side. They fed the net back on to the reel, and it was ready for setoff.

Everybody headed up to get a cup of coffee. They had another few minutes to go before they got up on the section of bottom Scanton was looking for.

Scanton said, "How bad is the net, Pat?"

"We've ripped it up pretty good, Joey, but you've done worse. The starboard wings shredded, and we should probably slug in most of the belly. It's not too, too bad though. What have we got for twine in the lazarette?"

Scanton said, "There's plenty down there. Why don't you go fill up some needles for us, Tom? There's a milk crate down on deck with a ball of twine and needles in it. Don't overfill 'em so we can't get them through the meshes. Pat, let's haul the doors up, so I can shorten the back straps a link. With the cookie sweep on there, I don't want to mud up."

Scanton left the boat in gear with the autopilot on. She was running at an idle. All four men headed down on deck. Before they left, Scanton took a quick peek at the radar screen to see if anybody was planning to run them down. He thought, *Thank God, nobody was.*

Chase and Scanton had to get the doors inboard so that they could shorten the back straps. He got to the port door first. This was always a dangerous process when there was a chop on. It was blowing about twenty, so the doors were going to slam around like a bastard while they tried to get them in.

"Pat, I want you to use a rope on that fuckin' door when I get it up. I don't want you losing any fingers. You won't be able to pick your nose anymore, and that would be disgusting."

Chase said, "Yep, it would . . . because you'd have to pick it for me."

He went back, tied a half-inch line on the towing bracket, and tied it off on a cleat on the side of the net reel. Scanton raised the door so Chase could unchain it. He lowered it just enough for Chase to get a hold with his half-inch line. The door was swinging and slamming around the gallous frames. He untied it from the cleat but left a single turn around it. He pulled hard enough so the door was inboard of the rail. Scanton lowered away until the door was resting quietly on deck. Reed was now back up on the deck. He climbed up from the lazarette with the bail of ready-made net. Chase and Scanton repeated the same process on the starboard door and got that rested on the deck.

Anderson had filled fifteen needles with twine. Chase sent him down to the engine room bench to get a medium adjustable and a set of pump pliers. When he was back with them, Scanton and Chase started on the back straps.

Scanton climbed back up to the wheelhouse to get ready for the setoff. When he stepped to the controls, he swung the boat back around to the west. He said over the hailer, "All right, ladies . . . let's get overboard. I'd sing you a song, but I'm afraid the sounds of my sweet voice might put you to sleep, you're all so dopey looking down there." A huge sea smashed over the starboard front rail, over the pilothouse, and crashed down on his men on deck. After the water cleared he could see that everyone was all right.

As soon as the boat was settled into her tow, Scanton called Anderson up to the pilothouse.

He said, "This is a simple tow. It's the same piece of bottom you towed this afternoon, only I moved two berths over. We're bearing 210 degrees, west southwest. Just like before, you really don't need to touch anything. Don't slow down or speed up. There's nothing down here but open bottom, so you can't hit anything. Keep an eye on the radar for traffic, and don't, whatever you do, fall asleep."

Anderson said, "Okay, Joe. Do you want me to sing a few tunes for you guys while I'm up here?"

He laughed. "Just run the boat and leave the singing to the professionals."

Scanton went back down on deck to start putting his rim-wracked groundfish net back together.

Charley Walker had been a patient teacher with Joey. He helped him learn not only what to do but also why to do it. Understanding how a net was made was key when you were looking at a pile of torn and tattered green twine lying on the deck of a boat.

Scanton bent down and started flipping through the net. The starboard wing was shot. He grabbed a mending needle and sorted his way back from the headrope. He stopped and tied a small piece of twine around a mesh and changed direction and worked toward the center of the net and tied another mark piece off. Scanton said, "Skip . . . strip out that marked section, and set it aside."

Scanton and Chase went to work on the belly. Chase had already started to strip out a huge section. The premade net bail was tied off in a bundle on deck. Scanton counted the meshes behind Chase as he began to strip out the mostly destroyed net. He let Chase keep at it.

They all mended in silence as the waves crashed over the bow, the pilothouse, and onto their backs. They were in the driving wind, rain, and rough seas; but it was where they belonged.

The hours wore on, the mending continued, and the net was beginning to take shape again.

Anderson was up in the pilothouse taking the ride of his life. He'd been out lobstering when the wind blew, but it was nothing like this. He was a hundred miles offshore at three in the morning, dead tired, a load of fish coming aboard, and at the helm. This was what he was looking for.

He glanced at the radar and his heart went into his throat. The screen was set on the five-mile range, and he could see they were steaming toward a huge piece of land. How the fuck could that be? The *Jubilee* was moving at a steady three knots. He thought, *Calm down, calm down.* This can't be happening. He hated to call Joey up to help him, but he had no choice. He grabbed the hailer mic, "Joey, I need you to come up and look at something in the radar right away." Scanton waved to Anderson so he'd know that he had heard him.

Anderson couldn't believe he didn't come immediately. A few minutes later, Scanton stepped into the pilothouse. His oil clothes were dripping water. He said, "Okay, what have you got, kid?"

There was a little panic in Anderson's voice. "It looks like we're headed for a big piece of land."

"No shit, if they moved some land out here in the last eight hours, we're in a lot more trouble than I thought we were." Scanton looked at the radar screen and adjusted the gain. "That's a line squall comin'. That thunderstorm late this afternoon drew this thing up on us. Bolt your socks on, kiddo. I'm going back down to finish mending the net."

Anderson was flabbergasted. "That's it? That's it? Bolt my socks on. What the fuck does that mean?"

Twenty minutes later Anderson knew what he had meant. He wished he could bolt his feet to the floor. The wind had picked up a good fifteen knots to over thirty-five and the seas out of the south were huge. The waves had gotten closer together and were coming at a rapid pace. He could see nothing out the front windows but breakers and foam, and the radar was a whiteout. Anderson looked out the rear window and couldn't believe the boys were still on deck. In the driving rain he really couldn't see them down there.

Now he understood how men got washed overboard and no one knew it had happened, until it was too late. His first thought was, *This is summertime. What are the winters going to be like with freezing cold, snow, and ice everywhere? Holy shit!* He was literally holding on with both hands to the rails around the pilothouse. He couldn't believe that with all the clutter and junk all over the place nothing seemed to fall off onto the floor. He was glad he'd bracketed the coffee pot down. For a second, he wondered if Uncle Charley was nervous. He looked down in the galley, and there she was, sound asleep on the table bench. She could have cared less. He was sure she had put in a lot harder weather than this.

Reed walked into the pilothouse with a green five-gallon bucket in hand. There were two large balls of mending twine and a dozen needles in the bucket. He walked over behind Anderson and pulled on the back of his pants. Anderson said, "What the fuck are you doin'?"

"Just checking to see if you'd shit yourself yet."

Anderson said, "You just continue to be the funniest son of a bitch I've ever known."

"Ya, I know. Aren't I a fuckin' riot? Joey wants you to fill these needles. He said for you to steady this boat down too. It's getting sloppy down there. Three of these needles have got to be doubles. Do you know how to do that?"

"No, I don't."

Reed showed him that you ran three and a half fathoms of twine off the ball, twice. Then you throw a half hitch in the end and start winding the twine onto the needle. Reed left Tom staggering around the pilothouse, trying to fill the needles. When he got done he was afraid to leave the helm unattended, so he got on the hailer. "The needles are full." Scanton looked up and, with a pissed look on his face, waved him down.

Anderson ran the bucket down and out on deck with no oil jacket on. Scanton said, "You too fuckin' scared to come out on deck in light breeze like this, for Christ's sake?"

"No, I didn't want to leave the helm."

"Good, then I think you should get your ass back up there then."

Anderson took off like a shot. Scanton looked at the other two guys and they all laughed.

Anderson rushed back up to the wheel. He was soaked to the bone and was still hanging on for dear life. There was a roll of paper towels up there, so he dried himself off as best as he could. The squall kept up about a half hour more, and suddenly it was just like driving out of a car wash. The rain stopped, the wind backed off, and the dawn started to break on the edge of the horizon. It was 4:50 a.m. The trawl clock had an hour and twenty minutes left on it. The seas were still rough but the storm had passed. He could see that the boys were wrapping up down on deck. He couldn't believe how one reality at sea changes for another in the wink of an eye.

The fifteen-fathom legs were pulled to the side and had to go back up on the reel first. Reed and Chase were guiding them on while Scanton ran the reel. They got the net back up in just a few minutes, and the boys were headed up. When Scanton came into the pilothouse with the rest of the deck gang, he said, "I'm some glad you ran right over that piece of land you saw on the radar. I sure as hell wouldn't want to explain to everybody how our green man ran us ashore and sunk us down here below Sigsbees."

They all thought that was about the funniest joke they had ever heard. Somehow the humor of it escaped Tom.

Scanton said, "Why don't you go get some breakfast together? We can tow another hour or so down this way. Where it's coming first light, we may do something."

Anderson headed down to the galley. He dumped the big coffee pot and started a new one. He had saved a big bowl of potatoes from when he made the fish chowder. He got bacon and sausage on the stove and made up a large bowl of scrambled eggs, a huge stack of pancakes, and some home fries.

Scanton was back on the helm. Anderson served up a big helping for him with a large mug of coffee and ran it up to him. "Thanks, kid, it looks great." By the time Anderson was back in the galley the crew was already speculating on the fish prices. Reed said, "The gray sole always brought big money. The dabs had been pretty high over the last month. The cod had been running about a buck a pound." They'd just have to see what would happen and hope for the best.

Scanton hollered down below, "Let's haul her back."

"*Jubilee, Jubilee,* this is the *Gloria Walker* on 16, Over."

"Ya, Dad, pick one."

"Seventy-three"

"Okay, 73."

"Hey Joey, where are you guys?"

"The bucket bottom. Over." Peter Scanton knew all about the lobster drop to Rusty Martin and exactly where his son was fishing.

"Yeah, finest kind, Joe. I'm just about ten miles east of catfish rock. Over."

"Where you headed, Dad? Over."

"Marshall and I are meeting up down on the coffee grounds. Over"

He knew the coffee grounds meant Tanners. Peter Scanton had almost fallen overboard there once trying to pass Marshall a can of coffee from boat to boat. That was almost ten years ago. "Ya, I got ya, Dad."

Peter hesitated a little and said, "Joey, I took Karen and Little Joey to Becky's for lunch yesterday. You know how he likes the toasted cheese and french fries down there. Well, we had a real nice talk. She's a good girl, just a little screwed up on her priorities right now. I think it went real well. Over."

Joey didn't say anything for a minute. He hated to have everybody into his personal business, but he knew he had started it himself by complaining to the old man about their situation. He knew his dad was just trying to help him out. He was very uncomfortable saying anything more over the VHF.

"Okay, Dad, I'm glad you had a nice lunch. Over." Peter Scanton got the message and changed the subject. He knew that half the fleet may be listening in on their conversation. He said, "Any fish going, Joe?"

"No, Christ, I couldn't catch a cold down here." Peter knew that his son and crew were doing big. That old line had been used between Marshall, Vern, Peter, and Uncle Charley for years.

"All right, boy, finest kind. I'll let you go. I see that old coot Marshall's down here. I'll give you a shout later. Over."

Marshall came on. "Who are you calling an old coot, you lousy poor excuse for a human being!"

Peter came back. "Well, Joey, I guess we know who's alive and well this morning."

"Yeah, Dad, catch you later. *Jubilee* back on 16." Joey knew that his dad and Marshall would carry on for the next half hour and probably drag Vern into it.

It was time for haulback.

They hauled back and had about 4,500 pounds of fish. There were thirty baskets of gray sole and eight baskets of dabs. The rest was mixed groundfish. There were at least sixty pounds of lobsters. That brought the *Jubilee*'s estimated catch to just over thirty-four thousand pounds. It was 7:25 a.m., August 7.

CHAPTER 21

S canton spun the boat around 180 degrees and headed back north by northeast, bearing thirty degrees, and the boys set the net off before they started getting the fish put away down below.

You could really start to feel the change in the boat with all this weight on board. The heavier she was, the wider she was. Her hull settled deeper into the water and the more stable she became.

Joey's uncle used to tell him that the ocean was a weird place. He'd say, "You can guess right and come out okay. You can guess wrong, and there's an empty place at the supper table at home. A lot of this shit is luck." Joey thought, *I guess that's what happened to you, Uncle Charley. Your luck just ran out.*

The seas had settled down, and it was another gorgeous day out on the Gulf of Maine. He didn't have to think about all that weather stuff right now anyway. He had sent the crew down to hit the bunks. There was a fine line between maximizing productivity and pushing men to dangerous exhaustion.

When Anderson crawled up into his berth he didn't even pull his dungarees off. He thought, *Ah, recess in heaven!* He was sound asleep before his eyes closed.

Scanton was sitting in his captain's chair, thinking. Things were going along pretty good. This Anderson guy was doing all right and anyway his food was great. It was a fun distraction too, bustin' his balls. It didn't hurt any to remind his other two that they were pretty good men. He took another swig from his coffee cup.

They had a lot of money fish aboard, but he couldn't wait to run up onto The Bunches again. There was just something about those huge bags of codfish that just turned him on. He liked working around in the rock piles. It was more exciting than just towing back and forth in the mud. He felt like a kid stealing a skin book out of the corner store. Just as long as you got out of there with a whole net and a big bag of fish. To him that's what this was all about.

The radio was loaded with traffic this morning. There were guys calling each other up just to shoot the shit and close friends talking in code to help each other out. He never chased other boats' calls up the band to listen in on them. He just didn't give a shit what other people had to say. He hated listening to all the fuckin' whining that went on and on over the radio. The lobster catchers were the worst.

For some reason those guys were always screwing with each other's gear and fighting with each other. He liked keeping his stuff with him.

"*Jubilee, Jubilee,* the *Jessica* callin'."

Joey picked up. "Yeah, Rusty, go to 88. Over."

"Eighty-eight."

"So you still on the bucket, Joey? Over."

"Ten-four, Rusty. We ripped up last night on the second tow, but we're back over on the flats now. Over."

"You doin' anything? Over."

"No, I couldn't catch a cold down here. Over."

"Yeah, I got you, Joe." Martin knew he was doing good, and he was glad for Joey. He needed a break. "How'd the new kid do when the blow went through? Over."

"I guess Skip checked his underwear, and he was okay. Over."

Rusty smiled to himself and said, "Ya leave it to Skip to be checking somebody's underwear, the pervert."

"Yes, Jesus. Yes, I know it. We were out on deck all night mending . . . the usual. I talked with the old man earlier. He and your old buddy Marshall were goin' at it. Over."

"Now that's something new. I never heard those two old bastards ever say anything unkind to each other. Over."

"I know it, I know it. How did you guys do in that little puff last night? Over."

"One thing for sure about this sled, she's a hell of a sea boat. I'd like to get her in some rough weather one day to see how she'd do. Over."

"I suppose that fifty knots you were caught off in last winter didn't count, right? Over."

"Shit no, it doesn't count. That blow was just a summer breeze, bub, summer breeze. Over!"

Scanton said, "How are you guys makin' out?"

"All right, I guess. We just hauled through the gear and we're almost set off again. The baits holding up good, and I'm getting ready to take a swing through the deck."

"All right, Rusty, I gotta go get a fresh coffee. Call me later. The *Jubilee*, clear with the *Jessica*."

"Finest kind, kiddo. This is the *Jessica*, clear with the *Jubilee*. Back to 16 and standing by."

Scanton towed until ten o'clock and then went down to wake his sleeping crew. They hauled back and had another six-thousand-pound bag. There were forty baskets of dabs and twelve gray sole, nine hundred mixed, mostly pollack and about forty pounds of lobsters. That brought her tally to about forty thousand pounds and about three hundred pounds of lobsters in the live tank.

It was 12:20 p.m. They had turned around, moved over a couple of berths, and set off again. When the boys came up, Scanton turned the tow over to Chase and headed down below. Uncle Charley got up and started talking to him. "I know, old girl, you want to take a spin around the deck. I gotta get some sleep. We'll go out this afternoon." Uncle Charley looked disgusted with Joey and flopped back down under the table.

Scanton was bone tired. He thought to himself, *How in hell did the old man do this all these years?*

CHAPTER 22

Anderson made a sandwich and sat back down at the galley table. Reed came down and slid in. He said, "Well, are you having any fun yet?"

"It's all so new to me. I'm really having a blast, but I'm sure to you guys, year in, year out, it gets to be old hat after a while."

"It's kind of funny. Once you go on one of these boats, it does get in your blood. It's hard to imagine not going. I do miss my lobster gear and the *Ruffian*. The problem is that lobstering is pretty seasonal."

"True . . . it is that."

Reed said, "Oh sure, you can pound offshore in the winters, but then you gotta fight the draggers. Small boats, out here fuckin' around in the winter . . . it's risky business. I'll tell you what I want to do though. I want to be rich. Filthy fuckin' rich and farting through pure silk, that's my goal."

"Well, Skip, you're two-thirds of the way there. You got the farting and the filthy part down. Now all you've got to do is figure out the rich part."

"I'm working on it. I'm working on it." Anderson thought, *I'm sure you are, Skip.* He headed back to his bunk. He figured they might have another long night ahead where they were going, so take the sleep now when you can get it. He had never been a guy that could take a nap ever in his life, but somehow out here, it seemed to work.

Chase came down and woke everybody up at about four o'clock. Reed had put on a pot of coffee, and they all grabbed their mugs and lit up their smokes. Scanton went back on the helm for the haulback.

The net came on board without incident. They dumped the bag, and it looked like around four thousand. The total catch was now up to forty-four thousand pounds. After the clip was pounded back in the cod end, they hauled the flatfish net back up on the reel and left it. He said, "Why don't you go down and get some grub going while we put these fish down? We're about an hour and half from The Bunches and I'm hungry." Anderson went up and on the way through the pilothouse. He asked Joey if he had anything in mind for supper.

"No, you're doin' fine by me. Whatever floats your boat."

Anderson hauled out three nice steaks. He made mashed potatoes and a big salad. He shook his head. Salad with no onions? That was unheard of at the Anderson household. He panfried the steaks and made a thick gravy. The steaks were seared and blood red in the middle. He made up his plate and went up. He told Scanton he'd take her so he could sit down at the table and eat. Scanton said, "Well, thank you, kind sir. I'll do that. Just keep her headed like she is."

The supper turned out great, but Chase fired up the stove and recooked his steak. He hated rare meat. After supper Scanton grabbed Uncle Charley and threw her up on his shoulders and headed out on deck for their tour. He sat down on the main fish hatch and lit up a Marlboro. He was watching the big cat. "Well, old girl, do you think we can get out of here without rim racking the net again?" She just kept on eating her fish. She was swinging her tail back and forth and back and forth.

Reed had the loud hailer mic in his hand and started singing (to the tune of "Oh Sola Mio"), "I'm Sal Scantini, oh Sal Scantini . . . I'm a going to breaka your fucking legs if a you don'ta catcha no a fishhh . . . La la . . . La la!" Scanton looked up at the pilothouse, shook his head, and started laughing. He could see Anderson and Reed looking down at him. He gave Reed the finger.

To get back up to the hard bottom they had been steaming a course of 270 degrees due west. They were just under a half hour away. It was 6:15 p.m. The sun was starting to go down, and the sky was clear. NOAA was calling for light and variable westerly winds. Scanton had saved his marks from his first tow up in there. He was going to do everything he could to get right back up on that same piece of bottom. The scanner was on. He had asked Reed to put a new roll of paper in the Kalvin Hughes. He had seen the light red mark across the paper a while ago, so he knew they were going to run out pretty soon.

After he got back up to the pilothouse, he checked, and the LORAN-C was coming up with new numbers. He watched them intently. Ten minutes later and he was on his marks.

Scanton hollered, "Let's get the net in the water, boys." The gang was down on deck in a flash, ready to set off. The doors were picked up, unchained, and hung on the wires. Chase was on the net reel paying out the net. Anderson could see the all new twine mended into the net. It impressed him the size and weight of the roller sections on the groundfish net as they came off the reel. Five massive pieces linked together to make up the bottom mouth of the net. The largest rollers were in the center section. It was still hard to envision that the majority of the fish caught pass over this one section.

The legs were off, the idler and the back straps were hooked, and the doors went over. Chase and Reed were winding out the wire. One hundred fifty fathoms and they were in business again. The brakes were set, and you could feel the *Jubilee* take on the bottom. She shook, she bucked, the wires popped, and the bollards snapped. Anderson could feel it. They were going to catch some fish on this tow and he knew it.

They came up in the pilothouse, and Scanton was totally focused on the helm. The tide was running hard just like last night, and he had to work the jog lever carefully to keep his course. The bearing was 170 degrees. Once again he had to steer up about ten degrees to hold the boat on course. The net and doors would hang up and then release. Nobody but the best could fish this bottom. He loved every second of it.

The boys went down to the galley. This tow would be all Scanton. The *Jubilee* was creaking from the stain. Her massive oak frames were being put through their paces. This Maine-built dragger was put together by some of the best craftsmen who ever constructed seagoing boats of this class and size. She was an absolute work of art. The *Jubilee* had three sister ships, and all of them were still in service. They had fished the North Atlantic for decades, keeping their men safe, while they harvested millions upon millions of pounds of fish.

Chase said, "Come on, kid. Sit down and let's have a game of crib. One on one."

"Oh, I don't know. Now if something bad happens and I get a dumb-luck hand and beat you, not saying that could possibly happen, but if it did, you're not going to rip up the galley table or kick a hole in the side of the boat or something, are you, Pat?"

"Just shut the fuck up and cut for deal." Reed was sitting there enjoying the show. In cribbage the deal goes to the low card cut. Although it doesn't determine the outcome of the game, winning the deal is a minor victory. Chase cut up a four. Anderson said, "A four? Oh crap!" and turned over a two.

"Go fuck yourself and deal!" Anderson dealt the cards and the normal banter began. Four, six, ten, and eight is eighteen, four is twenty-two. Seven is twenty-nine, is that a go? . . . Yes, go shit in your hat . . . The pegging, the counting, the insults, the abuse, the good hands, the bad—it was a good game. Fifteen two, fifteen four, fifteen six, and three are nine, and the right jack is ten. And in the crib Anderson had a pair of threes and two queens for four. They pegged their way around the track and were headed to the end. They were close. Chase was four holes from the end, and Anderson was five. The hands were dealt. Chase said, "Save your peggers."

The boat suddenly lurched as the port side hung up. Everybody held their breath. Scanton touched up the 1271 a little. She didn't free up with a pop; it was more of a slipping away. That could have been a rock rolling away or a wing shredding. They wouldn't have any idea until they hauled back.

The game resumed. It was Chase's deal so Anderson started. He played a four. Chase played a seven. Anderson played a six. The count was seventeen. Chase played a nine. The count was twenty-six. That's a go. He took a point. Anderson played a nine. Chase a six for two points. The count was fifteen. Anderson played a ten. The count was twenty-five. Chase threw down a six for thirty-one and two points, and he was out the winner.

Anderson said, "Well, the galley table and the boat are safe." Chase said, "Good game, real good game."

The *Jubilee* surged ahead with her nets in tow and made her way south. Chase went up to spend a minute with Scanton. He brought him a fresh cup of coffee. Joey said, "Things are going okay, but I'm anxious to see what kind of condition the net is in." They had another hour to go on the tow. Scanton said, "Pat, take a look at that paper." He pulled the bottom sheets off the machine. The heavy bottom line at fifty-four fathoms was thick and clouded with marks about two fathoms deep. Scanton said, "If that's what it looks like and the net's still together, this could be fun." They rode on in relative silence and the minutes crept by. The boat hung up a few more times, freed up, twisted, and turned. She fought the tide hard and continued steadily to the south. Anderson and Reed were playing cards. They watched, they waited, and they fished.

Scanton hollered down, "Let's haul back." The boys flew through the pilothouse and out on deck. Everybody was oiled up and ready to go in five minutes. Chase waved to Scanton to get the PTO engaged and the haulback began. The wires jumped and shook as the wire came back on to the winches. The *Jubilee* was literally being hauled backward. You could see a reverse wake beside her hull, illuminated by the deck lights. The marks came slowly, a single, a double, a single, as the wire rolled on to the drums. The one-hundred-fathom mark, the seventy-five, the fifty, the twenty, until the door markers appeared.

Slowly the doors were hung on the gallous frames, and the idler chain was clipped to the reel. The back straps were unhooked and hung. Then came the legs, and it happened—a massive wake appeared three boat lengths off the stern. No one could take their eyes off it. The gulls came. Chase yelled, "That's going to have to be split!" The bag was enormous. As the net came up onto the reel, no one could believe there wasn't a tear in it. It was as good as when they set it off.

Chase said, "Splitting this bag is a big deal." He pointed to the top of the net. "There's a line built into the net called a bull rope. It's worked into the twine on top of the net. When it's pulled tight, it closes around the top of the cod end like a hangman's noose. That forces half the fish up into the lengthening piece. The other half stays in the cod end." Anderson looked but didn't say a word. "With the net so full of fish you can't get it up the ramp, the bull rope lets us split the net in half and pull the cod end aboard. See, we pull the cod end right under the lengthening piece. It stays in the water. It kind of happens in a twisting motion."

The excitement on board the *Jubilee* was electric. Chase and Reed ran the jillsons, and Anderson followed the orders from Scanton that were coming over the loud hailer. The first part of bag came aboard and was at least five thousand pounds. After the cod end was released into the deck checker, the clip was replaced, and the cod end got set overboard again. The bull rope was relaxed, and the lengthening piece released six thousand more pounds of fish back into the cod end.

Scanton came down on deck. Everybody was laughing and congratulating him on the catch. Anderson was blown away. These were amazing fish. They were pure-market large codfish, all over thirty pounds each. Scanton said, "Well, are you guys going to screw around or put our fish away? We've got to get set out if we're going to catch any fish this trip!"

He headed up to the pilothouse and spun the boat around. The gang got the net off and Scanton pounded back toward the north. The fish were too large to use baskets. After the cutting and gutting they went into the wash checker and down into the fishhold. When all was said and done, the *Jubilee* now had approximately fifty-four thousand pounds of fish on board. It was 11:45 p.m., August 7.

CHAPTER 23

It took the crew a little over two hours to get all the fish put away and iced. They hosed off their oil clothes and headed up the stairs. It was coffee time, and Anderson went down to get a fresh pot on the stove. Scanton was hard at it. Just like all the other tows on this piece of bottom, it took his total concentration. The *Jubilee* was doing her part as she worked her way back to the north. It was just before midnight. There was very little wind, with gentle seas rolling from the south-southwest. The sky was clear and the stars were bright. The crew members were all standing behind Scanton. It was quiet.

Scanton spoke up and said, "Pat, look at that target on the six-mile ring." The radar screen showed a bright clear mark that had appeared. He adjusted the EBL and fixed it on the target. Within minutes you could tell that another vessel was moving rapidly in the *Jubilee's* direction.

Scanton said, "I'll bet that's one of those coastal tankers that runs up and down here all the time." He was watching the radar intently. You could see the boat approaching as it moved across the rings that divided the screen into one-mile sections.

Scanton grabbed a piece of paper and did some quick calculations that timed the movement of the vessel across the screen. After allowing for the three and a half knots that they were traveling, he calculated that the vessel was moving at about eighteen knots. That meant that the tanker would be within collision range in about twenty-three minutes.

"Tom, go down on deck . . . check and see if all our running lights are lit. Look at the towing light. It's the red one."

The *Jubilee's* towing light was located high in her mast. When it was lit, it signaled to other vessels that the boat was attached to the bottom and could not change her course. Anderson gave an okay from the deck. All lights were lit and shining brightly.

Scanton switched the VHF down to one watt. He still didn't want the world knowing where he was fishing. He grabbed the mic. "This is the fishing vessel *Jubilee* WBF 5658 on channel 16 calling the vessel approaching from the northeast. We are located in the area of Sigsbee Ridge north-northwest of Cashes Ledge. Come in, please." There was no reply. The vessel was tracking the EBL line and headed directly toward them.

Scanton said, "Come on, you bastard, pull off!"

Five minutes later the tension on board was growing. He grabbed the VHF mic again. The boat was too far away to hear a horn at this point.

"This is an emergency call . . . The fishing vessel *Jubilee*, WBF 5658, on channel 16 calling the vessel approaching our location of 13115 25545 from the north-northeast. You are on a collision course with our vessel! I repeat, you are on a collision course with our vessel. *Respond immediately . . . I repeat . . . respond immediately!*"

The air was totally silent. Chase said, "Joey, I've got a visual on her. I can see her running lights and her masthead. She's a small coastal tanker, just like you said."

Under his breath Scanton said, "Come on, you bastards, come on . . . pull off!" Now the tanker was within six or seven minutes. He was back on the radio.

"This is the *Jubilee* . . . answer your goddamn radio. If you're down near Sigsbees Ridge, answer your goddamn radio. Over!"

Scanton was holding back on trying to turn off his course. There was a very good chance that on this bottom, if he tried to make a turn, he would hang up solid. They could not afford to be anchored to the bottom with that tanker trying to run them over. His options were running out. He stared at the radar screen, praying the tanker would veer off. He thought about his uncle's words about guessing right, or guessing wrong. The thought that his luck had run out too was weighing heavily on his mind. Two more minutes ran off the clock.

You could see the tanker's bow and the wake she was kicking off as she bore down on them. He took the *Jubilee* off autopilot and switched to manual steering. He stepped up to the wheel and started a slow turn to port. He screamed into the mic, "WAKE UP, YOU BASTARDS! YOU'RE GOING TO HIT US! WAKE UP . . . GODDAMN IT . . . WAKE UP!"

He had just begun the turn and his heart sank. You could feel a shudder that ran from stem to stern. Just as he had feared, the net had hung up in the rocks. She swung slowly to the port and stopped dead in the water. The port door was hung.

He reached for the throttle and gave the 1271 full power. She revved up to 2,200 rpm. "Come on, old girl, come on. One more time, baby, one more time." Chase ran down into the galley and came flying back up with three cans of peas in his hands. Anderson looked at Reed with a questioning look.

"You'll see." Reed turned to Scanton and said, "Joey, the Givens?"

The Givens life raft was stored in a sealed container on the roof of the pilothouse.

Scanton said, "Get it ready, but don't deploy it. I'm not ready to give her up, not yet."

Scanton turned on the huge spotlight mounted on the roof of the boat and angled it so it was shining into the bridge of the tanker. Reed and Chase flew out on deck and up the ladder onto the pilothouse roof.

They were close enough to see into the bridge of the tanker. The quartermaster was slumped over in his chair, sound asleep. Suddenly, Scanton could feel a little give on the port side of the boat. The *Jubilee* was freeing up. He forced her to port.

Chase was up on the roof of the boat now. He reached back, like he was Nolan Ryan, and heaved a can of peas at the bridge of the tanker. It bounced high off the tanker's pilothouse roof. The second can though was a perfect strike! It blew the second to starboard front window. Broken glass sprayed all over the pilothouse of the tanker.

The man at the helm jumped up like he had been shot from cannon. When he saw what was happening, he jammed the jog lever on the autopilot to port. The tanker passed less than two feet from the end of the *Jubilee's* paravanes, on her starboard side. As she ghosted past them you could see the name on her stern, the *Harold B. Trenton, Boston, Massachusetts.*

Scanton slowed the *Jubilee* back to an idle until she was stationary in the water. He grabbed the mic and screamed, "This is the *Jubilee* to the tanker *Harold B. Trenton* on 16. Come back." To his complete surprise, the radio responded. "This is the *Harold B. Trenton* on 16 back to the *Jubilee.*" Scanton hollered into the mic, "You son of a bitch! You almost ran us over!"

"This is the *Harold B. Trenton.* Your vessel was not sufficiently lit or detectable on radar. Over."

Scanton screamed into the mic, "You lying bastard. You missed us by two feet!!"

There was no reply.

"This is the *Jubilee* calling the *Harold B. Trenton*! Over."

The radio was silent. Scanton couldn't believe what that prick had just done. He reached for a cigarette. His mind was still racing. He looked out the aft window and could see the tanker steadily disappearing from view. At least they were all okay. He slowly began to calm down. As he started to relax again he could only think of one thing. Now he had to figure out what kind of a mess he had waiting for him on the bottom. When the boys came back up to the pilothouse, he said, "Nice throw, Patrick!"

Chase took a drag of his cigarette. "I hate fuckin' peas."

CHAPTER 24

"**J**ubilee, *Jubilee*, this is the *Jessica* calling." Scanton switched the radio back up to twenty-five watts. "Go ahead, Rusty."

"Let's try 88."

"Eighty-eight."

Martin came on. "Hey, what's going on with you guys? I couldn't hear much. You were broken up. I figured you must have been on one watt. Over."

"Yes, Christ, Rusty, we had a close call with a goddamn little coastal tanker. We could see the son of bitch asleep at the wheel. We're all right though. I'm hung down pretty bad right now. I think I'm crossed up. I'll call you when we get squared away. Over."

Peter Scanton broke in, "Joey . . . is everybody okay?"

"We're fine, Dad. Your boy Pat blew out their windows with a can of peas though. I'll call you guys later. I've got to get the net up before it's nothing but rags. The *Jubilee*, clear and back to 16."

The gang headed back down on deck. Scanton put the boat up a notch, and they started to haul the wires in. They made some progress, and then he could see the wires narrowing off the gallous frames as they came up. He had to keep the boat off the wires. He had to slow the process down. He came over his hailer and told Chase to keep hauling the starboard side and for Reed to hold off on the port. They struggled and worked the winches back and forth for almost two hours. Raising and dropping the doors, jogging the boat ahead, and letting her settle back. The legs were wound into the doors and they came up in a ball. Everyone, including Scanton, was relieved that it was a calm night.

They had to use both jillsons twice and finally managed to get the net up to the ramp. The doors had crossed over and taken out the starboard wing. The belly of the net was three quarters torn out. They all laughed when the bag popped up, and it looked okay. Chase said, "Better than a sharp stick in the eye, ain't it?" They jillsoned the cod end up the ramp, and it looked like about four thousand pounds of large codfish. Scanton laughed when he saw it come on board. He came down on deck for a minute. "Skip, why don't you come up and run her over to the flatfish bottom? I'm spent."

"Ya, Joe, I'll be right up."

Scanton had gone without sleep the longest of anybody on board. He was dog tired and needed to take a break. It was five thirty in the morning, August 8. As Scanton passed through the galley he stopped to see Uncle Charley for a minute. He said, "It was another fine night on the *Jubilee*, old girl. Some asshole on a tanker tried to sink us. Can you fuckin' believe that?" He poured her a saucer of milk and turned in.

Reed headed back over to the flatfish tows. They were steering ninety degrees due east. It took Chase and Anderson about an hour and a half to get the fish down. By Chase's calculations they had about 6,500 pounds of codfish. There were eighty good-sized lobsters that should weigh about a 120 pounds. Anderson asked Chase how he could gauge the weight for the tally without using the scale baskets. He explained that he figured on the volume of tightly packed fish that were iced in the pens. "Basically I'm looking at a pen like it's a huge-scale basket. We've had enough fish on board before to make a pretty good estimate." Chase went up and wrote down the weight in Joey's daily logbook. It brought the estimated tally weight up to 60,500 pounds. The live tank was up to about 460 pounds of lobsters.

CHAPTER 25

It was 8:00 a.m. when they arrived back at the flatfish tow. Chase had a fresh coffee on, and he woke Scanton up. He came to. "Good, Pat, good, good, I'm up." He sat on the edge of his bunk and lit up a Marlboro. He grabbed a fresh cup of coffee on the way through the galley.

"Okay, boys, here's what we're going to do. We'll do two end-for-end tows down here, and then we'll head for Gloucester and take out. They pay quick down there, and I don't want to wait for our check."

Reed said, "Sounds good to me, Joe. Let's have at it."

They went down on deck and started setting off. When they raised the starboard door to unchain it, Anderson raised his arm and they stopped the winches. He called Chase back to the starboard gallous. He pointed out a shackle that appeared to have backed out a few turns where the main wire attached to the door.

Pat grabbed the large stillson wrench and tightened the shackle. He checked the port door, but it was fine. Apparently during the hang down with the doors crossing and slamming around, it must have backed off. Chase said, "Good catch, kid. Having a door come off is a huge pain in the balls. I've seen it before, and it sucks."

"Thanks, Pat."

The net was in the water in about a half an hour and they were underway.

"*Jubilee, Jubilee,* the *Gloria Walker* calling." They got shifted up to a channel.

Joey said, "All right, who's on this one? I don't want to have to tell this story fifty friggin' times. Over."

"We're all here." Scanton learned that everybody was there—Marshall Grimes, Vern Eldridge, Rusty Martin, his dad, and God knew how many others. He proceeded to tell the story of the near disaster with the *Harold B. Trenton*. He intentionally didn't leave out a single detail of the ordeal. He had a sneaking suspicion that the captain of the tanker was probably listening in as well. He'd bet good money that the guy who was asleep on watch had had his ass reamed by now.

Everybody loved the part where Pat had blasted the window out of the tanker with his can of peas. It had that sort of David and Goliath ring to it. Within forty-eight hours every free-rudder fisherman on the coast of Maine would know the story. Of course it would be embellished, to the point where Pat would have sunk that tanker with just one throw. Everybody fishing loved a good sea story, especially one with a good ending.

They got the dishes cleaned up and had a chance for a few hours of sack time. When Anderson hit the bunk, Chase and Reed were already asleep in their berths. He was thinking, *What was coming next?* He drifted off.

After a few hours Scanton called everyone to the deck, and they hauled back. There were four thousand pounds of flatfish by the time they had everything down. There were twenty-one baskets of dabs and thirty-four baskets of gray sole, bringing the tally to 5,600 pounds. There were only ten lobsters. It was noon on August 8.

The net was overboard for the last tow. Anderson was planning a great meal for the crew tonight. Up on the hard bottom there had been a half a scale basket of perfect large sea scallops. He had been shucking them out, and he had them packed away in the ice, down in the fishhold. Tonight there would be scallops for dinner.

The boat towed her nets over the mud bottom for the next three hours. It was four thirty in the afternoon when Scanton called for the haulback. They stepped on deck, oiled up, and were ready again. Even though this hadn't been a long trip, every one of them wanted to get things done, wrap up, and head ashore.

The haulback went well. The net came up without a hitch. Anderson got to tie off the clip line and release the cod end. They got the net back up on the reel and started working on getting the fish down. They had mostly dabs, about thirty baskets, and twenty-one of gray sole. There were ten baskets of mixed hake and pollack, bringing the *Jubilee's* grand total to approximately 65,000 pounds.

There was excitement aboard the boat. Dragger men called it channel fever. They had a great catch on board, and everything on the boat was working fine. The new reverse gear had been put to the test and had come through with flying colors. There's always a risk of vibration from a faulty realignment or poor installation with a job of that size. The boat was running smooth.

Chase went around and did a full boat inspection—deck to engine room. Since they were headed ashore, he had a notebook with him. He always put a list together for any parts he might need. Nothing agitated him more than getting caught offshore, trying to jury-rig a part together out of old junk.

Scanton was up in the wheelhouse putting his tally sheet together. Anderson was in the galley getting supper on, and Reed was on wheel watch in the pilothouse. He had his nose stuck in one of his pornographic adventure books.

Anderson had slipped Uncle Charley a bowl full of scallop rinds. He was building a big onion-free salad on the table and had made up a dozen homemade dinner rolls. He was making a dish called Scallops Casco Bay. It was Ritz crackers mixed with honey and a large amount of butter and sprinkled over the scallops and baked.

Chase came in and sat down at the galley table and hauled out a Marlboro. They were headed to Gloucester.

CHAPTER 26

66 *Jubilee, Jubilee,* this is the *Gloria Walker.*"

"Ya, Dad, Go ahead."

"Eighty-eight, Joe?"

"Eighty-eight."

"How's Babe Ruth doin'? Over."

"Jesus, Dad . . . Pat's getting old, but he's not that old."

"Is he up there with you? Put him on."

Scanton hollered down to the galley. "Pat, get up here. The old man wants a word with you."

Chase said, "Oh boy, here we go."

He came upstairs and grabbed the mic from Joey.

"Yeah, Pete . . . Go ahead."

"Jesus, boy, you got to tell me how it felt to nail that bastard with them peas. Over."

"No big deal, Pete . . . it was a lucky shot, I guess. Over."

"I'll tell you what, Patrick, I'd have pissed my pants laughin' if I'd seen you do it. I bet that kid at the wheel of that old tub ain't going to forget that in a hurry either. Over."

"Probably not. Over."

"Well, it's a good one, Pat. First time I heard of anything like that, in all these years pounding around out here. What are you fellas doing next? Over."

"Jesus, I don't know. Joey's right here, Pete. I'll put him on. Nice talkin' to you. Over."

"All right, Pat, finest kind. Good talkin' to you too, boy."

Scanton took the mic. "What's up, Dad?"

"Nothin' really . . . just checkin' in. Over."

"We're going to take a ride west southwest from the bucket bottom. Over." (That was code for going in to Gloucester.) A ride was always a long steam. When fish were around like this, the boats tried to land the biggest trip before the next boat got in. It could mean as much as fifty or sixty cents a pound more money.

Peter said, "Yeah, I gotcha. Give us a call tomorrow. Let us know how you made out. Marshall and I have scratched up a couple of trays between us. You know I think he's forgot how to catch fish. He's gotten so old and cranky."

Marshall Grimes broke in. "Cranky? Who's cranky . . . me? Why just the other day, my Grace was talkin' to your Gloria. She asked her if she ever woke up grumpy? She said, 'No, nowadays I just let the old bastard sleep.'"

Joey said, "All right, you guys, supper's on and it smells good. The green guy's made us up a bunch of scallops, and I can't wait to get at them. This is the *Jubilee*, clear with the fleet. Back on 16."

Marshall broke in. "Jesus, Peter, did you hear that? A scallop dinner? If we knew the captain on that boat we could maybe get us a site and have some of them scallop dinners. Over."

Peter said, "I know the captain on that boat and he'd never give you a site. You're too goddamn cranky. Over."

Scanton flipped back to 16. He thought to himself, *Those two should start up their own comedy show. They could call it* Peter and Marshall . . . The Floating Fruitcakes. *They could have Vern on every once in a while for guest appearances. He could talk about mending nets, hilarious moments in the fishhold, and codfish prices . . . look out, Johnny Carson.*

Scanton called down to the galley, "Those scallops ready yet?"

Anderson said, "Aye, aye, Captain. I'll bring some up!" Tom scooped out a big plate with salad and rolls. "What do you want to drink, Joey?"

"A milk would be great!"

Anderson brought Joey's plate up. "Jesus, this looks good, kid. How we holding out on grub anyway?"

Anderson said, "Really very well, actually. Of course I've tried to use the most perishable stuff first. We've still got some good meats buried in ice in the fish hole."

Scanton said, "Okay, I'm going to try and get out of Gloucester fairly quick and get back on the bottom. You think that meat will hold up?"

"It should be fine."

"Okay, kid, go eat your supper."

Chase got the boys to run the ripped-up groundfish net off the reel so they could get a jump on mending it. Once it was off the reel they jillsoned the groundfish roller sections forward. Anderson was anxious to learn what he could about this aspect of the job. Chase seemed in the right mood to spend some time with him. Chase said, "Skip, why don't you head up, and I'll teach boy wonder here some of the basics."

"Sounds good to me. You got a butt on you?"

"Yeah, I do. It surrounds my asshole."

"Very funny." Chase handed Reed a Marlboro. He walked off across the deck toward the companionway. After Reed was out of hearing range, Chase said, "Your buddy Skippy pulls that every fuckin' trip. We all buy our own butts on this boat and that's it. That cheap prick runs out every friggin' time and never replaces a pack. It pisses me off. Joey won't give him any more, it's gotten so bad. I know he brought two cartons of Marlboros on here just a few days ago . . . now he's out? Fuck him. He smokes yours and saves his for later, the shit bag."

Anderson thought, *We're headed in, and the shit between these two starts up again.* He couldn't blame Pat though. He'd had plenty of guys pull that crap with him, and he hated it too. Maybe that was part of Skip's big money-making plan. Rip off your friends' cigarettes and retire.

Chase and Anderson started to work on the net.

"It's very simple, really. The hardest part is looking at this pile of twine and having the imagination to see it in operation. Every part of the net is made based on a series of counts so that, when it gets destroyed and ripped up, you can duplicate it again from scratch. The meshes of a net, the square holes you're looking at, are what gets counted."

Chase said, "Now watch this." He grabbed a section of the net that had been ripped to shreds. "This was a wing." He started cutting the twine meshes until he reached a part that was still intact. I was counting while I was cutting that. It was forty-two meshes. When I go to put that back, I'll replace forty-two meshes."

Anderson said, "How the hell do you remember all the numbers?"

"Sometimes it's hard to. I write down the counts once in a while."

"I see. What about when there's nothing left to count?"

Chase said, "Then you have to know the counts and be able to lay out the net from scratch. Joey can do that. Peter, his old man, and Marshall are amazing at it."

"From what I'm beginning to understand, I'm not surprised."

"Okay, I'm going to bed now. You mend the net."

"You know something?"

"Whaaat?"

Anderson said, "This boat is full of fucking comedians. Is there like a dragger man school you graduate from, where they have maybe an annex for funny guys that couldn't make it on stage?"

"You may be catchin' on. Now get over here. You're graduating from nod man to nail man."

Pat told Tom that when he was a kid, hanging around the wharfs all the time, that the old-timers used to carry a nail in their pockets. Some green guy would be holding twine for a mender, and the old guy would say, "See this nail? I can pound it into a wall, hang the net on it, and replace you."

Anderson said, "See that's exactly what I'm talking about. Those old guys were probably like instructors, at the Dragger U comedy school."

"Shut up and hold this twine, shithead."

Chase worked along in silence for a while and then said, "I'm ready to be ashore for a couple of days with a good trip to sell. You got a girlfriend, kid, or are you going pussy chasing with Reed?"

"I do have a girlfriend, and I hated leaving her when we took off. I think it'll be a while before I see her though. If we go right back out and down east, who knows . . . we'll see."

"Let's wind this thing back up on the reel. We'll finish it up on the ride back out."

"Thanks for the twine lesson."

"No sweat, smart guy!"

It was just about ten o'clock when Chase and Anderson finally made it back up to the pilothouse. They headed down to the galley. Chase said, "I'm going to call my wife and see if she can come down and meet us in Gloucester for a day or two. You want her to call that girlfriend of yours? Maybe they could ride down together for a short visit."

"Yes, indeed. I'd like that." Anderson smiled immediately at that thought.

Reed said, "I bet you would, TTL."

Anderson ignored him. He was too excited about maybe seeing Kathy to pay any attention to Skip's bullshit.

"I'm going to go call Leslie. What's your girlfriend's name and number?"

Anderson told Pat how to reach Kathy and followed him up to the pilothouse.

Chase said, "Joey, I'd like to give Leslie a call, if you don't mind."

"No, Pat, go right ahead."

He took the mic. "This is the fishing vessel *Jubilee* JBF 5658 on 16 calling the Boston Marine Operator. Come in, please." A female voice answered back, "This is Boston Marine back to the fishing vessel *Jubilee*. Switch and answer on channel 24, and stand by, please. Over."

"The *Jubilee* switching to channel 24 and standing by."

You could hear the tail end of other calls already placed. After a ten-minute wait the operator came on.

"Fishing vessel *Jubilee* . . . this the Boston Marine Operator. How may I help you this evening?"

"I'd like to place a call to Maine at 207-773-4974. Over."

"I'll place that call for you, sir. Will this be charged to the fishing vessel *Jubilee* this evening? Over."

"Ten-four."

"Thank you, *Jubilee*. Please stand by for your call. Over."

"Standing by."

A couple of minutes went by and she came on again.

"*Jubilee*, your party is on the line. Please go ahead."

"Hi, Pat."

"Hi, Leslie. How are you, dear? Over."

"I'm fine . . . Muffin has been looking all over the house for you as usual, poor little kitty. Over."

Pat said, "I miss her too. We're headed up into Gloucester and should be there by three in the morning. I thought you might like to come down for an overnight. Over."

"Absolutely, my mother can take care of the cats and I'll be down. When do you think I should get there by? Over."

"Three thirty, four o'clock in the afternoon should be fine. We are going in to North Star Fisheries. Over."

"Great, honey, I'll look forward to seeing you. Over."

"Leslie . . . one of the crew members has a girlfriend in Falmouth. He'd like you to call her and see if she wants to come down. Her name's Kathy, she's at 781-4498. He thinks she will come if she can. Over."

"Okay, I'll try her. Have you met her? Is she nice? Over."

"Jeez, Les, I just met him. She could have three heads and one tooth. I don't know. Over."

"Okay, okay, I'll see you tomorrow then. Over."

"Okay, see you then, dear. Good night."

"The *Jubilee*, clear with the Boston Marine Operator. Thank you."

"This is Boston Marine, clear with the *Jubilee*. Have a good evening, sir."

Anderson was thrilled. "Thanks, Pat."

"You bet, kid. Want to lose another game of crib?"

Anderson said, "Ya, you kicked my ass so bad last time, I need to have another shot at you."

Reed came up the stairs and sat down in his favorite spot.

He said, "So did you guys get that all worked out? Is she coming down, TTL?"

Anderson said, "All right, I'll bite. What's this TTL shit I keep hearing out of you?"

"That stands for Tommy Tit Lapper."

Tom's face dropped and turned beet red. "Skip, you goddamn asshole. You were watching us?"

Scanton and Chase couldn't wait for this story. Joey said, "We gotta hear this one, Skip. We're all ears." Skip said, "Well, I was out back of my house taking a leak and smoking a butt. I heard Tommy boy here and his broad talkin'. Well, you guys know how friendly I am, so I walked up there to say hello. I look in the backyard and guess who's sucking as hard as he can on his girlfriend's titties. I didn't want to interrupt anything, so I stood there a minute. You know me. I didn't want to be rude."

At this point Scanton and Chase are busting a gut laughing. Anderson yelled, "You sick fuckin' piece of shit. I suppose you had your dick out, jerking off, while you watched."

Reed was laughing his ass off. "Who you calling sick? I wasn't the one sucking my girl's tits out in broad daylight for the whole neighborhood to watch. Besides, I just got my dick hauled out when her old lady came home and you guys quit. I bet if she hadn't shown up it would have gotten a lot better."

Anderson said, "You know what? Fuck you, Skip! Let's go play a game of crib, Pat."

They headed down below and Scanton said, "Jesus, you're something else, Skip. I'm some glad you're on my side."

"Hey, what are friends for? I'm telling you, she's got great tits."

CHAPTER 27

Scanton shook his head and picked up the mic. "North Star Fisheries, this is the *Jubilee* calling. Come in, please."

"This is North Star, go ahead."

"Let's go to 65. Over."

"Okay, 65."

"Hey, is Artie there?"

"Hey, Joey, this is Frank. I'll get Artie. Stand by a minute. He's out on the dock."

Artie came on. "Joey, my boy, you coming in to see your old friend Artie?"

"Ya, I couldn't figure out any other place to go, so I'm headed your way. Over."

"Good, good, you do anything?"

Fishing boats calling in a hail always have code language worked out with the dealer so their catch wasn't broadcast to the fleet. The dealers had to get set up for what the boats were bringing in.

Joey said, "Couldn't catch a friggin' cold. Over."

Artie turned to Frank and said, "Big trip. Write down what I tell you."

Artie came back on. "Sorry to hear that. There's always next time." Scanton started to report in. "Five and a walk, union. Over."

Artie said to Frank, "Write down '10,500 gray sole.'"

Artie came over the radio. "Go ahead, Joey."

"Five strike outs, brown. Over."

"Frank, write down ten thousand dabs."

"Yes, Joe"

"Three strikeouts and a walk. Tom Collins. Over."

"Frank, write down '3,500 mixed grounds.'"

Artie said, "Yes, Joe."

"Three home runs, five strikeouts, MCs."

Artie said to Frank, "God bless him . . . 35,000 large codfish."

"That a game, Joey?"

"No, two bozos'"

"Frank, he's got two thousand monkfish."

"Well, Joe, that's all right. You'll make expenses and a buck or two for the boys. You aren't going to nail them every time. Over."

"I know, Artie, but this shit is getting old. Over."

"When will see you poke around the corner?"

"Three a.m. or so. We want lumpers, and we need ice and fuel. Pat will want the fishhold set up. We'll sail in two days. Over."

"All right, Joe, we'll see you then. We'll take you out at three thirty. Over/"

"Finest kind, Artie. We'll see you in a bit. This the *Jubilee*, clear with North Star Fisheries. Going back to 16 and standing by."

"North Star, clear with the *Jubilee*."

Artie turned to Frank. "The kid's got about sixty-six thousand pounds."

Frank said, "Good for him."

Joey switched the radio back down to 16. He got up from his chair. "Skip, why don't you take her for a while. Get me up at around two thirty."

"Yes, okay, Joe. You have to admit the tit story was good."

"Yes, it was. Now I can't wait to meet her."

"Don't get too excited. She doesn't like our kind."

As Scanton headed below, he was thinking, *I was kind of hopeful that I'm a different kind than you.*

When he climbed into his bunk he laid there in the dark thinking about the trip he had aboard. He knew they would stock close to a hundred thousand dollars. There would be enough money to pay off the boat bills and leave him almost forty grand. They had done it. Turned things around . . . just like his dad said he could. As he fell asleep that night he felt the stress leave his body. He had a feeling that he could work everything out now, even the problems with Karen. They did love each, after all. As he drifted off he was thinking about Little Joey and looking forward to seeing him when they got back to Maine in a week or two.

CHAPTER 28

The *Jubilee* was headed to shore. Reed was at the helm and the rest of the crew was asleep.

He was thinking about his contact man, and he was nervous that there might be real trouble for him if he couldn't convince Joey to go ahead with his swordfish plan. You only live once, why waste it bustin' your balls? There were plenty of guys who knew a good opportunity when they saw it, and he was one of them.

Reed kept a sharp eye on the radar. He couldn't believe how close they were to getting sunk by that fuckin' tanker. That whole thing really pissed him off. The asshole practically cuts them in two, and then the bastard denies doing anything wrong. He could see how the real world worked—every man for himself. Those guys on that tanker would have run them down and never even called it in. They'd all be just another statistic. No one would have been around to defend them or report the facts to anybody if they had been hit. The money guys behind that tanker company would hire the best lawyers and beat the whole thing. That's assuming anybody survived to even try and sue the pricks. Plenty of guys in the winters had been hit by tankers and were lost.

These big companies don't give a shit about any of these fishing boats, or maritime laws either, for that matter. It's hard enough, playing around out here, trying to catch fish and then to get mowed over by a sleeping asshole on a goddamn tanker. It really sucked.

He spotted a few targets showing up on the screen. It was summertime, and the pleasure boats were all over the place out here. He was getting closer to shore now, so there would be more of them running around.

Nothing Reed saw on the screen seemed to present a problem to him as far as making headway into Gloucester. He really wanted to get in to make a few calls. There were people he needed to talk to, and soon. The big trip was going to be a problem, but he knew he could figure out a way to deal with that. He settled in and kept steaming.

The hours and minutes ticked away. Skip checked the ship's clock. It was 2:20 a.m. The radar was clear. He ran down forward and woke Joey and came back to the helm.

Joey grabbed a coffee on the way through the galley. He hopped up into his captain's chair and lit up a cigarette.

"Anything go on while I was down forward?"

"No, she was fine. Radio was quiet for a summer night. I'm going to go get some fresh coffee."

Joey grabbed the c.

"North Star Fisheries, the *Jubilee* calling."

"North Star back to the *Jubilee*."

"Sixty-five. Over."

"Sixty-five." They got up on the channel. "Who's this?"

"*Jubilee*, this is Frank. Go ahead."

"Hey, Frank, Joey Scanton here. We're about twenty-five minutes off your dock. Are you all set? Over."

"Ya . . . we're set, Skipper. The lumpers are here and ready to go. I'll let Artie know you're in. Over."

"Ya, finest kind then, Frank. I'll leave it on this one if you need me. Over."

"Okay, Skipper, we'll see you in a few minutes. Over."

"*Jubilee* standing by on 65."

"Skip, get everybody up. We gotta get the paravanes."

"Okay, Joey."

Skip went down forward and woke up the crew.

When he shook Anderson, he said, "Come on, TTL, rise and shine."

Anderson flew out of the bunk and grabbed Reed by the shoulders and arms and slammed him back against the bulkhead so hard his feet were lifted off the floor. He was no match for Anderson's strength, plus the fact that he was pissed.

"You listen to me, you little motherfucker. You ever call me that name again or make any of your nasty remarks about Kathy, and I'm going to break your fuckin' neck. I've put up with a lot of shit from you over the years because of our friendship. Now you've pushed it too far. You get me?"

The veins were standing out on Anderson's neck and his face was bright red. Skip knew he'd gone too far.

He said, "Okay, okay, calm down, lover boy. I was just having a little fun with you. I didn't know she was that important to you. I'm sorry, man."

Anderson put him back down and walked out and poured himself a cup of coffee without saying anything more. Skip made his way quickly through the galley and ascended the stairs back up to the wheelhouse. Chase came out into the galley and said, "Atta boy, Tom."

Once they were all topside, Chase said, "Come on, you guys, let's get the paravanes up. Let's go, Skip." They went out on deck. It was 3:00 a.m., August 9.

CHAPTER 29

Bertram Goldman was the head of the Drug Enforcement Agency for the state of Maine. He was a man of average height and stature. To describe him as an interesting personality would be an understatement.

He grew up in New York City. His dad worked in the garment district, and his mother was a second-grade schoolteacher. He had a twin brother named George. Goldman's mother cracked the whip over those two boys and made them do their schoolwork. She knew that if her sons were ever going to make anything of themselves, they'd have to have an education. She insisted on honor roll grades, and if they didn't deliver, there was hell to pay in her household.

Fortunately for Bert and George, they were very bright, and even though they were always running wild on the streets, schoolwork came easy for both of them. Bert's mother had often said to him, "Oh, Bert, just imagine what you could do if you only tried a little."

He would always reply the same way. "I know, Ma, but there are so many interesting things going on around here. I don't have time for it."

His mother would sigh. "You'll find time when you're sitting in a jailhouse somewhere."

Little did she know, at the time, how his adult life would eventually turn out.

Goldman's father died of heart attack when the boys were only fifteen. Sylvia Goldman did not give up on her dream to see her two boys go to college. Arthur Goldman had left her with a small life insurance policy, but mostly she scrimped and saved to put enough money aside for the boys to go get their educations. They were both enrolled at the city college and continued to live at home with her.

Bert was a very likeable street kid. A distant neighbor who ran into him might say, "I've seen you around, haven't I? Ain't you Sylvia Goldman's boy?"

"Yes, ma'am, I am. My name is Bertram Goldman, and I'm very pleased to make your acquaintance . . . and your name is?"

People would start talking to him, and before they knew it he would make them feel like an old friend.

It was during his junior year in college that Sylvia's sister Rose gave her a call. She told her that a golf resort, very near where she lived in New Hampshire, was looking for summer help. She thought Bert might want to get the job and stay with her for the summer.

Sylvia was thrilled. She hated Bert just hanging around in the city and thought he needed to have a real job. This one sounded perfect. When he arrived at home that night she announced, "You're going to New Hampshire to stay with your aunt Rose for the summer. You're going to work at a golf course up there. She's made all the arrangements for you. I got you a bus ticket. You leave at six in the morning. Go pack your stuff and go to bed."

Bert said, "Goddamn it, Ma, what do I know about golf?"

Sylvia gave Bert one of her most severe looks and said, "Don't you swear in my house! So . . . you know nothing from golf, so you go learn a little something new. It couldn't hurt, could it?"

Goldman knew this wasn't a rhetorical question. The discussion was over. He went up to the attic of the apartment and pulled out and old cardboard suitcase and packed up what he thought he'd need to be a golf course guy . . . whatever the hell that was.

At six in the morning, he was on that bus, ready for the eight-hour trip to New Hampshire. He was twenty years old and had never before left New York City. Everything was there. Why leave? School was great, there were exciting people, wonderful foods, entertainment, and fabulous women everywhere you looked. Why in hell would someone leave all that? He was getting his degree in English and special ed. Then there would be a job in the city teaching. He'd thought he would never leave.

Ah well, this summer thing would be something different, he thought. The city was starting to change. The drug world was expanding, and crime was at an all-time high. Maybe a change for the summer would be okay.

He watched the passing scenery and thought the countryside was absolutely beautiful. All he'd ever seen was skyscrapers and city streets. Oh sure, he'd seen this stuff on TV and pictures in books, but the real thing was amazing.

He started looking around the bus, wondering where all these people were going and why. He was a naturally curious guy.

Eight hours later and after several brief stops, the bus pulled into the station in North Conway, New Hampshire. His aunt was there waiting for him. After they greeted each other with hugs and kisses she drove him right to the little mountain resort.

Bert loved the job. It was so different from anything he had ever done before. The scenery was incredible, the weather was great, and he really did enjoy the work mowing the grass and keeping the place beautiful. He especially liked the look of the freshly mowed fairways and the beautifully manicured greens after he got done taking care of them. Spending the summer with his aunt Rose was a great idea.

One afternoon, when all his work was done, he was fooling around on the practice putting green. A gorgeous young blonde girl walked over, pulled her putter out of her bag, and dropped a few golf balls on the putting surface. She was taking some practice strokes. He had spotted this wonderful creature around the resort a number of times since he had been there. Goldman walked over to her and said, "Excuse me, but I would like to introduce myself."

In a smooth-as-butter Southern drawl, she looked up at him and said, "Well, go ahead, sugar, I'm not stopping you."

Bert never heard one word past "sugar." He was in love. There was something incredible about this girl that completely undid him. Her eyes were a deep clear blue color that reminded him of sapphires. He took a deep breath and plunged ahead. He felt like he was twelve years old.

"My name is Bert, Bert Goldman."

"Well, Bert, Bert Goldman, it's a pleasure to meet you, darlin'. I'm Ashley, Ashley Braydon."

Bert's heart raced. Wow, beautiful and a sense of humor too.

"Are you a member here, Bert?" Ashley asked.

"Oh yes." Bert said, "I have the only Jewish membership at the resort. After I cut the grass, weed the flower beds, and pick up all the trash, I can play all the golf I want . . . as long as it's after dark."

"Oh, Bert honey, you are so funny. You just crack me up!" Ashley was smiling at him.

Bert got up his courage and said, "Would you like to have dinner with me at my aunt Rose's tonight?"

To Goldman's total surprise, she said, "Sure, I would. Who's Aunt Rose?"

"She's my mother's sister, and she's going to love you. I know she will."

Ashley and Bert were inseparable all that summer. She was wild about this funny Jewish kid from New York City. He treated her like a queen. In fact, they fell so in love that summer that it would turn out to be enough for a lifetime.

They were married the next year, and he took her back to his beloved New York City. They rented a really great apartment. Ashley came from a wealthy family so they showered them with fabulous wedding gifts. There had been money too. Bert had finished his degree and was teaching in the city just like he had planned, but he was restless for something more. He wanted to give Ashley more than a teacher's salary could ever provide.

One night when he was riding the subway home from work, he was reading the evening newspaper over a guy's shoulder and spotted an advertisement that caught his eye.

"*United States Department of Justice* seeking applicants for a career in law enforcement as an agent of the federal government. Examination required . . . all applicants must be United States citizens and in good physical condition." The advertisement ran on with more details and more specifics about the offer. Goldman's first piece of investigative work was figuring out what paper that guy was reading so he could go get himself a copy.

After he bought it he rushed home to their apartment. When he came through the door, he called out to her in the kitchen. "Hey, honey, I've figured out what I want to do. I'm going to become a federal agent for the US Department of Justice."

"Sure you are, darlin', and I'm going to get me some of those cute little dancing slippers and try out for the New York City Ballet." Ashley didn't believe a word of it.

Goldman went to a designated government building bright and early the next Saturday morning and sat for the federal exam. He waited patiently for a month. There was no reply, so he took the exam again. It was a free test, and he really wanted to see this thing through. He waited another month; still no reply. He took it again and was halfway through when the monitor walked up to him. "Hey . . . Is your name Bert Goldman?"

"That's right, I'm him."

"Well, get the hell out of here, Goldman. You passed this exam three months ago!"

He scored in the ninety-eighth percentile in every category of that government test. He couldn't believe how easily the answers had come to him. He had always been smart in school, but this was different. It felt like the test was written for him personally. He thought it was weird. There were a lot of general questions, but the human logic problems were like fun puzzles, and he thought they were fascinating. The government finally did catch up with him. They called him in for interviews, physicals, and psychological tests. He wrote essays and answered endless questions about his background. They wanted to know everything about his childhood, his family, his friends, his enemies, his likes and dislikes. He met lots of the other candidates while he was going through the process.

Finally, after another two months of waiting, he was notified that he had passed every test. He was interviewed one more time. They wanted to know if he was interested in attending a special government school to be trained as an agent who would be assigned to the United States Federal Drug Enforcement Administration upon graduation. He had never considered that as a career path, but the more he thought about it, the more he liked it.

Goldman was very excited to tell Ashley about it. He sailed through the training with flying colors. His first assignment as a field agent was in Washington DC. In the years to follow he and Ashley would be transferred all over the country, living out what was to be a fabulous career in law enforcement. With his intelligence and his uncanny ability to entrap liars and criminals, it all came together. He was promoted rapidly through the system and became a special agent in charge at a very early age. He headed special task forces and enjoyed excellent professional relationships with his fellow officers.

Goldman couldn't believe the amount of crooked money and the extent of deceit and betrayal he witnessed every day in his job. But he loved the job. Unraveling the complex networks of lies and corruption that led to an arrest was fascinating. Drug trafficking had become a huge international enterprise of gargantuan proportions. The South American drug lords were infiltrating every facet of American life. No American family, wealthy or poor, was safe from the intrusion of narcotics into their everyday lives.

He served for over twenty-eight years all over the country. After his start in Washington they were assigned to places like San Francisco, Chicago, Tampa, Detroit, and Atlanta. He was involved in arrests and convictions that took place in the United States, France, Germany, England, and Sweden.

After all those years of service, his most recent transfer was to Portland, Maine, in 1975.

Goldman was assigned to head up all DEA operations for the entire state. He was glad to be back in the northeast. His fond memories of New Hampshire as a young man had stuck with him. For the past six years he had served in Maine, creating a large network of intelligence and surveillance operations up and down the coast. The Maine assignment could only be given to a man of his experience and skill.

The Maine coast is huge, extending from the New Hampshire border, with almost 3,500 miles of meandering coastline to Eastport, where it borders on Canada.

The network of hidden coves, outlets, inlets, and deepwater landing spots are almost too numerous to comprehend. There are winding rivers and hidden points that give perfect cover to maritime drug traffickers. In Goldman's opinion, the DEA could only be effective if a network of informants could be convinced to support the law enforcement efforts of his organization. A combination of state and local police, the warden service, both inland fish and game, and the marine patrol was the only hope he had of making any impact on the seemingly unstoppable flow of narcotics entering the state and transported throughout the northeast and beyond.

The public was a key part of Goldman's efforts. Under his training and influence, the officers of all branches of law enforcement were able to convince everyday citizens to join in the fight. Law enforcement officers passed out tens of thousands of cards and pamphlets encouraging people to be their eyes and ears. People all over the coast were participating in Goldman's efforts. Any suspicious activity at all, including idle conversation, could be the loose thread that caused an enormous international scheme to unravel. Make no mistake he was the top cop when it came to drug enforcement in the state of Maine. He took his job very seriously and was relentless in his pursuit of criminals, never getting distracted from his prime directive to see every guilty individual involved in drug-related illegal activities behind bars. There was only one man who knew everything that happened in that department of the DEA and his name was Goldman.

CHAPTER 30

The *Jubilee* passed Thatcher's Lighthouse, and the boat would land at North Star Fisheries in about ten minutes. It was August 9. Skip said, "Come on, Tom, let's get out the dock lines. We need the bow and stern lines and a bow and stern spring line. We'll set them up on deck."

Even though Reed's tone was friendly, Tom was still furious with him, but he knew he'd have to let it go. Scanton had enough to deal with without listening to squabbling crew members. He figured Reed was probably too scared to keep that little game going anyway. He should be scared. He'd meant exactly what he'd said about beating the shit out of him. One thing Reed had said was true. Kathy was very important to him. He couldn't stop thinking about her. He didn't know if she was going to come down to Gloucester to see him or not.

He was standing there daydreaming about Kathy when Chase yelled, "Wake up there, card shark, before I pop a can of peas off *your* head. You win two lousy games of cribbage, and you think you can just ride around on this boat half asleep! Get to work."

Anderson said, "Yes, sir. But lest you forget, it wasn't a couple of lousy games. It was one lovely, beautiful, gorgeous skunk, Mr. Chase."

CHAPTER 31

Back home in Maine the night before, Leslie Chase called Kathy Blackwell's house. After a few rings, Kathy's mother answered with an annoyed tone. "Hello, the Blackwell residence. This is Mrs. Blackwell."

"Hi, Mrs. Blackwell. This is Leslie Chase. Is Kathy there?"

"Yes, she is, but it's rather late at night to be calling, don't you think?"

Leslie, slightly embarrassed, said, "I'm sorry. Yes, it is."

"Well, just a minute . . . Kathy! It's for you. It's some Leslie person. I told her it was too late to be calling!"

"Oh god, Mother." She ran over and took the phone.

"Hello?"

"Hi, Kathy, you don't know me. I'm Leslie Chase. My husband, Pat, works on the *Jubilee*."

"Oh god, are they all right?"

"They're fine. Pat called me about ten minutes ago. They're headed into Gloucester, and he and Tom—is that your boyfriend's name?—they want us to come down to see them tomorrow afternoon." Kathy didn't hesitate a second.

"Yes, his name is Tom, Tom Anderson, and I'd love to do that. Do you want me to drive?"

"Sure, we can stop and get some lunch somewhere on the way down."

"Great, it sounds like fun."

"Pack your jammies. They want us to stay over."

Kathy smiled and thought, *I bet I won't need my jammies.*

She said, "Okay, Leslie, where can I pick you up and when?" Leslie gave her their address, and they agreed they should leave by noon. Kathy said, "Sorry about my mother. She's very old-fashioned. She really doesn't mean anything by it."

"It's okay really, I understand. When you live with a fisherman, there really aren't any normal hours to the days anymore."

"I'm sure there aren't. What do they say? Fishermen come and go with the tide. I'll look forward to meeting you tomorrow. I'll see you then. This is going to be fun! Bye, Leslie."

Leslie said good-bye and hung up. She thought, *I'm going to like her. I know I am.*

Kathy's mother said, "Who was that? What did she want?"

"That was Leslie Chase. Her husband works on the boat that Tom's on."

"What's that have to do with you?"

"That has to do with the fact that I'm going to meet her tomorrow, and I'm going to go see my honey!"

"Oh god, Kathy, we spent all that money on an education for you so you could have a good life. Don't wind up wasting it all on a guy like Tom Anderson. He'll never amount to anything. He's gone fishing with Skip Reed, for Pete's sake. What's the matter with you?"

Kathy just looked at her mother disgusted and said, "I'm sorry you don't like Tom, although I have no idea what that's based on. He's one of the sweetest men I've ever known. He's very loving and considerate to me. We've been special to each other, off and on, since we were just kids in the eighth grade. Please don't judge people you don't know. I'm going down to see him for a couple of days. I know this is hard for you to accept, but I'm a grown woman now, and I'll make my own decisions. I'll see you in the morning." Kathy went up to bed.

CHAPTER 32

Scanton steered the bow of the *Jubilee* in toward the unloading dock. He spun the wheel hard to port and threw the 1271 into reverse and hit the throttle. The boat shook and ground a little as her wheel changed direction. The *Jubilee* settled into her unloading berth. Reed tossed the bowline; Anderson got the stern line. They were landed, tied off, and ready to be unloaded.

Artie Valente had arranged for lumpers. Those men are the labor force that comes aboard fishing boats to unload their catch. Nine men, lumpers, had been hired for this unloading.

A crew member always had to be present to watch over the catch while it's being unloaded. There are different prices paid for different sizes and species of fish. The catch gets weighed, boxed, and iced in one-hundred-pound fish totes twelve to a pallet. It's pretty easy for a crooked man to slip four boxes of gray sole worth $3.50 a pound under eight boxes of dabs worth $2.00 a pound. Then the dealer pays for twelve boxes of dabs. It's a racket as old as buying fish.

The captain and crew have to protect their wallets. A watchful eye keeps everybody honest. A good lumping crew can unload a boat at a rate of ten thousand pounds an hour. The crew of men was quick to board the boat and get started.

Scanton was already up in the office when the boat started to offload. Reed was the first man on the culling table. He had a clipboard with him and was writing down the weights, the species, and the cull (sizing) of the catch. The lumpers started with the flatfish. The gray sole would be first. The loaded canvas baskets were beginning to be heisted out of the fishhold.

Scanton had told Anderson to get some breakfast going and leave it in the galley so the crew could eat in rotation.

Chase was in the engine room changing fuel filters, adding hydraulic fluid, and greasing bearings. The more of the mechanicals he got out of the way, the more time he'd have left for R & R.

It took about an hour for the gray sole to be unloaded. The lumpers were now attacking the dabs. Pat climbed the engine room stairs and headed down to the galley. He was sitting down and having a plate of eggs and sausage when a guy named Brian Ross came down into the galley. He sat down at the table like he owned the boat. He talked to Uncle Charley and rubbed her chin. He asked Chase if he could have some eggs and coffee. Chase introduced Brian to Anderson and told him to help himself to the food. Tom thought Brian and Pat seemed very friendly. He told Chase he had just come in on the *Margret Stone* and had quit his job on that boat. He asked him if he thought Joey might want to hire him on.

"Jesus, Brian, that's Joey's call. He's up in the office. You'll have to talk to him about it."

"Yes, okay. I'll do that. Joey and I always did great on this boat together. Hey, good grub there, Tom. You put cheese in these eggs? They're real good." Brian lit up a cigarette and hung around for about half an hour.

When Brian got up to leave, he said, "I'm going to go have a word with Joey. Thanks for the grub, and like I said, it was real good." After he left, Anderson asked Chase what the story was on him. He told him that he had fished with Joey off and on for years. He'd been with Joey's old man, and at some point or another it seemed like he had fished with everyone else too. He told him that Brian was a good man on the boat and an excellent twine man.

"We'll just have to see what Joey says. If you don't wind up staying on board, at least you can grab a ride back to Portland with Leslie."

Anderson couldn't believe that this would be the way of things on this boat. Trip by trip, somebody with more experience shows up, and you're on the wharf. He felt terrible. Chase could see the look of despair on Tom's face. He said, "Hey, we got a great trip of fish on board. You're going to get a big check for a rookie . . . what happens, happens. Let's go up and relieve Reed at the table." It was five fifteen in the morning when they left the galley and went up on the dock and took over for Reed.

Anderson could see Scanton standing and talking with Brian not too far away from the culling table. They were close enough so that he could hear what they were saying. Joey shook Brian's hand and said, "Okay, you've got a deal. Go get your stuff. We'll hook up later on."

Scanton walked toward Anderson and motioned to him to come over so he could to speak to him.

"I've checked out all the prices and we're going to do real good on this trip. I just want to tell you, you did real good with us this trip, real good. I'm going to have to let you go—"

A guy came out of the office, hollered down, and interrupted Scanton. "How much ice, Joe?"

He yelled back at him, "Fifteen tons." Anderson's heart sank. Scanton turned back toward Anderson. "What's the matter with you, kid? You look like you saw a ghost."

"Well, you just said you were going to have to let me go." Scanton started laughing.

"No no no. Not that 'go' as in 'fired.' I have to let you go, like *go* get the grub by yourself. There's an old gray van out back with the keys in it. They set up a temporary charge for us at the store. That Brian guy needs a ride in town. He's going to show you where the store is and walk to his motel. Christ, that shithead will be drunk and stoned for the next week. He tried to get me to take him with us. That bastard has fucked up more trips for me and other guys than you can imagine. His deal is this—he gets in from fishing, gets his money, and quits the boat. Don't get me wrong. He's a hell of a man out fishing. I'd only take him if one of us needed a trip off. Now go get the grub list and get going and stop being so paranoid, will ya?"

Anderson ran down the dock to get the list and his wallet so he'd have his license with him. He was practically skipping as he went back aboard the boat.

The van was out back, and Brian was waiting in it. He directed Tom to the store. Anderson was so happy to get rid of him that he gave him a ride all the way to his motel. He wanted to give him a chance to get started on his drink as soon as possible.

Anderson got everything they needed for food in about an hour. He made damn sure he didn't forget the onions this time. He got a big red Bermuda. He planned to make the crew a corned hake dinner later on, and the red onion was a key ingredient.

Anderson parked the van and started lugging the supplies down to the boat. He made about ten trips and had everything aboard. It was around eight o'clock, and the lumpers were now working on the codfish.

When Anderson came over, Chase said, "See what's going on here? They're breaking these cod down. We got some beautiful steakers this time. We should get a hell of a price for this whole trip. You don't have to worry about the cull on these codfish too much. Write down the weight and count the fish boxes as a backup, okay? I've gotta go have a piss and get a coffee. You want one?"

"No, I'm good. Joey didn't can me by the way, so it looks like you're in line to lose many more cribbage games."

Chase said, "Maybe I can go change Joey's mind. We haven't left the wharf yet. There's still time."

Reed had been up to the office to get some change for the phone. He walked up the street to find a phone booth. He had his little notebook with him. When he found a booth, he looked around to make sure nobody was watching him. He needed to make couple of long distance calls to Maine. The operator came on, and he slipped in the coins and dialed the number. On the third ring a deep male voice answered, "Yup."

Reed said, "We're in Gloucester. We had a good trip."

"You better hope it ain't good enough to cancel your big plans."

Reed could feel that same cold sweat break out on his forehead he always got when he was talking to this guy.

"I got a plan going. This trip isn't going to matter when it's all said and done." Reed was lying but he needed more time to work this thing out.

"You listen up. If you fuck this up and don't come through with this guy, your life ain't worth two cents."

Reed's hands were shaking as he lit up a Marlboro. "No, man, I got it worked out. We'll be there for the swordfish. I'll call you when we're in Rockland. Just get the propane ready."

The line went dead. Reed didn't know which was worse—this guy talking to him or this guy hanging up on him. He couldn't stop shaking. He walked over to a bench near the phone booth and sat down. His heart was pounding. He kept reminding himself that all he had to do was do this once. He knew he could pull it off; lots of guys had. When he calmed down he went back to the phone booth and placed another call to Maine. After a couple of rings, a soft female voice answered. It had a groggy, half-asleep tone to it. Skip could feel himself start to get excited just from the sound of her voice.

"Hello."

"Hey, sweetie . . . It's me."

"Oh hi."

"You sound sleepy, babe," Reed said softly.

"I am . . . I was dreaming about you."

Reed loved it when she said stuff like that. "We had a real big trip. We're in Gloucester. You should come down." She seemed to perk right up. "I can't come down this time."

Reed was disappointed, but she had already told him she didn't think she could come. "We're going to work back east. It'll put us in Rockland in five or six days."

"I'll make Rockland and I'll make it worth the wait . . . I promise."

Reed said, "We're close to what we want now . . . I gotta go." Skip hung up the phone and walked back toward the boat. He wanted something to eat.

Scanton was keeping an eye on things. He was kind of dragging his feet. He knew he had to call home and wasn't looking forward to it. He really hated fighting with Karen all the time. He went up to the office to use their phone. He asked Frank if he minded. "No, Joe, go ahead and use Artie's office. Close the door. You're all set," Frank said.

Scanton dialed home. Karen answered, "Hello."

"Hi, it's me."

Karen said, "Hi, honey. How you doing?" Joey didn't know what to expect when he called home, but this definitely was not it. Karen sounded like her old self again. "I'm okay. What's up with you?"

"I've been thinking a lot lately. I don't want us to fight anymore. I'm so sorry. This has been all my fault. I know you've been trying really hard for me and Little Joey. That reverse gear thing wasn't your fault."

Scanton could feel his heart melt. He said, "No, Karen, I shouldn't have lost my temper and hollered at you. I get so frustrated sometimes . . . I kind of lose my head."

"It's okay, Joey. Your dad came over and took Little Joey and me out to Becky's for lunch. It was really nice. We had a long talk, and he reminded me of how much I love you, baby."

Scanton was overwhelmed. He said, "Everything's going to be okay. We had a big trip. We should stock almost $100,000. We got a lot of back bills to pay, but after we get them squared away, we'll be fine."

Karen said, "Great, Joey! You're a super fisherman. Little Joey . . . Daddy's a super fisherman . . . hurray for Daddy!" He could hear his son in the background cheering for him.

Karen said, "Joey, I found the Ice and Fuel Services envelope in my car. It was in the glove compartment. I don't know how it got in there, but I sent it to Wally Dodge yesterday."

"It's okay as long as he got it. This month's boat payment is due, and we should pay Uncle Sal half of his money. That would be nine grand."

Karen said, "Okay, honey. I'm writing all this stuff down."

Scanton said, "Good. We got a new guy on board. His name's Tom Anderson. He's a friend of Skip's. He's a good kid and a hard worker. I want him to get a three quarter share. So pay the crew and catch up on the insurance too. I'm going to have Artie put the money directly into our account at Depositor's Trust. I think he banks with them so the money should be good right away."

Karen said, "Okay, I got it."

Scanton said, "You should come down. Leslie's on her way and maybe this Tom guy's girlfriend. We could have a night on the town."

"Oh, baby, there's nothing I'd rather do, but I can't. Little Joey has a doctor's appointment tomorrow to look at his ears. He's been getting those wicked earaches of his again. I'm sorry."

"It's okay. You take care of him. I'll call you when we get in. We should be back in Maine in five or six days."

"Okay, honey. We love you. Tell Daddy we love him."

He could hear Little Joey. "I love Daddy."

"All right, Karen, I've got to get down to the boat. We're still unloading. Bye, honey. I love you."

Karen said, "Bye, baby. I love you too."

Scanton came down out of that office feeling better than he had in months. A big trip, things all set with Karen, a night's sleep coming up—life was good.

They were about halfway through unloading the cod. He stopped by the culling table and asked Chase how they were doing.

"We're good, Joe. They're moving okay. When they unloaded the mixed groundfish, they tried to throw some of the cod in that batch with the seventy-cent stuff. Your boy Tommy here now knows why we watch the bastards so close now."

Scanton said, "Pat, you want a break?"

"No, Joey, you go ahead and get some breakfast. Skip's down there. We'll get this up here."

Scanton walked across the dock and down the ladder. When he got down to the galley, Reed was there having some breakfast. Uncle Charley came out immediately and started swarming Joey's legs.

"I'm sorry, old girl. I can't take you out there right now. Too much going on, you'd get stepped on, and then they'd get hurt when you tore them all up. The bastards would sue the boat for a lunatic cat attack, and we'd be screwed when we lost the case." Uncle Charley seemed to accept his explanation. She flopped down under the table and rolled over on her back.

Scanton said, "We've landed a good trip here, Skip, and I think I can square up with everybody and still have a good check. What I'm saying is forget this swordfish deal. We can work our way back to the east and make out good. I know I'm pushing my luck up on the fifty-fathom bunches, but the flats looked good all the way back up to the outer falls. If we hit them again like that, everybody's going to make out."

Reed said, "Okay, Joey. I understand where you're coming from. I hope things hold up like they are. The way the politics are, that swordfish ban is going to be in effect for a long time."

Scanton took a drag on his Marlboro. "You're right there. The way they've let the foreign boats come over here and pound Georges and the Grand banks like they have is unbelievable. I look at it this way though—all I can do is run my boat and catch as many fish as I can and let the chips fall where they may." Scanton had another bite of his breakfast.

"What are you planning tonight? I called Karen and had a great talk with her. She can't come down. She's got a doctor's appointment for Little Joey tomorrow."

Reed said, "I'm going to get a motel room at that same joint I always go to down here. I want to get cleaned up, have a nap, and then go out and get right friggin' sideways."

Scanton said, "Well, sir, that's about the smartest thing you've come up with in the last week."

Reed laughed. "You know it, brother."

Scanton finished his breakfast and walked back up to the office. He stopped by the culling table to check on Chase. Things were going pretty well. They had almost finished the codfish. The monkfish would be next. Then they'd take out the lobsters. Dragged lobsters could be sold in Massachusetts even though they were illegal in Maine. It being August, these offshore lobsters would command a high price. They were all hard-shell selects. They would be sold for cash and evenly divided up among the crew. That's a big reason fishermen rarely ate the lobsters that they caught at sea. They wanted the cash a lot more than they wanted the lobsters.

CHAPTER 33

Kathy found Leslie's house with no problem. She drove up in a pretty little blue MGB.

When Leslie saw it, she said, "Wow, what a great car."

"Thanks, I know. I love it. It's not practical at all, but I thought if I'm ever going to have one, it should be now. I spent everything extra I made after college on it."

"It's really cute. I don't know how we're going to fit the boys in here with us though."

"We'll let them drive, and we'll stuff ourselves in the backseat. That's why I didn't pack my jammies. I knew there wouldn't be any room for them."

"I didn't pack mine either, so we'll have plenty of room."

They both laughed. "Let's go. Does Tom know I'm coming?"

"I don't know how he would. I haven't talked to Pat since last night."

"Oh good, I love to be a surprise package."

"I think you already are." They both laughed again and started their drive down the Maine turnpike.

They had a great time talking girl talk. Kathy asked Leslie how she and Pat had met. She told her that it was a whirlwind summer romance. Her parents owned a summer cottage on one of the islands out in Casco Bay. Pat was one of those wild Maine boys.

"He was so handsome with his long brown hair. It had steaks of light tan from being bleached by the summer sun." Leslie said, "He was big and strong and full of himself. He had a confidence about him that showed in his eyes and his big smile. I knew from the moment we met that there was nothing he wouldn't do for me. We fell totally in love that summer. When we married, I was twenty and he was twenty-two. That was eight years ago."

Kathy said, "I can't wait to meet him."

"He's so funny. He's got this rough, gruff exterior, but this sweet loving little boy lives on the inside. Don't you ever tell anybody this, but my little niece calls him 'Uncle Pity Pat.'"

"That's adorable. Now I really can't wait to meet him."

Leslie said, "How about you and Tom?"

"Tom was always my special boy. I've loved him since I was fifteen. He doesn't know that though." Kathy said, "Of course, there were other boys in between but none like Tom. He always hung around with a really rough crowd growing up, but he stayed just as sweet as he was the day I met him."

"Oh, Pat did the same thing. It used to drive his parents crazy."

Kathy said, "Tom never really fit in with them. He always did so well in school. A lot of people were surprised that he wanted to go fishing so bad. No offense, please. I'm just scared to have him in danger all the time, but if that's what he wants . . . I'll support it."

Leslie said, "No offense taken. I knew when I married Pat that this was his life. Something happens to men once they try fishing—they can't stop. We're apart a lot, but it does make our time together more precious. I work, of course, but I've always had jobs where I can bug out like this when I want to."

Kathy said, "Don't you worry all the time in the winter months?"

"Yes, you do, but you get used to it after a while. I've trained myself not to watch the weather too much. It won't change anything. They're so far offshore most of the time the weather's different than what you're getting on the TV anyway."

Kathy said, "Tom and I have only been back together again as a couple for six months, but I really think this is going to be it. I just really love to hold him and have him hold me. It's kind of electric really. I'm sorry. I sound like a schoolgirl."

Leslie said, "No, honey, not at all. It's very sweet."

"Thank you. Where do you want to go for lunch?"

"How about that steak place in Saugus?"

"That's great with me. Do you think they've got a steak salad?"

"Oh yes, they do. That's what I always get."

They had a great lunch and motored their way south to Gloucester. Leslie said, "You're really going to like Joey. I doubt we'll see much of him this time though, but if Tom stays on this boat you'll get to know him. Pat always says he really likes working for him. We're saving for our own boat, but I'm pretty sure Pat will stay with Joey until we get it."

Then she said in a really deep voice, imitating Pat. "I respect the hell out of him." They laughed and Kathy said, "What about Skip?"

"You know Skip Reed?"

Kathy said, "Oh ya, I do. We all grew up together. He lives with his mother two houses away from me."

Leslie started laughing. "Skip Reed lives with his mother still?"

"Yes, why is that so funny?"

"Oh nothing, really. It's just the way he struts around like he's such a big deal. I think it's a riot that he still lives at home."

"I take it from your tone that you're not too fond of Skip."

Leslie said, "No, I'm not. There's something about him that just bugs me. He's always polite, but the way he looks at me, it makes me feel like he's sizing me up in bed."

Kathy said, "I know. Tom has been one of his best friends since they were little. He creeps me out too. Tom says I'm nuts, but that boy is a little weird."

"If he ever tried anything, Pat would kill him, and I mean that literally. He's got a serious temper. Skip would be awfully sorry if he ever made a move to act out one of his little fantasies."

They rode along until they saw the sign for Gloucester and headed down toward the harbor. Leslie directed Kathy to North Star Fisheries.

CHAPTER 34

S canton stopped at the office to meet with Artie. He went in, sat down, and lit up a Marlboro.

He said, "So, Artie, how did we make out do you think?"

"Well, let's see, Joe. The gray sole are $3.50 average. The dabs are going to bring $2.00. The cod are a $1.00 average. The mixed are 80¢, and you're going to get 70¢ for your monkfish. The lobsters are worth $2.25 a pound. By and large, you did damn good for a new guy."

Scanton didn't know what the final weight would be, but Chase's tally was always very close.

"One of those pricks tried to slide some of our cod in with the junk, Artie."

"Do you know which guy, Joe? I'll throw his ass off this wharf right now."

Scanton said, "Let it go . . . I know all these bastards try to pull that shit . . . just a heads-up."

Joey continued, "Are you banking with Depositor's down here still?"

"Yes, we are. You want Janice, my bookkeeper, to deposit your check for you?"

Scanton said, "That would be great. I've been tied up for a month and a half, and Karen's got some bills to pay for us. That money should be good immediately, right?"

"Yes, before you let your lines go, that money will be in Portland."

"That's great, Artie . . . we should be all set then. Now you'll take out the fuel, the ice, and the grub bill that Tom ran up at the store. Just show it all on the slip, will you? Karen's real careful with the money stuff. She used to do Janice's job in Portland. That's how I met her."

"Oh . . . impressing the young ladies, being an old salty captain."

"No, impressing the young ladies with my good looks and my beautiful singing voice."

Artie said, "No shit, really? The word around the wharf is that your men loved your singing so much that they cut off your speaker wires again."

Scanton said, "Yes, the pricks did. I can't believe you know about that. I'm going to figure out a way to get even with those bastards yet."

"I believe you will, Captain Scanton. I believe you will."

Scanton said, "We should be done unloading in a couple of hours. I'll see you then."

Artie looked up and smiled at his young friend. "Good, Joe."

Artie handed him an envelope with $1,400 cash inside to pay for the lobsters. He walked down the stairs and back over to where Anderson and Chase were working. He told Tom to go fill the water tanks and get ready to take on fuel.

"We should need about a thousand gallons per side. Get Skip to help you the first time with that fuel hose. That thing pumps so fast. If you don't do it right, it blows back and makes a hell of a mess."

Anderson said, "Okay, Joey. I'll get on it."

Scanton told Chase what the prices were going to look like. That put a smile on the big man's face.

Scanton said, "I know it's been a pain in the balls being tied up so long. I got a feeling though that things are going to turn for us real soon." There was no doubt about that. Things were going to turn.

They kept plugging away, and it wasn't long before the boat was empty and the lumpers were setting up the fishhold. They iced the pens exactly as Chase had told them to. Anderson gave his first order as a crew member on the boat. It wasn't a big deal really, but it felt big to him. He told the lumpers to hold off on any ice in the slaughterhouse until he could clean out the strainers. The man running the ice hose said, "No problem."

When Anderson lifted the slaughterhouse hatch covers, he was doubly sure to not turn one upside down. He'd never do that again.

Scanton came aboard and fired up the engine. They released the lines and slid her back a berth for the layover. He left the genset running for power and shut everything else down. He was buttoning everything up and the radio came on. Joey had left the radio on channel 65.

"*Jubilee, Jubilee.* This is the *Gloria Walker*. Over."

"Hi, Dad. How you doin? Over."

"I'm good. I tried you a few times, and then I figured you were unloading and had probably left it on a channel. I know you like 65 when you talking to the dealers. Over."

"Ya, I'm sorry. I never went back to 16 after we got in. Over."

"So how did you make out?"

"We did all right on price, but we were weak on volume. I guess we'll cover the grub bill okay."

Covering the grub bill was code that they were close to a $100,000 stock or over.

Peter said, "Ya, Joe, I know how it is. Marshall and I are barely making the fuel bill down here ourselves."

Scanton thought, *Great, they're picking some fish up inside.*

"How much longer are you and Captain Grimes out for? Over."

"At least two more days anyway. Then I got to take Marshall up to the nursing home and drop him off."

There was no response. That could only mean one thing. Marshall was on another channel going at it with Vern or taking a nap.

"Finest kind then, Joe. I'll talk to you later on then. The *Gloria Walker*, clear with the *Jubilee*, back to 16 and standing by."

"Okay, Dad. Thanks for the call. *Jubilee*, clear with the *Gloria Walker* and back on 16."

The crew got together in the galley. For the first time since he had been aboard the *Jubilee*, all four men were at the galley table together. Joey had the cat. "Don't worry, old girl. We'll take a turn around the deck before I head up the street."

Scanton pulled out the envelope he had gotten from Artie and gave everybody their $350 share of the lobster money. The gang sat there for a while, making small talk and smoking.

Scanton said, "All right, you guys. I'll button up here and you can head over to town. I'm going to grab a room at the Harbor Inn Motel. I'll see you here at 8:00 a.m., tomorrow morning. Skip, show Tom where we hide the keys. You'll need them if for any reason you need to get aboard, Tom. I'll see you guys in the morning then."

Everybody got up from the table and all seemed to speak at once.

"Yes, Joe. We'll see you in the morning."

"Yes . . . see you later, Joey."

"Have a good night, Skipper."

They climbed the ladder, but Joey remained on board. He went out on deck with Uncle Charley. She very quickly found a nice chunk of codfish.

The gang crossed the dock, and all but Skip headed up for the office. He borrowed the old van and drove it off without a word.

Chase and Anderson were out on the street side of the wharf when Kathy's little blue sports car pulled up. Tom was ecstatic. He was hoping she would come, but when he saw her he couldn't believe the feelings he had. Leslie and Kathy jumped out of the car, and Kathy ran over and threw herself in Tom's arms. She kissed him and then pulled away. "Oh god, Tommy, you stink!"

He said, "That's the sweet smell of success."

"No, that's the stinky smell of fish!"

She scrunched her face up. Tom laughed. "Kiss me again."

Kathy said, "Where's your clean clothes? We've got to get you in a shower."

"I like the sounds of that." He looked at Pat, who was holding a small gym bag. He smiled and sort of waved it at Tom. He obviously had his clean clothes in it. Anderson took off like a shot back aboard the boat. Chase hollered after him, "Come on, boy wonder, hurry up, will you?"

Anderson flew down the dock and was back in five minutes. Kathy had put the top down on her car. Tom said, "That bad?"

Kathy made another face. "It's worse than that."

When they finally got settled into the little car, they made their formal introductions. Kathy thought Leslie was right about the size of these two men together. As it was, they were packed in like sardines. Anderson drove, and when they got a little out of town they saw a little motel. "What about right there?"

Chase said, "Nope. That's where your buddy Skippy stays. Keep going."

Anderson drove about another half mile. There was a place called the Gloucester Twilight Motel. Chase said, "This is good. We've stayed here before. They're wicked religious here though. You better tell them you're married, or they won't let you in."

Leslie said, "They are not, Pat. Cut it out. Does he act like that on the boat too?"

Anderson said, "Oh yes, Leslie. It's been awful. Maybe you could have a little chat with him. That would be really wonderful."

Chase said, "Just park the car, shithead. Let's get in there."

Tom said, "You started it."

"Keep it up and I'll finish it too." They all laughed. "Whaaat?" Chase said.

After they checked in and were starting for their respective rooms, Tom said, "You want to meet back here at six or so and take the girls out to dinner?"

Chase said, "Leslie, you up for that?"

"Sure, I'd love to."

"Okay, we'll see you here at six," Chase agreed.

Kathy and Tom went into their room. She went right in and turned the shower on and grabbed a plastic liner out of the waste basket. "Strip and put your clothes in here."

"Yes, ma'am." That was an easy order to accept. He took everything off and stepped in the shower. He hadn't been in there two minutes when Kathy pulled the shower curtain back and climbed in with him. He looked at her naked body and couldn't believe how beautiful she was. She had been a champion swimmer when they were in high school and had a swimmer's shape. He had no interest at all in skinny, bony women. He liked them built like her—voluptuous. They had made love before, and he had seen her naked, but this was totally different. He took her in his arms, and she melted into him. They were like puzzle pieces, perfectly matched to fit into each other's bodies. Kathy looked up into his face with the warm water cascading down their nakedness. Tom was transfixed.

"Oh god, Kathy, I love you!"

She looked deep into his clear blue eyes. "Do you promise me, Tommy?"

He looked back and said, "Yes, I do. I promise that I really love you, Kathy."

She had the most wonderful hazel eyes he'd ever seen. She reached up on her tiptoes and whispered, "I love you too, my sweet, sweet Tommy dear. I do love you."

She took a facecloth and the soap and washed his body. Tom closed his eyes and felt the warmth of her gentle touch massaging his aching muscles. She washed every inch of him. It was so loving, so soft, and so perfect. She handed him a bottle of shampoo and said, "Wash my hair, darling."

He put some of the shampoo on his hands and ever so gently started to rub it into her beautiful blonde hair. He had never washed her hair before. It was all so intimate. He felt so close to her. He thought he was going to climax. She turned away from him so her back was now toward him. He kept moving his hands through her hair around in small circles. Kathy tipped her head back and closed her eyes, relaxing under his touch. She reached behind her back and took his penis in her hand.

"You *are* happy to see me, aren't you?"

She giggled and started moving her hand back and forth, back and forth. It felt so good. Tom closed his eyes. He couldn't help it; he came in an explosive wave . . . "Oh god!" he said. He leaned back against the wall of the shower and let the hot water pour over them.

After a few minutes he rinsed Kathy's hair. They got out of the shower. She said, "Go get in bed. I'm going to dry my hair really quick, and I'll be right in."

He went into the other room and dried himself off a little more and crawled into the bed. It felt like she took forever to come out of the bathroom. He pulled the covers back and welcomed her into the bed. He started kissing her and didn't stop. He kissed every inch of her body. He explored her nakedness with his tongue. She took deep breaths as he caressed the most intimate parts of her body. They made love ever so sweetly and ever so gently and fell asleep wrapped tightly in each other's arms in this heavenly place, Gloucester, Massachusetts.

A door away Pat and Leslie w ere basking in the afterglow of their own lovemaking. He was lying with his head up on the pillows. She had her head across his chest and felt now as she always had—safe and secure in her husband's arms. These little mini vacations were fun. It seemed like when the boat was in Portland, there was always something to do. Pat was always thinking about oil changes or parts that were broken or about to be broken. Here he was all hers. That's all she'd ever wanted. She was always anxious to come for these sleepovers. Not only was it happy times for them together as a couple, but she also knew that there would be no bar fights.

For some odd reason when a group of fishermen enters a bar, an unheard bell goes off. The die is cast and an alarm sounds . . . let the games begin. Being an exceptionally large man, he was always the target of some five-foot-eight drunken lunatic who thought that taking a swing at him was a really good idea. It never was. Even though he was a gentle person by nature, with enough alcohol and enough provocation, a brawl would ensue. The cops would come, and the damages to the bar would have to be paid. She really hated it. She would happily drive five hundred miles to be where she was, wrapped in her husband's arms, safe and sound. The dinner plans with their new friends was a bonus.

Leslie thought of something funny and started to laugh.

Pat said, "What's so funny, dear?"

"Kathy told me on the way down that Skip Reed lives at home with his mother!"

"You are kidding me, right?" Pat laughed. "He runs around telling everybody he lives on Falmouth Foreside and owns his own lobster boat. He's always playin' the role . . . Wow! What a riot. I can't believe it. How does Kathy know about that?"

Leslie said, "She lives next to him and his mother. They all grew up together."

"Really. I knew Tom and he were friends. Is she pals with him too?"

"No, she can't stand him. She thinks he's a jerk."

Pat said, "She has no idea."

Pat told Leslie about Skip watching Tom and Kathy in Kathy's backyard.

Leslie said, "Oh my god. I don't know her very well. We just met, but I think she would kill him if she found out about that. How did Tom handle being teased like that in front of you and Joey?"

Pat said, "He was pissed. Later on Skip made another remark about it when he woke Tom up to come out on deck. Tom picked him up and slammed him hard against the bulkhead and told him to shut his fuckin' mouth. I think Reed was scared. He sure as hell hasn't mentioned it again."

Leslie said, "I hope *you* didn't laugh when Skip was telling his little story."

"Of course not, dear. You know I wouldn't laugh at someone else's expense like that."

Leslie laughed and said, "Yeah, I bet!"

She knew damn well he had probably been laughing the hardest.

Pat said, "Okay, its nap time. I need my beauty sleep if we're dining out with our new friends from Falmouth."

"Just go to sleep, Pat."

"Whaaat? Why are you always picking on me?" He was still chuckling when he and Leslie drifted off.

CHAPTER 35

S canton had his clean clothes in a small bag when he came up the ladder to get off the boat. He ran up the stairs to the office. Artie was still there working on some paperwork.

He said, "Hey, Artie, mind if I use the phone to call a cab? I want to get over to the Harbor Inn and get cleaned up."

"Joey, go right back there. There's a nice shower unit with some fresh towels already. Carol made me put that shower in a few years ago." She was Artie's third wife, and she hated him coming home smelling of fish. Civilization comes to the waterfront. Artie said, "I don't give her any shit like I did my first two wives. Now I just say, 'Yes, dear, yes, dear.' It's so much better than, 'How much alimony did you say I owed?'" Joey laughed. Artie said, "Look, you go get cleaned up. Carol's going to meet me down at Maria's for dinner. You come out with us for dinner, my treat. Carol hasn't seen you in months."

Scanton said, "All right, Artie, if you twist my arm. I'd really enjoy that, thanks." He went back to the bathroom. Artie was right. It was a nice bathroom. All tile shower, very fancy. Artie wasn't suffering any for money, that was for sure. Joey had his shower. It felt great to get the scales and the salt off. While he was in there he thought about Karen and how he wished she had come down. He really wanted things to work out. He missed Little Joey terribly when he was away.

He got all cleaned up, shaved, and put his fresh clothes on. He took his fish clothes and wrapped them up in a ball and brought them out with him.

Artie said, "Here, give me those and that towel." He walked back toward the bathroom and opened a closet door. There was a small stackable washer dryer in there. He stuffed the dirty clothes in, threw in some laundry detergent, and pulled the start button.

"Wow," Joey said, "Carol really has got you towing the mark."

"When you marry a broad fifteen years younger and as hot as Carol, you've got to behave. I'm telling you."

Scanton said, "It helps that she's blind as a bat, don't it?"

"Just for that you're buying the drinks tonight."

They locked up the office and left in Artie's dark-blue Cadillac. Maria's was about a fifteen-minute ride.

CHAPTER 36

Sometimes, when he was in Gloucester, Reed liked to stay at a place called Dan's Cabins. It was a run-down dump really. It was probably one of the last of its kind down there. There was an old gas station with six dilapidated cabins out back. Reed knew the owner. The real Dan had been dead for twenty years. This guy's name was Ralph, but everybody called him Dan. He didn't give a shit if they called him Fuckface as long as they paid him the twenty-five bucks for their room and didn't wreck the place.

Dan's was perfect for Reed. He didn't want anyone to know where he was. He'd told everybody he was going to his regular motel. He just wanted a place to sleep and get a shower. He had people to see, and it was private business. Dan usually had a little dope for sale too. The place was exactly what he wanted.

If he'd been able to talk his girlfriend into coming down, it would have definitely been somewhere else. He lay back on the bed, rolled himself a joint, lit up, and was enjoying the buzz. There was a bar within walking distance called Red's. He loved that old hole in the wall. There was a fat broad named Brenda who hung out there and would suck his dick for him after he bought her a few beers. She was always over there. He'd invite her over after he'd had a few laughs with the locals.

There was another reason he liked Red's. He had met the guy there that turned him on to the swordfish connection. Sammy D. was what everybody called him. No one seemed to know what the *D* stood for. No one really wanted to know. Sammy was the one who had given Reed the guy's number up in Maine.

At first he had been scared to call the guy. He had never seen the man face-to-face. It took him quite a while to get the balls to make the call. When the guy found out the size and range of the *Jubilee* and Joey's money problems, they had set up a deal. Reed's biggest worry was that you don't just "talk" about a deal like this. There was big money and big risk involved when you started making plans with these people. If you committed and didn't follow through, they'd fuck you up royally. He knew about a guy who had done just that. The guy made big promises and didn't make good on any of them. He'd been found later on in a dumpster, deader than a doornail. Reed knew all too well the potential consequences of his actions. He just wanted to pull it off because his girlfriend really wanted it. He'd admits there is an adrenaline high to all this stuff, a hell of a lot more than a big bag of fish while some goddamn asshole tried to run you over with a tanker.

Reed finished his joint, got up, and headed over across Brown Street to Red's. When he got there, the place was packed. He worked his way through the crowd to a back table. Sammy D. was sitting back there with a couple of other creeps. They were dressed in slacks and fancy dress shirts. They had their sleeves rolled up a turn on their forearms. Their shirts were open in front, and you could see gold chains hanging around their necks. Reed was sure that these guys thought they were chick magnets. He thought they'd have better luck drawing flies.

When Sammy saw Reed coming toward him, he told the guys to get lost. That move made Reed feel like a big deal. Sammy smiled a cold smile. "Well, if it ain't Skip Reed, in from the sea."

"How you doin', Sammy?"

"Good, Skip. How about you?"

Sammy was fat. Not just regular fat either. He was huge. At six feet tall he must have weighed 350 pounds. He always thought he'd like to get him on the scales down at the wharf just to see.

He knew Sammy was nobody to screw around with. He was a bad guy. He had gray lifeless eyes that were sort of rheumy when he looked at you. There was no doubt about Sammy's intelligence, but you couldn't read him at all. Skip thought he was a guy who could kill you and never think twice about it. He was absolutely sure he was right about Sammy.

Reed said, "I'm doin' good. We had a big trip. I think around a $100,000 stock. They're still down there unloading. I don't have time for that shit myself anymore. I talked the captain into hitting some hot spots I knew about down by Sigsbees. They paid off big . . . What can I say?"

Sammy said, "How you making out up north? How's that broad you're tappin' up there?"

A cold chill ran down Reed's spine. Nobody knew about his Maine girlfriend, nobody. How did this fat fuck know anything about her?

Sammy said, "You had any conversations with the man up there?"

Reed said, "I had a nice chat with him today, as a matter of fact."

Sammy's eyes narrowed. "Now you listen to me, motherfucker. Nobody has a nice chat with that fucker. You didn't have a nice chat with him and you know it. That propane is dangerous stuff if you don't know how to handle it. I mean a guy can blow himself up if he's not careful. Now you go have a nice beer with Brenda. You make sure you're ready to get those swordfish when you leave Rockland. You understand me?"

There was fear in Skip's voice. "Yes, I understand."

Reed wandered away from Sammy's table in a daze. He thought about her, back in Maine, remembering the night before he left for this trip. He knew exactly what she wanted from him. He knew that he had to do what she expected or it was over. This was his one chance to break out of this mess and be with her. She was not the kind of woman that would put up with any excuses. She was so beautiful that he couldn't believe he even had a chance with her, but he had his chance, and he wasn't going to blow it, not for her or himself. Just stick to the plan, that's all it took.

He was so scared that he had to laugh at himself. He felt better, at least for the moment anyway. If Skip Reed knew one thing, it was how to live in the moment. He walked over where Brenda was sitting. She had her back to him and hadn't noticed him coming in. He put his arms around her from the back.

"How you doin', baby? Did you miss me?"

Brenda was a big girl. She wasn't homely, but she always tried to do too much with too little. Her jeans were so tight that they really took all the guesswork out of it. Her hair was bleached blonde, curly, and loaded with hair spray. She always wore way too much makeup. Her bountiful breasts were pushed way out there on full display. There was no doubt in anybody's mind that met Brenda, what it was she had for sale.

She worked at North Star Fisheries for Artie in the packaging room. It was shift work, of course, and she dreamed of finding a man to take care of her. It wasn't working out though. The men she met were mostly self-indulgent creeps out for a quick piece of ass. She lived in a trailer park with her aunt Shirley and kept on dreaming.

It was clear that Brenda believed that the way to a man's heart was through his penis, and she was always willing to accommodate. She liked this guy Skip. He was always generous with his money, buying her drinks and food. The thing she liked best about him was he didn't hit her.

Brenda turned around and said, "Hi, stranger, sit down and take a load off. You want something to eat?"

Reed said, "Yes, I would."

Brenda called one of the waitresses over. Reed said, "Bring me a cheeseburger, some fries, and a large Bud on draft."

The waitress said, "You want anything on it?"

"Mustard, relish, and some raw onions. I have a huge appetite for raw onions for some reason."

The girl said, "What?"

Reed said, "Never mind . . . it doesn't matter."

"Okay, darlin', I'll be right back with your order."

When his food arrived he was relieved to see Sammy was leaving Red's. The guy made Skip very nervous. That other guy he always talked to on the phone from up in Maine, Mickey, was intimidating; but Sammy was just plain scary.

Reed thought as he watched Sammy leave, *What the fuck did you really expect when you got wound up with these guys? They handle a huge amount of illegal money . . . they aren't the Boy Scouts.*

Just the same, Reed was happy for the moment that Sammy had left the place. He had a few more beers and picked up the tab for the table. He said, "Come on, Brenda, you want to get out of here?"

She said, "Sure, Skip. You over at Dan's?"

"Yes, let's go." He left Red's with Brenda and walked over to Dan's.

After Sammy Dalton left Red's, he went to a pay phone and called Maine. The phone was answered quickly.

"Yup."

There was a pause and Sammy said, "Mickey, its Sammy."

Mickey hollered, "No names, goddamn it!"

"Yeah, yeah, I forget."

Sammy didn't forget anything, but he got a real kick out of busting Mickey's balls. "Look, I just saw your boy off that Portland dragger. I'm at Red's bar down here. If I read him right, I think he'll make things happen. I scared him pretty good. I told him that propane is a very dangerous thing." Sammy laughed at his own joke.

Mickey said, "Yeah, so what?"

"I'm just keeping you informed. You better have one of the boys keep a close eye on that broad of his up there. She's the glue to this deal. This kid Reed, he don't think much past his dick."

Mickey said, "Okay."

"I'll call you later, Mickey." Sammy hung up and laughed. He said to himself, "No names? Fuck him, no names."

Reed was on the bed at Dan's with Brenda doing her best to keep him entertained. He was watching Brenda, but all he could think of was his girlfriend, her beautiful brown hair and her amazing green eyes. It wasn't long before he came hard, and it was over. He rolled over on his side and went to sleep. He didn't give a shit if Brenda stayed or left. It was funny that it never dawned on him that his girlfriend in Maine could be using him, the same way he was using Brenda.

CHAPTER 37

I t was dark and damp when Andy made his way down the hill to the float. To say he was nervous cannot begin to describe how he felt. He looked around to see if anybody was around watching him. There wasn't. He quickly got aboard the *Ruffian* and started the engine. He hauled the two crates of lobsters up on the rail and turned the small VHF radio on to channel 8. He cast his lines off and pulled slowly away from the dock.

He ran off to where Danny's boat was moored and tied his lobsters off the stern of his boat. It was time to go. When he pulled away he checked the compass and steered a course of 147 degrees, just like Danny had said. It was a straight shot from Overset Island to the Mud Buoy, just about twelve nautical miles. He knew that the *Ruffian* had a steaming speed of about eight knots. He figured that he should be in the area where he would get a call in about an hour and a half. When he passed Overset Island, the seas out of the south started as a gentle roll. Gradually, they increased in size until Andy was starting to feel a little queasy. He thought to himself, *You could spend all the time you wanted up in the bay . . . outside was different.* There was practically no wind that night and the seas were steady. As the bottom started to deepen, the seas began to subside a little and spread out some. Andy wasn't sure if it was seasickness or his nerves. He started to throw up and couldn't stop. He heaved so hard that it brought tears to his eyes. As sick as he was he was still able to keep an eye on the compass so he wouldn't run off course. He threw up until there was nothing left, and then he threw up some more. The pain in his stomach and throat was worse than he had ever experienced in his life. It really only lasted about five minutes, but Andy would have bet money that it was more like an hour.

He was glad he was alone on the boat. Fishermen all agreed on one thing—getting seasick was a sign of weakness. Some guys who really wanted to go to sea just couldn't because of this affliction. People that didn't suffer from it were always kind of curious as to why it happened at all. One known fact about seasickness is the harder you fight it, the worse it gets.

Andy was shocked that after all that heaving was over, he felt really great. His nerves were gone, his stomach was fine, and he didn't mind the rolling of the *Ruffian* at all.

He didn't own a watch, but Reed had a cheap digital hanging off the wires that powered the radio. He took a good look at it. It was ten to twelve. He thought he had to be pretty close to the Mud Buoy by now. He stared out the pilothouse window.

He noticed that the starboard side window was on a hinge with a slide rig that let you open the window and keep it open. Once that window was up, he had a much clearer view. He kept steaming along, and then he saw it. The Mud Buoy was quite a way to the starboard, but he could see the yellow flasher blinking in the distance. Of course, when he told the story, he'd tell Danny that he made the buoy dead-on.

He took a visual of it and steered for it. The deck hose was still running in the blue barrel. He'd remembered to keep a dozen lobsters in there so he could get his free bag of pot. He fished out the hose and sprayed the deck down. He didn't want the suppliers to think they'd hooked up with a seasick guy.

The buoy was farther away than he had thought. He checked the watch again; it said twelve fifteen.

Oh Jesus, Andy thought, *I hope I didn't frig up and miss the whole goddamn thing.* Just as those thoughts were flashing through his mind, a voice came over the radio. All he heard was the word "thirty"

There was a pause and the voice came on again. "Thirty." It was a foreign accent. Andy had no idea what kind of foreign accent, but it was definitely foreign to him.

He turned the *Ruffian* to thirty degrees and held his breath. He maintained his speed and waited. The minutes dragged by and Andy had to take a leak. He pulled down his fly and pissed. He grabbed the wash-down hose and ran some water over the deck and kept on steaming. He checked the watch again. It was twelve twenty-five, and he felt like a bug under a microscope. He knew damn well he was being watched. He kept on steaming.

Suddenly the *Ruffian* was completely lit up. He had seen a movie about space aliens once, and that was exactly what it was like. The light was so intensely bright that he couldn't see a thing. The boat that pulled up alongside him was enormous. It was a beautiful oceangoing yacht.

Andy guessed that she was over a hundred feet long. He couldn't imagine how much something like that must cost. He was standing there staring when the side of the yacht opened and he could see inside. The staterooms were gone. The boat was a giant floating warehouse, and he could see people and stacked bales of pot. He had no idea how much there was, but it was definitely thousands of pounds.

Andy stood there staring with his mouth wide open. A beautiful girl was standing at the open door, motioning him closer. He put the *Ruffian* in gear and slid her up tight against the yacht.

Two young men appeared at the doorway and threw lines around his boat. The girl jumped aboard and motioned for Andy to put his hands up on the dashboard. She quickly patted him down. He'd seen this done on a million cop shows on TV, but the real thing was completely different. He hoped it would be kind of sexual, but it wasn't. The girl quickly got off the *Ruffian*. She said nothing.

Andy pulled the deck hose out of the blue barrel. He reached in the barrel and took out the dozen lobsters and put them in a five-gallon bucket and handed them to one of the guys on the yacht. They loaded the ten bales aboard the *Ruffian* in less than five minutes. They threw a blue tarp over the bales stacked on deck and tossed Andy a Ziploc bag full of marijuana.

He said, "Thanks." No one answered. The doors on the *Invincible* slammed shut, the lights went out, and the boat disappeared into the darkness.

Andy took a deep breath. Now he had to figure out where he was and how the hell to get back. He checked the compass. He deduced that the opposite of 30 degrees was 210 degrees. He started steaming in that direction. He thought he would be able to see the Mud Buoy in twenty minutes or so. Soon after he was underway, he felt the *Ruffian* take a strange lurch. All it could be was the wake of another boat traveling very fast past him. He couldn't see a thing, but in the distance he could hear the loud roar of a diesel engine at a very high rpm. He knew he wasn't out here alone on this August night. The thought of someone screaming by him, unseen like that, made him shudder.

He kept on going. It seemed like forever, but within a few minutes he had a visual on the Mud Buoy. Now, an experienced man that was headed for Bug Light Point would change course and steam past Ram Island Light, run up the ship channel, and sail right into their destination. Andy didn't qualify. He reversed his direction and headed back for Overset Island. He steered a course of 327 degrees. The other way did flash through his head, but he didn't want to take any chances and get turned around and lost. If these guys wanted Andy Brown to smuggle pot for them, they could just wait.

He ran up the Hussey with the seas on his stern. The little Novi surfed her way back. Andy thought this must have been what it was like for the rum runners back in the day. He was having a ball.

He kept on going up past Cow Island, on in between Peaks and Diamond. He crossed the outer harbor with Fort Gorges on his starboard side and slid right over to Bug Light Point.

There was a lobster truck there waiting. It had lettering on it that said, "Lively Lusty Lobster Co. Little River." He slid the *Ruffian* up to the dock, and three men were there waiting for him.

They took the bales off his boat in less than three minutes. They handed Andy a small paper bag and pushed him off. He pulled the boat into reverse, turned his wheel hard to starboard, and hit the throttle. The *Ruffian's* bow swung to port, and he rolled the wheel back hard to starboard. He put her in forward, hit the throttle, and she turned in her own length. Andy Brown was headed home. He couldn't believe that this whole thing was so easy.

He couldn't wait to look in the bag at the money. There it was, just as promised, more money than Andy had ever seen in his life—$5,000 cash, in $100 bills.

CHAPTER 38

Joey and Artie pulled up to Maria's about twenty minutes from the wharf. The place was mobbed. They had about a half-hour wait. Scanton noticed an empty table at the back of the place, and he asked Artie why they weren't offered that table. Artie just shook his head no and didn't answer the question.

They were only there a few minutes when Carol, Artie's wife, came through the door. She gave Joey a kiss and a hug. She hugged Artie too. They waited together for their table.

They were seated almost exactly when they were promised to be. Joey loved Maria's. It was old-fashioned Italian, right down to the red checkered tablecloths. They ordered some drinks. Scanton had a whiskey and ginger. Artie was a scotch man. Carol had a chardonnay.

It seemed like everyone who came through the door knew Artie. He hired a lot of people in town to work at his wharf. His entire crew was over one hundred people, and his processing facility ran twenty-four hours a day.

Carol was just what you'd expect as the third wife of a fish dealer. She was pretty but not in a glamorous way. She was a little glitzy looking. She worked hard at watching her weight and had a great figure. Men paid a lot of attention to Carol. She paid no attention to them. Artie was her hero and the love of her life. He had saved her from a horribly abusive husband who nearly killed her. Joey really wished Karen was here to enjoy this great evening with their friends.

They ordered and were enjoying their meals when an overly large man walked in. He was immediately escorted with two other guys to the empty table in the rear of the restaurant. A waitress practically tripped over herself to bring a bottle of wine and a glass to the table.

She completely ignored the two hoods with him. Joey said, "Who the hell is that?"

"Keep your voice down, Joey. That's Sammy Dalton, or Sammy D. as most people know him. He's real bad news, that one. I have nothing to do with him. You know I know some guys, and nobody has a line on him. I'm not so sure what he does, but he ain't clean."

"I bet maybe he knows my uncle Sal. Maybe they room together at the annual crooks' conventions."

"Joey, don't joke about that bastard. There's nothing funny about him."

"Okay, Artie, I get it." They changed the subject, but a couple of times Joey felt a cold hard stare coming his way from Dalton. This guy was definitely creepy. Joey noticed that he had these dead gray eyes that made your skin crawl. Joey thought to himself, *Fuck this guy. He don't know me, and I don't know him. He's not wrecking my night.* Joey decided to change the subject. "How are Carol's boys doing, Artie?"

Artie lied, "Good, Joey, good. They've been working hard over at the wharf. They're okay, those two."

Carol had left the table to go to the ladies' room. Artie motioned to Joey to move closer to him.

"Now you listen to me, Joey. I heard some stuff around that's making me uneasy. I've been told that your boy Reed has been seen a couple of times talking with Sammy over there. I can't prove nothing, but I'm pretty sure that he's involved in smuggling swords. There's a big underground market for them Canadian fish, and he's tied into it somehow. I've seen some of this shit going up over my own friggin' wharf. Boats show up with crews that don't know a long line from a clothesline, show up with thirty, forty thousand pounds of swordfish. It ain't right. I won't touch 'em."

Joey just listened and didn't say anything. Artie continued on. "One day these guys are going to get caught. They're going to tag these fish with electronic shit or something, and it's going to be all over except for the shouting."

"Maybe I should go over there and ask that fat pig what Reed's been talking to him about."

Artie grabbed Joey's arm. "No, Joey. I know you got big balls, kid, but there's a lot a dead guys with their big balls stuffed up their asses. You stay the fuck away from that bastard, promise me."

Joey said, "Okay, Artie, if you say so."

"I know you've heard it a million times, but your uncle Charley, your dad, and me all graduated from school together in this town. It don't mean shit to you now, but someday those things will. You wait and see."

Joey said, "I know, Artie, the old man's told me a million times about you guys back in the day."

"Joey, you just go catch the fish, and leave all this other crap alone. Everything's going to be okay if you do that. I heard about you needing money for your boat and getting a loan from your uncle Sal Scantini, that rat bastard."

Joey said, "Jesus Christ, does the whole East Coast know my business?"

"No, Joey, not everybody knows your business."

"Well, why don't you tell those two old ladies over in the nursing home, and then everyone will know!"

Artie said, "Those old ladies already know, but there's a couple over in the next town that were away on vacation. They haven't listened to their answering machine yet."

"Very funny, Artie."

"Just stay away from all that shit, and keep Skip Reed away from Sammy too. He'll be one sorry bastard if he doesn't. I'm telling you."

"Okay, Artie, I'll speak to him."

"You've just had a great trip of fish. You got plenty of money to get clear with Sal. I still can't believe your old man let you do that. He knows better."

"He tried to stop me. I didn't listen." Artie reached over and hit Joey in the back of the head.

"Jesus, Artie, that hurt."

"If Charley Walker was still alive, he'd have really kicked your ass for you!"

Joey said, "I know, I know. Everybody has been on me. Even your old pal Jimmy Desanto was mad at me."

"Jimmy? How is he? Is he still running his store up in Portland? I haven't seen him in years. How about that little girl of his, Teresa? How's she doing?"

"They're all fine. We still get our grub there."

Thankfully for Joey, Carol was back. She had stopped to visit with friends when she saw Artie and Joey were in a serious discussion. Carol stepped up to the table, and Artie immediately jumped up and held her chair. When Carol was seated again Artie asked if anybody wanted any dessert. Carol and Joey both agreed that they were more than satisfied with what they had already eaten and didn't need anything more.

Joey said, "Artie, how about taking me back to the boat? I don't need to stay in any of these overpriced dumps around here."

"Joseph Scanton, watch your mouth. These are wonderful New England accommodations designed for your sleeping comfort."

"Like I said, Artie, take me back to the boat."

They all laughed. Artie paid the bill and refused to let Joey even pick up the tip. As they headed out, Joey quickly glanced toward Sammy Dalton's table. He was surprised to see that Sammy was staring at him. Joey gave Sammy a nod and a little wave. Sammy didn't move.

Artie drove back to the wharf, and Joey got out of the car. Carol hopped out and gave him a kiss and a hug good night. He thanked them profusely for the dinner and the wonderful evening.

Artie said, "My pleasure, Joey. You be careful out there on your trip back east. I'll see you here again in a month or so maybe."

"Okay, Artie, sure thing. Thanks again."

"Say hi to your mom and dad and Jimmy D when you get home, boy. Take care."

Scanton turned and made his way down the ladder to the *Jubilee*. He unlocked the main companionway and walked down to the galley.

Uncle Charley was there and very happy to see him. He poured her a saucer of milk and headed for his bunk. As he got undressed, he wished Reed was aboard so he could put this swordfish crap to rest for once and for all. He climbed into his bunk and flipped off his light.

* * *

Pat and Tom took the girls to a seafood restaurant in downtown Gloucester called Barnacle Billy's. The place was packed with tourists, but it was still a fun place.

After the meal, the waitress asked if they wanted coffee. Tom said, "No, thanks, we need to get back." Tom was anxious to get Kathy back to the room for obvious reasons.

She said, "I'd like some coffee, Tom."

"Maybe we should get some to go."

Kathy said, "Don't worry, stud muffin, we'll get back to the motel soon enough."

Pat said, "Stud muffin!" He started laughing so hard everyone thought he was going to have to leave the table. He looked up at the ceiling. "You can take me now, Jesus, because I've heard it all . . . stud muffin!"

"I don't know what's so funny. When you got it, you got it, and I got it," Anderson said.

Pat said, "Well, I hope I don't get it then, whatever it is you got."

Kathy and Leslie got their coffee. Tom waited patiently while they drank it. They drove back to the motel and said good night. After Kathy showed Tom how to put the top up on her car they went into their room. Kathy headed for the bathroom. Tom could hear the shower running.

Kathy came in from the bathroom with nothing on. She snuggled into Tom's lap with her arms around his neck.

Kathy said, "Tommy, will you write me some love letters while you're gone?"

Anderson said, "I can try, but I doubt they'll be worth reading."

"Oh, they'll be worth reading all right. I'm going to save them too. So we can look at them a long time from now and remember how it was."

He said, "Oh, Kathy, I love the sound of that . . . I love you so much."

She kissed Tom with her soft sensuous lips, and he nestled his head into her neck.

He said, "Let's go climb in that bed, so I can show you just how sweet I can be."

"Go get a shower, stud muffin, then show me your best stuff."

Pat and Leslie were cuddled together in the room next door. Leslie asked Pat if he had had a good time at dinner.

"Sure, I did, but I'm not going to get too close to this guy. He's just a passerby. Tom's a real smart guy. He's been to college. This fishing thing is just window shopping for him. He's got options. It's not like it is for the rest of us. Guys like me and Joey, and even Reed . . . this is the life we were born into. We'll never do anything else. Tom can do lots of other things. He won't be around long, you watch and see."

"Maybe he'll open a stud muffin shop and sell stud muffins."

He said, "Very funny, Leslie."

Leslie was concerned about Pat's negative feelings about himself. "Pat, you're really smart too. When you get your own boat, you're going to be a great captain. Let's just enjoy Tom and Kathy for who they are, okay? You're my stud muffin, you know." She kissed Pat good night. They drifted off to sleep.

The alarm in their room went off in what felt like ten minutes.

The couples met in front of the motel and loaded themselves into the car. They started the drive back to the wharf. When they drove past the motel Reed was supposedly staying in, Chase looked in but didn't say anything. They arrived at the wharf in about twenty minutes and pulled up in a parking spot out in front of Artie's building. They got out and Kathy reached up to Tom and kissed him. "Is it always going to be sad like this when you leave to go fishing?"

He said, "I hope so. I'd hate to have you happy to see me go." He hugged her tight. They all said their good-byes and Kathy opened her trunk. She handed Tom a bag of clean and folded clothes.

"Thank you, sweetheart. When did you do this?"

"When you were asleep. I spotted a Laundromat across from the motel."

"That's so great. Thank you."

Kathy handed a bag to Chase and said, "I didn't forget you, sweetie!"

He said, "Jeez, Kathy, I can't believe you did that. Thanks."

Kathy said, "Leslie and I had it all planned. She left your stuff outside the door in a plastic bag. We were just very lucky that none of the other guests called in the Gloucester pollution control team while they were out there."

He said, "Very funny, Kathy."

Chase kissed Leslie good-bye and turned to Anderson. "Come on, stud muffin. We gotta get out of here before Joey leaves without us."

They turned and walked down the wharf and boarded the boat. Kathy said, "You want to watch them leave?"

Leslie said, "No, they'll be a while before they take off, and it's bad luck to watch your loved one steam away to sea. Pat will go through all the engine room stuff anyway, and Joey will inspect the deck before they leave. Let's go home."

Just as Kathy was starting her car, Reed pulled up in the old van. He drove right past them and never paid them any attention. The girls drove off and started their drive north, back to Maine.

Scanton had the boat running and the coffee on when they met down in the galley. They sat at the table and lit up their cigarettes. He said, "I got the numbers from Artie, and we weighed in at just under 63,000 pounds. We got a good price for the fish. I had the check deposited to the boat account, so your checks will be ready in a day or so. You can have them when we get into Rockland or have the women pick them up from Karen. I'm going to pay Tom a three-quarter share." Anderson was beaming.

"When we leave, I'm planning to head down toward Wilkinson basin and fish our way east. Tom, why don't you get a breakfast on and we'll get underway. Let's go hit 'em again." It was August 11.

CHAPTER 39

Scanton told Chase he had already done his deck check and had been through the engine room. Chase and Reed went out on deck and handled the dock lines. They spun off the stern springer and headed out to sea.

Anderson made his usual breakfast. Chase lowered the birds. Reed threw a half-inch line around them and guided them back onto the deck. They lowered the paravanes as they started the steam down toward Thatcher's Island.

Joey was at the helm. Chase brought him a breakfast plate and went back down below. They were headed east as the sun came up. It was a great-looking morning. Scanton finished his breakfast and picked up the VHF mic.

"*Jessica, Jessica*, this is the *Jubilee* calling on 16. Over."

"*Jessica* back to the *Jubilee*." Scanton recognized Skip Cathcart's voice immediately.

"Go to 88, Skip."

"Eighty-eight, Joey."

When they were up on 88, Joey said, "Hey, Skipper! How are you, boy?"

"I'm good, Joey. How's about yourself?"

"Finest kind, Skip . . . where's old Rusty? Down in his stateroom pounding his pillow?"

"No, Joey. He's down in the galley having breakfast and bustin' the crew's balls."

Scanton said, "Really? Who's he after now?"

"Well, you know about his work release deal he made with the prison. He's interrogating prisoners. He's relentless with these poor bastards. They're all scared to death of him. He's been telling them that the state told him he could keelhaul anybody that doesn't do what he says."

"No shit? You gotta be kidding."

"One poor guy asked what 'keelhaul' meant. He explained that he was going to tie a rope on him, throw him off one side of the boat, and pull him up on the other. We got nine guys on here from jail, and half of them believe everything Rusty tells them. Over."

Scanton started laughing. "That's my boy!"

"He wants to know everything about their crimes and their trials. He asked one guy if he was a criminal when he was a little kid or did he work his way into it gradually. Over."

Scanton said, "He better watch it. You guys are going to have to go ashore sometime."

"There won't be two of these guys that will last over one trip. We got three guys on here that are in for murder. Rusty says he's going to try for some muggers and rapists next round. He thinks they may be a little tougher crowd and more suited to fishing on this boat. Over."

"You getting to know any of these guys? Over."

"Yeah, there's one guy named Butch on here that's kind of a sad story. He was about twelve when his parents dumped him on an uncle who had a farm over in Turner. They ran off and just left him there. The uncle started putting it to the kid once he got him. He worked him half to death on the farm and went after him sexually all the time. The kid put up with it until he was about eighteen. Apparently he was getting some size to him by then. He caught his uncle splitting some wood and went up behind him and let him have it between the shoulders with a splitting maul. He put the old bastard in a wheelchair for the rest of his life. He told me he was trying to get him in the head, but the old bastard bent over just enough at the last second. The judge gave Butch fifteen years for assault with a deadly weapon and attempted murder."

Scanton said, "Wow! That's horrible."

"Butch said he wasn't mad with the judge. He said it was definitely a deadly weapon, and he was attempting to murder the son of a bitch. Over."

"How's he doing on the boat? Over."

"He told me that prison was like summer camp compared to being on this boat. Not that Butch ever went to summer camp."

"Jesus, that is sad. I hope that prick uncle of his suffers every day for what he did to that kid. Over."

Cathcart said, "Me too."

Scanton said, "Hey, how's that Hacksaw guy doin'? Over."

"Oh Jesus, Joey, he's a seasick guy, that one. Did Rusty tell you he was huge? Christ, the guy killed somebody in a bar fight. He looks like Arnold the weight lifter. Well, anyway, Rusty puts him on the bait table. Between the rolling and the smell of the mackerel we're using for bait, he starts heaving. Of course, the line slows up and Captain Rusty gets pissed. The guy keeps puking and Rusty won't let him off the table. Rusty is getting more and more pissed, so he goes down to the galley and gets a bowl of chili and eats it in front of him. The poor bastard has to watch Rusty fire down that stuff. I swear, Joey, I've never seen anybody that sick on a boat, ever. Over."

"Who was the sick one? Hacksaw or Rusty?"

Skip laughed. "I don't know, Joey. Rusty finally let him hit the bunk after about twelve hours of that shit. Next morning, Rusty ate pancakes in front of him when he staggered into the galley for some coffee. He started heaving all over again. When we get in, that guy's going to run back to jail. He'll probably get five more years for breaking and entering the prison just to get away from Rusty."

"Jesus, I believe you. I'm going to get going. I got to plot out my course . . . all right, Skip, finest kind then. Good talkin' to you. Have Rusty give me a shout when he takes a break from harassing his crew, will you? Over."

"Will do, Joe. Good talking to you, man. We'll probably see you in Rockland, won't we? At least that's what Rusty tells me. I'll buy you a beer. Over."

"Finest kind, Skip. This is the *Jubilee*, clear with the *Jessica*. Back to 16 and standing by."

"Good, Joe . . . *Jessica*, clear with *Jubilee* and back to 16."

The deck crew went out and started pulling the groundfish net off the starboard reel. They jillsoned the net forward so they could get at it to mend it. Chase had already tacked most of the replacement twine in place. Anderson filled the needles, and they started working.

Chase said, "So, Skip, how did you make out last night?"

"Oh, I stayed at my usual motel over town there. I was kinda tired so I just stayed in and had some Chinese. I haven't got a regular broad like you guys, so I just hung out in the room."

Chase said, "You must have ordered up some of that porn shit you like so much."

"You bet I did. They got some great stuff over at that joint."

They kept working for about an hour or so. Chase had Anderson mending some of the straight shots while he and Reed did the more complicated jobs. They were fairly close to being done, and Chase said, "Go ahead up, Skip, if you want. I'll show Tom how to tie back the wings to the head rope, and we'll put her back up on the reel."

Reed said, "Okay. Are you sure? I'll help finish if you want."

"No, that's all right. We're all set here."

After Reed left, Chase said, "That lying piece of shit. I've been fishing with that guy for over two years. Not once in all that time did that man ever leave this boat with a pocketful of shack money and stay in his goddamn room eating Chinese food and jerking off. That bastard's up to something. We went by that place he stays at four different times yesterday, and that old van was never there."

"What do you think is going on?" Anderson asked.

"I really don't know, but he keeps talking about big money and all that. I just don't trust him any further than I can throw this boat."

"I'm starting to feel that way myself. It's weird, you know. I've been around him all my life, but he's changed a lot in the last year. You can bet your ass there's a woman involved somewhere in all this. For all his bullshit, women can make him do anything they want him to."

"Well, he isn't all alone on that score," Chase replied.

"No, it's worse with him. I think the right broad could talk him into some real bad shit if they played him right."

Chase thought a minute. "Maybe so. I really don't give a shit what he does as long as it doesn't involve me."

"I know. I'm the same way," Tom said.

When Reed came up to the pilothouse, Scanton said, "Skip, hold on a minute I want to ask you something."

"Sure, Joe. What's up?"

"I had dinner with Artie last night, and he told me something interesting."

Skip looked a little concerned and said, "What's he saying now?"

"He pointed out this big bastard who came into Maria's. Artie said the guys name was Sammy Dalton, and he told me that he was some kind of a crook. You know anything about him?"

Skip looked very uneasy at that question. He reached in his pocket for a cigarette and lit it up. Scanton could tell he was stalling for time.

Reed talked in a halting tone. "No, Joe, I don't know a Dalton guy. Who's he supposed to be?"

It wasn't a total lie. Reed never knew until that moment what Sammy's last name was. Scanton was furious. "Goddamn it, Skip, don't you fuckin' lie to me. You been seen at Red's talking to this guy. No one can miss this bastard, and you know it."

Reed shifted in his seat. "Oh, that Sammy. I didn't know his name was Dalton. Yeah, he's a guy I know down here. I just talk to him once in a while. We're kind of friends."

Scanton looked even angrier than he had been before. "That motherfucker has no friends and especially not you. He's a goddamn gangster, and you know it. Now tell me what you're talking with him about."

"Okay, okay. He's one of the contact people on the swordfish deal. I told him we were out of that and wanted no more to do with it," Reed replied nervously.

"So what did this fat fuck Sammy have to say about that?"

"He said okay. Don't worry about it. I dealt with it."

The fire was coming out of Scanton's eyes. "If I ever hear another word about this swordfish crap, you're done. You'll get your shit and get your goddamn ass up the wharf, and don't ever think about coming back. You got it?"

Reed put his hands up. "Okay, Joey. I hear you. It's done."

Joey lit up another cigarette and looked away from Reed out the forward window. Reed went down to the galley and got himself another coffee. When Chase and Anderson passed through the pilothouse, Joey still had an agitated look about him. Chase said, "Everything okay, Joe?"

"Yes, I'm all right. The net all set?"

"She's all set, Joey, ready to set off." The boys went down to the galley and got out the cribbage board.

Scanton was still very unsettled about his discussion with Reed. He kept thinking about that Sammy guy looking at him, but he had to forget about that now. They were headed offshore for a trip, and no one was going to make him do anything he didn't want to. He settled back in his chair, ready for a long steam, when channel sixteen came to life.

"Mayday, Mayday. This is the fishing vessel *Black Magic* calling the Coast Guard. Come in please. Mayday! Mayday!"

"This is the United States Coast Guard Group Boston to the fishing vessel *Black Magic.*"

"Coast Guard, we got a guy on board that's stove his arm up real bad. We're going to need some help here right off. Over."

"*Black Magic*, this is Coast Guard Group Boston. Please switch and answer on channel 22 Alpha."

"Ten-four, Coast Guard, 22 Alpha."

"*Black Magic*, give us your exact location."

"We are at 14250 25440. Just south of Fippennies Ledge. Over."

"Thank you, Skipper. Please describe the nature of the man's injuries. Over."

"We were hauling back, and the idler chain got inboard of the starboard towing door. It was hanging from the gallous frame. He reached down to flip it outboard, and the boat took a roll. The door swung and crushed his arm up against the hull. It smashed it up real bad. The bones are sticking out of his forearm, and he's bleeding a lot. We ran him up into the galley area, and we got a towel around it. He's in awful pain. Over."

"Skipper, this is the officer on deck, Lieutenant Marks. We have a medical officer on the way in to advise. Please give us your name."

"I'm Manville Wallace. Over."

"We will be back with you shortly. Please stand by."

The *Jubilee* was on the air, and Scanton was listening intently as were all the other boats in the area. Scanton switched back to 16, knowing there would be an announcement soon. The Coast Guard came on.

"Pan pan, pan pan. Hello, all stations. This is the United States Coast Guard Group Boston reporting an accident at sea. Any vessels with trained medical personnel aboard in the immediate vicinity of 14250 25440, south of Fippennies Ledge, please respond on this channel. Coast Guard Group Boston out."

About three minutes went by, and the Coast Guard was back on the air on 22 A.

"Fishing vessel *Black Magic*. Coast Guard Group Boston. Come in, please."

"*Black Magic* to Coast Guard. Over."

"Captain . . . this is Chief Medical Officer Morton. We are going to instruct you in the application of a tourniquet. Is there any person on board with medical training? Over."

"We got a deckhand that's on the ski patrol winters, and he's got his first-aid training. I think he's putting one of them tourniquet things on the guy now. Over."

"Good, Captain. Please put him on the radio once he has the bleeding stopped. Over."

"Ten-four on that."

"*Black Magic*. There is a Coast Guard jet aircraft approaching your location. This aircraft will make radio contact with you momentarily. They will be dropping an emergency medical kit. They will overfly your vessel and release a buoy and line across your deck. You simply retrieve the medical kit by hauling in the line. In that kit you will find a morphine injection syringe to be administered to the injured man as soon as possible. Over."

"Coast Guard, here's the guy that put on that tourniquet thing." Manny had called his deckhand Bill Savage up to the pilot house so he could talk with the Coast Guard.

He spoke into the mic. "This is Bill Savage. I put the tourniquet on John. Over."

"Roger that. Has the bleeding stopped? Over."

"Yes, I got another guy holding it in place. It's hurting him real bad, but I know we've got to keep it on him if we're going to have any chance to save that arm. I got it below the elbow. Over."

All four men of the *Jubilee* were up in the pilothouse now. Scanton turned and pointed out the aft window. They were all looking as a jet came screaming across the ocean in their direction at an extremely low altitude. It flew over the *Jubilee* so close that the crew thought it was going to hit their antennas.

"This is Coast Guard Group Boston Airborne to the fishing vessel *Black Magic*. Over."

"*Black Magic* back to Coast Guard Airborne. Over."

"Captain, we will be arriving in your immediate area in approximately two minutes. We will be dropping emergency medical supplies to your vessel by overfly drop and tag line. Please keep all personnel clear off the deck area until the drop is completed and we have left your immediate area. Over."

"*Black Magic* back to Airborne. We've got that. We'll be ready for you."

The jet laid a perfect strike across *Black Magic*'s deck. Savage was out there hauling that kit aboard within seconds. He tore the package open, ran for the galley, and administered the morphine shot to John Poor. His pain began to subside within a few seconds. Savage hollered up to Wallace to let the Coast Guard know that things were stabilized, at least for now.

Wallace got on the radio. "*Black Magic* to Coast Guard Group Boston."

"This is Coast Guard Group Boston back to the *Black Magic*. Over."

"The drop was perfect, and the boy's got his shot, and we're doing pretty good now. Over."

"Coast Guard Group Boston back . . . Roger that, Captain. A rescue helicopter has been deployed and is flying in your direction and will make radio contact shortly. They have an ETA of approximately fifteen minutes. Over."

"Ten-four, Coast Guard . . . We'll be standing by."

Wallace was shaken by the accident. He was from the tiny midcoast fishing village of Port Clyde, down a peninsula south of Rockland. At fifty-nine, he had grown up on boats and was a fourth-generation fisherman. His oldest son, Manville Jr., was fishing off the Grand Banks for swordfish. Wallace had been in the wheelhouse for almost thirty-five years. When he was in his late twenties, he lost a man overboard in a February gale. He never got over it. They were chopping ice in a thirty-mile-an-hour northwest wind. A sea took the guy overboard before anyone knew what happened. A rogue wave almost rolled the boat. They were on the eastern edge of Georges Bank, and there was nothing he could do. The man he lost had a wife and two little ones. She was remarried now and the kids were grown, but Wallace really still couldn't look her straight in the eye when he saw her around town.

Wallace sold his boat back then and tried to work ashore. His life was miserable. He ran a backhoe for a while. He drove a truck interstate for a mover. He even tried carpentering, framing houses for a guy he had grown up with. He was a lost soul. Finally, his wife put her foot down and told him it had to stop. He needed to go back to sea.

He bought a dragger out of Boothbay and within a week was fishing again. He had owned several different boats over the years.

Five years before, he turned his old boat over to his younger brother and went to Texas after the *Black Magic*, a Southern shrimper. She was a seventy-two-foot steel dragger at the time named the *Arlene Rose*. He named her *Black Magic* and re-lettered her before he left Texas. Some guys thought it was bad luck to rename a boat, but Wallace didn't believe in that stuff. He spent a lot of money on her conversion, and she was worth it.

The kid who got hurt today was a Port Clyde boy. His name was John Poor. He was twenty years old, and his wife just had a baby boy. Wallace said a prayer that the Helo boys would be there in time to save his arm. That tourniquet could only stay on for an hour. After that, the arm would have to be cut off. He knew how it would be.

Everybody in Port Clyde would rally around Johnny Poor and his wife. No one would blame Wallace for the accident, but eventually some smart young lawyer would show up with a lawsuit. The kids would be very reluctant at first to do that to Wallace and his wife, but the lawyer would ultimately convince them that it was nothing personal. He'd tell them that the insurance company would pay.

Wallace would understand. It was nothing personal all right, until the vicious bastard lawyers started working him over in one of those depositions accusing him of all kinds of stuff. They'd make you feel like you went out on deck and took a pipe to the kid's arm. Not one of those pricks had ever been on a dragger in their miserable lives. They had no respect for the situation on a boat at sea.

There was no doubt that this was a dangerous business. What pissed him off the worst was that anybody who went knew that. Wallace's attitude was that if you can't handle the risk just stay the fuck ashore. It never worked out that way though. Somebody gets hurt and all bets are off.

"*Black Magic*, this is Coast Guard Group Boston. Come in, please."

"This is *Black Magic* back to the Coast Guard."

"Could you give us the name of the injured man and any contact information, please? Over."

"His name is John Poor and we hail from Port Clyde. He lives on Brown Tree Road. The family's all there. Over."

The crew of the *Jubilee* was still hanging out in the pilothouse, listening to the communication. A look of recognition crossed Chase's face. "That's Willy Poor's little brother. I saw him in Boothbay a few months ago. He said something about Johnny getting a site with Manny. Manny's such a good shit you hate to see that stuff go down on anybody's boat, but it just kills him."

Scanton said, "Here comes the chopper."

Once more the overflight was so close they could see the color of the pilot's eyes. Anderson said, "Holy shit!" as they went through. The chopper rattled the rigging.

"*Black Magic,* this is Coast Guard Group Boston Helo Airborne. Come in, please."

"*Black Magic* . . . back."

A strong and confident voice began to speak. "I'm Lieutenant Commander Bob Garnett of the United States Coast Guard Group Boston Helo Airborne Division. I'm the chopper pilot headed your way. Here's what we're going to do, Skipper. You got any gear overboard at this point? Over."

"No, sir. We got everything aboard now. Over."

"Good, Skipper. All I need you to do is keep the old girl headed up into the wind at a steady straight jog. I'm going to bring this bird right over your deck. My boys will lower a basket to you. Skipper, make sure that no one touches that basket before it hits your deck. It will be loaded with static electricity that can electrocute a man if it gets grabbed before it grounds out."

"Okay, sir, I'll let my man know."

Garnett said, "You fellas load that boy into that basket. I'm going to snatch him right up here with me, and we're going to fly him into the hospital in Boston. The docs are waiting there to get him fixed up. Over."

"It sounds good to me, sir. We'll be standing by, and thanks for getting down here so quick and all. Over."

"You're very welcome, Skipper. Let's make this happen."

Bob Garnett had been flying choppers for the Coast Guard since he graduated from flight school in 1966. He began his career in Vietnam. After he made it home in one piece he had run rescue operations all over the East Coast and at one point had done a couple of stints on the Bering Sea. He was one of the best in the business. The guys all said Garnett could snatch the shine off a shark's tooth and never even piss off the shark.

He was good and he knew it. He lived for this job. The chopper settled in over the *Black Magic*.

"*Black Magic* . . . take her out of gear now for a little bit."

Wallace came back. "Ten-four."

The only way to describe the sequence of events that took place next was "perfectly orchestrated." Johnny Poor was in the basket and off that boat in less than five minutes.

Poor waved to Wallace as he was lifted up past the pilothouse. Garnett came on one last time. "Okay, *Black Magic*, we got your boy up here with us, and we're on our way to Boston. Good job, Captain Wallace. This is the United States Coast Guard Group Boston Helo Airborne Division, clear with the *Black Magic*."

"Thanks for everything, fellas. *Black Magic*, clear with the Coast Guard."

The *Black Magic* swung around and headed back to the east. Wallace picked up his mic and placed a call.

"Boston Marine Operator, this is the *Black Magic*. Come in, please."

"Boston Marine back to the vessel calling. Please switch and answer on channel 24." Wallace switched to 24. "*Black Magic* to Boston Marine. Over."

"Boston Marine back to the *Black Magic*. Over."

"Boston Marine, this is an emergency call to Port Clyde, Maine. I don't have the number, but the party's name is John and Susan Poor on Brown Tree Road, Port Clyde, Maine. Over."

"Boston Marine to *Black Magic*, please stand by. Attention: this will be a priority call ahead of all other traffic."

A lawyer named Dumont was furious. He had a boatload of guests from the Boston Yacht Club aboard his custom sport fisherman, and he'd already been waiting fifteen minutes to place his call.

A few painfully slow minutes passed while Wallace thought over what he was going to say to Susie when he got her. He loved that girl. She used to come down to his dock and play when she was a little girl. She'd say, "Can I help you, Big Manny? I'm a good helper, just you wait and see."

Wallace would take one look at her with her farmer overalls on and her blonde pigtails, and he was all hers. Manny and Betty Wallace had two teenage boys who were always off tearing up the harbor in their flat-bottom skiffs and raising holy hell in general.

That little girl was a pure joy to Wallace. Susie would fetch wrenches, pass bolts, and get clean rags. She'd stay until her mother would call her home for lunch or supper, depending on the time of day, of course.

When she got to be a teenager, she didn't come around as much as she had, but she was still just like a daughter to him. He was thinking about those days when the Boston Marine Operator came on again.

"Boston Marine to the *Black Magic*, we have your party standing by. Go ahead, please."

"Susie, are you there? Over."

"Yes, I'm here, Manny. What's going on?"

Susie knew when she heard Wallace's voice this was no social call. Captains never called crew members' wives unless it was something bad. You could hear the fear in Susie's voice. Wallace cut right to the chase.

"Johnny's been hurt, Susie. He's alive, and there's no danger he ain't he going to be. His arm got smashed up pretty bad. The Coast Guard airlifted him into Boston a few minutes ago. Over."

You could hear the tears in Susie's voice. "Oh god, Manny. Is he in bad pain? Over."

"No, honey. They dropped us a morphine kit from a jet. Billy Savage gave him the shot. It worked real fast on him. He waved to me when they lifted him off the deck. Over."

Susie said, "Jesus, Manny, we don't have any health insurance. With the baby and all we just couldn't keep it up. Over."

"It'll be all right, Susie. You go over and see Betty right after we get off this call, and she'll go down to Boston with you. She'll take care of whatever Johnny needs. Over."

"I'll get my mother to take the baby. Where is he? Over."

Wallace said, "They didn't tell me where they were taking him, but if you call the Coast Guard base in Boston they'll let you know. Over."

"Okay, Manny, I got to get going. Over."

"All right, Susie. I'm awful sorry this happened, honey. We're headed to the east. Call us when you know what's going on. Over."

"Okay, Manny. I'll get Betty, and we'll talk with you later."

Susie hung up. Wallace said, "Boston Marine, thanks for the call."

"You're welcome, *Black Magic*. We'll place this call on your account. Boston Marine Operator clear with the *Black Magic*, back to channel 16 and standing by."

Five minutes passed and a call came on 16. "Fishing vessel *Black Magic*, fishing vessel *Black Magic*. This is the Boston Marine Operator. Please switch and answer on channel 24 for traffic."

Wallace grabbed the mic. "*Black Magic* back to Boston Marine, switching to 24." He quickly changed channels.

His heart was racing.

"This is *Black Magic*."

The marine operator said, "Go ahead with your call, please." Betty Wallace was on the line. "Hello, Manny?" Wallace was so relieved that it was Betty. He was scared to death that something had happened to Johnny. He was standing there shaking.

"Betty, did Susie get over to our house yet? Over."

"No, Manny, that nice boy Rusty, who runs the *Jessica*, called me on our shore radio. He's fishing down here to the eastard, and he heard the whole thing, so he gave me a call. Over."

Wallace replied, "Okay, I see. He must be just on the edge of hearing us and being able to get you. I'll call him in a little bit and thank him. So you know what's happened then? Over."

"Yes, he filled me in. Is Susie coming here? Over."

"That's the plan. I figured you could drive her down to Boston. Please bring the checkbook. Them kids have got no insurance. I want him to get the best of care. Jesus, Betty, they got to save his arm. Over."

"Okay, dear. I'll take care of everything. We all need to pray for Johnny. Reverend Grant will rally the whole town when he gets wind of this. Over.

"Oh, Manny, there's Susie's car out front now. I'll call you when we get down there. Try not to worry. Johnny's going to get the best care possible in the big city hospital. I'm going to call Carol Valente and see if Susie and I can stay with her and Artie while we're down there. Over."

Wallace said, "That's great. I'm sure they'll be happy to have you two. Now drive careful, will you, and call me. I'll be right here waiting. I love you, Mother."

"I love you too, Daddy. I'll call you. Bye."

Betty hung up. Wallace said, "*Black Magic*, clear with Boston Marine. Thanks for the call."

"You're welcome, sir. Boston Marine, clear with the *Black Magic*."

The boys on *Black Magic* had already started putting the fish down. Within an hour the net was back in the water, and they were fishing again. It may seem strange that Wallace didn't head in to Boston to be there waiting for Johnny. Someone might think he didn't care. The reality was he cared very much. Betty Wallace and Johnny's wife would come down from Maine. He'd be paid his full share for the trip. There was nothing Wallace or the crew could do for him. They kept on fishing. That's what fishermen do . . . they keep on fishing.

*   *   *

The men of the *Jubilee* had another three hours to steam and they'd be fishing again. No one could get Johnny Poor out of their head. Reed went up on deck and lit up a cigarette. Even he was thinking about that kid. It just strengthened his resolve that he needed to get off this boat and out of this way of life as soon as he could. Chase was thinking about what had happened too. He knew that Johnny Poor should have used a gaff to get that idler chain clear of the door. He'd reached overboard himself and done the same thing a thousand times. You were always in a rush. Nobody ever ran up to get a friggin' gaff. Maybe he would next time, but he doubted it. When no one was watching them there was a time when all four men looked at their own forearms.

CHAPTER 40

Andy Brown was on top of the world as he steamed for Falmouth. It was an easy shot from here. He could see the strobe lights on the Cousin's Island power plant, and he headed that way. He was too excited to even think about smoking a joint. He just kept going. *I could do this twenty times. I'd have almost a hundred grand. I'd never work another day in my life. That might not be too bad, not ever working again,* he thought to himself. He was hooked; he was now a full-blown drug trafficker. Cool! The trip back to the landing flew by, but it was three in the morning, and he was getting tired.

He ran into the town landing float. The dock there was always all lit up. He saw a man standing up on the dock, leaning on the rail with a fishing pole. It was normal to see these guys. It seemed to him that there was somebody there fishing for mackerel twenty-four hours a day. He left the boat running and ran up the dinghy dock and grabbed Reed's punt. He heard a *click, click.* He figured the guy fishing was probably snapping a Zippo lighter closed after lighting up his cigarette.

Andy threw the punt's bowline around his davit and ran off to Reed's mooring. He put the *Ruffian* on her mooring and shut the engine down, closed the seacock, and turned off the battery switch. When he climbed into the punt to row back into the float he thought he saw that Kathy Blackwell broad walking up the dock. Now that was weird. What was that chick doing out here this time of night? She was so hot. He'd always wanted to nail her. Now that he had a load of money, maybe he could. Broads love money. That was an irrefutable fact.

CHAPTER 41

J oe Lamb had worked for Bert Goldman ever since he had entered
the service of the federal government. He was twenty-seven
years old and had grown up in Haverhill, a suburb of Boston. He
was the son of a retired military officer from Pennsylvania. He had
a Japanese mother who had grown up in California and had served
in the military herself, as a nurse. Lamb graduated third in his class
from the University of Rhode Island with a degree in criminal justice
and a minor in psychology. Everyone said that the minor must come
in very handy, working with Bert Goldman. When Lamb started
working for Goldman he had no idea what he would be in for. The
United States Justice Department operations training manuals were
not written with that guy in mind.

Goldman had devised a giant network of undercover agents that
extended over the entire coast of Maine. He treated everybody but
the crooks with respect and appreciation. His best helpers though
came from the public. They were his spies. His drug task force made
a point of letting the general public know that they could serve their
government and their communities by helping ferret out the crooks
and seeing them locked up.

This was definitely the case with Nettie Sherman from Edgecomb,
Maine. Nettie was seventy-one and sharp as a tack. She had served
her country during World War II in the Bath Iron Works shipyard
as a welder. She was a tough-minded woman back in those days,
and she was a tough-minded woman today. The love of her life, her
husband George, had passed away from a vicious lung disease caused
by the asbestos from the shipyard five years before, and she missed
him terribly. In those days no one knew much about what had caused
his death.

Nettie would be the first to admit that she had a lot of time on
her hands now with George gone. She was an avid reader and a news

addict. She knew all about the government's drug enforcement task force operating in Maine. She was determined to help. She studied up on the lingo of the drug world so she could be alert to any tip-offs that managed to come her way. She knew about reefers and joints; and she'd heard about speed, smack, and horse. They transported grass in bales and measured cocaine in kilos. Nettie considered herself quite an expert.

When Goldman's task force got a call from her, they sent Special Agent Joe Lamb out on the case. Lamb drove down US Route 1 to the turnoff for the town of Edgecomb. He had an appointment with Nettie bright and early on a Tuesday morning.

When Nettie had called in, she told Lamb that she was always up by four thirty in the morning and wanted to know if he could make it by six. He managed to convince her that nine o'clock would work just as well for him. She explained, in no uncertain terms, that once her vital information was received, there was very little doubt that Mr. Lamb would want to have the perpetrator she was going to reveal safely behind bars by noon.

When Lamb arrived at Nettie's house, he was overwhelmed by the wonderful aroma of a homemade Maine apple pie. The coffee was on the stove, and two places were set at her kitchen table. When Nettie answered the door, she took one look at Lamb's oriental features and almost slammed it in his face. She thought better of it though. "So I figure you must be that Mr. Lamb from the DEA. When did your kind join up on our side?" Lamb wasn't the least bit upset. He had encountered all different levels of prejudice ever since he was a little boy. Nettie Sherman wasn't about to rattle him.

He said, "They started letting us in about ten years ago. It was just an experiment in those days, and I guess it worked out okay."

Nettie picked up on the sarcasm. "Don't be a smart ass in my house, young man."

"Yes, ma'am." He answered, knowing it would be a pointless exercise in futility to pursue this matter any further.

Nettie said, "Well, sit down over here and have a cup of coffee and a piece of my apple pie."

"Yes, ma'am. It looks delicious." His suspicions were correct. The pie was fabulous. After he had taken a few bites and complimented Nettie on its splendid flavor, he said, "So what do you have for us at the DEA, Mrs. Sherman?"

Nettie was thrilled. The question was put just exactly the way they always said it on TV on those cop shows she loved to watch.

"Well, here's what's up." She began. "There's a suspicious character who's been operating in this area for years. I've had my eye on him now for a very long time. I haven't said nothing to nobody about it until I was real sure what he was up to. Just like it says to do in them investigative books I've been reading. Even the most hardened criminals will eventually screw up and make a mistake. This one did, and he had the misfortune to do it right in front of me."

Lamb pulled out his notebook. He started writing a few things down. Nettie plunged ahead with her story. "I was at this social gathering, and I overheard the whole thing. I've been sure as sin that this bum has been growing that wacky weed on his farm up near here for years. I heard him making a deal for ten bales of the stuff, right there in front of me."

Nettie had Lamb's undivided attention. "Who is this character, and how do you know him?"

"His name is Corliss Bracket, and he's married to my sister Margret. He has been for forty-nine years. There ain't been one of those days either that he's been worth the powder to blow him straight to hell."

Lamb had all he could do to keep from laughing. Things were starting to take shape now.

"All right then, our perpetrator is your brother-in-law, and he lives near here?" he said.

"That would be right," Nettie said. "The place is right over there." She pointed out her window at the farm next door.

"I see, Mrs. Sherman. I really appreciate this lead, and I'm going to check it out immediately."

Nettie was beaming from ear to ear. "Good, but you should probably have another piece of pie and a fresh cup before you go lock that bastard away for the rest of his miserable life."

"Thank you, ma'am, but when we're on the trail of a likely suspect of this magnitude, we can't take time out for personal pleasure, such as your incredible pie." Lamb said while trying to maintain a straight face.

"I appreciate the compliment and respect your decision," Nettie replied.

He excused himself from the table and thanked Nettie for her report.

Lamb was almost out the door. "Just one more question, ma' am . . . you mentioned a social event where you overheard this suspicious conversation. What was the nature of that social event?"

"Oh, that was my sister Maggie's birthday party."

It was hard but Lamb managed to keep the smile off his face. In the most serious tone he could muster, he said, "Yes, I see." He assured her his investigation would be thorough and immediate. He left her house after the normal good-byes and walked over to the Bracket farm next door.

Lamb found Corliss Bracket out in his barn working on an old tractor. He walked over to him, and after introducing himself, he pulled out his badge. The gold shield of the United States Department of Justice Drug Enforcement Administration was an impressive thing indeed. Corliss Bracket looked at it and laughed.

"Well, the old girl's finally flipped her wig, has she?"

Lamb said, "Are you referring to Mrs. Sherman?"

"Well, Christ, boy. She's the one that sent you over here, ain't she?"

Lamb couldn't help but smile. "Mrs. Sherman did suggest that it might be in our best interest to have a chat with you."

Corliss started laughing so hard that he had to hold onto one of the hayloft support posts to keep from falling over.

Mr. Bracket said in a very confident tone, "Well, son, there ain't no goddamn pot or drugs of any kind on this godforsaken farm.

Nope, hold on now, my old lady's got some mighty potent pain pills that Doc Wheeler gave her three months ago for her bad back. You ain't goin' to lock her up for that, are you? I've had her around a good long time, and I'd kind of miss her if you were to throw her in the jailhouse."

Now Lamb started laughing.

Agent Lamb said, "Just out of curiosity, what has made Mrs. Sherman so angry with you?"

"Well, son, back during WW II, her sister and I started seeing each other a little. That was when I was home here on leave. It was back when I was getting ready to head overseas to fight them German bastards. Things got a little out of hand between us, so to speak, and I got her in a family way. I was gone afore I ever knowed what had happened. When Nettie found out about it she got really pissed off. Maggie, my wife, was her little sister and all, and she never forgave me. Things weren't that bad when her husband, George, my brother, was around, but after he passed on she hasn't said a civil word to me since. Maggie and I had three other children, and exceptin' for the fact that she's a goddamn Democrat, we've had a pretty good run at it now for almost fifty years."

Lamb had a half smile on his face and said, "I see."

"Exactly how much pot did she tell you that you were going to find over here anyway?"

"Ten bales," Lamb replied.

Corliss Bracket started laughing again.

"Wow! Ten ten bales, huh? Well, if that don't beat all. Jesus H. Christ, I could retire if I had that kind of stuff around here. I'm seventy-four years old. Don't you think that kind of money would last me and the old girl till we kicked the bucket?"

Lamb didn't say anything more. He just reached out to Corliss and shook hands with him as he was leaving.

As Lamb turned to walk off, Corliss said, "If I was a young buck like you in your line of work, I would check on the goings-on down at Little River in East Boothbay though. You might be kinda interested in what them fellas is up to."

"Thanks, Mr. Bracket. What kind of goings-on are you referring to? What do you think is going on down there?"

Corliss Bracket looked at Joe Lamb with a very serious expression on his face. "That's somethin' a bright young fella like you can figure out on his own. You don't need an old shit kicker like me explainin' nothin' to you."

CHAPTER 42

Andy slowly made his way up the hill at the town landing and over to the trailer park where he lived. It was quarter to four in the morning when he finally put his head down in his own pillow. His cash was carefully stashed in a shoe box underneath his bed. He was finally home and he was exhausted.

It was two thirty in the afternoon before he woke up again, but he felt a lot better. He immediately looked under the bed to make sure his shoe box was still there and then stumbled out into the kitchen. There was a two-day-old Portland paper lying there on the counter. He had a thing about reading newspapers. He mostly didn't do it. Part of the reason for that was because he was barely literate, and part was because he didn't give a sweet crap what went on with the rest of the world. There was a headline that did catch his eye though. It read, "DEA makes major drug trafficking arrest in the midcoast city of Belfast." It had a picture of two guys being led off in handcuffs with two men in DEA jackets holding them by the arms.

Andy didn't connect himself to that scene. He figured those guys didn't have a foolproof system like he had. They were probably just a couple of dumb guys who didn't know what they were doing. He read some of the article, and it was full of some gobbledygook about illegal transportation of narcotics with the intent to sell and distribute. Blah, blah, blah . . . he couldn't have cared any less. It had nothing to do with him.

He kept thinking about the money under his bed. He knew that he wasn't supposed to spend any of it for at least six months, but goddamn it, he'd earned it, and it was his money. They could go fuck themselves.

What Andy needed was a truck. Not a fancy truck, just an old beater, so he could get around. What good was the money anyway if he couldn't spend it? He needed a shower and some clean clothes. He had been in his clothes for at least four days. He probably smelled of lobster bait pretty bad.

He stripped down, turned on the water in the shower, and climbed in. He kept some Clorox in the tub to use to scrub his arms to get the bait smell off them. After he was done showering, he got dressed, got into his shoe box, and pulled out $500 of the cash and stuck it in his pocket. He still had a bunch of money left from the lobsters he had sold over the last couple of days.

He walked up to the Landing store and went in and bought a soda. The guy who ran the store hated to have people hang around after they had bought their stuff. He really never liked Andy, and he was pretty obvious about it. Thankfully he wasn't there.

Mark Peterson, a guy Andy knew, walked into the store. Everyone called him Petey.

Andy said, "Hey, Petey. What's up?"

"Oh nothing, really. What's up with you, Brown?"

Andy puffed his chest out a little. "Same old shit, different day. I'm doing real well lobstering though. I'm thinking of buying Skip Reed out. Hey, how about giving me a ride up to Villacci's? I want to buy myself a truck."

Mark said, "Sure, I'm just hanging around until tonight. I'm going to the movies with my wife and her sister. I'll give you a lift up there."

Villacci's was the local used-car dealer. He sold everything from nice cars to rolling pieces of junk that just qualified for an inspection sticker. Brown was much more in the latter category. He got his ride up to the little car shop up on the Middle Road.

Gene Villacci was in his office. He had his reading glasses tipped back on the top of his head. Villacci had been around this lot all his life. His dad had opened the business when he and his brother were just little kids. He sold his first car when he was eighteen.

When Andy walked into the office, Villacci said, "Hi, Andy Brown. How are you doing?" His friendly smile and the happy tone in his voice was his best stock in trade.

"Hi, Gene . . . I'm here to see if you have a truck you might want to sell me."

"Sure, I do. What are we talking about for money?"

"I've got $750."

He laid the cash on Villacci's desk.

"Well, Andy, let's see now. Come on out here a minute."

They walked around to the back of the garage. There was a 1968 Chevy C10 pickup.

"This old truck has 120,000 miles on it. It's got a three speed on the floor. The body's got some rust, but the cab is in good shape. My brother Bob has an old stake body that I'm sure he'd sell you cheap when the time comes that you need it. It will fit on this frame, and we'll put it on for you. The truck runs pretty well, but it's old and tired. You've got to baby it along, Andy, but it will do the job for you if you take care of it."

The Chevy truck was bright red. Villacci pointed out that it had good tires on it and a new sticker. He said, "You have a valid license, Andrew?" Brown pulled out an old beat-up wallet with a picture of Mickey Mouse on it. No one ever asked him about the wallet, but if the truth were to be told, it was the last thing his dad had given him for his birthday before he left him and his mother more than seventeen years ago.

He pulled out a driver's license and handed it to Gene. "Okay, Andy, let's take her for a spin, shall we?"

Villacci snapped some dealer plates on the back and passed Andy the keys. He had never driven a stick shift before, but after a few stalls and jerky takeoffs, he started to get the hang of it. There were no mean jokes or wise cracks made. It wasn't Gene's style. He gave Andy some quiet encouragement, and before long they were cruising down Middle Road.

Villacci turned the radio on. The previous owner had replaced the standard speakers with some new ones that probably cost the guy a third of what he was selling the truck for. He smiled. "How about that, Andy? Great sound!"

Andy had never owned a car or truck in his life. He used his mother's old cars when he needed one. In a strange way, he had really led a very sheltered life. Driving down the road in this old pickup truck, he was smiling from ear to ear.

They turned around and headed back to the garage. After they got there, Villacci filled out all the necessary paperwork. He called a local insurance man whom he'd done business with for years and got Brown covered. He put some temporary plates on the truck, and Andy was ready to go.

Villacci got really serious for a minute and said, "Andy, you've got to listen to me now. This is an old truck. If you get it in the saltwater or lug a bunch of traps and bait in it, take a minute to rinse it out. Change the oil every four thousand miles or so. Don't forget to pay for your insurance, because you'll need your card to register this truck."

"Okay, Gene . . . Thanks."

"Drive carefully and call me if you have any troubles of any kind, okay, Andy? Good luck."

Brown headed down the road. He was on top of the world. He decided to run in town and get his bait for the next day. It was a hell of a lot faster than running the boat in. He wanted to get an early start in the morning.

He was driving along toward Portland when he spotted Crazy Mary from the trailer park, walking along the road, eating a Popsicle. He pulled over. Mary looked up. "Hi, Andy, you got a pretty new truck!" Mary wasn't what they called, in those days, totally retarded; but she was very close. Andy said, "You want to go for a ride in town with me, Mary?"

"Oh yes, Andy. Mary would like to take a ride in your pretty new truck."

She climbed in, and they took off. Andy had the radio on and Mary was smiling.

She looked over toward Andy. "Does Andy want Mary to play with his pee pee?"

He thought about it for a minute. "Not right now, Mary. Maybe later."

"Okay, Andy. Maybe later, okay."

They pulled in at Portland Lobster after just a few minutes. He drove up near the rear overhead door and got out of the truck. He told Mary to remain put and to not talk to anyone. Mary made the locked signal over her mouth and smiled. "Okay, Andy!"

He went in and found a guy running a forklift and told him he needed three fish totes of redfish. Andy thought it was weird that the Oriental guy was still hanging around the place, snapping pictures.

The kid driving the forklift loaded the bait into the truck for him. He and Mary headed home. He dropped her off near the little store and drove down over the hill to the town wharf. He dragged his bait down the dock and rowed out to the *Ruffian*. He brought the boat in and put his bait aboard. After everything was done and the *Ruffian* was safely back on her mooring, he went home, had some supper with his mother, and went to bed.

CHAPTER 43

The *Jubilee* had been fishing hard for over thirty-six hours. The captain and crew were tired. They had started fishing below Fippennies Ledge and had worked to the eastard, through most of Wilkinson's Basin, and were now headed back toward Sigsbee's. Scanton was chomping at the bit to get back to the fifty-fathom Bunches and go after some of those large codfish they'd had last trip. They had about forty-five thousand pounds of fish aboard. There were a lot of flats and a healthy amount of gray sole. Everybody was feeling good except for Reed. He was restive, nervous, and seemed to be constantly on edge.

Anderson had made a chicken and rice casserole for supper, and it was nearing midnight when they finished eating. Chase was on the wheel; Scanton and Reed had hit the bunks and were both sound asleep.

Chase had brought out the old speaker he had found down in the engine room. Scanton had been going hard at it over his loud hailer all this trip again. The deck orders were driving him crazy. He knew that the biggest reason Scanton was on that thing all the time was because of wheelhouse boredom. The singing and the music played on deck was funny as hell, but he couldn't let him know that.

The pilothouse on the boat was not neat and organized, to say the very least. There were papers, old charts, used and outdated pieces of electronics, and tools everywhere. Chase had a plan to raise some hell with Joey, and the mess was a key part to the practical joke. Nothing could compete with the nod man prank, but this was going to be close, real close. He found the output lead wires from the hailer and wired the extra speaker into the system. He put it up on the aft shelf about head height. He covered it up with magazines and papers so the speaker was aimed right at Scanton's left ear. When he started yapping on the goddamn thing, he was going to get it right back at him, full bore. He was chuckling to himself. This was going to be *grreeat.*

He got back to the wheel and checked the sounding machine. It looked like fish to him. There were another three hours to go on the tow, and he settled in.

At three thirty Chase spun through the fo'c'stle and woke up the crew. There was a pot of coffee on the stove, and he fired it up on the way by. The gang was up in the pilothouse and ready to go in ten minutes. When they left to go down on deck, Chase said, "Joey, turn up your hailer a little. We couldn't hear it that well last set off."

Scanton should have known something was up. Chase wanted him to turn up the hailer? When the boys were oiled up and out on deck, Chase made the sign and Scanton slowed the *Jubilee* down and engaged the PTO. The haulback began. Anderson was taking a turn running the starboard winch, and Chase was standing back toward the rail, waiting for the first big announcement over the loud hailer. When the door marks showed, Anderson and Reed slowed the winches. The doors broke water and Captain Joseph Scanton made his move. All he said was, "Hang the . . . *what the fuck!*" Chase could see Joey rip the extra speaker off the shelf and yank the wires out of the back of the hailer.

He came out the starboard pilothouse door and threw the speaker at Chase, who was laughing so hard he almost forgot to duck when the speaker came flying at him. "Fuck you, Chase!" he screamed. The speaker bounced off the deck and smashed up against the main hatch cover. Chase hollered back, "Hey! You wrecked my extra speaker!" Reed and Anderson couldn't see Scanton from where they were under the shelter deck, but they knew this was a winner.

The haulback went fine. They transferred the doors to the net reel by moving the idler chain. It went perfectly. Now every time anybody looked at those idler chains, they thought about John Poor from the *Black Magic.*

The bag came aboard, and it looked like a least five thousand pounds. Joey popped in one of his favorite selections—"I don't care too much for money! Money can't buy me love!" Scanton was dancing around up in the pilothouse. He looked pretty ridiculous but he didn't give a shit. He was a 110 miles offshore with three other morons.

The boys set off, put the fish down, and came up into the wheelhouse.

"Very fuckin' funny, Chase. You almost blew my ears off!"

He laughed. "I thought it was great! Now you know what it sounds like on deck!" They were all laughing and fooling around when the radio came up.

CHAPTER 44

"*Jubilee, Jubilee*. The *Gloria Walker* calling."

"*Jubilee* back to the *Gloria Walker*."

"Joey, go to 88." Joey switched up. "Hey, what's up, Dad?"

"Where are you guys?"

"We're about two hours west of the bucket bottom. Over."

"You towing, Joe?"

"Yes, we just set off."

"Switch down to one watt. We're pretty close to you."

Scanton lowered the power on the VHF. Pete Scanton obviously had something to say he didn't want anybody else to hear. He said, "Marshall, you on here." Marshall came on. "Yes, I'm right here, Pete."

Peter said, "Go ahead, Marshall."

"I'm about twenty minutes up inside of you, Joey, and I've got the net in the wheel. I've got some things goin' on here, Joey, that I don't want to call for a particular kind of help."

Joey knew that Marshall's boat was old and tired. He didn't want the Coast Guard boarding him and inspecting everything. There was nothing serious that would threaten the boat. It was just a lot of little stuff that probably would get him tied up for a while. Everybody fishing put off a lot of maintenance shit in the summer that would be done in the fall before winter fishing started.

Marshall's boat was a fifty-nine-foot eastern-rigged dragger. They were a dying breed. Eastern-rigged boats were very different from the setup on a boat like the *Jubilee*. Those old boats all hauled their nets in on the starboard side instead of up over the stern. The winches were placed just ahead of the pilothouse and centered on deck. Then they are rigged with deck bollards, which guide the wire to the doors that hang off two gallous frames. The gallous frames are mounted parallel just inside the rail up the starboard side of the boat.

Hauling back on an eastern-rigged boat can be very difficult. The trick is to always have the wind off the starboard side when you haul back. A sudden shift at the wrong moment on the port side and the boat will drift. The net winds up in the boat's propulsion wheel. Marshall was dead in the water a hundred miles offshore and did not want any help from the US Coast Guard.

Marshall Grimes said, "Joey, your dad says you've got a diver aboard. We're pretty good right here for a while. I was wondering if we could get the guy off your boat, and maybe he could get me straightened out."

Peter Scanton came on. "We aren't fishing right now, Joe, but we're down here. I'll come get your man and bring him back up to Marshall, if you fellas are willing." With the mic off, Joey Scanton turned to Anderson and said, "You ain't got to do this, Tom. No one is going to be pissed at you if you turn them down. It's not your problem. Going overboard down here, it's not like going over up in the bay. I've known Marshall all my life. He's my dad's best friend, and I'm telling you right now, I wouldn't do it."

Anderson thought about it for a few minutes. Hell, he figured, he didn't have to dive that deep. He guessed he'd go down under, take a look, and if it was too fucked up, Peter Scanton could always tow Marshall in. He told Joey he'd get his dive stuff together and go give them a hand. Scanton hit the mic, "Dad, he's willing to take a look. Why don't you get your guys to set your aluminum skiff and outboard overboard? They can run it up our ramp. We'll put Tom and his stuff aboard." Peter came back. "Sounds good, Joey. We gonna call this the dive bottom from now on?"

Joey smiled. "Yes, we are!"

"Hey, Marshall, you got a bag of fish hanging?"

Marshall came back. "Yes, I do, Joe."

"You seen any fins?"

"No, Joe, no. I wouldn't put that boy over if I had."

"Okay, Marshall, we'll be standing by."

Anderson went down on deck and got things organized. He checked over everything before he was ready to go.

A few minutes later the *Gloria Walker* was at hand. They pulled up on the port side of the *Jubilee*. The little twelve-foot aluminum boat came over and slid her bow up the *Jubilee's* ramp. A guy named Harry Stone was running it. He gave the outboard a quick turn on the throttle, and it popped almost out of the water. Harry had been a deckhand on Pete Scanton's boat for at least three years.

Anderson loaded his tank, weight belt, and dive bag aboard. Chase wished Tom good luck and gave the skiff a hard shove. They backed away and headed over for the *Gloria Walker*. This was the first time Anderson had seen the boat, and he was impressed. She was a fifty-eight-foot beauty, perfectly maintained and outfitted to the nines. He went up to the pilothouse to introduce himself to Joey's dad. "Glad to meet you, Tom," Peter Scanton said with a big friendly smile. "I appreciate you doing this for Marshall."

"No problem. I'll have to see how bad it is. If I hook a line into the bag you may be able to pull some of the weight off the net, and I can free it up without cutting the shit out of it. We'll see when I get overboard. I've done some salvage work for the boatyard with a lot of weight involved, but this may be different."

Within a few minutes Peter had run down to Marshall's boat. Tom put his wet suit on, out on deck. He installed his regulator on his tanks and opened the valve that supplied the air. He watched the pressure gauge climb to 3,200 pounds. The hose stiffened as the air filled the line. He squeezed the diaphragm plate on the front of the regulator and allowed a quick shot of air to escape. He put the regulator in his mouth, inhaled a large breath of air, and exhaled it. The air was clean and cool as it filled his lungs. He closed the regulator valve when his test was complete.

The buoyancy control device (BCD) was attached to the backpack, ready to flip up over his shoulders and onto his back. He was suited up and ready to go when Peter Scanton pulled up beside the *Teresa Lynn*.

Anderson would get to meet Marshall Grimes for the first time. The *Teresa Lynn* was a classic. Her lines were sleek and beautiful. She had her pilothouse toward the stern and a central mast that was used to jillson the bags of fish up and onto the deck. There was a forward companionway that lead down to the fo'c'stle and the galley. For a boat built in 1947, she looked to be in great shape.

Anderson and Harry Stone loaded his gear into the skiff and pulled away from the *Gloria Walker*. The sun was up now, and it was a clear bright day. There was a brisk northwest breeze of about ten knots. Just enough, Tom thought, to be a real pain in the ass. The small chop was lifting and dropping the *Teresa Lynn* like a bouncing ball. Harry brought Anderson up alongside so he could chat with Marshall Grimes.

"I'm Marshall Grimes, and who might you be, young man?" the old captain said. Anderson could see the big friendly grin on Marshall's face, and he knew immediately he was going to really like him. "I might be Tom Anderson." Grimes laughed out loud. "Good boy, good. You think you can unsnarl an old skipper that can't run his boat worth a shit this fine summer morning?"

"I'll sure try for you, sir, and I'm real doubtful you can't run your boat. I'm going to flop overboard and take a look here in a minute. Then I'll come up and we'll make a plan."

Marshall said, "Finest kind then. I sure do appreciate you doin' this for me, Tom."

Anderson had his flippers and his diver's hood on. He stood up and fastened his weight belt around himself. He reached down with both hands and grabbed the tank by the backpack and then flipped up in one smooth motion over his head and down onto his back. He moved his shoulders around a little and strapped the webbed band closed around his stomach. He took his mask, spit in it and rubbed the saliva around on the face plate, and then rinsed it overboard. Saliva is a perfect natural cleanser that keeps the mask from fogging up while he's in the water. Anderson had a razor-sharp knife attached in a holster fastened to his leg. He had Harry turn on the air supply to the regulator for him and made him double-check it to be sure it was wide open. He swung around and sat on the starboard gunwale of the skiff and flipped over the side backward and into the cold offshore water.

He took a deep breath, and the cool clean air flowed freely into his lungs. He returned quickly to the surface. As the ice-cold ocean seeped into his wet suit, he treaded water and checked his gauges. Everything was in perfect order. The crew of the *Teresa Lynn* had hauled the doors on board; they were hanging on her gallous frames. The ground cables were hauled, and the roller sections were aboard and on deck. They had the first strap attached to the jillson. The wings were up, and the lengthening piece was hung tight against the hull, running back toward the stern. The net was wound in tight.

Marshall had tried to jog the boat from forward and back to reverse to try and get the net free. It hadn't worked, and the net was wound tighter and harder into the propulsion wheel than it had been when the accident first occurred.

Anderson swam up under the *Teresa Lynn's* hull. The boat was rolling and bobbing around. It was very difficult to not get hit in the head by the movement of the boat and driven down under. Anderson made his way back to the stern.

He could see it now. It was a huge ball of net wrapped around the wheel and rudder. This twine mess was at least five feet across. There was no way to figure out whether the snarl was wound to the right or left. He worked back to the rudder and held on for dear life as the boat rose and fell with the chop. He flipped some of the twine off the rudder and was able to get some slack as the boat settled down into the water. The first section of net dropped like a boulder off a cliff when it was freed up. Anderson pushed himself back quickly so he wouldn't get caught in the twine and sucked down with the net as it fell away.

He cleared as much of the net as he could and turned and swam for the surface. Harry was there waiting when he broke the surface. Anderson was relieved to see him. The majority of diver drownings happened on the surface, not under the water. Harry was a good man and had positioned himself directly over Tom's air bubbles as they were breaking the surface.

Anderson detached his weight belt while he was in the water and passed it up to Harry. With the regulator still in his mouth, he slid out of his backpack and passed it up to him. Once Harry had both hands on the air tank, Tom spit out the regulator and hung on the side of the skiff. A couple of powerful flips and he was in the small boat sitting on the forward seat. He pulled off his mask, flippers, and hood and stood up ready to get aboard the *Teresa Lynn*.

Marshall was waiting on deck and gave Anderson a hand as he stepped up onto the dragger.

"Well, boy, how'd she look down there?"

"Pretty bad, sir. She's wound in there hard, and the damn boat keeps bouncing around, so it's tough to get a hold of anything down there." Anderson hesitated for just a second and said,

"There's something I don't understand. Every time I free up some net it drops hard."

Marshall said, "We've been towing up on the hard bottom. My guess is we got a bag of rocks."

Anderson said, "There's something I want to try that could help. Is there any way you can slowly turn the shaft so I can see which way she's wound on?"

Marshall was glad he could do something to help. "Sure can, son. I'll get my deck man to put a large stillson on the shaft and roll her over that way."

Anderson said, "Okay, have him roll her a full turn to the right and then a full turn to the left." Grimes said, "Finest kind, Tom. We can do that. Yes, sir, we can."

He smiled at Marshall. "Let me get together my dive stuff and get my ass overboard and then let them have at it."

"Okay, Tom, okay. We'll do her up good, up here. Yes, we will."

Anderson said, "This is my plan. If I can start cutting some of the twine with all the weight rising and falling, I may be able to take advantage of that and get her free with minimal damage. Worst-case scenario, I'll put a line on the bag and cut the net right off so you can pull it aboard. Then I'll just whack out the other snarled twine section of the lengthening piece and you'll be good to go. I'm going to try to free it up without doing that though."

Marshall said, "Don't you worry about that twine none. Me and the boys can mend that old net up in a flash. Yes, we can, son. In a flash, I'm telling you. You do what you can, but be careful down there, will you, boy?"

He promised he would and climbed back aboard the skiff with Harry. Anderson was back overboard and under the boat, and the wheel started to turn to the right and then to the left very slowly. He saw exactly what he needed to see. The *Teresa Lynn* had a skeag that extended from the bottom of the keel aft and supported the rudderpost. He hung off the skeag with his right arm and was able to slowly unwind the net. On every rise and fall of the boat, he pulled one section of snarled twine off the wheel.

As he freed the net, it dropped hard toward the ocean floor, foot by foot, yard by yard. Anderson noticed a quick motion of some kind. It was really just a flash on the very outside edge of his field of vision. He dismissed it as a phantom shadow. The twenty-foot mako had other things that he was more interested in at that moment because he moved on to something else.

Slowly and carefully Anderson worked at freeing the net from the wheel. He was sure he banged his head about ten times against the hull of the boat as she rolled up and down in the chop. He was glad he had on a soft rubber hood that was absorbing most of the impact. He was breathing hard. He stopped working for a second and checked his pressure gauge. It read just below five hundred pounds. He didn't have much dive time left before he would run out of air. He had been in the water over thirty-five minutes already. Finally, he worked through the entangled twine all the way down to the wheel. There was the final knot. If he cut one small section, the net should be free and the net would drop away from the shaft.

He stopped to catch his breath and rest a second before he made the final cut. He reached down to his holster and pulled out his knife. He couldn't believe he had cleared 90 percent of this mess away without having to make a single cut. The short steady chop of the ocean was what had made it so hard to do, but it had also made it possible.

Up on deck, Marshall Grimes was as near to being in a panic as he ever got. He could see the breaker coming toward the boat, and there wasn't a goddamn thing he could do to warn Anderson about it. He just stood there watching it come like an impending train wreck. Anderson, underneath the boat's hull, was taking a break. He was thinking about Kathy and how much in love with her he was. He was so completely comfortable in the water that it probably saved his life. For him this was just another labor-intensive task that was almost done. He reached up to make his final cut. He sunk his knife into the last knot. In an instant the weight of the bag came down full force. A section of twine grabbed his flipper and suddenly he was violently spun upside down and drawn directly into the falling mass of twine. That breaker had raised and dropped the *Teresa Lynn* three and a half feet in a split second. Anderson's tank was caught in the net, and he was pulled down at an incredible free fall rate. His mask was ripped off, and the seawater was being driven up his nose. He was choking to death.

He was still barely conscious and had the presence of mind to bite down hard on the regulator so he could still breathe. The claustrophobic sensation was terrifying. He had to fight to breathe through his mouth only. One mistake and he would suck seawater into his lungs and he would drown. When the net stopped falling, he had been dragged down over twenty feet in a matter of seconds. He was trapped in the net and fighting for his life. It was only a matter of seconds before a strange sense of panic overcame him. He was angry and trapped. *This isn't fair. This isn't the deal. I'm young and strong and I need to have more time. I need to be with Kathy. I need to live.* He began to feel weak. He was suddenly back at home in Falmouth at the dinner table with his mother and dad and his sister Joanne. The picture was fading quickly and everything began to get dark. When Tom Anderson lost consciousness he was no longer afraid.

Up on deck Marshall saw that the net was free, but he couldn't see Tom's bubbles anywhere. Harry screamed at the top of his lungs, "HAUL THE NET, MARSHALL! HAUL THE NET NOW!"

Grimes engaged the winch and started the jillson as fast as he could. Within seconds, he saw Tom's body breaking the surface and snarled up in the net. He wasn't moving. Marshall's heart raced. When the net came up above the rail, he and Harry pulled it aboard the boat by hand. The boy's body was snarled into the net, hanging upside down. Marshall could see that he was unconscious. He wasn't close enough to tell if he was still breathing or not. They yanked him aboard, untangled him from the net, and laid him down on the deck.

Harry ripped the dive gear off him as fast as he could. He tore open his wet suit and put his head down on Tom's chest. Harry screamed, "I can't hear a heartbeat. He's not breathing. Harry started pressing hard on Tom's chest and giving him mouth-to-mouth resuscitation. Between breaths he screamed, "Come on, Tom, Come on!"

Marshall watched for what to him seemed like an eternity. Suddenly Tom choked, coughed, and puked out a mouthful of seawater. Marshall yelled, "Thank God!" when Tom's eyes blinked opened. Harry rolled him over on his side, and he threw up hard. He must have heaved four times before it stopped wracking his body.

Tom sat up and wiped his face. Marshall said, "Well, are you all right, boy? You scared the shit out of us!" Tom laughed and coughed. He was as weak as a newborn kitten. "Now you bastards are going get on the radio and make fun of the green guy getting seasick and pukin' all over your deck. I know how it works!" Marshall laughed. "If that don't beat all. I don't think we'll be doing that. No, sir, we won't."

Tom laughed a little and lay back down on the deck. Marshall said, "If you feel up to it, why don't you go down and stretch out on one of the bunks for a few minutes, and we'll get you back to the *Jubilee*. Thanks a hell of a lot, son. Thanks a hell of a lot. I'm sure glad you're all right."

Tom staggered down forward to the fo'c'stle. He found a towel and dried himself off, grabbed a bunk with a blanket on it, and climbed in. He was surprised how weak he felt. He guessed that it had been a pretty close call. He really didn't remember anything past the feeling of being hauled toward the bottom upside down. He lay back in the bunk and closed his eyes. He was only there a few minutes when Harry came down with his clothes. He had run over to the *Gloria Walker* and gotten them. He threw them up on the bunk and let Tom sleep undisturbed.

The *Teresa Lynn* made her way back toward the *Jubilee*. Marshall got on the radio. All three boats' radios were still down on one watt, so the conversation was relatively private.

Marshall came on the air first. "Well, fellas, that was a close one. Apparently, when Tom got us free there, the bag had a lot of rocks in her. I think that's probably why I got her screwed up to begin with. I ain't makin' no excuses for my poor captainin' now. Anyhow when that friggin' small breaker came through, the damn bag dropped. That bitch breaker came down on us at exactly the wrong time. Well, the net caught Tom by the back of his diving rig and yanked him down deep. If you can believe it, he was upside down. 'Cause of Harry's quick thinkin', we hauled that kid up with the net off the jillson and yarned him aboard. We pulled him out of that net. He was in there like a hung-up haddock. Harry gave him a poundin' on his chest 'cause the poor kid had lost his consciousness. He coughed up half the goddamn ocean and then started breathin' again. He's a good boy and a right tough one. I'm real glad he didn't get drownded on us. Thank the Lord he seems pretty good right now. He's restin' up down forward."

Joey Scanton came on. "How's he look? Is his color all right? You think we should get him airlifted in?"

Marshall said, "He's a little pale, really."

Scanton said, "Of course he is. He's a friggin' Norwegian. They're all that color."

"I ain't no doc, of course, but he seems to be okay to me. He's a pretty tough kid."

Scanton said, "We're still towing, but I'm about ready to haul back if you don't mind waiting for a bit before we take him back aboard."

Marshall said, "No, Christ, no. Harry says your boy is sound asleep right now. We'll just hang off here till you get squared away. Try not to get your net in the wheel. I think your diver is out of commission for a bit."

"Thanks, Marshall . . . I'll try to keep that in mind."

Peter Scanton was pretty rattled. The older he got, the less tolerance he had for this kind of shit. He didn't want to talk about what just happened. He just lay off a ways with the *Gloria Walker* and waited.

The *Jubilee* had a lousy tow. After the haulback they only had about 1,500 pounds. It took about an hour to get everything aboard the boat. Harry pulled over in the skiff with Tom and his dive equipment.

Before he got out of the little boat, he said, "I really want to thank you for saving my ass. My chest is a little sore from the beating you threw on me, but I do appreciate it."

"No sweat, kid. Thanks for helpin' out Marshall. He's a hell of good old shit. You can buy me a beer next time we're ashore together. Good meetin' you." Harry waved as he pulled away and buzzed back to the *Gloria Walker*. Marshall had tried to give Anderson a hundred-dollar bill before he got off the boat. He pulled his hand back like Marshall was trying to pass him a red hot piece of coal.

When Anderson climbed aboard, Chase and Reed grabbed his dive gear. Chase said, "Well, if it ain't Lloyd Fuckin' Bridges. You all right, shithead? Don't you start thinking you can come aboard here with a bunch of lame-ass excuses about how you can't count a cribbage hand accurately now on account of oxygen deprivation."

Anderson said, "Nice to see you too. I can't seem to remember how much three of a kind is worth, now that you mention it."

He turned and walked rather slowly up to the pilothouse. When he got up there Scanton said, "How are you feeling, Tom?"

"I'm all right." Scanton studied Anderson's eyes to see if his pupils were dilated or uneven. "How's your head feel?"

"I've got a fierce headache," Anderson said.

Scanton said, "I'm not surprised. Go hit the bunk. Take three aspirins before you do. I don't want to see you for at least four hours."

"Okay, Joey." Anderson went down, got the aspirins, and crawled into his bunk. He lay back, and to his total surprise, Uncle Charley came in, jumped up into his bunk, and curled up around his neck. "Did you come to take care of me, old girl?" Uncle Charley didn't say anything. She closed her eyes and stayed snuggled close, purring to Tom.

CHAPTER 45

Danny was three quarters drunk by the time he staggered into his little house out on Green Island. Tammy was nowhere around, and it really pissed him off. He wasn't a guy who got angry much, but he had been really stressed lately, and it was getting a lot worse. He'd been hearing a lot of stuff that was making him very nervous. That Goldman prick who ran the DEA was starting to get to people. Maine might have a long coastline, but it had a very short and fast underground communication network.

That Steve Warner guy at Barnesy's had told him a few things that had him all worked up. He had seen the paper with the article about the guys getting busted up in Belfast. Even though he wasn't lugging pot anymore, he was scared to death that someone would be showing up on his doorstep any minute. He had convinced himself he was out of it, but he knew that you're really never out of it. Danny wanted no part of jail. He had grown up out here on the island, and the thought of confinement absolutely terrified him. He was already a prisoner in his own mind, and he hadn't even been busted yet.

Now he just wanted something to eat, have a smoke, and try to figure some things out. Where was that bitch anyway? He slammed around the house a while and then decided to take a hike down to South Beach to see if he could find her. It was a while before sunset, and he figured she'd be sitting down there, staring out toward Portland Harbor. He grabbed another beer for the walk down there. It took him about fifteen minutes to make it down the old gravel road that leads to the beach. He tossed his beer can on the side of the road.

The island was beautiful this time of year, but Danny didn't even notice. To him the island was the island. When he reached South

Beach, Tammy was sitting in her favorite spot on the beach all by herself.

He walked up behind her. "Why aren't you home! I want some supper, bitch."

Tammy said, "You want supper? Go make it yourself, asshole." Danny was shocked. Tammy had never spoken to him that way. She always put up with his nastiness until she finally broke down and cried and then he'd back off a little. That's how it always been before now. They'd been together a long time, and she had never once talked back to him. He was so taken aback that he didn't get mad or even know what to say. With his typical sarcastic tone and an aggressive set to his jaw, he said, "What's the matter with you anyway?"

"It's my birthday tomorrow," Tammy said.

"Yeah, so what? What do you want me to do? Get a cake and sing you a song?" Tammy had a hurt look on her face as she turned toward him. "Why do you have to be so mean? You've never asked me once about my family or anything about me. You treat me like I'm a stray you picked up on the street, and I hate it!"

Unfazed, Danny said, "Well, if the shoe fits, wear it."

Tammy was really pissed now. "I'm turning thirty tomorrow, and from now on everything is going to be different."

With a dismissive ring to his voice, Danny said, "Ya? What are you? Going through that mental pause shit already?"

"No, you prick, I'm not! Fuck you, Danny! What you don't know, smart ass, is that I had a real family of my own once. This will shock you, but I grew up rich. My father is a big-time lawyer in Connecticut, and my mother came from money too. I went to private school and everything."

Danny said, "No shit, really?" He was suddenly interested now.

Tammy was crying a little. "I was really bad. The family tried everything to straighten me out, but I was a real pain in the ass. They sent me to drug and alcohol rehab and tried to get me sober. That's why I only smoke pot now. I did it all, Danny. You name it, I did it." She wiped her nose on her shirt.

Danny said, "No shit, I never knew about this crap."

"That's what I'm talking about. You never gave a shit enough to even ask me about anything. All you wanted do was screw me and treat me like shit. And you know what, Danny? The screwing isn't all that good."

To Tammy's total surprise, Danny said, "I'm sorry, Tammy." That was another first. Tammy never talked back, and Danny never ever apologized for anything he said or did.

"So what's going to be so different from now on? You had it with me and getting off the island?" Danny said.

Tammy took a deep breath. "I hadn't planned to. What's going to be so different is the money. When I was so bad, my family cut me off, and believe me, I had it coming. They disinherited me and threw me out for good . . . all except for my grandfather. He left me a trust fund."

"Christ, Tammy, we been living on SpaghettiOs for years now, and you got a fuckin' trust fund?"

"I couldn't get one dime of it until I turned thirty. Tomorrow I do . . . so now I get the money."

Danny was shocked; he couldn't believe what he was hearing, "How much money are we talking about anyway?"

"I don't know really, but I think it's a lot."

"A lot like several thousand?"

Tammy said, "A lot like a hundred thousand."

Danny fell over backward on the beach. "Holy shit! That really beats all. I'm going to wind up in jail, and you're going to be rich!"

"Why are you going to wind up in jail? What are you talking about?"

Danny hadn't verbalized his fears until now. "I'm not absolutely sure, but I'm really scared. There's a lot of talk around that that Goldman asshole is starting to figure a few things out, and the shit is going to hit the fan and soon. People start talking when they get busted, and then everybody rats out everybody else, and we all go down. It's always the little guys like me Goldman gets first. Then he works his way up."

Tammy hadn't even thought about that. She figured once Danny wasn't running pot anymore, he was all set. She had been straight for a couple of days, and her brain was now starting to reengage.

"Maybe we should get the hell out of here while we can, but if we do, you're going to have to change your nasty attitude toward me," Tammy said.

Tammy's new attitude toward Danny was getting old quick. He held his tongue though. His options had run out, and he knew it.

"I know damn well if I don't get out of here, my ass is going to wind up in jail. Nobody believes one of the Brown boys could earn enough money lobstering to buy a new boat and traps. There are guys on this friggin' little island that have been running their mouths about it already. They all wish they had the balls to do it, but instead they're out to get me."

"Okay, okay, tomorrow I'll get the ferry and go in town. I'll go see the lawyer who has the money and get what's mine. Then we'll make a plan and get out of here. It's time for a change anyway," Tammy said.

"Okay, Tammy, you're calling the shots." Tammy was so different when she was straight. He guessed everyone was. They walked back to the house and went to bed. Danny and Tammy had always had sex, but they made love for the first time in years. Tammy felt much better. Things were going to be different from now on. She went to sleep.

CHAPTER 46

I t was just before dawn and low tide when Andy got in his new truck and drove down to the dock at the town landing. He pulled into one of the places reserved for the commercial fishermen. He got out and walked down the parking lot and headed for the dinghy he had tied up on the lower float. He was a little surprised to see the harbormaster in his office on the pier. He gave Andy a short wave as he started rowing out to the *Ruffian*. The Falmouth harbormaster was a retired Coast Guard man who ran things with an iron fist down at the town landing. His name was Sonny Wilkins, and he was a royal pain in the ass if he didn't like you, and he didn't like Andy Brown.

Andy boarded the *Ruffian* and started her up. He let the engine warm up and turned on the deck hose and filled the lobster barrel with seawater. The *Ruffian's* front windows were wet with morning dew. He opened the one in front of the wheel and climbed up on the bow and let the mooring line and the dinghy go. He jogged into the, float and after he had tied up, the harbormaster hollered down to him, "Hey, Brown, is that your truck?"

Andy hollered back with a very sarcastic tone, "Well, Sonny, you just saw me get out of it, didn't you?"

Wilkins said, "There isn't a Falmouth town sticker on that truck."

"Jesus, Sonny, I just got that truck yesterday afternoon."

Wilkins shook his head and gave Andy a condescending look. "Not my problem, boy. It's yours."

"Goddamn it, Sonny, I've lived here all my life, for Christ's sake. Give me a break."

Sonny Wilkins fired back, "Young man, I am a retired Coast Guard officer. You will not talk to me with that tone of voice."

Andy said, "Settle down, old man. All I want to do is park my fuckin' truck. I don't want to join the service."

Sonny was now one angry fellow. "You either get a sticker for that truck or I'll have it towed." Andy just shook his head. He shut down the engine on the *Ruffian* and got off. He checked his dock lines and started walking up to the parking lot. When he was almost to the end of the dock, Wilkins yelled out to him, "Brown, can you read? That sign right there says 'Dock Rules . . . twenty-minute tie-up limit,' and you know it."

"Jesus, Sonny, there isn't a soul down here but you and me!"

"It doesn't matter. The rules are the rules."

Andy took a deep breath and went down and climbed back aboard the *Ruffian*, started her up again, and ran her off to the mooring. He tied off and rowed back in. He got out of the dinghy and climbed the ladder back up onto the dock. When he walked past the harbormaster's office he said, "Thanks a lot, Sonny."

Sonny smiled a nasty smile at Andy. "Oh . . . you're very welcome."

Andy thought to himself, *Yeah, fuck you too, Sonny, you prick!*

He got in his truck and headed over toward the town hall. Then it dawned on him that it was only around six o'clock in the morning. The town hall wouldn't be open until nine. He decided to go over to McDonald's and get something to eat while he waited. He went in and ordered an Egg McMuffin breakfast sandwich and a cup of coffee with cream and sugar.

He was sitting at one of the booths when Junior Butland walked in. Junior was a Falmouth town cop. Andy Brown hated him with a passion. Junior was a kid with a chip on his shoulder. His father's name was Frank Butland Sr. He was a local businessman, an accountant, so everybody in town just naturally called his son Junior. If the truth was to be told they all called him Junior Butthead behind his back. Junior knew about it and hated it. He was always being picked on. He wasn't smart, athletic, or rich; and in this town that was three strikes against you. All he was, in reality, was a big pissed-off kid with a badge and a gun. It's funny that Andy and Junior didn't get along. They really had a lot in common.

Junior Butland loved to use his authority against guys like Andy Brown. He felt it was his duty to bust balls. Young Frank just wasn't that smart. He had to take his police exam three times before he passed it. He was twenty-eight years old and had been one of Falmouth's finest now for three years. To watch him walk around you'd think he was the chief of police.

He nodded his head to Andy as he walked past him but didn't speak. Andy just looked at him with total disdain as he went by. Junior ordered some breakfast and sat down by himself at a booth near the back. A few minutes later three Maine state troopers walked in. Junior smiled and waved. He thought they might come over and sit with him. They didn't. In fact, they didn't even acknowledge him. He pretended it didn't matter.

Andy had time to kill. He couldn't believe he was still sitting here. He should have just walked to the landing like he always did. He finally finished his coffee and walked out to his truck. He opened the door to climb in and somebody said, "License, registration, and proof of insurance, please." It was Junior Butthead. Andy couldn't believe it. "Oh Christ, Junior, will you give me a break? I just got the truck from Gene Villacci's yesterday. It has temporary plates on it. I haven't picked up the insurance card yet because their office isn't open this time of day."

Junior said in an overly loud voice, "Step away from the vehicle and place your hands on the hood, where I can see them." Andy had no choice but to comply. Junior proceeded to pat him down. Andy couldn't believe it. He was very relieved when he remembered he'd left his bag of pot aboard the *Ruffian*.

Junior got on his handheld radio and called in this major case. He asked the dispatcher to run a check on Andrew Brown for any outstanding warrants. Andy Brown had never even been in a cop car in his entire life. Junior checked all through the paperwork that Gene Villacci had prepared for Andy.

He said, "Everything appears to be in order. However, before you can move this vehicle, I'll need to see your proof of insurance."

Andy shook his head and said with his teeth clenched, "Junior, it's only seven thirty in the morning. I just told you, they're closed."

Junior said, "That's not my problem. If you move this vehicle without proof of insurance, I'll arrest you, and please refer to me as Officer Butland."

Andy said, "Okay, Junior." Andy walked over and stepped into the phone booth beside the McDonald's and called Gene Villacci's. After all, Gene had said to give him a call if he had any trouble. This was definitely trouble. Andy got Gene on the line. He explained what was going on. Villacci told Andy to put Junior Buthead on the phone.

Andy didn't know, and he would never know, what Gene Villacci had on Junior, but it had to be something really good. Junior's face turned bright red, and his forehead started sweating profusely. He stepped out of the phone booth and handed Andy his sale documents.

"I'm going to let you go this time. The next time I see you, you'd better have that insurance card. A word to the wise—keep your nose clean." Junior said this with a very officious tone.

Andy thought, *Keep my nose clean? Go clean your own nose, asshole!*

The state troopers were watching this performance out the window. They were all laughing.

Andy finally got in his truck and headed for the town hall. If people wondered why Andy smoked pot, this is why he smoked pot—because of the Junior Buttheads of the world.

He drove over to the town hall and sat there in the parking lot and waited. About eight o'clock, a car pulled into the parking lot. It was Joan Jensen. Joan was an old friend of Andy's mother. When he got out of his truck, she said, "Hi, Andy. How are you?"

"Oh, I'm fine, Mrs. Jensen. I'm trying to get a town sticker for my truck so I can park down at the landing," Andy replied.

Joan said, "We don't open until nine, but I think I can make an exception for you and get you a sticker. Have you got $10?"

Andy gave her a ten-dollar bill. She came back out in a few minutes with Andy's sticker. He thanked her and promised to say hi to his mother for her and drove back to the landing. He found a space and walked across the parking lot. The harbormaster came out of his office. Andy pointed to his sticker and gave him the finger. It was after nine thirty, and Andy hadn't left the dock yet.

There was a kid hanging around the landing named Roger Bishop. He was about sixteen. Andy knew him from seeing him around down there all the time. He had a lobster license, a skiff, and seventy-five traps of his own.

"Hey, Roger, you want to go haul some gear with me? I'll pay you for the day," Andy hollered.

"I'm not going anywhere in that skiff of yours, Andy. I don't want to drown."

"No, I'm fishing Skip Reed's boat for him while he's out dragging, and there's nothing wrong with my skiff."

"No, nothing a good boat burning wouldn't fix."

Andy thought, *The little wise-ass prick*. He didn't say anything though; he really needed a helper. "Do you want to go or not?"

"How long are we going to be out? I got to go call my mother and see if she paid up my life insurance first."

Andy said, "Very funny, wait here. I'll go get the boat and pick you up at the float."

"It's a good thing because I wouldn't get in that piece of shit dinghy of yours either."

Roger grabbed his oil pants and boots that he had stashed under the wharf building and went to meet Andy down on the float. One of the other kids, standing on the wharf watching, yelled, "Hey, Roger, when you don't make it back, can I have your skiff?"

Roger said, "No, but you can kiss your two sisters and your mother good-bye for me!"

Andy picked Roger up, and they headed out to haul.

Andy never had anyone work for him before. It was kind of overwhelming for him really. Roger had been stern man for enough other guys, so he knew more about it than Andy did. Roger started setting up the deck of the *Ruffian* as soon as they steamed away from the dock toward Clapboard. He stacked up the bait trays so that they were easy to reach. He filled three bait irons and put some bands and a measure beside a cull box. There were some new cotton gloves in a cardboard box down forward, and Roger put on a pair.

Andy was impressed, but he acted as if this was all expected. He turned on the radio and started the sounding machine. He didn't expect any calls, but he wanted to look cool in front of the kid. The radio was still on channel 8 from the other night, so he turned it back to 16.

Andy had already decided not to haul any of his own traps. He didn't want little Roger here to be running his mouth all over town about how lousy his traps were. They steamed past the west end of Clapboard and started off in the eight-fathom water. To his amazement the first string came up with a dozen nice select lobsters.

Roger was good at tending traps. Andy picked out the big lobsters. Roger cleaned out the shorts, rebaited the traps, and swung them around to the stern in a row to be set off.

When the last trap was up, ready and on the rail, Roger said, "Where are we shifting this one to?" Andy hesitated a minute. He'd really never shifted his traps very much. He had a philosophy that you set the traps overboard, and the lobsters came to you. That's what the bait was there for. Did the friggin' lobsters expect him to do everything? Andy turned the *Ruffian* away from where he hauled it and headed south. He started to push the first trap off, and Roger looked at him like he had three heads. Andy said, "What's wrong with you?"

"Well, for starters, you're getting ready to set across three other guys."

Andy had always fished single traps, so where you set them didn't matter to the other fishermen. These strings were different. There were rules when you got away from the islands. All the lobstermen set their gear northeast-southwest to avoid setting over each other. Andy had no idea about any rules.

He spoke to Roger in a very defiant tone. "What are you talking about, kid?"

Roger said, "Your boat, your traps, set them wherever you want to, but there's going to be some very pissed-off guys out here if you do what you're planning to do."

"Well, Mr. Smartass, where would you set them off?"

"Well, Captain, it isn't the where—it's the how. Haven't you ever noticed that all the strings are set in the same direction from end to end?"

Andy said, "Of course I know that. You think I'm stupid or something?"

Roger thought to himself, *Or something is right!* He decided to let it go. He couldn't believe that this guy had tried to make a living at this shit and could be so far out of it. "The rule off away from the islands is you set northeast-southwest." Andy Brown didn't even own a compass. The first time he had steered anywhere with one was on his pot run.

"I know that, for Christ's sake. You distracted me with all your goddamn questions."

Andy swung the boat around and headed to the northeast. He got ready to push off the first trap and said, "Will *this* be okay with you, kid?"

"Like I said . . . your boat, your traps."

They kept on hauling. There were a few messes but not really too bad. Out of the skiff, Andy had put the traps back overboard in the exact same spots for the most part. He started thinking about his efforts down in the Hussey and started to get a little nervous. He'd have to deal with that later. They hauled about seventy-five traps for 125 pounds of lobsters. Andy was trying hard not to set over any of the other guys' traps. He took the *Ruffian* out of gear at about noon. He went down forward and got his bag of pot. He rolled a joint and brought it back up to the wheel. He lit it up and took a hit. Roger watched him and thought, *That clears up a lot of questions.*

They kept hauling until about two o'clock. They had worked their way down into the Hussey Sound. The strings around Cow Island were in one huge mess. Andy had set across every lobster catcher that fished that piece of bottom. The radio came to life.

"*Ruffian, Ruffian,* You on here, Skip!" Andy thought, *Uh oh!* He picked up the mic.

"Hello, this is the *Ruffian.*"

"Go to 73. Over."

Andy didn't like the sound of that voice. It sounded really pissed off. He switched the radio up to 73.

Andy said, "This is the *Ruffian.*"

The caller said, "Who the hell is this?"

"I'm Andy Brown. Over."

"This is Joel Carter on the *Warrior.* Where is Skip?"

Andy said, "He's out dragging on the *Jubilee.* I'm tending his traps for him while he's gone."

"Is this Quarter Pound Brown? For Christ sake that explains it . . . you friggin' moron. You set over me three times down here. Everybody fishin' gear down this way has been trying to raise Reed on the radio. They're all ready to kick his goddamn ass. So now I guess they'll have to kick your ass first and then kick his for letting you make all this goddamn mess down here! What the hell is wrong with Reed letting you haul his traps?"

Andy said, "I'm sorry, I didn't mean to set over you. I'm new at this type of lobstering. Over."

"I think you should go into another line of work or get your dumb ass back up in the anchorage and haul your singles. You'd better get things straightened out down here now. Don't you cut anybody's rope but Reed's either, you hear me, Quarter Pound? You tell Skip Reed I want to see him when he gets in."

Andy said, "I hear you. I'll take care of things."

"This is the *Warrior* clear with the *Ruffian.*"

After that Andy and Roger had quite an afternoon for themselves. The traps were all in huge balls. They had been towed together. There were doors open, end lines with loops tied in them, and snarls with other people's traps twisted into them.

Roger was even getting a little frustrated. "You're paying me double for this bullshit, or you can run me up to the landing right now."

Andy had no choice. "All right, all right, I'll take care of you."

The hauler on the *Ruffian* strained and popped. They parted off some of the end lines and dropped a few traps. It was backbreaking work. Andy was getting a lesson called Lobster Fishing 101.

He was careful to only cut Reed's lines when he hauled through the gear. He never would have been able to pull this off without young Roger aboard. They finished up about four thirty in the afternoon. There were another 150 traps to haul, but Andy was exhausted, and so was Roger.

They headed back to the landing. Roger grabbed the wash-down hose and cleaned the boat up. He scrubbed the overhead, washed the engine box down with Dawn, and hosed out the bait trays.

Andy, for the life of him, couldn't figure out why. He'd just go again tomorrow and get the boat all filthy again.

Andy dropped Roger off at the town landing dock. He asked him if he wanted to go again tomorrow. Roger told him he was going to haul his own traps in the morning, but he'd go half a day for twice the pay. Andy said, "See you at noon down here then. We'll finish up the other 150. I'll pay you tomorrow."

Roger said, "No, you'll pay me now if you want to see me tomorrow." Andy pulled out two twenty-dollar bills and handed them to Roger. As he pulled away from the dock and headed for Portland, he wondered how a young kid like Roger Bishop could outsmart him like that. As he steamed off, he pulled out his trusty Bic and got his joint going again. After a couple of fresh hits he was still puzzled.

It took him about a half hour before he was tied up at the unloading float at Portland Lobster. He had about 250 pounds of lobsters on board. He told Harland Barnes they were all Reed's lobsters. Out of a $565 stock, he got $200 after bait and gas. He stuffed the cash in his pocket.

He loaded two trays of bait aboard and headed off toward Green Island. He was steaming across the bay when the sky started to cloud up. He thought the wind was kind of funny. It seemed to shift from the north to the northeast as he ran along. He looked back at the Falmouth shore, and it was getting really dark. The wind lifted, and the first crack of lightning was so close he could smell the ozone. The wind began to come on hard . . . probably twenty knots or so. Even up in the bay like this, it was starting to get rough. The rain fell in sheets across the water. A huge seagull landed on the *Ruffian's* stern and stared at Andy with that weird look they all had. It was just like in that movie by that fat guy Alfred Hitchcock . . . *The Birds.*

Maybe it was the dope, but Andy was pretty creeped out by this whole scene. The sky all around him was green. The rain was now driving down even harder and there was hail too. He couldn't see anything. The visibility was reported as zero. He didn't have a compass course, but he figured he may as well head east-southeast and see what happened. He slowed the *Ruffian* down to a crawl. He was jogging along when a huge sailboat came out of nowhere and was bearing down on him under full sail. He tried to turn off to starboard as quickly as he could. The sailboat pulled toward Andy's port side and just missed him. The boat was full of Yacht Club people out for the Thursday-night races. They all screamed at Andy to get the fuck out of there. Two more boats were right on their stern, and they all started yelling. How the hell should Andy know that they were running around out there in a goddamn thunderstorm? He headed south to get away from them. Now he was really lost. He kept jogging forward. He had the sounding machine on, and it was getting shallow fast. He was only in about three fathoms of water. He watched the machine like a hawk. It was getting even shallower. He slowed the boat to an idle and stepped back to the stern. He stood there listening. He could hear a boat with a big diesel engine coming at him at full tilt, and he was paralyzed with fear. A few seconds later he could see the bow of a thirty-eight-foot lobster boat headed right at him. The name painted on the bow in huge letters read, "*Warrior.*"

The boat slowed down a second before broadsiding him. Joel Carter looked at Andy from around his pilothouse. "You fuckin' lost down here, Quarter Pound?"

"Yes, I seemed have gotten turned around in all this rain and fog, Mr. Carter."

"Did you get through all that gear down here, numb nuts?"

Andy said, "No, but I'll finish up tomorrow."

Joel Carter said, "You better. Guys like you have been known to disappear down this way in the fog and rain, you know!" Andy didn't say a word.

"You're just on the north side of Cow. Head 120 degrees and you'll hit Green. You and your asshole cousin can hang out together down there," Joel said as he touched off the *Warrior* and was out of sight in about five seconds.

Andy did as he was told and headed 120 degrees and slid the *Ruffian* over toward Green Island. To his great relief, fifteen minutes later, the sky had cleared and the Green Island town dock was in plain sight. He was very happy to tie up. The seagull had flown away from him a long time before. The gull knew where he was going.

CHAPTER 47

By the time Andy made it up to his cousin's house, both he and Tammy were sound asleep. He thought it was strange, but everything was strange tonight. He flopped down on the couch and turned on the old TV. He put it on the channel 8 news. They had the usual crap about a bus driver in Hollis who drove into a telephone pole with a bunch of kids on the way to a summer camp. Everybody was fine except for one little fat kid with a broken arm.

He was half looking at it when a report came on about the drug arrest in Belfast. Two bozos busted for pot smuggling. They were clam diggers from Northport who tried to lug some shit out a woods road through a field. One of the nosy neighbors heard them laughing as they dragged the shit up a hill to the back of their house. These two assholes were stoned to the hilt when the cops showed up. They tried to convince the cops that the pot floated in on the high tide. They said they were bringing it in to turn it over to the cops. When asked why they were in a near-comatose state of cannabis inebriation, they replied that they had to test their discovery to see if it was the real thing. They didn't want to waste anybody's time if it was the fake stuff. One observer remarked they were still laughing when the cops piled them into the car to take them off to jail. The reporter commented that he doubted they were still laughing now. Andy thought, *Pure genius, those two.* Thank God he was working with professionals.

He started looking around and found Danny's stash out on the kitchen counter. He grabbed some papers and rolled himself a joint. *Jeopardy* or one of those shows was on. He hated that shit. It was all rigged anyway. He knew it was, or he would have known some of the answers to the questions, and he didn't know a one. He flipped the channels around a while and finally settled on a movie about some babysitter that went nuts and tried to kill the baby's mother so she could run off with the kid's father.

He watched that flick for quite a while and then dozed off to sleep. About two thirty in the morning Danny wandered out of the bedroom and staggered across the living room and headed for the bathroom. Andy woke up and said, "Christ, you guys went to bed early." Danny looked over at Andy. "I didn't know you were here."

"I came in about seven thirty. That was some thundershower that came through last night."

Danny said, "What thundershower? Tammy and I must have slept right through it. I was a little tanked up when I got home. Hold on a minute. I got to take a leak." When Danny got back he sat down in an easy chair and lit up a Marlboro. Andy said, "I want you to hook me up for a run tomorrow night."

Danny said, "I want to talk with you about that. I'm hearing some stuff around that the heat's starting to come on. That Goldman guy that runs the DEA is figuring things out. They got those guys up in Belfast. I'm not sure it's smart to keep doing this shit." Andy was pissed. He said, "Boy, if that isn't the fuckin' dying end. You goddamn get everything you want. Boat, traps, a new start . . . I just get going to catch up and you lose your balls. Well, I haven't, and you can just make that fuckin' call for me. I'm going again and that's it, you prick!"

Danny said, "All right, all right, I'll make your call. But I'm telling you, you'd better not push it, Andy. You'll be one sorry bastard."

Andy said, "Well, cousin, it's none of your fuckin' business what I do, so you can shove your advice right up your ass for all I care!"

Danny just frowned and said, "Okay, big time, but don't say I didn't warn you!" Danny went back to bed and shut the door. Andy curled up on the couch again and went back to sleep.

It was ten o'clock when they all woke up. It was Saturday morning. Andy had a bowl of cereal and walked down to the float and got aboard the boat. There was a note on his dashboard that said, "NO OVERNIGHT TIE-UPS AT THE MUNICIPAL FLOAT. GREEN ISLAND

HARBORMASTER. FINE: $25. Please pay all fines at the Green Island Town Hall. Open every third Tuesday of the second month after the full moon except in August." Or something like that.

Andy said to himself, "These assholes must meet somewhere and dream this shit up to drive people crazy."

Andy folded up the ticket and stuck it up under the radio bracket. He never would pay that fine. Andy fired up the *Ruffian* and headed over to Falmouth to pick up Roger. The day was clear, and a light breeze was blowing out of the northwest, as it so often did after a low-pressure front moved through.

It was eleven thirty when Andy pulled into the float at the town landing. He saw Roger sitting on one of the benches up by the harbormaster's office. He waved to him, and he came down the float with his oil pants over his arm. Roger said, "Hi, Andy. Half a day, twice the pay, forty bucks, right?"

"Get aboard, kid. You'll never make it in this business with that attitude."

"Drop me off! I don't have to go, you know. I can stay home and screw half the girls on that beach by suppertime."

Andy shook his head. There were only five girls on the beach, and two of them were young mothers with little kids, but it sounded good anyway when he said it. This kid was amazing!

They ran right down to the Hussey. Things weren't any better today than they were yesterday. There was just a hell of a lot more guys out hauling to watch him screw around.

He and Roger worked their asses off all afternoon, and at least nobody stopped to yell at them.

The other guys just ran by and gave him dirty looks. Mostly, they passed him and Roger with as much wake as they could muster. Whatever gear they had on the rail fell off, and they had to pull it back on board. They still managed to catch about 175 pounds of lobsters.

Andy ran Roger back up to the float. He asked Andy if he was going in town to sell. He said he was.

"How about if we pick up my lobsters, and I'll go with you, so I can sell mine too?" Roger asked.

"Sure, we can do that. How many traps you got, kid?"

Roger said, "Seventy-five."

"So what you got? Twenty-five, thirty pounds?"

"Yeah, about that. I sold the ones I had two days ago." They ran up the anchorage to Roger's skiff.

It was a beauty. A seventeen-foot flat-bottom, chine-built skiff, painted dark green with a red copper bottom. It was a tan color inside and had one of those slick little electric haulers. She was as clean as a whistle with a fairly new twenty-five-horse Evinrude outboard. There was a name painted on the stern . . . *Mr. Money Bags*. There were two crates floating off the back end of the skiff. Roger told Andy there were eighty counters in one and sixty-three in the other. They pulled the crates aboard.

"Pretty good, kid. It looks like you're catching on now that you've been out with me."

"Oh yes, Captain. I've learned a huge amount from you."

Andy said, "Good, good, I'm glad you have."

Roger thought to himself, *What a fuckin' idiot.*

They ran up into Portland Harbor. Andy had his traditional joint. He let Roger drive for a while after he had cleaned up the boat. Roger would admit that he really did get a kick out of running Skip Reed's little Novi. He was only sixteen after all, and this was a great rig. They went into the unloading float at Portland Lobster. That tourist guy was there again with his damn camera snapping away. Andy waved to him. He wanted to look good in the *Ruffian*. The last time he'd taken a picture of him he was in his old ratty skiff. He told Roger that he thought the guy was probably working on a calendar, and he thought he would be one of the featured lobstermen, so Roger waved too. They unloaded, sold, and fueled up. After they got paid, Roger had $290. Andy had $180 dollars. Roger plucked forty bucks out of Andy's cash for his stern man pay.

Andy thought, *No shit, he is Mr. Money Bags!*

He ran Roger back into the landing and dropped him off. Roger waved and said, "See you in the funny papers Andy. I got to go catch up on what I missed all afternoon while I was out with you." There was no one on the beach.

Andy looked up in the parking lot and suddenly realized his truck was gone. He spun around wide open and went back to the float. He tied up and ran up the dock. He burst into the office and said, "What's the story, Sonny? Where's my fuckin' truck?" Sonny didn't even look up from his desk. "Go read the sign." Andy stormed out and walked over; and there, sure as shit, in red letters, it said, "ALL NIGHT PARKING BY PERMIT ONLY. No overnight parking in commercial parking zones. All vehicles will be towed at the owner's expense." He went storming back up to the office and said, "Goddamn it, Sonny! Who's got it for Christ's sake?"

Sonny said, "You'll need to check in with Officer Butland. The towing fee is $65. I believe it may be at Villacci's yard. By the way, you only have ten more minutes at the float."

Andy walked out of there so pissed the steam was coming out his ears. He ran down the dock, down the gangway, and jumped aboard the *Ruffian*. He untied and backed away at full throttle and steamed out the fairway the same way. Sonny Wilkins was very tempted to go ticket Andy for speeding in a no-wake zone, but he figured Andy might flip out and try to kill him, so he let it go. Sonny thought, *Run your nasty mouth to me again, kid, and we'll see what's up.* Sonny chuckled to himself. He locked up the office and went home for the night. It had been a long day.

CHAPTER 48

A ndy steamed for Green Island. He had never been as angry in
his entire life as he was that moment. It didn't make any sense.
Andy knew he was the laughing stock of the bay and probably the
whole goddamn asshole town of Falmouth. That didn't bother him.
He just went along minding his own business, smoking his pot, and
living his life. Now that he was catching lobsters, running a nice
boat, and trying to get ahead in the world, he was having a worse
time than he did before. That kid Roger made more money than
Andy did, and he'd practically taught that kid everything he knew.
Roger had admitted he learned a lot from him, just today. Well, screw
these people. He was going to make some quick money lugging pot,
get himself set up, and they could all kiss his ass.

Danny and Tammy were having some cheeseburgers when Andy
arrived at the house. Tammy made one for Andy, and they sat outside
on a rickety old picnic table and ate them. They had a few beers and
a joint and watched the sun go down. Green really was a great little
island. Andy felt more at home there than anywhere else he had ever
been.

Andy said, "Okay, cousin, what's the deal for tonight?" Danny
drummed his fingers on the table and took a drag on his cigarette.
He finally said, "No talking you out of this, is there?" Andy looked
Danny straight in the eye and said, "No fuckin' way!"

Danny kind of shook his head. "You're supposed to go down to
the Mud Buoy just like before. They'll give you bearings on channel
8. Then you got to take the stuff up to a private dock in Yarmouth.
It's on the inboard side of Cousin's Island. It's right by the power
plant just inside of where they bring the tankers. The night guys at
the plant are all in on this, so there won't be any trouble. The place
is all fenced off, so it's a perfect pickup spot."

Andy said, "What time am I supposed to meet them for the pickup?"

Danny said, "Be at the Mud Buoy at one o'clock!" They walked into the house. Danny helped Tammy pick up the dishes and clean up the table. Andy couldn't believe his eyes. Danny was helping out? Andy went in the house empty-handed, as usual, and flopped down on the couch. He could hear Tammy and Danny talking quietly in the kitchen. This was getting too weird. Ah well, fuck them. He laid there watching the TV and didn't pay them any more attention.

He fell asleep before he remembered to tell Danny about the asshole harbormaster in Falmouth or the bullshit with Junior Butthead. Danny shook him awake at eleven thirty. Andy said, "You got any lobsters overboard? I forgot to save some out from my haul for the trade for my personal pot."

"Yes, there's a crate on the stern with forty or so in it. By Jesus, you replace them though, goddamn it!"

Andy said, "Calm down, cousin, calm down. I'll put them back." Of course, he never would. He trudged down the hill and got aboard the *Ruffian*. He slid over to the Frayed Knot and grabbed a dozen lobsters out of Danny's floating crate. Maybe that broad on the *Invincible* will be nicer to him this time. He headed down and out the Hussey, steering 147 degrees. The run was about an hour and a half to the Mud Buoy just like it had been before. The night was clear and still. He made the yellow flasher on his starboard side. It was twelve forty-five. He turned the radio to channel 8. At one o'clock on the dot a voice came on the radio—"185, 185"—and clicked off. Andy adjusted his course to 185 degrees. He steamed for about fifteen minutes.

As clear as it was that night, once again the *Invincible* still seemed to appear out of nowhere. Andy wasn't as nervous this time as he had been before. The giant spotlights were on, and the side of the boat was open. He was snapped in and tied up in an instant. The same girl came over and frisked him, checking for guns or wires. Andy moved toward her and said, "How about I have a turn now?" The girl looked at him with ice-cold blue eyes and slapped him across the face, hard. He started to move toward her a little. It was perceived as an aggressive move. Out of the corner of his eye he saw a handgun pointed at him by one of the guys on the crew. Andy put his hands up defensively and said, "I guess not, huh?" The crew member returned a look that made Andy's blood run cold. They had him loaded in a few minutes. Andy remembered the lobsters. He got a milk crate and passed them over to a deckhand. The guy turned the milk crate upside down, dumping the lobsters overboard. He slammed the door to the boat shut, and they took off. Andy was a little stunned. It was never like that in his porn movies.

He spun the *Ruffian* around and steamed back up the Hussey. It was about 3:00 a.m. when he made it to the power plant. It was an easy run. The chimney at the plant was always lit up like a Christmas tree. The dock on the northwest side was dark as a pocket, but he was able to slide up to it.

High up in, near the shore, was the same small truck with "LIVELY LUSTY LOBSTER CO." painted on the side panels. It looked just like the one that had picked up the pot at Bug Light Point. Two guys had the ten bales in the truck in minutes. They handed him his bag of cash. One tall, very-nasty-looking guy grabbed Andy by his shirt. "Never, and I mean never, talk to or try to touch one of our girls again. You understand me, motherfucker?" Andy swallowed hard, "Yes, sir. I understand." He pushed Andy away from the dock and went back up the gangway, got in the truck, and drove off.

Andy crossed over to the northwest inboard of Sturdivant Island, through the anchorage past Perry's point, and back to the *Ruffian*'s mooring. He rowed in and trudged up the hill headed for home. Andy could swear he heard a click. There was no one around. He was sure he must be hearing things.

When he got home to the trailer, he put his five grand in his shoe box and went to bed. Almost ten grand in hundred-dollar bills—this was great. Andy felt flush for the first time in his life. He slept like a baby. It had been a really long day for Andy Brown too.

CHAPTER 49

Agent Lamb began the drive down toward East Boothbay from Edgecomb. He was driving down Route 27. He stopped and walked back into the woods a little and quickly changed his clothes. He had on an ankle holster with his service revolver tucked in it. He put on his tourist outfit, including his I Love Maine ball cap.

The ride down to Little River was beautiful. After leaving the main drag in Boothbay, he turned left and followed a long winding road east. After a couple of miles, he looked to the right at one of the most beautiful anchorages he had ever seen. There were a dozen lobster boats lying at anchor in the river.

Lamb snapped over forty pictures of the place. He got the wharf, the floats, the buildings, and the lot. The deepwater landing, the seclusion, the truck activity at all hours of the day and night—it was a perfect cover for drug distribution. Lamb drove back to the Portland office. He enjoyed the gorgeous afternoon drive. It was a truly grand late summer day after all. He thought about Nettie Sherman and smiled.

CHAPTER 50

Kathy was having a hard time sleeping. Her poor, sweet heart was breaking. She really needed to talk to Ronny, and she had no idea where he was. It had been over eight months. She was worried and feeling helpless about her situation.

Kathy had met Ronny at school in Denver. He was a handsome guy and funny, and he came from a lot of money. His father was an investment banker in Connecticut and grew up in a mansion in Mystic. Kathy had gone home with him once over a Thanksgiving vacation and had not fit in at all. A poor middle-class girl from Maine was considered quaint at best. There was a weekend party, and Ronny's friends and neighbors said things like, "Oh, you're from Maine. How delightful. Do you know Gary Merrill? He and Bette Davis live up your way in Maine. Do you see them often?" Kathy just smiled and said, "Yes, I've seen him in our little store trying to buy beer in his trench coat and clamming boots on Sunday mornings. He's really very charming when he's sober." She was pretty sure Bette Davis had divorced Gary Merrill years ago. She kind of got a kick out of all the phony arrogance of these people.

In spite of all that, Kathy was completely swept off her feet by Ronny Stockton. They dated for about a year and were practically inseparable. Ronny was a senior and in her class. He told Kathy he was completely in love with her. He was always telling her about his big plans for business and how successful they were going to be.

In the spring of the year she went over to his apartment to see him after class one afternoon, and everything was gone, including Ronny. There was an envelope with her name on it on the window sill.

Dear Kathy,

I'm sorry to end us this way. Dad has ordered me home. I'm going to marry the daughter of one of his partners. I've known her all my life. There's big money to be protected by merging the families, I guess. I'm going to be a multimillionaire.

I'm sure you understand it has nothing to do with you. I'll still be able to keep seeing you. We can buy a faraway place somewhere, and I can be with you whenever I can get away. You'll never have a worry in the world for the rest of your life. I do love you. I wish it could be different. Please don't call me, but I'll call you as soon as I can.

Love,
Ronny

Kathy sat down on the floor and burst into tears. Her heart was broken. She was angry with herself and confused about how she could have been so wrong about him. Her parents had always been after her about how trusting she was, particularly her mother. She never gave Kathy credit for any judgment of her own. She was thinking, *Mother would have a field day with this one.* And she would have, if she ever heard about it. Kathy had no intention that she ever would.

She sat there on the floor of the little apartment, wanting to just die. Eventually, she left and went back to her dorm. Her roommate barraged her with questions about what was wrong. She simply said that she had decided to break up with Ronny. She asked her to please leave her alone for a while, and they could talk about it later.

The days and weeks went past, and eventually she came to realize that she really would never have fit into Ronny Stockton's life. She knew that if he had married her, there would have been some other woman hidden away somewhere that he would be visiting whenever he could. She was coming to the point where she was at peace with the whole thing. Kathy knew that it was all part of growing up and that she had to get on with her life. She threw herself into her studies and was feeling a great deal better.

That was until she found out she was pregnant. In the beginning she was sick first thing in the morning, and she thought it was the flu. She went to the campus infirmary, where they did a blood and a pregnancy test. The results were positive . . . she was shocked. There were three more weeks before her graduation. All she could think of was that her family was coming out for it, and here she was in more trouble than she ever had been in her whole life. She went back to her dorm and got into bed and didn't leave her room for two days. All she thought about was what she was going to do. She knew she would have to call Ronny, so she did.

She got his mother on the phone and learned that Ronny was on his honeymoon in the Bahamas. His mother, in a very snotty tone, said, "Why are you calling, dear? Can I help you somehow?" Her intonation was so full of disdain that if Kathy hadn't just thrown up, she would have then.

Kathy said, "I think you should have Ronny try to reach me as soon as he can. It's important."

His mother said, "If you want me to give your message to Ronny, you'd better tell me what you want, young lady."

The condescending authoritative attitude came through loud and clear. Kathy never was great at holding her tongue. "If you don't give him my message, you'll all be very sorry, old lady!" Kathy hung up the phone.

She was pretty sure that Ronny wouldn't be getting her message. She sat down and thought about things. Then she remembered something important that Ronny had told her once when they were talking about their bright future with each other. His father's brother Gerald had a fabulous beach house in the Bahamas. She called the international operator and got the number through the information services. She thought, *What the hell*. So she called. It was three o'clock in the afternoon in Denver so it should be around five there. The phone rang and a woman's voice answered. "Hello?"

Kathy said, "Hi, is Ronny there?"

"Who's calling, please?" The voice sounded very concerned about who was calling. Kathy thought, *You have no idea, you poor thing.*

Kathy said, "I'm a friend of Ronny's who couldn't make it to the wedding. My name is Kathy Blackwell." Ronny's wife covered the phone. Kathy still could hear her. "It's a Kathy Blackwell. Do I know her, Ronny?"

Ronny didn't answer her and grabbed the phone. "Hello."

"Hi, Ronny. Congratulations on your wedding. I just called to let you know that I'm pregnant and I'm having your baby." Ronny hung up the phone without another word. His wife said, "What did *she* want?"

"Oh nothing, honey. It was just some crazy bitch I knew in school. Let's go to the beach."

With the hang-up, Kathy had her answer. She was on her own.

Graduation came and went. Kathy kept it all inside. She never said a word to her mother about the pregnancy. Her dad seemed somehow a little suspicious that something was up. She managed to keep him off track too. She had always been good at that. She loved her father more than anyone else in the world, and she couldn't bring herself to tell him what she'd done.

Kathy graduated with honors and got a great job at an advertising agency in Denver. She started working. It was a big firm that hired her. They represented most of the Western ski areas. She was able to be part of a great marketing team and really loved her job. She bought herself a used wedding band from a pawnshop and told everyone her husband was in the service, stationed in Germany.

It worked really well. No one bothered her. There were a few flirtatious attempts from a couple of guys she met, but very pregnant and apparently very married women were left alone for the most part.

The baby was born in January. It was a beautiful healthy baby boy. Kathy named him Matthew Robert Blackwell and called him Matty. They lived in a great little apartment in Denver. The company had day care, and they did fine together. She had to make up a few stories about where her husband was, but for the most part she just blended in as much as she could.

As far as coming home to Maine was concerned, she had a list of excuses about work and other commitments that always seemed to arise at just the right time to keep her safely in Denver.

One day when her mother called her at work, she told her that she and Kathy's father were getting a divorce. Kathy wasn't totally shocked. Her mother gave her an angry and lengthy explanation as to how everything that had gone wrong in the marriage was Kathy's father's fault. She listened with very little comment and hung up the phone after that bomb and tried to process the whole mess.

A week later she called her dad and asked him to fly to Denver and stay with her awhile. Bob Blackwell was on the next available plane, and she met him at the airport. Matty was with her. He had just recently turned one. When her dad met him for the first time, of course it was love at first sight. Kathy explained the whole gruesome story of what had happened between her and Ronny Stockton.

At first, her dad was mad as hell about the whole situation. He couldn't imagine anybody being so hateful to his little girl, but then after a while he calmed down.

He and Kathy spent the happiest month together that they had ever had. They truly enjoyed each other's company, and Matty was the frosting on the cake. They did find time to talk about the pending divorce. They both knew it had been coming for a long, long time. Bob accepted much of the responsibility as Kathy knew he would. But Kathy knew they were both to blame. Her father was surprisingly rather philosophical about the whole thing.

After their stay together Bob went home to Maine, with the absolute promise that the baby was to remain a secret. Before he left, he told Kathy that she knew damn well that she was going to have to tell her mother soon and that holding it back was ridiculous.

Kathy said, "I know, I know, Dad, and I will . . . someday."

Kathy did feel pretty guilty about the secret, but the longer it went on, the harder it got. Over three years went by. Matty was growing up to be a smart and funny little boy. Then out of nowhere,

Ronny Stockton showed up. He came knocking on Kathy's door completely inebriated. He demanded to see his son. Of course the to-be-expected fight ensued, but eventually, after a number of battles and slammed doors, Kathy broke down and let Ronny see the baby. He told her that he was divorced (big surprise there), and he wanted to be a father to his son.

Kathy was angry and confused. One thing for absolute sure was that she had no feelings at all for Ronny Stockton. All she had to do was to take a good look at him to realize she never really had. The thing that bugged her the most was that she kept having these dreams about being at home in Maine and being with a boy she knew from school, named Tom Anderson. He was constantly in the back of her mind. She hadn't seen him in over five years. It was too, too weird. He was probably already married with kids of his own.

For a few months, Ronny hung around. He still had lots of money, of course, and he gave Kathy ten grand to help out with her expenses. She put the money away for Matty's college. She didn't expect Ronny to be around all that much longer. He was drinking a lot and totally bored. She never let him near the baby when he was like that. She kept thinking, *Why doesn't he just go away and leave us alone?* Once during a fight he asked her if she was sure that the baby was his. She slapped him across his face and told him to get out.

This back-and-forth situation lasted awhile longer, and then one day Ronny just left—only when he did, he took Matty with him. Kathy went crazy. She called the police. They were no help at all. She hired a private detective. The answer was always the same—"It's a big country out there, lady, and he is the baby's father." She couldn't imagine where he could have gone with their child. With his money and influence it was much easier for him to totally disappear like that than it would have been for a normal person. She tried to contact Ronny's parents. They denied knowing anything about a baby. They insisted that if she tried to harass them about it anymore, they would have her arrested. The long and short of it was, Ronny had vanished with Matty, and he was nowhere to be found.

As the months wore on, Kathy was so distraught she couldn't work, she couldn't think, and she couldn't stay. Eventually, she packed her bags and went home to Maine. She kept her secret from everyone except her father.

There was nobody in more pain than Kathy. She felt like a liar and a fool. For months she stayed around her mother's house and didn't do anything. She was suffering from mild depression. Eventually, she did start seeing Tom. It wasn't long before she knew what the old dreams were about. She was deeply in love with him. How could she tell him about Matthew and what had happened? She didn't believe that anybody could love her enough to accept her with all her baggage, not even Tom Anderson. Night after night she cried for her baby. She cried for her screwed-up life. She cried for fear she'd lose Tom, but she mostly cried for herself.

One night, just like she had done every night since Matty had been taken away from her, she prayed, "Dear God, please bless and keep my Matty safe and bring him home to me. I love him so much, and he needs to be with his mommy, as soon as you can, Lord." She finally drifted off into a fitful sleep. When she woke up in the morning the pain was still there. Her secret burned in her heart. She suffered as only a mother does who has been separated from her child.

She thought about Tom a lot. The trip to Gloucester had been perfect, and she had been able to forget about the mess her life was in for a little while. She did love Tom, but how would she ever make this right between them? She began to reconcile that it couldn't be done, and maybe she should just go back to Denver. She even thought about talking to her new friend Leslie about it, but she decided against it. Kathy was feeling depressed and totally discouraged when she got up that morning.

About ten o'clock she was having a coffee with her mother at the kitchen table when a black Mercedes pulled up in front of their house. A man Kathy had never seen before got out and opened the back door of the shiny new car. She thought, *Oh god, what now? This can't be good.*

Kathy's mother said, "Good lord! Who is that, Kathy?"

Kathy sighed and said, "I don't know, Mother." Just then a little boy got out of the car and stood there by the driveway, crying. Kathy flew out the door; it was Matty. She grabbed him in her arms and held him like she would never, ever let him go again. His tears stopped immediately once he was in the loving embrace of his mother's arms. He said, "I misted you, Mommy!" Kathy, through a torrent of tears, said, "Oh, Matty, I misted you too!" She spun around and around, soaking up the pure joy and love that came from her wonderful little boy. Kathy looked toward heaven and said, "Oh thank you, God, thank you!"

Without saying anything, the man handed her an envelope. She put Matty down for a second and tore it open. There was a neat, clean typewritten note inside.

> *This kid's not mine. I almost fell for it, you bitch. Don't ever try to contact me again! Ronny*

There was a legal document inside that gave her full parental custody of the child and a check for $100,000. Kathy was stunned. Even with all the emotions that were running through her mind at that time, it did strike her as interesting that he had a lawyer draft custody papers for a child he denied was his own. She suspected that the hateful hand of Mrs. Stockton was at the bottom of this matter. The "bitch" thing in the note was perfect. No one could have been happier to be called that under these circumstances.

It was an end, a wonderful end. She was being bought off, and it was great because she already had all she ever wanted. She had Matty. She had never wanted a dime of the Stocktons' money, but for Matty's sake, she would take it. It meant she would be able to give him a better life. She picked him up again and stood there in the driveway for a while, holding her baby boy.

Her mother had been watching intently from her kitchen window. Eventually, Kathy carried Matty into the house and said, "Mother, I'd like you to meet your grandson, Matthew Robert Blackwell." Matty just looked at his grandmother and blinked his beautiful blue eyes.

CHAPTER 51

After things settled down following the diving event, Scanton decided to head up toward Pecks Ledge and try their luck there. They steamed west-northwest. It would be about four hours before they made the bottom.

The fog had started rolling in thick as a wall around the *Jubilee*. You couldn't see anything. Like the weatherman says, "The visibility was zero." It had been a long day already and it was only ten after two. Scanton turned the boat over to Reed with the new course bearings and went down below. Anderson was asleep in his bunk, still recovering from the dive. Chase went down and out on deck. He wasn't ready to hit the bunk yet, and he wasn't about to hang out with Reed up in the pilothouse. He walked back to the stern.

For all of his wise-ass fooling around with Tom Anderson, he was pretty shaken up by the near disaster that had occurred over on the *Teresa Lynn*. He liked Tom, and he couldn't imagine himself explaining to Kathy or Leslie what had happened if things had turned out differently. He didn't even want to think about it.

He was leaning up against the starboard rail, back in the corner of the stern. He had a Marlboro going, and he was standing there just sort of daydreaming. He was watching the wake and propwash falling away behind the boat. The fog was so thick he couldn't see the pilothouse less than twenty feet away.

Out of the fog bank, coming from the starboard bow side, he heard men's voices. They were shouting at each other. He couldn't make out what was being said, but he could hear sail canvas flapping and the squeak and rattle of old-fashioned wooden blocks straining as rope lines were pulled through them. A strange chill ran through his body. He stared out into the blank wall of fog.

The voices were getting louder as they got closer. Suddenly a shape began to appear. It was an old sailing vessel. She was huge and she was sailing right past them. The rails were almost underwater. She was at a close haul on a broad reach. Chase could make out the men on board now. The crew must have been actors from one of those maritime museums or something. *What the hell were they doing way down here?* He thought. They were dressed in old-fashioned seamen's apparel like in the antique paintings he had seen from the late 1800s.

The boat was a beautiful barque with three giant masts. He could see that the main and foremasts were square-rigged, and the mizzenmast was fore and aft rigged. He couldn't believe his eyes. This was not a restored training vessel from one of those floating colleges; this was the real thing, but it couldn't be. He counted at least fifteen men on deck. None of them seemed to be aware that the *Jubilee* was even there. Chase could see her clearly now as they passed close by on his starboard side. Not one crew member even looked in his direction. They just kept running the deck as if they were all alone on the ocean. Pat grabbed the rail and watched her cut through the water. The vessel was less than twenty feet away. He figured she had to be going at least ten knots. She was close enough now that he could read the name on her bow. In beautiful gold sculptured letters, it read, "*Evan Stevens.*"

As she sailed by he could see a boy of about twelve standing behind the enormous wheel. The captain was directly behind him with his hand on the young man's shoulder. He was a handsome kid with wild blond hair and a very stern expression on his face. It was pretty clear to Chase that the boy was being taught how to stand a wheel watch. As they passed by, the captain turned and looked Chase straight in the eye. The man looked to be at least sixty. He had a perfectly trimmed beard. His hair was snow white, at least what you could see of it from under his cap. His eyes were as black as coal. He was the only man who seemed to know that Chase was even there. He nodded his head without expression and turned back again, looking forward off the bow. The *Evan Stevens* disappeared within seconds. The sounds of the ship and the voices of the men softly vanished back into the Dungeness's thick fog, and Chase felt strangely alone. A slight shudder ran through his body.

He turned and ran for the pilothouse as fast as he could. Reed was sitting there as calm as a cucumber. Chase checked the radar screen. It was set on the five-mile range. To his total disbelief, the screen was clear. He switched down to the mile range. It hadn't been five minutes since the *Evan Stevens* sailed past them; nothing showed. He switched up to the twenty-five-mile range. He saw the same blank screen—not a boat or a mark of any kind to be seen anywhere. He stood there a few minutes, completely mesmerized, watching the sweep of the radar showing nothing at all.

He was just standing there, staring at the radar, when finally Reed said, "What the fuck are *you* looking at, Chase?" He turned away without answering Reed and went down below. He crossed over to his bunk and climbed in. Every fisherman who's been out to sea for any number of years had a story like this one. The truth was no one shared these tales for fear of ridicule and humiliation from their shipmates. Chase never told anyone about what he had seen, ever.

Reed sat there at the wheel, wondering what had just happened. That goddamn asshole's been out here too long. His brain's starting to go bad just like the rest of these jerks. He couldn't believe all the fish they were catching. If he had any chance of getting this boat down below the Hague Line, he had to figure a way to force Joey into port without outright sabotaging the boat. The more money they stocked, the less likely he would be to pull this thing off. He really didn't want to do anything mechanical though. He didn't know enough about that shit to be confident that he wouldn't do real damage. He didn't want the boat disabled. He just wanted to drive her ashore as soon as possible.

He sat there thinking about what he should do, and then it dawned on him, and the timing was perfect right now. He checked the radar, and there wasn't a thing out there showing up on the screen. The boat was running on autopilot. He ran down through the galley. All three men were sound asleep. He raced back up through the pilothouse, down and out on the deck. He lifted off the main hatch cover and climbed down in the fishhold. He grabbed a shovel and pitched away the ice that was over the slaughterhouse deck hatches. He lifted two of them off and set them to the side. He put his hand down into the bilge and could feel the air flowing toward the engine room down through the fish hole. It would work just like a chimney in reverse, if he left the main hatch cover off. With these deck hatches open, the dense fog, full of moisture, would rot the fishhold ice so fast you could practically see it melt.

He scrambled back up on deck. In three short hours his problem would be solved, but just one more thing. He climbed the ladder mounted up under the shelter deck that led up to the overhead. There were two one-hundred-pound propane gas tanks lying side by side and strapped down in a wooden cradle to keep them in place during rough weather. He bent down and opened the valve on the number two tank. The propane started to rush out. He went back down the ladder and back to his watch at the wheel.

He grabbed one of his skin books and settled back in the captain's chair. "Horny high school girls who need older men to be satisfied." There was a picture of a bare-breasted teenager supposedly named Betty Bidwell. Betty was saying, "No underclassman for me. They just don't have what it takes."

Reed laughed a little and thought to himself, *Good stuff . . . really good stuff.*

The time seemed to drag by for Reed on that watch. He listened in on a radio conversation from Marshall Grimes to Vern Eldridge about Tom's diving heroics. Frankly, Reed thought the whole thing was stupid. There was no way in hell you'd see him going overboard in these shark-infested waters for some old asshole like Marshall Grimes or anybody else for that matter. Tom would be the big hero now for a while, until he fucks up, and everybody on a boat fucks up.

Reed laughed as he thought about who would get blamed for the little stunt he was pulling. At the two-and-a-half-hour mark, he ran out on deck again. He climbed up on the overhead and shut off the propane gas valve. He listened to the valve. There were no hissing sounds. The gas had all leaked out as planned.

Then he was down in the fishhold in a flash. He put back the hatch covers, spread a little ice around, and climbed back up on deck. Mission accomplished. He replaced the main hatch cover, and he was done. Back up to the wheelhouse like nothing had happened.

Fifteen minutes later he woke up the crew. They would set off again as soon as everybody was up and Scanton had the helm. Joey had a fifty-fathom edge that he wanted to try. There was a hard gavel piece on Pecks, and considering how they had hit the cod on The Bunches, he thought the fish might be there as well. Once he was back at the helm and had everything under his control he told the boys to set off the groundfish net.

With the relatively shoal water, the net was down in twenty minutes. The fog had hung in, and you couldn't see the forward stays from the pilothouse window. Like on all the other hard bottoms, the *Jubilee* was popping, yanking, and shuddering her way along. Reed went down forward. It was his turn to hit the bunk. He slept in total comfort, knowing that his plan was well on its way to fruition.

Anderson went down forward and got out some steaks for supper. He peeled some potatoes and put the pot on the stove. He turned on the burner, and within two minutes it flickered and went out. He tried it again and nothing happened. Scanton and Chase were up in the pilothouse, talking about nothing. Anderson climbed the stairs and said, "Joey, it looks like we're out of gas."

Chase said, "Bullshit, the number two tank is full. Maybe it got shut off somehow. I'll check it out." He went down and up onto the overhead. He was back in about two minutes.

"The fuckin' thing is empty, Joey. I can't believe it. I was running off the number one. Maybe during the long layover in Portland, it bled off somehow. I don't fuckin' know."

"Shit happens. Cold food for a while, I guess," Scanton said.

Tom went back down to the galley and made a plate of sandwiches. They would really miss their coffee. Scanton and Chase both knew the propane on the boat was Chase's responsibility. He was surprised and angry at the same time. He decided to just let it go. Anderson brought the sandwiches up to the pilothouse. Scanton asked him how his head was feeling.

He said, "I feel some better, but there is still a little headache bothering me." They both knew that he was a very lucky young man. Not only because he hadn't drowned when he was trapped in the net, but also because being hauled to the surface that fast could easily have caused an air embolism. That could have given Anderson a stroke and left him paralyzed. Neither man wanted to think about it. It hadn't come down that way, thank God.

The tow lasted about two and a half hours. Anderson went down to wake up Reed for the haulback. When he woke him, he seemed in a much better mood.

"So . . . How you doin', Tom? That was real nice thing you did for Marshall. I heard you got pulled down by the net."

"Yeah, that's what happened, I guess. It was so fast that I don't remember it at all. They tell me I passed out."

Reed spoke with a convincing air of concern. "No shit, man. I'm glad you're okay. We've been best friends for a long time, and I'd kind of miss you."

Anderson hesitated a little and said, "Thanks, I guess." They went out into the galley.

Reed said, "Any coffee on?"

"No, we're out of propane."

"Really? Out of propane? Chase will get his tits in a wringer for that one. That pisses Joey off, when shit like that happens. I guess your new buddy Mr. Engineer, know-it-all Chase isn't so fuckin' perfect as you thought he was."

Tom thought, *For a minute there I heard the old Skip I knew.* But it was very short-lived, "Whatever, Skip."

They hauled back and had a beautiful seven-thousand-pound bag of pure large cod. They had to split the bag. Joey adjusted to the eastard, and they set off again. The deck checkers were full. Joey fired out, "It's been a hard day's night . . . I been workin' like a dog . . . But when I get home to you . . . I find the things that you do . . . They make me feel all . . . right!"

The boys out on deck did get a kick out of that one. Chase said, "Hey, Tom, give Joey a nod and the okay sign." Anderson did as ordered. Joey laughed and gave them all the finger.

Chase said, "You have to admit it, dipshit, you made a great nod man."

"I guess you got me there. It seems like a million years ago now."

Chase said, "Yes, ain't it grand? Life on a fishin' boat adds a lot to your day, don't it?"

They all three started cutting and gutting. The deck hose was running to clean the fish. After they had a thousand pounds or so dressed, Reed walked over and took the main hatch cover off.

"Hey, Chase! You know how you were just saying life on a fishin' boat adds a lot to your day? Well, your day just got a fuck of a lot longer."

"What are you pissing about now, Reed?" Chase walked over and looked down into the fishhold. He couldn't believe his eyes. The ice in the hold was down to next to nothing. He climbed down in and started looking around. There were seven pens that were near deck level when they put the last 1,500 down. There were six inches of ice on top of every pen. Now the fish were now fully exposed. He couldn't imagine what had happened. None of this shit made any sense to him—the propane gas loss and now the ice. Of course the ice loss was ten times worse than no gas. They were onto the fish big time. Now the trip would be cut short, and they'd have to go in. The expenses were paid in full. Leaving seven-thousand-pound tows to go home was more than brutal. These fish would be pure profit for everyone.

Chase was second-guessing himself now. He knew he would be able to juggle things around and save the fish they had on board, but they would have to haul back and head for Rockland now.

Chase climbed out of the hold and started up to the pilothouse. Anderson said, "What's up, Pat?" He just put up his hand and said nothing. Reed said, "We've lost our ice. Your pal fucked up again. We're going to have to cut the trip short and go in."

"Wait a minute. I shoveled that ice on the top of those pens myself. Everything was covered, and I know it. Chase checked it out when I was done."

Reed said, "That fishhold is Chase's responsibility. If he can't handle it, Joey's better off with that motherfucker off the boat."

"I don't know what happened here, but something did. This is completely fucked up," Anderson said.

"You're goddamn straight you don't know what happened. You've been on this fuckin' boat for two weeks, and you think you got it all figured out. You don't. You don't know shit from Shinola on this thing or about fishing for that matter. You should just keep your mouth shut."

Anderson was blown away by this diatribe from Reed. Half an hour ago they were on top of the world; now they were at each other's throats. Reed was standing there with his jaw set in a very defiant and aggressive pose. He was clearly looking for a fight, and Tom was not going to engage. Reed was no match for Tom, and Reed knew it. Things weren't adding up.

Chase came into the pilothouse. Scanton said, "What's up? Why aren't you putting fish down?"

Chase's voice got really quiet, "We've lost our ice, Joe. I don't know what happened. We had the fish covered perfectly when we put down the 1,500 tow. Now the motherfuckers are exposed. I can't explain it. I couldn't believe my eyes when I went down there. I just don't believe you can lose four tons of ice in four hours."

Joey grabbed his hailer mic. "Tom, come on up."

When Anderson made it up, Scanton said, "Take her, Tom. Stay right on this bearing. If the net hangs up, don't do anything. I'll be right back up. Come on, Pat. Let's go have a look."

They crossed the deck and climbed down the fishhold. Joey was pissed. The first thing he did was to grab a shovel and clear some of the rotten ice off the slaughterhouse deck. The hatch covers were all in place. He threw the shovel and started yelling.

"Goddamn it, Pat. This is your area of the boat. I never check it out. I didn't think I had to. Haul back the fuckin' net. Get these fish down. We've got to run for Rockland."

Chase had a pained expression on his face. "Jesus, Joey, I don't know what happened."

"I don't want to hear about it. I told you what to do, so just fuckin' do it!" Scanton yelled. He climbed out of the hold and headed back for the pilothouse. Chase climbed out and started heaving the dressed fish down. Reed just stood there watching with a smug, satisfied smile on his face and then he started in. "What did you do, Chase? Short us on ice so we could go home early?" That was it. Chase went over and grabbed Reed by the oil pants and lifted him up against the net reel frame.

"You keep your goddamn mouth shut, asshole, and help put these fish down, or I swear I'll break your fuckin' neck right here and now!"

Reed didn't look the least bit afraid. He actually had the balls to smile at Chase. "Just calm down there, big fella. I didn't melt your goddamn ice. Let's follow the captain's orders and head back to shore before we lose the fish we got."

Reed couldn't have been happier. Everything was working out perfectly. They were headed ashore, and no one suspected he had anything to do with it. Seven hours from now they'd be in, and he couldn't wait. She had promised him that she would meet him in Rockland. Just the thought of seeing her was making his dick hard. Anderson came back down on deck. They hauled back. There were about one thousand pounds of fish in the net. Scanton didn't play any music; the deck was silent.

After they got the fish down and iced as best they could, they took their oil clothes off and went back up to the pilothouse. It was just past midnight, and they were headed for Rockland Harbor.

CHAPTER 52

Scanton grabbed the VHF mic. "Sunny Breeze Seafood, Sunny Breeze Seafood, come in, please. This is the *Jubilee* calling. Over."

After a minute or so, a lady's voice responded. "This is Sunny Breeze back to the *Jubilee*."

"Hi, Florence. Where to?"

"Sixty-five, Joey." They both switched channels, and Florence Handly came on the air.

"Hi, Joey. How are you, babe? You coming in here to see your best girl?"

"I sure am, darlin'. We'll be at your doorstep in about six, six and half hours. Over."

Florence and her brother, William Handly, owned Sunny Breeze Seafood. She was sixty-seven years old. She and William inherited the fish dealership from their father when he died almost twenty-five years before. She lived for this business. It was after midnight and Florence was still manning the radio. Joey didn't believe the woman ever slept. "Florence, don't you ever go to bed? Over."

"Is that a question or an invitation, you sexy thing?"

"Just a question, Florence. I wouldn't dare sleep with you. I'd be scared of a heart attack. Over."

"I look at it this way, Joey. If you die, you die. I'll find another one just like you."

Florence coughed a few times and said, "What's the hail look like, Joey?"

Joey was so pissed about being forced in he didn't really give a shit who heard what on the air. Florence knew, by prior agreement with Scanton, to triple whatever he told her. "We're looking at about sixteen, mostly tires, and a few more. You can handle it."

Florence knew he was talking about forty-five thousand flats. "Joey, there's been some guys around here all day asking questions about you. There were two suits and at least one slimy-looking hood. Over."

Joey said, "I don't know what that's about." He dismissed that report as nothing and reached for a cigarette.

Florence said, "That's how I knew you were coming. I'll see you when you get in here, hon."

"Okay, Flo. See you in the morning then. *Jubilee*, clear with Sunny Breeze Seafood."

"Sunny Breeze Seafood, clear with the *Jubilee*, back to 16 and standing by."

Scanton thought that was weird. Not just the part about the guys asking questions. He had either sold fish, or been aboard boats that sold fish, to Florence and her brother for as long as he could remember. Not once in all those years did she ever forget to ask in advance if he needed fuel and ice after they were unloaded. That really gave him the creeps. The only reason he could think of was if she thought he wouldn't be going out again. He really wished he could have a coffee about now. He said to Chase, "Don't forget to order propane for when we get in." That was a shot at Pat, of course. Joey knew damn well he wouldn't forget the propane. Chase didn't say anything. "Take the wheel, Pat. Call me back when we make the Mussel Ridge. I'll take her from there." Scanton left the pilothouse.

"Finest kind, Joey." He settled up into the captain's chair.

The fog had lifted. Chase could see the stars. Reed was down forward having a sandwich, and Anderson was writing a letter to Kathy. A promise is a promise.

My Dearest Kathy,

How's that for a start? I'm doing pretty good, huh? You don't know this, but I'm an old hand at writing really mushy, sloppy love letters, so I don't want to waste all my best stuff on this first one.

I haven't spoken to one other female, except for Uncle Charley, since I saw you last.

That proves my absolute loyalty and devotion to you. I did listen to an old lady trying to get our captain to have a fling with her on the radio. She's a fish buyer in Rockland. She sounds pretty hot. I don't think I'm her type though. I think she really has a big thing for Joey. I'm pretty sure she's on the other side of eighty by the sounds of it.

I had a fun offshore diving experience yesterday that I may tell you about later on. I made a new friend named Marshall Grimes. He's a wicked downeaster. I thought I could hear the islands in his voice.

I'll tell you this. Your old stud muffin misses you so bad his heart just about breaks when he thinks about you. I've never been so in love with anyone in my entire life. Unless you count Penny Thompson from third grade, and that was because she had one of those hot-looking Brownie uniforms on all the time. You don't have one of those kicking around, do you?

We're headed in early. It seems funny to me that I'll be in your loving arms again before you read this letter. I know you wanted me to write this so you'd know I was thinking about you while we were out here. Believe me I don't think about anything else. I'm looking forward to reading it again with you some time in the distant future.

I'll bet you right now that I'll think I was unbelievably funny. My plan is to call you in about six hours.

All my love,
Tom

PS. I was going to send you twenty bucks for gas money for the drive up to Rockland, but I had already sealed the envelope.

Nobody on the *Jubilee* had harbor fever accept Reed. While Chase was on the wheel, Rusty called from the *Jessica*. He wanted Joey to know he'd be seeing him and his crew in Rockland. Pat thought, *Oh boy, this will be fun. Maybe Leslie should try and come up for the second day.* He, Rusty, Skipper Cathcart, and Joey had been on some great drunken tirades together.

Chase stayed on the wheel till they rounded Allen Island. It was just before 4:00 a.m. Anderson came up and Chase had him take the helm. They would make the Mussel Ridge in about forty-five minutes. He was going down forward to read for a while.

Scanton came up about thirty minutes later. They had over six hundred pounds of lobsters on board. He grabbed the VHF mic to give his old friend Charley Perkins a call.

"*Charley's Pride, Charley's Pride*, the *Jubilee* calling."

"Yeah, Joey, 70?"

Joey switched up to 70 and said, "Charley! How you doin'? You old drunk!"

"I'm good, Joey boy, I'm good, but you're confused though. It's my twin brother that's the drunk. Hell . . . I had all I could do to lug his sorry ass out of the bar just tonight. Over."

Joey said, "I always do forget that. You two look so much alike."

"Yes, sir, that bastard has had me in trouble, all my life he has."

Charley, of course, was an only child. The imaginary twin was Charley's way of not facing any of his life's problems. It was much easier and a hell of a lot more fun to blame things on his imaginary evil twin than to face any of his own demons.

Scanton said, "You home, Charley?"

"Yes, sir, Joey, I am. You got reason for me not to be?"

"No, I just was checking in on you. We'll see you maybe sometime tomorrow."

Charley came back. "Finest kind then, Joey, finest kind."

There was only one reason for Scanton to call Charley at this time of night. He wanted him to run some lobsters in for him. Dragged lobsters were illegal in Maine. Scanton told Anderson to go get Chase and tell him that he had talked to Charley Perkins.

Chase came up from below. "Come on, Tom, we got a little something to do. Let's hit the deck."

When the boys left Gloucester, Chase had put seven lobster crates aboard the boat when no one was paying any attention. They were covered up by a piece of blue plastic tarp. He grabbed a crate and started putting lobsters in it from the live tank. Anderson jumped in and helped. Scanton was watching the job being done from the pilothouse window. Chase had turned the deck lights off.

After the crates were full, Joey slowed the boat down. He had the hailer on low and said, "You see it, Pat?" Chase waved his arm and grabbed the gaff, hooked a single red lobster buoy, and pulled it up. He started tying the crates together. He said, "Come on, Tom, help me get these overboard." They launched them one after the other as fast as they could. When they were done over Joey put the boat back up to full steam. Chase lit up a cigarette and offered Anderson one. They stood there a minute and watched as the sun was starting to break the horizon. There was that soft eerie light you sometimes get just before dawn. Chase pointed over toward the northeast. Tom could make out a lobster boat coming their way, and it was flying. He had never seen a lobster boat move like that. Chase said, "That's *Charley's Pride*. That guy that owns it is named Charley Perkins. He's got a souped-up eight-cylinder Cat diesel with a turbo charger in that thing. She really screams, doesn't she?"

"It sure as hell does," Anderson said as he watched the boat move across the horizon.

"Charley is an old buddy of Joey's. He'll sell those lobsters to his dealer like he caught them. Then he'll have our shack money for us later on today. He's a lifelong bachelor and lives alone down on Clark Island. He's a wicked good shit. He really just lives for his lobstering and his beer and not always in that order."

Anderson said, "I got it now. Do we give him a share of the shack money for selling these for us?"

"Yes. We'll split it up five even shares. It's still good money and a hell of a lot better than throwing them overboard and making nothing. We should get about $225 apiece, and we don't go into the wharf with any lobsters aboard for the marine patrol to find."

"Sounds good to me," Tom replied.

"Not to change the subject, but is Kathy coming up?"

"I'm sure she will. I'll call her when we get in. How about Leslie?"

"I think so. I'm planning to call her later on though. I might want to blow off a little steam up in here before she comes up. I don't know how long we're laying over."

It hadn't been ten minutes since they started watching, and they could see Charley getting those crates aboard his boat.

Chase laughed and said, "Wait till you catch this guy's act. He's worth the price of admission."

They got back up to the pilothouse. Chase asked Joey for the mic.

"Rockland Propane, Rockland Propane. *Jubilee* calling. You on here, Gary?"

"That you, Patrick? Pick one."

"Eighty-eight, Gary." Pat and Gary Gasner had been friends for years.

"Is that you, Gary Gas?" Pat loved calling him that. "Gary, we got to have two one-hundred propanes if we could. We ran out this trip, so there's two empties. We'll be off-loaded by two thirty, three o'clock if you can come by."

"Finest kind, Pat. I'll be there. You going to free up for a cold one after?"

Chase said, "We'll see. I'll be around."

"Okay, Pat. Rockland Propane clear with the *Jubilee*."

Chase signed off. "*Jubilee*, clear with Gary Gas."

CHAPTER 53

They steamed up past Mosquito Island. They were steering seventeen degrees on a straight run for the Mussel Ridge channel. The sunrise was magnificent this early September morning. Summer was just a few days gone, and there was already a little fall bite in the air. The angle of the sun had changed just enough to give the ocean a slightly different color and look.

Scanton stayed at the wheel. He had turned thirty-one just a few days before, but he didn't tell anyone on board. His mother and dad had called to wish him a happy birthday (his mother from home, his dad from the boat), but there wasn't anybody up in the wheelhouse with him when they did. He thought it was kind of funny that he didn't hear from Karen. She probably got busy with Little Joey and just forgot—no big deal. Things felt different to him this morning. It was strange. He felt a bizarre kind of nostalgia for the ending of the summer. He couldn't put his finger on it, really. Maybe it was just passing the thirty-year mark, he wasn't sure. He always looked forward to the fall and the winter fishing. This sense of loss was brand new to him, and he didn't like it. He had looked in the mirror when he was in the head this morning. He was starting to lose his hair. A small bald spot was beginning to appear. Jesus H. Christ, he was only thirty-one. After he noticed it he pulled his ball cap back on. He always wore it with the brim forward. He brushed his teeth and hadn't looked in the mirror since.

The atmosphere on the boat that morning was okay. They were going to land a good trip of fish even though it had been cut short. The ice thing had really gotten to him. He still couldn't figure out what had happened. One thing he knew for an absolute certainty, Pat Chase did not screw up the fishhold. It didn't happen, not this time, not anytime. Anderson was working with Pat right steady, so he didn't do it. He was pretty sure he didn't do it himself, unless he had started sleep walking. That left Reed. Why in the fuck would Skip Reed want to come off fish like that? They were catching enough to load the boat, and he hadn't hit the places he really wanted to go yet; it made zero sense. The hell with it. They had a great trip into Gloucester, and they had a good fifty-six thousand pounds on board. Things were going to be all right. He started feeling a lot better, at least for the time being.

They were steadily making their way up the Mussel Ridge. They passed Spruce Head Island and were almost to Owls Head. The day was gorgeous. The *Jubilee* was running perfectly. Scanton called Chase up to the wheelhouse. He said, "Let's throw together a list of maintenance stuff we want to do while we're in here. I figure we should plan on a three-day layover. I want to change all the filters, top off all the lube oils, and check this fishhold out completely before we blow ice aboard again."

"I know, Joey. That ice loss thing is driving me crazy. I can't figure it out."

"Pat . . . Look, I know you didn't mess that up. I'm sorry I was pissed at you. I got my thoughts on what happened, but I don't want to talk about it right now. Don't worry about it. Let's get the fish unloaded and get ready to head out again."

"Finest kind, Joe. I think I should pick up a spare float switch, and I want to replace the circuit breakers in the main panel after our little flameout. I used the extra float switch I had when we were in Portland. I forgot to mention it to you. Do you think I should pick up an extra loud hailer speaker since you broke my other one?"

Joey laughed and said, "Get the fuck out of here!"

Twenty minutes later the *Jubilee* had rounded Owls Head and was making her way up into Rockland. They could see the breakwater protecting Rockland Harbor.

Joey picked up the mic. "Sunny Breeze Seafood, the *Jubilee* calling. Over."

"Sunny Breeze back to the *Jubilee*."

"Where to, Flo?"

"Try 65, darlin'."

"Sixty-five."

"How you doin, Flo? We're about to round the breakwater in about fifteen minutes. You ready to take us on?"

"Oh, I'm always ready, but I'll have to take you on one at a time. Over."

"Jesus, Florence, do you talk to everybody like that?"

"No, just you, honey, just you."

"We'll be right along. Is the unloading dock open?"

"Sure is, Joey. We'll see you in a minute. You've got company waiting here."

He thought to himself, *Great*. He asked, "Is Karen there, Flo?"

Florence came back with a serious tone in her voice. "No, honey, it's not Karen."

Joey said to himself, *What the fuck? There must be something up.*

He slowed the boat down while the boys raised the paravanes. Chase and Anderson broke out the docking lines. Reed was ready on the stern. Joey swung the *Jubilee* into the dock and turned hard to the port. He popped the boat into reverse and nailed her. The black smoke rolled out of her exhaust pipe in a heavy cloud. She waltzed sideways into the floating camel. The dockhands were there, ready to tie her up. He shut down the 1271 but left the genset running. He came down from the pilothouse and crossed the deck.

"Pat, go ahead get started unloading. I need to go up to the office for a few minutes. You're in charge, just you."

"Okay, Joe." Chase thought something has changed here. The tone in Scanton's voice was serious. If Joey was going to count on him to run the unloading, that was fine.

Scanton climbed the ladder and made his way up to the office. When he walked in, he saw Bobby Crosby standing there with another guy he didn't recognize. Joey smiled when he saw Florence. She came over and hugged him. She looked absolutely horrible. Her hair looked like straw after a fire. Her face was a wrinkled mess from years of overexposure to the sun and three packs of Lucky Strikes a day. She reminded him of one of those Sharpies. The false teeth and the bright-red lipstick really brought the whole package together.

"You look gorgeous, Florence. How do you do it?"

"That's why there's no future for me and you, Joey. You're a wicked liar. It'll just have to be wild sex for us, just like it's always been, and you're going to have to accept that fact."

Scanton turned and put out his hand to Bobby Crosby. "How are you, Bobby? It's good to see you. What's up?"

Crosby worked for Maine Coast Marine Finance. Scanton knew him because he was the guy that had made him the loan on the *Jubilee* when he bought her. He was from a fishing family himself. His grandfather and father had both fished offshore. He had two brothers that were fishermen as well. They were all from Bath. He had been a real smart kid in school. He graduated from the University of Maine with a degree in finance and managed the southern branch for the marine loan company that financed a large portion of the fishing fleet. He was only a year older than Joey. He said, "It's good to see you too, Joey. I wish it were under different circumstances."

Scanton said, "What circumstances? What's wrong, Bobby?"

He said, pointing to the stranger, "Joey, this is Ben Berry from Hyland, Berry & Morse. Ben's our lawyer. We've got a serious problem here."

Scanton said, "What serious problem? I don't know what you're talking about, Bobby."

Attorney Berry had heard enough. "Mr. Scanton, you know perfectly well why we're here."

He opened a folder. "You have been notified by certified mail three times and served with a court summons. I have written receipts for the notification letters right here. I think it's pointless to continue this ridiculous charade. Trying to pretend that you don't know anything about this is ridiculous."

Scanton's face was scarlet. "Show me these letters." Ben handed the copies of documents to him. Berry continued on. "You're four months behind on your boat payments. This is a default notice for breach of your promissory note for failure to pay. The boat is collateralized and will be seized and auctioned by a marshal's sale immediately, of which the proceeds will be used to satisfy your debt."

"What the fuck are you talking about, asshole? I've never missed a boat payment since I've had that boat."

Berry said, "Please refrain from talking to me in that foul and derogatory language. It will not help your situation. I'm Mr. Berry, and you will address me as such."

Scanton took the letters and read them quickly. "Notice of delinquency" was the headline on three letters. He checked the dates, which started in May. He looked at the court summons but really didn't understand all the language in it.

"I'm telling you I never saw these letters."

Berry said, "That's so typical of you people in the fishing business. You think you can just stand there and deny the truth? Well, not this time."

He handed Joey four of those green cards used for certified mail. "Every one of these cards is signed by Karen Scanton." The lawyer continued, "Your boat has also been liened by Commercial Fuel and Ice Services of Portland LLC for failure to pay on a signed note. They are charging you with theft and deception for landing and selling fish across state borders in breach of an agreement to land and sell at a Portland fish dealer, where they had a hold on your catch. The city of Portland reports that you failed to pay your excise tax on the boat. Your insurance company has suspended your coverage as well for failure to pay. The boat is tied up until further notice by the authority of the State of Maine District Court."

Scanton's heart was racing and so was his mind. He said, "Slow down here a minute. I just landed a $100,000 trip in Gloucester and forwarded the money to our account in Portland. My wife paid everything."

Berry said, "Mr. Scanton, please allow me to inform you that we are well aware of your recent success in Gloucester. You creditors are very anxious to learn what you and your wife have done with their money. Can you answer that question, Mr. Scanton?"

The nasty, condescending, arrogant tone of this prick lawyer was more than Joey could stand. He wasn't a violent man, but he had thoughts about breaking this bastard's head for him.

He said, "Bobby, you better get this guy out of here before something happens we're all going to regret, especially him."

Berry said, "Are you threatening me?"

Crosby intervened and said, "Back off, Ben. Let's take a walk for a few minutes. Joey probably would like to make a few calls. I'm sure this has come as quite a shock to him."

Berry looked at Bobby Crosby like he had to be the most naive individual he had ever met. "Fine, you're paying for my time. I've dealt with a lot of these deadbeats before, and this one is no different. They all have stories, but if you're willing to listen to him . . . that's your business."

The deadbeat line almost sent Scanton over the top, but Florence came over to Joey and said, "Honey, it's going to be all right. You and old Flo are going to figure this thing out. I'm just as rich as I am beautiful. It's going to be okay, I promise." After Florence intervened, Joey did relax a little. In his heart he knew that everything would be all right. All he had to do was get a hold of Karen, and things would get straightened out. Christ, she had enough money to pay off all this shit.

He really didn't want to kill that lawyer anyhow. He would wind up in Thomaston State Prison. Then ultimately he'd find himself fishing on Rusty's boat on his hire-a-killer program. He'd rather just let the little prick live.

Scanton said, "Can I use the phone, Flo?"

Florence said, "Of course you can, honey. I'll step outside here and have a Lucky. You just go right ahead."

He grabbed the phone and dialed his home number in Portland. The phone rang and rang unanswered. He thought that was weird. It was only eight thirty in the morning. Karen was never an early riser. He couldn't imagine where she was. Joey called his mother next. She picked up after the second ring. "Hello."

"Hi, Ma, how are you?"

Gloria said, "Oh hi, honey. I'm fine. How are you?"

"I'm fine, Ma. I'm kind of in a rush though. We're in Rockland unloading. Have you talked to Karen recently?"

"Gee no, Joey, I haven't in over a week. I was going to try her today. I really wanted to get Little Joey for a while. Dad's home, and I wanted to have him over so we could take him out to lunch somewhere."

Joey said, "There's some kind of trouble, Ma. There are some guys here that say I owe boat payments and a bunch of other bills. I can't get her on the phone. Dad probably told you we did big last trip, so I don't know what's going on. I sent her all the money."

Gloria said, "Just relax, Joey. I'll find her and call you back. Daddy and I have money put away if you need money. It'll be all right."

"Ma, I got my own money, okay? I just told you that. Please just find Karen and call me back as soon as you can. I'm at Florence Handly's. You know, Sunny Breeze Seafood up here. Dad's got the number."

"Okay, Joey. I'll call you in a few minutes."

"Ma, you're still signed into our account at the bank. Call over there and ask for Cindy Pinkham. You know her. See what's in there for money. I may have to have you write some checks for me. I got to go."

Gloria said, "Okay. Bye, honey, don't worry now."

On the rear of Florence's office there was a back door that led to a little deck. Joey stepped out there. She was out there sitting at a small table, smoking. You could see the unloading operation going on from there. Chase looked up and spotted Joey watching him. He gave him the thumbs-up and smiled. Joey returned the wave, but he didn't smile.

"I don't know what's going on, Flo. My mother's going to check things out and get back to me. Karen always pays the bills. At least we had a good trip and the price of fish is up." Florence looked down a little. "You haven't talked to anybody, have you, Joey?"

"No, I haven't. What's going on?"

"The fish prices, Joey. Everybody's catching fish. The big boats are in from the Grand Banks and George's loaded with groundfish. The price dropped $1.25 a pound in the last four days. I don't know what the Boston auction's paying. The Portland fish exchange is the last I heard from."

"Are you shitting me, Flo? Goddamn it. I wish my mother would hurry up and call back. I'm going down on the dock for a minute. I'll be back."

Scanton went down the stairs and passed Bobby and Ben Berry.

Ben said, "Are you ready to give us some answers, Mr. Scanton? I really don't have all day."

"No, but I do have a question for you though, Mr. Berry."

"What's that, Mr. Scanton?"

"Why don't you go fuck yourself?" Crosby knew that was going to do it. Berry walked off and headed for the car. After he was gone Joey said, "I'm sorry, Bobby. That prick is such a jerk."

Crosby said, "I know it feels like that to you, but he's just doing his job. What do you think you need for time?"

"I got almost sixty thousand pounds of fish on board. I know Florence will cut you a check for all four boat payments. I'll get my mother to take a check to the insurance people. Just keep that lawyer away from me, okay?"

"Look, Joey, why don't I take Mr. Berry out for breakfast, and we'll come back and see what we can do. I don't think this thing is quite as simple as you think it is. Okay, Joe?"

"Okay, thanks, but I still think you run with a lousy crowd of people."

"I know, Joey."

Scanton went out on the dock to see how the unloading was going. Chase told him they were doing fine. "Where's Skip anyway?"

"I don't know. Tom and I have been on this since we started. He's watching the fishhold. We got about nine thousand off so far. Everything all right, Joey?"

"Oh yeah, just fucking grand." Chase looked up and pointed toward the deck off the office. Joey turned and saw Florence waving him up.

He ran up the stairs and was out of breath when he picked up the phone. Gloria Scanton was sobbing.

"Ma, what's wrong? Is Karen and the baby all right?"

"I . . . I don't know, Joey. She's gone."

"Ma, stop crying. I can't understand you. What do you mean she's gone? Gone where?"

"Gone . . . gone. I used the key you gave me for emergencies to get in your apartment. There's nothing left of hers at your place. All her clothes are gone. The baby's stuff is all gone. Karen's gone. She's run away, Joey, I know it."

"Maybe she's with her sister. She can't have taken off. Where would she go?"

Gloria finally started to calm down, but she was still crying. "I called Cindy Pinkham. There's no money, Joey. She withdrew all of it. Karen didn't pay anybody anything. She transferred the whole check that you got from Artie, except for $50. There was nothing Cindy could do about it. Karen's a cosigner on that account. You know how that works."

Joey said, "That fuckin' bitch!"

"I'm so sorry, honey. I don't know what to say. How can I help you?"

"Now I get it. She stole the trip and ran off. I'll have to call you back, Ma. Oh, one thing you can do is have Dad go over and get the insurance placed back on the boat. That bitch didn't pay that either. I'll call you in an hour or so. Thanks, Ma. I love you."

Gloria started sobbing again. "What am I going to do if she won't let me see my Little Joey? Oh please, God, no."

"Try to calm down, Ma. Karen's not going to hurt that baby. Don't worry, we'll find him."

Gloria fought through her sobs. "Daddy's right here. He wants to talk to you." It always drove Joey crazy that Gloria referred to his father as "Daddy."

"Hi, Dad. How long have you been ashore?"

"We got in yesterday. By the way, Marshall really appreciates what you guys did for him off there."

"I know, Dad, I'm sure he does. I've got some more serious problems right now myself."

"Your mother tells me that Karen ran off with the baby and the money from your Gloucester trip?"

"That about sums it up. The worst part is she's been keeping other money away from me too that I didn't know about. She's been paying all the bills on that boat since I've had her. You remember the fuel and ice bill I had in Portland? I told you I wrote that check. She never sent it in so she could keep the money. What a sucker I am! This is real bad. I owe almost $30,000 to the crew for the last trip, and the bitch hasn't been paying the boat payments either. Bobby Crosby from the boat loan company is down here with an asshole lawyer trying to sticker the boat."

"Oh god, Joe!"

"I got friggin' served by the bank's lawyers. She signed for all the papers and never told a fuckin' soul."

"Joey, we can help out some, but we don't have that kind of cash available. Maybe we could sell some stocks, but it would take time."

"No, Dad, you're not doing that. If I lose the boat, I lose it. She had me completely fooled. I knew she wasn't happy, but I never dreamed she'd do something like this."

"She had us all fooled, son, all of us."

"Christ, with all I owe, I'm so screwed. I don't know what I'm going to do."

"Call Terry Norton and tell him what's going on. He's been taking care of this family forever. He'll know what to do. He's your lawyer for your boat corporation, isn't he?"

"Yes, he is. I haven't talked to him in three years though. He probably won't even remember me."

Peter said, "Don't worry, Joey. He'll remember you. Hang on a minute while I get you the number." Peter put the phone down. Joey thought, *That's what I need, a goddamn lawyer bill on top of everything else.* Peter came back on the line. "It's Norton, Ferris & Bowen. The number is 775-2010. You got that, Joey?"

"Yeah, I got it. Something else, Dad . . . I think Uncle Sal sent my cousin Vito down here to strong-arm me for the money I owe him. That slug is probably in bed with some whore down here, but I expect to see him show up anytime. I've really got to go. I'll call you later on, Dad. I'll talk to you later." Joey hung up the phone.

He went back aboard the boat. He had to think for a minute. He sat down in the captain's chair, put his feet up on the wheel, and lit up a cigarette. He pulled out a piece of paper and a pencil. The number one priority was the boat. Any chance he had of replacing the money Karen had just stolen he will get back by fishing. The boat payments were $1,600 a month and some change, so four months came to about $6,400. The insurance was taken care of. The excise tax his mother could go pay was about a grand. The crew was due $28,000 from Gloucester. This trip they would share out at about $16,000. The Portland Fuel and Ice bill was about $5,300, and he had to have at least $9,000 for Uncle Sal. He needed at least $64,000 dollars to get off the wharf. The total stock was only going to be around $59,000. In a word, he was fucked. How could Karen do this to him? "YOU GODDAMN BITCH!" he screamed in a total rage.

Reed was in a phone booth. He dialed the number for Rockland Propane. He was ready to hang up if that Gary guy answered; he didn't. A fairly youngish female did. Reed said, "Hi, this is Pat Chase from the *Jubilee*. I'm calling to cancel the propane order for the boat that was to be delivered today. Somebody had already ordered it from someone else, so we're all set. Thank you. Sorry for the inconvenience."

The girl said, "No problem, sir. Thanks for calling."

Reed thought, *One down and one to go.* He dialed the number. Three rings and the phone was answered. "Yeah?" He heard that same nasty gruff voice as every other time.

Reed said, "It's me. We're in Rockland. I'll call you in a few hours. Send the gas." This time Reed hung up without waiting for a reply.

Scanton went back up on the wharf. Chase and Anderson were there. Chase told him that they had about thirty thousand pounds off the boat so far. Reed finally showed up and Scanton said, "Where the hell have you been?"

"I had to make some calls, but I've been right around watching the scale.

Chase looked incredulous. He thought, *You haven't been watching any friggin' scale.* But he didn't say anything.

Scanton said, "Skip, you give Pat a break on the table. Are you all right at the hatch for now, Tom?"

Anderson said, "Yeah, I'm fine, Joey." Scanton ran back up to the office and sat down at Florence's desk. He called Terry Norton's office. The receptionist answered. "Norton, Ferris & Bowen . . . how can I help you?"

"Yes, this is Joe Scanton. I need to talk to Terry Norton, please."

"I'm sorry, Mr. Norton is in with clients. Can I take a message, please?"

"Yes, tell him to call me please. It's important. The number here is 833-7869. It's Joe Scanton. It's real important."

"I'll make sure Mr. Norton gets your message as soon as he's free."

Joey thought, *That'll be the day, a free lawyer.* He said, "Thanks," and hung up the phone.

The receptionist at Norton's office returned the phone to its cradle said to no one, "It's always important, honey, always important."

Scanton was sitting there when Crosby and Berry came back into the office. "Well, Mr. Scanton, have you had time to make your phone calls?" Berry said.

"Yes, I have. I think I have a handle on things. We are halfway through unloading. I think I can have a check for all the back payments for you within an hour or so."

Berry laughed. "The back payments? I don't think you understand, Mr. Scanton. You're in default on your loan. I have been to court and gotten a judgment against you. The entire balance of your loan is due now, sir. I already have a call into the sheriff's department. They are going to seize your boat and secure it within the next few hours. This will happen after the vessel is unloaded, unless you can pay the entire balance due, plus the costs of collection."

Scanton said, "How much is that exactly?"

"$71,912 to be exact." Ben smiled at him and said, "Who can go fuck themselves now, big shot?"

Scanton's face was completely expressionless. His hand shook as he reached for his cigarettes. Crosby was the first to speak. He said, "Look, Ben, why don't you give Joey and I a minute, please?"

Berry snapped, "That's totally inappropriate under these circumstances. You should not have any discussions whatsoever with this man regarding the matter at hand without your attorney present."

Crosby said, "Ben, leave us alone please."

Berry walked out of the office, but before he closed the door, he said, "You're paying for my time, Mr. Crosby!"

"Yeah, yeah, I know. We're paying you for your time."

After the lawyer left, Crosby said, "Okay, Joey, what really happened?" Joey told Bobby everything, including the fact that he had a call into Terry Norton. Crosby just shook his head. He had been through a divorce himself a few years ago. It was nasty, but it was nothing like this. He said, "I knew that you had blown a reverse gear recently. My brother that fishes on the *January Gale* told me about it. I thought you were going to call me for a rewrite of your loan. The payments were already showing delinquent by then, and I thought you were ignoring me. I should have come to see you, but honestly I got real busy. You know how that happens. I'm sorry, Joe."

"I swear to you, Bobby, I had no idea that Karen was pulling this shit."

Crosby said, "I believe you. My problem is what do we do now? I'm the manager of the office, but the guy I report to is all about the lawyers. How good is your guy? If he can convince Berry that this isn't the slam dunk he thinks it is, maybe you'll have a chance."

The phone rang on Florence's private line. Joey picked it up and said hello.

"I'm looking for Joseph Scanton. This is Terry Norton calling."

"Hi, Terry, it's Joey. How are you?"

"I'm fine, Joey. The question is . . . how are you, my friend? My receptionist said it was important."

Scanton explained in detail what had happened. Crosby had excused himself from the room when he knew who was on the line. He had all the copies of the documents in front of him, so he read and described them to his lawyer. Terry said, "This is an extremely important question. What's your relationship with the loan manager like? Friendly or hostile?"

He said, "Very friendly. He's a hell of a good guy. That lawyer is a son of a bitch though."

"I know Ben Berry. You let me worry about him. Break down the current available cash you're getting out of this trip."

Scanton went over the numbers. Norton said, "Have someone there go get Ben Berry, and tell him I'd like to speak with him, please."

Scanton told Crosby that Terry Norton wanted to have a word with Berry. Berry walked into Florence's office with the air of a matador headed in for the kill. Scanton wasn't buying into it though. He was thinking this could become very interesting.

Berry picked up the phone. "Berry here."

"Hi, Ben. This is Terry Norton. How are you?"

"I'm fine, but I think your client has a real problem."

"Well, I appreciate that, Ben, but you and I have a few things to discuss." Terry proceeded to inform him that he had made a major error in not providing notice to his office on the default claim. His firm was the registered clerk of the LLC that owned the fishing vessel *Jubilee*. He told him that Li'l Joey LLC was an active, registered, Maine limited liability corporation and that he had every legal right to notice as the corporate clerk. He also informed him that his client had, just today, learned of his delinquency relating to the boat loan due to the negligence of a shareholder of the corporation. He also just learned of an embezzlement of funds from the corporation by a shareholder. Norton informed Berry that he would not hesitate to use the federal bankruptcy court's protection to sort out these matters before he would allow any sale of the *Jubilee* to proceed. He was ready to prepare an emergency request for a stay from sale with the court. Then Norton asked Berry if his client might not want to discuss the possibility of a cash debt reduction offer today with an accompanying agreement that the loan would be reinstated immediately.

Scanton was watching lawyer Berry squirm in his seat. After a short hesitation, he said, "What kind of offer do you have in mind?"

"I'll propose to my client that he offer $1,000 today, catch up all the back payments, and cover your collection expenses."

Berry became instantly red in the face. "Don't be ridiculous. Your client has violated all the terms of his loan agreement and the promissory note. He is not going to reestablish credit with this company under any proposal of less than five figures."

That was just exactly what Norton was hoping to hear. All his statements about insufficient notice and embezzlement were 99 percent hot air. He knew no one can be guilty of embezzlement when they're signed into the checkbook and authorized to have access to the funds. The last thing Norton would ever do would be to file his client into bankruptcy. Norton asked Berry to put Joey on the line.

Scanton picked up. "Hi, Terry. What's up?"

Norton said, "Joey, here's where we are. Karen has put you in a terrible spot. After the courts have awarded a judgment against you it's, for all practical purposes, impossible to get it overturned. A no-show at a foreclosure hearing is the worst defense strategy known to man, and you, through no fault of your own, were a no-show."

Scanton said, "I get that."

"I want to offer them $10,000 to reinstate. Do you think you could get the crew to let you square with them next trip?" Norton continued.

"Jesus, Terry, do you know what you're asking?"

"Yes, I do, Joe. If we don't reach agreement with the loan company, they're going to tie up your boat right now . . . and yes, they can."

"With the expenses I got to pay, including that money, I'll have to ask the crew to carry the whole ten grand. Then I got to get the dealer here to carry me on fuel and ice. I'm assuming that little prick won't do this deal without a check for Portland Ice and Fuel Services."

"That would be correct. They attached the boat, and he'll never allow this deal to go ahead without that paid," Norton said.

For the first time all day Joey felt some hope. "Go ahead, Terry, make the offer. I'm sure the boys won't let me down."

Norton and Berry hammered out the details of the agreement. Crosby called the main office and got the deal approved. He had really stepped up for Scanton. Crosby's boss had never reinstated a bad loan. Crosby had made a great case without sounding like he was too sympathetic to the borrower.

Scanton signed some more documents, and Florence gave Berry two checks adding up to $15,300. The old fuel bill was paid and the *Jubilee* was free to sail.

Scanton was pleased that something had been worked out, but he wasn't looking forward to talking with the crew about what had happened to their money.

The unloading was going well. Florence had promised to give checks cut directly from Sunny Breeze Seafood to the crew for their previous share from the Gloucester trip. That was a big deal. She had to trust Joey that his accountant would file all the correct paperwork so as not to create a tax nightmare for her and her brother. When they were all done, Joey shook hands with Crosby and thanked him for his help. He didn't acknowledge Berry. When they parted, Crosby said, "What are you going to do about Sal's money?"

Scanton said, "Bobby, trust me, you don't want to know."

CHAPTER 54

Ten minutes later a gold Cadillac pulled up in front of Sunny Breeze Seafood. Vito Scantini got out of his car. He personified every negative thought you could ever conjure up about a two-bit hood. He was fleshy, pale, and dressed in an outfit that was so cliché that he must have stolen the ideas for it out of the old gangster movies.

Scanton walked over to him and said, "Hey, Vito . . . how's the mob doing without you around today?"

Vito tried to give Joey a tough-guy look. "Don't fuck with me, Joey. Dad wants to talk to you. He said you should make the call from a pay phone."

"Jesus, Vito, this is just a reverse gear loan, not a major crime conspiracy."

"Just call him before you piss me off."

"Settle down, you fuckin' creep. I'll call him."

Scanton walked over to the pay phone and dialed his uncle Sal.

"Uncle Sal, it's Joey."

"Joey, Joey, Joey. How's my favorite nephew?"

"I'm okay, Uncle Sal."

"Joey, you and me we got some business to finish up, right?"

"Yes, we do. I got a payment for you today."

"How come you don't pay in full? I hear you had a big trip of fish down in Gloucester. You don't want to pay your uncle Sal like you said you would? You holding out on me, Joey? I don't like guys that hold out on me."

"No, Uncle Sal. You're not going to believe this, but Karen took all that money out of our account and left me."

That sounded funny to Joey. Of course, that's what had happened, but when he said it out loud, it sounded so weird.

Sal said, "Believe, not believe, it don't matter. I don't want to hear no stories. I want my money. You understand me, Joey?"

Joey was starting to fidget. Sal said, "You got a week to get the rest of my money. You understand, Joey? No stories . . . just the money. Okay, boy?"

"Okay, Uncle Sal. I'll give Vito a check for the first $9,000."

"No, Joey, no, you give cash. You understand me now? Cash, boy."

"Okay, I'll get you cash. Please tell Vito to stay out of my face until I give him the money."

"I wish you and Vito could be close like me and your dad. That would be my wish. Family, that's what it's all about, Joey, family."

"Yeah, Uncle Sal, family." Joey was thinking, *My father hates you, has always hated you, will always hate you, you lousy rotten bastard.*

Sal said, "Your aunt Mary sends her love to you."

He hung up. Vito walked over to Joey after he saw him leave the phone booth. "You got the money for me?" Vito said.

"Get the fuck away from me, you cocksucker. Come back at five o'clock. There will be a bag with the money in it in the mailbox outside there."

Joey pointed to one on the side of the building they were in.

CHAPTER 55

Chase gave Anderson a break from unloading. He ran for the phone booth and dialed Kathy's number. She picked up on the second ring. Kathy had been debating about how she would explain Matthew to Tom. Neither of them had talked much about their pasts. She thought that Tom really didn't want to know about it. He liked pretending that he was the only man she had ever been in love with. That was okay; it was really very sweet. Finally, she decided that she would take a chance and just have them meet for the first time, face-to-face. Kathy would be able to tell by the look in Tom's eyes how he felt. Roll the dice and be a winner! Kathy answered the phone.

"Hello."

"Hi, darling . . . your fisherman is home from the sea."

"Hi, Tommy dear. How are you?"

"I'm good but I'm missing you bad!"

"Oh, you are, are you?"

"Awful bad. I want you to come up to Rockland, if you can, this afternoon."

"I think I can do that. I won't be coming alone though."

"Is Leslie coming with you again?"

"No, Tom. It's somebody else. Somebody really important. It's a surprise."

"You're not going to tell me who's coming?"

"Nope."

"Are we going to need two rooms for tonight?"

"Nope."

"Kinky, huh?"

"Very kinky."

"Oh wow. I love kinky."

"I know, big boy, I know."

Tom gave Kathy directions to Sunny Breeze. They said all their "I love yous" and their good-byes. He was on top of the world. After he hung up with Kathy, he called his sister Joanne. She lived in Yarmouth, not far from where they had grown up.

"Hey, sis. What's up?"

"Oh hi, Tommy, I thought you were out rolling around in the big blue ocean somewhere."

"Well, I was, but we have to come home every once in a while to get more food."

"Why don't you just eat that awful fish you catch?" Tom knew Joanne was making a face on the other end of the line.

"Hey, how about doing your loving sweet brother a big favor?"

There was a short pause. "What do you need now, brother dear?"

"I want you to go over to the house and go in my top drawer and get that box I keep in there and bring it to me in Rockland." Joanne waited a minute and said, "I know what's in that box, don't I?"

"I bet you do. Can you do it?"

"It'll take me about three hours to get there, but I'll come. Very exciting!"

"We'll see. It could be." Tom gave her the directions she'd need to find him, and they hung up.

Scanton was back up in the office with Florence explaining his need for $9,000 in cash. Florence said, "What, are you crazy? Nine thousand dollars in cash? The IRS is watching everybody on cash transactions because of all the drug running going on. If you withdraw $9,000 in cash, the bank reports that, you know." He explained the situation with Uncle Sal to Florence. He was relieved when he learned she didn't already know about his loan. He thought she must have been out on her deck having a Lucky when the word went out, so she got left out of the loop.

"Nine thousand dollars cash . . . $9,000 cash . . . you think I'm a goddamn bank?" Flo turned to a small safe behind her desk. She opened it, reached in, and pulled out a stack of $100 bills. She counted out $9,000 and handed the cash to Joey.

"Thanks, Flo. Now I've got to go speak with the crew."

"Good luck with that one. I don't envy you. Their checks are in that envelope there. You owe me a big roll in the hay for all this, you know."

"I can't wait, you old slut."

"I really am an old slut, aren't I?"

CHAPTER 56

The unloading was just about done. The *Jubilee* would weigh out at 58,700 pounds. They had stocked $59,000. The prices had dropped to $1.00-a-pound average from a $2.00 average in just five days. Chase had gone in town to a marine parts store and picked up his supplies. He was going through all his mechanicals when Joey climbed down aboard the boat.

Anderson was giving Chase a hand greasing bollards and getting the deck reorganized. They had checked the fishhold; the disappearing ice would remain a mystery for now.

A propane truck showed up and backed down over the wharf beside the boat. Chase was surprised and curious that it wasn't his friend Gary. The truck looked the same, but the driver was a guy he'd never seen before. Reed was right there like he had been waiting for the guy. He was up on the wharf taking charge. He hollered down to Chase, "I've got this, Pat. I'll get it swapped out for you."

He went aboard the boat and was up on the overhead in a flash.

Chase thought, *That's the fastest I've seen Reed move in the last two years.*

The gas truck was rigged with a small retractable boom that allowed enough extension to easily move these small tanks from the boat to the truck and back again. Reed had a wrench with him and unhooked the regulator from the top of the tanks. He unstrapped the webbed belts that held the tanks in place. The driver extended the boom with a rope bridle on the end, attached by a small hook. Reed wrapped the bridle around the tank marked number one. He gave the driver the sign to lift the tank. The boom easily plucked the empty gas tank out of its cradle and quickly retracted it to the truck. He unhooked the bridle and repeated the process for the number two tank. Within a few minutes the new tanks were aboard the boat, and the number one tank was hooked back to the regulator. Reed turned on the gas.

Chase was watching the whole thing. He said, "Tom, you better run down forward to the galley and make sure that the stove isn't on. That stupid prick could blow us all to kingdom come."

Anderson took off like a shot, not remembering if he had turned the burner off or if it just flickered out on its own. When he got down into the galley, he could smell the raw gas. He quickly turned the burner off and opened the hatch cover in the galley overhead to clear out the air.

Chase had already gone down into the fishhold and opened a deck hatch. Propane gas is heavier than air and flows down to the bilge of the boat. *Disaster averted*, he thought.

When he came out of the fishhold he was headed up to blast Reed for what he had just done. He looked up on the wharf and spotted something strange. The gas truck driver was handing Reed something. It looked like a small key with a tag on it. The guy said something that looked kind of aggressive. Chase couldn't hear what was said. He decided he wouldn't confront Reed about the gas fuckup down in the galley. Reed would only blame it on Tom. After all, he did leave it open.

The guy in the gas truck drove off. Chase watched Reed hide the key in his cigarette pack. It was a pack of Marlboros, and he slid the key between the box and the aluminum foil and put the pack in his shirt pocket. Reed didn't notice that Chase was watching him.

Anderson came back out on deck, and Chase told him about the way gas goes down into the bilge and not off into the sky.

"I'm sure glad you were paying attention. I'll never leave that burner on again like that." Pat was glad that Tom was willing to take responsibility for the mistake and not blame it on Skip.

Scanton came out of the main companionway with Uncle Charley under his arm. He dropped her on deck, and she tore off after her fresh fish treats. The deck was pretty well cleaned up and hosed down. He had a cigarette going and was sitting on the main hatch cover. The dock crew was getting ready to blow the ice aboard.

Scanton told Anderson to fuel up. He wanted a thousand gallons in each side.

"Skip, come on up above with me a minute, will ya?"

"Sure, Joey." They sat down up in the pilothouse and Reed said, "What's up, Joe?"

It was hard for Joey to talk about what happened, but he spit it out. "Well, for starters, Karen stole the Gloucester trip. I deposited the money in our account while we were down there. She took out every dime and didn't pay anybody."

Reed said, "That fuckin' bitch! She stole the crew share too . . . everything?"

"You got it. I'm so fucked it's unreal. I'm sure you saw the suits running around while we were unloading. I was four months behind on boat payments, and they were here to seize the boat!"

"Holy shit, Joe," Reed said.

"She's run off somewhere and taken little Joey with her, and my mother can't find her." Joey took a drag. "I goddamn hate to ask you this, but is the swordfish deal still out there?"

"I don't know. I imagine it is. I'll have to call." Skip fought to keep the look of satisfaction off his face.

Joey said, "You go ahead and make that call. As you know, we hold ninety thousand pounds. I figure if we're going to do this, we may as well do it right. Tell them we'll take sixty thousand pounds of swords."

"Now you're talking, Joey. We'll get everything straightened out with that kind of money."

"Skip, don't mention this to Pat or Tom. Let it stay between us."

"You bet, Joey."

"I want to fish our way off there. I'm not going to steam straight for the Hague Line. It would draw too much attention."

"Yes, I got you, Joe, whatever you say. I'll go make the call. You figure four days before we meet up with the swordfish boat?"

"Make it five. I want to leave here at dawn, day after tomorrow. Tonight I'm going to get drunk and celebrate my upcoming divorce."

"Jesus, man, I'm sorry about you and Karen. I guess it was coming though."

Joey was a little surprised at Reed's response. "What makes you say that? She was as sweet as pie when I talked to her from Gloucester."

"Oh nothing. It's just that you guys had a blowout when we were leaving Portland."

"Yes, you're right. I had forgotten that everybody knew about that."

Reed practically ran up the dock. He was surprised to see Tom's sister walking across the fish-buying building toward him. "Hi, Skip. How are you?" She smiled at him when she spotted him.

"Hi, Joanne! What are you doing down here?"

"Brother dear called and wanted me to bring him something from home."

"Well, aren't you nice? He's down on the boat. He's out on deck, so just yell to him. He'll come right up. I'd take you down, but I got to make an important phone call. Nice to see you, Joanne."

Reed hurried off. He liked Joanne. He thought about all the great times he'd had at their little house when they were growing up, but that was a different time and a different life.

When he got in the phone booth, he was so nervous he fumbled around and dropped two quarters on the floor. He finally got them stuffed in the thing and dialed the number. Like always, he had this creepy feeling he was being watched, but he ignored it. The phone rang. "Yup." That same caustic, nasty-sounding voice. Reed said, "It's me." Without any hesitation he continued. "He's on board. We'll be there at midnight in five days. You got the bearings?"

"No . . . call me tomorrow."

The line went dead. Skip's confidence was growing. Fuck these guys. They needed him now.

Joanne found Tom. He came up on the wharf and got the box from her. They hugged, and he thanked her for coming. Joanne said, "Good luck. Let me know how things turn out for you down here."

"I will, Joanne. Thanks again."

Joanne said good-bye and left. He went back down aboard the boat. They were all fueled and iced. He needed to get some grub, but he figured he'd wait on that until Kathy got there. She's coming with a mystery guest. How much fun is this going to be!

When Reed made it back down to the boat, the rest of the crew was sitting at the galley table. There was hot coffee again and he sat down. He knew what was coming, but he really didn't give a shit. Scanton started out, "Boys, I got a huge problem. My wife fucked me over, and she fucked you over in the process." He explained what Karen had done and handed everybody their checks. They were short by a total of $10,000. It was about four grand for Pat and Skip and three for Tom.

Chase said, "Well, fuck her, and fuck this shit. I'm out of here! I don't work for nothing for nobody." He got up from the table and went into his bunk, grabbed his gym bag, and started packing his stuff.

Reed said, "Jesus, Pat . . . come on. What are you doin'? Joey's been great to you, for Christ sake."

"Mind your own fuckin' business, Reed. I'm not letting anybody steal from me and then stay on their fuckin' boat!" Chase walked back through the galley. On the way up the stairs he said, "You still owe me the money." He pointed his finger at Joey. Everybody was silent.

Scanton finally said, "Just let him go. I wish I could storm off the boat mad myself."

Chase had fished a long time and been through this kind of crap before. He was pissed, and no one could blame him. Reed was thrilled to see him leave the boat, and he hoped it would be permanent.

After they sat there a while, not really saying anything, Anderson got up from the table. He said, "Anybody hungry?"

Joey said, "Yes, as a matter of fact, I'm starving."

"Breakfast or lunch?"

Skip said, "Breakfast would be great."

Anderson got the stove going and threw on some bacon. They were all still at the table when they heard a voice coming from up in the pilothouse. "Hello below!"

Scanton said, "Come on down, Charley, and have some breakfast."

Charley Perkins came down into the galley. He was loaded to the hilt and he staggered down the stairs. "How the *fuck* are you, good people?"

"We're all good. How the hell are you, Charley?"

"Jesus, Joey. I'm good, real good."

Scanton had a smile on his face. "Wait a minute. Is that you, Charley, or your twin brother?"

"Jesus, Joey, did that bastard follow me aboard this fine boat of yours? Throw him right straight overboard if you catch him, will ya? He's been doin' nothing but raisin' hell for a week now, and I'm goddamn sick of it!" Charley pulled out a Camel and a huge wad of cash. After he lit up he started counting out five separate piles of money. He was dealing it out on the table and licking his fingers as he counted.

Charley said, "Where's that big fella Pat, anyway?"

"He's having his period so he went to the store after some tampons," Joey said.

Charley smiled at that one. "Is that right? Well, I hope that clears up for him. I like that fella, yes, I do, goddamn it."

Charley gave everybody $250. He kept the same for himself. Scanton picked up Chase's share.

Charley joined the crew for a breakfast of eggs, home fries, and bacon. He ate enough for himself and his imaginary twin brother. They finished up their food and got ready to leave the boat. Charley said, "I'm feeling kind of tuckered out after that fine meal. You mind if I stretch out down forward for half a minute, Joey?"

"Christ no, go ahead," Scanton said. "Stay as long as you want to, Charley."

"Thanks, Joey."

"Come on, Skip, let's slide the boat back into a berth and tie her up." Anderson and Reed went out on deck. Joey fired up the boat, and they moved her back a slot and tied her off. He left the genset running for shore power.

Anderson went down forward and packed a few clean clothes in a duffel bag and left the boat.

Joey just left. He was headed for the bar and he was going as is. If somebody didn't like how he smelled they could kiss his ass.

CHAPTER 57

Reed brought some stuff with him. He had called a cab this morning to pick him up and take him to his hotel by three o'clock. The cab was there waiting at the prearranged time. He had a regular room in one of the local places in downtown Rockland. As soon as he got there he checked in. There wasn't anybody around. It was September. He had the whole second floor to himself. He went into his room, left the door unlocked, and hopped into the shower. The water felt great as it poured down over his head and shoulders. He put shampoo in his hair and scrubbed out the salt and grime. He let the water cascade down over his body.

His eyes were closed when she slipped into the shower behind him. She put her arms around his waist and pulled her naked body into his back. He could feel the shape of her perfect breasts as they touched against him. He became immediately erect. His dick was so hard it was painful. He turned to look at her. It had been a few weeks now since he'd seen her, and she was so beautiful he couldn't believe it. He kissed her full on the lips. She slid her tongue into his mouth and moved it around in a slow sensuous motion. When she pulled back she looked him straight in the eye and, without looking away, dropped to her knees. She took his penis in her mouth and started sucking him. He couldn't take his eyes off her. She had the soap in one of her hands and was gently massaging him. She slid her finger up into him and he almost fell down on the shower floor. She was still watching him when he came in her mouth. She didn't stop sucking until he had completely finished. Those eyes, those beautiful deep green eyes, he'd never forget how they watched him while he came. She stood up and he took her in his arms and said, "I love you, babe. I really do."

"I know you do." She had gorgeous dark-brown hair that fell long over her shoulders. They got out of the shower, toweled off, and went out into the bedroom. She got dressed and said, "How's everything looking, Skip?"

"It's all on track. It won't be long now."

"Good, I'm sorry but I can't stay. I've really got to get back. Call me when you can."

She was out the door and gone before he could say anything. He laid down on the bed after she split and lit up a joint. He stayed there for about a half hour. He felt himself get erect again so he jerked himself off. When he did all he could think about was what she had just been doing to him. After he came he rested quietly for a while and fell asleep. He stayed that way until about seven thirty.

CHAPTER 58

When Kathy pulled her car up to the wharf, Tom was standing there waiting. She jumped out and flew into his arms. She held back and didn't comment on how he smelled this time. While he was holding her, Tom was thinking how great it was to be in love.

"Hey, where's this mystery guest of yours? I don't see anybody."

Kathy took Tom by the shoulders and pushed him back away from the car.

"Now you just stand right here a minute, Tommy dear."

Kathy went over to the car's passenger side and flipped the seat forward. She reached in the back and unbuckled Matty from his car seat. She pulled him out and took his little hand, and they walked around the car together. Kathy said, "Tommy, this is my little boy Matty."

A huge smile came across Tom's face when he saw this handsome little man.

Matty said, "Are you Tom?"

"I sure am."

"My mommy really likes you. She says I'm going to really like you too. I really like football. Do you like football?"

"I sure do, Matty. Maybe you and I can play sometime."

"Okay, Tom. When?"

Kathy said, "All right, Matty, we gotta give Tom a chance to get cleaned up first."

"Mommy, why does Tom smell so bad?"

"He's been working on a big boat that catches fish. We'll get him smelling good again in a little while."

"That would be good, Mommy." He scrunched up his face and held his nose. Kathy and Tom laughed until they were both in tears.

Matty said, "What's so funny?"

"You are, baby boy, you are."

They went over to the car and Tom said, "Can I help you get in, tough guy?"

Matty said, "Sure, tough guy."

"We're both tough guys, aren't we, Matty?"

"Yup!"

Kathy said, "Where to, Tom?"

"I don't care. Just drive downtown and pick a place. It's September, there's plenty of vacancies." "Okay." As they drove away from the fish dealer's, Kathy looked over at Tom with a half smile and raised both eyebrows. She didn't have to say anything because her look said it all. Tom started to laugh when their eyes made contact. "Well, when you bring a surprise guest, you really bring one."

"Uh huh." She nodded her head. "So what do you think?" She was anxious for his answer.

"I'm thrilled, but I can't wait to hear the story behind this one."

"Are you really thrilled, Tom?"

"Absolutely." Tom looked over at Kathy. She had tears running down her cheeks. She choked a little and said, "You promise, Tommy?"

He reached over and put his hand on her arm and said, "Oh yes, I promise. I love you so much, Kathy . . . everything is all right."

"Oh, I love you, Tommy."

"I have a big surprise for you too, Kathy."

Kathy sniffled a little and wiped her eyes and said, "You do?"

"Yes, I do! And it's even better now."

"I can't wait to hear what it is. Tell me."

"You'll have to hold your horses for a little while."

Kathy made a face. They drove downtown and found a nice-looking motel on the main street and pulled into a space. Tom looked into the backseat, and the little boy was sound asleep. He looked over at Kathy and nodded back toward him. She whispered, "Long day for little cowboys."

"Can I get him?" Tom said.

"Sure you can. I'll run right in and get us a room." He let Matty sleep in his seat and waited by the car.

While he stood there he thought, *Wow, this is huge.* He loved Kathy so much, and he was already in love with her little boy. When it's right, its right, and he couldn't wait to get into their room. Kathy was back in a few minutes with the room key. They were only two spaces away from their door. Tom reached in the back and unbuckled Matty and pulled him out of the car. He didn't wake up but he curled into Tom's neck and chin. He was sucking his thumb, sound asleep. Kathy's heart was about to explode with love for these two.

When they got into the room and when Tom put Matty down on one of the beds, he barely stirred. Kathy pointed and whispered, "You, in the shower." Now she made a face and held her nose. Tom smiled and very softly said, "Okay, I get it." He went in the bathroom and got undressed. Kathy followed him in with a large clear plastic bag for his fish clothes. She had to laugh at him when she saw him standing there with an erection. He looked down and said, "I can't help it."

"I'm glad. Now get in the shower." The shower felt great. He scrubbed his arms and hands with a nail brush until they were bright red. He shampooed his hair and rinsed it under the wonderful-feeling hot water.

Kathy climbed in and said, "We've got to be quick. Matty could wake up any second." They were quick. It didn't matter to Tom. He couldn't remember when he had been happier or more excited in his whole life. He hopped out of the shower and toweled off. He went out and got into his fresh clothes. Kathy stayed in the shower and washed her hair.

Tom stretched out on the second bed and was asleep in an instant. Kathy came out of the bathroom, got dressed, and curled up with him. They woke up about six thirty.

Matty came over and climbed in bed with them and snuggled down with his mother. He laid there, staring at Tom with a half smile on his face. Tom said, "Hi, little guy."

"Hi, stinky guy."

Tom laughed and said, "Hey, are you hungry, Matty?"

He said, "Yes."

"If you could have anything you wanted for supper, what would it be?"

Matty answered immediately, "A hot dog!"

"Okay, a hot dog it is!" Tom said with a big smile.

They got ready and went out for a walk and found a little a family restaurant called Watson's. The place had tables and chairs along a wall of windows overlooking Rockland Harbor. It wasn't fancy but it was nice. They had small glass candles on the tables with red-and-white checkered tablecloths. The waitress brought over a booster seat for Matty, and they ordered their drinks and dinner. Kathy ordered a chicken mushroom dish, Tom a double cheeseburger, and Matty got his hot dog with french fries.

Tom was very fidgety. He didn't seem to be able to sit still. Kathy said, "Tommy, what *is* the matter with you?"

"Okay, I can't stand it anymore."

He reached in his pocket and pulled out a little black heavily worn jewelry box. He said, "Kathy, I love you. Will you marry me?"

Kathy's mouth popped open and her eyes got big. She jumped out of her seat, came around the table and climbed onto Tom's lap, and threw her arms around his neck.

"Yes, yes, yes, I'll marry you! Of course I'll marry you!" They hugged each other and kissed. Matty said, "Am I getting married too?"

Tom said, "Yes, you are if you want to, Matty."

"I will if Mommy wants to."

"It's a deal, Matty." The other people seated around them applauded.

They had a great time together that night. The ring had belonged to Tom's grandmother on his dad's side. It was a small antique diamond set in a silver band that had been given to her back in Norway. Kathy loved it. She thought it was the most beautiful ring she had ever seen.

They finished their dinners and had some great homemade ice cream. They walked back toward the motel, and Matty kind of dragged behind, pulling on Kathy's hand. She said, "What's the matter, honey?"

"Can I ask you something, Mommy?"

"Of course you can. What is it, Matty?"

"Is Tom going to be my new daddy?"

"Yes, he is, darling." Matty had huge tears in his eyes and said, "Will he take me away from you, like my other daddy did?" Kathy swept him up into her arms, held him close to her, and started to cry. She couldn't believe that her decision to allow his real father into his life could have put this perfectly innocent child in such peril.

She said, "No, honey, no. No one will ever take you away from me again, ever. I promise."

"Okay, Mommy, then I want to marry Tom too."

"Okay, baby, okay. We will." She showered him with kisses until he squirmed and turned his head away and said, "Cut it out!"

CHAPTER 59

W hen Scanton climbed off the boat he had a paper bag in his hand with $9,000 in cash in it. He put it in the mailbox outside the fish building and closed the lid. He looked around to see if anybody was watching. No one was. He decided to walk to his favorite Rockland bar, the Thorndike. He knew Pat would be held up in the place drinking away his anger and sorrows, and he wanted to see him.

When he walked into the Thorndike, the place was rocking. He looked across the packed bar room, and there they were. A pre-jail group if he had ever seen one—Pat Chase, Rusty Martin, Dave Wilson, Charley Perkins, and Skipper Cathcart, all sitting at a big table over by the back wall. This was going to be trouble with a capital *T*.

When Chase saw Joey coming, he tried to get up and leave.

Rusty said, "You sit the fuck down, Pat, or I'll have my new best friend Hacksaw come over here and straighten your miserable ass out." Pat was stuck between Rusty and Dave. He was pinned in his chair up against the back wall. He was going nowhere. He had already downed four shots with two beer chasers, and he was feeling no pain.

Chase said, "All right, I'll drink with him, but I ain't going to have any fun, goddamn it." Rusty and Dave laughed.

Skipper Cathcart said, "There by Jesus, Pat, that'll show him!" They all laughed some more. Even Pat chuckled a little. Joey grabbed a chair, sat down, and said, "Charley, where's your twin brother at?"

"We locked that prick in Rusty's truck. He's been thrown out of here so many times in the last month you wouldn't believe it. I didn't want him wreckin' our evening of socializing!"

Scanton said, "Where's the waitress anyway?" Skip Cathcart hollered to a pretty girl who was waiting tables near them, "Hey, Judy, Joey needs a cold one."

Judy Carlson worked at the Thorndike because this is where she could make the most money in what she saw as a godforsaken hole of a town. The fishing guys treated her okay, and they tipped her really well. In the summer months the tourist business was pretty good. Then everyone in town went back into survival mode for another ten months. On a few rare occasions Judy would ask her mother to keep her son overnight. Then she would favor one of these young studs with a night of lovemaking. She thought her life really sucked, and for the most part, it did.

Scanton convinced Chase to come over to the bar with him, where they could talk alone. Chase complied reluctantly. Once they were seated he handed him his shack money. Joey said, "I'm really sorry about your crew share of the money from this trip. You do know two things though, Pat. Number one, I didn't screw up and lose the fuckin' money—I had it stolen from me. Number two, I'll pay you all of your money if it's the last thing I do."

Chase said, "If I didn't know that you and Karen had been having such a hard time with each other, I'd think you were part of this bullshit!"

That statement hurt, but Joey took the accusation in stride. He knew Chase was angry and worried about his paycheck. Anyone would feel that way and Joey didn't blame him. He figured that cruel remark from Pat was mostly the booze doing the talking anyway.

Scanton turned toward Pat and looked him straight in the eye. "I'll make you a deal, Pat. You come back, and I'll have all your back money when we get ashore. Then I'll kick Skip Reed off the boat." Pat looked at Joey and pulled his head back just slightly in total surprise. He thought seriously about dragging things out a little longer to teach Scanton a lesson. He wasn't about to be taken advantage of by anybody, but this was too good.

Now Chase had a huge grin on his face. "You serious about shit-canning that asshole?"

Joey said, "I think he's been manipulating things to get what he wants. He's been trying to use me, and I know it. Well, the user is about to be used."

Pat took a swig from his beer. "I have absolutely no idea what you're talking about."

"It's probably better that you don't know . . . trust me."

"All right, goddamn it, it's a deal! Can I fire him, Joey?"

"No, that's my job to fire guys off the boat."

"Pleeease?"

Scanton laughed, "We'll see, Pat, we'll see."

They tapped their beer bottles together to clinch the deal.

Pat and Joey were sitting there enjoying their beers and talking about nothing when they overheard a guy dressed in a blue blazer, white slacks, and a pair of penny loafers playing the big-time sea-dog role. He was holding court in a loud voice for a couple of hard-looking bimbos decorated in multicolored tramp stamps. The one on the left had a lovely rose on her left breast, and the other had a Harley insignia across her back just above her tight jeans. The three of them were sitting directly across the bar from the boys. The women were totally enthralled with this guy, or at least they appeared to be.

Joey and Pat overheard the guy say, "Yes, I graduated from the Maine Maritime Academy at Castine, and I was at the top of my class." Joey rolled his eyes and thought, *Lie*. The brunette with the big tits said, "So what are you doing now?"

"I'm the quartermaster on board the coastal oil tanker *Harold B. Trenton*. We hail from Boston.

When Scanton looked at Chase, he knew the shit was going to hit the fan. This was the asshole that had almost run them down at sea off Sigsbee Ridge. Chase stood up and walked around the end of the bar and stepped in close behind him. The self-promoting tanker admiral turned around and said, "Excuse me, but can I *help you*?"

Chase said, "Yeah asshole. You can give me back my fuckin' can of peas before I kick your goddamn ass!"

When the guy looked at Pat and figured out who he was, his face turned stark white. He knew he was in line to get one hell of a beating, and he was terrified. He jumped down off his bar stool, ran, and pushed his way through the crowd to get out of the bar. He almost knocked Judy the waitress over while she was carrying a tray full of beers. He got very lucky for a second time and didn't bump into her. He ran out the front door of the Thorndike and down the main street.

Chase and Scanton went back to sit down at their table with the boys. Rusty said, "Who was that guy, Pat? What did you do? Ask him to dance?" Scanton told the story. Everybody in the group already knew about the coastal tanker almost hitting the *Jubilee*. They couldn't believe that guy had the dumb ass luck to show up in this bar on a night when Joey Scanton and his crew were in town.

Everyone at the table had a big laugh about it, and for a short while, Joey was feeling like himself again. The loud music blasted away, and they got drunker and drunker. Nothing of any great consequence happened that night except for Skipper Cathcart making a great pass at Judy about an hour before closing time. She had brought another round of beers to their table, and when she served them she came within what Skipper Cathcart liked to call a "striking distance." Cathcart was undoubtedly what women referred to as extremely handsome. He was a little over six feet tall and was about 225 pounds of solid muscle. He had grown up in Massachusetts and had done very well in school, and it came through in his manners and his speech. He had a nice way about him and spoke without using vulgarities constantly to get his point across. Skipper had very fine light blond hair that made some women jealous. When Judy bent across in front of him to place the beers on the table, he reached out and slipped his arm very gently around her waist. She felt his embrace and pulled back a little. Skipper said, "What do you think, Judy darling? You and me tonight?"

She thought, *That's not what you'd call a clever pickup line, but it was direct.* She looked at Skipper's big blue eyes and leaned down and kissed him right on the mouth. "I'll call my mother. I'll see you at closing time, darlin'." She went back to waiting on the other customers.

The boys at the table were impressed as hell and came out with a collective "Wow!" As Judy walked away from their table, she thought, *Could I possibly be a bigger idiot? Hey, baby, you look like nothing but trouble, want to come to my house for overnight?* She still called her mother though. Her son would be spending the night at grandma's house.

Later on Pat called Leslie. As soon as she heard his voice, she knew he was drunk. She said she'd be down in the morning and hung up.

CHAPTER 60

Bert Goldman said, "Another big day . . . at the DEA." His team had made an arrest just outside of Damariscotta. They got a guy they had been watching for a long time. He had been picked up on Route 1, headed south, in a gold Cadillac at about six o'clock. His name was Vito Scantini. The guy was the son of a mob-related, old-school crook named Salvatore Scantini. Goldman and his team of investigators were pretty sure that Vito had been acting on his own, outside the family business, dealing heroin and cocaine. They had reason to believe that he was trying to make some extra money dealing drugs apart from his regular income as a strong-arm collections enforcer for his father. The older generation guys like Salvatore Scantini didn't like the drug trade as a part of their normal criminal activities. The elder Scantini was a relatively small-time loan shark who also dealt in bookmaking and prostitution activities. Drugs were too complicated. They involved too many outsiders of a different ethnic background than he liked to do business with. The reasoning behind that choice was because these drug guys, for the most part, used drugs themselves; so they couldn't be trusted to do what they were supposed to do. He saw them as unreliable. Goldman believed that the Salvatore Scantinis of the world liked total control over their businesses.

When the arresting officer, one of Goldman's top field agents, accosted Vito Scantini, he was a complete whimpering coward. This schoolyard bully was nothing. The sloppy fat punk that had threatened and humiliated other human beings for a living was a sniveling wimp when he finally got caught.

A surveillance team had been tailing him for over six months. Down in Rockland they had observed him removing a large sum of cash from a mailbox at a fish-buying operation. When they pulled him over and searched the vehicle, they found $9,000 and approximately $3,000 worth of cocaine in a plastic baggie. In the trunk they discovered an unregistered semiautomatic handgun and a shotgun with seven slugs in the chamber. Scantini kept saying, "I need to call my father!" The arresting officer assured him that he was most anxious to have him contact his father. They would be very interested in having a conversation with Salvatore Scantini at his earliest convenience. Vito Scantini was immediately booked and confined at the Androscoggin County Jail, where he would await questioning.

Goldman's office was busy. There were a lot of things going on, as usual. When the call came in informing him of the Scantini arrest, he stuck his head into Agent Lamb's office. "You up for a little overtime work tonight? I think I want to ride down to Androscoggin County Jail and meet Mr. Vito Scantini. He sounds like a fun person that I'd like to get to know better."

"Sure, Bert . . . your car or mine?"

"Let's take that cool little BMW you've been running around in all summer."

CHAPTER 61

V ito Scantini had never been as scared of anything in his life
as he was of the mess he was in now. They had booked him
for illegal possession of firearms and possession of cocaine with the
intent to distribute, conspiracy, and a host of other things that he
didn't understand. There was some crap about an illegal business
and concealed weapons. When they arrested him, they read him his
Miranda rights and cuffed him. They forced him into the back of a
government car. He was so upset he didn't know exactly who had
arrested him, but he was pretty sure it was drug enforcement guys
with backup from the Maine state troopers. When they got him to
the county jail, they strip-searched him, fingerprinted him, and
threw him in a cell. He was terrified.

After about an hour passed, they let him make a call to his father.
He was pretty sure they were monitoring the call, but he wasn't
positive. When he finally reached his father, he said, "Dad, it's Vito,
and I'm in real trouble." The line went dead. His father had hung up
on him. Vito started to shake uncontrollably. They took him back to
his cell and slammed the cell door shut.

He sat there on the bunk, still shaking. He waited about another
three hours, and finally, one of the guards came and got him. They
chained his feet and hands, and he was shuffled down a long corridor
past other inmates to an interrogation room. There were two guards,
one on each shoulder. The room was about ten by twelve with a
large mirror that Vito knew was an observation mirrored glass that
allowed, God knows how many people, standing on the other side,
to watch and hear what he had to say. He was only there about five
minutes when two men entered the room. One guy was a younger
Oriental-looking man and the other was a medium-sized older man.

Agents Lamb and Goldman walked around the table and sat
down. Goldman took one look at Vito and hollered out to the guard,

"Are these chains and handcuffs absolutely necessary? If not, please remove them from this gentleman right away." Goldman had used this tactic a million times. He had ordered them to be put on the prisoner himself. Vito relaxed a little after the chains were removed. He thought, *At least this guy's going to treat me with a little respect.*

Goldman introduced himself. "I'm Agent Goldman, the senior special agent in charge for the United States Department of Justice, Drug Enforcement Administration of the State of Maine." Both agents were wearing their federal badges on chains hanging from their necks. "This is Special Agent Lamb. I would like to ask you just a few questions . . . if that's all right," he continued.

Scantini mustered what little bit of courage he had left and, in a weak and shaky voice, said, "I ain't saying nothing." Goldman smiled one of his best winning smiles and said, "Vito—do you mind if I call you Vito?"

Vito answered defiantly, "That's my name."

Goldman didn't hesitate, "Vito, I respect your right to not talk to us. I really do, but I think you might want to reconsider your position when I enlighten you about your potential upcoming future in the federal prison system."

Goldman explained in detail what Scantini was facing for charges and the likely sentences that would be imposed against him. The man sat in his chair trembling. Goldman told him that he would probably be looking at a minimum of fifteen years in a federal prison.

Goldman's prisoner interrogation strategy was to bring a folder of photographs taken by his agents of the suspect. He spread twenty nine-by-eleven pictures on the table in front of Scantini. His eyes got big when he looked at the pictures and saw himself in every one. Sweat beads began to appear on his forehead. There were restaurant shots, street pictures, photos of meetings he'd had in cars, and a whole lot more. He couldn't believe that someone had taken all of these without him knowing it. He looked up at Agent Goldman and said, "Holy shit, I'm fucked!" Goldman smiled and replied, "In a couple of words, yes . . . you're fucked."

He convinced Scantini that he might be able to get his charges dramatically reduced if he cooperated with him in his investigation. Vito decided that cooperation was the right choice. He gave up and verified suspects that Goldman and Lamb had been working on for at least a year. They were both amazed that this not-too-bright, small-time gangster had as much information as he did. Goldman was listening to him spill his guts and betray everyone from the small-timers to the midlevel organizers. Most of the information that Scantini was coming up with was already known to Goldman and Lamb, but confirmation of information was key to helping close the loop on some other open cases.

They were almost finished with the interrogation when a guard knocked on the door. Agent Lamb got up and opened it.

"Agent Goldman," the guard said, "excuse me, but there's an attorney out here that says he represents Vito Scantini." The attorney marched past the guard and into the interrogation room. When he entered the room he said, "Mr. Scantini, my name is Brewer. I'm an attorney and have been retained by your father to represent you in this matter. I'm hoping you haven't said anything up to this point in time."

Scantini was pissed. "Too late, asshole. Tell my father thanks for hanging up on me when you talk to him again."

Brewer said, "Goldman, this interview is over. I need to meet with my client alone, immediately."

Agent Goldman smiled and pushed back from the table. "Agent Lamb, I think you and I are done here. We should be seeing you again a little later on, Mr. Scantini. As a matter of fact, I'm absolutely sure of it." Goldman and Lamb left the room.

After the federal agents walked out and closed the door, Vito Scantini had never in his entire life felt as alone as he did then.

CHAPTER 62

When Tammy and Danny woke up in the morning they got dressed right away and went down to the dock to get the on the early ferry into Portland. Tammy had placed a call from the store on the island and left a message with a law firm that she was coming into town and wanted to see her attorney, Richard Sanders, as soon as she could.

This was the first time she had been off Green Island in almost a year. They stood up in the bow of the ferry alone as it steamed across the bay. It was still warm enough to be comfortable out on deck, and she hated to be around a bunch of nosy islanders. They got off at the ferry terminal in Portland and walked up to a twelve-story office building located on Congress Street, where Richard Sanders practiced law.

When they approached big fancy glass doors to the building, Danny asked Tammy if it was okay if he stayed out on the street. He found the whole situation totally intimidating. Tammy said, "Sure . . . What the hell." Danny sat on a bench outside and smoked one cigarette after another while he waited.

Tammy went in and found the elevator and rode up to the eleventh floor. She thought, *This is one high-class expensive law firm.* She could see Green Island from the windows in the reception area that overlooked Portland Harbor. She wanted out of this place as fast as humanly possible. The receptionist was a cute, little, snotty twenty-something who looked at Tammy like she was trailer trash. Tammy had worn a pair of jeans with holes and rips on the knees and an olive-green T-shirt with no bra. She considered this outfit island chic, but the receptionist was unimpressed. The girl called Attorney Sanders's office and let his secretary know that a Ms. Carlson was there.

Tammy waited about ten more minutes and Richard Sanders rounded the corner. The receptionist was a little taken aback. Mr. Sanders never left his office to greet any clients unless they were extremely important. He always sent that nasty bitch secretary, Mrs. Peters, instead.

When he approached her, he said, "Hi, you must be Tammy Carlson. I'm Richard Sanders, but please call me Rick." For reasons she couldn't put a finger on, Tammy immediately liked this guy. He exuded a level of confidence that impressed her, and she felt immediately comfortable with him.

Attorney Sanders escorted her back to his office and offered her a seat. Mrs. Peters looked in and asked her if she would like a coffee or anything else to drink. Tammy thought, *I'd like a hit on a joint if you got one of those going, lady.* She declined the offer of coffee. Sanders started out the conversation. "Well, Tammy, I kind of expected you to come in to see me today . . . happy birthday."

She smiled and said, "Thanks, Mr. Sanders—I mean Rick." No one had said happy birthday to her in many, many years. Even though she knew this was business, she was still a little touched, but she wanted to get right to the point of today's meeting. "You know I'm here about the money. Do I get it now?"

Rick couldn't help but smile at Tammy's directness. "The trust money is now available to you, and you can do anything you want with it. Under the terms of your grandfather's will, you've had your thirtieth birthday, and you may now have it all."

"I don't even know how much money it is."

Sanders pulled out a folder and opened it.

"As of this morning the balance in the trust account is $741,062.51." Tammy suddenly took a deep breath. She said, "Holy shit!"

He smiled and said, "It is quite a large sum of money. I hope you appreciate that this firm has done a very good job managing this trust for you and that you will continue to allow us to represent you in the future."

Tammy said, "Yeah, whatever. When can I have the money?"

"That depends on how much you want and how you want it."

"A friend of mine and I want to go away for a while, and we need some money to do that. How about $20,000? Could I get that, like today?"

Very quietly, Sanders said, "Tammy, you can have whatever you want. I'll be happy to cut a check as trustee for you. Whatever financial needs you have, in terms of cash or credit, all you need to do is contact my secretary, Mrs. Peters. She will notify me, and your money will be available to you almost immediately."

Tammy was very excited. "No shit? Cool!"

Rick and Tammy spent at least another hour together reviewing and discussing her trust fund. He called a friend of his at a bank that did a lot of business with his firm and made an immediate appointment for her to get a checking account and a charge card. The bills for her expenses, from this day forward, were to all be sent and paid for through his firm. When they finished, he escorted Tammy to the elevator. They shook hands and she thanked him for all his help.

He said, "Good-bye, Tammy, and good luck. Don't hesitate to call me with anything you need." Tammy promised she would as the elevator door closed.

Sanders watched her leave and thought, *I'd rather have shot the money out the window as paper airplanes than do what I just did.* He went back to his office. Mrs. Peters let him know there were three other clients waiting to see him.

CHAPTER 63

When Tammy came back out and onto the street, Danny was there waiting for her. He said, "Well, how did it go?" Tammy had a serious look on her face like she was worried. "If you mean did I get the money, the answer is yes." She screamed a little and danced around him in a circle laughing.

Danny said, "Way to go, babe!" He hadn't called her that in years. Tammy thought, *It's funny what a big load of money can do to improve a relationship, particularly if it's yours.*

She said, "Danny, we've got to go next door and meet with a banker. I've got to get a checking account open and a credit card."

Tammy made it through the appointment and deposited her $20,000 check. When they left the bank, Danny said, "Exactly how much money is there anyway?"

"It came out to about $75,000."

"Wow! We're set for the rest of our lives with that kind of money!"

Tammy wasn't about to tell Danny how much money there really was. She didn't trust him at all after how he had been treating her all these years. They walked up Congress Street together hand in hand. Tammy spotted a little travel agency, and she went in and bought two one-way tickets to a place very far away from Maine and Green Island.

They caught the afternoon ferry back, packed a few personal items, left a note on the kitchen table for Andy, and closed the door to the little house. They rode the ferry back into Portland, got a cab to the airport, boarded a plane, and flew out. Tammy and Danny never set foot in Maine again. No one but Richard Sanders knew where they were or whatever became of them.

CHAPTER 64

Andy Brown had spent the past few days hanging around Falmouth. He bailed his impounded truck out from Villacci's. He and Gene had a few laughs over what a total asshole Junior Butland was. He still refused to tell him what he had used on Junior to get him to leave him alone down at McDonald's that morning.

Andy took the *Ruffian* out and hauled through some of the traps and caught a few lobsters. The gear was all straightened out now, so the hauling went a lot better. The pounds per trap had dropped off severely. He hated to admit it, but Skip Reed was a good lobster catcher. He hadn't seen or heard from his cousin Danny in at least three days. When he hauled down around Green Island, he could see Danny's boat on its mooring. He was planning to make another pot run soon. He figured he'd better get down there and get his instructions. That afternoon when he went down to the town landing, he went on foot. He wasn't going to have that asshole harbormaster Sonny tow his truck again. It was three thirty.

As he approached the island there was a fog bank rolling in from the southwest. On the way in, he ran past Danny's boat. It looked like no one had been aboard in a few days. The dead giveaway was the seagull shit all over the pilothouse roof and the decks. He ran the *Ruffian* into the island town dock, tied her off, and climbed the hill toward Danny's house. When he got there things looked totally abandoned. They weren't around. Hell, maybe they were down at the beach, but for some reason he didn't think so.

He walked into the house and yelled, "Hey! Anybody home!" No one answered. Then he noticed that on the kitchen table there was a note there addressed to him.

Dear Andy,

Tammy and I have left town. You can do a pot run if you want to but I suggest you don't. If you want to know when, you can go just turn on channel 65 and say, "Does anybody know when the Red Sox play again?" Somebody will come on and tell you, but that's just because people are helpful. That's not them answering. What you do is switch to 8 and listen. Somebody will come on the air and say a number. You deduct two from that number and that will be your time. You really shouldn't do this run though. That DEA asshole Goldman is closing in. We are gone and I'm not telling you where. The boat and house are yours now to keep. There is a map of where my gear is. You can have all my traps too. The keys to the boat are aboard under the radio bracket. Be smart and just live there and forget about the drug money. I probably won't ever see or talk to you again. Have a good life.

Danny

"Holy shit!" He couldn't believe it. Danny was the biggest pussy of all time. What the fuck was wrong with his head? Andy really couldn't have cared less though. The house, the boat, and traps were all his now. He was the king of the world. He had almost ten grand socked away under his bed and now all this. Life was great Wow, his own place. He sure as hell was going to do one more pot run. Why not? He could put the money into fixing up this old wreck of a house. He had standards after all. He loved the island and couldn't wait to live here full time.

Andy went over and opened up the refrigerator. There were some cold cuts in there and a loaf of bread on top of the counter and even a jar of mustard.

"Thanks, cousin, a free house and a free meal." How can you beat it? Andy had his sandwich and left to go back down to the dock. He got aboard the *Ruffian* and ran out to Danny's mooring. He loved his cousin's boat.

He figured he'd make his run in that boat tonight. It was a lot faster than this old tub of Reed's, and he was getting a little tired of it anyway. He was only borrowing it anyway, and Reed would take it back as soon as he showed up. Besides, he should move up in boats . . . he deserved it. He climbed over to Danny's boat. The first thing he planned to do was to get rid of that stupid *Frayed Knot* name and name her *Andy's Dream*.

He found the keys and started the boat up. He pulled out the wash-down hose and started spraying the seagull shit off the boat. If there was anything Andy hated, it was a dirty boat. He'd taught that to that Roger Bishop kid. After he got the boat cleaned up he turned on the radio and put it on 65.

"Anybody know when the Red Sox play again?" Two or three people answered with the game time. Andy switched to channel 8 and listened. Suddenly a voice said, "Fourteen."

Andy said to himself, "Well, all right. Eleven o'clock it is! No no no . . . midnight!" He swapped mooring lines from Danny's boat to the *Ruffian* and ran the boat into the dock.

The fog was so thick he couldn't see it at first, but he made it in and tied off *Andy's Dream* to the town float. He walked back up to the house. The place felt different now that it was his. He started poking around a little. They had left virtually everything. Danny's clothes were still in his closet and drawers. Andy was about the same size as Danny, so that was also good news. He would take all the junk he didn't want to the dump once he got his truck out here. It was only six thirty, so Andy flopped down on the couch and broke out his baggie of pot. He rolled a joint and lit it up.

Andy had never thought about his life in terms of happy or sad. Life just was. He felt a little uneasy about the fact that things were going well for him. He didn't want to trust what was happening for fear that it would all be taken away. He took another hit and tried to just let all that shit he was thinking about melt away in a cloud of exhaled smoke. It really worked pretty well. That was the beauty of this stuff . . . you could really avoid some nasty shit by staying stoned most of the time, and that was just fine with him.

He figured he had to be out of there by ten o'clock at the latest. He went into the bedroom and found an alarm clock beside the bed and set it. He lay down and pulled a blanket over himself and fell asleep. When the clock woke him up he looked outside. It still looked pretty foggy. He put a jacket on that he found in the kitchen hallway and walked down the hill to the dock. He got aboard the boat and started it up. He remembered that he had to steer a course of 147 degrees to get down to the Mud Buoy.

Danny's boat ran a lot quicker than Skip's. Andy was starting to get nervous. He had no idea where he was. He kept jogging along, getting more anxious by the minute. He could feel the change in the roll of the sea, so he knew he was outside the Hussey by now. He kept steaming, and then he slowed down to a crawl. He kept thinking about Danny's advice to call it good and quit the pot-lugging deal. Those doubts about whether to just turn around and go home kept running through his head. The harder he tried to figure out where he was, the more anxious he became. For the first time in Andy's life, he felt like he had something to lose.

He slowed down and pulled the boat out of gear. He was just plain scared and he hated the goddamn fog, particularly at night. He listened to the ocean. The wind was out of the east, and the waves around him were starting to break. He said to himself, *Fuck this . . . I got no one to prove anything to. These drug guys would just have to make it on their own without the help of Andy Brown.*

He swung the boat around and headed home. He ran up the Hussey and almost ran ashore on Cow Island. He turned off in just the nick of time when he heard the breakers on the southeast side of the island. After he got his bearings again, he did pretty well until he was up in the anchorage where he bumped up on York Ledge. Luckily he was able to back the boat off and pick his way back to Reed's mooring. In his whole life he had never been so happy to kill an engine as he was that night. He rowed ashore and walked home to his mother's trailer. It was 2:00 a.m.

CHAPTER 65

When Andy woke up, it was two o'clock in the afternoon. He had a lot of stuff to do. He had some canned spaghetti for lunch and got started with his packing. He was going to move to Green Island to his new house. There was a ton of junk he wanted to get rid of. He started loading his truck with it and headed to the dump. It was after five and he was only half done. On the way home he spotted Mary walking down the road. He stopped, pulled over, and asked her if she wanted to help him for a while. Mary said, "Sure, Mary will help Andy! What's Andy going to do?"

Andy said, "I have to take some things to the dump and pack my truck. I'm moving out to Green Island." Mary laughed and said, "All the islands are green. Andy is silly!"

Andy thought, *That's great when trailer park Mary thinks you're silly, you've pretty much struck the bottom.* He took Mary back to his trailer, and they started working on getting his stuff out. They loaded the truck with the things he wanted to take to the island first, and the rest for the dump went on top. He left a note for his mother and promised to call her later.

They headed for the dump. When they got there Andy threw the junk off his truck and climbed back in the cab. It was starting to get a little dark. He had brought his whole pot stash with him. His shoe box with the ten grand in it was stuffed under his seat. He was ready to move on with his life. He rolled a joint, laid back, and lit up. "Mary, I'll take you down to McDonald's and buy you a cheeseburger if you'll do the thing I like best."

"Okay, Andy. I'll do it. I like cheeseburgers." Andy unbuckled his pants and pulled them down. Mary got busy earning her cheeseburger.

Andy put his head back and took another deep hit on his joint. He was completely relaxed. So relaxed in fact he didn't hear Junior

Butland walk up beside his truck. Junior tapped his flashlight on Andy's window, and Mary started to scream. When Andy saw who it was he hollered, "Jesus, Junior, what are you trying do for Christ's sake?" Junior pulled his gun out of his holster, aimed it at Andy, and told him to step out of the vehicle. Mary was completely losing it now. Andy said, "Mary, calm down it's just Junior Butland. You're all right."

Junior got more aggressive, "STEP OUT OF THE VEHICLE!"

Andy said, "Back off, Junior!"

That did it for Junior. He opened the truck's door, reached in and pulled Andy out, and threw him onto the ground. Andy yelled, "For Christ's sake, Junior, take it easy!"

Andy was at a complete disadvantage. First of all, Junior was a big guy and Andy wasn't. Second was the fact that Andy's pants were down around his ankles. Junior cuffed him there in the dirt of the Falmouth town dump and called in for backup.

Junior had already spotted Andy's bag of pot. He still had his service revolver trained on Andy as if he were going to jump up with his pants down around his ankles and overthrow him. Andy's greatest fear was that Junior was so nervous that he might shoot him by mistake. He was lying on the ground with half his face in the dirt when he heard the sirens of the approaching police cars coming toward them from Middle Road. The sound made his stomach tighten.

"For god's sake, Junior, let me get up and pull my pants up, will ya?"

"Don't move, asshole, or you'll be sorry."

Andy started laughing. "Don't move or I'll be sorry? Jesus, Junior, that's a beauty!"

Mary was still sobbing uncontrollably, and the oncoming sirens were making it worse. She kept saying, "Mary's a good girl, not a bad girl. Mary's a good girl, not a bad girl." Junior yelled at her to shut up. It was less than five minutes before two more cruisers from Falmouth PD drove into the parking lot with their blue lights flashing.

Andy said, "Thank God, the backup has arrived." There were two officers in each vehicle, so now there were five cops to try to subdue Andy Brown and his mentally impaired girlfriend.

One of the cops grabbed him and snapped him to his feet. They pulled his pants up and threw him in the backseat of one of the cruisers. One of the men knew who Mary was. He got her calmed down by telling her she was a good girl. He said he'd give her a ride home. She asked if she was still going to get a cheeseburger at McDonald's. The cop said, "Sure, Mary, we'll get you a cheeseburger." The officer in charge told him to go ahead and take her home. Mary was thrilled. She waved good-bye to Andy as they drove her away in the cruiser.

The guy in charge was named Glen Morrison, a member of the Falmouth Police Department for more than ten years. He was experienced, knew his job, and how to do it. He began searching Andy's truck. The large baggie full of pot was more than enough for probable cause to proceed without a search warrant. Morrison had to admit that he was pretty surprised to find a cardboard box with almost $10,000 cash in it. The rest of the stuff in the truck was full of personal property, mostly junk.

"Andrew Brown, I hereby place you under arrest for possession of illegal narcotics in an amount sufficient to warrant arrest for drug trafficking with the intent to sell to others."

He read Andy his *Miranda* rights and put him back in the police car. After he closed the door he acknowledged Junior Butland.

"Good job, Officer. I'm taking this guy into Cumberland County Jail. Notify the guys over at the DEA. I think Special Agent in Charge Goldman will be interested in this guy." Junior Butland was ecstatic. He was going to get to notify the DEA about his collar. He was on his way right to the top. There was no doubt about it.

Andy Brown couldn't believe what was happening to him. One minute he's on the top of the world with a new house, a boat, a gang of traps, and a blow job, and the very next thing he's off to jail for a bag of pot. He really didn't think this was going to be that big a deal. The money in the shoe box worried him some, but he'd just tell them that it was lobster money he'd been saving up. Nobody could prove where that money came from. The bag of pot wasn't a big thing either. He'd known all kinds of guys that had gotten a slap on the wrist for a bag of pot. He was surprisingly relaxed about the whole thing. Maybe the joint hadn't completely worn off yet.

By the time they arrived at the Cumberland County Jail, he wasn't as relaxed as he had been back at the dump. They were pretty rough with him when they booked him. He'd seen it on TV plenty of times, so he was sort of prepared for what was going to happen. Just like when they patted him down on the *Invincible,* that big pot boat, it looked a whole lot easier on TV.

They made him put on one of those orange jumpsuits and threw him in a cell with a guy who looked like a killer. He waited about two hours before a guard came and got him. They took him in chains to a small square room and left him in there by himself for about another half hour.

Finally, two guys came into the room. The older man didn't look familiar to him, but the younger one did. He couldn't place him to save his life. The older man said, "Mr. Brown, I'm the senior special agent in charge for the United States Department of Justice, Drug Enforcement Administration for the State of Maine. My name is Agent Goldman." He showed his badge before introducing Agent Lamb. He spoke softly, "This gentleman here is Special Agent Lamb. How are you doing this evening, Mr. Brown?"

Andy had his head down when he spoke. "Not too good."

Agent Goldman said, "No, I can imagine being arrested on a fine evening like this is not a good thing to have happen to you. Not that I've ever had that experience myself. I can only imagine what it must be like." Andy thought, *This guy is nuts.*

"Mr. Brown? It's Andy, isn't it? Do you mind if I call you Andy?"

"Sure, I guess."

"Andy, Agent Lamb and I work for the Justice Department. Our specialty is drug enforcement. Now you know that you are entitled to an attorney if you want one, or you can answer a few questions for us now. Would you care to answer some questions for us?"

Andy still thought he didn't have anything to worry about. "Sure, I'll answer your questions."

"They arrested you in Falmouth, is that right?" Goldman began.

"Yes, I was at the dump."

"They found a plastic bag full of marijuana in your possession. Could you explain to us how you happen to have that marijuana in your truck?"

"It was just some pot I had for my own use. It's no big deal."

"I agree with you, Andy. By itself, a baggie full of pot, for personal use, is no big deal. That's true. However, if it's just a small part of a bigger picture, then it can be a big deal. Do you know what I mean?"

"I guess so."

Goldman said, "There was a box full of cash in your truck, almost $10,000. That's a lot of money to me. Can you explain where all that cash came from?"

"That's my lobster money. I've been saving it for a long time."

"Who's Quarter Pound Brown? Is that someone you know? A relative or something?" Goldman said this with a puzzled look on his face.

Andy was a little embarrassed to have this guy bring that up. "That's a nickname some of the guys at the wharf call me. It's kind of a joke."

Goldman smiled. "Oh, I see . . . a joke. What does it mean anyway, this joke? Do you eat more quarter pounders than the other guys down at the wharf or something?"

Andy thought, *This guy really doesn't get it.* "Yeah, Yeah, that's it. I love quarter pounders."

"Good, Andy. If this interview takes a long time maybe we can send out for some quarter pounders. I bet you'd enjoy that, wouldn't you?"

"Yeah, I guess."

"You've been doing a lot of guessing during this interview, and I have a question that you can't guess about, okay, Andy?"

"I guess."

Goldman just let it go. He started again. "Now you're absolutely sure that all that money was lobster money, Andy?"

"Yes . . . I saved it up."

"How long does it take for a lobsterman to save up that much money?"

"A long time."

"I bet you're right. I bet it would take you a very long time to save up that kind of money."

"I guess."

"Who is Danny Brown? Is he a relative of yours?"

"Yes, he's my cousin."

"Do you know his whereabouts?"

"His what?"

"Do you know where he is . . . where he might be at this time?"

"No, I don't. I think he went on vacation."

"Do you have any idea where he might have gone on vacation?"

"No, I don't."

"I have a few photographs I'd like to show you. Would you mind explaining what's in them for me, if you know, Andy?"

"I guess."

Goldman laid out thirty different photographs of Andy, the *Ruffian*, Andy in his skiff, Danny in his new boat, Danny in his old boat, the wharf, Danny unloading big white plastic-covered bales at night. There were shots of Andy unloading big white plastic-covered bales too, from the *Ruffian*.

Andy started to sweat. Goldman said, "Are you all right, Andy? Is it too hot in here for you? Because if it is, I know these guys who run this place, and I'll get them to turn the air-conditioning up for you. Do you want me to do that?"

Andy shifted in his seat. "No, I'm all right,"

"Are you sure, because I don't want you to be uncomfortable, Andy."

He shook his head no and just kept staring at the pictures.

Goldman pointed to the photograph of Andy unloading the bales. "What's in those white plastic square bags I see you working with there in this picture?"

"That's seaweed in those plastic wrappers . . . it's seaweed." Goldman turned to Joe Lamb.

"Well, Agent Lamb, that explains it. All along you and I have thought that there was marijuana in those wrappers, and Andy here has cleared that mistake up for us—it's seaweed."

Goldman raised his hands and had kind of a confused look on his face. "I'm relieved to know that that stuff is seaweed because, Andy, you would have been in a lot of trouble if that had been marijuana, but seaweed is no big deal. No big deal at all."

Andy started to feel a little more confident. "Yup, it's seaweed."

Agent Goldman took a deep breath. "Good, Andy . . . good. But I have a problem, and Agent Lamb here does too. That truck there in the picture that says 'Lively Lusty Lobsters' on it? Agent Lamb had one of our other agents follow that truck down the road. He pulled it over for a routine check. You're not going to believe this, Andy, but we found that those white plastic wrapper things were not full of seaweed at all. They were full of marijuana. I'm sure you're shocked to learn this information, just as we were."

"I thought it was seaweed, really," Andy stammered.

"Okay, Andy, I have to tell you something. If we are right and that really is marijuana in those pictures, you could be facing up to ten years in federal prison for drug trafficking."

Andy's hands began to shake. "But I really thought it was seaweed in those bags,"

Goldman pressed on. "I'm sure you did. I don't want you to be too upset. Prison isn't going to be that bad for you. When they arrested you, they told me that at that time you were getting a blow job from your girlfriend. Is that true?"

Andy said, "Well, yes, but she's not my girlfriend."

"But you do know her, right?"

"I guess."

"Do you like getting blow jobs, Andy?"

"Yeah, doesn't everybody?"

Goldman said, "Yeah, I guess . . . but in prison, the big difference there is . . . that instead of getting the blow jobs, you'll be giving them."

Andy looked at agent Goldman and turned stark white. The reality of his situation finally sunk in. He pushed back from the table and threw up all over himself.

Goldman called a guard. "Hey, come get this guy out of here, get him cleaned up, and bring him back afterward. I'm not done with him yet. Also send somebody out to get some quarter pounders. I think my prisoner may be hungry when he gets back."

Goldman looked over at Joe Lamb, smiled, and said, "I think this is going rather well, don't you?"

He and Agent Lamb took a walk around the jail and visited with a few people there on duty that they were friendly with.

By the time the guards bought Brown back to the interrogation room, he had had enough time to think things over and was fully aware of the seriousness of his predicament. He had only been sitting there for a very short time when Goldman and Lamb walked back into the room and sat down.

Agent Goldman said, "Are you feeling better, Andy?"

"No, not really. I'm in a lot of trouble, aren't I?"

Goldman's jaw clenched a little and he nodded his head. "Yes, you are, Andy. But maybe we can help you out, if you tell us all about everything you know about what you did and what else is going on out there in the bay."

Unfortunately for Andy, he really didn't know much. He explained in detail how the transfer of bales of pot from the *Invincible* to the lobster boat worked. He told them about the Mud Buoy and how you got bearings on channel 8. While they were talking, Andy stopped suddenly and said, "I know you now." He was looking at

Agent Lamb, "You're the guy taking all those pictures down at the wharf. I thought you were making a book or something."

Lamb said, "Guilty as charged." Goldman started laughing. "Now that's funny." The humor of that line escaped poor old Andy. They continued on and learned the code for getting pickup times. Goldman thought that it was very clever yet simple. They continued on for another hour. When things were finally winding down, Andy said, "Mr. Goldman? What's going to happen to me? I told you all about the *Invincible* and everything. They're the bad guys here."

Goldman said, "Well, Andy, it's like this. Last night at about 2:00 a.m., the United States Coast Guard boarded and seized the very boat you're talking about. They arrested the entire crew. They were all from South America, so they're under federal detainment in Portland right now. Your problem is that you didn't have anything of any significance to offer us. The overwhelming evidence against you and the federal warrant for drug trafficking and conspiracy to distribute creates a big problem for you."

Andy Brown looked like he was near tears. "What happens next?"

"First off they'll appoint a public defender for you, unless you have money for your own lawyer. Then they'll have an indictment hearing. If you're indicted, which is very likely, then after a while you go to trial. Then we see where it goes from there."

Andy didn't say anything. When they came to take him back to his cell, Andy said, "Thanks for not making fun of me, Mr. Goldman."

Goldman said, "Sure, Andy, sure."

Bert Goldman dealt with a lot of criminals in his day-to-day life, but as he walked away Senior Special Agent in Charge Goldman felt sad for Andy Brown.

CHAPTER 66

After the Thorndike closed for the night the gang broke up and headed back to their respective boats. Pat and Joey walked back to the dock. Charley Perkins decided to stay ashore and sleep it off on Dave Wilson's tug. Scanton knew that 90 percent of the reason Pat Chase had decided to come back aboard was to see Skip Reed get fired. Well, that was going to have to wait. He went up forward and hit the bunk and was out for the night.

The crew showed up about ten the next morning. Scanton said, "There are just a few things we have to do. Then you all can have the day to yourselves. We'll plan to meet back here and leave the dock at ten tonight. I'd like to be down to the Outer Falls before dawn and go after some of those flats down there."

"Where do we go for grub up here, Joe?" Anderson asked.

"Go see Florence. She's got a little pickup. I'm sure she'll let you use it."

Anderson headed up the dock but was back in about five minutes.

"Joey, Florence told me to let you know that your Uncle Sal called and wants you to call him from a pay phone," he said.

"What does that prick want now?"

When Sal Scantini answered the phone, he said, "Joey, you little bastard, I think you got my boy Vito in some big trouble. He's been arrested and he's in jail because of you!"

"Hold it, Uncle Sal. Why's he in jail?"

"They got him with the nine grand you gave him and some other shit. It don't matter. I think you called the cops on him because you don't like him, that's what I think."

"You're right on one count, wrong on the other."

"What the fuck are you talking about, Joey?"

"I don't like him, you're right about that. But I didn't call the cops on him."

"You been selling him coke?"

"You're losing it now, Uncle Sal. What did they catch him with?"

There was a long pause. "This ain't over, Joey, it ain't over. You still owe me the first nine grand too." The phone went dead.

Joey called home. When his mother answered the phone, he said, "Hi, Ma. How you doin'? You find Karen yet?"

"No, Joey, I haven't, and I'm so upset I can't stand it. I think she's really taken off. I cry all the time. Daddy's ready to throw me out."

"Is he there, Ma?"

"He's right here, honey. I won't let him go fishin' until we find my baby boy."

Peter picked up the phone. Joey said, "You talked to Uncle Sal recently, Dad?"

"No, Joey, I haven't. What do I need to talk to that prick about?"

"He just called up here raving about Vito getting arrested on some kind of drug charges. He was so nuts I really never got what it was about. He thinks I set Vito up. He told me it wasn't over, like he was out of the friggin' *Godfather* or something."

Peter was really getting pissed now. "What's this got to do with you, that piece of shit Vito getting arrested?"

"I don't know. Uncle Sal made me give Vito his nine grand in cash. If that fat fuck got picked up with a load of cash, a bag of coke . . . plus if he was packin' some kind of weapon he's screwed. Those three things are going to fix his ass for a long, long time, depending on what he had on him for dope."

"I'll deal with Sal about any threats to you. I can put that motherfucker in jail alongside his slug of a son!"

"Jesus, Dad, don't you get in any trouble over this shit. You told me to stay away from him, and I didn't listen."

Peter said, "Don't you worry about that, son. There's only one guy around here that Sal's really afraid of. That's Jimmy Desanto. I don't know what Jimmy's got on him, but I think it's pretty big. He won't fuck with you if he steps in. The best part of this is that the cops have got your nine grand, not Sal."

"Okay, Dad, I'm not arguing with you. Ma's got you tied to the wharf, I guess. Let me talk to her again."

Gloria picked up the phone. "Ma, let Dad go fishin', will ya? He's not a goddamn private eye. Karen's around somewhere. This is just some stuff between her and me. She loves Little Joey as much as I do. It'll be all right. Just give it a little time. I'm coming home to Portland after this trip. I'll get it straightened out then."

"I know, Joe, I know. All right, I'll let him go fishing. I just get so worried. You know how I am."

"I know, Ma. I love you. I've got to go."

"Okay, honey, call us when you're getting near Portland, okay?"

"All right, Ma, I will."

Scanton walked back down to the boat. Anderson had gone over to get the grub. Leslie Chase was standing on the dock, looking down at the *Jubilee.*

"Hi, Les." Joey gave her a hug. "I'm sure Pat must have told you what happened to me."

Leslie said, "Yes, he did. I'm so sorry, Joey."

"You know I'll get Pat his money no matter what, Leslie."

"I know, Joey. He's really been screwed before on other boats, and he's never gotten over it. It's really not personal against you, but I'm sure it feels that way."

"Thanks for that. Want me to get the old man off the boat for you?"

"That would be nice. Kathy wants us to go to lunch with she and Tom, you're included. I've got the keys to their room so Pat can get a shower."

Scanton said, "I've never met Kathy."

"Oh, she's great. You're going to love her. When Tom gave me the keys to their room, he was acting like the cat that swallowed the canary. I don't know what's up with those two."

"Huh? I don't know. I'll go get Pat. He's in the engine room."

When Scanton found him, Pat had all his mechanicals straightened out and was all set to go.

"I'll see you back here at ten and we'll sail," Scanton said.

"Finest kind, Joe. Hey, can't we complete our little deal now?" Chase was looking right at Skip Reed filling the freshwater tanks.

"Get out of here!"

Chase laughed and headed up the ladder.

CHAPTER 67

An hour later Anderson showed up with Florence's little truck, loaded with groceries. They got everything put away quickly. After they were done Reed spoke up and said, "I'm planning to hang out down here today. I'll see you guys tonight."

Scanton looked surprised. "All right, Skip, we'll see you then. If you want to warm up the boat around nine thirty, go ahead."

"Finest kind, Joey. You guys have a good day."

Scanton climbed the ladder thinking, *That's a first. Skip Reed wants to stay aboard the boat on a day off? Maybe he's sick and didn't say anything, still very weird.*

Reed couldn't wait for everybody to get the hell off the boat. He waited no more than ten minutes and walked up to the phone booth. He got into the phone booth and dialed his call. When the phone was answered he said, "I need the bearings." The man on the other end of the line said, "25375 12700." Skip repeated the bearings and wrote the numbers in his notebook. The voice said, "Four days gone, midnight" and hung up. Reed ran back down to the boat and pulled out the chart and hunted for the spot where the 25375 line crossed the 12700. It was on an edge of the Truxton Swell just to the east of the Hague Line.

He put a pencil mark on the chart where the bearings intersected and tossed the pencil up on the dashboard. He sat back in the captain's chair with his hands folded behind his head with a big smile on his face. This was all going to work. He pulled out the bag of things he'd bought last night at the pharmacy. The toothpaste and all that stuff spilled out of the bag plus a bottle of high-dose, over-the-counter sleeping pills. He was glad to have bought some new porn magazines to read today. He wouldn't leave the *Jubilee* tonight for all the tea in China. What he didn't know was that there was a guy hidden from view watching the boat to make absolutely sure he didn't.

CHAPTER 68

When Anderson and Scanton were up on the dock, Tom asked Joey to join him and Kathy for lunch. They were going to go to the Wayfarer Restaurant.

Joey said, "Sure, I'd like that. Do you want to see if we can keep Florence's truck for a while or walk down there?"

"She said I could keep it as long as I needed to. She has boats coming in and isn't going anywhere."

When Joey and Tom showed up at the restaurant, Kathy was already there with Matty. When Tom walked up to the table, Matty jumped down and ran to him. Tom scooped him up in his arms.

Joey said, "Who do we have here?"

Tom said, "This is Matty. He's Kathy's little boy."

"Well, how about that? I'm Joey. How are you, Matty?"

Matty tucked his head into Tom's shoulder and said, "I'm fine."

They sat down with Kathy. Joey hadn't met Kathy before. With a big smile he said, "How are you, darlin'? What do think of Rockland?"

"Glad to meet you, Joey. I'm well, thank you. This place is very nice, especially looking out at that breakwater."

The waitress came by and the boys ordered beers. Kathy was having white wine, and Matty was enjoying his favorite, chocolate milk. They sat there talking for a few minutes when Leslie and Pat walked through the door. Leslie spotted them immediately and came over to the table. She saw Matty and said, "Oh my gosh, who are you?"

Matty said, "I'm Matty, that's my mommy, and Tom's going to be my new daddy!"

Leslie was a little taken aback, but a big smile appeared on her face. "Is that so? I can't wait to hear all about it from your mommy."

Kathy jumped up. "So much for my big surprise . . . I know he's a pretty big one, Leslie, but look at my diamond!" Leslie screamed and she and Kathy hugged. Pat and Joey congratulated Tom. After things settled down a little, Joey said, "When's the big day?"

Tom said, "We don't know yet. A few months, I guess."

Joey said, "That won't work. We'll be fishing then."

Kathy shook her finger at Joey. "Don't you start with me!"

He put his hands up defensively and cowered a little. "Okay, okay, don't hit me."

They had a great lunch. Joey was starting to feel human again. They spent a good two hours there. Tom and Kathy had promised Matty that they would go to the movies that afternoon. There was a kid's show on about some animals that had gone wild in a park. Matty loved that stuff. Kathy told them all that they were first on the guest list for the wedding. Everyone said their good-byes when they left the restaurant and headed in different directions.

CHAPTER 69

S canton took a walk down to the major commercial wharf just
north of the restaurant. The *Jessica* was tied there. He climbed
aboard looking for Rusty and found him up in the pilothouse. Skipper
Cathcart was there with him. Joey said, "Well, Mr. Skipper, how was
your night of fun and games with Judy?"

"A gentleman never tells."

"Yeah so, just how was it?"

"It was great, to tell you the truth . . . sweet lady."

"Well, good for you."

After a few minutes, somebody pulled out the cribbage board,
and they played a few games of three-handed cutthroat. Rusty had
a cooler full of Buds going and the afternoon was on.

Dave Wilson and Charley Perkins showed up eventually. Joey
told the boys about cousin Vito getting locked up and how pissed off
his uncle Sal was.

Joey said, "When are you letting the lines go, Rusty?"

"A day or two. I've got to go over and visit the boys that run that
prison. You're not going to believe this, but some of them fellas quit
me after this trip. They said I was too hard on them. Can you believe
that? I got me a bunch of hardened criminals, killers no less, aboard
here that think I'm too hard on them. By god, that confuses the hell
out of me."

Everybody laughed. "I suppose you bastards are all on their side.
Jesus Christ, I give these guys a chance to reintegrate into lawful
society, enjoy a life at sea, on what amounts to a luxury liner, and
here I am the subject of laughter and ridicule from my own best
mates."

This was too much. Everybody was laughing so hard listening
to Rusty describing himself as a social humanitarian that Skipper
Cathcart and Dave Wilson had to leave the table.

"Hell, just like I was telling Skipper here, this next trip, I'm going after some muggers and rapists to see if they're a little tougher crowd and can stand up to the rigors of a life at sea."

Joey was laughing so hard that the beer came out his nose and he had to wipe his face.

"Jesus Christ, Rusty, it isn't the life at sea that's made 'em quit—it's the life at sea with Captain Crazy, Rusty Martin."

"Well, I'm personally offended and hurt by the suggestion that I'm anything but sweet and nice to these boys."

Joey was still laughing hard; the tears were coming down his face. "Well, I'm sorry to have offended you there, Captain."

Somebody started asking Charley Perkins a few questions about his days in Vietnam.

When Charley turned nineteen his dad had convinced him it was time he saw a world outside of the island. After some convincing, Charley joined the navy and after boot camp he was assigned to what they called a PBR, Patrol Boat River, in Vietnam. PBR duty was one of the most dangerous assignments a sailor could draw. His job was to navigate the rivers deep in the jungles in search of Vietcong fighters. The relative mortality rate on those boats was high. Charley was good at it and eventually earned his way up to first-class petty officer and captain of the boat.

He survived and served there for two years when they talked him into staying for another tour. He didn't want to let anybody down, so he signed on again.

Charley never talked about the bad stuff that gave him so much pain. Fourteen men had been shot to pieces while serving with him on three different boats he had run. At least four had died in his arms. Charley was a real honest-to-god war hero, but most everybody had forgotten that, and to folks around here, he was just an aging drunken lobster catcher.

That afternoon Charley told the boys the story about getting a piece of shrapnel in his leg from a mortar rocket that exploded near him while he was eating lunch at a riverside army camp. He told them at the camp he couldn't wait to get back to what he considered the safety of his boat, so he left without being treated. It was only a small piece of metal, so he pulled it out of his leg by himself with a pair of pliers.

The gang hung out drinking and having a grand old time until about five o'clock. They broke it up, and everybody headed back to their respective boats. Charley Perkins's lobster boat was still tied up at the town dock. He jumped aboard and took off for his house on the island.

Dave Wilson had to run his tug back up to Boothbay. Rusty told Joey to give him a shout when they made the Outer Falls. As Joey went up the ladder, Rusty came out on the wheelhouse balcony and said, "Have a good safe trip, Joey. We'll be watching for you as we work to the eastard."

"Finest kind, Rusty, same to you. Hey, did your man Hacksaw quit?"

"Jesus, no, Joe, he didn't. He's turning out to be a good man. In fact, I'm thinking of firing Skipper Cathcart and making old Hacksaw first mate." Joey just smiled at Rusty, waved, and walked up the wharf.

CHAPTER 70

Tom, Matty, and Kathy went back to their room after the movie. They had some pizza on the way back. When they got there, Matty turned on the TV and was watching some kid show. Tom was sitting at the little table in the room, and Kathy came over and curled up in his lap. She had her arms wrapped around his neck and was looking into his eyes.

She said, "Are you happy, Tom?"

"Oh, Kathy, I've never been happier in my entire life." They kissed each other. They looked over at Matty, and he had his hands over his eyes. Kathy said with a big smile on her face, "Cut that out, you little brat!" Matty made a face and shook his head no.

"Are you going to give us trouble, buster?"

Matty said, "Yes, I am!"

Tom grabbed his wallet and took something out and passed it to Kathy.

"Here's my check. Take it over to my mother's for me, will you?"

"Don't you think you should tell her about us first?"

Tom had a big smile on his face. "Yes, let's call her right now!"

"Don't you think you should let her know about m-a-t-t-y?"

Matty turned around. "I'm Matty!"

Kathy said, "Oh no, he's too smart for me already, and he's only four."

"I'm four and a half, Mommy."

Kathy shook her head. "I give up."

Tom grabbed the phone and dialed home. Frances answered and Tom said, "Hi, Ma! Guess who?"

His mother said, "Well, I have no idea who it might be. There are so many options to choose from."

"Funny, Ma, funny. I'm in Rockland and I have big news."

"Are you going to quit that awful boat and come home and get a real job?"

"No, Ma. I'm going to get married to the most beautiful, wonderful girl in the world!"

"Is it Kathy Blackwell?"

"Lucky for you, yes, it is!"

"Oh thank God, she'll talk some sense into your thick head. I'm thrilled. Is she there with you now?"

"Hang on, Ma, she's right here!"

Kathy's eyes got big; her face grimaced when she took the phone. "Hello, Mrs. Anderson."

"You can call me mom or Frances, darling. Welcome to our family. You and I have a lot of work to do to get that boy you're marrying straightened out."

"I don't know. I really like him pretty well like he is."

"I'm glad you do. I'm so happy for you both. Come over to see us for supper when you get back to Falmouth."

"I'll call you tomorrow . . . Here's Tom."

He took the phone back and told his mother that they were headed back out to sea. They'd be gone about a week and then they'd be back in Portland. He told her he was crazy in love with Kathy, and they'd all get together as soon as he got in. They said good-bye.

Kathy said, "Matty, Tom and I are going to go out on the deck for a minute. You stay here and watch your show, and we'll be right there if you need us, okay, honey?"

"Okay, Mommy. I'll be right here if you need me too." Tom and Kathy went out on the little balcony deck overlooking Rockland Harbor. Kathy explained everything to Tom about Matty and Ronny and the whole mess from start to finish. She cried a few times while she was telling him. She explained that Ronny had come from a big money family. She pulled the papers out of her pocketbook that said she had total custody of Matty and told him about the check the driver had given her with papers.

"I'm so sorry to have not told you everything from the start. I was afraid you'd leave me and not want me. I didn't even know where my own son was." She started crying again.

"Kathy, I love you. I'll never leave you, ever! We'll give Matty brothers and sisters to play with, okay?"

Kathy came over and climbed into Tom's lap. "You promise, Tommy dear, do you promise?"

He held her tight. "I do. I promise, forever."

Kathy knew it was going to be all right now. They went back into the room after a little while, and the three of them curled up on the bed until it was time to take Tom back to the boat. It was about seven o'clock. Kathy wanted to get Matty home to Falmouth at a reasonable hour. She and Matty dropped Tom off at the wharf. When they said good-bye, Kathy looked into Tom's eyes and had a terrible overwhelming sense of foreboding. She kissed him and said, "Be safe, my darling. Please be safe."

Tom looked into her eyes. "Of course I will be, sweetheart. I'm on the best boat with the best crew in the state of Maine!" He really believed that.

He watched Kathy and Matty drive away. He went over to the phone booth, got in, and called home. His mother answered when he said, "Hi, Ma."

"Twice in one day? What's wrong?"

"Nothing's wrong, Ma. I just needed to tell you something."

"What is it, Tommy?"

"Kathy has a little boy. His name is Matty. He's really a great little kid, a total ball of fire. We're going to have a great life together."

"A child . . . Oh, I don't know, Tom. Bringing up another man's child is no easy job. You may think it is, but trust me, it isn't."

"Okay, Ma, I understand. I'm in love with Kathy and her little boy. We are going to be a family. I just wanted you to know from me, before one of our nosy neighbors spilled the beans and got you all upset."

"I don't know, Tom. I really don't know."

"There's nothing for you to know, Ma. The crew's waiting for me down aboard the boat. Good night."

"All right, Tom, good night."

Tom hung up the phone. He was thinking and hoping that his mother wasn't going to be a royal pain in the ass about this little boy. He wouldn't tolerate it. He called his sister Joanne and told her the news about Kathy and about Matty. He mentioned their mother's negative comments.

"Brother dear, don't worry about Mumma. I'll take care of her. I'll try and call Kathy and make a lunch date soon. Congratulations. I'll see you when you get home."

CHAPTER 71

When Anderson got aboard the *Jubilee*, the engines were running and the deck lights were on. She was ready to sail. Everybody was down at the galley table having coffee and shooting the shit about nothing. When he came down the stairs, Joey said, "Hey there. It's the new daddy-to-be. What a great little kid. When we get home and I find Little Joey, we'll get them together."

"Great, Joey . . . No word from anybody about where she is yet?"

"No, but she's around. Karen's wicked stubborn. She's bustin' my balls. She knows I'll wring her neck when I catch up with her for stealing the goddamn trip, so she's hiding out. She'll slip up. Somebody will spot her. You wait and see."

Anderson said, "I hope you're right, Joey."

"Oh, I'm right, all right. I know it for a fact."

"Good," Anderson said.

Chase and Reed didn't say a word on the subject. Scanton told Anderson to go ahead and get some supper on. They all wanted to have a good meal before they let the lines go. Joey told them he was planning to go down around the Outer Falls and work that bottom for flats toward the southard and then fish over to the east toward Truxton Swell.

It was about nine o'clock when Scanton said, "I'm going up to say good-bye to Florence. I'll be back in a few."

Reed said, "Don't let that old broad rape you now, Joey!"

"I'll try to not let that happen, Skip." He climbed the ladder and walked up the stairs to Florence's office. She was sound asleep on a couch with a blanket pulled up over her. Joey turned to leave, and suddenly she coughed her way back into consciousness. When she sat up she grabbed a Lucky and offered Joey one. He took it and they lit up.

413

"I just wanted to stop by, before we headed out, to say thank you for everything, Flo."

"It's okay, darlin', but you owe me some big-time lovin' when you get back here next time."

"I won't think of anything else until I see you again."

Florence laughed that raddled smokers' laugh. "I know how it is. You'll suffer for quite a while, but eventually you'll get over it till you see me again."

"Seriously, Flo, I really do appreciate everything."

Florence looked at Joey and nodded her head. "I talked to your old friend Artie from Gloucester late this afternoon. I'm shipping him some haddock. He heard about what your wife pulled on you and wanted you to know how sorry he was about it."

Scanton's face turned bright red. "Jesus H. Christ! Welcome to the Fisherman's Network, all the news twenty-four hours a day. I can't believe this shit is already up and down the goddamn East Coast!"

"I'm sorry, Joey. I have no idea how he heard about it." Florence had been the one that had given Artie all the gory details.

"I got to go, Florence. We're planning to go back to Portland after this trip, but I'm sure I'll see you before the end of the month."

"Okay, Joey, have a safe trip. Keep an eye on the weather. There's something big comin' up the coast. They're calling for some big winds." Joey walked over and gave her a hug and went back down the stairs and boarded the boat.

"Okay, boys, get her off the dock. Let's get the fuck out of here!"

CHAPTER 72

They pulled out of Rockland Harbor, lowered the paravanes, and headed out to sea. It was nine forty-five as they began their run out around Owls Head and down the edge of Penobscot Bay.

Anderson sat down in the pilothouse, and Joey said, "What's up, Tom?"

"Did you hear anything about how that kid made out on the *Black Magic* after he got flown in?"

"Let's give them a call and find out."

Scanton grabbed the mic and hit the button. "*Black Magic, Black Magic,* the *Jubilee* calling."

"This is the *Black Magic* back to the *Jubilee.* Eighty-eight?"

"Eighty-eight."

"Go ahead, *Jubilee.*"

"Hi, how you doin', Manny? We were just to the west of you, down off Gloucester, when you had your accident on deck. We were just wondering how young John Poor made out. Over."

"Finest kind there, *Jubilee.* You're Pete Scanton's boy, aren't you?"

"That's right, Manny, it's Joey."

"Yes, Joey. Thanks for askin' about Johnny. Them docs down in Boston did one hell of a fine job on him. Yes, they did. He's back up home in Port Clyde restin' up. He's still got his arm on him, and by Jesus, he can move his fingers!"

"That's great news, Cap . . . great news. We're just headed out of Rockland to go fishin', and we thought we would check in with you."

"Well, thanks for that. I'll let the boy know you were askin' about him when I do talk with him again. It looks like we are going to see some weather down this way, son. Have a safe trip, Joey. Over."

"Finest kind then, Manny, we'll be standing by on 16. *Jubilee*, clear with the *Black Magic*."

"Thanks for the call . . . The *Black Magic*, clear with the *Jubilee* and back to 16."

Tom said, "That's pretty damn good news."

"You got that right. We need some of that aboard here." He reached for a cigarette.

Anderson said, "I'm going back down below. Thanks for making that call for me, Joey."

"No sweat."

Scanton was still at the wheel when Reed came up to the pilothouse. He rolled back the chart and showed Joey the mark he made on it. He told him that the plan was to meet the Canadian swordfish boat at midnight in four days at that location.

Scanton had a concerned look on his face. "They going to be all set with sixty thousand pounds?"

"Yes. It may not be all fish from one boat. It doesn't matter to us. That's their problem. We get paid per pound for what we land. The dealer pays the Canadians. I don't want to know any more about it and neither do you."

Scanton said, "You have no idea how much I don't want to do this. If that fuckin' bitch I'm married to hadn't screwed me over there's no way I'd be agreeing to this little deal."

"I know, Joey. It really sucks what she pulled with you. That bitch will get hers one day, you wait and see."

"I really want to fish hard on the Outer Falls until we get down there to Truxton's. Who are we supposed to sell these swordfish to anyway?"

Reed said, "I thought you wanted to go to Portland with this trip of fish. So I've got a deal set up in Boothbay to get rid of the swords on the way through. Then we'll just head for home and sell our own catch down there."

"Pat will have to ice our fish pretty heavy," Scanton replied.

"I'm sure we'll be fine on ice. That was pretty weird last trip how all that ice melted away."

Scanton didn't look at Reed. He said, "Yeah, pretty weird. You may as well go ahead and hit the bunk. I'll get everybody up for setoff. We should be down on the bottom in about four hours."

After Reed went down below, Joey grabbed the mic to the VHF.

"*Charley's Pride, Charley's Pride*, you on this one? The *Jubilee* calling."

"*Charley's Pride* back to the *Jubilee*."

"Sixty-five, Charley?"

"Okay, Joey, 65." They switched channels.

"How you doin', Charley? You home? Over."

"Yes, sir, Joey, I'm home. I'm okay, but my goddamn brother has been complainin' about chest pains half the night."

Joey was immediately fully alert. "What are you talkin' about chest pains, Charley?"

"We hauled four hundred traps the other day, and he bitched all day long. I think he has indigestion from the terrible way he eats."

"All right, Charley Perkins, you listen to me now and you listen good! No more bullshit about your goddamn imaginary twin brother! You get down that rickety old dock of yours and get your ass into Rockland Hospital right now! I'll give you one hour. You call me and tell me your there, or I'll send Rusty and Skipper C. down to get you. They'll haul your sorry butt in town to that hospital themselves. You hear me, old man? I ain't foolin' with you!"

"All right, all right. I'll do it. Please don't send Rusty after me. If I was to die he'd be so goddamn mad he'd probably kill me for it."

"For Christ's sake, Charley, call me when you hit the dock."

Joey flipped back to 16, knowing it would take Charley some time to leave his house and get down aboard his boat. He wanted to place a call before Charley was on the radio listening.

"*Jessica, Jessica*, the *Jubilee* calling!" Rusty was sitting up in the pilothouse watching TV when the call came in.

"Hey, Joe . . . I'm right here."

"Go to 88, Rusty!"

"Eighty-eight, Joe." They switched channels.

"Rusty, I just talked to Charley and he's having chest pains. He's headed to the Rockland town dock. Have an ambulance waiting there for him, but tell them to leave their lights out. If he sees those lights flashing on that thing, he'll know it's for him, and the bastard will never pull into the float!"

Rusty said, "Charley's having chest pains? We just saw him this afternoon, for Christ's sake."

Joey said, "I know, I know. He told me his brother has been complaining about them when they're out hauling! That crazy bastard. I gave him holy hell here just two minutes ago. Tell those guys running the ambulance that you're his brother and ride to the hospital with him. Getting him into the hospital should be no problem. They'll probably move him to the Togas VA facility if it turns out to be serious. I hope he's all right with the folks at the hospital. You know how nuts he is!"

"Don't you worry, Joey. Skipper and I will take care of him. I'll call you when I know what's going on."

"Okay, Rusty. Thanks."

"No sweat, man. We all love old Charley too."

Joey flipped back to 16. After about ten minutes had passed, he went back on the air. "*Charley's Pride, Charley's Pride* . . . you on here?"

"*Charley's Pride* back."

"Sixty-five, Charley."

"Okay, 65, Joe."

"You on your way, Charley?"

"Yes, sir, I am, Joey." Joey could hear the scream of Charley's huge Caterpillar engine cranked wide open over the radio.

"Good, Charley . . . how you feelin'?"

"I'm okay, Joey. Like I told you, it's no big deal, really. I'm doing what you said though. I ain't been in a hospital since Nam days. I wonder if them nurses over at that hospital place will be good-lookin' and sweet to old Charley. Over."

"I can guarantee it, Charley. Pay attention to where you're going and give me a shout when you hit the dock, and, Charley, take care of this thing so you can be healthy and be around a while longer, will you?"

Charley said, "Finest kind, Joe. I'll call ya."

Charley was headed in the opposite direction from Rockland. He was going south, southwest . . . straight for Monheagan Island where he could hole up with a few of his old drinkin' buddies. No goddamn doctors were going to get their hands on him, not if he had anything to say about it.

CHAPTER 73

S canton turned to the NOAA weather channel. NOAA radio was reporting a tropical storm moving at a rapid pace up the East Coast of the United States. The storm system, named Debby, was gaining intensity and dumping huge amounts of rainfall with sustained high winds along the Florida coast. It was headed for the Carolinas. Winds approaching forty-five knots and higher in gusts were being reported. Seas of fifteen to twenty feet offshore, with severe beach erosion and heavy surf were anticipated. The storm system is expected to reach the northeast by noon time Wednesday, eastern standard time. Then they gave the current conditions from Eastport to Block Island. Scanton said to himself, *Forty-five and gusts?* Not great but he'd been through it plenty of times during the heart of the winter. This was no big deal, but he'd keep an eye on it just the same. Offloading sixty thousand pounds of swordfish from boat to boat was going to be a huge pain in the balls if it got rough. They'd have to feed them over on boat-to-boat lines one at a time. It could be done. Who knows, it could be flat ass calm by then anyway.

The radio came to life. "*Jubilee, Jubilee,* the *Jessica* calling."

"*Jubilee* back to the *Jessica.*" They switched up to 88.

"How's Charley doing, Rusty?"

"How the sweet Christ should I know? The old bastard never came in!"

"You gotta be kidding me. Where the hell is he?"

"I don't know. He probably got scared of the hospital deal and all and ran offshore somewhere."

Joey said, "Goddamn his ass! You been trying to raise him on the VHF? I know he was aboard his boat because I could hear it over the radio!"

"I've been calling him steady. We sent the ambulance back. The guy was pissed about it. He's known Charley for years, I guess. He wanted to know who he was supposed to pick up Charley or his invisible twin brother. Then the prick said maybe Charley's brother was standing right there in front of us, and we just couldn't see him. The bastard gave me the finger when he drove off. Don't that just beat all? I don't understand why some folks down this way are just downright disrespectful to me. Over."

"Maybe he had a brother serving time in Thomaston prison, and he heard about you. I've been listening to the NOAA forecast, so I didn't hear you trying to reach Charley. Well, if that goddamn idiot wants to go offshore somewhere and have a friggin' heart attack and die, there's nothing you and I can do about it. Thanks for trying."

Rusty said, "I'll try him in the morning and let you know. What's the weather calling for anyway?"

"There's a tropical depression named Debby headed our way. They're calling for forty-five, higher in gusts."

"Light breeze, son, light breeze."

"Yeah, I know, Rusty, I'll call you after the first tow. See ya later."

"See you later. Get fishy! *Jessica* out!"

Scanton couldn't believe Charley Perkins had pulled that shit. He knew that these downeast islanders were a different breed though.

CHAPTER 74

The *Jubilee* steamed east-southeast for another five hours, and Joey woke up the crew. When they all made it up to the pilothouse with their coffee, the dawn had just broken. The sea was flat calm and the sky was blood red. Scanton said, "Okay, boys, let's set off!"

They were going after flats in ninety fathoms of water. The bottom was pretty smooth, and they were dragging to the south-southwest toward Jeffery's Ledge. Tom was down in the galley making a big pancake breakfast with sausage when Peter Scanton called on the VHF.

Joey said, "Well, Dad, it sounds like your old lady let you off the dock finally."

"Please don't refer to your mother as my old lady."

"Okay . . . sounds like Ma let you off the dock finally."

"Very funny, Joseph. Your mother tried to file a report stating Little Joey to the police as a missing person. They completely dismissed her. They said with you at sea they could only assume that the child was under the care and supervision of his mother with your full consent."

"Well, technically that's right, Dad. I told Ma to just wait until I got home to deal with it. Over."

"You know your mother, and you know how much she loves that grandson of hers. She just can't stay put and wait. Over."

A strange voice broke in on their call and said, "What a soap opera. What is this? *Days of our Lives?*"

Neither Joey nor Peter recognized the voice, but Joey was pissed. He hated talking about this shit on the VHF, and he'd told his father that a million times, and he still got sucked in.

"Dad, I really don't want to talk about this now. Over."

The voice said, "Thank God!"

"I got to go. Whoever is busting in on us, mind your own business."

The voice said, "Fuck you, Scanton." Joey was so pissed he could barely see straight. He shut off the VHF and threw the mic against the dashboard. He hollered down to the galley and asked Anderson to bring him a fresh coffee.

Anderson came up with breakfast and his coffee. Joey had him take over while he ate. The sounding machine was showing fish. They towed for a full four hours. The ocean was so still it was creepy. The exhaust from the *Jubilee* lay over the water in a soft black cloud. You could hear every creek and groan of the wires and bollards as they hauled back. The boat seemed heavy in the water, and everything felt like it was in slow motion. The bag had over five thousand pounds of flats and gray sole. The fish were still here. Joey set up for another tow and they set off the net.

You could detect a slightly different smell and feel to the air though. Chase said to Anderson, "There's a storm coming, there's no doubt about it." Scanton told Anderson to take the boat. He was going to hit the bunk. He'd been up all night.

They fished hard for the next two days. They had mixed it up between flat fishing during the day and the hard bottom for groundfish at night. They had about thirty thousand pounds aboard by eight o'clock the night of their third day at sea. The weather was starting to deteriorate, and Scanton had the VHF on the NOAA station.

The weather was being reported over the station.

"The weather forecast from Eastport to Block Island and all waters 125 miles offshore. The National Marine Weather Service has posted severe storm warnings with winds in access of forty knots from the east-northeast with seas gradually building from fifteen to twenty feet. All mariners be aware of gale force and higher winds with gusts approaching fifty knots. Heavy rain and fog will be limiting visibility to one-quarter mile and less. Tropical storm system Debby may be raised to hurricane category-one status by late tonight. The system is moving rapidly across the southwest portion of Georges Bank and will strike the Gulf of Maine within hours."

Scanton flipped back to channel 16. The pilothouse was silent. The boat had been gradually working its way south-southwest toward Truxton's Swell. They were still fishing in ninety fathoms of water, and they had just set off. They were towing to the north-northwest, steering 340 degrees. The seas were hitting then side to and had begun to build from the east. For the first time since Chase had been fishing with Joey, he questioned his judgment. Of course, he knew that Scanton was under huge financial pressure, but that was no reason to stay off in severe weather conditions.

The paravanes were down with the birds in the water. The seas were about four feet and gentle. Scanton had the helm. Anderson was in the galley with Chase. Uncle Charley had jumped up on the galley table and was pacing back and forth, crying. Chase shook his head. "That ain't good. When Uncle Charley acts like that, you can bet your ass it's going to get rough."

Anderson had never been offshore in a boat like this, or any other boat for that matter, in a real storm. He remembered very clearly what the squall was like when they were down at the bucket bottom. He had a feeling that this was going to make that look like what Rusty called a summer breeze.

They were towing the groundfish net and the seas were building. Scanton was watching the radar. He said, "Skip, look at this." There was a wall of white crossing the screen on the twenty-five-mile range, and the heart of the storm had to be at least thirty miles further to the south. Reed said, "Holy shit, Joe, that looks like a beauty, doesn't it?"

They had been towing on gravel bottom for a long time, but things were going along pretty smoothly. The rain was coming down so hard you couldn't see anything. The wind had lifted to over thirty knots, and the seas were starting to break over the starboard side of the boat. There were long troughs between the breakers, and when they struck down over the *Jubilee*, they came with a thunderous force. Scanton hollered over his hailer to close the engine room door and secure it. The wind and rain were so fierce no one could hear him. The door was left ajar. There was a surreal screaming sound as the wind ripped through the rigging. Anderson had never heard such an eerie sound in his life. He'd never forget what it was like. Chase and Reed were focused on the stern of the boat. They started the winches and began the haulback.

Chase said to Anderson, "It really doesn't matter how much power you have or how much experience. When you're hung down, side to the sea, this fuckin' boat will wind up drifting with her stern into the wind when we go to haul back."

The seas were going to come in mountainous waves up over her back side. Scanton worked the full power of the 1271, and she didn't budge. The bow swung, and her stern was now fair wind and wide open to the oncoming seas. They all held their breath when they saw the first wall of water building behind the boat. Everyone hung on. Anderson looked up at the fixed boom mast twenty-five feet above decks. The crest of the first wave was above the net reel and gallous frames. When it crashed down on them, the weight and sheer force of the wave drove the three men straight to the deck. Chase was the first man to his feet. He looked back toward the pilothouse and realized that the wave of water had rolled down the decks and had poured down into the engine room. He ran across the deck and grabbed Anderson by the back of his oilskins and pulled him to his feet. The screech of the storm was at a fever pitch. No one could hear anything. Chase looked up at Scanton. He was waving his arms and yelling into the hailer. Chase closed the companionway door.

Scanton never panicked on the boat, ever, but Chase could see the stress on his face. He had been in tough situations with him many times and understood what his captain was trying to tell him. Reed was on his feet now, and Chase pointed to the winches. He quickly spread his arms to the side. Reed knew that Chase was giving him the signal to free the winches. The wire was holding the *Jubilee* like an anchor, and the seas were breaking over her stern every fifteen seconds. As soon as the winches were released, the wire flew off the drums. The *Jubilee* was free. Chase ran aft a few steps and looked up at Scanton. He had his back to him and was concentrating on getting control of the boat. He pushed the 1271 to full throttle, running away from the hung-down gear. He was trying to turn the boat up into the wind before she swamped and sank. Chase literally dragged Anderson with him down into the engine room. Anderson saw that the water had flooded the engine room, and the starter would soon be underwater. Chase motioned forward. There was a small engine that Anderson hadn't noticed before. It sat up on a platform that was high and dry. Chase screamed, "THAT'S THE LISTER! WE'VE GOT TO START IT!" There was a hand crank on the front of the engine. Chase shut off the engine's main generator switch. With the starter almost underwater he didn't want to have any electricity flowing through the boat's systems. There were two levers on top of the engine that released the compression on this small diesel. Chase pulled them back and screamed, "CRANK IT, TOM, CRANK IT!" Anderson rolled the crank as hard as he could once. Nothing happened. He did a second time—still nothing. On the third crank the Lister sputtered and coughed. The little engine caught hold and ran. Chase pushed the levers forward, and it smoothed out and came up to full rpm. He ran back to the Mersa pump manifold, switched over to the engine room setting, and engaged the pump.

Anderson remembered from his first tour of the engine room Chase saying that he hoped he'd never have a reason to see that pump work. It was a beautiful sight right now. The water dropped below the starter in less than two minutes.

Chase quickly raised his hand with his thumb up toward the ceiling. Anderson knew he was telling him to go let Joey know they had things under control. He ran up to the pilothouse. "We got the Lister running and the big pump is working!"

"Good, good. I told you guys to shut that engine room door, goddamn it."

"It was my fault, Joey. I was the last man out the companionway door, and I didn't secure it. I should have known better."

Scanton didn't say anything. He was concentrating on getting the net free. They were not out of the woods yet, and the winds were increasing. He had to try the most dangerous move he could possibly make on a night like this, and he needed Chase and Reed to help him try and pull it off. He sent Anderson down to get them up to the pilothouse. Chase had shut down the Lister and had switched over from the Mersa pump to the normal bilge pump system.

"Here's what I have to do, boys. When I give you the signal, I want you to start the winches and haul back. I'm going to run the boat up into the wind and hold her. While you haul the wire, I'm going to drift down over the net and pray to God I don't get it in the wheel."

Chase said, "Jesus, Joey, in this wind that's goddamn near impossible!"

"I haven't got a choice. Since you deaf bastards can't hear me, I'll use the boats horn to signal you. One blast, you haul back. Two blasts, you stop. Three blasts, you release the winches." Chase said, "What happens if there's four blasts?"

"That means I've pissed my pants and you need to come up here and take over."

Reed and Chase went down on deck. Scanton told Anderson to stay up in the pilothouse and watch what was going on out on deck so he could concentrate on keeping the boat headed up into the wind.

He carefully positioned the *Jubilee* above the gear and hit the horn once, and the boys started the winches for haulback. Nothing gave. He carefully worked the boat around from three different angles. Still nothing freed up. That was exactly what he was afraid would happen. He hit the horn three times and pulled away from the net and centered the boat right above the wires. He hit the horn once, and they started the winches again and carefully jogged the boat in and out of gear as the boat gradually drifted backward. He held his breath, knowing that one false move, and he would hear a horrible grinding sound as the main wires were sucked into the wheel. It didn't happen. As the boat passed backward over the net, what he was trying to do worked. The net released with a sudden smooth lift.

When the boat freed up, Joey let out a full breath of air. He hit the horn three times. The winches spun free and the wire flew off. He put the boat in forward and opened the 1271 full throttle. After he was a safe distance away he slowed the boat and hit the horn with one blast. The haulback began and the doors were coming up.

Scanton turned to Anderson. "Well, are you going to stand there looking, or are you going to get down there and put my fish away?"

Anderson raced down to the deck. He couldn't wait to see the doors hung and the net come on board. The seas and wind had increased to a fierce velocity, and no one on board seemed to notice. When they finally got the net on board, it had over eight thousand pounds of beautiful large codfish, and the net was in perfect shape. Only the starboard door had been hung down. The bag had to be split, and that was no easy task in the seas and wind.

When they were all back up in the pilothouse, Scanton said to Anderson, "The fishing is always big during a storm, Green Guy."

Anderson said, "No shit?"

"No shit."

They didn't set the nets again that night. They jogged into the winds and rode out the hurricane. The *Jubilee* showed once again what a great sea boat she was. She climbed the walls of black and relentless water to slide down into deep troughs, plunge her bow, and rise again. It was a long and tension-filled wait for the dawn.

The boat sustained minimal damage, but things on board got pretty shaken up. After about four thirty in the morning, Chase took a look down into the galley. Uncle Charley was sound asleep on a galley chair. He knew then that they had made it through.

Debby turned out to be a category-one hurricane with sustained winds of fifty knots and gusts over sixty-five. It made land in Nova Scotia one day later and did significant damage to several small fishing villages there.

As quickly as the storm had come down on them, the skies cleared and the wind shifted to the northwest. It blew almost thirty-five knots for four hours. The huge seas flattened out, and it turned out to be a beautiful early fall day.

They were gradually working their way down toward Truxton Swell. Anderson and Chase were down on deck. Scanton was talking to Reed. "We're getting closer. We should make the bearings by midnight with no problem."

Reed said, "It sure looks that way. The weather should be decent too."

"Do you think they laid off during that friggin' storm? Maybe you should give them a call." Without hesitation Reed said, "I have no idea what channel they hang out on. I'm sure with all that weight aboard, they wouldn't run for it."

"Well, we're going to see tonight, won't we?" Scanton said.

"Definitely, we'll see tonight."

Scanton had a serious tone in his voice. "I've told you from the beginning, I don't want Pat and Tom knowing anything about these swordfish until we're back in American waters."

Reed said, "I've got it covered. Work those two guys hard enough, and they'll sleep through the whole thing."

Scanton said, "I hope you're right. You just caught the flu."

"You're right. I'd better hit the bunk right now."

When Anderson and Chase came up to the pilothouse, Scanton told them Skip was down in the bunk sick as a dog. He hated to lie to Pat. He had never done it before, and it almost made him sick. "You guys are going to have to haul back and put the fish down yourselves."

"No problem. How much time before we haul back, Joe?"

"I'd say thirty minutes or so. You guys want something to eat?"

Anderson said, "I'll go put something together."

Joey said, "No, you take the wheel. I'll make us something."

Anderson had never done the whole haulback two-handed before. He was a little nervous about it. They had a three-thousand-pound bag, mixed flats and groundfish. Chase was surprised when Joey told them to set off the groundfish net.

It took about two hours to get the fish down with just the two of them working. When they got back up to the wheelhouse, Scanton said, "I want you guys to put the roller section back into the flatfish net." Chase looked surprised at that request. They'd been up for over twenty hours at this point. Scanton said, "Go ahead, get a coffee, and then let's get it done."

It took about an hour to get the roller section back on, and it was time to haul back.

They had just over four thousand pounds. Chase thought that things were getting weirder by the minute. Why the fuck would Joey have them put the roller section on and not set that net off? By the time they had the fish down it was just before ten o'clock. Chase and Anderson could barely stand up.

Reed had laced the coffee pot with eight sleeping pills and had snuck back into his berth. When the boys got back up to the pilothouse, Joey told them to go ahead and hit the bunk.

Chase could not remember feeling so tired ever before. Neither of them even pulled off their clothes. They crawled into their bunks, and it was lights out in less than a minute.

When Reed was sure they were asleep, he got up and went back topside. Scanton was agitated to say the least. He had never deceived his men before, and the whole situation pissed him off. He moved around in his captain's chair constantly.

"Well, Skip, I hope you're satisfied now. This is what you've been hoping for since we left Portland. You're all about the easy money. This fuckin' thing better work out to be what you've been telling me, or you and I are done, permanently. You understand me, you little prick?"

"Hey, take a deep breath, Joey. It's all going to be just fine."

"Is that why you're sweating like you are, because it's all set?"

Reed said, "Its fine, Joey. You'll see."

"I don't trust you one little bit. Too much bullshit has gone on during these last two trips, and I know something is up."

Reed avoided Scanton's look. "Let's just steam down, get our fish, and go home, okay?"

CHAPTER 75

The night was still. The aftermath of Hurricane Debby had blown through, and the stars and the skies were bright and clear. Scanton had left the wheel and gone out on deck to have a smoke and to get away from Reed. He wanted to survey his boat. After the kind of pounding the *Jubilee* had been through during the storm, he was pleased to see that everything seemed to be okay. He sat down on the main hatch cover and lit up a Marlboro.

He sure as hell was having some last-minute doubts about going after these swordfish. The part about smuggling them didn't bother him. There were hundreds of thousands of pounds going through this country every friggin' year. He wasn't scared of getting caught either. Every fisherman took risks. Once he had the swordfish into US waters, there was nothing anybody could do to him. The part that was getting to him was deceiving his crew. He felt bad about Tom, but lying to Pat was killing him.

If he just kept on fishing he'd catch enough fish to square away his debt, but then he'd have to pay all the expenses too, on top of that. This was quick money, and he needed a bunch of cash right now, not later.

Fuck it! he thought, *we'll have these fish on board and be back across the Hague Line before anybody is the wiser.*

He finished his cigarette and tossed his butt overboard. He stretched his aching shoulders and had just started to walk across the deck when he heard the roar of a jet engine. He looked up and saw a Coast Guard jet scream across the sky, flying directly over them. The pilot had buzzed them close just like they always did. He ran up to the pilothouse and heard the radio call from the plane coming in.

"*Jubilee Jubilee*, this is the United States Coast Guard Airborne Unit. Come in, please." Scanton grabbed the mic and said, "This is the *Jubilee* back to the Coast Guard."

"Captain, please switch and answer on 22 alpha."

"Twenty-two alpha." After he switched up, he said, "This is the *Jubilee*. Go ahead."

"*Jubilee* . . . just a quick check on your status, Cap. How did you weather the storm? Over."

"We came through it real good. There were a few tense moments but we're all right. Over."

"What are your intentions from here, Captain? Have you been fishing today? Over."

"Yes, we have. We're shifting bottom and expect to resume fishing within about four hours. Over."

"What species of fish are you harvesting? Over."

"Northeast multispecies. Over."

"What's your plan for returning to port? Over."

"Within a day or two. Over."

"How many men aboard your vessel, Captain?"

"Four men and a mean old cat. Over." You could hear the radio man chuckle.

"All right then, Captain. Thanks for your time. Have a safe end to your trip. United States Coast Guard Airborne, clear with the *Jubilee*."

"Finest kind, Coast Guard, *Jubilee* clear, back to 16 and standing by." The jet was long gone.

Scanton looked at Reed. "You still think nobody's watching?" Reed didn't say anything, but the look on his face told it all. They kept steaming for their mark.

It would be another hour before they would be far enough to the east to be able to make visual contact at the 25375 12700 line. Even though the night was clear, Scanton had the radar on the five-mile range. They steamed toward their destination. They had been going about half an hour when Scanton slowed the boat and pulled out of gear. Reed thought, *What the fuck is up now? Is this asshole going to change his mind when we're within minutes of pulling this off?*

Scanton said, "Well, Skip, don't you think we should take up the paravanes before we tie up with these guys?" Reed sighed with relief.

He said, "I guess we should. I'm a little nervous here myself."

They went down on deck, raised the paravanes, and got the birds back on board. Scanton returned to the wheel. They steamed for another thirty minutes, and he spotted a target on the radar. He said, "Skip, look at this. There's something wrong here. This thing I'm looking at is too big for a swordfish boat."

Reed said, "Jesus, Joey, calm down. They said they were going to bring us swordfish from more than one boat. How the hell should I know what their brining it on? Let's go get our fish and get out of here."

A few minutes later Scanton had a visual on the boat. This wasn't a swordfish boat; it was a small freighter. They were very close, and Scanton was feeling leery about this whole thing now. The size of this boat didn't make any sense to him. There was something terribly wrong about this picture. His muscles started to tighten and his heart began to race.

Reed said, "I'll run down and get the lines ready and put some poly balls off, so we can tie up to them."

"Yeah, go ahead," Scanton said absently. He estimated that this freighter was a little over a hundred feet long. She was white with blue trim and was in good shape. He had made his swing to pull up alongside. Now his heart was up into his throat. The name lettered on the boat's stern was *Juanita*. She was a Columbian vessel, not Canadian. He was suddenly feeling real panic.

There were a few low deck lights lit on board. He could tell that the main engine was running. There was a soft green glow coming from the pilothouse. The light was being refracted from the lit instrument screens running on board the boat. His instincts told him to pull away, but before he could back off, Reed had thrown the lines, and they were tied off to the freighter. He felt instantly trapped.

There were three deckhands working the lines aboard the freighter, and one of them jumped aboard the *Jubilee.* The guy was wearing a shoulder holster that held a heavy-caliber handgun. Scanton stepped out from the upper pilothouse door into cool night air.

A short heavyset man with dark complexion stepped from the freighter's wheelhouse onto the balcony of the small ship. There was a soft deck light burning over him. Scanton could make out that he was wearing a white shirt and an old worn captain's hat that was stained with sweat and grease. There were two other men with him, making the count six in all. At least that Scanton could see anyway.

The man had a jet-black beard and cold hard eyes. He hollered to Scanton in a thick Spanish accent, "Hey, Gringo! You ready to get your swordfish?" They all laughed hard, especially him. He had a small cigar in his mouth. He took it out, blew some smoke, and spit off the rail. Scanton just stared at this man. Before he could move, the Columbian that had boarded the *Jubilee* earlier was standing behind him with a gun firmly planted in his ribs. He spoke to Scanton very softly, "Done move and you done get hurt."

The captain hollered, "Where's this Skip Reed, the captain of this boat?" Scanton thought, *What the fuck is going on? Skip Reed, the captain?* Reed stepped out of the shadows into the faint light of the deck and hollered, "I'm right here."

The captain shouted back, "Where's my fucking money?"

Reed replied with a nasty tone, "Don't worry about it. It's all right here."

The captain's face contorted with fury. He wasn't used to having anyone talk to him with such disrespect. He screamed, "YOU MOTHERFUCKER, DON'T YOU TELL ME WHAT TO WORRY ABOUT! YOU GET ME MY MONEY, YOU PIECE OF SHIT!" There were three guns pointed at Reed. He thought he was going to be shot right then and there.

Scanton was forced by gunpoint back into the pilothouse. He knew now that the *Jubilee* had just been seized by a Columbian drug trafficker.

CHAPTER 76

Two men with guns trained on Reed boarded the boat. One followed him down into the engine room. When they returned Reed had a high-speed grinder and an extension cord with him. The power source was down below, and he fed the extension cord up the ladder. The armed men followed him up beside the companionway and onto the overhead. When Reed was topside, he quickly unstrapped the propane tank that wasn't hooked into the boat's gas system. He pulled it back onto the overhead deck and started cutting the end of the tank off with the grinder. The Columbians backed away in fear. With sparks flying, Reed cut his way into the tank. They thought this crazy American bastard was going to blow them all straight to hell. They both kept their guns aimed directly at Reed's head.

The new weld was soft and cut away easily. It had been done that way so the end of the tank could be removed quickly. After the cut was made, the end fell off, exposing a clear plastic bag that had been stuffed into the cylinder. Reed grabbed it with both hands and pulled. The bag was packed tightly with one-hundred-dollar bills. It was $9,000,000 jammed perfectly into that empty cylinder. Very few people in the world have ever seen that much cash in one place. The three men stood there, staring at it for a few seconds.

The two Columbians grabbed the bag and quickly got it down on deck. From Scanton's vantage point he could see what it was. He had no idea what had been going on above his head, but now it all made sense. He couldn't believe that he had a fortune in cash aboard his boat and never knew it. Everything started to add up to him now, at least almost everything. That fucking prick Reed had set this whole thing up. He had started sucking him in way back in Portland before they had even left the wharf. He was so pissed at himself that he got sucked into this mess because of his own stupidity. The question was could they come out of this alive. One thing for sure though, Reed didn't pull of any this shit together by himself. The brains behind this were far beyond his mental capacity. He'd scammed his way into this, and there was no way out for any of them now. He thought about his two crew members asleep down below and how his actions had betrayed their trust in him. It made him feel sick.

Scanton was still watching the deck of the *Juanita* from the pilothouse. The Columbian captain had come out to inspect the cash and seemed satisfied. They took the bag in through the companionway. He was sure that once inside, every bill would be counted. He was still watching when he got the shock of his life.

A huge man walked out from the companionway of the freighter. He came around the corner and out onto the deck. He was wearing a shoulder holster with a handgun in it. It was that Sammy Dalton guy he'd seen at the restaurant with Artie Valente, the gangster from Gloucester.

One of the deckhands from the *Juanita* placed a fish tote on the deck of the *Jubilee*, so Dalton could get his large body through a side door, over the rail, and down onto the deck. For such a big man, Dalton moved with a certain grace. He knew his way around boats and Scanton could see that.

Dalton turned and motioned to the deckhands and gave them a loud order in Spanish. Scanton couldn't understand what was said, but the message was clear. The men began passing hundred-pound closed fish totes from the freighter over to the deck of the *Jubilee*. There were eight of them in all when they were done. Scanton turned to his armed guard and said, "What's in the totes there, Juan?"

Scanton's arrogant tone angered the gunman. "My name is Carlos, and that's pure Columbian cocaine you fucking pig."

Scanton said, "Holy shit!" He did a few mental calculations and figured those totes had to hold almost 350 kilos of coke!

Dalton ordered the totes stacked up against the back of the pilothouse just under the shelter deck. They looked very natural stacked that way and would cause absolutely no unwarranted attention.

After the cocaine was aboard, Dalton hollered to Skip Reed, "Come here, you." Reed walked slowly over to Dalton. He said, "Now listen to me, motherfucker. Your part of this shit is done. I don't need you no more. If you want to live, you'll do exactly as I tell you. You fuck around with me, and I'll blow your goddamn head off and feed you to the sharks. I'll kill every last motherfucker on this boat too. Do you doubt what I'm saying to you?" Reed was scared shitless. This is not how he thought things were going be at all. He had figured they would just get the cocaine and take it in themselves. He would have a chance to explain everything to Scanton and cut him into the deal.

Reed had heard Dalton's question. He had no doubts whatsoever about Sammy Dalton being a killer. He said, "No, I don't doubt your word."

Dalton smiled a totally mirthless smile. "Good. We are going to steam this boat up into a place called Little River in East Boothbay. You know where this Little River place is?"

Reed swallowed hard and said, "Yes, it's on the western side of the Damariscotta River. I was in there a couple of times a long time ago. There's a tricky entrance to the place. There's a bell and a spindle with a day marker on it. They call it the bull. A huge ledge guards the entrance to that hole. You have to run straight toward the shore and then cut back to the east or you'll run aground."

Dalton was sitting there smoking a cigar, looking at Reed like he was talking garbage. He said, "I don't give a fuck about that shit. You want to keep those brains in your head you make sure we get up in there safe and sound. You understand me?"

"Yes, I understand."

"We got to land in there around 10:00 p.m. tonight. Do you know how many hours in this piece of shit boat it will take to get up in there?"

"I'll have to check the chart with Scanton. He does all the navigating on the boat, but I can do it myself."

"Well, what is it, big time? You got to check with this guy Scanton to run this boat or not?"

Skip caught himself. "I can do it."

"Good, because I don't think you get this thing we're doing at all. You see, Reed, you lied to us. Do you know how fuckin' stupid it is to lie to people in my line of work? I've been known to kill people for that kind of shit. You kept telling us that Scanton was all in on this deal. I can see now that you set him up. That asshole thought he was really here for swordfish. That's why that Columbian captain up in the wheelhouse thought all this was so fuckin' funny. He knew by the looks of things Scanton had been set up. I'm different though. I don't think anything is funny. I know now that I got three assholes aboard this boat against me now. Then I got you, see? If you can't control these boys completely, we're going to start out with you, in the elimination department. I really don't give a shit what happens."

Reed was shaking again. Dalton said, "You get up there to the wheelhouse and figure out the where and when of all this shit. I don't have no more patience for you. Get away from me."

Reed said, "I'm sorry, Mr. Dalton."

"You're the sorriest piece of shit I ever saw, Reed." He walked over to the main hatchway and sat down. Then he hollered, "Reed! Any duct tape on this slab?"

"Sure, we got some down in the engine room." Dalton rolled his hands out to his side. "You stupid fuck! You think I'm going down there and get it?"

"No." Reed ran for the main companionway.

Dalton said, "Like I said, Reed." When he brought it back up, Dalton said, "Go tape up Scanton, hands and feet. Where are them other two jerks anyway?"

Reed said, "They're asleep down forward."

"Asleep down forward? What did you do, drug the fuckin' cocksuckers?"

"Well, yes, sort of."

"Reed, I met a better class of people in federal prison than you. Get the fuck away from me!" Reed turned to leave. "Don't forget. You duct tape Scanton," Dalton snarled.

The longest walk Skip Reed had ever made in his life was up to that pilothouse. When he went in, Joey Scanton was sitting there with a gun pointed at him that was being held by a very jumpy Columbian thug.

"Well, Skip, you fuckin' bastard. You met my friend Carlos here. He's one friendly son of a bitch. If I didn't think I would get shot trying, I'd rip your fuckin' throat out of your body right now."

"Listen to me a minute, Joey. All our lives are going to depend on it. I figured we'd be picking up the drugs ourselves and running them in. I never thought they were going to take over the boat."

"You never thought about anything, you stupid prick. You set us all up, you motherfucker!" Scanton screamed.

"All right, have it your way!" Reed walked over to Joey and told him to put out his hands. Carlos raised his gun to Scanton's head to make sure he complied. Reed wrapped his hands in the duct tape. He said, "Get your ass down in the galley." Scanton went down the stairs. He sat at the galley table. After he got him down there, Reed duct taped his feet together.

"You should be some proud of yourself, you bastard. You've screwed everyone on this boat including your lifelong friend. How the fuck can you live with yourself?" Reed didn't respond to the question.

"If you're smart you'll keep your mouth shut and cooperate with these men." Reed left and went back up to the wheelhouse. Dalton was sitting there. "All right, Reed, let's get underway. How much longer do you think the other two will sleep?" he asked.

"At least ten hours."

"Good, cast off and get this piece of shit moving."

"All right, but I need another hand here to cast off the lines."

Dalton said, "Go ahead, Carlos, give him a hand. Let's get underway."

Dalton gave a short wave to the Columbian freighter captain. The *Jubilee* was released from the *Juanita* and began her eighteen-hour steam for East Boothbay. Reed was at the helm.

Scanton sat bound in the galley, knowing that he had lost control of his boat and his life. His destiny and that of his crew rested in the hands of two desperate criminals. Uncle Charley jumped up and put her head on Joey's lap. The long steam was underway.

CHAPTER 77

Seven hours had passed. Scanton had been quiet and had made no attempt to resist. Dalton knew this guy Scanton was smart. He was just stupid enough though to let that scumbag Reed con him into the worst disaster of his life. He had heard about Scanton's old lady ripping off the big Gloucester trip. Dalton knew there had to be more to that story, but he really didn't give a shit. He decided to let Reed take the duct tape off Scanton. Dalton figured Scanton wasn't going anywhere anyway. Dalton knew that fuckin' Carlos creep working this job with him was a born psycho killer. If there were any trouble, he'd take Scanton out in a heartbeat just because he could. Dalton just wanted to get his ass into Boothbay and get off this boat and get his money. It was crystal clear to him that Reed had lied and deceived every man on this boat and probably had been doing it for a long, long time.

Dalton had grown up on boats in the New York area. Back in the day his whole family had been in the fishing racket. When he got the chance twenty years ago to get out, he did. Sammy Dalton was a cagey guy. Nobody knew what he knew or what he didn't know. He had put in his days at sea on boats just like this one, but that was a different time.

Dalton was standing a wheel watch when the *Jubilee* began to lose power. She dropped from 1,800 rpm down to nothing and stalled. The engine alarm bells were ringing full tilt. Dalton hollered, "What the fuck! Scanton, get your ass up here!"

He came up the stairs. "What's up, fat man? Did you fuck up my boat?" Scanton said.

He reached over and turned the ignition key off, and the bells stopped ringing. Dalton turned purple. Nobody ever had the balls to talk to him like that. Then he started to laugh. "You stupid Ginny cocksucker. I've killed guys for a whole hell of a lot less than what you just said to me. I will admit you got some guts to run your mouth like that."

Scanton said, "I'm not impressed, and I really don't give a shit either. You got me fucked over pretty good here. What am I going to do? Run from you? You want to shoot me? Go ahead, but you're going to look pretty stupid when the Coast Guard shows up in their 41-footer and you're stalled in the middle of the North Atlantic. I guarantee you, fat man, that the Coast Guard will be overflying us within at least two hours, so you got a big problem right now."

"All right, all right, you and me . . . we gotta make peace. You want to live to break Reed's neck, and I want to get ashore. You help me and I'll promise you, Reed will pay dearly for his bullshit. Deal?" Dalton said.

"What have I got to lose? If the Coast Guard comes, we're all fucked the way I see it. They're going to arrest me sure as hell. They did a flyover last night, and they knew which way I was headed. They find drugs aboard here, and they'll assume I was in on it. So we have a deal."

Dalton pointed at Scanton. "Don't call me 'fat man' again or I will shoot you. I'm Sammy."

Joey mumbled, "What the hell." Scanton pulled out a Marlboro and lit it up. He knew that as soon as they landed in East Boothbay Sammy was going to kill them all anyway. Scanton said, "I'm going down forward and wake up my engineer. Chances are that during that hurricane we kicked up a bunch of sediment from the bottom of the fuel tanks and the main Racor is plugged solid. I'll need his help to get things changed over so we can start the engine again."

Dalton knew that was a huge lie. He didn't need any help to change that filter.

"Go ahead and get him up, but I'm sending Carlos down below with you. Don't screw with that bastard. He's a fuckin' crazy Columbian killer and a coke addict—bad combination. Don't fuck with him, I'm telling you, Scanton."

Scanton didn't say anything. He went down forward. Reed was sitting at the galley table. Carlos was sitting across from him. His handgun was on the table in front of him. Reed didn't look up at him when he passed by. He went up forward to wake Chase. The big man was practically comatose. He shook him hard, but he rolled over away from him. Scanton figured Chase had been out almost ten hours by now. He shook him again and called his name. Chase coughed a few times and opened his eyes. "What the fuck do you want?"

"It's time for school, and Ma says you gotta get up."

"Yeah, well, tell Ma I ain't going today."

"Get up, big boy. We got a major problem."

Chase said, "I heard the alarm bells going off. We sinking?"

"No, it's worse than that."

Chase rolled his legs out of the bunk and stared at Joey with bloodshot eyes. "What time is it? Where the fuck are we? Why isn't the engine running?"

Scanton gave Chase the short version of what had happened during the time he'd been asleep.

Chase said, "That's it. I'm breaking his fuckin' neck right now."

"Slow down, Pat. Take it easy for a minute." They went out into the galley. Chase saw Carlos and the gun. He saw Reed sitting there across from him.

Pat Chase was ready to kill. "What the fuck have you done now, Reed?" Carlos grabbed his gun and trained it at Chase, and he backed away.

Scanton said, "Come up with me. We got to get this boat going or we're all screwed."

Chase followed him up above. Dalton was sitting in the captain's chair.

Scanton said, "I'd like you to meet my new best friend Sammy. He's a drug trafficker and a self-admitted killer. Try not to call him 'fat man.' He hates that and he'll probably shoot you for it."

"Very funny, Scanton," Dalton said.

Chase said, "Jesus, Joey, tell me we don't have drugs aboard here, and that miserable weasel Skip didn't set us all up!"

"You figured it out," Scanton said.

"Goddamn him. That's what happened with the ice. He was trying to force us ashore. We were catching fish, and he needed to drive us home. What about the fuckin' gas though? I knew I didn't run out. What was the deal there?"

"Skip got those tanks swapped around somehow. He smuggled a huge sum of cash aboard in one of those tanks to pay for the drugs we picked up offshore."

Chase said, "Are you shitting me? What have we got on here for drugs?"

Finally, Sammy lost it. "You two assholes can catch up on all this shit later. Start this fuckin' boat before I lose my patience with you two jerks and start doing my thing!"

Sammy hollered down below, "Reed, get your ass up here. Carlos, you come too!"

When they got up to the pilothouse, Dalton said, "Carlos, these guys got to change a filter. You watch them. If you got to kill one or the other, I don't care. Don't kill them both though. Hurry up, Scanton! Get this piece of shit boat started."

When they got down into the engine room and started swapping out the filters Joey explained all the rest of the gory details. Chase was getting madder by the second. He couldn't believe that Scanton would be so stupid as to agree to a swordfish smuggling scam without telling him about it to begin with. Then they wind up with a boatload of cocaine instead. He felt completely trapped. He hadn't done a goddamn thing but go fishing, and now he could killed as soon as they touched the shore. He had to figure out a way to get the control of the boat back from these guys. He was sure that none of them would make it out of this alive if he didn't. He had always hated Skip Reed, and now it was ten times worse. For the first time in his life he truly wanted to kill another human being with his bare hands.

They got the filter changed and bled the injectors on the 1271 and got the engine started. Carlos never took his beady eyes off them the whole time they were working on the engine. Chase thought,

Smart to keep an eye on us, bub. If I had a second to do it, I'd shove that fuckin' gun right up your ass.

They all went back up to the wheelhouse. With the boat ready to run, Dalton told Joey to take the wheel. He wanted something to eat.

Chase said, "I'll wake Tom up. He'll be happy to learn about what his best friend Skippy has pulled on this boat."

Reed said, "Fuck you, Chase."

Carlos turned toward Skip. He aimed his gun right between Reed's eyes. "Shut up. I'm very tired of your voice."

They started steaming again toward East Boothbay.

CHAPTER 78

Mickey Varney had grown up dirt poor on the Back Narrows road in Boothbay. His mother had been a drunk. He had two brothers and a sister who were as wild as anyone had ever seen down this way. His sister, Carly, started having sex with every boy that she could by the time she was fifteen. She was still a total slut to this day. His two older brothers had left the state and were both serving sentences for armed robbery somewhere in the South. His father was serving a thirty-five-year sentence at the state prison in Thomaston for involuntary manslaughter. He would never live long enough to get out. He had beaten a man to death over a stolen outboard motor. Old man Varney beat the thief to the point where the man's dead body was unrecognizable. Mickey was just like his father—one mean bastard.

Varney got into lobster buying when he was pretty young. When he was a kid, he had hung out down at the wharfs in the harbor all the time. He was mean as hell, but one thing he was that his old man and his brothers weren't was smart. He started shoveling bait for the lobster boats early on and eventually worked his way up to running the scales. Lobster catchers, not unexpectedly, watch the scales like a hawk. If there was ever a hint of deception detected, the guilty man would be banned from the job for life. Varney was as clean in that department as anyone you could ever find. He worked his way up to being a lobster buyer by the time he was twenty-two. He made some pretty good money and bought himself a little house. He worked hard for a number of different major fish dealers over the next ten years, and he lived alone.

Mickey Varney was gay. No one in Boothbay Harbor had figured that out. They all thought he was just too nasty a temperament to ever have a girlfriend. He never had any relations with anyone within a hundred miles of that town. He never communicated personally with anyone in his family because he hated them all, and they hated him.

Not only was Mickey mean and smart, but he was an opportunist of the highest degree. On one of his out-of-town junkets, he had run into a very interesting man in a gay bar in Boston. They became friends, or at least what passed as a friend to a man like Mickey Varney. After a few months, when the man got to know him better, he suggested an interesting business proposition. The man was involved with some very wealthy businessmen that might be interested in expanding their business interests in Maine. They wanted to buy some oceanfront property in a secluded area for the purpose of landing and transporting illegal narcotics. This was right up Mickey's alley. He wanted desperately to make some big money and leave Boothbay in the dust. He couldn't believe his good fortune. When his friend said that the resources for a purchase were unlimited, Varney couldn't wait to get back to Maine to start looking around for property. His friend told him that a business, such as a small restaurant or a motel, would be great. Varney asked what they might think about having a combination lobster-buying facility and a restaurant. The guy thought it would work perfectly.

His friend asked him if he would like to come to his place for the night. Mickey had been there a few times before. After they got there, the man made a call. When he got off the phone he said, "Mickey, it's all set. If you can find a place like we discussed, please try and buy it. My contacts will provide you with whatever capital you need for this purchase."

Mickey was gay but he had always hated it. He and his friend had angry sex, forcefully delivered by Varney. After he was finished, he dressed hurriedly, left, and drove home to Maine. Two days later he got a phone call from his friend, who told him he did not want to see him ever again. The man was scared to death of Mickey.

He gave Varney the name of another contact that he could talk to about the deal up in Maine. The new contact was from Gloucester. His name was Sammy Dalton. The man warned him that Sammy was not gay and that Mickey should keep that part of his life, as he had always done, a secret. He called this Sammy Dalton guy and obtained assurances that he should try to move ahead with a purchase.

Mickey knew the owners of the Little River lobster-buying and clambake restaurant operation. Everybody in a small fishing touristy place like that knows everybody else. They had been there running the place for a long time. The owner and his wife were old and tired. He was a lobsterman, and his wife ran the food service. The old man couldn't haul many lobster traps anymore because of severe arthritis, and the rest of the business was wearing them down. Mickey dropped over to their place one night. His first question was, "How would you two like to move to Florida and be rid of this place?"

The deal was negotiated almost immediately. The couple didn't need to be asked twice to be out of there. Thirty days later, a closing was held, and the elderly couple was on their way. Their first real stop was Disney World.

That was just over a year ago. The drug-trafficking gig had been an incredible success in such a short period of time. Mickey had $2,000,000 dollars already socked away in a foreign bank account. After tonight's landing of cocaine and everything they had held over in the barn was shipped, he would add another $2,000,000 to his stash. After that no one would ever see him in Boothbay ever again. All he had to do was wait a few more hours. He had his passport ready and a one-way ticket to Greece. He had absolutely no idea why he had chosen Greece. It didn't matter; it wasn't the Back Narrows Road in Boothbay.

Everything was set to go. There were three tractor trailers on route from Massachusetts. Everything in the barn would be loaded into those trailers and be out of Maine in less than an hour and a half. The entire crew would be here tonight and ready to load the truck with the bales of marijuana. He was paying those guys a thousand bucks each tonight for their efforts—chump change!

Mickey knew that Sammy Dalton would be on the boat. Mickey hated Sammy with a passion. He would be glad to be done with that fat bastard after tonight. He had a speedboat tied off at the float ready to go so this Carlos guy and Dalton could get back to the freighter. The bosses had told him to make sure that the boat had plenty of fuel aboard to get them back out to sea. One of the Columbians that was sent to work with him checked out the mechanicals on the boat early yesterday. He had been the one that had put the propane gas tanks aboard the *Jubilee*. Varney had taken him to the jetport in Portland the previous night. He was at home in Columbia by now.

CHAPTER 79

Chase went down forward and woke up Anderson. Carlos made Reed go down in the galley and sit at the table again. He was thinking, *If I am to kill one of these Gringos, I pray to Jesus that it can be this one.* Anderson had a hard time waking up. He had a wicked headache and couldn't figure out what had happened. He felt like he was trying to swim in honey. Chase brought him a coffee. After he explained to him what was happening on the boat, Anderson said, "No, Jesus, no. It can't be."

"I know how you feel. I can't believe it either," Chase said.

"Where the fuck is Skip now?"

"Easy, Tom, he's out at the galley table being guarded by a Columbian. That bastard is nuts. Don't make matters worse. We'll deal with Skip later on, if we live through this. I spotted this Carlos guy taking a few hits of coke when he didn't think anyone could see him. He'll make a mistake. You'll see."

Anderson was starting to regain his senses. "Where are we going?"

"A place called Little River in East Boothbay."

"I hate to ask you this, but the guy in charge wants food. Can you put something together?"

"Sure, I guess so. It's my job." Anderson made up a platter of sandwiches and took them up to the pilothouse. Scanton was at the helm. Dalton was standing by watching. He devoured the food like he hadn't eaten in a month. They steamed toward Boothbay.

The hours peeled away slowly. Time seemed to stop. It was dark now and they were getting closer. Scanton had turned the VHF off. He didn't want any calls that might draw attention to them. The closer they got to shore, the more the tension was building. Carlos was jazzed on coke. He had the three crew members down at the galley table. He was sitting in a chair rocking back and forth. He was tapping his foot constantly on the deck. Over and over, *tap, tap, tap*—it was driving everybody crazy. This guy had a weird look in his eyes. He was right on the edge. They had been sitting there saying nothing. Reed pulled out his pack of Marlboros and pulled one out. Before he could do anything, Chase grabbed the pack out of his hands. Reed said, "Hey, what the fuck do you think you're doing?"

Chase said, "I'm having one of your cigarettes, asshole. What about it?"

Reed looked totally panicked. "Give those back to me, Chase. Get your own!"

"Fuck you, Reed. You've been smoking my cigarettes all friggin' year."

Then Chase remembered something. Reed had hidden a key of some kind in this pack of butts. He slipped the pack under the table and felt in between the foil and the box. There it was. He slid it out and jammed it up under one of the brackets underneath the table. He took out a cigarette and threw the pack back at Reed. Reed didn't make a move to look for the key. He just put them away in his shirt pocket with a relieved look on his face.

Chase couldn't believe it, but this stupid coked-up Columbian hadn't even noticed that Uncle Charley was down here in the galley. According to Scanton, that fat bastard up in the wheelhouse hadn't moved out of there in seventeen hours. He'd been pissing in a cup and throwing it out one of the pilothouse window. He didn't sleep.

Chase was being watched like a hawk by Carlos. Chase reached into a bag of chocolate chip cookies, took one out, and bit off a piece. He dropped the rest of the cookie on the deck near the end of the table where Carlos was still tapping his foot.

Uncle Charley made her move. She spotted that cookie and was on it like a shot. She started devouring it and swishing her tail back and forth, back and forth. Chase couldn't see her under the table, but exactly what he was hoping for happened. Carlos smashed his foot down right on Uncle Charley's tail. The cat screamed bloody murder. She sprang up and planted her front and back claws deeply into Carlos's leg. When she sank her teeth into his flesh, he screamed like a little girl. When he jumped back from the cat, his chair slipped out from underneath him and he fell over backward. Uncle Charley wasn't about to let go. She was beating her legs as fast as she could go and was tearing the hell out of him.

Chase made his move. He jumped up and landed on top of Carlos. His huge hands were around the Columbian's throat in an instant. You could see the powerful muscles in his arms as he tried to squeeze the life out of the Columbian. Carlos's face turned bright red. Pat's arms were shaking from the sheer force of the anger and fury he was feeling.

Carlos was being choked to death when the gun went off. The sound was deafening. The look of pain and fear on Chase's face was terrifying. His arms gave way, and he let Carlos go and rolled off him onto the deck. He had been shot in his side. Dalton flew over to the stairs and looked down. Carlos was choking and gagging. He was struggling to his feet, trying to get his gun aimed at Chase to finish him off. Dalton hollered, "STOP!"

Carlos looked up at Dalton and trained the gun back at Chase's head. Dalton yelled, "I TOLD YOU TO STOP!" Carlos slowly backed off and let the gun drop to his side.

"You there . . . See how bad he is." Dalton was pointing at Anderson. Chase was lying on the deck, groaning in pain. Anderson got him rolled over onto his back and pulled up his shirt. Luckily it was just a flesh wound. Anderson ran for the first-aid kit. He put a compress on the wound. The bleeding slowed within a few minutes. He sprayed an antiseptic on it and made a bandage to cover the spot where the bullet had torn the flesh away. Chase was in pain, but he'd be all right.

Anderson helped him over to his bunk. When he was in it, Anderson said, "Well, Pat, that was stupid, brave but stupid. You almost got yourself killed."

"I had to try, goddamn it. They're going to kill us all when we get in anyway."

Anderson said, "I'm not so sure. That Dalton guy could have let Carlos kill you just then, and he didn't. He stopped him for some reason. Just relax. I'll call you if you and Uncle Charley need to take another run at overthrowing the boat."

Anderson went back out into the galley and up to the pilothouse.

They had steamed up inside the White Islands just outside of East Boothbay now, and you could see the bell at the mouth of Little River in the radar. They were close.

Scanton said, "Sammy, what's going to happen when we land?"

Dalton's demeanor had changed. It was like night and day. That nasty look that Scanton remembered from Gloucester was on his face.

"Shut up, Scanton. You do what I tell you when I tell you, and you might live."

Scanton didn't respond. He lit another cigarette and kept steaming. He was so angry to have this bastard take control of his boat he could feel his blood boil. The seas were calm, but there was a huge roller breaking at the mouth of Little River. It was dead low water. The *Jubilee* was a big boat to try and make it up through that opening between the two massive sections of ledge that guarded the entrance to the river.

After Scanton passed the bell, he angled the boat to run just past the spindle, leaving it on the immediate port side. If his memory was right, there was about twelve feet of water at low tide beside the spindle. The tough part was that the opening between the ledges was less than twenty feet wide. The hurricane had left a huge breaker, creating giant curling swells of water for the boat to steam through. This was going to be a real first-class roller-coaster ride. Dalton might have had a lot of experience at sea, but he had never seen anything like this before. This ledge was breaking forty feet across. When he saw what they were going to have to do to make it in there, he raised his voice. "Scanton! You sure this is right? This don't fuckin' look right! You run this boat ashore to fuck this deal up and I *will* blow your head off!" He had his gun out, cocked and placed firmly behind Scanton's head. Joey stepped away from the wheel. "You want to take her in, Sammy? Go ahead."

Scanton didn't have to say another word. Sammy lowered the gun and uncocked it.

Scanton stepped back to the wheel and was concentrating on what he had to do to get through this little hellhole. The timing was everything. He plunged ahead past the spindle.

When the breaker caught the *Jubilee*, she started to surf. He pushed the 1271 wide open. Dalton's eyes got huge. He hollered, "Jesus Christ, what are you doing!"

Scanton remained absolutely calm at the helm. He could not let the sea take control of the boat. He throttled up so she wouldn't get turned sideways and smash into the ledge that extended underwater on the inboard side of the spindle.

He did take a deep breath. The boat's hull speed was only eight knots. They were doing at least twelve when they made it through the ledges and up inside the mouth of Little River. You could feel the *Jubilee* settle back down to her normal speed.

"Okay, Sammy, what did you think of that?"

Dalton ignored the question. He was too busy looking up the river to answer. He could see a large dock on the right-hand side of the inlet with floats off it. This had to be the spot they were looking for. There was no one around. It was deadly quiet.

Agent Goldman and all the law enforcement officers he had called in were hidden from view. They had spotted the *Jubilee* coming through the entrance to the river. They had Mickey Varney and his entire crew already under arrest. They had three tractor trailers, the drivers, and their helpers. So far the total was fourteen people. He had seized a barn full of marijuana. He figured that there was a street value of at least $2.2 million.

There was a group of ten officers and agents left on the scene to deal with the *Jubilee*. Mickey had been taken away screaming his head off. He was sure he had been set up by one of his partners so they could steal his share of the money. He wanted his lawyer. He wasn't going to put up with any of this shit. He yelled at Bert

Goldman as they were putting him in a state police car to be taken to Portland, "Do you know who I am, you motherfucker!"

Senior Special Agent in Charge Goldman said, "Yes, I do, as a matter of fact. Yes, I do." He laughed as he slammed the door on the patrol car waiting to transport Varney to jail.

CHAPTER 80

S canton couldn't believe there was nobody around. Carlos was up in the pilothouse now. He had forced Chase up there under gunpoint. You could see the dark stain of blood coming from under his shirt. It was flowing steadily. He was white as a ghost and couldn't stand without holding on to something. All six men were looking in at the dock. They could see a speedboat tied up at the float with its bow headed back out to sea. Dalton said something to Carlos in Spanish. He grabbed Reed and pushed him out the door. They were going to have to get the dock lines ready. Dalton looked over at Anderson. He could see he was thinking about making some kind of move.

He said, "Don't even think about it, asshole. You'll all be dead before you take another breath." Anderson knew there was nothing he could do but stand there and watch. There was no doubt in his mind that Dalton could follow through with his threat.

The river's surface was absolutely calm. The water was as smooth as glass. Scanton pulled the *Jubilee* into the series of floats and backed her down. Carlos jumped off the boat, grabbed the docking lines from Reed, and tied her off. Carlos immediately ordered Reed to start passing him the fish totes full of cocaine. They had the eight totes off the boat in less than five minutes. Carlos opened one of the totes just to see that everything had made it ashore in good condition.

That's all it took. Agent Goldman stepped forward out of the shadows with ten officers, all with weapons trained on the *Jubilee*.

Goldman had a bull horn. "Raise your hands high in the air! You are all under arrest by the order of the United States Department of Justice. I am Senior Special Agent in Charge Goldman. All of you remain where you are! I have an arrest warrant from the assistant United States district attorney of the federal government."

The agents and police, with weapons pulled, swarmed the boat. Dalton said, "Don't anybody move."

Scanton, Anderson, and Chase were all standing there with their mouths open. This shit happened on TV, not in real life. They had Carlos disarmed, cuffed, and lying face down on the float. Reed was forced to lay flat on his stomach with his hands cuffed behind his back.

Three agents scrambled up to the pilothouse. Goldman stayed up on the dock and watched. He was getting too old to jump around boats like a kid.

When the agents came into the pilothouse, Dalton dropped his weapon with no attempt to resist and put his hands in the air.

Scanton was completely relieved. He said, "Thank God you guys are here!" A tall thin agent said, "Are you Joseph Scanton?"

"Yes, I am," he replied

"Turn around. You are under arrest for drug trafficking, conspiracy to distribute narcotics, illegal possession of narcotics . . ." The list went on forever.

"You have the right to remain silent. Anything you say can, and will be, held against you in a court of law. You have the right to an attorney. If you cannot afford one, an attorney . . ."

Scanton didn't hear a word that was being said to him; he was in a daze. There were DEA agents everywhere, all over the boat. They arrested all of them and ordered everyone off the boat and down onto the floats.

They lined up the whole crew, including Reed; all were handcuffed. There was no ramp to get up on the dock, just an old steel ladder that was attached to the pilings that lead up to the wharf. Agent Goldman made his way down the ladder. He wanted to have a firsthand look at his prisoners.

Anderson's head was reeling. He couldn't believe what was happening. He thought about Kathy and Matty. He couldn't help it. A tear seeped out of his eye and ran down his cheek. He turned away ever so slightly so Chase couldn't see him. They were all still under gunpoint. The agents were going to have to uncuff them to get them up the ladder. Chase was the first one to go. Anderson could see the blood running out from under his shirt. He couldn't believe he hadn't passed out by now. He could hear a siren coming down the road. He hoped it was an ambulance for Chase. He was next up the ladder. They put the handcuffs back on him as soon as he got up on the dock.

Reed was next. When one of the officers took the handcuffs off him, he made his move. He spun away. It all happened so fast that he was out and running down the float before anyone could do anything. Three agents raised their weapons and hollered, "STOP OR WE'LL SHOOT!"

Law enforcement officers are trained not to shoot an unarmed man trying to flee from an arrest unless he demonstrates life-threatening capability.

Agent Goldman hollered, "Let him go!"

Reed sprinted over to the speedboat, jumped aboard, and started the engine. He threw it in gear and opened it wide open. When he took off, he tore the docking cleats off the float. They all stood there watching him as the boat flew down the river wide open. The boat had a sixty-knot capability and was at full plane within seconds. For just an instant, Reed looked back at the wharf. He raised his left arm with his middle finger fully extended and was at the end of Little River in less than three minutes. Everyone stood watching him as the boat began the turn at the mouth of the river.

Just as he approached the Little River spindle, the boat burst into a giant ball of fire that lit up the sky. It looked like a tiny mushroom cloud. Two seconds later the sound of the explosion reached the wharf. The flames flew fifty feet into the still night air. The light from the blast showed pieces of the burning fiberglass falling from the sky in a spectacular display of flames and smoke. It looked like a fireworks display. Everyone watching was totally mesmerized by the spectacle of the explosion

Chase was the first to speak. "Holy shit!" When his mind processed what he was seeing, he said, "See you later, Skippy!"

Anderson couldn't believe his eyes. They were all staring at the flames leaping out of the hull as it continued to burn.

Sammy Dalton and Carlos looked out at the glowing wreck and realized that they were looking at what was supposed to be their destiny. It flashed through Dalton's mind that the Columbian captain must have weighed anchor and left the area as soon as the *Jubilee* was out of sight.

The Columbian sent to help Varney out had planted the explosive device on the speedboat before he left. The bosses gave him a $200 bonus for doing it. He wasn't going to do it without a reward—after all, Carlos was his first cousin.

The ambulance pulled up into the parking lot beside the dock. The agent who was holding Chase's arm said, "Come on, Chase, your transportation has arrived."

Chase said to Anderson, "I'll talk to you when we can."

The agent said, "Shut up and move ahead, Chase!" He shoved Chase toward the ambulance. They got him inside, strapped him to a gurney, slammed the doors, and drove off.

The officers and agents forced Scanton and Anderson into a cruiser and took off for Portland with lights on and sirens blasting. They were headed for Cumberland County Jail.

"What do you think is going to happen to us, Joey?" Anderson said.

"It isn't good. I'm sure they'll book us on these drug charges. They're going to put us in jail. We'll have to come up with some money, which none of us have, to pay lawyers to try and get us out. Don't say any more right now, and we'll try to figure something out. Try to stay calm. We didn't do anything wrong here. Just remember we were set up."

Scanton and Anderson talked about Skip Reed and how fucked up all that was. They had seen him blown to kingdom come with their own eyes and still couldn't believe it. A million things were going through Scanton's mind. The boat would be stickered now and go under federal impound. The fish on board would be sold by the feds, and they'd keep the money. No matter what, he wouldn't be able to keep up his boat payments, and that fuckin' Ben Berry asshole would get his pound of flesh. He had no idea where his wife and child were. He felt a knot in the pit of his stomach when he thought of something else. What would happen to Uncle Charley?

CHAPTER 81

The agents inspected every inch of the *Jubilee*. They took pictures of everything. They began inspecting the cocaine-loaded totes that had been removed from the *Jubilee*. This was the biggest drug bust in the history of the state of Maine. To say that Agent Bert Goldman and his men were pleased with this one would be a major understatement.

It took just over an hour for the DEA agent who had Scanton and Anderson to reach Portland with his prisoners. Scanton thought it was weird the kind of things that went through your head during a time like this. When they passed other cars going down Route 295, he saw people looking at him in the back of the government car. He thought about how he always did that when he saw a cop or a sheriff driving a prisoner. It was natural to wonder what the guys being taken in had done. Now it was him who was headed to jail. This really sucked. Knowing Reed was dead didn't relieve any part of the anger and hate he felt for him . . . not one little bit.

Anderson and Scanton were booked and put in separate cells. The night wore on, and neither of them slept at all. It was 5:00 a.m. when the guards woke up all the prisoners in the jail. They ate breakfast in a dining hall with all the other prisoners and then were returned to their cells by seven o'clock.

Anderson sat there wondering if anyone knew what had happened to him. He had never been so depressed in his life. A guard came in and put him in ankle chains and cuffs. They walked him down to an interrogation room. He waited about ten minutes before Agent Goldman and Agent Lamb came in and sat down. Goldman went through his usual routine of introducing himself. He had Anderson freed from his restraints.

After Agent Goldman gave him his speech about having an attorney present for the questioning, Anderson said, "Would you

461

explain to me again what I'm being charged with?" Goldman ran down the list charges from illegal possession to conspiracy to distribute illegal narcotics.

Tom Anderson turned white when he realized the extent of criminal violations he was facing.

Agent Goldman said, "Mr. Anderson, can you explain to me exactly what your role was in these drug-trafficking activities?"

Anderson said, "Absolutely nothing."

Goldman laughed a little and said, "Absolutely nothing, huh?"

Anderson said, "That's right. We had made it through a hurricane and had been fishing again. Pat Chase and I were working the deck alone for over twenty hours straight. I was exhausted. When our deck watch was over, the captain told us to hit the bunk. When I came to, all this shit was happening. I think Skip Reed drugged us, by the way I felt when I woke up. We had been taken over by that Sammy Dalton guy and a Columbian named Carlos. I still have no idea how all this stuff came about."

Agent Goldman pulled back in his chair. "Now, Mr. Anderson, do you expect Agent Lamb here and myself to believe that you were 135 miles offshore in a sixty-five-foot dragger with three other men, one of which was a lifelong personal friend of yours, a Mr. Arnold Reed—Skip Reed, I think you just called him—and you had no knowledge or any part of trying to smuggle 350 kilos of Columbian cocaine into the United States? All this took place aboard this boat you're working on, and you knew nothing about it because you were asleep?"

"That's the truth, Mr. Goldman."

Agent Goldman said, "Well, that's an interesting explanation. Don't you agree, Agent Lamb? I think it's very interesting indeed."

Agent Lamb spoke for the first time. "I don't believe one word of it, sir."

"Now why don't you believe Mr. Anderson's explanation, Agent Lamb?"

"Because the statement makes no sense to me. This type of thing takes very careful planning, and I don't believe anyone could pull it off without everyone on board that boat being aware of what was happening."

Agent Goldman said, "By our calculations there had to be nearly $9,000,000 in cash aboard that boat to pay for all the cocaine that you smuggled into Maine. I don't think the Columbians we've been dealing with in the recent past would allow you to put that kind of money on a credit card. Do you, Mr. Anderson?"

Anderson said, "No, I don't."

Agent Goldman said, "Good, I'm glad you agree. So you admit you had the $9,000,000 cash on board to pay for the cocaine."

Anderson became noticeably upset. "No, I didn't say that. I don't know about any cash or any payments made to anybody."

Agent Goldman smiled and said, "Oh yeah, that's because you were asleep the whole time. Is that right?"

"Yes. That's right. I know it sounds crazy, but it's the truth."

"No, Mr. Anderson, it sounds crazy because it is crazy. Are you familiar with what a federal indictment is, because you're facing a federal indictment for illegal activity on at least seven different charges. If we're successful in prosecuting you on these charges, which I believe we will be, you'll serve at least twenty-five years in federal prison. Now does that sound crazy to you?"

Tom Anderson was now very afraid. He said, "I'd like to have an attorney present from now on, Mr. Goldman."

Agent said, "That's definitely your right. However, if you were to start telling us the truth, we might be able to help you out and get some of the charges against you reduced, and maybe you'll get less time in jail."

"I really want to talk to an attorney now, Mr. Goldman, if you don't mind."

"I don't mind at all. Have it your way. Guards take this prisoner back to his cell. Put him back in chains."

The guard said, "Sure thing, Mr. Goldman."

They walked Anderson back to his cell just like Bert Goldman wanted—in chains. He was allowed to make a phone call home. His mother answered the phone. "Hi, Ma, it's me."

"Oh thank God. What's going on, Tommy? It's been all over the radio and TV about you guys getting arrested."

He said, "Try not to panic, Ma. I've been arrested, and I'm here in Portland in Cumberland County Jail."

"Oh god, Tommy, no. What happened?"

"This is going to be hard for you to believe, but Skip got us involved in a drug-trafficking mess. It's real serious, Ma. We're all in big trouble. I might go to jail for a long time."

Frances started to cry. "Oh, Tommy, no. We'll get a lawyer."

"It's going to be too expensive, Ma. I don't know what to do."

"They said on the news that Skip Reed was killed in an explosion. How did it happen?"

"I'll have to tell you about it later. They are going to make me hang up. Call Teddy Atherton and get him to recommend a good criminal lawyer. Please call Kathy for me. They only let me have one call."

The guard came over to him. "That's it, Anderson!"

The grabbed the receiver from Tom and hung up the phone.

"Back to your cell." It was only eleven o'clock Tuesday morning. Anderson felt like he was going to have a breakdown. He sat there in his cell, alone and afraid.

At noon they moved all the prisoners back out to the dining hall for lunch, and Anderson spotted Pat Chase. He got his tray and walked over to his table and sat down. "How are you doin', Pat? How's your side?"

He said, "Oh, I'm all right. They stopped the bleeding and put me on some antibiotics. They only booked me about half an hour ago. Have you talked to anybody yet?"

"That guy Goldman questioned me. He told me we're being charged with a whole shitload of things. Pat . . . he said I could go to jail for twenty five years," Anderson said with fear in his voice.

"Tom, we didn't do anything. You know it, I know it. The motherfucker responsible for all this shit is dead. He got his, and I'm glad about it. Somehow we'll come out of this," Chase responded.

"I hope you're right. Look . . . here comes Joey."

Scanton walked over to their table and grabbed a chair. "Well, if it isn't the men of the *Jubilee*. How's your side, Pat?"

"I'm all right, Joe. The bullet just trimmed down one of my love handles. I'll be back to normal in a couple of days."

Scanton took control of the conversation. "Look, boys, we've got to make some decisions here. I called my old man, and Jimmy Desanto has a criminal defense lawyer coming in here to see me. I think we can all use the same guy in the beginning of this shit if you want to."

Anderson said, "Has Goldman questioned you yet?"

"No, he hasn't yet. What about you?"

"Oh yeah, he did. You'll just love your little chat with him."

"You don't have to agree to be questioned by him at all, you know."

A guard came over to the table. "All right, girls, lunch break is over. Move it out."

Anderson said, "Let's share the lawyer if we can."

"I got to call Leslie from the hospital. They didn't restrict my call. I told her everything I know about what happened. They wouldn't let her in to see me though."

The guard hollered, "I told you assholes to move it out!"

Scanton shot back, "Oh, you meant us assholes. I thought you meant some other assholes."

Chase said, "Shut up, Joey. We got enough crap going on without pissing off the guards."

"I know, I know. I'll cut it out."

Anderson was in his cell for about an hour when a guard walked up and said, "Come on, Anderson, you got an appointment." Anderson was escorted down a hallway and into a small conference room. He was pretty sure that there weren't any two-way mirrors in this room. Chase and Scanton were already seated at the table. A tall broad-shouldered man that looked like a weight lifter greeted Anderson. He put out his hand. "I'm Jim Kelley. I'm an attorney, and I've been retained by Mr. Scanton to represent you, if you agree to that plan."

"I'm glad to meet you. I'm Tom Anderson." They shook hands. Strangely Tom suddenly felt a whole lot better. This man had enormous presence, and he exuded a lot of confidence. Tom said hello to the boys and sat down at the table.

Attorney Kelley began, "Here's what's going to happen, fellas. You are required to appear before a federal magistrate for a hearing. This first part isn't about the facts. This is where they charge you. My job will be to listen to what they have to say, and I will plead you innocent to all charges, unless somebody wants to plead guilty and save the government the expense of a long trial."

Kelley looked around at everybody and said, "I didn't think so."

Scanton said, "When is this going to happen?"

Kelley replied, "This afternoon at three o'clock. They'll take you guys over to the federal courthouse, and I'll be there when you get there. You'll appear before a federal magistrate. After that happens we'll argue for bail and try to get you out of here. I'll warn you right now that this isn't going to be easy. We need to talk about what you've got for money. Does anyone own their own homes?"

Chase said, "My wife and I just bought our place a year ago. We made a real small down payment on it. It isn't worth much more than we paid for it. I've been saving money for my own boat though. How much are we going to need?"

"I don't know right now, but you all need to talk to your families and try and raise what money you can. The assistant US district attorney will level the charges against you. You're going to hear a lot of things being said that will upset you. Try to remain calm and let me do the talking.

Okay, fellas? This isn't a trial. Nothing will be decided today except whether or not we can get you released on bail."

Anderson said, "When do we get to tell our side of things?"

"They'll be plenty of time for that, Tom."

Scanton said, "Should I agree to talk to Goldman?"

"No, you've got nothing to offer him. Right now he believes that you guys are guilty as hell. You aren't going to dissuade him of that today. When they ask you to see him, just refuse. Look, boys, I got to get prepared for your appearance. I'll see you in court. Try and stay calm." Attorney Kelley shook everybody's hand and left. The guards came and escorted them all back to their cells.

Just after two o'clock, the guards removed all three prisoners from their cells, placed them in chains, and escorted them down the long hallway to an exit at the back of the jail. They passed through the security lockdown chambers and finally out into the light of the fall afternoon. There was a white van parked, ready to take them to the federal courthouse. No one spoke a word. There was silence for the ten-minute trip from the Cumberland County Jail. Three armed officers were waiting when the van pulled up to the rear entrance to the massive gray granite building. The guards walked all three men into a small waiting room, removed their chains, and told them to be seated. All were dressed in orange jumpsuits with Cumberland County Jail stamped across their backs. They talked in low voices to each other as the two guards watched. The guards never took their eyes off them. Everyone was on edge. No smoking was allowed. There was a look of fear on each man's face. Finally, a bailiff entered the room at said, "It's time, gentlemen. Let's go." They walked slowly into the federal courtroom. It was an old building, and as the men looked up at the grandeur of the room, it emphasized the seriousness of their situation. Tom Anderson looked over the crowd and spotted his dad first. Martin Anderson was sitting there with his back straight and his jaw tight as he watched his son cross the room. Martin was sitting beside Kathy and holding her hand. Tears streamed down her face. Tom had never been so ashamed in his entire life. He hung his head. Pat Chase saw his wife, Leslie. She was sitting beside Kathy, and she was crying too. Her head was bent slightly forward. She was taking short breaths and trying not to sob.

She looked so tired. Pat knew she hadn't slept since this whole thing happened. She didn't want anyone looking at her. Two rows back, Gloria and Peter Scanton watched. Peter was stoic; Gloria was not. There was no way her mind could accept what her eyes were seeing.

The bailiff marched the three prisoners over to a large flat table where James Kelley and another man stood waiting. Kelley extended his hand to each of them. "Okay, fellas, just take a seat and try to relax. Tom, this is Peter Green. He's here to represent you." Peter was a tall man of medium build. He had a friendly but authoritative look about him.

Peter shook Tom's hand. He said, "I'm Peter Green. I've been retained to defend you. I'll be working very closely with James to give you the best defense possible, with your permission, of course."

Anderson said, "Good to meet you, Mr. Green, but who's going to pay for all this?"

Attorney Green said, "It's Peter, and we'll talk about that later. The proceedings are about to begin."

The bailiff, in a loud practiced voice, said, "Hear ye, Hear ye. All rise for the Honorable Judge Carl Branton, United States Federal Magistrate." A small heavyset balding man in his early sixties entered the room. He moved with certain quickness, ascended the three steps, and sat down behind the bench. He smacked his gavel. "Ladies and gentlemen, members of the court, let these proceedings begin." He peered down at the stenographer and said, "Are you all set, Mary?" She looked up and said, "Yes, thank you, Your Honor." Without hesitation, he began. "I'll start with the government. Please go ahead."

A man sitting across from the boys at a similar table stood up. "Thank you, Your Honor. I'm William Howerton, the assistant United States district attorney. I'll be representing the federal government in this matter."

Judge Branton said, "Thank you, Mr. Howerton, and for the defense?"

Attorney Kelley got up and said, "James Kelley, Your Honor. I will be representing Mr. Joseph Scanton and Mr. Patrick Chase."

Attorney Green spoke next. "I'm Peter Green, Your Honor, and I'll be representing Mr. Thomas Anderson."

Judge Branton said, "Very well, gentlemen, let's begin."

CHAPTER 82

The tension at the defendants' table was almost too much to bear. The judge had finished his speech and was ready to begin the hearing. The judge turned to William Howerton and said, "We'll begin with you, Mr. Howerton. You may proceed."

The assistant district attorney began. "Thank you, Your Honor. The United States government brings the following charges against the defendants Joseph Scanton, Patrick Chase, and Thomas Anderson."

The three defendants were all charged with possession of illegal narcotics with the intent to distribute, conspiracy to distribute illegal narcotics, the transportation of illegal narcotics across international boundaries, and finally the operation of an illegal business enterprise in the state of Maine.

All three men sat there in silence, listening to the charges being leveled against them. Chase growled, "This is total bullshit!" Jim Kelley looked over at him and raised his finger with a disciplining look designed to silence Chase. It worked.

Judge Branton spoke next. "Is that all the charges, Mr. Howerton?"

"Yes, it is, Your Honor." The judge turned toward the accused. "Do you understand the charges that have been brought against you?"

Jim Kelley and Peter Green briefly discussed what was now happening to their clients. Jim Kelley spoke up and said, "Yes, Your Honor. My clients understand the charges being brought against them." The judge asked the same question of Peter Green.

"Yes, Your Honor. My client understands the charges brought against him."

Judge Branton said, "Thank you, gentlemen, and how do you plead?"

Jim Kelley said, "Mr. Joseph Scanton pleads not guilty to all charges, Your Honor. Mr. Patrick Chase pleads not guilty to all charges."

"Thank you, Mr. Kelley. Mr. Green, how does your client plead?"

"Mr. Thomas Anderson pleads not guilty to all charges, Your Honor."

"Thank you, Mr. Green. This court, having heard the plea of innocence, moves on to the bail portion of this hearing. We'll hear from you first, Mr. Howerton."

"Your Honor, due the seriousness of these charges and the likelihood that these defendants may try to flee, the district of Maine recommends that bail be set at one million dollars for each defendant. These defendants have actively participated in the largest single criminal attempt at the transportation and sale of illegal narcotics in the history of the state of Maine."

All three defendants were horrified. Kelley whispered, "Calm down, boys. We're just getting started."

The judge said, "Mr. Kelley, how do you respond?"

"Your Honor, we believe the government is being unreasonable. These men have no criminal records. They are all family men except for Mr. Anderson, who is currently engaged to be married. We contend that these men are responsible citizens who pose no flight risk whatsoever. We respectfully request that bail be set at $25,000."

Bill Howerton jumped up and said, "Your Honor, this arrest is the result of a yearlong investigation by the DEA and represents significant time and expense on the part of the Justice Department."

Judge Branton said, "I appreciate that, Mr. Howerton. However, it is my position that this case may be more extensive than just these particular defendants. I tend to agree with Mr. Kelley that the bail at $1,000,000 may not be reasonable. Mr. Kelley and Mr. Green, what is the financial status of your clients?"

"My clients are both working commercial fisherman of modest means, Your Honor. Mr. Scanton's boat has been seized and is under impound by the federal government. However, his father, Mr. Peter Scanton, has agreed to guarantee the presence of his son and will allow him to be employed on the family fishing boat while my client prepares for trial.

Mr. Chase has been offered interim employment by a Mr . . . . excuse me, Your Honor"—Kelley looked quickly at his notes—"a Mr. Marshall Grimes on his commercial fishing boat."

Peter Green then spoke on Anderson's behalf. "My client, Mr. Anderson, has been offered a job at a local grocery store, where he was previously employed, while he prepares for trial."

Bill Howerton was agitated and it came through in his voice. "Your Honor, these defendants were apprehended with approximately $29,000,000 in illegal narcotics aboard their boat."

Judge Branton said, "I understand that there are two other individuals that are being charged that were aboard that vessel at the time of this arrest. I think there could be extenuating circumstances involved here. It is my sworn duty to not presume guilt upon any defendants that appear before me in this court before they have had a fair and impartial trial. I will not impose bail based on a presumption of guilt. However, bail will be determined only on a presumption of risk to society. I hereby establish bail for all three defendants at $100,000 each. This bail will be extended under the following conditions. The defendants will be restricted to remain in the state of Maine. They must surrender their passports. Mr. Scanton, you may engage in fishing activities, but only aboard your father's boat. There will be specific restrictions that will be provided to you, in writing." The judge directed his attention to Chase. "Mr. Chase, should you decide, you may choose to engage in fishing activities with Mr. Grimes but may only do so with the restriction that the vessel remains and conducts its fishing activities within the waters of the Gulf of Maine. Mr. Anderson, you are remanded to your own custody in the event that you are able to post the required bail. This hearing is concluded."

There was a loud crack of the gavel. Judge Carl Branton had ruled and immediately left the courtroom. The hearing was over.

Agent Goldman who had been watching from the back of the courtroom, but if he was concerned you could not tell from his demeanor. He left the courthouse and headed back to his office without talking to anyone.

Scanton said, "What happens now, Jim?"

"You guys go back to Cumberland County, and we should have you all out before five o'clock tonight. Your mother and father are posting your bond, Joey."

Anderson said, "I don't see how I'm getting out. We don't have $100,000 for bail. I'm completely screwed here."

Attorney Green said, "We only have to raise 10 percent, just ten grand in actual cash. Your parents have agreed to post their house in Falmouth to guarantee your bond."

"Jesus Christ, I don't want them doing that."

Green added, "And that beautiful young lady over there had already agreed to post your $10,000 in cash if we pulled this off." Tom looked over at Kathy. She gave him a little wave and smiled a brave smile.

Chase said, "That leaves me. Leslie and I don't have anything to guarantee my bond. So I'm going to be in jail for a while."

"Well, Pat, actually you're not. Peter Scanton, Jimmy Desanto, and Marshall Grimes are all ready to step up for you and guarantee your bond."

"Are you shitting me? Is that so? Why would those guys do that for me? I'm not their family."

"You'll have to ask them that question. It's pretty obvious to me, gentlemen, that a lot of people out there believe in you and your innocence."

Peter Green said, "They only lose their money if you try to run." Chase shook his head. He couldn't believe what he had just heard about those guys being willing to trust him like that. Nobody ever had done anything like that for him before.

Attorney Kelley said, "We all are going to have a lot of work to do to get ready for the trial. Mr. Green and I will see you in two days so we can get your story about what happened aboard the . . . what is it . . . the *Jubilee*?"

Scanton said, "That's right, the *Jubilee*."

Before leaving, Kelley said, "Listen to me. Don't discuss this trial or what happened with anyone but your immediate families. You get talking about this mess, and it could really backfire on you. I couldn't be more serious, okay, fellas?" All three men agreed.

The Cumberland County driver that had brought them over to the courthouse was there to take them back. They had to stay in chains until they were inside the facility and escorted back to their cells.

To everyone's surprise, they really were processed out and released by seven thirty. When they stepped out into the twilight of the late afternoon, they all felt like the whole thing was surreal.

They all immediately lit up cigarettes. Five hours ago they didn't know if they might remain locked away for months in this hellhole, waiting for a trial. Now all three of them were standing on the sidewalk, watching their loved ones running toward them.

Anderson saw his sweet, sweet Kathy leading the pack. She threw her arms around him and held him in a fierce embrace.

As he took her in his arms, he said, "Oh, Kathy, I'm so sorry."

"Don't be sorry. I don't know what happened, but I know you didn't do anything wrong. I'm so glad to have you out of that awful place. Nothing else matters now."

He said, "I love you so much."

"I know. I love you too, Tommy. Let's get you home."

"Where are we going?"

"It's a surprise. You'll see."

As he got into her car, he said, "You are my surprise girl, that's for sure."

Kathy smiled weakly. "I am that, aren't I?"

Gloria Scanton and Peter were there to greet their son. Gloria hugged him and Peter shook his hand. "We'll get to the bottom of this thing, Joey."

"I don't know what's going to happen, Dad. This thing is so complicated. Can we just go home? I'm exhausted. You know anything about where Karen is, Ma?"

"No, Joey, not a word. I can't come up with anything."

Pat and Leslie were the last ones standing there. Chase walked over to Peter Scanton. "I really want to thank you and Marshall for helping me out, Pete."

Peter Scanton said, "Pat, son, you're like family to us. We know you would never let us down. Marshall said to tell you to take whatever time you need. Just give him a call when you're ready to make a trip fishing. He's got a guy on the boat he doesn't like. He's going to fire him whenever you're ready."

Chase said, "Okay, Pete, thanks again. Joey, I'll talk to you tomorrow."

Joey said, "Finest kind, Pat. We'll talk in the morning. I'm going to want to take a ride up to Boothbay and check on Uncle Charley. I'm kinda hopin' she hasn't attacked any more Columbians while we've been gone."

Kathy and Tom drove out to Falmouth. He said, "Where's Matty?"

"My mother's got him. I thought you'd want to talk tonight. I'll get him in the morning."

He said, "How's he doing?"

"He's fine. He can't wait to see you."

She drove them out on Route 88, turned down over the hill at the town landing, and pulled into a driveway. Tom said, "What are we doing?"

"You remember Mrs. Woodworth that ran the lunch program at school and owns this house?"

"Yeah, she's had it for as long as I can remember."

"Well, what you might not know is there's great little apartment downstairs in this house. I rented it. I thought it would be great for Matty and I, so close to the beach. I didn't know you'd be coming home to us so soon."

"This looks great. Did you go see my mother?"

"Yes, and we need to call her. I haven't got a phone here yet."

"We can go over there in a little bit. I'm starving."

"I knew you would be. I'll make something quick, and then we'll go over to your parents."

They never made it. Tom told Kathy everything he knew about what had gone on while they ate their supper. She knew what a rat Skip Reed was, but this was way more than even she could comprehend. He told her he had no idea what they were going to be able to do to defend themselves. He explained to Kathy what the DEA guy, Goldman, had said to him during his interrogation.

"Kathy, you know I could be sent to prison for a long time."

"No, you won't be. That's not going to happen."

"Kathy, I was there. If they convict Joey, I can get nailed as an accomplice."

Kathy started to cry. "This can't be happening. It can't." He took Kathy into his arms. "I know, honey. I'm worried though. We've got to think about Matty. Right now he's not that attached to me, but I know that won't take anytime at all. I already love the little guy. I don't want to break his heart. He's already been through so much."

Kathy was sobbing, "What are you trying to say?"

"I don't know if we should be together until we know what's going to happen."

"Oh no, Tommy, you promised you wouldn't leave us . . . you promised."

"I don't want to, Kathy, but if they send me way, I'll ruin your lives. I can't do that."

"If you leave me now, our lives are already ruined. Don't do it, Tom. Have faith, please. We'll get through this. I know we will. Promise me you'll see what the lawyers have to say before you decide anything."

"Okay, I promise that's what I'll do. I'm really worried about the money to pay the lawyers. I don't have anything except the eight grand you gave my mother. That won't last anytime."

"Do you love me, Tom?"

"You know I do."

"Then you have to let me help you. I've got all that money from Ronny. We'll use that."

Tom reacted negatively. "That money is for Matty. We can't do that."

"We can do that and we will do that. You promised to be Matty's new daddy, and you have to do that."

"I'll try, Kathy." They curled up on the bed in each other's arms. There would be no lovemaking that night. They finally fell into a fitful sleep.

CHAPTER 83

S canton got up early and tracked down his station wagon. It was still there in the parking lot where he'd left it when they took off from Portland a few weeks ago. He went down to the dock where his father tied the *Gloria Walker*. His dad was already aboard doing an oil change. Joey gave him a hand. They hadn't talked about what went on yet, but Peter knew his son, and he also knew that when the time was right everything would come out. It was only seven thirty when they finished with the engine, so they decided to go over to Becky's for breakfast. When they walked in, it felt like every person in the place turned and stared at them.

There was a guy there named Roscoe Townsend sitting at the counter with some other fishermen. Roscoe was a drunk, and he was already loaded even this early in the morning. He growled at the Scantons as they walked by, "Hey, if it ain't the high and mighty Scanton boys. Now I know how you fellas always had the best of everything on them boats of yours. It's goddamn friggin' drug money, ain't it, Peter? Well, you guys finally got caught, didn't ya? I knowed something weren't right and I knowed it for a lot of years!"

Peter turned to Roscoe. "Roscoe, you goddamn prick of misery. You mind your own business before I lay your ass out right here and now!"

"Well, well, Mr. Peter Scanton, we'll all see now, won't we? Yes, sir, we'll all see." Joey knew this asshole was just the beginning of the shit he and his family would be subjected to. Tom and Pat will get the same kind of crap from jerks just like this one. They got a table way down at the end of the diner. The waitress brought the coffees right away. They ordered the egg and sausage special. One of the girls who knew Joey and his dad was waiting on them. "Don't you guys pay any attention to Roscoe. He's a drunken bum and everybody knows it."

"Thanks, honey," Peter said, smiling at her.

Their breakfast came and Peter said, "When are you guys going to get together with your lawyer again?"

Joey said, "I think it'll be tomorrow afternoon sometime. Shit, Dad, I don't know what I'm going to do for money to pay for any of this."

Peter said, "I know, son. Your mother and I don't owe anything on the house, and the boat's free and clear too. She's meeting with the bank today to get a loan, so the money will be there."

"Dad, I can't let you do that. This is my screwup. The house is yours. This is awful. Jesus Christ, this is awful."

"Joey, let me ask you something. Did you try to run drugs with Skip Reed?"

"Christ no, Dad. I'll tell you later on how this whole thing happened, but no, absolutely not."

"Good, that's what I thought. Now if it were your mother and I that were in this kind of trouble, what would you be willing to do to help us? Would you sell your boat?"

"Of course, I would. I would give you my last dollar and borrow another one for you."

"I know you would, son. Let's not talk about the money again."

They were eating their breakfast when Pat Chase walked into the restaurant and made his way to their table. When he walked past Roscoe's, the nasty drunk took a deep breath and was all ready to make a remark, but before he did he took a good look at Chase. He decided to keep his mouth shut. Smartest thing old Roscoe did that whole day. Pat came over to the table and sat down. The waitress brought him a cup of coffee.

Peter said, "Morning, Pat."

Pat took a drink of his coffee. "How you guys doin' this morning?"

Joey said, "I was thinking you and I should take a run up to Boothbay and see if we can find Uncle Charley and bring her home.

I have no idea if she'll agree to a car ride or not. You know I've never taken her off that boat since she's been running things."

Pat said, "Yeah . . . I'd like to go up. There's some shit I'd like to get off the boat, if they'll let me."

"With a federal sticker on her, I don't think they'll let us even go aboard, let alone take anything. I'm kinda hopin' that Uncle Charley will be an exception."

After breakfast they said good-bye to Peter and left the diner. It took them about an hour and a half to drive to East Boothbay and Little River. On the way they had their first chance to talk about what had happened to them.

Joey said, "I know it won't matter, but I couldn't be any more sorry about getting you guys into this fuckin' mess."

"I know the pressure you were under," Chase said, "but I'm surprised you didn't talk to me about his swordfish deal."

"I really wasn't going to do it. I thought with the fish we were catching, I could bring us out of it. Then when Karen stole the trip and the boat was being taken away from me, what the fuck else was I going to do? I owed over twenty-five grand when we left the wharf in Rockland."

Chase said, "You never told us about the back boat payments and them being after the boat."

Scanton said, "Karen had been getting served with the delinquency papers. She signed for them and then threw our copies out in the trash, I think."

Chase shook his head. "Jesus, Joey."

"That bastard Skip manipulated the whole thing right up to the end. I didn't get it. I was real stupid. What can I say?"

Chase lit up a cigarette. "I'm anxious to see what these lawyers have to say about our chances. I'm so goddamn mad about it I can't see straight."

"I know, Pat, me too. I'll bet you that one of the strategies the prosecutor will use is to try and get us to go against each other. We've got to stick together on this shit, or we'll all go down."

"I know." Chase said, "I'm wondering what they'll try to pin on me and Tom. We were sound asleep through the whole thing."

"I know . . . the problem is the one guy, other than me, that could testify to that is nothing more than ashes at the bottom of the mouth of the river now."

CHAPTER 84

W hen they pulled into the parking lot at Little River, the whole place was vacant. There was crime scene tape kicking around the parking lot, but no one was around anywhere. There were huge padlocks on all the buildings and federal No Trespassing stickers on everything. Scanton said, "Let's head over to the harbor and see what we can find over there."

The first place they stopped at was Coastal Fishing Enterprises. Scanton figured that they probably took the *Jubilee* there to unload her. The fish buyer there was a guy named Ralph Abbott. He had been buying fish there for at least twenty years. He was a Boothbay native, born and bred. Scanton hadn't sold a lot of fish to him over the years, but he had more than a few times. Ralph Abbot was a fellow who loved to talk. He had an old bassett hound that followed him everywhere. He came out on the dock as soon as he spotted Joey and Pat get out of the car. Scanton asked Ralph if they had taken fish out of the *Jubilee* at his place. "Sure enough, Joe. They unloaded here the next day after they arrested you fellas for lugging all them drugs into Little River." Ralph spit some tobacco juice on the dock. "They went and took your boat over across the way to the Stample's Yard."

"How much fish did we have, Ralph?"

"Jesus, Joe, it came into just over forty-two thousand pounds. You would have got good money for 'em. Them prices jumped back up again here a few days ago. I got a check ready for your uncle Sam for $67,000."

There was a look of pain on Joey's face.

"Thanks, Ralph. I appreciate you letting me know that."

Ralph said, "I guess that drug-runnin' business must pay wicked good to beat a check like that, huh, Joey?"

Scanton said, "There's more to it than what you've heard, Ralph. A lot more to it, trust me."

"I don't doubt that, Cap. No, sir, I don't doubt that at all." Ralph spit again. "Jesus, I was sorry to hear about Skip Reed getting his ass all blowed up like he done. They's folks around saying you fellas are going to get charged with his murder. That's what I heard."

Scanton said, "Jesus, Ralph, we had nothing to do with that."

"I ain't saying you did. I was just saying what I heard. I've only known one other killer in my life, and you ain't nothing like him."

"Well, thanks for that vote of confidence, Ralph. I appreciate it very much."

Ralph cocked his head a little to the side. "No problem there, Joe. When do you guys have to go to jail anyways?"

"We aren't guilty, Ralph. I know that's probably a huge shock to you, but it's the truth."

Ralph laughed and said, "I guess almost all of them fellas coolin' their heels up in Thomaston didn't do nothing either, the way I hear it."

Chase was really about ready to rip Ralph Abbot's head off, and Joey knew it was time to move on. He said, "Hey, Ralph, I keep a big black cat aboard the boat. You don't know what happened to her, do you?"

"Yes, by Jesus, I do. That cat's the goddamn spawn of Satan in my book. One of them fellas hired to bring your boat around tried to take that miserable friggin' banshee off your boat. I want to tell you, she bit the living shit out of that guy's arm and clawed the hell out of his leg too. He threw that fuckin' thing on the wharf and grabbed a bait fork and tried to kill it. That godforsaken cat got away though. I ain't seen it around here since, but if I do I'll break its miserable neck."

Joey and Pat both started to laugh. "Yup, that would be Uncle Charley. Good luck trying to break her neck. You better be heavily armed, old man."

They walked up the wharf still laughing. They got in Scanton's car and drove off toward Stamples.

Scanton said, "Old Uncle Charley will either turn up or she won't. I'm just glad she's not trapped on that boat. And at least she didn't get herself forked to death by that guy she beat the shit out of."

"I hope she can fend for herself out on the loose." Chase said, "She's been awful pampered on that boat."

"I know . . . Let's go over to Stample's and check out the *Jubilee*."

When they got over to the yard, they almost wished they hadn't come. They found the boat down on one of the lower floats. She was completely chained up. There were "NO TRESPASSING stickers by order of the United States Federal Government" on the windows. They were standing there looking at her and a man yelled, "Hey! What are you guys doing down there! Get away from that boat. That's the property of the US government!"

Scanton said, "I'm the owner of that boat."

"No, you ain't. That's government property now, and you stay the hell away from it, I warn you. If you don't take leave of this place immediately I'll get the sheriff here to arrest you!" The boys started up the dock. "All right, calm down. We're leaving."

On the way back to Portland, the reality of what was happening began to sink in. They were pretty quiet. Both men were thinking about their plight. The remarks made by Ralph Abbott really pissed them off. They knew he was an agitator and was trying to get them stirred up, and he had succeeded. It was not going to be easy to keep emotions in check. Joey hoped that Pat would stay out of the bars until this shit was over. With his temper and some guy starts running his mouth with him three-quarters mulled, it would become very nasty. He didn't want to think about it. He knew that bringing the subject up with Pat wouldn't change the outcome one iota.

CHAPTER 85

Tom and Kathy woke up about six in the morning. He wanted to go see his mother and dad. Kathy said, "Why don't you take my car? My mother has a great time with Matty in the mornings anyway. I've got a lot of stuff to do around here. Bring some clothes back with you, okay?"

"I thought we agreed that we should wait to hear what the lawyers say before we figure out what we should do."

"You may need to figure out what you need to do. I know what I want to do. You have to have faith if you want to beat this thing. Stop doubting yourself, and go home and get some clothes. Matty's going to be calling you stinky Tom all the time."

"Thank you, Kathy, for being so strong. I love you so much."

"Get going. I think you have a football game to play this afternoon. See this?" She pointed at her engagement ring. "It's mine and you're not getting it back."

Tom went over to his mother's. It was sad. Frances had a hard time with all the information, but she was absolutely convinced that Tom would be freed. He didn't say anything to dissuade her from that notion. He figured there was no point in doing that. He was learning that he had to be positive, if not for himself, then for others. He got some clothes together and hugged his mother good-bye. He told her he loved her and that everything would be all right. He didn't believe a word of what he just told her.

When Tom got back to Kathy's, he decided to go take up some of his lobster traps. The fishing was over in the bay pretty much, and he didn't want to leave the gear off any longer. Kathy gave him a kiss and told him to have a good time.

He went down to the town landing float and got his punt and rowed out to his skiff. Teddy had taken care of everything. He hoped that he had enjoyed hauling his traps. He was such a good friend.

God bless Teddy, the skiff was as clean as a whistle and the gas tank was full. His oil pants were neatly folded under the trap table.

The outboard started up first pull. He found his first row of traps and started loading gear aboard.

The skiff held about fourteen traps. Luck would have it that it wasn't quite high water yet, so he'd be able to get a good bunch in before he ran out of tide. He had a great spot on the Falmouth shore that he had been able to use for winter storage of his traps for years. He got five loads ashore before he had to give up and call it a day. He had a crate of lobsters, so he decided to clean up the skiff and run into Portland Lobster and sell them.

When he made it to the wharf, the float was open. He tied off his skiff and called for a basket. A stranger was working the scales. He filled the wire basket when it was lowered to him and climbed the ladder to go see Harlan Barnes. He was in his office.

"Hey, Tom, how you doing?"

"I'm fine, Mr. Barnes."

"Now, Tom, you and I both know that's not true. Your best friend has been killed, and you've been arrested for drug trafficking. That's not fine and you know it."

Anderson said, "I was just being polite. Where's Steve Warner anyway?"

"Last I heard he was fishing with Marshall Grimes."

"No shit, really? It couldn't be for very damn long. We just saw Marshall a week ago, and he hadn't lost his mind at that point."

"I'm sure that arrangement will be very short-lived." Harlan hesitated, as one would when beginning an uncomfortable conversation. "What really happened to Skip anyway? I really always liked that boy. He was about eight when he sold me his first five lobsters. He was such a good kid. He loved catching lobsters. He should have stuck to that."

"Nothing personal, Mr. Barnes, but we can't talk to anybody about what went on with this mess. The lawyers have us under strict orders."

"I understand, Tom. You know Andy Brown got arrested for lugging pot, right?"

"No, I didn't. Andy Brown? How was he doing it? Not in that old half-sunken skiff of his?"

"He was hauling the pot in Skip's *Ruffian*. The DEA grabbed the boat. She's stickered and hauled over at Handy's."

"Jesus, no. Where's Andy Brown now?"

"They have him locked up in Cumberland County. They say he's pleading guilty to all charges and that he's going away for a long time."

Anderson didn't say anything. He just wanted to get his lobster money and go home. Harlan paid him $200 for today's lobsters and gave him another $515 for the lobsters Teddy had been bringing in.

Harlan said, "Teddy refused to take a share from those lobsters. He took home probably a half dozen over the whole time you've been gone. He said he liked to make lobster rolls for his dad once in a while."

Tom said, "Thanks, Mr. Barnes . . . thanks for everything."

Barnes said, "Hey, Tom, call me Harlan, will you?"

Tom really wanted to get out of there. "Thanks, Harlan. I wish I could have told you more. You'll know all about it before too long. I'll see you in a couple of days. I've got another forty to take up."

"Okay, Tom, good luck with everything. I'll see you in a couple of days then." Anderson took off and ran back to Falmouth. He had a big football game he had to get ready for.

They had a quick supper. Tom got up from the table and said, "How about some football there, Matty boy?"

Matty looked at his mother. "Can we?"

Kathy said, "You sure can. I'll do up these dishes. Then I'll come out and watch."

Matty said, "Cheer for me, Mommy!"

"Always." Kathy went over to the front window and watched Tom and Matty running and falling in the sand. Matty could catch the ball really well as long as it was thrown underhanded. Then he would turn and run away as fast as his little legs would carry him.

Then it would be Tom's turn. Matty always caught up with him and took him down with the ease of a great defensive back.

As Kathy watched from the window of their little apartment, her heart swelled with love for these two men of her life. She was terribly afraid, but she believed in her soul that things would be all right. She prayed every night for Tom just like she did to get her Matty back. She walked outside to the beach.

"Mommy, I takeled him! I did it. Did you see me!"

CHAPTER 86

Joey dropped Pat off at Becky's when they got back from Boothbay. He went home to his mother's house. When he got there, Gloria told him that Jimmy Desanto had called and wanted to meet him for dinner down at The Village. He got a quick shower, changed into some good clothes, and headed down there.

Jimmy was at the bar when Joey came in. He greeted him with a hug. "Joey, how are you? You hangin' in there, boy?"

"I'm all right, Jimmy. Thanks for backing me and Pat the way you have. I really can't thank you enough."

"It's okay, Joey. I've been checking around with some people. I know you boys were set up by that asshole Reed. Jim Kelley is the best guy around when it comes to this kind of defense work. You're going to need some luck to go your way to get you out of this one."

"That's what worries me, Jimmy. I haven't had shit for luck lately, you know."

Jimmy said, "The hard part of this, the way I read it, is that with Reed being dead, we can't make him admit to what he did to you guys."

"I know, Jimmy. That little bastard is a pain in my balls, even dead."

"How did he get all that cash aboard the boat to pay for that much coke without you knowing it?"

Scanton explained about the propane tank trick. Jimmy said, "Pretty clever, really. I doubt that came from him."

"Oh no . . . this thing is way bigger than it looks."

"I heard some little jerk from Falmouth, Brown or something like that. He got busted lugging marijuana in Reed's lobster boat."

Joey said, "Andy Brown? Is that the guy's name?"

"I think that's it. I'm not sure. Who is he?"

"He's a moron that Skip had hauling his traps for him while we were fishin'. No shit Andy Brown. Maybe Skip was bigger in this drug-dealing stuff than I thought."

"We better hope that Kelley figures a way to distance you from Skip Reed's actions. He tells me there were two more guys arrested with you, besides your crew. What's the deal there?"

"That's the guy that worries me the most. His name is Sammy Dalton. He's one scary gangster. He's really the one that seized our boat. If he decides to throw us under the bus for some kind of a plea deal, we're done. That Carlos guy was strictly a Columbian thug."

"There would have to be one hell of a lot more than offering up you guys to justify a deal for this Sammy guy. Let's face it. In their minds, they already have you."

Joey was contemplating that statement when Teresa, Jimmy's daughter, walked over to them.

"Hi, Daddy. Hi, Joey." Joey looked at her. She was so pretty. Her blonde hair and blue eyes were captivating. In fact, he was staring at her so blatantly Jimmy said, "Jesus, Joey. That's my little girl you're ogling there!"

"I'm sorry, Jimmy. Hey, are you going to join us for dinner, Teresa?"

"Can I, Daddy?"

Jimmy said, "You're a grown woman. You can do whatever you want to."

Teresa slapped her father playfully. "You know what I mean. Am I interrupting you guys?"

"Yes, you are, but don't let that stop you."

Teresa said, "Okay . . . I won't. Let's get a table. I'm starving." They were seated in the back at a corner table.

Jimmy said, "You want a drink, Joey?"

"Sure, I'll have a beer."

Teresa said, "Me too, Daddy."

The waitress came and they ordered a round of beers. Jimmy had her bring some calamari as an appetizer. They had a great Italian meal. They didn't talk about the trial anymore. Joey asked

Teresa how things were going at the store. Teresa said they were busy as always.

"How's Olivia? She's such a beautiful little girl. I could hold her forever, I swear."

"She's great, Joey. You should come visit her sometime. She loves you too, you know. I'm sure she'd be thrilled to spend some time with you."

Joey said, "I will. That sounds great."

Jimmy said, "Oh god, here we go!"

Teresa said, "What, Daddy?"

"Don't you 'what daddy' me. You know what." Teresa and Joey both looked a little embarrassed.

Joey decided to change the subject. "Man, I wish I could find Karen though."

Teresa hesitated a second and then said, "I know where she is, Joey."

Joey's jaw dropped. "You know where she is. Nobody's heard a word from her in almost three weeks now."

"I've seen her. I think she cut her hair real short and is wearing a wig. She's driving a different car. I've seen her alone though. She hasn't had Little Joey with her."

"You gotta be kidding. Where did you see her?"

"The last time I did, she was going into the back door of a ground-floor apartment on State Street. You know me, I can't keep my nose out of other people's business. She parked her car about two blocks away on Ting Street and walked back over to State."

Jimmy said, "Jesus, Teresa, you never said anything to me about this."

"I didn't really think it was a big deal. I was planning to tell Joey when I saw him. I didn't know they were having any trouble until she didn't pay his boat bill at the store."

Jimmy said, "What were you going to do? Collect our money from her?"

"Daddy, I knew she was holding out on Joey, and it really pissed me off. So I did a little spy work. I'm Daddy's little girl. It's really your fault."

Jimmy rolled his eyes. "Oh brother, it's my fault."

Joey said, "Teresa, can you take me there?"

"Sure, Joey. You want to go now?"

"I'd really like to, if we can."

"Let's go. Daddy, pay the bill. I'll call you later. I love you." Teresa kissed her dad on the cheek and grabbed Joey's arm, and they were gone. Jimmy sat there and said to himself, *Daddy, pay the bill!*

It was less than five minutes to the place where Teresa had seen Karen the other day. They had decided to take her car. They figured that if Karen saw Joey's station wagon she'd hide in the apartment. They parked on the street. Teresa said, "Good luck. I'll be right here."

"Thanks for all this, kiddo. I really appreciate it." Teresa, in a very soft voice, said, "You're welcome, Joey."

He walked around the corner of the building. It was eight thirty. If Karen had Little Joey, she'd be home this time of night. He found the door Teresa was talking about. It was a metal fire door with no window. He knocked on it, but no one came. He was sure that someone was in the apartment. Even though the window shades were pulled down he could see a soft light behind them. He pounded on the door even harder, and eventually he heard footsteps. The door opened against a safety chain. He could see Karen's face.

When she saw who it was, she slammed it. Joey pounded furiously. He yelled, "Karen, open this door, goddamn it, or I'll get the cops over here! I want to see my son."

She didn't respond. "Open up right now, Karen, or so help me God . . ." The door opened against the chain. "You're not going to call the cops. The last thing you need is a domestic violence charge against you, and your sorry ass will be back in jail again."

Joey said, "Karen, please, I really want to see Little Joey. Whatever is happening between you and me, we shouldn't let it ruin Little Joey's life."

"I'm afraid of you, Joey. I'm not going to let you beat me up."

"I never laid a hand on you in my life."

"Not till now you haven't."

"I'm not going to touch you. I just want to see my little boy. Please let me in."

Karen slid the safety chain off and backed her way into the apartment. He went inside. It was nice. All the furniture were new—a new TV, a white leather couch, and a beautiful mahogany dining room table.

"Nice stuff, Karen. I guess the Gloucester trip money really came in handy."

Karen started yelling, "Don't you start with me, Joey. You owed me that money. You always got what you wanted. You had your boat, all your fishing buddies, even that stupid ugly cat of yours got more attention than your own family. You refused to buy me a decent house when you could have. You were making good money on deck with your old man when you inherited all that money from your uncle, but oh no . . . you had to have your own boat and be a big shot down at the wharf. Well, where's all that got you now? You're going to jail and your best crew member is dead. Way to go, asshole!"

Joey was furious. Maybe beating the crap out of Karen wasn't such a bad idea. He had never realized the hate she must have been carrying around in her all this time.

"You set me up real good, Karen. Spending all our money, letting the boat go into foreclosure, playing real sweet to me when I called you from Gloucester. You conned me as smooth as could be. I really believed your bullshit."

Karen said, "You're so selfish and self-centered. You have no idea what goes on right in front of your stupid ugly face."

Joey hesitated for a minute and looked at Karen closely. Her eyes were dilated. Her hands were shaky. There was something about her voice tone. Then it hit Joey like a ton of bricks. "Karen, are you high?"

"Fuck you, Joey!" He ran over to the kitchen table and grabbed her pocketbook and dumped it out."

Karen screamed, "Leave my shit alone!"

An aluminum foil wrapper fell out of her purse. He opened it, and there was at least an ounce and a half of cocaine inside. Joey looked at Karen. He was just about to speak when their little boy walked into the kitchen, rubbing his eyes. "Daddy, is that you?"

Joey swooped his son up into his arms. "It's me, little boy. How are you doin'?"

Little Joey said, "Daddy . . . I'm a big boy."

Karen said, "What are you doing out of bed? I told you to go to bed and not come out of your room until morning!"

Joey said, "No, Karen, it's over. My son is not going to stay here with you doing that garbage. You understand me? I'm taking Little Joey to my mother's until you get straightened out."

Karen screamed, "Your mother, your mother. That fat old meddling bitch can leave me and my baby alone."

Joey said, "No, Karen, this is not going your way. How long have you been into the coke?"

"How long have I been into the coke? I'm not into the coke. I just have a little bit now and then to help me deal with my life. I don't even need it at all."

Joey smiled. "Okay, then you won't mind if I get rid of this stuff." He opened the foil pouch up and poured it down the sink drain.

Karen screamed, "No, you bastard!"

Joey said, "That's what I thought. I'm leaving with my son. Let's go get some of your things, Joey. I'm going to take you to Grammy's house. Grampy Petey's there and he can't wait to see you."

Little Joey said, "Oh boy. Can Mommy come too?"

"No, not this time. Mommy will see you later. Let's go get some of your things now, okay?"

"Okay, Daddy."

They went into his room and picked out some clean clothes, sneakers, and jackets and threw them into a sheet and wrapped them up. When they walked back into the kitchen past Karen, she was crying.

Karen said, "Go ahead, take him. He's a lot of trouble, you'll see. I've got some things to do for a couple of days anyhow. I need a break. Then I'll be back to get my son, goddamn you!"

"Okay, Karen. We have to leave now. Call me when you're straight."

"Fuck you, Joey!" She slammed the door on them and locked it.

Joey hurried out of there and walked quickly over to Teresa's car. She jumped out and opened the door for them. They threw Little Joey's stuff in the back, and he climbed in beside it. Joey said, "Take me to my mother's, will you? I'll get my car tomorrow."

"Sure . . . How are you, Little Joey?"

"I'm fine. Are you Olivia's mommy?"

"Yes, I am."

"I know Olivia from the play place at the park."

"Yes, you do, honey. Maybe we can all play together there again real soon."

"Can we, Daddy?"

"We'll see." They drove over to Joey's mother's house and Teresa pulled up in front. They got out.

When they said good night, Joey thanked her profusely for her help. Before she got into her car, she kissed Joey ever so softly on his mouth. She said, "You're welcome. Good night, Joey. I'll see you later."

Joey's head was spinning. What a crazy night. He had to give some serious thought to his old friend Teresa.

Gloria Scanton was out of her mind with excitement when Little Joey came through the door. "Hi, Grammy! It's me."

She ran to him and swept him up in her arms. She squeezed him so tight he said, "Grammy, I can't breathe."

"I'm sorry, honey. I'm just so glad to see you." The tears were pouring down her cheeks.

"Me too, Grammy. Where's Grampy Petey?"

Peter wandered out into the room in his pajamas and said, "I'm right here, buddy boy. Come give me a bear hug!"

Gloria stood there for a minute. "We've got to get you to bed, little boy. It's way past your bedtime."

"Okay, Grammy."

Gloria took him upstairs to the bedroom where he always stayed when he came for sleepovers. When she was tucking him in, she stood there looking at this handsome child.

"You have your mother's beautiful green eyes."

"No, Grammy, Mommy has her own eyes. I saw them with her today."

"That's right, sugar. Those beautiful green eyes are just yours." She kissed him good night and turned off his light.

When she got downstairs Joey and Peter were having a cup of coffee and talking.

Gloria said, "How did you ever find him?" Joey explained how Teresa had spotted Karen. He hated to do it, but he also explained that he had caught Karen with cocaine.

Gloria gasped, "Oh, Joey, she's a drug addict. She can't have our grandchild ever again. I'll contact child protective services. I won't have my Little Joey with a mother like that!"

Joey said, "You've got to calm down, Ma. Karen may or may not be addicted to cocaine. For right now we have him, and we'll have to see what happens from here. I can't afford the distraction of a big fight with her right now. Just help me with him, and enjoy it. Okay, Ma?"

"You're right, Joey. That's what I'll do."

Joey said, "I'm going to see the lawyer tomorrow. I hope that we will at least get to tell our side of the story."

Peter said, "How did you make out up in Boothbay? Did you find your cat?"

"No, that sweet old girl tore some guy's arm half off, and she ran from a bait fork. I don't know if we'll ever see her again. If you guys don't mind, I'm going to take a walk down to The Village and get my car."

Gloria said, "Go ahead, dear. We're just fine here."

Peter said, "I might want to go fishin' tomorrow night. We'll go three-handed if you're up for it."

"I don't know, Dad. Are you sure you're going to be okay out on deck at your age?"

Peter said, "Get out of here, you bum!"

Joey walked down to The Village, had a beer at the bar, and watched the ball game. The Sox were at home and won four to two over Baltimore. He got his car and went back to his old apartment and looked things over. He planned to move back there within a day or so. The lights had been turned off. He had no idea whether the rent was paid or not. He'd call the landlord tomorrow. He was flat ass broke, and he'd have to deal with that problem in the morning too.

The Scanton household was up at seven thirty in the morning. Joey came downstairs, and grandmother and grandson were having pancakes for breakfast. Peter was already gone. Gloria was acting a little funny. Joey poured himself a cup of coffee and sat down. He turned over the morning newspaper and saw why.

PORTLAND MORNING HERALD

Four local men arrested in drug-trafficking bust in East Boothbay. Three survive and one man dies.

Arnold Reed of Falmouth died in a mysterious explosion as he tried to elude arresting officers in the largest drug-trafficking arrest in the history of the state of Maine. Reed was killed as the result of an explosion aboard a speedboat he was driving in an attempted escape from a small ocean/river outlet known as Little River.

Reed, according to authorities, was part of a cocaine-smuggling attempt thwarted by the Federal Drug Enforcement Administration officers and other law enforcement officials headed by Bertram Goldman, senior special agent in charge of DEA operations in Maine.

As part of the United States Drug Task Force arrest, the suspects were taken into custody at just after midnight Tuesday. Joseph Scanton of Portland, Patrick Chase of South Portland, and Thomas Anderson of Falmouth were all arrested and have been formally charged by Federal Magistrate Justice Carl Branton. All three men have been released on bail and remain in the Portland area.

In an interview, Agent Goldman said that this arrest was the direct result of a yearlong investigation conducted by the DEA. Also arrested were Michael Varney of Boothbay and a number of others, still unnamed, from various locations, including three tractor-trailer drivers all from outside the state of Maine.

Varney is the purported drug distributor. There was a large amount of marijuana seized that was in storage and scheduled to be transported the night of the arrest.

Scanton, Chase, and Anderson were arrested with approximately 350 kilos of Columbian cocaine with an estimated street value of $29,000,000. The fishing vessel *Jubilee*, owned by Scanton, was seized by law enforcement when it attempted to land at a lobster-buying facility owned and operated by Varney.

Patrick Chase was the victim of a mild gunshot wound and was transferred to a nearby hospital for treatment. Chase was later released and remanded into custody at the Cumberland County Jail.

Also arrested was a Columbian, Carlos Raphael, and Samuel Dalton of Gloucester, Massachusetts. According to authorities, based on early questioning, Raphael and Dalton came aboard the fishing vessel to assist in the transportation of the narcotics into the state of Maine. Allegedly the drugs were purchased by the crew of the *Jubilee* from a Columbian freighter. That vessel, allegedly, was met by the accused drug traffickers, at a point at sea, east of the Hague Line, the offshore boundary between the United States and Canada. The Hague Line was established by a treaty written in the International Court of Justice in the Hague, the Netherlands, dividing United States territorial waters from Canadian territorial waters. For more on this story, see tonight's *Portland Evening Herald*.

There was a large photograph of Scanton, Chase, and Anderson in their prisoner jumpsuits being escorted into the courtroom. Off to the side of the article there was an inserted picture of Skip Reed. The photo was taken of him standing at the dock at Falmouth town landing. He was wearing his fishing boots, oil pants, and a big smile on his face. He had the classic look of a Maine fisherman. Joey wanted to rip the paper into shreds. He sat there shaking his head. Little Joey had finished eating his breakfast.

He said, "Daddy, where's Kip?"

Joey wasn't paying any attention to his son. He said, "What, Joey?"

The little boy, with a somewhat frustrated tone, said, "Where's Kip?"

"I don't know Kip. Who is Kip?"

"He's Mommy's friend, Kip. He comes to my house sometimes to be friends with my mommy."

"I still don't know who you're talking about, pal."

"Kip, you know Kip." He pointed to the picture of Skip Reed in the paper.

Joey's heart almost stopped. He turned scarlet when he realized what had been going on behind his back. He yelled, "That fucking bitch!"

Gloria said, "Joey, don't talk that way in front of him, please."

"I'm sorry, Ma. I gotta leave for a while. I'll be back later on." He slammed the door on the way out.

He got in his car and drove over to Karen's apartment. He was so angry he didn't know what he'd do to her when he found her. The thought of his wife having sex with Skip Reed was more than he could comprehend. How long had these two been doing this? Karen was right when she said he didn't know what was going on right in front of his stupid ugly face. The goddamn bitch had some big questions to answer. He parked his car and went around back. He pounded on the door. No one answered. He banged harder and yelled for Karen to open up. She didn't come. Joey screamed, "Goddamn it, you bitch, open this door!"

A neighbor hollered, "Hey, shut up down there before I call the cops!"

Joey wanted to tell the guy to go fuck himself, but he couldn't afford that luxury. He had to calm down. He got in his car and drove off. He knew his dad was probably down at the boat getting ready to go. When he got there, the boat wasn't in her berth. He headed over to Ice and Fuel Services. He could see the *Gloria Walker* at the fuel dock when he drove in.

He parked and made his way down to give his dad a hand. He needed a distraction. The pain of being made into a complete fool was worse than the legal charges he was facing. He was totally humiliated, and the guy he wanted to deal with was dead.

CHAPTER 87

Karen Scanton had picked her sister up early. They were going to go to Boston and have a great day. Karen loved having a day free from Little Joey, plenty of cash, and a lid of coke. She had bought a two-year-old black Mustang with the some of the money from the Gloucester trip. She had already had a couple of hits this morning, and she was feeling no pain.

She was pretty upset about Skip getting killed. She could have cared less about him, but he was due for a big payoff if they hadn't completely botched the drug deal. She didn't hate Skip, but there were a lot of things she'd have rather done than suck his cock to wind up with nothing in the end for her effort. She should have known that asshole she was married to would screw up her plans. At least she had a good portion of the Gloucester trip money socked away.

She pulled into her sister's driveway and honked the horn. Her sister came out. "Hi, Karen. I'm ready to go!"

"Great, let's do it," Karen hollered back. She drove them over to the turnpike toll booth and headed south.

She told her sister about Joey showing up at her apartment and making a big scene. She wondered how he found out where she was, but it really didn't matter to her. He knew now, he had the brat, and she was free. The last thing she wanted to think about today was that asshole. They made idle chitchat for the next forty-five minutes. Then she pulled over into the breakdown lane by the Kennebunk exit.

Butch Harris had been driving tractor trailers for ten years. He hauled for a grocery chain out of Bangor. He didn't make a fortune, but he did okay. He had a wife and little girl and a new baby on the way. He was listening to a Willie Nelson tune on his tape deck. He spotted the black Mustang up ahead in the breakdown lane. The emergency flashers weren't on. He couldn't see the passengers. He was going seventy miles an hour.

Karen said, "Give me that lid in the glove compartment."

Her sister said, "Jesus, Karen, you're already flying. Wait till we get to Boston and I'll do a line with you."

Karen said, "Don't tell me what to do, bitch. Give it to me." Karen chopped a line on her little mirror. She had a glass tube and snorted the coke hard up her nose. She laid her head back as the magical powder shocked her system. She screamed, "Wow!" She threw her head back, put her car in low, revved the engine, popped the clutch, and pulled out directly in front of Butch Harris's truck. Butch laid on his horn and hit his brakes. He missed Karen's car by inches. Unbelievably all three lives would go along without change.

CHAPTER 88

The meeting at Jim Kelley's office was set for two o'clock. The guys all met in the lobby of the law office. All three men were anxious to have somebody hear their side of the story. Attorney Kelley walked out of a private office and escorted the boys into a large plush conference room. Peter Green was already there waiting. Jim shook hands with the boys as did Peter. Jim said, "First off, we have to get independent representation for you, Pat. Under the rules, even though we can collaborate on your defense, each defendant is required to have his own counsel."

Chase said, "You got any recommendations of somebody that will work cheap? I haven't got any money."

Kelley said, "I'm not sure you want a public defender for this trial."

"I don't know what to do about it." Pat said, "How much is this thing likely to cost?"

"It's going to be at least thirty grand," Kelley said, looking directly at Pat.

Chase laughed. "Well, pick out my cell, boys, because I ain't got it. I've saved for five years for a boat of my own, and I've only got a little over twenty grand. If they convict me after spending all that money, there will be nothing for my wife to live on. I ain't doin' it. Maybe they'll give me a plea bargain or something."

Scanton spoke up. "If you confess to something you didn't do, we're all screwed, Pat."

"I didn't screw anybody. The guy who screwed everybody here is dead."

Jim Kelley said, "Pat, that's exactly why you need a lawyer of your own to sort through these issues. I can recommend a good defense attorney from another firm."

"Pat, we'll work this out." Scanton said, "Let Jim call him. We can't let Skip Reed get away with this. We'll come up with the money. We aren't going to jail."

Anderson finally said, "Come on, Pat. We're in this together. Let Mr. Kelley here call this guy."

Chase decided to give in. "I hear you, guys. I don't look that good in stripes."

Scanton said, "You don't look good, period."

"Yeah, and you're a beauty queen. All right, call the guy."

Jim Kelley stood up from the table. "Excuse me a minute. When I get back, I've got some good news for you guys." He was gone only a few minutes,

"The attorney I called is a man named Walter Farley. He's got a good background in this type of work, and I think he'll add to our efforts very well. He can be here in twenty minutes. I was lucky to catch him. He's read about the case in the paper. Nice story, huh, boys?"

Scanton said, "The bastards have got it all figured out. What's the good news, Mr. Kelley?"

"Well, I think you'll like this one." He pulled a check out of his briefcase and slid it over to Scanton. The check was for $67,800 made payable to Joseph Scanton F/V *Jubilee.* Signed by William Howerton, assistant Unites States district attorney.

"Holly shit, Jim. How'd you get this?"

He said, "The attachment of those funds is a civil matter, not criminal. The government would have to prove that the money was a result of the crimes that were allegedly committed and not the result of a legitimate commercial enterprise. They weren't, so I requested their release. Agent Goldman said he had photographed all the fish on board the boat for evidence, so he authorized Howerton to release the money. Goldman is a straight shooter. This isn't a favor. It's what's right."

Scanton said, "Well, Pat, this will help. We'll figure out the share for this last trip and pay you the four grand I owed you from the Rockland trip."

"Jesus, that is good. I'm surprised Goldman didn't try to fuck us out of this money."

Kelley said, "I'm telling you guys, Goldman doesn't play games." He reached into his briefcase, pulled out some documents, and spread them out on the table.

Attorney Peter Green said, "We have to agree that there isn't any information shared here that implicates guilt of one individual over the other. We have to watch the prosecution carefully. With three defendants they will be looking for any opportunity, during discovery, to access information we might not want them to have. Some things we could say in a group situation may not be subject to client-attorney privilege. Consequently, Mr. Kelley and I have agreed that we are going to meet with you separately to hear your versions of what went on with each of you. I'm confident that Walter will agree as well."

There was a knock on the door. A large man walked into the room. Jim Kelley spoke up. "Here's Walter now." Jim introduced Walter Farley to Tom and Pat.

Chase said, "I'm the guy whose ass you need to save from jail."

Attorney Farley said, "I'll do what I can."

CHAPTER 89

It was nine o'clock in the morning when Agent Goldman and Agent Lamb were set up for their meeting with Bill Howerton. Howerton had worked as a prosecutor for the government for over ten years.

He had a degree from Bowdoin College and had applied to law school right after graduation. He was accepted and graduated from Boston University Law School, high in his class.

This was the biggest case of his career. It would bring him national recognition if he gets all these guys behind bars. He had worked a lot of cases with Goldman, and they always had a lot of success. In fact, they had only lost one major case for the government in the last five years.

Granted, a lot of cases went to plea bargains or outright confessions. This Scanton case was one he really wanted. He could practically taste it. He knew that these guys were into this thing up to their eyebrows, and he was going to prove it. He had spent the last few days reviewing the evidence. There was a definite connection between Vito Scantini and Joey Scanton. The tapes of phone calls and photographs clearly implicated Reed as the main contact connecting the entire crew of the *Jubilee* to the crime. He loved the fact that he had everything he needed to convict the dead man, and he was sure the same evidence would nail his buddies.

This Thomas Anderson guy was a little confusing though. A totally inexperienced man comes aboard a money-making dragger out of the clear blue. Then they're busted in a huge drug-trafficking crime? He was sure pretty sure that Anderson and Reed were in this together. They had been lifelong friends. Anderson was smart; Reed wasn't. Anderson probably planned the whole thing. This Chase guy would be easy. He had engineered the propane tank vehicle for transporting the cash needed to pay off the Columbian supply boat. No way in hell could anybody pull that off without the full cooperation of everyone on board. Chase was smart and experienced. Howerton had solid proof that no one on that boat ever dealt with propane, ever, except Mr. Patrick Chase.

As for Scanton, he had him dead to rights. There were four or five recorded phone conversations when Reed told Varney that Scanton had agreed to transport the drugs. They used the code word "swordfish," but the jury would have to be brain dead not to see through that. They had a chart where the location of the pickup had been plotted by Scanton. The Coast Guard had flown over them and positioned them on the way down and on the way back from crossing the Hague Line to and from Canadian waters.

There was no way Scanton wouldn't see thirty years in federal prison when the judge, His Honor Robert J. MacFarland, got through with him. MacFarland had been assigned the case within hours of the pleadings before the federal magistrate.

Howerton's ace in the hole was Mickey Varney. The deal he made with Varney's attorney to negotiate a witness-protection plan in exchange for his cooperation was perfect. This deal was not only for assisting in convicting the crew of the *Jubilee* but nailing Varney's out-of-state partners too. He was exposing all the Columbian connections as well. Varney's cooperation had so many people in the queue for arrest that the numbers were staggering.

Varney was one happy guy. He'd have testified against the pope if it got him off without jail time. The assistant United States district attorney in Massachusetts had arrested the three major drug distributors that had funded Varney in East Boothbay. They were apprehended at the airport as they were on their way out of the country the morning after the bust. DEA had confiscated $3,000,000 in cash and drugs, as well as houses, boats, and a bunch of luxury cars. There was no doubt the government had to put Varney in a witness-protection plan. He wouldn't survive a week in federal prison. A lot of guys would be serving time when he got done ratting them all out.

The Scanton and Chase convictions were solid. He'd get Anderson on aiding and abetting criminals in the act of a known federal crime. The larger arrests were taking precedent in his mind when Agent Bert Goldman came into his office for their meeting.

Goldman got along okay with Howerton; he had to. They were both federal employees on the same side of the law. The senior agent didn't like him though. Howerton was a very arrogant man. He was always talking to Goldman and his agents in a very condescending tone. It pissed him off to see how much more interested Howerton was in advancing his career than actually seeing justice done.

If the truth were to be known, it really didn't matter all that much to Bert Goldman anymore. After this case, he was retiring. He and his wife had already picked out a destination town in North Carolina that they really liked. There was a big golf course there, and he was really looking forward to being done with this chapter of his life.

When he arrived at Bill Howerton's office with Agent Lamb, it was just turning nine o'clock in the morning. Howerton got up and extended his hand. "Well, Agent Goldman, I see you're right on time. I think that's smart, on your part, considering I'm about to prosecute the largest drug bust in Maine's history."

Goldman thought, *Oh yeah, Howerton, and you're doing it all by yourself too!*

Howerton said, "I've really got things pretty well sewn up here on this one. I honestly don't think I need much more input from you boys, but I'm willing to fill you in on how I'm going to do this."

"I'd hate to waste your valuable time, but I'm somewhat curious about how you plan to convict all these people," Goldman said with a pleasant smile on his face.

"I appreciate that, because I really don't have all that much time," Howerton said, "but I can give you a brief overview. Then I really have to move on with some other very important matters."

Howerton never looked at Goldman when he answered. He plowed forward and laid out his plan of attack against Scanton,

Chase, and Anderson. He explained the basics to Goldman like he was speaking to an eighth grader from a middle school. He kept saying things like, "Not to get too technical with you boys but . . ."

After he was finished, Agent Goldman said, "That's very well thought out, but you have one major problem with your plan." Howerton became immediately defensive. With an angry look on his face he said, "No, Mr. Goldman, there are no major problems with my plan, and I know exactly how this is going to play out. I don't have time to sit here and listen to your famous homespun humor about interviewing stupid scared criminals and how clever you are at getting them to confess. I just don't need it. I've got these guys dead to rights."

Goldman accepted Howerton's hostile nasty tone without showing the slightest sign of concern. "Fair enough. That's quite a statement, Attorney Howerton. I didn't realize until now that you saw my contributions in exactly that way. Because you have everything completely figured out and under your control, my associate Agent Lamb and I will be leaving now."

"Nothing personal, Goldman, you're department does an excellent job. I'm just very busy, that's all."

Goldman said, "Nothing personal taken. You have a nice day. We'll be in touch. Agent Lamb here will assist you in any way he can."

The two federal agents left the assistant DA's building and walked out on to Congress Street.

Lamb spoke first and said, "What an asshole! As much as we deal with that guy, this one has really got his head swelled more than usual."

Goldman smiled and said with a sarcastic tone, "I think the term 'asshole' may be a little harsh, don't you? Maybe 'condescending prick' would be more appropriate."

Agent Lamb said, "What was it you were trying to tell him?"

Agent Goldman said, "It was something fairly important, but he didn't want to hear it, and you know me. I always respect the wishes of my fellow crime fighters. For now, it's better that you simply proceed with this case by supporting Mr. Howerton's efforts." Bert Goldman put his hand on his fellow agent's shoulder as they walked away. "Let's go get something to eat. My treat, Joe."

CHAPTER 90

Anderson had promised to stop by the supermarket. Kathy needed to have him pick up a few things. As he was leaving the checkout counter, Sally Reed, Skip's mother, walked in, and she was drunk. She was wearing a black dress and high heels. She staggered a little as she walked up to Tom. She stood in front of him for a minute just staring at him.

"Hi, Mrs. Reed."

Sally screamed, "Don't you 'hi, Mrs. Reed' me, you bastard!" She slapped Anderson hard across the face. He turned away in pain.

"I buried Skip today. There wasn't anything to bury, but I had a funeral service for him anyway. I can't believe you didn't care enough to even show up. After all my Skip did for you, how can you live with yourself?"

The other customers were all staring at Sally Reed, sobbing uncontrollably.

Tom said quietly, "It's not what you think, Mrs. Reed. Stuff happened between Skip and I and the rest of the crew. You don't understand."

Sally said, "The crew and you? Don't you make me laugh. You would never have gotten near that boat if it hadn't been for Skip, and now he's dead. He was trying to run for help to save you guys, and he was murdered. I think you were all in on it."

Anderson said, "No, Mrs. Reed, you weren't there. He was trying to escape from the police."

"That's a lie. My Skip never ran from anything in his life. He loved you, Tom, and you guys got him killed. All he ever wanted—"

Tom didn't say anything. He looked away from Sally Reed.

"I'll tell you something else." She said, "I'm going to get Skip's name up on the fishermen's memorial too. He deserves to be there."

"Oh please, Mrs. Reed, don't do that. Let him rest in peace. Save yourself from a lot of embarrassment. You really don't want to do that."

Sally Reed said, "I am going to do it, and don't you try and stop me either."

By then everyone within earshot was listening in on their conversation. This small town scandal stuff could be really fun! Things were really just getting started. Sally Reed turned away. She asked the clerk to get her some cigarettes. Anderson walked out the door of the supermarket, got in his car, and went home to Kathy.

CHAPTER 91

When Joey Scanton got home to his mother's, she was sitting at the kitchen table. She asked him to sit down with her for a minute. As he sat down he reached in his pocket and pulled out the check he got from the lawyer's office and tossed it to his mother.

Gloria said, "What's this?" He explained where it had come from.

"At least I can pay off the crew what I owe them. I ain't paying Skip's mother a friggin' quarter for his share. She can chase me for it."

"I'll get it deposited, and we'll figure out what you owe everybody." Gloria said, "I'll set Skip's money aside in case you change your mind about things."

"You can do that, but I'm not changing my mind about anything. That sleazy bastard got us in this horrible mess, and he can help pay to get us out of it."

Joey's dad was chafing at the bit to go fishing again. They were leaving to head offshore at three thirty in the morning. Joey hadn't talked to Chase, but he knew he would before too long. That man couldn't hang around ashore any more than he could. He knew that pretty soon they would be spending a lot of time with the lawyers getting ready for trial. Attorney Kelley had already told him that if they didn't file any motions for continuances they would be in court by the first or second week of January. He was ready as he'd ever been to let the lines go and be back fishing. He wanted to do some work instead of hanging around worrying about all this shit. Depression was starting to set in.

Scanton had decided to move back into his old apartment. He got a hold of the landlord and called the electric and phone companies after he left his mother's house.

He had to figure out a way to get someone to take care of Little Joey while he was out fishing. He really didn't want the child to be raised entirely by his grandmother, although she would be thrilled at the prospect. Little Joey was already in school half a day now. He kept thinking about how to make plans when every place his mind turned to there was a looming disaster. Finally he gave in and set his alarm clock for eleven o'clock and went to bed. Peter Scanton was planning to set sail at 4:00 a.m.

Joey was woken from a sound sleep by a ringing. As he came to he knew it couldn't be his alarm clock because it felt like he'd only been asleep for a few minutes. He woke knowing that he had had a bad dream, but he couldn't remember what it was about. The phone was ringing. It was 2:00 a.m. when he answered the phone.

"Hello?"

"This is Paul . . . man." The voice on the line belonged to a young guy who sounded like he was loaded to the hilt.

"Who are you?" Scanton said.

"I'm a friend of your old lady, man. You need to come over here. She's in bad shape right now. I think we need a doctor. She won't like . . . wake up."

"Jesus Christ! Did anybody call 911!" Scanton yelled into the phone.

"We tried to, but nobody knew the number." The line went dead.

Scanton called for an ambulance, threw his clothes on, and drove to Karen's apartment building.

By then time he got there the EMTs were parked out front of the State Street building and were on their way in with a stretcher. He ran toward the door. The place was packed with people. Everybody was either drunk or stoned. When he finally forced his way in, he could see Karen lying on the living room floor, unconscious. He said, "Oh god, Karen. What have you done to yourself?"

They had her on a stretcher and out of there in less than five minutes. Scanton grabbed one of the EMTs as they hurried out past him. "Is she breathing?"

The EMT answered, "Just barely. We'll have her at Maine Med in about five minutes."

Scanton followed them to the hospital. When he got there, there was nothing he could do. He called his mother and let her know what had happened. He told her so she could let his dad know what was going on and to not expect him at the boat.

He waited only about forty-five minutes when a doctor came out and told him that Karen had died. They just couldn't bring her up. They were sure that her death had been caused by a drug overdose. Joey put his face in his hands and started to cry. He couldn't believe what was happening. The grief he felt was completely overwhelming. As he sat there in the waiting room, trying to reconcile it all, he was totally confused about his feelings. He was so angry at Karen that he really couldn't understand where all this pain was coming from, anger and sadness merging like a train wreck. He felt like he should be able to walk away satisfied that she got just what she deserved, but that's not how he felt, not at all.

When he got up and left the hospital he was in a state of shock. He kept thinking, *How in hell do I explain something like this to a five-year-old boy?*

When he got home and climbed the stairs at his mother's, Gloria was sitting quietly at the kitchen table. Peter had decided to stay ashore until he knew what was going on and stayed there with her. They could see by the look on their son's face that something terrible had happened. As he explained they sat there in total silence. Gloria got up and poured them all a fresh cup of coffee.

"You're ready to go, Dad, and there's nothing you can do here. Why don't you just head off, and we'll give you a call later on through Portland Marine. I'm going to stay ashore and deal with this mess."

"Okay Joey, I suppose you're right about that, but I feel kind of funny just leaving you all here."

"Don't worry about it, Dad. You're better off where you belong. Go catch some fish. That's what we do."

Peter Scanton said good-bye to Gloria and left.

Joey finished his coffee and went upstairs to bed.

The days following Karen's death were absolutely bizarre. Her parents were from Connecticut and requested that Karen's body be released to them for burial at home. Joey agreed. He had no intention of attending her funeral anyway. This way her parents could pretend that things were different than they really were. By now he could have cared less. Even though her death was a shock, the betrayal of their marriage and her relationship with Skip Reed was more than he could comprehend. It was so hard to accept how much she must have hated him. She was willing to risk his life and everything they had for what she thought was going to be a big money payoff. The bitch was dead, and he was glad she was. Karen was permanently out of his life.

CHAPTER 92

P at and Leslie Chase were struggling with the pressure of the pending trial. He had so little real information on how this horrible situation began. Every time Leslie asked a question about it, he reacted with anger and would almost take her head off. He was frustrated and worried. Everything Leslie said seemed like a challenge of some sort. He kept blaming himself. He thought he should have seen what was going on and done something about it. He was imagining that Leslie was seeing his predicament like the prosecutors did. He was drinking a lot, and it didn't help the situation at all. In fact, it had gotten so bad with him being completely overly defensive, Leslie had shut down and wasn't talking to him about the trial at all. She didn't mean a single word the way Pat was taking them. She knew he was simply not equipped to deal with this mess, and it saddened her to watch him suffer so. He resented the situation he had been put in, and he resented the money that was being spent on the lawyers.

He didn't trust any of them to begin with. Pat Chase was an angry and confused human being. Adding to his frustration was the simple fact that he had no control over his own destiny.

Leslie really wanted him to go fishing with Marshall as soon as he could. She knew that there was something else that was bugging him, but he wouldn't tell her what it was.

It was nine o'clock on Saturday when Chase walked into the Portland Library. He approached the librarian and she said, "Can I help you?"

"Yes, please. I'm looking for a book on old sailing vessels of the mid-1800s. There's one I'm looking for in particular, and I'll know it if I see it."

"I think I may have something for you. Wait just a moment, please."

"Thank you." She was back in about five minutes with a file number. She directed him to a section of the library that had several large volumes on old sailing ships. He pulled down the book she had recommended and took it over to one of the large old oak tables. He sat down and opened it very carefully.

It was entitled *Sailing Ships of the North Atlantic*. There were pictures of sailboats dating back to the 1300s. There was one depicting the Norwegians sailing to Maine from Norway across and below Greenland in a small open sailboat with a single sail. He'd have to keep this information away from Tom or he'd never hear the end of it.

He kept looking. The paintings, the pen-and-ink drawings, and photographs were fascinating. When he got to the 1800s, the clipper ships began to take a dominant role in the book. There was a fleet of eighty-five of them. All but two were captained by men from Maine. There were pages and pages of wonderful pictures of these magnificent vessels. Then he spotted her.

There she was, The *Evan Stevens*! He slowly read the description. She was a barque, just a little smaller than a clipper ship rigged with three main sails instead of five.

She sailed from Nova Scotia to Maine and on to Boston, delivering wood, coal, and sometimes building materials. He stopped his reading immediately. What he was seeing made absolutely no sense at all, and his pulse began to quicken. He hadn't had a thing to drink all day, so he couldn't blame it on that. The *Evan Stevens* had sunk in August 24, 1842. That was 140 years before he saw that boat sailing beside the *Jubilee* in the thick fog. There was a picture of the captain. He was standing as straight as an arrow, facing forward with his black coat, and his captain's hat placed squarely on his head. There was no doubt in his mind this was the man he had seen at the wheel of the ship. The square jaw, the perfectly trimmed beard . . . it was him.

There was a young boy in a separate picture. He was the blond boy Pat had seen at the wheel of the boat. The article underneath the pictures said that the *Evan Stevens* had been lost at sea in a late summer gale in the general vicinity of Sigsbee Ridge. The captain's name was Joseph F. Homer. The young man in the picture was Nathaniel Homer. He was the captain's son. The boy was thirteen years old when the photograph was taken. They were returning to Portland from Canada. All hands of the fifteen-man crew were lost, including the captain and his son.

Chase had heard a lot of tales like this one over the years from old salts, half drunk, telling stories in bars.

He thought they were all bullshit. Now that it had happened to him, he felt very differently. He decided he wouldn't tell anybody about this one, ever.

Chase decided he had to go down to the waterfront and see if he could hunt up Marshall Grimes. It was time to go back fishing. He needed to find out if Grimes really would fire his man to take him on.

When he got down to the section of the wharf where Marshall had always tied the *Teresa Lynn*, there she was, sitting there. He walked down the wharf and stood there a minute watching. Marshall was talking to a deckhand and had all but lost his temper. His voice was raised to a loud volume.

"Jesus H. Christ, Warner, can't you do anything? All I wanted you to do was grease a few fittings, and you got the shit all over everything. Didn't your old man ever teach you how to work a goddamn grease gun?"

"I didn't have an old man. He took off when I was eight."

"He was probably getting to know you by then and decided leaving was a better option than murdering you."

Marshall happened to look up and see Chase standing on the wharf. "Patrick, tell me you're here to take a site on this boat with me."

Chase said, "If you still want me to go."

Marshall turned around and said, "Warner, the lord has gone and intervened on my behalf. Get your shit off this boat and get up the wharf. There will be a check for you from this last trip in a day or so. Pick it up at the office."

"You can't just up and fire me like that. It isn't fair."

"What ain't fair is you coming aboard this boat pretending to be a fisherman. Get the hell off my boat now!"

Warner grabbed his oil pants, climbed the ladder, and said, "All right, old man, but you'll be sorry."

Chase walked over to the ladder and grabbed Steve Warner by the shirt. "Are you threatening my friend Marshall, asshole?"

"No, man, no. I just don't like being treated like that, that's all."

"This is your lucky day because I'm not in the mood to beat the shit out of you right now. So just get out of here before I change my mind."

After Chase let Warner go, he ran up the wharf.

He hollered back at Pat, "You bastards are crazy!"

Chase thought, *Worse than that jerk off . . . I even see ghosts.*

Chase climbed down the ladder, walked over, and shook hands with Marshall.

"Well, Patrick, you scared the crap out of that useless waste of humanity . . . I appreciate it. My days as a pugilist are over."

"No sweat . . . Marshall, I haven't ever fished on an eastern rig before. I hope I can catch on."

"Christ, Pat, you'll love this old girl. She's a little tricky on the haulback, but you know Corliss Holmes that's been with me for the last hundred years? He'll show you everything you'll need to know."

Chase said, "Okay, Marshall, I'm looking to get out of Portland for a while. I'm some sick of this shit around here. When you planning to let the lines go?"

Marshall said, "We're going to take on fuel and ice her in about two hours, then we'll sail about midnight. Peter says there might be something going down around Three Dory Ridge."

Chase said, "I'll head over to the house and let Leslie know what I'm up to. I'll grab some clothes and some butts then come back and help you guys get fuel and ice. I couldn't get my oil clothes and boots off the *Jubilee*, so I got to get some. Why don't I meet you over at Fuel and Ice Services in a couple of hours?"

"Finest kind, Pat. Don't you rush now. Corliss and I have done this job a thousand times together. I'm looking forward to having you aboard, son. Corliss is by far the worst cribbage player to ever cut up a jack in the history of the game. I'm hankering for a good hand or two with ya."

Pat smiled. He felt a lot better than he had in the last two weeks. His gunshot wound had healed up, and he was ready to go fishing.

CHAPTER 93

Scanton and Chase went fishing, of course. Anderson stayed ashore and enrolled in a class at the university. He worked and he studied. The weeks dragged by. The case investigators were out there in full force. There were meetings with the lawyers, some separate and some with everyone together. It was a tedious process, and it was wearing everyone down. The same questions over and over. The endless rehearsing of answers to the questions that would be asked by the prosecutors had everyone on edge.

There would be very hard decisions to make. They had to figure out whether to allow any of the three men to testify in their own defense. Practicing in front of your own lawyer was one thing; being on a witness stand, with everyone watching and having antagonizing questions thrown at you by a nasty prosecutor, was something else.

The attorneys were all worried that if Chase got really pissed off this could go from a drug trial directly to a murder with a courtroom full of witnesses watching him do it and cheering him on while he did.

The paperwork was mounting. Regrettably, so was the evidence against the boys. The lawyers wanted to meet with everyone in a couple of weeks. There was an overwhelming gray cloud of fear and despair controlling the emotions of the group.

CHAPTER 94

Life on the *Gloria Walker* was pretty normal. The old days of fighting between father and son were over. Joey loved fishing with Harry Stone. Harry had been on deck with Peter Scanton a long time, and he was like part of the family. They were catching fish. Peter liked getting down on deck for a few haulbacks to break things up. He didn't stay out to put fish down though. Joey was getting in shape, and the boat was making money. They were fishing down around Fippennies. Joey was standing a wheel watch. Harry and Peter were asleep. It was just after 2:00 a.m.

"*Gloria Walker, Gloria Walker,* this is the *Jessica.* Come in, please."

Joey grabbed the mic. "Yeah, right here, Rusty. Where to?"

"Go to 88, Joey"

"Eighty-eight."

Joey had talked to Rusty Martin a few times since the arrest, but Rusty hadn't been ashore anywhere so they could get together face-to-face.

Martin said, "What's going on, Joseph? I figured they'd give you the twelve to four. You're the low man on the totem pole on that boat now."

"That's right, Rusty. They make me cook too. The old man hasn't had a decent meal aboard here in weeks. Over."

"I'll be ashore again in about two weeks. I'm going to take a few days off, and I'd like to see you."

"Finest kind, Rusty. I'll be around. You coming to Portland?"

"Yes. I haven't seen the old lady in a while. I'm pretty sure she misses me, but I'm not positive. This trip fishing shit is hard on a marriage." There was a pause.

Joey said, "You don't have to tell me."

"Oh shit, Joe, I'm sorry. I wasn't thinking."

"No sweat, man."

"All right, Joey. I'll give you a shout later on then. I'll see you in a couple of weeks. Over."

"Yeah, Rusty. Finest kind then. Talk to you later. *Gloria Walker*, clear with the *Jessica* back to 16."

"*Jessica* out!"

After Rusty Martin got off the radio, he was sitting in his pilothouse worried half to death about his friend. He had every son of a bitch he knew tell him that Joey was guilty as hell. They were saying that he and Skip Reed had been planning this deal for months. They had heard rumors about millions of dollars of cash hidden aboard the *Jubilee*. This trial was the talk of every waterfront bar from Eastport to Kittery Point. One asshole captain talking to Rusty said, "By Jesus, nobody could put millions of dollars on my boat without me knowing it. I'd have just taken the money and steamed for parts unknown. Fuck them Columbians and their cocaine. Scanton was in on it, sure as shit he was."

Rusty got so pissed he snapped at the guy, "You don't know a goddamn thing about it. Keep your fuckin' mouth shut and mind your own business." Rusty had slammed his way out of that bar.

As angry as Rusty was about it, he had to admit he had his doubts too. The whole thing didn't make sense to him either. He hadn't been able to talk to Joey other than a short phone conversation and a few chats on the VHF. There was no way they were going to talk about anything serious on the Maine Public Fishermen's Network, channel 88. The belief amongst the fishing community was the guys on the *Jubilee* were guilty as hell and would be going to jail for a long, long time.

A few minutes later the radio came up again. "*Gloria Walker, Gloria Walker*, the *Teresa Lynn* calling.*" It was Chase. Joey answered back and they switched up to 88. He was glad to hear his friend's voice.

"What's going on, Pat? How they treating you on that boat? Over."

Chase said, "They're good as gold to me. This is a great old boat, but I do have to admit I miss Tom's grub. This Corliss guy is a hoot, I gotta tell ya. He's a real downeaster. His sense of humor is something else. And then when Marshall and Vern Eldridge get going after each other on the radio, sometimes I think I should write down the shit they say. We've been listening to it for years, but I could make a fortune with their material. Probably no one would think it was that funny though. Just a bunch of crazy old loonies from Maine yapping on the radio to each other. Over."

Scanton said, "How do you like that eastern rig? Some different, isn't it?"

"Sure as hell makes turning to starboard easier. But you can see how Marshall got that net in the wheel that time. If the wind shifts during haulback and you lose the wind on the starboard side . . . you're screwed. You blow down right over the gear. What a pain in the ass. Over."

"You doin' anything on the fish? Over."

"Half of our last one before Rockland."

"Yeah, I see. We're about in there too. The volume's down but I heard prices are all right. You all set for the next meeting?"

"Yes."

A strange voice jumped in on the conversation. "Hey, you boys got any extra cocaine aboard this trip? We could use a good snort down this way."

Scanton said, "Time to go. *Gloria Walker*, clear with the *Teresa Lynn*."

"*Teresa Lynn* out." Pat said to himself, *Goddamn assholes.*

CHAPTER 95

Attorney James Kelley was meeting with two female associates who had been helping him prepare for the trial. Peter Green and Walter Farley joined them in the big conference room. Kelley started things out. "Well, ladies and gentlemen, we are due shortly to have a meeting with our clients and inform them as to the status of our defense strategy. Have you all had an opportunity to review the documents and photographs that have been sent to you from the prosecutor's office?" Peter and Walter said they had looked at everything.

Kelley said, "How do you see the prosecutor's case?"

Attorney Green responded, "They clearly plan to establish that Reed had been working the deal to transport the cocaine for at least a year. They have Varney's testimony that he had been actively planning the crime with Reed. Varney has worked out a deal with Howerton to turn his testimony for the prosecution as a federal witness. He's doing it in exchange for the witness-protection program. It's pretty apparent that he's going to testify that Scanton and Chase were in on this crime along with Reed. Their plan is that Anderson will be convicted as either an accomplice or on aiding and abetting or both. They will try to tie Reed and Anderson as tight as possible. The evidence shows that Reed helped Anderson get a job on the boat and that they had been best friends since childhood. The fact that Anderson denies any knowledge of Reed's drug-related activities isn't very compelling.

"They'll also try to connect Anderson to a guy they busted, named Andrew Brown. Brown's a weak character. He's terrified and will do and say whatever they tell him. He's already confessed to a drug-trafficking charge and is facing some serious time. He's hoping for a reduced sentence for his cooperation. Poor bastard won't get it from Judge MacFarland. Brown was using Reed's lobster boat to smuggle marijuana that wound up at our crime scene in East Boothbay. I still say that's going to be a little bit of a weak connection for Howerton. I should be able to undo any testimony from Brown on cross-examination.

"The problem is that the jury is going to hear one story after another about close associations with our clients and known drug offenders."

James Kelley said, "I agree. I received final confirmation that at the time of her death, Karen Scanton had large amounts of cocaine in her system and, in fact, did die from a drug overdose. We have to convince the jury that Mr. Scanton knew nothing of his own wife's drug use. From what we now believe, it appears that Karen Scanton was in fact an accomplice of Reed's, but we can't prove it."

Kelley continued on, "So in review we have Reed working on the *Jubilee* for two years, eventually to be blown up attempting an escape from federal authorities while under arrest for drug trafficking. We cannot and will not object to his guilt, because it's the basis of our defense."

The evidence in this case and how it would be presented to a jury was weighing heavily on the entire defense team. Karen Scanton, the defendant's wife dying . . . loaded on cocaine. Vito Scantini, the defendant's cousin, awaiting trial for possession of cocaine, illegal weapons. There was a large sum of cash that was coincidently provided by their client. Add one other confessed drug trafficker, Andrew Brown, awaiting trial and sentencing. Brown was also a lifelong acquaintance of one of the defendants, Tom Anderson, as well as an associate of Reed's. Anderson, Reed, and Brown all graduated from high school together and were considered by witnesses as friends. It wasn't looking good for the boys and the lawyers all knew it.

Walter Farley said, "From my research they are going to try to tie Pat Chase to the cash they used to pay off the Columbian supplier. We now know that the amount was around $9,000,000, courtesy of information provided by Varney. From the photos we received from the DEA and the information from Varney, we know the cash was put aboard the *Jubilee* in Rockland in a sealed propane tank. They have records that implicate Chase, because all propane gas orders came through him as the boat's engineer. That included an order placed while the boat was headed into Rockland to unload. That tank order was allegedly cancelled, although Chase says he didn't cancel it. The prosecutor's office is saying it was a ruse to create confusion. If that's the case, they have certainly accomplished that. They confused me.

"The prosecutor's office has been trying to implicate the owner of Rockland Propane. He's a very good friend of Chase's. They think he was part of the action, although there has been no arrest, as of yet.

"That's one thing Varney isn't forthcoming on. He stated the amount of cash that was to be paid the Columbians for the coke, but that's it. He won't talk about the propane switch or any other details related to it. Howerton doesn't care. He has twenty photographs of the tanks being loaded on board the *Jubilee* that were taken by DEA investigators. No one can figure out why Varney won't talk about it. He says he doesn't know anything about that part of the deal. All he did was ship the drugs for a fee. We know he's lying, but I'm not sure that helps us any."

James Kelley said, "Anything else, folks?"

"My greatest concern is that the star witness for the defense is dead." Peter Green said, "We certainly have enough understanding of how this deception was accomplished. How in hell do we make a dead man confess to his crime?"

Walter Farley said, "What's being said about Reed's death?"

"They say that another Columbian, who was assigned to work the onshore side of things, must have planted a bomb at the request of the Columbian freighter captain. He apparently flew home to Columbia the night before the bust. Clearly, the captain of the freighter didn't want to wait for his own crew member or this Samuel Dalton guy to return to the mother ship. Reed was just in the wrong place at the wrong time."

James Kelley said, "What do we know about Dalton?"

"My people say he's the main out-of-state contact between Varney and the money guys. He's apparently a major criminal player. Varney hates the guy and can't wait to burn him at his trial. Dalton should see at least thirty-five years."

Walter Farley continued, "I agree this one is tough because there are so many drug-related connections to our clients. We have to convince twelve jurors that our guys are innocent bystanders to the biggest drug bust in the history of the state of Maine. The irrefutable facts are they loaded $9,000,000 in cash aboard the boat, and they crossed the Hague Line and picked up 350 kilos of cocaine from a Columbian freighter and brought it in to East Boothbay. The captain, our client, was at the wheel when the DEA arrested the entire crew. There is no unbiased uninvolved witness that can testify in their defense. Has anyone thought about a guilty plea for a reduced sentence?" Green and Kelley agreed that it had to be a consideration. This case looked like a fairly certain conviction to all the members of the defense team.

Kelley said, "Gentlemen, I think we should all meet with our respective clients privately before Tuesday's meeting. Please let me know if we have any further developments in the meantime. Thank you all for coming."

James Kelley walked back to his office. He sat down at his desk and folded his hands behind his head and stretched. The stress of this case was wearing on him. He truly believed the boys were innocent, and the frustration of not being able to get to the truth was taking its toll. He sat at his desk thinking, when he happened to looked down. There was an unaddressed white envelope lying there. He picked it up and tore it open.

Dear Jim,

I think it may be in your best interest to contact me to set up a meeting. Please call me on my private line to do so. 775-7898 is the number. I need to have this communication remain absolutely confidential. That includes the other attorneys involved in your current case or anyone else in your office.

Bert Goldman

Kelley read the note several times. There was no way this was a setup. He had watched Bert Goldman run the DEA for years. Generally speaking, DEA guys and prosecutors hate defense attorneys. Goldman's whole office worked their asses off to arrest criminals, and then the defense guys come along and set them free. He was most anxious to meet with Agent Goldman. He immediately dialed the number written on the note. On the first ring the phone was answered, "Bert Goldman here."

"Hi Bert, Jim Kelley. I received a note from you and was responding to it."

"Great, Jim, do you have a minute when we might grab a cup of coffee?"

"Sure, where would you like to meet?"

Goldman said, "How about a diner in Lubec?"

Kelley laughed. "Someplace where we wouldn't be recognized, is that it?"

"That would be what I have in mind, yes." Goldman hesitated a minute and said, "I'll tell you what. I'll pick you up in front of your office in twenty minutes. I'll drive one of the unmarked cars I have available, so no one will think you've been picked up by the narcs."

Kelley said, "That would be nice. I would prefer that be the case."

Agent Goldman had been expecting this call and was ready to leave his office immediately. "I'll see you in a little bit."

Goldman pulled up in front of Jim Kelley's office in a gray Volvo station wagon. When Kelley spotted him, he thought, *When this guy says unmarked, he means it.* He got in the car.

"Okay, Bert, what's on your mind?"

They were gone for almost an hour. When Goldman dropped Kelley off and he was getting out of the car, he looked at Goldman and said, "Are you absolutely sure that I can rely on what you told me today? Is it all true, Bert?"

"One hundred percent. At the end of the day, right is right, whether we like it or not," Goldman said.

Kelley was deep in thought. He didn't say good-bye. He just closed the door and looked around to see if anyone was watching him. As Agent Goldman drove off, Kelley walked slowly up to his office thinking about how he would handle what he had just learned.

CHAPTER 96

When Anderson walked into their apartment, Kathy said, "We got a call from your mother. She said that your lawyer Peter Green called their house looking for you. He wants you to call him a soon as you can." She immediately saw a worried look come across his face.

He said okay and grabbed the phone and dialed Peter Green's office.

"Tom Anderson calling for Attorney Green, please."

"One moment," the receptionist responded.

There was no delay . . . Peter Green answered the line.

"Hey, Peter, Tom Anderson. My mother called and said you were looking for me."

"Yes, I am, Tom. Look, we need to have a talk before our meeting with the rest of the group."

"You sound pretty serious, Peter. Should I be worried?"

Peter didn't answer his question.

Green simply replied, "When can you come in? I've got an eight o'clock in the morning tomorrow open."

"I'll be there, Peter."

"Okay, Tom, I'll see you in the morning then."

When Tom hung up the phone Kathy said, "What's the matter? You look upset, Tom"

"I don't know, honey. Peter sounded very concerned. It wasn't exactly what he said. It was how he said it."

"Are you sure? Sometimes you tend to read into things."

"I don't think so, but I guess we'll see tomorrow."

"If you're going in the morning, I'd like to go. My mother will take Matty."

"Of course you can come. It's better that way. I don't think I always repeat what goes on accurately."

It was a sleepless night. They got up in the morning and drove into Portland early and had breakfast at Becky's. The fishing crowd was there but no one said anything to them. Anderson figured it had to be mostly because Kathy was with him that people were able to control their mouths. Plus the fact that, just like everything else, the newness had sort of worn off.

Anderson knew that Chase and Scanton were both ashore. He had hoped he might run into them. Kathy and Tom enjoyed their breakfast and were about to leave when he saw Agent Goldman walk into the diner. Tom's heart ran to his throat. He couldn't help it; Goldman was the enemy. He was working to destroy his life, and he hated him with a passion. Tom and Kathy were on their way to the register. He didn't know how to react. Bert Goldman solved that problem. When he saw them leaving he said, "Hello, Mr. Anderson. I hope you enjoyed your breakfast." Anderson was so stymied he said, "Thanks, Mr. Goldman. It was good." What he had wanted to say was, *Fuck you asshole. Eat shit and die!*

After they left the place, Kathy said, "Who was that?"

"That was Agent Goldman, the head of the DEA that arrested us all."

"He seems nice."

"Jesus, Kathy, he's trying to put me in jail!"

"I'm sorry, Tom. I didn't know who he was. He looks just like any other man to me."

"Well, he isn't. He's a rotten bastard and I hate him."

"Okay, Tom, I understand. I'm sorry. Let's get up to your lawyer's office and see what he wants."

Anderson said, "I'm sorry, Kathy. I get really upset when I see that guy."

"It's okay, dear. It's understandable."

The receptionist at Peter's firm escorted Tom and Kathy into his office as soon as they came in. Tom said, "Peter, this is my fiancé, Kathy."

Peter extended his hand to her. "Hi, Kath. I've met her before. She hired me to defend you." Tom had forgotten that.

Green continued, "Tom, this isn't going to be easy. As you know, the prosecutor's office has now supplied us with the complete file of evidence. We know what their plan of attack is. I have to tell you the case against you is very serious. We have all concluded that Skip Reed being dead poses the largest threat to our defense case. We understand that he manipulated this entire scenario, but with him gone we can't prove what he did. The prosecution has cut a deal for the witness-protection program with Mickey Varney in exchange for his testimony."

Anderson said, "Can they do that? Why wouldn't he lie to make a deal for himself? I never even met this Varney guy, and he's going to testify against me?"

Peter nodded his head. "That's how it works. We'll try our best to repudiate his testimony on cross-examination. That's only one of the issues. How do you know Andrew Brown?"

Anderson said, "He's an idiot that went to school with us. He lives in a trailer park with his mother. He's a big pothead. Somebody said he was arrested for smuggling pot. What's that have to do with me?"

Green said, "Howerton is going to try and make a case that you and Skip Reed were accomplices of Brown's."

Anderson's face got bright red. "That's total bullshit. I barely know Andy Brown. I told Skip he was nuts to make a deal with him to haul his traps while we were gone. I didn't know anything about pot smuggling!"

Green said very calmly, "I know, Tom, but the big picture is there are so many drug connections to all of you that proving you guys innocent is going to be—there's no other way to put this—practically impossible."

Anderson's heart began to race and so did Kathy's.

He raised his voice. "What are you trying to get at here, Peter?"

"It's my duty to discuss the possibility of a guilty plea for a reduced sentence with you."

Kathy put her hands to her face. "Oh god, no."

Tom said, "Well, fuck that. I didn't do anything wrong at all here. It's your job to get me off, not help out Bert Goldman and have me confess to something I didn't do."

Green said, "You have to be prepared. If you lose, this federal judge—MacFarland is his name—has a reputation of being very hard on drug offenders. You could see a minimum of ten years and a maximum of twenty-five." Everyone was silent for a minute while that bit of information sunk in.

Kathy started to cry. Peter said, "I'm so sorry, guys, but this thing looks very bad right now. You need to carefully consider a plea bargain. We could possibly get it down to five years."

Kathy said, "Oh god, you can't be serious." The tears were streaming down her face.

"I've never been more serious about anything," Peter green said very softly.

Anderson said, "I don't need to talk with the other guys before I decide what to do. I'm not going for any plea bargain. When those jurors hear our side, we'll be all right. You better get on board with us, Peter, goddamn it, or I'll fire you and get someone who believes in us."

Peter Green withdrew slightly. "I'm sorry that that's what you think. I've worked defending people for over fifteen years, and these trials don't go the way you think they do."

Tom was unyielding. "Well, Peter, just figure out how to prove three innocent men innocent. That's your fucking job. Now do it . . . no stories. Come on, Kathy, we're leaving. I assume I'll see you at Kelley's office this afternoon. Let's hope he hasn't given up on us too."

Green was still trying to get Tom and Kathy to understand. He said, "You're getting this all wrong, Tom."

"No, I'm not getting this all wrong, Mr. Green . . . you are." Tom and Kathy left the law office without another word.

CHAPTER 97

That afternoon at two o'clock the three defendants were sitting in the reception area of Jim Kelley's office. It was apparent that their attorneys were early and waiting in one of the conference rooms. Anderson said, "Did you guys get the same line from your lawyers as I did about a guilty plea for a reduced sentence?"

Chase said, "I did, and I haven't told my guy about what I think about it yet. I'm going to in about two minutes. How about you, Joey?"

"Kelley talked about it some, but he knew my answer just by looking at my face. He keeps trying to figure out a way that he can show the jury how goddamn stupid I was to believe Skip's bullshit. I never thought it would be important for me to prove my ignorance. I told him that it had always come to me naturally. I never had to prove it to anyone before." The receptionist got a buzz on her phone. She looked up and said, "You gentlemen can go into the conference room now, third door on your left."

Two of the attorneys, Peter Green and Walter Farley, were sitting and chatting with two women whom the boys hadn't met. They sat down and went through the usual greetings. Attorney Green said, "We're here today to fully discuss our defense strategy for the upcoming trial. Mr. Kelley will be in here in just a minute. Is there anything we need to discuss before we begin, guys?"

Chase said, "Yes, I have something I'd like to say." He was just about to start when James Kelley walked into the room and placed a rather large file folder down on the conference room table. "Sorry to interrupt you, Pat, please go ahead."

"All right. I gotta tell you guys something and especially you there, Wally." His tone of disdain was nearly palpable. "All three of you guys are really pissing me off. I know every one of you assholes have been talking to all three of us about giving in to these bastards and trying some plea deal for a lesser sentence. Well, you can shove that idea right up your asses. You pussies need to come out on the boat with us some winter night with it blowing forty and the boat making ice. Afterwards you might not be so anxious to talk to three innocent guys quitting on themselves. Where we spend our lives, giving up when things get bad is not an option. If it starts to come off real nasty, you have to calm down, take a deep breath, steady out, and get through it. You can't run around like a bunch of chicken-shit bastards, go hide under the bunk, and hope you make it through. If you jerks can't step up and figure out how to get the three of us proven innocent, you're worthless as goddamn lawyers, and you ought to go into a different line of work. I'm sorry if you don't like what I had to say. That's how I see it."

You could hear a pin drop in the room. Attorney Kelley was the first to speak. "Well, Pat, don't hold back. I guess you had a right to get that off your chest. Please understand we have an obligation to inform you, as our clients, of all your options under these serious circumstances."

Scanton said, "Yeah, Jim? We call that '*you* covering your own asses.' We are probably just a bunch of stupid, uneducated fisherman to you smart guys, but we are hoping that it's going to be people just like us on that jury. Nothing works like telling the truth and we'll tell it. You guys need to believe what we told you and make the jurors believe it too."

Walter Farley said, "Mr. Chase, I apologize if I haven't conveyed the right attitude to you, which I clearly haven't. I think we would all be better off if you had different counsel."

Chase shook his head in disgust. "You really can't take it, can you? I agree with you. I need another man. Don't let the door hit you in the ass on the way out, Wally boy." There was total silence in the room as Attorney Walter Farley gathered his files and left the room.

After he was gone, Chase said, "That guy and I . . . it was never a match."

James Kelley said, "That may have been the biggest mistake of your life, Pat, and it was totally uncalled for. Walter Farley is a very talented defense attorney, whether you like him or not. There was no need for you to be rude to him like that."

Chase said, "I'll take the risk. I'll find someone else. My life is on the line, and so are these other guys', and that man has no balls. I don't care what you say. Do you all need me to leave now? I gotta tell you something though, before I leave. As for being uncalled for . . . this whole goddamn thing was uncalled for. That rat bastard Skip Reed screwed everybody here, and I'm glad that little prick is dead."

Peter Green said, "No, it won't be necessary for you to leave. Please sit down and let's figure out where we're going from here."

Chase said, "I'll just sit back here and keep my mouth shut."

Things settled down some after that. Tempers on both sides flared a few more times, but for the most part, it was a productive meeting. They examined and reexamined all the photographs and tried to remember the exact circumstances and what was being talked about at the time each one was taken. They went through the list of defense witnesses and decided that all three men should testify on their own behalf. Chase said if he did wind up in jail, he would feel a whole hell of a lot better about it if he at least had a chance to tell his part of the story anyway.

Chase said with a big smile on his face, "Don't worry, boys, I can be wicked charming when I want to. Ask my wife."

Attorney Kelley was holding something back, and Peter Green could sense it. After the meeting was over he hung back and talked to Kelley about what he'd been sensing.

Kelley said, "I'm not at liberty to tell you about what's on my mind. It would break a promise that I made, which could have terrible repercussions for our clients and others if I did. You'll have to trust that I'm making the right decisions and let it go at that." Peter Green was frankly annoyed but agreed to let it go, but he was definitely intrigued by Kelley's statement. Kelley could see that look on his face.

"Peter, please don't be distracted by this thing I've got going on. Let's focus on the evidence and win this case."

Green said, "I hope Chase chooses a good lawyer and does it quickly."

"I'm not recommending another one, I'll tell you that."

Green nodded his head in agreement but said, "I do know a guy out of Lewiston named Philip Davis that's very good. I think he'd like these guys. He's handled a ton of tricky drug cases. Lewiston, that's a tough city, you know."

Kelley said, "I've heard of Phil Davis. I know him by his reputation. Get a hold of Mr. Chase and see if you can set it up. I know I can work with that guy."

Peter Green called Chase the next morning, and he agreed that he'd be willing to drive up to Lewiston to meet with this lawyer if Green could set it up. A meeting was arranged for three o'clock that afternoon.

When Chase arrived at Morgan, Davis, & Pratt he had no idea what to expect. Nothing could have prepared him for Attorney Philip Davis anyway. The office was on the first floor of an old derelict building on a dumpy section of Lisbon Street. He parked his car and walked into the building. The place was practically falling down. The receptionist was a woman of about fifty trying very hard to be thirty-something. Bleach blonde, slathered in red lipstick, with her breasts stuffed into a tight blouse displaying a lot of cleavage. She had on so much perfume it almost made you pull away. Chase took in the scene. "I'm Pat Chase and I have an appointment with Mr. Davis." The receptionist had a nameplate on her desk. It said "Marilyn" in bold letters; he wondered if that was her real name.

Marilyn turned around and yelled, "Hey, Phil! Your three o'clock is here." Marilyn turned to Chase and said, "Sorry about that, darlin'. The intercom thing has been broken for the last couple of years."

He said, "That's okay, sweetie. I hate those things anyway."

"I hate 'em too." She smiled at him, and for reasons he couldn't explain he liked her and suddenly felt comfortable.

Chase heard someone coming toward him. He turned and watched a semibald man, about five foot nine, in his late fifties, and at least thirty pounds overweight, walking toward him. He was wearing dark-blue pinstriped trousers, supported by black suspenders, and a bright white shirt. His sleeves were rolled and he was smoking a short cigar. He said, "I'm Phil Davis, kid. Come on in here a minute."

Chase followed him into what passed, in this office, as a conference room. Mr. Davis said, "Sit down right here. They tell me you fired a real good lawyer down there in Portland because you didn't like him. That was stupid . . . you're probably not going to like me either."

Chase said, "It wasn't just that I didn't like that guy. He was trying to get me to agree to a plea bargain. That's what pissed me off."

Davis said, "Now you listen to me a minute, kid. It don't mean nothing, that plea bargain shit. They make us lawyers tell you guys that so you won't bitch about it after you lose in court and wind up in jail. I'll tell you right now this law shit is not a personality contest. You don't strike me as the kind of guy who graduated from charm school yourself."

Chase laughed. He had definitely found his attorney. Davis said, "Let's talk about what went on with these charges. I've had a chance to read through the file quickly, mind you. I don't give a shit whether you're guilty or not by the way. My job is to beat those bastards on the prosecution side and get you off. I've freed a lot of guilty guys over the last thirty years doing this job."

Chase said, "I didn't do anything. Neither did the other guys on the boat, except for that piece of shit Skip Reed that got his ass blown up." Phil Davis listened intently to the whole story without comment.

After Chase was through, Davis said, "I'll take on the case if you want me to. I don't know or care about the other guys. You, I'll probably figure a way out of this mess for. You got about a fifty-fifty chance of not seeing jail time. If you can live with those odds, I'll move ahead."

Chase swallowed hard. "I'm not liking those odds at all. At least I know you won't try to sell me on a plea bargain to make it easier on yourself."

Davis laughed and said, "That's an absolute fact. I've never made it easier on myself. I'm ready for this if you are."

They talked about the case for about an hour and a half. Davis concluded that the prosecution's case against Chase seemed to be based on guilt by association more than anything, which is no small thing in a criminal enterprise of this size. He would have to prove that Chase had no knowledge of any drug-trafficking conspiracies during an almost-one-year time span that led up to the arrest. Proving that would be the greatest challenge an attorney could ever face. Once a jury listens to all the facts laid out for them, they would ask themselves, *How could this guy not have known what was happening?*

After they finished talking about the case, Chase signed a document agreeing to retain Davis as his counsel. A large check would be sent to Mr. Davis's firm.

Phil Davis told Chase he would be in touch with the other attorneys soon. They shook hands, and as Chase walked out the door, Davis said, "Anytime you feel like making rude and insulting remarks to me, feel free to go for it. I can take it, and I won't quit afterward either."

Chase laughed. "Thanks, Mr. Davis, I'll keep that in mind if the urge strikes me."

As Chase made the drive back to Portland he felt much better. Phil Davis hadn't made him any promises about how this was going to turn out, but he was starting to feel a little more confident. He wished he'd had this guy on the case sooner. The waiting for the trial was driving him crazy. He never thought that he would be anxious to go to a trial where he could be sent to jail for the majority of the remainder of his life.

He bought a twelve-pack on the way home. It was gone before midnight. Leslie went to bed about ten o'clock. The worrying was taking a terrible toll on her.

CHAPTER 98

The days and weeks before the trial dragged on. Nothing of any significance had changed. The lawyers worked together to try and put together the best defense possible for their clients. The prosecution, under the direction of Attorney William Howerton, prepared for the conviction of all three defendants. Howerton and his team had worked hard too. They had interrogated everyone with a possible connection to the men of the *Jubilee*.

The investigators talked to Harlan Barnes. They intimated that he had arranged for Andrew Brown to use Skip Reed's lobster boat for drug transportation. They told him that he could be charged with conspiracy to transport narcotics illegally. They thought they if they could connect Reed and Anderson with Barnes they'd tighten the case. By subpoena, they did a major review of all his financial records. They were looking for a large deposit that might prove to be a drug payoff. They reviewed his relationship with Steve Warner, the guy he had working for him on work release from Cumberland County Jail. They were speculating that with Warner's criminal record, there might be a connection that would lead them somewhere. They found nothing. Harlan Barnes was just exactly what he appeared to be—a lobster buyer, nothing more, nothing less.

Howerton's office had the Massachusetts DEA do a full-blown investigation of Artie Valente, the fish dealer from down in Gloucester. They tore his business apart limb from limb. What they really wanted was to find a connection between Artie and Sammy Dalton. They already had proof of Scanton's close relationship with Valente. They found nothing. There were a few cash transactions on his books that were questionable but nothing substantive. Certainly nothing that rose to the level of what they were looking for. They were pretty sure Artie had transferred a fair amount of swordfish across his dock for a piece of the action, but they couldn't prove anything.

The Sammy Dalton thing was driving Howerton's office crazy. There were all kinds of rumors about Dalton's connection to swordfish smuggling but absolutely no hard evidence to support the allegations at all. Artie had never touched a swordfish that had anything to do with Sammy Dalton. Howerton was fascinated by the fact that a criminal was using one imaginary criminal activity to front and cover up another criminal activity. Clever or stupid, he couldn't sort out which. The whole town of Gloucester believed that Dalton's thing was smuggling swordfish, but no one was surprised to hear about the drug-trafficking arrest. It all seemed to make perfect sense, now that the truth about him was out.

The DEA guys had more stuff on this guy Dalton than he could comprehend. What pissed Howerton off so much was he couldn't find any past information on him. He seemed to appear from nowhere. Howerton knew that that wasn't all that uncommon in the drug underworld. Just like a corporate transfer. Keep moving from one location to another. Establish business, and if the heat gets too close, move on. None of that past history stuff really mattered at all.

Howerton learned that none of the four—Reed, Scanton, Chase, or Anderson—even had a possession arrest until they got caught with three 350 kilos of cocaine aboard the boat.

The prosecutors pushed hard to tie up the source of the $9,000,000 cash used to pay off the Columbian freighter captain. Mickey Varney had never changed his position on the cash. The two men who had been arrested and believed to be the financial source for the entire enterprise were refusing to talk under the advice of counsel. They were under arrest by the Massachusetts DEA and under the assistant United States district attorney's jurisdiction.

Howerton was convinced he could prove that Chase had gotten the money aboard the *Jubilee* with the help of his pal up in Rockland at Rockland Propane. It really didn't matter. The cash came aboard. They had the photos of the whole thing. They had the empty tank. They knew how much money was required to buy that amount of cocaine. They had Pat Chase.

William Howerton was ready. It was only a matter of time now.

CHAPTER 99

O n the home front the stress was unbearable. Thanksgiving at the Andersons was sad and quiet. Kathy tried her best to lift everyone's spirits with her positive attitude. The whole family, including Kathy, was scared. The best part was Matty. They all loved him, especially Tom's sister, Joanne. He loved to look at books, and she was in her glory reading to him and talking about what Tom was like when he was a little boy. When all of them thought about Tom and who he was, it just added to the frustration and anger. It was the twilight zone. Nothing made any sense anymore.

The story was pretty much the same at the Scanton household. Joey was starting to spend a lot of time with Teresa Desanto. She and Olivia were invited to dinner with the family. Little Joey and Olivia ran around the house and played. The distraction was great, and Gloria had a nice day in spite of all the worry.

The Chases went to Leslie's brother's house. Things were quiet but pleasant. If the truth was to be known, everyone was dreading Christmas.

The weeks went by and the holidays passed. Anderson finished his fall class. He made enough money working here and there at the store to contribute to some of the household expenses. The money he had made on the *Jubilee* was still holding out. The big legal fees would come later. Kathy and Tom had a nice first Christmas with Matty. Pat and Joey kept on fishing. It was countdown to the trial day, January 10, 1983.

CHAPTER 100

Attorney James Kelley had a meeting scheduled for two thirty on Thursday afternoon. It was set up at a motel in Kennebunk. He would be there alone with a crucial witness for the defense. He had been a lawyer for twenty-two years, and he was just as nervous about this meeting as he had been the first time he spoke in open court. When he arrived at the motel, he already knew the room number. There were no cars around and the parking lot was barely plowed. It was a summer resort motel, and the place was empty as a ghost town. He found the room and knocked on the door. A voice said, "Come on in."

When he entered the room a man stood up and said, "You must be Mr. Kelley."

CHAPTER 101

January 10,1983, had finally arrived. It was trial day. The beginning of a federal trial is a tediously slow and cumbersome process. It all begins with jury selection. The three defense attorneys and the prosecutor participate in choosing the jury. One of Attorney Phil Davis's great strengths, as a criminal defense lawyer, was his ability to select jurors who would be sympathetic to his clients. They made him the lead man for the defense team. Mr. Davis was a colorful and animated man whom people related to easily. Consequently they became very communicative with him. Much of selecting the right jury is instinct, and the choices had to be made quickly. He always relied on street smarts. He joked, smiled, laughed, and looked the prospective jurors straight in the eye when he asked them questions. The better glimpse he got of their personalities, the easier it was to choose the right people. Jury selection to him was a huge chess game with very specific rules that he had to follow. The prosecution was looking for one thing and he was looking for another. It took seven days for the lawyers to finally agree on the jury. Now the long-awaited trial could begin.

The opening day of the trail was a cold Maine winter morning. The courtroom was full of spectators. Seated directly in front of the judge's bench on the courtroom floor, the defendants were at a table facing the judge on the left. The prosecutor William Howerton, his female assistant, and Agent Lamb of the DEA were on the right. Everyone was fidgety and the place was noisy. The boys were dressed in sport coats and ties. Pat Chase kept pulling on his like it was a noose around his neck. Joey Scanton was wearing one of his dad's sports jackets. It was too big, and he wished that they weren't making him wear it. Tom Anderson looked the best of the three; his clothes fit him perfectly. Kathy had taken him shopping. Her plan was that she wanted him to look like the all-American boy he was, and she had succeeded. He looked as much like a drug trafficker as Ritchie Cunningham from *Happy Days* looked like Charles Manson.

They didn't have to wait very long and the bailiff spoke up in a loud voice, "Hear ye, hear ye . . . all rise for the Honorable Judge Harold MacFarland, of the federal district court." Judge MacFarland swept into the room. He was a tall man, just over six foot two. He was a fairly thin man and wore glasses with black frames. He had a full head of snow-white hair. The boys had seen him before, but today he had a completely different demeanor. During jury selection he seemed less than interested. He was reading pretty much the whole time. Now the business before the court had his undivided attention.

Judge MacFarland said, "Good morning, ladies and gentlemen of the jury. We are here today to begin trial case number 147. The federal government versus Scanton, Chase, and Anderson. We will begin today's proceedings with opening statements from the federal government and then from counsel for the defense. Assistant United States District Attorney Howerton, you may begin."

"Thank you, Your Honor. Ladies and gentlemen of the jury, my name is William Howerton. I am the assistant United States district attorney. I work as a prosecutor representing the federal government. My job is to try and convict criminals that break federal law and see that they are sentenced to prison for their crimes. My colleagues and I work very closely with the Federal Drug Enforcement Administration, which is part of the United States Department of Justice. You'll hear them referred to throughout this trial as the DEA. The DEA is a law enforcement division of the United States government that—through careful, well-planned observation and investigation—arrests perpetrators of criminal acts. After a process called an indictment my office investigates all the evidence and ultimately brings the defendants before a jury just like you, for trial. My role in this procedure is to present evidence to you, that after you have heard it, you and only you will decide the guilt or innocence of the parties we have brought before you."

Howerton was a very calm and strong orator. He stopped speaking and took a drink of water from a glass on the prosecution's table. As he delivered his opening remarks he had the undivided attention of every person in the courtroom.

Attorney Howerton continued with his very forceful tone. "The DEA spends an enormous amount of time and money, putting forth a superb professional effort, to bring criminals to justice. It is my personal opinion—and you may or may not share this with me—that drug-related crimes are the number one legal tragedy of our society today. The trafficking of illegal narcotics is only part of the horrific byproducts of the trafficker's endeavors. The underworld activities of these criminals include addiction, theft, prostitution, and even murder. A murder was the unfortunate result for one of the individuals that participated in the crime that we have before us for trial today. The man was actually arrested with these very defendants but did not survive to come to trial. As citizens of this state, country, and even the world, we have a sacred responsibility to fight back against the evils of drug-related crimes. We need to protect ourselves, our children, and our grandchildren from these acts that are counter to the very well-being of human life everywhere. In this case I will prove that these three men, Joseph Scanton, Patrick Chase, and Thomas Anderson, did—with full knowledge and willful intent—organize and carry out part of a well-planned effort to transport and sell the largest amount of cocaine ever attempted in the history of the state of Maine. Had it not been for the incredible investigative work performed by our DEA drug task force, they may have been successful in this endeavor. But the DEA stopped these individuals, folks. They stopped them dead in their tracks in East Boothbay as they were trying to unload their boat and load onto all of us their brutally addictive poison. It is now your responsibility and privilege to serve your government and your country by participating in a trial that will bring these three men to justice. Listen to the facts and find these three men guilty as charged, so they can be removed from society and imprisoned where they can do us no further harm. Thank you, ladies and gentlemen."

Attorney Howerton walked back to his seat at the prosecution table with the swagger of a tailback after a touchdown.

Judge MacFarland said, "The defense may now make its opening statement." Even though James Kelley was the lead attorney for the defense a decision was made to have Phil Davis make their opening remarks. Attorney Davis had already removed his jacket. He was dressed in dark-blue pin-striped trousers, a white shirt, a tie, and jet-black suspenders. He had reading glasses that were hung on a chain around his neck most of the time. He got up from the defense table, looked directly at the three defendants, and winked. He turned and walked toward the jury box, smiled, and began.

"Thank you, Your Honor. Ladies and gentlemen of the jury, I don't know about you but I'm impressed. I chatted with most of you a little before you were chosen to serve on this jury. My name is Philip Davis, and I'm just a country bumpkin lawyer from Lewiston, Maine. When the prosecutor, my esteemed colleague, Mr. Howerton, started throwing around all those intimidating titles, like federal this and that and United States Department of Justice, et cetera, I looked around and thought, 'What am I doing here? I'm completely out of my league.' That's how impressed I was. But after some thought, I concluded I'm here to defend those three men over there with the help of those other two lawyers. They're very sophisticated attorneys, and they're going to keep me straight on course during this trial." Davis walked slowly back and forth in front of the jury.

He continued on, "Mr. Howerton, in his opening remarks, made statements that implied that our three clients were being charged with, and are guilty of, everything from drug trafficking, theft, deception, prostitution, and even murder. I may be confused at this point, but I thought they had only been charged with drug-trafficking crimes, and none of those charges have yet been proven to be true. Attorney Howerton made it sound like it was your patriotic and moral duty to protect yourselves, your children, and your grandchildren by convicting these three men and that the very future of human life as we know it is hanging in the balance. I think that's how he put it. Nothing could be further from the truth. Mr. Joseph Scanton, Mr.

Patrick Chase, and Mr. Thomas Anderson were, in fact, victims of a well-thought-out web of deceit and manipulation that put them, and their boat, in a position to be seized. They were taken over by outside criminals and forced as captives, not perpetrators, to be on board the boat when the narcotics were landed in East Boothbay.

"Ladies and gentleman, these men were pawns in a complicated and carefully orchestrated plot to smuggle cocaine into the United States. We will show you that, in fact, Mr. Arnold Reed was the only member of that crew who was guilty of any crime at all."

Attorney Davis paused just long enough to allow his allegation about Skip Reed to settle in with the jury.

"Mr. Reed was, in fact, killed, trying to escape arrest by the federal agents. We all understand that he is not on trial here today and that these three men are. It is an absolute fact that dead men cannot speak. The true perpetrator of this crime cannot be tried here today. We on the defense team wish with all our hearts that Mr. Arnold Reed were here now to answer for what he did to these men and how he did it. He is not, and we'll all have to live with that fact. I ask you to listen to all the facts carefully and, then and only then, draw a conclusion as to the guilt or innocence of these three men. Thank you all for your attention."

He walked slowly back to the defense table and took his seat.

CHAPTER 102

The courtroom was relatively silent and all eyes were on Judge MacFarland. "Mr. Howerton, if you're ready, you may call your first witness."

"Thank you, Your Honor. The prosecution calls Mr. Michael Varney."

Varney got up from his seat and walked slowly toward the witness stand. The bailiff extended a Bible. He instructed Varney to place his left hand on it and to raise his right hand. "Do you solemnly swear to tell the truth, the whole truth, and nothing but the truth, so help you God?"

"I do."

The bailiff pointed and said, "You may take the witness stand."

After Varney was seated, Attorney Howerton approached him. "Would you please state your name and address for the record?"

"Michael Varney, 25 Green Hill Road, Boothbay Harbor, Maine."

"What do you do, Mr. Varney?"

"Well, up until recently, I ran a lobster-buying and small restaurant facility. The place was a front for a drug racket. It's located down on Little River down in East Boothbay. Then I got arrested by the DEA for drug trafficking." The response was obviously highly rehearsed. The jurors all looked shocked.

"Well, Mr. Varney, for today's purposes we are most interested in discussing the drug business. Would you mind answering a few questions about that?"

"No, not at all . . . shoot."

"Tell us about the drug business. What did you do, and how did it work?"

Varney shifted slightly in his seat. "I purchased large amounts of marijuana from a Columbian trafficker. The pot had been brought in by boat to Portland and other locations. I transported and stored the marijuana in my barn until I accumulated a large enough amount to transport it out of state for distribution."

"You were aware that this was an illegal activity, a federal offense in fact."

"Definitely. I ain't stupid. I made a huge amount of money before I got caught at it."

"Explain to us about the cocaine part of your business."

"The coke, that was the big one, the big payoff. We had enough cocaine coming in on that boat to retire. The street value of it was around $29,000,000."

The jury and the rest of the courtroom gasped.

"What went wrong, Mr. Varney?"

Varney shifted again in his seat. "The DEA was onto us and busted up the whole thing and arrested everybody involved."

"Are you facing federal charges right now yourself?"

"No, I struck a deal for the witness-protection program with you, in exchange for my testimony." There was a murmur that ran through the courtroom. Howerton ignored it.

"How did you become part of this big cocaine delivery?"

"It was all set up by a crook named Sammy Dalton. It started with another guy, but then Dalton took over. He made a deal with a guy named Skip Reed out of Portland to bring the stuff in from offshore on his boat."

"Did you think the boat belonged to Skip Reed?"

"I don't know. Reed was the contact man, but he told me all them guys were aware this thing was going down. He told me a dozen times, over almost a year, that they all knew about it."

"Who are you referring to when you say 'they all knew about it'?"

"Scanton and the other two over there." Varney pointed toward the defendants.

"How exactly did you begin to communicate with Mr. Reed?"

"It was by phone always. He would call me, and we would discuss the details of when and where this deal was going to go down."

Attorney Howerton said, "When was your first contact with Reed?"

"I don't remember exactly, but it was at least a year ago."

"Tell us what you remember about that first conversation."

Varney looked directly at Howerton. "The guy calls me and tells me he got my number from Sammy Dalton. I blow my stack. I know I'm dealing with an amateur because nobody uses names when we talk on the phone."

"Why's that?"

"Wire taps. Them DEA guys use wire taps and all kinds of sneaky shit to spy on you. Anyway, he starts like bragging to me about how he can move large amounts of product around and wants a shot. He tells me that he's hooked up with a broad that's married to the captain of this boat and him and her could control things on that boat."

"By 'control things,' what do you think he was referring to?"

"According to Reed, she controlled the money for the boat, so they'd be able to encourage, so to speak, the captain to willingly participate in the little venture."

"This little venture you're referring to was worth a lot of money for all participants. I take it Mr. Reed and Mr. Scanton's wife were in anticipation of a large share of that money, were they not?"

Varney started to pull at his tie like the thing was choking him. "I don't know nothing about that part of it. All of them kind of details were handled by Sammy Dalton."

"When you were told by Reed that a decision had been made to go pick up the cocaine, what did you do?"

"Everything is always talked about in code. We used the word 'swordfish' instead of 'cocaine' when we were talking about the deal. I got a call from Reed when they landed in Rockland. I heard that Scanton's wife had taken all the money from their previous trip and ran off with it. Smart broad, too bad she's dead. She knew that her old man would have big bills mounted up, and he'd be desperate to do the drug deal. The whole crew was in on it because they weren't going to get paid with her stealing all the money from their last trip."

Attorney Kelley spoke up. "Objection, Your Honor. The witness is drawing conclusions based on his opinion with no substantiating facts."

Judge MacFarland responded immediately. "Sustained." He spoke directly to the witness, "Keep your responses limited to actual conversations that occurred and not things you think may have occurred as a result of other conversations. Do you understand?"

Varney said, "Yes, Your Honor." He was being very respectful. The last thing he wanted was to piss off the judge.

MacFarland said, "You may continue, Mr. Howerton."

"Thank you, your honor. Mr. Varney, did you make the arrangements yourself, as to the exact time and location of the pickup for the cocaine?"

"Oh no, I never talked to any of them Columbians. That was way out of my league. All the arrangements for pickups were handled by some other people. I was what you call a glorified warehouse boy. I was just a shipper. As far as I know all that kind of scheduling was done by a guy named Frank Matson, from down in Massachusetts. I heard you guys arrested him as he was about to go on a little vacation abroad?"

There was a small wave of laughter that ran through the courtroom. Howerton said, "So Frank Matson coordinated the time and location for pickup with the Columbians. Do I have that right?"

"Yes, that's right."

"Who told Mr. Reed the specifics about where to be and when?"

"I did. They gave me the bearings offshore for the pickup, and I gave them to Reed and Scanton."

James Kelley spoke up again. "Objection, Your Honor. Mr. Varney has not stated that there were any direct conversations between himself and Mr. Scanton."

"Overruled. You may continue, Mr. Varney."

Varney cleared his throat. "As I was saying, that's how they knew exactly where to go and when."

Howerton walked away from Varney and turned toward the jury. "I'm curious about something. Where did they have to go to meet up with the Columbians transporting the cocaine?"

"They had to go down into Canadian waters."

Howerton turned back toward his witness. "Why did they have to go so far?"

"That's easy. They had go to east of the Hague Line to stay out of US Coast Guard jurisdiction. The Coast Guard can't patrol down there in them waters."

"In your opinion, Mr. Varney, could any captain of a fishing vessel like the *Jubilee* mistakenly travel to place like the pickup point while the boat was engaged in fishing?"

In a booming voice, Varney said, "Absolutely not."

James Kelley jumped up and yelled, "Objection, Your Honor. The prosecution is leading the witness. The witness's testimony draws conclusions and speculates!"

The judge said, "Sustained. Please strike that last statement from the record. The jury will ignore that statement as well. Mr. Howerton, you know better."

Howerton was unfazed. "I apologize, Your Honor. Mr. Varney, you have stated for this court that you believe that Mr. Reed and the entire crew of the *Jubilee* knew about this drug deal. Is that correct?"

"Yes, that's true. Reed told me repeatedly that they were all in on this deal."

"So when you were told that by Reed, did you believe him?"

"What's not to believe? I've been around fishin' boats my whole life. You ain't going to run 130 miles offshore, go get 350 kilos of coke on a boat that size and not have everyone know about it. Can't happen."

Attorney Howerton said, "So it is your opinion that all three defendants knew about the deal to transport the cocaine."

Varney was now becoming very agitated. "Maybe you didn't hear me. I just told you they all knew about it, didn't I?"

Howerton wasn't the least bit put off by Mickey Varney. "I just wanted you to be clear for the jury."

Varney leaned a little forward, looked straight at the jurors, and said, "All three of them guys over there were part of the deal. They all knew about the cocaine. Okay, Mr. Howerton?"

"Yes, thank you, Mr. Varney. Can you please tell me what you know about Skip Reed's death."

Varney settled back in his chair. "It's pretty clear to me that Reed wasn't supposed to get blown up in that boat. That was set up for someone else."

"Who exactly do you think was supposed to get blown up, if not Mr. Reed?"

"I think it was supposed to happen to the Columbian that came ashore with these guys and that fat bastard Sammy Dalton."

The judge said, "Mr. Varney, please refrain from using vulgar language in this court."

"Yes, Your Honor."

Howerton continued, "Why do you think that was the case, Mr. Varney?"

"I think the captain of the freighter had his money, and why should he split it with the other Columbian and that prick Sammy?"

James Kelley said, "Objection, Your Honor, total speculation."

The judge said, "Sustained. The jury will disregard the last statement. I warned you once about your language, Mr. Varney. One more time and I'll hold you in contempt. Knock it off."

"Yes, Your Honor."

Howerton said, "I have no further questions of this witness at this time, but I reserve the right to redirect."

CHAPTER 103

Judge MacFarland spoke. "Your witness, Mr. Kelley."
Attorney Kelley rose from the defense table and walked over toward the witness stand. "Mr. Varney, my name is James Kelley. I am part of the defense team representing the defendants, and I'd like to ask you a few questions, if I may."

Varney had a smart and defiant look on his face. "Go ahead, ask away."

"Mr. Varney, you have stated, for the record, that you ran a drug-trafficking racket. I think you called it 'operating in East Boothbay.' Is that correct?"

"Yes, it is."

"You also stated that you had reached a bargain agreement with the assistant United States district attorney, Mr. Howerton, exchanging testimony for a witness-protection program. Is that correct?"

"Yes, it is." Varney had a big smile on his face.

"What did Mr. Howerton tell you would be expected of you to comply with this agreement?"

"If I helped him nail these guys he would get me out of these charges, a new identity, a job, and I'd be free to live my life."

"So let me see if I understand this arrangement. You help Mr. Howerton convict these defendants, and in exchange you would be set free in a new community with a new job and a new life. Is that right?"

"That's the way I understand it. Yes."

"That's quite a deal, really. You have a lot of incentive there to help Mr. Howerton, don't you?"

"Yes, I do, but I'm telling the truth about everything here. I ain't makin' shit up to get myself a better deal. These guys are all part of this thing. I'm just doing what's right. I'm telling the truth."

That was just the kind of outburst Kelley was hoping for. He knew from experience that when a witness starts making explanations and covers statements before a question was asked, it makes them look like a liar to a jury. In Varney's case it had worked perfectly. No one in that courtroom had any doubt that Mickey Varney was a liar.

Kelley said, "No one here has questioned your integrity. I'm sure integrity is one of the key character traits required to be a good drug dealer."

Howerton said, "Objection, Your Honor."

Judge MacFarland said, "Overruled. But go easy, Mr. Kelley."

"Yes, Your Honor." Kelley began again. "Mr. Varney, you have testified repeatedly that all three defendants were fully aware of the drug-trafficking plot that was worked out with Mr. Reed. Is that correct?"

"Yes, that's true."

"Did you ever have any direct communications with Mr. Joseph Scanton?"

"No, I did not."

"Did you ever have any direct communications with Mr. Patrick Chase?"

"No, I did not."

"How about Mr. Thomas Anderson? Any conversations with him?"

"No, I did not."

"Mr. Varney, you have testified under oath and just reiterated that all your statements were truthful—that all three of these men were part of this drug-trafficking plot—yet you never have even talked to one of them. Can you explain that to me?"

"I don't have to talk to them about nothing. These guys were all part of this deal."

"Tell me how you know that. What specifically happened that tells you these men were part of this crime?"

Varney had an angry edge to his voice when he answered. "For a guy that's supposed to be a smart lawyer, you ain't too smart. These four guys—Reed, Scanton, Chase, and Anderson—they all work together. Reed gets a bright idea that instead of fishing with the boat they can lug dope with it. They all need money just like everybody else. Reed hooks up with this guy and signs on to transport some coke. They figure out a way to get $9,000,000 cash on board their boat in broad daylight. They go all the way down past the Hague Line and pick up 350 kilos of coke, with all hands on board. They steam back to Maine, and the Scanton guy is running the boat when they land. They all get arrested, and you ask me how I know they were all involved? How the hell could they not all be involved? You tell me."

Kelley pressed on, "Very interesting answer, Mr. Varney."

"I'm glad you liked it."

"The only problem I have with it is this. I didn't ask you whether they were present during the crime. I asked you to support your testimony that these men knew about it and were involved in the crime before it happened."

Varney laughed. "I guess you had to be there."

Kelley turned and smiled at the jurors and said, "I think that's true, and you, sir, were not there."

Kelley walked back to the defendants' table.

Attorney Davis stood up. He said, "I have a few questions, Your Honor."

Judge MacFarland responded, "Proceed."

Attorney Davis approached Varney.

"Mr. Varney, I'm Phil Davis. I represent Mr. Chase. I have a few brief questions for you."

"Fine."

Davis said, "Have you ever spoken to my client, Mr. Chase?"

"I told the other guy. No."

"I understand, but I'm asking the questions now, and you'll answer them for me. Have you ever supplied any directions or information of any kind to my client, Mr. Chase?"

"No."

"Did you supply any money or propane tanks to my client?"

"I don't sell propane."

"Let me be absolutely clear with you. You are under oath. You are a witness testifying, and you will answer my questions. Now did you ever supply any money or propane tanks to my client Mr. Chase?"

"No, I did not."

"Did my client, Mr. Chase, negotiate the transportation of any narcotics to be landed at your location in East Boothbay?"

Varney was quiet for a minute and finally mumbled, "No, I guess not."

Davis said, "Would you repeat that so the jury can hear you, please."

Varney sneered at Davis, "No, I guess not!"

"That's all, Mr. Varney."

Peter Green stood up. "Your Honor, I have a few questions for this witness."

The judge said, "Go ahead."

Attorney Green began. "Mr. Varney, I'm Attorney Peter Green. I represent Mr. Thomas Anderson. You stated in your previous testimony that you knew that my client knew about this drug deal and participated in it from the beginning. Is that correct?"

"Yes."

"That's an interesting allegation. Did you ever speak with my client?"

"No, I did not."

"Did Mr. Anderson, to the best of your knowledge, ever speak to Mr. Sammy Dalton or Mr. Frank Matson?"

"How would I know who your guy talked to?"

Green smiled and said, "Precisely, Mr. Varney. Answer the question."

"No, not to the best of my knowledge," Varney said.

"Were you ever told of any conversations between my client and anyone else involved at any level with this crime that we are trying here today?"

"No. I was not."

"I'll ask you the same question Mr. Davis asked, as it relates to my client. Did my client ever negotiate the delivery or sale of any narcotics of any kind to you?"

"No, he didn't."

"That's all I have for this witness, Your Honor."

The Judge MacFarland said, "Mr. Howerton, anything further from you?"

Attorney Howerton said, "No, Your Honor."

The judge looked down at Mickey Varney. "Mr. Varney, you may step down. Ladies and gentlemen of the jury, it's been a busy morning. We will break for lunch, and I'll see everyone here at one o'clock this afternoon. Thank you all."

He tapped his gavel and quickly disappeared from the courtroom.

CHAPTER 104

A s the room cleared, the boys hung behind for a minute. Scanton said, "How did we do so far?"

Phil Davis answered, "We were okay. It's hard to read a jury. We know the truth, so it clouds our perspective on how they may be reacting. Hang on a minute. I'll have an answer for you that you can rely on." He went to the back of the courtroom. Marilyn, Phil's secretary, was standing there. She had on a way-too-short black skirt and a skintight top.

They chatted for a minute and Davis came right back. "Marilyn says we did okay but not great. Too many questions raised by Varney. She says the jury doesn't care about the planning and phone conversations. The worst part is the boys were all there the whole time. She sees a problem that there's nobody independent to testify on your behalf. Varney was effective with his description of sequential events."

Scanton said, "And why do we care about what Marilyn thinks?"

"Because she's never gets it wrong, Joey . . . ever."

The lawyers closed up their briefcases. Peter Green suggested that all go over to Anthony's Italian Kitchen across from the courthouse and get a sandwich. Everyone agreed that that was a great choice. The girls were all waiting, including Teresa. They crossed the street and went down to Anthony's. There was a line but it was moving quickly. Tony was standing there, just like every day, with a huge smile and a handshake for his best customers. When the group approached the counter, Tony said, "How's it going Jim, Peter, and I don't know you?" He was looking at Phil Davis. "I'm Phil Davis, glad to meet you." He shook hands with Tony.

Tony said, "I'm glad to meet you. So the big trial started today, huh?"

Kelley said, "Yes, it did."

Tony looked over at the boys and said, "Don't you fellows worry now. If you're innocent, these fine men will prove it to the jury, and you'll be free. They are the best there is in the business. What's everyone having for lunch today?"

Tony's smile and his warmth were infectious, and everyone felt better. They ordered their sandwiches and had a great lunch. Nobody talked about the trial. Kathy and Leslie looked like they had been put through the mill. Tom kept his arm around Kathy all through lunch. One of the things that Tom loved so much about her was her combination of incredible strength and vulnerability. He found it so endearing. When they finished, they walked slowly back to the courthouse. No one was anxious to go back there.

As soon as the courtroom settled down and the bailiff announced the judge, everyone took their seats. Judge MacFarland began the afternoon session. "Mr. Howerton, you may call your next witness."

"Thank you, Your Honor. The prosecution calls Andrew Brown." Andy Brown walked up to the witness stand and was sworn in. He had on a cheap-looking blue suit and a clip-on tie that somebody must have sent one of the jailers out to buy. He looked miserable and afraid sitting in the witness stand. Attorney Howerton said, "Please state your name and occupation for the record."

In a very shaky voice Andy said, "I'm Andy Brown and I'm a lobsterman."

Howerton said, "Okay, Mr. Brown, I have a few questions for you. How do you know the defendants?"

Andy Brown said, "I've known those guys all my life except for Joey Scanton. I know him but not all that well."

"Okay, which one of the defendants do you know best?"

"That would be Tom Anderson. We went to school together."

"Are you friends with Tom Anderson?"

"Kind of friends . . . Tom's a little snobby. He was smart in school so he thinks he's a big deal."

Howerton said, "Mr. Brown, you were recently arrested. Can you explain to the court the nature of that arrest?"

"I got busted for bringing pot into Portland in a lobster boat."

"Whose boat was it?"

"It was Skip Reed's boat. He set up a deal for me to use his boat and carry the pot in for a bunch of guys that paid me money to do it."

"Was there anyone else that was part of that arrangement?"

"Yes, Tom Anderson was. He was Skip's best friend, and he was in on the whole thing."

The jurors were all looking at Tom. He couldn't contain himself. He shouted out, "That's bullshit . . . goddamn it!"

The judge rapped his gavel and yelled, "Mr. Green, control your client."

Attorney Howerton continued, "Mr. Brown, when you said Tom Anderson was in on the whole thing, what did you mean by that exactly?"

"All the bearings and times to meet the big boat were all coming from Tom Anderson."

"Slow down. Please explain what you mean by all the bearings and times."

Andy Brown felt kind of important explaining about bearings and times to a smart man like Attorney Howerton, and his chest puffed out a little. "When you go off to get the pot you have to have a time to be there down by the Mud Buoy. And you need bearings to tell you where to steer to get there."

Howerton said, "What's the Mud Buoy?"

"That's a place offshore away. You have to go to the Mud Buoy at a time they tell you. Then they call a compass bearing to you on channel 8, and you steer that way. Then after a while they show up with a big yacht and put the pot on your boat. You take it in where they tell you. Some guys take it off your boat, and they give you five grand."

Attorney Howerton said, "Mr. Brown, can you tell us how Anderson was involved in all this?"

"He gave me the times and bearings and all that over the radio."

Peter Green was on his feet. "Objection! Mr. Anderson is not on trial for being involved with Andy Brown's pot-smuggling arrest! This is ridiculous, Your Honor."

Judge MacFarland said, "I agree with you, Mr. Green. I wondered how long you were going to let this go on. Objection sustained. The jury will disregard this testimony. Mr. Howerton, you need to bring your line of questioning back to this trial. Is that clear?"

"Your Honor, I have a witness here that will testify that Thomas Anderson had a direct connection to the same drug traffickers that were involved in the East Boothbay arrest. All of these narcotics were being funneled through Lively Lusty Lobster operated by Michael Varney."

Judge MacFarland said, "Find another path to accomplish that goal or have Mr. Anderson arrested and charged with the new crime you just introduced to this court. Is that clear, Mr. Howerton?"

"Yes, Your Honor. I have no further questions for this witness."

The judge said, "Your witness, Mr. Green"

Green stood up and walked toward Brown. "Mr. Brown, I'm Peter Green. I have some questions for you." Andy Brown became very tense. He said, "Okay, Mr. Green."

"It sounds like you have been through quite a lot recently, Mr. Brown. You've been arrested for drug trafficking and are facing a trial and a possible conviction with a potential for jail time. Is that right?"

Brown's head dropped. "Yes, that's right."

"You testified earlier that Thomas Anderson and Skip Reed were involved in some of your drug-related activities."

Brown looked down at his hands and said, "Yes, I did."

Attorney Howerton was getting a little fidgety watching his witness up on the stand. He didn't like Andy Brown's voice intonation. It was soft and he was becoming almost withdrawn. He said, "Objection, Your Honor, this line of questioning has already been ruled by you as unallowable."

MacFarland said, "Overruled, Mr. Howerton. I'm interested in what this witness might tell us all. You started this. Please continue, Mr. Green."

"Thank you, Your Honor. Mr. Brown, who was it that arrested you?"

"A Falmouth cop named Junior Butland. But Mr. Goldman handled things after that."

"What did Mr. Goldman tell you?"

"He said I was going to jail for ten years for what I did. I pleaded guilty, and they haven't gotten around to my trial yet."

"That's a long time, Mr. Brown, ten years. Did you reach an agreement with them of some sort? How come you're here to testify against Mr. Anderson?"

Howerton spoke up. "Objection, Your Honor. This questioning has nothing to do with this trial."

Judge MacFarland said, "Overruled. It must be going somewhere or you wouldn't be so nervous. Continue, Mr. Green."

"Thank you, Your Honor. Mr. Brown, my question is this. Again, why are you here to testify against Thomas Anderson?"

"Mr. Goldman said I was getting such a long sentence because I didn't have anything to offer him. Like if I knew somebody that was more guilty than me, I could get a shorter sentence maybe."

"Did Mr. Goldman offer you some kind of deal?"

"No, Mr. Goldman didn't."

Peter Green turned and looked at Attorney Howerton. His face looked flushed. Attorney Green said, "Andy, tell me how this happened."

Andy Brown started to explain himself. "I was talking to some guys over at Cumberland County Jail. This real smart guy over there told me I should try to make a deal with Mr. Howerton."

Attorney Green said, "Were you able to do that?"

"Yes, I was. I told him all this stuff about Tom and Skip, and he told me he'd help me at my trial. It's all I had."

"Did you lie to Mr. Howerton?"

Brown was sweating profusely. "Yes, I did, Mr. Green. Mr. Howerton seemed so happy to hear what I had to say . . . he didn't really question anything. He thinks Tom's guilty. I figured that me helping him and all that, I might have a chance."

"Did you lie in court today about Thomas Anderson's involvement in your crime, Mr. Brown?"

A tear ran down Andy Brown's cheek. "Yes, I did, Mr. Green. I'm real sorry, Tom. I shouldn't have done it."

"So none of the bearings and directions you talked about coming from Mr. Anderson, they really didn't, did they?"

"Yeah, that's right . . . he didn't have nothing to do with it."

"How do you know that for sure, Mr. Brown?"

"Because I know Tom's voice, and the people who talked to me on the radio wasn't him."

"Are you absolutely sure, Mr. Brown?"

"Yes, I'm sure."

Green said, "That's all for this witness. Thank you, Mr. Brown."

The judge said, "Any further questions, Mr. Howerton?"

Howerton said, "No, Your Honor."

Judge MacFarland said, "You may step down, Mr. Brown. We will take a brief recess. I want to see all four attorneys in my chambers."

Judge MacFarland stepped down from the bench, turned, and exited the courtroom. As soon as he entered his chambers, he took off his robe, hung it on a coat rack, and took his seat behind his large oak desk. All four attorneys came in within minutes.

"Please take a seat, gentlemen. I invited you boys in here to express my dissatisfaction with some of the conduct I'm seeing in my courtroom. Mr. Howerton, exactly how many more criminals do you expect to present to the jury to aid you in your prosecution effort? Perhaps during your illustrious career, you haven't noticed, but criminals sometimes don't make the most credible witnesses." The judge could have cared less about who Howerton brought forth. He wanted to set a tone of authority for this little meeting.

"I'm through with them, Your Honor."

"Fine . . . You other three need to be mindful of the rules for examination and cross-examination. I expect you to control your clients. No more outbursts from any of them. You need to prepare them that they may hear things being said in court that they don't like."

They all mumbled, "Yes, Your Honor."

"All right then, gentlemen. Who's your next witness, Mr. Howerton?"

"I'm calling Agent Bert Goldman."

"It's two thirty. I'm going to call it a day for today. I'm assuming that Agent Goldman's testimony will take a long time, and I don't want that broken up. Let's head back into court."

The judge announced the end of the court day. The jurors were given their instructions. They were not to discuss the trial with anyone, and they were ordered to refrain from reading newspapers or watching television news that may have reports on the trial. The courtroom emptied.

When they were out on the street, Phil Davis said, "Jim, when the judge started talking I asked myself if the guy had lost his marbles. That meeting was about nothing. I think it did send a message to the jury that he was upset with Howerton. I think that really helped us. So often these judges are in the pocket of prosecutors. I guess I'm impressed."

Kelley said, "I think he really didn't like Howerton's deal with Brown. He just didn't do his homework. He's so sure he's going to win this thing that he's not paying attention."

Peter Green said, "I agree. That was weird though. We need to be mindful of the rules of examination and cross-examination? Maybe old Harry has been trying out some of the pot Andy Brown was bringing in."

Phil Davis said sarcastically, "You boys should be more respectful of judges. You may be appearing before the Honorable William Howerton one of these days."

Peter Green said, "There's no doubt that's what that guys aiming for. He's all about the glory. We're going to wreck his plans though."

"That's exactly what I have in mind," Phil Davis said as he lit up a fresh cigar.

No one could really ascertain how they had done in court that day. Everyone had an opinion of course, but that's all they were. Gloria asked Joey to come home to her house for dinner. Her sister had been taking care of Little Joey all day, so he was already there. They got home, and Joey's dad pulled a couple of cold beers out of the refrigerator. They sat out on the back deck, even though it was bitter cold, so Joey could have a smoke.

Peter Scanton said, "What did you think about today?"

"Shit, Dad, I don't know. The lawyers say you can't read a jury. I guess the best thing we can say is that nothing really bad happened." They talked for a while and then went into the house for the rest of the evening.

In the morning the story was the headline in the paper.

PORTLAND HERALD

Drug-trafficking trial gets underway

Assistant United States District Attorney William Howerton, before a packed federal courtroom, presented evidence in the case brought against defendants Joseph Scanton of Portland, Patrick Chase of South Portland, and Thomas Anderson of Falmouth. The three men are facing federal charges for their involvement in the purchase and transportation of 350 kilos of cocaine from international waters into the state of Maine aboard their fishing boat.

The men were arrested by agents of the Federal Drug Enforcement Administration in East Boothbay in the largest drug bust in the history of the state. The arrest occurred a little over three months ago. A fourth named accomplice in the alleged crime, Skip

Reed, was killed in a still-unexplained explosion during an escape attempt aboard a high-speed boat. The DEA seized the narcotics from the fishing vessel *Jubilee* owned and captained by Scanton.

Assistant United States District Attorney William Howerton began with a key witness for the prosecution. Michael Varney, 52, of Boothbay Harbor, the former owner of a lobster-buying and outdoor restaurant facility located on Little River in East Boothbay. Varney turned and testified as a prosecution witness as part of a witness-protection program agreement with the prosecutor's office. Varney was arrested the same night as the defendants and has admitted to running the drug-trafficking operation from the Little River location.

During today's testimony Varney testified that all three defendants were directly involved not only in the transportation of the narcotics, but also in the planning and purchase of the drugs.

The defense lawyers, led by James Kelley, a Portland attorney, supported by Peter Green of Portland, and Philip Davis of Lewiston, challenged Varney's testimony during cross-examination and raised questions about the involvement of the three defendants.

Jurors listened intently to the testimony that placed the captain and crew of the *Jubilee* present at every step of the crime. Defense attorneys, during an interview, claim that the planning and execution of the crime was in fact perpetrated by Arnold Reed, the fourth crew member who died in an explosion while attempting an escape at the time of the arrest.

A second witness was called, Andrew Brown of Falmouth. His testimony was inconclusive based on some technical rulings made by the presiding judge, Harold MacFarland. Through some well-placed objections by defense attorney Kelley, it appeared that Brown's testimony lost some of its impact on the jury. Howerton was effective in establishing that all three defendants were present during the time that the drug-trafficking crime was planned and executed.

Today's proceedings were brought to a close at about two fifteen this afternoon, shortly after a meeting in the judge's chambers called by MacFarland. Undisclosed sources told reporters that the purpose of the meeting was to further instruct the defense team on proper courtroom procedures. The trial will resume tomorrow morning at 9:00 a.m.

Joey put the paper down in total disgust. He said, "I hope the jury follows the judge's instructions and doesn't read this shit or we're screwed."

CHAPTER 105

At nine o'clock in the morning the federal courtroom was packed with spectators and reporters. The bailiff called the court to order and Judge MacFarland took his seat at the bench. He rapped his gavel to silence the room.

"Good morning. Ladies and gentlemen of the jury, we will begin today's testimony with the first witness to be called by the prosecution. Mr. Howerton, you may begin."

"Thank you, Your Honor. The prosecution calls senior special agent in charge, Mr. Bertram Goldman." Goldman walked to the front of the court. The bailiff, Robert Dixon, had known Agent Goldman for all seven years that he had been the senior special agent in charge of the DEA. Dixon was friends with and really enjoyed Bert Goldman.

As he approached the witness stand, Dixon said, "Good morning, Mr. Goldman."

"Hello, Robert. How are you this fine morning?"

"I'm fine sir, thank you." After he was sworn in, Goldman took the witness stand.

He was very comfortable in court. A major portion of his job involved testifying during trials. Attorney Howerton said, "Good morning, Agent Goldman."

Goldman smiled and said, "Good morning, Mr. Howerton."

"Agent Goldman, would you mind stating your name and your profession for the court."

"No problem there. My name is Bertram Goldman, and I'm the senior special agent in charge of the Federal Drug Enforcement Administration for the state of Maine. I report to the United States Department of Justice. I'm the head of the narcotics division. They might refer to me as the head narc."

Everyone laughed except Attorney Howerton. "What are your responsibilities for the Drug Enforcement Administration?"

"I supervise the Federal Drug Crime Task Force here in Maine. I have thirty special agents that report to me. I also enlist the services of the state police, local police, the marine patrol, the warden service, and private citizens to help me in the surveillance and investigation of criminal activity involving the illegal use and trade of narcotics."

"That's an impressive job."

Goldman smiled. "I do what I can."

"How long have you been an agent with the federal government?"

"Over twenty-two years."

"That's a long time."

"You're telling me. I'm about to retire here shortly."

"Well, Agent Goldman, before you do, there are some questions I'd like to ask you regarding these three defendants sitting across from you."

"Fire away, I'm ready."

"Could you give us a history of the investigation that led to their recent arrest in East Boothbay?"

"Certainly . . . Our department became aware of certain communications between a Mr. Arnold Reed, also known as Skip Reed, approximately one year ago. This information came to us through an unnamed informant. Reed began telephone discussions with Michael Varney of East Boothbay. We knew of Varney's connections to major out-of-state drug traffickers before we were able to identify the exact location of his operation. The transportation and sale of narcotics is a major marketing network. It runs almost exclusively underground. There are many levels of involvement in, what has become over time, an enormous enterprise. Through the relentless pursuit of information, technical assistance through electronic surveillance, and old-fashioned luck we are able to apprehend a large number of criminals. For an example, the Little River location was finally discovered because of an old lady who was trying to have her innocent brother-in-law, a simple farmer by the way, arrested as a drug dealer. She was mad at him and had been for over fifty years and was trying to settle an old family score. He was the person that tipped us off about the Little River location." Everyone in the courtroom laughed again.

Goldman continued, "After we became aware of Reed's initial negotiations with Varney making a deal to transport drugs, we simply began a constant surveillance effort to see if and when they would make their move."

Attorney Howerton said, "These three men—Mr. Joseph Scanton, Mr. Patrick Chase, and Mr. Thomas Anderson—were they all part of your surveillance effort?"

"Oh yes, most definitely."

"What did you collect for evidence during this effort?"

"We have phone conversations, photographs, eyewitness observation by agents, video tapes, and the actual arrest. We seized their vessel and have detailed photographs of the boat, its condition at the time of the arrest, and the narcotics that were transported on the vessel. We have possession of all the drugs that were confiscated from them."

"I guess you could say you caught them red-handed with all these drugs in their possession," Howerton said rather smugly.

"Yes . . . all of the drugs were aboard the fishing vessel *Jubilee* when they were arrested."

Attorney Howerton said, "The drugs that were aboard the boat, do you have reason to believe that they were purchased before they were transported into Maine?"

"Yes, I do. We have photographs and testimony that prove that there was approximately $9,000,000 in cash placed aboard the boat for the purchase of these drugs."

Attorney Howerton said, "How did they get that amount of cash aboard the boat?"

"It was quite clever actually. It came aboard concealed in a propane tank. The boat was tied up in Rockland, and two replacement gas tanks were delivered to the boat, one full of propane, the other filled with the cash."

"Did a member of the crew place the tanks aboard the boat?"

"Yes, we have pictures of Skip Reed placing those tanks in their receptacles on the roof of the boat."

"Where does the propane come from to supply the boat and who buys it?"

"We have records extending back over a two-year period that show that Patrick Chase, as engineer for the fishing vessel, was responsible for all propane orders for that boat. The records indicate that all propane was purchased through Rockland Propane, a small local gas company."

Howerton was feeling great momentum. "Thank you, Agent Goldman. Can you tell the jury how you knew exactly where and when the drugs would be landed?"

"We had the assistance of the United States Coast Guard in tracking and observing the activities of the *Jubilee* immediately after they left the dock in Rockland. The Coast Guard was under strict orders from me not to interfere with them. There was, in fact, a radio conversation with Captain Scanton and the Coast Guard just before they headed further east for their rendezvous with the Columbian freighter."

"Can you tell us the nature of that conversation?"

"The captain, Joseph Scanton, reported on their fishing activities, his men on board, their destination, and their estimated anticipated time to return to port."

"Did they follow the itinerary that Captain Scanton reported?"

"No, they did not. They traveled directly to the east, crossed the Hague Line, the ocean boundary between the United States and Canada, where they met up with a small Columbian freighter. We have testimony from another individual involved in the arrest that the drugs were transferred to the *Jubilee* and transported to East Boothbay."

A brief look of surprise crossed Bill Howerton's face. "Who is this other individual?"

Agent Goldman replied, "He's a foreign national that has been deported to Columbia under an agreement made by the International Crime Division of the Department of Justice."

Attorney Howerton said, "To sum up this entire event, would it be accurate to say that the drug activities relating to the entire crew of the *Jubilee* were observed and monitored for at least a year? That there is sufficient proof that, in fact, $9,000,000 in cash was put aboard the fishing boat. That Captain Scanton, with his entire crew aboard, steamed to a destination point east of the Hague Line into Canadian waters. That they took possession of 350 kilos of cocaine and transported those drugs back into Maine waters, where the boat and crew were arrested by federal agents of the Drug Enforcement Administration."

Agent Goldman said, "That would be correct."

The courtroom was totally silent as the weight of Goldman's testimony sunk in.

Howerton said, "Thank you, Agent Goldman, that will be all. Your witness, counselor."

Judge MacFarland said, "Ladies and gentlemen, we'll take a short recess before the defense begins its cross-examination." The judged rapped his gavel and left the bench. The lawyers on the defense side and the boys all left the room. They grabbed a small conference room for a minute. Chase was the first to speak. "That son of a bitch screwed us to the wall."

Attorney Davis said, "Relax, Pat. It didn't go as badly as you think it did."

James Kelley said, "Don't be too quick to condemn Goldman. His testimony was very broad and, for the most part, nonspecific. You'll see, and so will the jury, when we get back at it."

Peter Green said, "Did anyone hear anything that was totally inaccurate?"

Scanton said, "Yeah, every fucking thing he said. I've got to go take a leak. I hope you guys are worth the money we're paying you."

Phil Davis said, "Way more than that, man. Go take your leak. I hate having my clients wet their pants in court."

Everyone filed back into the courtroom and settled in. The bailiff spoke.

"All rise for the Honorable Judge Harold MacFarland." Court was back in session.

Agent Goldman was back on the witness stand, and James Kelley was ready to start the cross-examination for the defense. "Agent Goldman, I'm sure I don't have to remind you that you're still under oath."

Goldman said, "You probably don't have to remind me that I'm still under oath, but I sure do appreciate it. I've been known to forget things from time to time."

There were snickers throughout the room.

Attorney Kelley said, "Agent Goldman, you stated for the jury that you began to have suspicions of criminal activity based on your department's becoming aware of certain communications between Mr. Reed and Mr. Michael Varney. Is that correct?"

"Yes, it is."

"Now did you, or any of your agents, observe or have any information from the witness Mr. Varney regarding direct communications with Joseph Scanton?"

Goldman said, "No, they did not. Mr. Scanton was mentioned during those conversations as a willing, available participant in any future arrangements that might be made."

"My point is this, Agent Goldman—all those statements were being made by Skip Reed, not the defendant Mr. Scanton. Is that correct?"

"That would be correct. However, it has been my experience in these matters that normally one person is the negotiator for whoever may be ultimately involved."

"Once again, Agent Goldman, do you or your agents have any taped or videoed or directly overheard conversations with Mr. Scanton or either of the two other defendants?"

"No, I do not."

"Thank you, Agent Goldman. Do you or your agents have any photographs or videos or recordings of any kind with the three defendants and any other suspects, drug dealers, or any party that was involved in any criminal activities at all prior to their arrest?"

"No, I do not."

"Then let me see if I have this right. All of your surveillance work seems to implicate Skip Reed as the perpetrator and not the defendants."

Attorney Howerton jumped up. "Objection, Your Honor. This question calls for a conclusion on the part of the witness."

Judge MacFarland said, "Sustained."

"Let me rephrase the question, Agent Goldman." Kelley responded, "The surveillance reports all implicate Skip Reed. Is that correct?"

Goldman said, "My job is to collect information and arrest suspects based on that information. Mr. Reed was definitely implicated and arrested based on that information."

"Thank you, Agent Goldman. Was defendant Joseph Scanton directly implicated by any surveillance reports?"

"Yes, he was. He was implicated by Mr. Reed and his actions."

"Was Joseph Scanton implicated by any other person or action, other than the statements made to others, by Reed?"

"No, he was not. He was, however, implicated by his actions. He was observed by the United States Coast Guard piloting his vessel into Canadian waters from United States waters."

"Objection, Your Honor. I move to strike the answer as nonresponsive. There are no photographs or witnesses that show exactly who was piloting the fishing vessel during its voyage into Canadian waters."

"Sustained. The jury will ignore the last statement."

"Do you have specific photographs or an eyewitness who can testify, before this court today, that they saw Joseph Scanton actually at the helm piloting the fishing vessel *Jubilee* across the Hague Line from the United States into Canadian waters?"

"No, I do not."

"Thank you, Agent Goldman. Just one more question. In your experience, do you think an individual can manipulate another into an illegal act without their knowledge?"

Agent Goldman was slow to answer.

"Yes, I do."

Attorney Howerton said, "Objection, Your Honor. This question calls for total speculation on the part of the witness."

"Overruled. The question that was asked was based on the witness's experience as a professional law enforcement officer. I'm going to allow it."

Attorney Kelley said, "Thank you, Agent Goldman. That's all I have for this witness."

Attorney Davis came to his feet and approached the witness. Davis said, "How are you doing, Agent Goldman?"

"I'm good, Mr. Davis."

Davis said, "You know I represent Mr. Chase over there. I'd like to talk to you about the propane tanks."

Goldman said, "Okay."

"You mentioned, in previous testimony, that there were photographs of propane coming aboard the *Jubilee*. Is that correct? And that there was a large sum of money—approximately $9,000,000, I believe was the figure—that was smuggled aboard the boat. Is that correct, Agent Goldman?"

"Yes, it is."

"Could we take a look at those photographs, please?" The clerk brought them over to Attorney Davis. They were marked as exhibits 6, 7, and 8.

"Agent Goldman, would you take a look at these photos and tell me which tank has the propane in it and which one has the cash."

Agent Goldman looked carefully at the photos. "I don't know which one has the money and which one has propane."

"I'm confused then, because I thought you said that you had conclusive evidence that there was $9,000,000 in cash in one of those tanks."

Goldman smiled. "I guess you got me there. You can't tell which tank has money in it or if either one of them does. You see, we were told by that Columbian that we arrested and deported that that's how the money was smuggled aboard the boat. Of course, we have the top of the propane tank lying on deck in this photo that substantiates that contention."

Attorney Davis said, "It's interesting to me that you used the word 'smuggled' to describe how the cash was put aboard the boat. Now to me, Agent Goldman, 'smuggled' would imply that the money was put aboard without anyone's knowledge. Is that what you meant?"

Goldman smiled. "No, I meant that's how the cash got aboard the boat in broad daylight."

"Agent Goldman, now that you brought it up, in your expert opinion as an investigator, is it possible that Skip Reed and the gas deliveryman could have placed that tank aboard the boat without the captain and the rest of the crew knowing about its contents?"

Howerton jumped to his feet. "Objection, Your Honor. This question calls for speculation and conclusion on the part of the witness."

The judge said, "Based on Mr. Goldman's expertise in these matters, I'm going to allow it. Go ahead, answer the question, Agent Goldman."

He said, "There is little or no doubt that, properly planned, that gas transfer, concealing the cash, could have been accomplished without the knowledge of anyone but the two people directly involved."

There was a murmur that ran through the courtroom. Howerton gave Agent Goldman a vicious stare. In classic Goldman form he raised both hands with a "what can I say?" expression.

Attorney Davis continued, "Let's take a look at the photos of the gas truck that delivered the gas to the dock where the *Jubilee* was tied in Rockland. I want to see if you notice some of the same things I do." The clerk brought the pictures Davis had asked for over to the witness stand. There were no objections from the prosecutor. All of these pictures had already been accepted into evidence.

"Agent Goldman, when you look at those photographs with the gas truck in them, do you see anything unusual?"

Goldman glanced at the pictures. "No, not really."

He carefully studied the pictures a second time and started to smile.

Attorney Davis said, "You see it now, don't you?"

Goldman said, "I'm surprised I didn't notice it before."

Judge MacFarland said, "Excuse me, gentlemen, but do you think you could include the rest of this courtroom with your brilliant discovery?"

"I'm sorry, Your Honor. Agent Goldman, what have you noticed that's unusual in these pictures?"

"None of these photographs with the gas truck in them have any lettering on the trucks that say Rockland Propane. There are gas decals indicating that the truck stops at railroad crossings but no logos or company lettering."

Davis said, "What do you think that might mean?"

"It may indicate nothing, or it could indicate that the truck was not from Rockland Propane at all."

Davis said, "Your Honor, I would like to introduce a piece of evidence at this time that might shine a little light on this subject."

He passed a copy of a letter to the prosecutor and the judge.

The judge said, "Any objections, Mr. Howerton?"

Howerton said, "No, Your Honor."

Davis handed the letter to Goldman. "Agent Goldman, would you take a look at this letter and tell the court what it says, please."

"This letter is a sworn affidavit from the owner of Rockland Propane. It says that there are no unlettered trucks in its four-truck fleet and that the driver shown in the photograph is not an employee of Rockland Propane and the truck shown is not his."

"Thank you, Agent Goldman. That's all I have for this witness."

Attorney Peter Green stood. "I have a few questions for Mr. Goldman, Your Honor."

Judge MacFarland said, "Please proceed."

"Agent Goldman, did you collect any evidence of any kind that implicates my client, Mr. Thomas Anderson, in this crime?"

Goldman said, "The fact that Mr. Anderson was present during all phases of the purchase, transfer, and transportation of the narcotics implicates him in this crime."

"Does any of the evidence generated by your investigation, other than his presence, indicate an active role in this crime by Mr. Thomas Anderson?"

Howerton rose and said, "Objection, Your Honor. The witness has already answered that question."

The judge said, "Sustained."

Peter Green continued, "Allow me to rephrase the question. Prior to his arrest, do you have any photographs, tapes, wiretaps, eye witnesses that implicate Mr. Thomas Anderson in this crime?"

Bert said, "No, I do not."

"So . . . to be perfectly clear. There is no evidence that demonstrates that Tom Anderson had any direct communications with Mr. Varney, Mr. Dalton, Mr. Vito Scantini, or any other individuals with the exception of his crew members Reed, Scanton, and Chase. Is that correct?"

"Yes, it is."

"Thank you. I have no further questions for this witness, Your Honor."

The judge said, "You may call your next witness, Mr. Howerton."

Attorney Howerton said, "No further witnesses your honor. The prosecution rests."

Judge MacFarland said, "Thank you, Mr. Howerton. It's eleven forty-five. We are going to recess for lunch. I'll expect everyone back here at 1:00 p.m. sharp. I'll remind the jury to not discuss anything that has been said in this court today with anyone including fellow jurors. Thank you, all." He rapped his gavel and the courtroom emptied.

CHAPTER 106

James Kelley said, "I've got a conference room for us. I'd like to order in for lunch so we can have just a few minutes to prepare for this afternoon." Everyone agreed, and they went to the designated room. They ordered various sandwiches and drinks. Chase said he wanted to go outside and grab a quick smoke. Scanton headed out with him. Anderson stayed behind with the attorneys.

Peter Green said, "Tom, we're going to put you on first. Try to stay calm and answer the questions clearly. You do not need to address the jury. Just look at me and answer the questions. When Howerton starts his cross-examination, he will try to engage you in a confrontational manner. Listen carefully to his questions, answer them, and don't lose your temper."

Anderson said, "I'll try. If the guy starts trying to set me up, I'm not putting up with it."

"Now listen to me carefully, Tom. That's exactly the wrong attitude. If he can get to you, he'll tear you up. The man is an extremely accomplished interrogator. He knows every trick in the book. You will lose if you try to engage with him. Do what I told you and simply answer the questions as asked. Don't try to second-guess him or read anything into his line of questioning. Remember we're there to do that. If he gets out of line, I'll object. Just trust in the system. Are we clear on this, Tom?"

Tom nodded his head. "Yes, we are. I'll do my best."

Chase and Scanton walked back into the room. Just after the lunch arrived, Phil Davis said, "Patrick, I'm going to give you the same speech Peter Green gave Tom while you were out getting your nicotine fix." Davis went through the same lecture that Tom had just heard. He said, "I'm very concerned about you during cross-examination, Pat. You cannot afford to display any anger or disrespect toward the prosecutor. As good as that might feel at the time, it will only work against you. The jury will see you as combative and aggressive and will think you have something to hide."

Chase said, "What am I supposed to do? Sit there and let that asshole try to make me say that I did shit I didn't do?"

"No. Listen to the questions, take your time, and answer them."

"All right, all right, I'll try . . . I'll try not to jump out of that witness stand and break his fucking neck."

Davis smiled and said, "Yeah, Pat . . . that would be good."

Attorney Kelley said, "You've heard it all, Joey. You'll be last, so you'll have a chance to see what the other guys have been through."

Scanton said, "We'll all do the best we can."

Then Kelley said, "Boys, you've all got to listen to me a minute. This is serious stuff today. We all know you weren't part of this thing. Go out there and tell the truth. This is going to come out better than you may think. Let's get back in there."

CHAPTER 107

A s soon as everyone was back in the courtroom, Judge
MacFarland called the court to order. "Ladies and gentlemen
of the jury, we are now going to begin the defense part of this trial.
Mr. Kelley, you may call your first witness.

Attorney Kelley rose from his seat. "Thank you, Your Honor.
Mr. Green will be calling the first witness for the defense."

Green stepped forward. "The defense calls Mr. Thomas Anderson."

Martin Anderson and Kathy were watching from the seats just
behind the defense table as Tom was sworn in. Kathy said to herself,
"Please, God, help him through this. I love him so much."

Attorney Green began. "Please state your name and occupation
for the jury."

"My name is Tom Anderson, and I'm a commercial fisherman."
Anderson had never said those words out loud before and had to admit
he liked the way they sounded. He was proud to be a fisherman.

"Thank you, Mr. Anderson. Can you please tell me about how
you came to have a job fishing?"

Anderson said, "I grew up with Skip Reed. He and I were best
friends ever since we were little kids. He was a little older than me,
but we were in the same class. He was the one that vouched for me
to get a job on the boat. At least he said he did."

Attorney Green said, "What do you mean by that?"

"He told me I had a job all set. We went in town to where the
boat was tied, with me planning to just get aboard and go fishing.
When we got there, the captain, Joey Scanton, hadn't agreed to take
me on at all."

"Well, how did you get the job then?" Green said.

"I guess I talked myself into it. Part of the reason was because
Joey was so mad at the way Skip had handled things. He decided to
give me a chance."

"Was this typical behavior for Skip Reed? Is that how he normally treated you?"

"No, I was real surprised at him doing that to me. It was very embarrassing to say the least."

Green pressed on. "Things did work out though. You got your job and went fishing on the boat in question, is that true?"

"Yes, it is."

"You've been charged with a very serious crime, drug trafficking. If you are convicted, you could to be sent to prison for a long time."

Anderson looked down at the floor. "I know that."

"The prosecution and its witnesses have alleged and testified that you were an active, fully informed participant in this crime. What do you have to say about that?"

"That's not true . . . any of it. I had no knowledge or any part in this crime."

Attorney Green turned toward the jury and looked at them. "Could you please explain for the jury how that's possible?"

Anderson took a deep breath. "I came aboard that boat to learn to go offshore fishing. I'm still what they call a green man, a rookie, a newcomer. I had to learn everything from the ground floor up. That's what I did. I did my job on that boat. I cooked all the meals and did all the grunt work aboard. I didn't know anything at all about a drug deal. We were finishing a five-day trip when we came into Rockland. We left for fishing again after a few days. We got into a hurricane offshore and survived that in pretty good shape. We started fishing again after the wind let go. We were down around a piece of bottom called Truxton's. Pat Chase and I had been on deck for about twenty hours. Skip Reed was supposedly sick with the flu. Finally, Joey told Pat and me to hit the bunk, and we did.

"When I got woken up, that's when I found out the boat had been taken over by some crooks and that we had cocaine on board."

Attorney Green said, "Mr. Anderson, you expect this jury to believe that you had no knowledge of anything to do with drugs and that you were sound asleep when they were put aboard the boat. Is that correct?"

"Yes, sir. That's the truth."

"After you were woken up, what did you do?"

"They told me to make some food for everybody, which I did. That's when I found out that Skip was in on the whole thing. Pat told me about it. I think Reed drugged Pat and I so we wouldn't make any trouble."

Attorney Green wanted to slow Anderson down a little. "What do you mean trouble?"

"You know, fight back and maybe not let them get the drugs on board."

"Who do you mean by them?"

"There was a Columbian named Carlos and a bastard named Sammy Dalton."

The judge said, "Mr. Anderson, refrain from that type of language in this courtroom."

"I'm sorry, Your Honor. I hate that guy, that's all."

The judge said, "Control yourself, young man."

"Yes, Your Honor. I'm sorry, sir."

The judge said, "Continue, Mr. Green."

Attorney Green resumed. "After you were awake, did you try to resist the takeover of the boat?"

"No, but Patrick and Uncle Charley did."

"Who is Uncle Charley?"

"That's our cat." Everyone in the courtroom started to laugh. The judge hit his gavel several times.

"Could you please explain for the jury how Mr. Chase and a cat tried to take the boat back?"

"This Carlos guy had Pat, Joey, and me at gunpoint down in the galley. We were sitting at the table when somehow Pat managed to get Uncle Charley, that's our cat, to come out of her bunk. I think he did it with a cookie, and then that Carlos guy stepped on Uncle Charley's tail . . . big mistake." The courtroom was in gales of laughter at this point. The judge cracked his gavel again. "Order in the court!"

After things got quieted down, Anderson continued, "Uncle Charley jumped the Columbian and bit the living hell out of his leg. She was slashing him up real good. That's when Pat made his move." By now the room was total chaos. The judge was banging away, trying to get things to calm down. A couple of minutes passed, and Attorney Green continued with his questions.

"Just out of curiosity, did you say 'she,' referring to Uncle Charley?"

"Yeah, that's right. Uncle Charley's a female cat. It's a long story. Anyway, that's when Pat Chase jumped the Columbian and started to choke him to death. He almost got it done, and then the guy somehow managed to get at his gun and shot Pat in the side."

"Then what happened?" Green said.

"Then that very delightful fellow, Sammy Dalton, got us all under gunpoint again. He let me try to get Pat fixed up with some bandages we had aboard and into his bunk. Pat stayed there until we were almost into Little River."

Green said, "Would you say that you, Mr. Scanton, and Mr. Chase were trying to resist Carlos and Mr. Dalton?"

Bill Howerton spoke up and said, "Objection, Your Honor. This question calls for speculation on the part of the witness. He has no possible knowledge of Mr. Scanton's intentions during this altercation."

The judge said, "Overruled. I'm going to allow it. Mr. Anderson was present, and I want to hear his opinion."

Attorney Green said, "Go ahead, Mr. Anderson."

"In my opinion, that was an attempted takeover. It all happened so fast Joey and I didn't have time to jump into the fray."

"Just a few more questions. Did you ever have any discussions with Skip Reed, Michael Varney, Sammy Dalton, or anyone else about smuggling cocaine into this country aboard the *Jubilee*?"

"No, sir, I did not."

"Were you aware of any conversation or meetings that occurred between Skip Reed, Sammy Dalton, Patrick Chase, Joseph Scanton, or anyone else regarding the purchase or transportation of any narcotics of any kind into this country or anywhere else aboard the *Jubilee?*"

"No, sir, I was not."

"Just one more question. Did you have any knowledge whatsoever about the drug-related activities of one Andrew Brown of Falmouth?"

"No, sir, I did not."

"Thank you, Mr. Anderson . . . your witness, Mr. Howerton."

CHAPTER 108

The jurors all seemed very engaged in this trial. One of them was a young man named Dennis Waters. He was thirty years old and was a life insurance salesman at his dad's agency. He was really glad to be picked for jury duty because he hated selling insurance and was happy to have a legitimate reason to be out of the office. The place bored the crap out of him. He did the job because he probably couldn't get one anywhere else and because he eventually wanted to own the company. Then he could go play golf and be drunk most of the time like his old man did.

He was married, but he saw his wife as nothing more than a pain in his ass. She was always after him about his friends and was constantly on his case. He thought it was funny that he had gotten chosen for a cocaine-trafficking trial. He loved coke. All recreational, of course, but he hated these tight asses that were all holier than thou about a little nose candy. If these guys on trial had been able to get away with all that dope they would have had enough money to have it made for the rest of their lives. Dennis thought, *The more power to them*. He was enjoying the trial.

The courtroom was silent as Attorney Howerton stepped toward Anderson to begin his cross-examination. "Mr. Anderson, you stated for the record that you and Skip Reed had been best friends since childhood. Is that correct?"

"Yes, it is."

Howerton had taken on a very aggressive tone. "Do you expect us all to believe that Mr. Reed perpetrated this drug-smuggling scheme alone, and you had absolutely no knowledge of it at all?"

"That's right. Skip never mentioned a word to me about his plan to do this."

"What puzzles me, Mr. Anderson, is why would he expose you to arrest and imprisonment for involvement in a crime of this magnitude and never tell you what you were in for. That doesn't strike me as what a friend would do to another friend."

"I don't know why he did that, and he's not here to answer for himself."

Howerton said sarcastically, "I think that may be lucky for you, Mr. Anderson, because I believe that he would admit that you were along to help him with the entire crime and that you would be paid a handsome share of the take afterward."

Anderson immediately bristled with the accusation. "But that's not true. I went for the fishing job. That's all."

Howerton looked directly at Anderson. "Then explain why they would hire a complete novice with no experience whatsoever to go fishing aboard that boat."

"I don't know. You'll have to ask Joey Scanton that question. He hired me."

"Oh, I will, Mr. Anderson. You can count on it."

Howerton clasped his hands loosely behind his back. "Do you do drugs, Mr. Anderson?"

"No, I don't."

"Not even a little pot from time to time, to calm the old nerves?"

"No, I never got into it. I smoke some cigarettes and drink a few beers, but that's pretty much it for me."

"How about Skip Reed? Was he a pot smoker or cocaine user?"

"I've seen Skip smoke some pot once in a while, but I never saw him use coke."

"That's strange to me. We have you boys dead to rights, busted with 350 kilos of cocaine, and the mastermind was a casual pot smoker. Is that right?"

Anderson said, "I guess so."

"So you admit that we have you dead to rights and that Skip Reed was the mastermind of this crime. Is that right, Mr. Anderson?"

"No, that's not right. That's not what I said."

"All right, Mr. Anderson, if Skip Reed didn't mastermind this crime for you men, who did? Was it Joey Scanton over there?"

"No, it wasn't like that. I don't know what happened."

"Well, Mr. Anderson, you've just stated under oath that Mr. Reed didn't mastermind the crime all of you are on trial for. Would you kindly tell the jury who did?"

"I don't know. I was just a crew member. I went fishing with these guys. We were way offshore somewhere. I was told to turn in. When I got woken up, there were guys that had taken over the boat. That's all I know."

"I don't believe you, Mr. Anderson. Admit to this court that you and all the rest of the crew had planned this drug-smuggling escapade from the beginning. Save us all a lot of time and start telling the truth now!"

Peter Green jumped to his feet and hollered, "Objection, Your Honor! Mr. Howerton is badgering the witness!"

Judge MacFarland said, "Sustained. Mr. Howerton, you will refrain from that tactic in this courtroom."

Attorney Howerton said, "I'm through with this witness, Your Honor."

The judge said, "You may step down, young man." And just like that it was over. Anderson walked away from the witness stand. His hands were shaking. He was sweating profusely. He looked over at Kathy and she gave him a weak smile. Her cheeks were stained with tears. He went over and sat down at the defense table, and Phil Davis put his hand over Tom's forearm. He said in a very low voice, "You did all right, kid. You did all right."

*   *   *

Pauline Wallace watched and listened from the jurors seats. She was shocked when she learned that she had been picked as a juror for this trial. She was fifty-three years old and had worked at a local bank since she was in her early thirties. She wasn't married and lived alone in a house that she had inherited from her mother who had died fifteen years earlier.

She had dated a few men from her church years ago, but it had always gotten down to the same thing, the sex stuff, and she didn't want any part of that foolishness. Her life was fairly simple really and this trial was a very exciting and interesting event in her otherwise boring life.

These guys on trial seemed awfully rough to her and might be capable of doing anything. She didn't know much about drugs, other than the fact that people involved with them should be in jail. Her sister had a teenage son who had been caught smoking pot. It made her mad that kids could get a hold of that stuff to begin with. She thought the prosecutor was doing a good job. Polly believed in the government. That was the side he was on, and so was she. She promised to listen to the evidence, try to keep an open mind, and find them all guilty.

CHAPTER 109

A ttorney Davis stood up and said, "The defense calls Mr. Patrick Chase, Your Honor." Chase got up slowly and made his way over to the witness stand. He was sworn in and took his seat. He looked very uncomfortable and kept pulling at his tie. The jury was taking its first good look at this rather formidable man. Davis said, "How you doin', Mr. Chase?"

"Oh, I'm all right, I guess. There's places I'd rather be, to be honest with you."

Davis said, "I understand. Would you please state your name and occupation for the record?"

"My name is Patrick Chase, and I'm a commercial fisherman, out on bail."

There were a few snickers from the courtroom.

"Mr. Chase, my records indicate that you worked for Joseph Scanton aboard the *Jubilee* for approximately two years, is that correct?"

Chase said, "Yes, it is."

"Was Arnold Reed a crew member when you came aboard that boat?"

"No, he wasn't. He came about a half a year after me."

"How did you get along with him? Was he a good man on the boat?"

"He did his job fishing, but I didn't like him at all. He was an arrogant little know-it-all, and I never trusted a thing he said."

"Why was that?" Davis said, "Can you give us a specific example of what made you feel that way about him?"

"He'd lie about stupid little shit all the time. Like where he'd been when we weren't aboard the boat. He was constantly bumming cigarettes from me and never replacing them. I just didn't trust the guy, that's all."

"Did you ever observe him talking to a Mr. Varney or a Mr. Dalton?"

"No. I never saw any of those guys before that jerk Dalton had me at gunpoint, and I had never seen that Varney guy either, until this trial."

"Mr. Chase, were you ever suspicious that Reed was involved in a drug-smuggling plot?"

"No, I wasn't. I thought Reed was a pain in the ass, but this cocaine deal was way over the top, even for him."

"Mr. Chase, do you do drugs?"

"Hell no, I'm a drunk. I never liked that stuff." The courtroom broke out in laughter.

Davis said, "How about Joey Scanton? How do you get along with him?"

"Finest kind . . . he's a real good skipper and has been a good friend. He's a semidrunk. He doesn't do any drugs either, that I know about."

"How about Reed? Did you ever see him using drugs?"

"Skip Reed was a casual pot smoker as far as I know, but I never saw him doing it out on the boat. Joey would have thrown his ass off if he'd caught him with that shit on board."

Judge MacFarland spoke up. "Mr. Chase, could you please refrain from the use of vulgar language?"

"Sorry, Judge. I'll try to clean it up for you."

"See that you do, Mr. Chase. Please proceed."

"That seems strange to me. You guys are arrested with almost eight hundred pounds of cocaine, and you seem to describe this as drug-free boat."

"That's easy. That cocaine wasn't ours. That deal was engineered by Reed and the rest of us were all dragged into it at gunpoint."

"We'll get into that some more later on. You are stating that there was a no-drug policy aboard the boat."

Chase smiled. "Clean boat. Always was, since I was aboard her."

"Are you trained in all aspects of navigation and the full operation of a fishing vessel of the size of the *Jubilee*? In other words, could you run the fishing operation yourself?"

"If you are asking me if I could step up to the wheelhouse, the answer is yes."

Davis said, "By that you mean you could become captain of a boat this size, based on your experience and knowledge, is that correct?"

"Yes, I could."

"Have you gone captain on other vessels before?"

"Yes, I have. I ran a boat for Terry Dawkins out of Kennebunkport and one for Albert Wakelin, out of Portland."

"What happened to those jobs? Why did you leave?"

"The cheap pri—sorry, Your Honor. They refused to spend money to properly maintain their boats. I don't fish on boats that aren't safe. End of story."

"Does Joseph Scanton maintain the *Jubilee*?"

"Definitely . . . Joey takes real good care of her."

"Recently, you were tied up for an extended period of time. Could you explain what happened to cause that?"

"Shi—I mean, stuff happens on a boat like that. We got a net in the wheel and blew out a reverse gear. We had to replace it. Joey and I did all the work ourselves, and it still cost him over nineteen grand."

"Did Mr. Reed help out with that work?"

"No, he didn't. I didn't care about that either. That guy could break an anvil. He was lousy around the mechanicals."

"What was the financial situation after that breakdown?"

"It was bad. We had a fairly decent trip going when we got messed up and had to be towed in. Joey told me he had to borrow money from his uncle, Sal Scantini, to pay for the new gear. We were tied up for over a month with no money. It was bad . . . there was no doubt about it."

Attorney Davis said, "If I understand correctly, you went fishing again and did pretty well."

Chase said, "We did have a great trip. The boat stocked a $100,000. Then Joey's wife stole the trip."

"What do you mean she stole the trip?"

"Joey sent her the money to pay everybody, and she took the money and ran off with it."

"Do you think that there might have been a plan to put Joey under huge financial pressure?"

Howerton spoke up. "I object, Your Honor. How would Mr. Chase have any idea of any plan placing Mr. Scanton under financial pressure?"

Judge MacFarland responded, "Overruled. I'd like to hear Mr. Chase's answer. Please continue and answer the question."

"I don't know. I really don't . . . all I do know is that we got back out fishing. We were out there about three days, and we went through a hurricane. Then just like Tom said, we were fishing pretty hard. We'd been out on deck pretty near twenty hours. We came off, hit the bunk, and I woke up with the boat headed back to Maine with two crooks—actually three, including Reed—running things."

Attorney Davis said, "We are going to talk about that trip a little later."

Davis changed the line of questioning. "Mr. Chase, let's talk about the propane gas situation. Did you order more propane for the boat when you were headed into Rockland?"

"Yes, I did. We ran out at sea. I called in the order through Camden Marine Radio. Rockland Propane took the order over the radio. Rockland Propane is where I always get our gas. A friend of mine named Gary owns it. When the gas came though, it was from somebody else. We were all busy aboard the boat, and Reed handled the swap out. I really didn't pay that much attention to it. I thought it was funny that my friend Gary didn't show up. We were supposed to have a beer together after he dropped off the gas. They told me one of those tanks had $9,000,000 in cash in it. You could buy a lot of beer with that kind of money. Gary usually doesn't have nine bucks on him."

Everybody laughed.

"So you don't think Gary supplied the money then?"

"No way in hell. I believe Reed must have had that all set up with somebody. That's how he fooled all of us, including Joey, and got the money on the boat. I'll guarantee you Reed did it, but I bet he didn't think up that idea."

"Why do you say that?"

"Because there's no way that Reed was smart enough to think up something that clever. All that Reed was, was a sneaky nasty little creep that deceived other people and manipulated them for his own gain. He wasn't smart."

"Did you have any knowledge of a deal to transport 350 kilos of cocaine aboard the fishing vessel *Jubilee*?"

"No, I did not."

"Did you participate in the transportation or purchase of 350 kilos of cocaine aboard that same boat?"

"No, I did not."

"Thank you, Mr. Chase. On the trip in from the Hague Line you got into a fight. Tell me about getting wounded."

Chase said, "I'll tell you this—it hurt like holy hell."

Everyone laughed.

"I'm sure it did, but I was curious as to how it happened."

"Tom explained it better than I can. Just like he said, we were being held at the galley table under gunpoint. We got a cranky cat on the boat named Uncle Charley that was under the table, out of sight. Well, I managed to get Uncle Charley close enough so that that Carlos guy stepped on her tail. When he did that, Uncle Charley nailed him good in the leg, bit the living hell out of him. That really distracted the guy, and I jumped him. I had him pretty good but somehow he managed to shoot me in the side. That's pretty much it."

"What were you trying to do?"

"I was trying to kill him, actually, but I wanted to get his gun and try and take the boat back from him and Sammy Dalton."

"What about Skip Reed? You'd have to fight him too, wouldn't you?"

"There wouldn't be no fight there. Reed was a coward. I wasn't worried about that little jerk. That Sammy guy though, he was a different story. I'm still a little surprised he didn't blow my head off when I was choking his Columbian buddy Carlos to death. I guess me and Uncle Charley didn't have what it takes to overthrow a Columbian and a fat guy, that's all."

"Did anyone else join in to try and help you?"

"No . . . I think it was all over so fast they didn't have a chance. No one knew I was going to try it, including Uncle Charley."

"Thank you for that, Mr. Chase. Tell us about the arrest."

"We landed the boat in East Boothbay, and the entire place was loaded with cops and DEA agents. We were all thrilled to see them there. We all figured 'hooray for the good guys' until they came on board and arrested us all. That was the biggest friggin' shock of my life. Hell, I'd been shot by one of these bastards, and I was going off to jail with him. Go figure."

"Tell us about Mr. Reed's death."

"Now there's the best part, and the worst part, all at the same time."

"What do you mean by that?"

Chase was dying to get outside and have a cigarette. "Okay, by then Joey, Tom, and I knew he had set all this stuff up. The little bastard had been lying to all of us. He was guilty as hell, so he ran off when they were trying to get him up the wharf ladder. He grabbed that speedboat, made a run for it, and it blew up on him."

"Do you think it was accidental or intentional?"

Howerton interrupted, "Objection, Your Honor. This witness has no idea what the circumstances were of that explosion."

The judge said, "Sustained. Rephrase the question."

Attorney Davis said, "When you witnessed the explosion, what were your thoughts at that time?"

Chase said, "That's where the good news and bad news comes in. I was glad to see him get his, after what he had done to all of us.

The bad news was he wasn't around to take responsibility for all the stuff we're going through now."

"I understand." Davis said, "If in fact the explosion was planned, do you think Skip Reed was the intended target?"

"I've thought about that. I think it was intended for Carlos, the Columbian, and Sammy Dalton. That was supposed to be their ride back to the mother ship. I bet that freighter was underway one minute after we were out of radar range. I never even saw that boat. I was out cold in my bunk sound asleep at the time."

"I have no further questions for this witness, Your Honor."

The judge said, "Your witness, Mr. Howerton."

Attorney Howerton rose slowly and walked over to the witness stand. "Mr. Chase, I'm curious about something. You have admitted to ordering the replacement propane, correct?"

"Yes."

"We have established that the cash to acquire the cocaine was placed aboard the boat and transported in those propane tanks. Is that correct?"

"I guess so. I never saw any of that money."

"Oh yes, that's because you and Mr. Anderson were asleep, how convenient. Let's, for the purposes of this questioning, assume that the money was transported in one of those propane tanks, all right?"

Chase said, "You can assume anything you want to."

"Thank you. You have also admitted that you didn't cancel the propane you ordered, correct?"

"Yes, I guess so."

"Mr. Chase, 'you guess so' is not good enough. Did you or did you not cancel the propane?"

"No, I didn't. But they read a paper from Rockland Propane that the order from them was cancelled."

"That may or may not be relevant. Did you witness two cylinders of propane being delivered?"

"Yes, I did."

"Now for the record, you ordered propane, you've admitted that you saw the propane arrive, you've admitted that one of the cylinders was full of cash that was ultimately used to pay for the cocaine. Could you please tell this court where you got the tank with the $9,000,000 hidden inside?"

"I didn't. I have no idea where the cash you are all talking about came from. And I never saw any cash come out of any propane tank."

"Mr. Chase, if you don't know where it came from, who would? You ordered the tanks from somewhere, and certainly you knew they were carrying the concealed cash."

"I had no idea there was anything in those tanks but propane."

"You have previously testified that Mr. Reed unloaded the tanks and put them aboard the boat. Is that correct?"

"Yes."

"Then you testified that you thought it was strange that your friend from Rockland Propane didn't come to deliver the gas. Is that correct?"

"Yes, it is."

"Yet even though the gas deliveries for the boat were always your responsibility—ordering, accepting deliveries, and placing the gas aboard the boat physically—this one time you didn't do it. Is that correct?"

Chase said, "Yes."

"And you stood by and let that happen and never said a word."

Chase was losing his patience fast. "For Christ's sake, it was just propane."

"No, Mr. Chase, it was not just propane. You know it now and you knew it then. You were allowing Mr. Reed to accept those tanks to try and divert attention from yourself. It was clever to say the least. Tell the court where you acquired that money. Was it from Varney or Dalton or some other place? You're under oath, Mr. Chase. Answer my question."

"I don't know."

"You don't know whether the money came from Mr. Varney or Mr. Dalton?"

"I don't know anything about that money." Now Chase was starting to get angry. His face was getting red. His huge hands were gripping the railing in front of the witness stand, and his knuckles were white. Phil Davis leaned toward Jim Kelley without taking his eyes off Pat and whispered, "Hang in there, big fella, hang in there."

Howerton said, "If you weren't part of the propane and cash delivery, would you please explain why it was relegated to Mr. Reed?"

"He just kind of took over and did it."

"And you stood there and let that happen for the first time in two years of gas deliveries on that boat. I don't believe you, Mr. Chase. It's time to start telling the truth about what went on here."

"I don't give a shit what you believe. It's the truth. That's what happened."

Judge MacFarland spoke up immediately. "Language, Mr. Chase." He raised his hand as to signal stop. Chase looked down and said nothing.

"Mr. Chase, this alleged fight you described to the court. Weren't you, in truth, trying to overthrow the boat and get control of it to be able to take advantage of the $29,000,000 in cargo aboard? That way there could be more money for you and your accomplices?"

"Yeah . . . that was it, me and Uncle Charley, we had cut a deal, but she was taking her share in fresh fish guts though. You figured it all out, big time." The courtroom broke out in laughter. This time it was Attorney Howerton that was angry.

"You think this is joke, do you, Mr. Chase? Trust me, there's nothing funny about where you'll be spending the next twenty-five years."

Phil Davis jumped up and hollered, "Objection, Your Honor!"

Judge MacFarland said, "Sustained. You know better than that, Mr. Howerton, and you, Mr. Chase, refrain from the nonresponsive answers or I'll hold you in contempt. You understand me?"

"Yes, Your Honor."

Howerton said, "You testified that you were surprised that a Mr. Dalton didn't shoot you when he found you and this Carlos man engaged in an altercation. Is that correct?"

"Yes."

"Was that because of your relationship with Mr. Dalton and perhaps a prearranged deal that you already had with him?"

"No, I had never seen that Sammy Dalton guy before in my life, until I woke up in a haze and had the privilege of meeting him. I better not ever see him again."

"Mr. Chase, you were involved aboard the *Jubilee* from the beginning negotiations of this crime. You had, and have, a personal relationship with all of the perpetrators of this crime, including Mr. Reed. You have admitted in court to ordering the propane tanks that contained the cash used to purchase the drugs. You have aided and enabled yourself and other parties to smuggle 350 kilos of cocaine into this country from international waters. Those are the facts, yet you sit before us now, stating under oath that you had no knowledge of any drug-smuggling activities at all, that you were asleep, in fact. Is that your testimony here today?"

Chase looked Howerton square in the eye. "Yes it is."

"Well, Mr. Chase, I don't believe that the jurors or anyone else has been put to sleep by you, sir. I have no further questions for this witness."

The judge said, "You may step down." Chase stood and walked back to the defense table. Howerton made sure he was back in his seat and that he was out of his reach when he went by. Scanton laughed a little when he saw Howerton so obviously intimidated by his friend Chase. Hell, it was kind of funny. The prosecutor was very nervous about what Pat might do to him. After he took his seat, Phil Davis said, "Good job, Pat, you didn't hurt yourself at all."

"That prick doesn't know how lucky he was that I didn't hurt him."

Judge MacFarland spoke up and said, "I'm going to end this for the day. I'll once again remind the jury to not discuss this trial with anyone, including each other. Please avoid radio, television, and newspapers. We'll reconvene here at nine o'clock tomorrow morning. Have a good evening, ladies and gentlemen." He rapped his gavel and court was over for another day.

*   *   *

Juror Dennis Waters was glad to be out of the court with a long night ahead of him. His wife had left just before the trial started for a few days with her sister in New Hampshire. He was ready to get together with his friends, do a few lines of coke, and get out on the town for the night. His kid was at his mother's so he was free as a breeze. His buds were going to get a kick out of all this trial shit. He couldn't wait to tell them all about it.

Juror Pauline Wallace went home and had a nice long bath. She got on her nightgown and went straight to bed. She didn't dare turn on her TV for fear she would hear or see something on there that would go against the judge's orders. She lay there a long time, wide awake. She was still lying there when her clock read three fifteen. Then finally, she slept.

CHAPTER 110

T om and Kathy were exhausted after the long day in court. He said, "How do you think it went?"

"I thought you did great. I was so upset when that Howerton guy was trying to bait you. I think you're going to be okay. There's a lot more going to happen tomorrow when Joey goes on."

Tom said, "Let's pick up Matty and go out to the movies. There's a good kid's show over in Westbrook, and then we can get a pizza or something."

"Sure, I don't want to hang around worrying all night."

* * *

By the time Joey got home to his apartment, Teresa and Olivia were already there. He and Little Joey came into the kitchen. Teresa had dinner already on. They were having meatloaf and mashed potatoes. Teresa said, "How did it go today? I'm sorry I couldn't come. I had to work at the store all day."

"It's okay. They had Tom and Pat on the stand today, tomorrow is me. I'm feeling real anxious about it."

Teresa came over and put her arms around his neck. "Of course you are, Joey. You'll be okay. I'm going to be there to watch you. You know you didn't do anything wrong. Just answer the questions."

"The thing that makes me sick is I did do something wrong. I let Skip Reed talk me into going after swordfish. At least I thought it was swordfish. Lugging those fish is illegal, and when I admit it it's going to make me look bad. There's a woman on there that I know hates us. I can see how she admires every word that comes out of Howerton's mouth."

Teresa said, "It takes all of them to convict you, not just one old bitch. My dad says you guys are doing okay so far."

"I know. You're right. Thanks for being here with us."

"My pleasure, Captain." She kissed him sweetly on the lips and went back to making supper.

*   *   *

Pat and Leslie were sitting at their kitchen table. Pat was having a beer. Leslie said, "Pat, I think you did fine today. I wish you hadn't tried to antagonize that Howerton guy. I guess it's over though."

"I know, but the guy's such an asshole. You know me . . . I used to do the same shit in school when we were kids. Oh, that's right, you missed all that while you were out in Kansas living with Dorothy."

"Ha ha." She'd heard that line a billion times. She got serious and said, "This is going to sound awful, but I'm going to say it anyway. Do you think they could find you and Tom innocent and Joey guilty?"

"Don't even think it, let alone say it."

"It's just that he did agree to go way down there with the boat. He kept it all from you and Tom. He left you out on deck all that time intentionally and worked you into exhaustion. Whatever he wanted to do, swordfish or drugs, you were being left out of it, and his deal was with Skip."

Pat took a deep breath. "You think I haven't thought about that? When we were in the engine room getting the fuel filters straightened out so we could get the boat started again, I confronted him with that."

"And what did he say?"

"He told me that he kept us out of it for our own protection, and I think he meant it. He was so ashamed of himself for agreeing to go down there in the first place. He screwed up."

Leslie said, "This is all going to come out tomorrow on the witness stand. I hope it doesn't hurt you and Tom."

"We'll see. I still believe Joey got totally worked over by Skip. You know what Joey told me when we were out having a butt at lunch?"

"No, what?"

"Skip was screwing Karen."

"No! You're kidding me. Why would she get involved with him?"

"Joey thinks Skip was in for a big cut of the drug money, and they were going to take off together with it. He said he caught her with a coke stash when he went to get Little Joey away from her. You know she died of a coke overdose, for Christ sake."

"Oh my god! So Karen was manipulating Skip, and he was working Joey over. This whole mess is sicker than I thought."

"We'll see what comes down tomorrow, I guess."

Leslie and Pat went to bed and held each other until they fell asleep.

* * *

Joey was up by eight, and Teresa was getting the kids going. She promised him that she would drop Little Joey off at his grandmother's, and then she was going to take Olivia over to her mother's. Joey was feeling sick to his stomach. He would ten times rather be back in the middle of that hurricane than doing what he had to do today.

He thought to himself, *There isn't shit I can do about this now. What happens, happens.* He went down and got into his car and headed toward the courthouse. He hadn't eaten anything, but he was going to stop and get a cup of coffee from one of those little places on Middle Street.

CHAPTER 111

E veryone arrived in court just about the same time. Once again it was standing-room only. Scanton spotted Goldman standing near one of the doors leading into the courtroom. He looked very casual leaning against the wall. Joey resisted the urge to give him the finger. After everyone was seated, the judge entered and called the court to order, and things were underway quickly.

James Kelley stood and said, "The defense calls Mr. Joseph Scanton." Scanton walked over and was sworn in. He took his seat on the witness stand and Attorney Kelley began.

"Would you please state your name and occupation for the record?"

"Joseph Scanton, commercial fisherman."

"How long have you been a commercial fisherman, Mr. Scanton?"

"Twenty years. I started helping my dad summers when I was ten. I was only allowed to go on short trips while they were fishing up inside. My mother would only let me stay out just one night. The old man used to leave about midnight though, and we'd get back at maybe eight or nine o'clock two days later. He'd work as much time in as he could."

"Did you always like fishing, Mr. Scanton?"

"I didn't like it, I loved it. I would have stayed aboard that boat 24-7 if my mother would have let me. She did make me finish school though, and I am glad for that."

"Mr. Scanton, you own the *Jubilee* that we have heard so much about, is that correct?"

"Yes, I do."

"Are you the captain of that vessel?"

"Yes, I am."

"How long have you had the boat?"

"It's a little over four years now."

"How did you buy it?"

"My uncle, Charley Walker, died at sea fishing, and he left me the insurance money from his boat sinking. He was my mother's brother."

"We've all heard about the cat on board your boat. Is that why she's named Uncle Charley?"

"You've got it."

"How's it been going financially since you bought the boat?"

"It's been all right. She needed a bunch of stuff when I bought her. I put some paravanes on her, some new electronics, we did some hull work. I had to get a boat loan, plus the money I got from Uncle Charley, to get her going the way I wanted her."

"So things had been going along pretty well, and then I understand you had a breakdown of some sort. Could you tell us about that?"

"Yeah, we were towing down to the southard a little, and I screwed up and got the net in the wheel. When that happens, you usually try and jog her in and out of gear a little. Sometimes it works, sometimes it doesn't."

"How about this time?"

"This time it didn't work, and I blew the reverse gear."

"Just for clarity, from the perspective of the mechanically impaired like myself, did you break the transmission on the boat?"

"Yes, I did, and we had to be towed into Portland by the Coast Guard."

"Then did you have to repair the boat?"

"Yes, I did. It took almost a month and a half and cost almost twenty grand."

"Did you have that kind of money saved so you could pay for the needed repairs?"

"No, I had some from that trip, but after paying the crew and all the other expenses, I had to borrow money from my uncle, Sal Scantini."

"What specifically was his relationship to you?"

"He's my dad's brother. He's a small-time gangster. He lends money to people like me that are in trouble. He charges big interest under what you'd call hard terms."

"Go ahead and explain for the court what you mean by 'hard terms.'"

"With Uncle Sal, your loan collateral is your body as a first and your life as a second. You know what I mean?"

Attorney Kelley said, "Borrowing from Mr. Scantini was your only alternative?"

"I thought so at the time. Now I know better. What's done is done."

"How much money did you borrow from him?"

"I needed nine thousand to get the new gear."

"Thank you, Mr. Scanton. We'll get back to that subject again later. Can you please tell the court when you came in contact with Arnold Reed?"

"I've known Skip Reed for years. The fishing crowd all know each other. Me and the old man took him quite a few years ago on the *Gloria Walker* for a few trips. We were shrimping out of Boothbay winters. He was a pretty good man on deck. I'd had the *Jubilee* about two years when he showed up again and wanted a site on the boat. So I took him. I had fired a guy and had a spot open at the time."

"When you say a 'site' do you mean a job?"

"Yeah, sorry."

"How did it work out with him on board?"

"He did his job. He and Pat Chase didn't get along to good though. Reed liked to make himself out as big deal, and Pat hates that shit." Joey looked quickly toward Harold MacFarland and said, "Sorry, Judge." Judge MacFarland just looked back at him.

"How would you compare the two men as crew members?"

Scanton said, "No comparison. Pat's five times the man Skip Reed could ever be, no question."

"Joey, when you had the breakdown and the money pressures were on, did Skip Reed make a proposal to you of some kind?"

"Yeah, he did. He told me he had some connections and that we could lug some Canadian swordfish into Maine and make some quick cash. I've known a bunch of guys that had done that. There's an embargo on Canadian swordfish, supposedly because of mercury content, but them fish get sold all over the world."

"Did you agree to transport the swordfish?"

"Well . . . not at first. We were strapped for money, but there were a few flats around, so I figured I'd take my chances and try to fish my way out of my problem. I refused Reed's offer on the swords and decided to go for the flats."

"By flats do you mean flatfish, like flounders and that type of fish?"

"Exactly. We get good money for them, and I had a brainstorm going where I thought I could go and catch a few fish."

"So that decision was made by you, before you left Portland in August. Is that correct?"

"Yes, it is."

"Tell me about hiring Tom Anderson."

"Well, Skip just shows up with this kid out of the clear blue, looking for a job. He was a green man. No dragger experience at all. I don't take green men. I think they're dangerous on board the boat. It's not that they're stupid or anything. When things happen on a boat, you gotta know what to do, or you can get yourself killed or somebody else."

"But you did decide to hire him and take him with you, is that correct?"

"Yes, I did. I knew friggin' well that Skip had promised this kid a site, and he was counting on it. I was so mad at what Reed had pulled on him, I hired him to make things right. That probably sounds nuts now that I hear myself say it, but that's what I did."

"How did it work out with him on the boat?"

"Oh, finest kind. Anderson was a quick learner. He had been lobstering and around boats his whole life. He and Pat became good friends after Tom trimmed him at the cribbage table a few times."

"I understand that Tom and Skip Reed had been close friends since childhood. Is that correct?"

Howerton spoke up, "I object, Your Honor. This is all very fascinating, but does the counselor have some point in mind?"

The judge said, "Overruled, Mr. Howerton. This is an important trial. You'll have every opportunity to cross-examine this witness for as long as you need. It is this court's opinion that the relationships between these men are critical to understanding the total picture in this case. Please proceed, Mr. Kelley."

"Thank you, Your Honor. Did Skip and Tom continue to remain close friends, in your opinion, aboard the boat?"

"Not really. Skip made some nasty remarks about Tom's girlfriend, and he was pretty mad. At one point I thought Pat was going to have to break them up, but then I figured Pat would probably be happy to see Reed get the snot beat out of him."

"You did leave Portland then and were out fishing when these conflicts between Mr. Reed and Mr. Anderson occurred. Is that correct?"

"Yes."

"How did the trip go in general?"

"Great. We stocked just over a hundred grand, and we were set. I had money to pay all the back bills. I had nine grand toward my debt with Uncle Sal. The crew was all going to make big money. Tom was catching on as to how to do his job pretty good. Things were looking up."

"Then what happened?"

"I didn't know it at the time, but my wife stole the whole goddamn trip!"

The judge said, "Mr. Scanton."

"Sorry, Your Honor."

Kelley began again. "Explain what you mean by saying that 'she stole the trip.'"

Scanton cleared his throat. "She and I talked on the phone after we got into Gloucester. She had been so nasty to me when we left Portland, it was unbelievable. Then she's all sweetness and love all of a sudden because I got a slammer boatload of fish on board. I was stupid. I didn't want to believe the marriage was over. I deposited all the money from that trip into an account that she handled. She transferred all the money out, moved out of our apartment, and didn't pay one single bill or any crew member their share."

"When did you find that all out?"

"When we got into Rockland after the next trip. The lawyers, bankers, and my cousin Vito, my uncle Sal's strong arm, were all there waiting for me."

Jim Kelley turned away from Scanton and walked slowly in the direction of the jury. "What did you do?"

"Do you mean after the heart attack cleared up?" Everyone laughed. "What the hell could I do? My mother found out about it and told me the details of what Karen had pulled. My dad's lawyer straightened things out with that creep lawyer Barry, who was working for the bank. I scraped together everything I had and, with the help of the crew, settled up as best I could, and we went fishing again."

"Explain what you mean with 'the help of the crew,' please."

"These guys don't have to go fishing with me. They get off the boat and that's it. It might not have been my fault, but you're there asking guys to go break their backs for you, and they just got screwed out of a trip's pay? That's a big deal to ask for on a fishing boat. They went fishing without being paid for the last trip."

Attorney Kelley nodded. "But everyone agreed to do this, including Skip Reed. Is that correct?"

"Oh yeah, Skip was all about helpin' out. He was real sympathetic to how bad Karen had shafted me. He felt bad for poor Joey. I didn't find out till later that my pal Skip Reed had been sleeping with my wife for the past year. They were both in on this whole scam together." Kelley didn't speak for a minute to allow that revelation to resonate with the jury.

He began again. "Do you think Mr. Reed knew earlier that Karen had 'stolen the trip,' as you put it?"

Attorney Howerton interrupted the questioning. "Objection, Your Honor. Mr. Scanton has no idea what Mr. Reed knew or did not know."

The judge said, "Sustained."

Kelley said, "I'll withdraw the question."

He looked at Scanton. "What happened next?"

"I was flat broke. I had given out every dime I had. I even got the fish dealer to give me $9,000 in cash that I left for Vito in a mailbox at the fish building."

"Was that money part of the money due you from the fish you sold that dealer?"

Scanton said, "Yes it was, but I was going to be leaving the dock $25,000 in debt. I didn't know it at the time, but I had been set up."

Kelley said, "What did you do next?"

"I made the biggest mistake of my life. I told Skip Reed to contact his guy and tell him that I would agree to go get sixty thousand pounds of swordfish and smuggle them back into Maine."

"Where did you expect to go to get these swordfish?"

"Reed told me we'd get bearings for a location below the Hague Line down in Canadian waters."

"Would transporting those fish be an illegal act in your opinion?"

Scanton very quietly said, "Yes." The courtroom was silent.

"Did you follow through with your agreement and take the boat to the location you had been given?"

"Yes, I did. We fished a few days and went through some fairly nasty weather, but ultimately I took my boat down to the coordinates I'd been given."

"By nasty weather, you're referring to Hurricane Debby that went through, is that correct?"

"Yes, that's right."

"And did you, in fact, find any swordfish aboard the boat you met?"

"No. It was just before midnight so I was running on radar. When I saw the size of the boat on the screen I wanted to pull off. It was a freighter, not a swordfish boat."

Kelley said, "Where was the crew at this time?"

"Pat and Tom were asleep down forward, and Reed was standing right beside me in the wheelhouse."

"Did you express your concerns to him at that point?"

"Yes, I did. Then I did another really stupid thing. He convinced me that the freighter was carrying the swordfish for several other boats. I remember it as clear as a bell. He said, 'Let's just go get our fish, and get out of here.'"

"Then what happened?"

"I pulled the boat into their port side and they tied us off. When I looked at her letters and I knew she was a Columbian, I knew right then that I was screwed. They came aboard and held me at gunpoint and took over my boat."

The courtroom was silent. Only Kelley was close enough to Joey to see it, but a tear had escaped his eye and was running down his cheek.

Scanton took a deep breath and started to speak again. "The captain of that freighter came out on his bridge deck and made a joke in Spanish about me coming to get swordfish. They all laughed their asses off. Then he started screaming he wanted his money. I was taken into my own pilothouse at gunpoint by a guy named Carlos."

"Did you have his money on board?"

"Reed made some smart remark to the Columbian captain. I thought he was dead right then and there. That guy was some ugly-looking nasty bast—guy."

"So did Skip get the money?"

"He grabbed a grinder out of our engine room. He cut the top off one of the propane tanks, and there was the cash. They tell me it was about $9,000,000."

"What happened after they got their cash?"

"That was when they had to put a couple of fish totes down as a kind of steps so this guy, Sammy Dalton, could get aboard the *Jubilee*."

Attorney Kelley said, "Who was Sammy Dalton?"

"I saw that guy once down in Gloucester. I was out to dinner with friends down there, and he waddles into the place like some big-time hood or something. Turns out he was one. My fish dealer down there, Artie Valente, told me Skip Reed had been seen talking to him. Artie said the guy had a big reputation as a swordfish smuggler. I challenged Skip about having any talks with anybody about any swordfish smuggling."

"Did you ever speak with Sammy Dalton directly at any time before he boarded your boat?"

"No, I couldn't stand to even have him look at me as I left the restaurant. Of course, I had a lot of talks with him while he had me at gunpoint aboard my own boat."

Kelley said, "Skip Reed was told in no uncertain terms that you were not going to be involved in any swordfish deals after you left Gloucester. Is that correct?"

"Yes. There was no reason to do it. We knew where the fish were and we had a huge stock. I know now why he didn't try any of his usual arguments. He and my wife had already figured out a way to make me cooperate with their plan. He wasn't the least bit worried. As I look back at it now, I think he was more scared of the drug dealers than he was that I wouldn't go for his con job."

Kelley said, "Your boat had been seized, the cocaine is loaded aboard, and you're steaming back toward US waters. Correct? What happened next?"

"The fuel filters clogged up and the 1271 quit," Scanton said.

Kelley said, "English please."

"Sorry, we had been through a little heavy weather, and sometimes sediment in the fuel tanks can clog up the filters, and the engine will stop running."

"What did you do to restart the engine?"

Scanton said, "Pat was still asleep down forward. I told Dalton that I needed to have Pat's help to get the engine going. He told me to go wake him up. When Pat and I were headed down to the engine room to get things going, he sent Carlos down to guard us. He told him not to shoot us both, but if he had to shoot one of us, he didn't care which. That's when I knew that he was a fair-minded killer. This was only business to him, nothing personal."

"Did you get the engine started right away?"

"It was a simple deal. I only woke Pat up so we could figure out a way to try and take the boat back."

"Were you able to make such a plan?"

Scanton shook his head no. "No. Carlos had a close watch on us at all times. He was a scary guy. He was hitting the coke pretty hard all the way in."

"Tell me your recollection of Pat's attempted attack on Carlos."

"It was pretty much like you heard it before. Looking back at it, we all think it was Uncle Charley that talked Pat into giving it a try. If Pat hadn't jumped Carlos, that Columbian would still have that cat's teeth planted in his leg to this day."

Kelley said, "There has been some questions raised, Mr. Scanton, about why you and Mr. Anderson didn't try to jump in and give Mr. Chase a hand."

"Have you taken a good look at Pat? That Carlos guy was just one skinny little Columbian. He was just real lucky he got off a shot, or he'd be snorting coke with his dead amigos right now. It's a good thing Tom or I didn't make a run at it, because one or more of us would have been killed."

Kelley said, "Another question has been raised. Why do you think Mr. Dalton didn't shoot Mr. Chase when he had the opportunity?"

"I have no idea why. I've wondered about that. I'm real glad he didn't though."

"Thank you, Mr. Scanton. There have been some statements made about you being at the helm when the boat arrived at Little River. Please explain that situation if you could."

"The Bull at Little River is a real hellhole after a storm. It breaks right across the opening of the river. There's practically no water there at low tide. If you didn't know what you were doing you could put a boat ashore there easy and tear it up. Make no mistake . . . these two guys, Sammy and Carlos, they were a pair of armed and dangerous killers. I wanted to get my ass, Tom's, and Pat's ashore alive. So I ran the boat up in through the Bull and up to the dock."

"What was Skip Reed doing through all of this?"

"To tell you the truth, I think he was scared to death that he was going to be killed before this was all over. That Dalton guy hated Reed. You could see it in his eyes. Skip had screwed all his friends, and this deal was way over his head. I wish I could have told him to his face that the bitch I was married to wasn't worth it . . . I know." Scanton waited to get his head taken off by the judge but he remained silent. He probably agreed with the statement.

Kelley waited a few seconds for Scanton's testimony to settle in with jury. Then he said, "When you landed the boat, the DEA and the police were all there waiting. What was your reaction?"

"Just like Pat said, we were all thrilled to see those guys, except for Reed and the other two creeps. We couldn't wait to have them come aboard and arrest Dalton and Carlos. I don't think we could have been more . . . more ah . . . more naive. It never entered my head that we would all be arrested and thrown in jail. But you see, we all knew what had really gone on aboard the boat, and no one else did."

"Tell us about Mr. Reed getting killed from your perspective."

"I think he knew damn well it was all over for him anyway, no matter what happened to any of us. I've thought about him a lot since this happened. I've never felt so much hate for another human being in my life, and that includes my dead wife. He just got in way over his head though. He had betrayed everyone he knew, and it was all coming down on him at once. He thought he had this big deal all worked out. As much as I hate to admit it, part of that was being with my wife. He knew damn well that everything was over with her if he didn't pull off the drug deal. Pat Chase said it best when he said Skip was a coward. Cowards always run, and that's what he did, he ran. That boat was rigged to blow up, and just like Anderson said, he was in the wrong place at the wrong time. I guess we all were really."

"Your Honor, I have no further questions at this time. I will reserve the right to redirect. Thank you."

Judge MacFarland said, "We are going to break for lunch." The judge gave his routine instructions to the jury to not discuss the case. The courtroom emptied. The defendants dispersed with their respective families. No one wanted to talk about the trial. Joey asked if it was okay if he got a sandwich by himself. Everyone understood.

CHAPTER 112

When the court reconvened Howerton stepped toward the witness stand. He had the look of a gladiator moving in for the kill when he approached Joey Scanton.

"Mr. Scanton, that's a pretty amazing story that you shared with us earlier, and I think it has some elements of truth in it too. Like any great lie it has to have some truth in it to sound even remotely plausible."

Kelley was on his feet. "Objection, Your Honor! Mr. Howerton is pontificating, not questioning."

The judge responded, "Sustained. Mr. Howerton, proceed with a question if you have one."

Attorney Howerton continued unfazed. "Yes, Your Honor. Could you please explain something to the jury, for me, Mr. Scanton? You've admitted to making a deal with Mr. Reed to smuggle swordfish illegally into this country. Is that correct?"

Scanton said, "Yes, I did."

"You've admitted that you did that because of the extreme financial pressures you were facing that originated with a mechanical breakdown. You also decided to borrow money from, in your own words, a small-time gangster, your uncle Sal Scantini. Is that correct?"

"Well, partially."

"Mr. Scanton, answer the question. Yes or no?"

"Yes."

"Nothing had changed, as it related to your financial situation, that enabled you to pay off that debt, which I'll remind you, based on your own testimony, could be life threatening. Is that correct?"

"Well, that's not so . . . I—"

"Yes or no, Mr. Scanton?"

There was a look of frustration on Joey's face. "Yes."

"In fact, according to your testimony, the situation worsened. You were falling behind on boat payments as well. You had outstanding debts up and down the coast for things like insurance and even the basics like fuel and ice. Is that correct?"

"But that wasn't my fault . . . Karen—"

Howerton interrupted. "Mr. Scanton, no one is assigning blame here. Simply answer the question. Yes or no?"

"Then yes."

"Mr. Scanton, are you familiar with the concept of 'code words' that are used to deceive authorities when criminals communicate with each other?"

"I'm not sure what you're asking me."

"Oh, I think you do, Mr. Scanton. It's been stated in previous testimony that the word swordfish was used as a code to cover for the word 'drugs' during the planning and the investigatory phase of this crime. Now do you understand what I'm asking? Wasn't all this swordfish talk merely a ruse to throw off law enforcement people while your drug deal was being planned and negotiated?"

Scanton didn't know if Howerton meant a code word used by him or other people. That guy Varney said that was the code. Joey hesitated for a second and said, "I don't know."

Howerton pounced. "You don't know what, Mr. Scanton? You don't know if it was a ruse or if you are trying to mislead this jury. When the plan was being made to smuggle the drugs found aboard your boat, did you use the word 'swordfish' as a code for 'drugs'?"

Scanton looked cornered and confused. He said, "No."

"No what, Mr. Scanton? No, you aren't sure? No, you're not going to try and mislead the jury any longer? During the planning did you and Reed use some other term? What is it, Mr. Scanton!"

Attorney Kelley was on his feet. "Objection, Your Honor. The prosecutor is badgering the witness."

The judge said, "Sustained. Ask a question and give the defendant a chance to answer, Mr. Howerton."

He continued, "Mr. Scanton, you have testified that you were under great financial pressure, and based on that, you agreed to rendezvous with a boat to commit an illegal act involving international transportation of a banned swordfish product into this country. Is that correct?"

Kelley was up again. "Objection, Your Honor. My client is not on trial for swordfish smuggling. This line of questioning is irrelevant for the purposes of this trial."

The judge said, "I'm going to allow it, counselor. It goes to intent. Answer the question, Mr. Scanton."

"Yes, I agreed to go get some swordfish and bring them back to Maine."

"Are you familiar with the serious legal ramifications of swordfish smuggling? Did you understand the consequences of being arrested for the international smuggling of contraband, Mr. Scanton?"

"Objection, Your Honor. Mr. Scanton is not an attorney or a law enforcement official. This question is beyond being reasonable for a layperson to answer."

"Sustained. Get back on track, Mr. Howerton."

Howerton did not back off at all. "Did you or did you not, under your own free will, pilot your boat to a prearranged destination across the Hague Line into Canadian waters and knowingly bring your vessel into contact and tie off to a foreign vessel?"

Scanton looked down for a moment and then said, "Yes, I did."

"Mr. Scanton, now listen carefully. Did you in fact tie off to this foreign vessel, and then one of your own crew members produced and delivered to that vessel cash in the amount of approximately $9,000,000?"

Scanton said, "When you put it that way, yes."

"There is no other way to put it, Mr. Scanton, because that's what happened. Then, in fact, approximately 800 pounds or 350 kilos of cocaine were loaded aboard your boat. Is that correct, Mr. Scanton?"

"Yes, but I was at gunpoint. I didn't want them doing that."

"Mr. Scanton, there is no conclusive evidence that has been presented by you or anyone else that proves what you wanted or didn't want. Did those drugs get loaded aboard your vessel?"

Scanton was now fidgeting in his seat. "Yes, they did."

"Then did you and your crew members pilot your vessel back into United States waters until the vessel was landed in Maine, at a location referred to as Little River in East Boothbay? Please answer yes or no, Mr. Scanton."

Joey looked at his attorney before he answered. "Yes, but—"

"That's all for that question, Mr. Scanton. Do you have any idea what kind of money was going to be paid to you and your crew had you been successful in this drug-smuggling operation and not been arrested?"

"No, I don't know."

"Are you admitting to this court that in fact you and your crew were to be paid and you're unsure as to how much?"

"No."

"So you were sure how much you were to be paid. Can you please tell the court how much money was to be your share?"

"No, goddamn it! We weren't part of this. None of us were part of this. It was Skip Reed. You're twisting everything around here. Not one of the three of us did anything wrong."

Attorney Howerton smiled. It was exactly the type of reaction he had been trying to invoke.

"Mr. Scanton, there was plenty done wrong. Are you now recanting your previous testimony that Mr. Reed was the perpetrator of this crime? Was it someone else we haven't heard of yet, someone different that was piloting the *Jubilee* and not you? Was there some unknown or unidentified person aboard the boat that made that infamous rendezvous with the Columbian freighter? Is that it, Mr. Scanton? We're all waiting to hear this new testimony."

"No, Skip Reed was running things. It was Skip's plan from the beginning."

"No, Mr. Scanton, you have already testified here today that it was you that piloted your own boat to pick up those drugs, no one else. Can you name some other person that was running that boat other than you?"

"No, but I was doing it against my will."

"I don't think so, Mr. Scanton, I don't think so."

Joey began to raise his voice. "I was set up, and so was the rest of the crew."

Howerton responded with a very skeptical look on his face. "I believe if anyone set up your crew members, it was you. You've already admitted to working them into such a state of exhaustion that they slept, by my calculations, almost twelve hours. Did you do that to minimize fighting over the money you were to be paid? Were you trying to avoid an altercation like the one started by Mr. Chase?"

"No, it wasn't like that."

"Do you or do you not agree with the testimony that was made before this court that you worked your men, Thomas Anderson and Patrick Chase, almost twenty hours and that they were asleep during the time that you met up with the Columbian freighter and took the drugs aboard your boat?"

Scanton's head was reeling. He didn't know what was right or wrong anymore. He was confused and frustrated. Nothing was coming out how he meant it or how it had happened. He was staring at the floor thinking.

"Mr. Scanton, will you please answer the question?"

"Oh yeah, I guess so, yes."

"Thank you, Mr. Scanton." Scanton had no idea what he had just answered yes to.

"Mr. Scanton, when you finally reached your destination in East Boothbay and landed, there were federal agents and state authorities present when you were attempting to unload your cargo of cocaine. Is that correct?"

Attorney Kelley was on his feet. "Objection, Your Honor. My client has testified repeatedly that his boat had been seized and that the narcotics were placed aboard his boat without his consent. The prosecutor, however, continues to try and make my client admit to the possession and transportation of drugs that were not his. He has not denied that the drugs were aboard his boat and were transported into this country illegally. He does, however, state that his cooperation was forced under gunpoint and that he was being threatened with death to himself and his crew."

Judge MacFarland said, "Objection sustained. I agree with your assessment of Mr. Scanton's testimony. You will strike Mr. Howerton's question from the record. Mr. Howerton, you may continue, but I order you to cease and desist from badgering this witness. Am I clear?"

Howerton took a deep breath. "Yes, Your Honor. Mr. Scanton, just one more question. Did you or did you not, of your own free will or otherwise, transport 350 kilos of Columbian cocaine aboard your boat into this country from Canada?"

Scanton said, "Yes I did, but it was against my will."

"We are going to have to let the jury decide that very question, Mr. Scanton. I'm through with this witness, Your Honor."

The judge said, "Mr. Kelley, any redirect?"

"No, thank you, Your Honor."

The judge said, "Mr. Scanton, you may step down."

Joey walked away from the witness stand completely drained, but he was glad it was over.

He crossed the room to the defense table with his head down. He took his seat and whispered, "I probably just got us all sent to jail."

Attorney Kelley said, "It was rough. The jury will decide your fate. The trial isn't over yet. Hang in there, boys."

The judge said, "There are no other witnesses on your list. Does the defense rest, Mr. Kelley?"

Kelley said, "I would like to call a meeting in your chambers, if it pleases the court."

Judge MacFarland said, "Granted. Ladies and gentlemen of the jury, we'll have a brief recess while we meet." He rapped his gavel and disappeared from the bench.

By the time Kelley and Howerton entered the judge's chambers, he was already seated behind his desk. "What's this all about, Mr. Kelley?"

"Well, Your honor, I have another witness I wish to call for the defense. He was unavailable, but I managed to find him today." Mr. James Kelley was taking the biggest gamble of his entire career.

Howerton said, "I object, Your Honor. I need sufficient time to prepare. Who is this witness?"

Kelley handed the judge and Howerton each a piece of paper. Howerton grabbed it and read it quickly. "This is your witness? Your honor, I have no problem with this witness. No objection whatsoever."

Judge MacFarland said, "I certainly have no objections to this witness with the full consent of counsel. I'm going to call it a day when we get back out there, gentlemen. Is that all, Mr. Kelley?"

"Yes, Your Honor, it is. Thank you." William Howerton laughed to himself as they left judge's chambers. *This has got to be the stupidest move I've seen since I've been practicing law. What could this guy be thinking?*

Attorney Kelley had a fresh spring to his step when he returned to the defense table. Phil Davis cornered him immediately. "What was that all about?"

"I'm still not at liberty to tell you . . . tomorrow morning though, my friend, tomorrow morning."

Pat, Joey, and Tom all had questioning looks on their faces. Kelley said, "Have a little faith, boys. Tomorrow you'll see why. Here comes the judge."

MacFarland was back up on the bench. He hit his gavel and brought the court back to order. He announced the end of the day and gave his nightly instructions to the jury. He stated that court would reconvene at nine o'clock in the morning. It was over for the day, and everyone went home with their thoughts about what had happened.

When the courtroom emptied and everyone was out on Congress Street, Polly Wallace took a deep breath and walked to the parking garage to get her car. She was tired. It had been a long day, and she had so little sleep the night before. The testimony had been interesting but tedious. She had a little advice for the defendants though. The ad they ran on TV said it all—just say no to drugs. If these young men didn't want to go to jail, they should have stayed away from all these types of people and situations that can get you into trouble. They seem like pretty nice young men, really, now that she had heard them all speak. Maybe a little time in jail would teach them to stay on the straight and narrow. That's what she had always done herself. She was going home, bake a nice hamburger patty, make a green salad, and go right to bed after supper. Tomorrow will be a very important day and she wanted to be ready for it. She was going to decide the fate of these three young men. She was doing her civic duty.

Tom and Kathy got into the car and started the short drive back to Falmouth. "I think it went okay today. I hated the way that Howerton guy kept twisting everything Joey had to say. You just don't know how the jury is going to react to what they're hearing."

Kathy said, "I know. We're very prejudiced in our reactions because we know what happened. Did you notice Teddy was there for a couple of hours today?"

"No, I didn't. Did you get to speak to him?"

"No, I spotted him and waved. You should give him a call tonight. I'm sure he is worried about you."

Tom said, "I know you're probably right. I'll admit it, I'm scared. I asked Peter about what would happen if they convict Joey. He said that if they do, we're all likely to get convicted as accomplices, and we will all go to jail."

"Don't say that. I'm worried too, honey, but I can't think that way. I still have faith it's going to be all right."

Tom said, "I'm glad you do."

Joey Scanton really wanted to go get drunk. That Howerton guy had really sent him over the edge. He hated his arrogant, condescending attitude, the way he had twisted everything and made him feel so stupid. He tried to take his time and answer the questions, but they were worded so cleverly that no matter what you said, it was wrong. He had always thought, up until now anyway, that the purpose of a trial was to determine guilt or innocence based on the truth. He knew now that the only thing the prosecutor cared about was getting a conviction. The man didn't have the truth on his side. All Howerton was after was to discredit him as a defendant and try to screw up his story.

He wondered about jail. He had lived his whole life free at sea, and he couldn't imagine being locked away in a prison for years and years. This was all wrong, and he didn't know what to do. He pulled into a waterfront bar and went in. It was after midnight when he called a cab and went home to his mother's. He didn't feel one bit better, but he was drunk.

The emotions were running high at the Chase household. Pat was frustrated and angry. "Goddamn it, Leslie, I ought to just take off."

"Oh, Pat, you can't do that."

"I'm telling you that bastard Howerton put the nail in our coffin today with his last question to Joey."

Leslie was trying to remain calm. "I know it looks bad, but he really can't prove anything."

"He doesn't have to prove anything. They caught us with a boatload of coke. They figured out how that fuckin' piece of shit Reed pulled off the money to buy it with. I think we're going down."

"You don't know that. Don't they say something about it being circumstantial evidence or something?"

"The circumstances are what's killing us all right now. Reed was the only one who could have proven us innocent, and he's dead, and he's lucky he is."

"Why do you say that?"

"Because if he wasn't I'd kill him."

"Pat, sit down and have a beer and I'll make you your supper. Kathy and I still think it's going to be all right."

"You two aren't on the jury unfortunately."

CHAPTER 113

In court the next morning the tension in the air was so thick you could cut it with a knife. The jury had been escorted into the courtroom and had taken their seats. The boys were seated at the defense table. James Kelley had still refused to tell them what was going on. Phil Davis and Peter Green must have known what was up because they seemed very relaxed. The bailiff announced the judge, and in seconds the courtroom was called to order.

Judge MacFarland said, "Mr. Kelley, you may call your witness."

Attorney Kelley stood and said, "Thank you, Your Honor. The defense calls Mr. Samuel Dalton." Scanton turned around and watched as Sammy Dalton made his way to the witness stand. He said in a low voice, "Are you bastards crazy bringing that piece of shit in as a witness?"

Kelley leaned over toward Joey and said, "Just relax, Joey. You're going to love this."

Dalton stepped up to the bailiff. He said, "Place your left hand on the Bible and raise your right hand. Do you solemnly swear to tell the truth, the whole truth, and nothing but the truth, so help you God?"

Dalton smiled and said, "I do."

Joey was thinking, *Here it comes. This is the end for us. What could Kelley be thinking?*

The bailiff said, "You may take your seat." He sat down in the witness stand.

Attorney Kelley walked over to Dalton. "Could you please state your name and occupation for the court?"

"My name is Samuel R. Dalton, and I am employed by the federal government, United States Drug Enforcement Administration."

Attorney Howerton jumped up. "Objection, Your Honor!"

The judge said, "Under what grounds are you objecting?"

Howerton was furious. He knew he had been had. "I was not informed that this witness was employed by the DEA."

The judge said, "Overruled. You know it now. Sit down, Mr. Howerton. Mr. Kelley, you may proceed."

Kelley said, "Mr. Dalton, could you share with this court your educational background?"

Dalton said, "I graduated from John Jay College, School of Criminal Justice in New York City. That was in 1965."

"Thank you, Mr. Dalton. You have stated that you are employed by the federal government. Can you tell me in what capacity?"

"Yes, I'm a paid informant for the Drug Enforcement Administration. I am what is called a created agent of the federal government. I operate under the authority of a contract I have with Senior Special Agent in Charge Goldman."

Howerton was furious. He turned to Agent Lamb and said, "Did you know about this?"

Lamb said, "No, I didn't. In fact I can't believe it." He had a slight smile on his face. This was going to get very interesting.

Attorney Kelley said, "Mr. Dalton, how long have you known Mr. Goldman?"

"As far back as I can remember. I was just a kid when I first met him in the city."

"What city is that, Mr. Dalton?"

Dalton said, "There's only one city, Mr. Kelley, New York City."

Kelley continued, "Could you please describe for the court your professional relationship with Mr. Goldman."

"Certainly, I have worked for Special Agent Goldman on major drug cases for over eighteen years. I have been on the inside of several large cases in various parts of the country."

"Mr. Dalton, are you an undercover agent?"

"No, no, I'm an independent, paid for hire. They call my position a created, documented informant."

"Why don't you work as an agent?"

"Too restrictive. I enjoy much more freedom than an agent, and I would never ever work for anyone but Agent Goldman."

"Freedom to do what, Mr. Dalton?"

"There are countless rules and regulations that apply to special agents that don't apply to me. For example, an undercover agent can never be left alone with a criminal or several criminals. It's for own their safety, of course, but I have no such restrictions. It allows me to more completely infiltrate the criminal activity and become far more knowledgeable about the crime."

Kelley asked, "Isn't that more dangerous for you?"

"Oh, I'm sure it is, but the pay's much better. I'm a high-risk, high-reward kind of guy."

"Mr. Dalton, how much money will you be paid for your role in this particular arrest?"

"I've worked on this case for almost sixteen months. I get all my expenses and a fee at the end. Agent Goldman is always tightfisted with my expenses. He and I have had some lively discussions about my dining habits. It's not cheap for me to maintain this fine figure."

There was quiet laughter.

Dalton smiled. "The final fee for this case came to $780,000."

The courtroom gasped.

"I've risked my life frequently during this case, doing my job. The folks I deal with have no sense of humor when it comes to people in my line of work. I'm retiring after this. In fact you were lucky to get me to testify today. This is outside my typical responsibilities. Normally I just disappear into the sunset. I have no contact with anyone but Agent Goldman at the DEA. They have no idea that I even exist."

Kelley said, "I'm sure we are all fortunate to have you here today. How did you begin this particular case?"

"I had been out of the loop for a few years. Goldman and I had worked most recently on a case in Miami, Florida, in 1978. He was in Maine, and I was his contact there in Florida. It was small plane transportation of cocaine. I posed as the owner of an airstrip. Agent Goldman bought it for me. Well, I should say the government did.

They made me give it back though, after the case was closed. I was Fredrick Waterman down there."

"Is your real name Samuel R. Dalton?"

Dalton smiled and said, "What's in a name anyway? For the purposes of this trial it is. I have all the necessary identification, if you need to see it."

Dalton smiled again. He looked at Agent Goldman standing in the back of the courtroom. He had his arms crossed over his chest and was leaning against the wall.

Dalton continued, "Anyway, Agent Goldman contacted me and wanted me to move to Gloucester, Massachusetts. He asked me to get on the inside of a case he was running. I had a family background in the fishing racket, and it sounded like fun." Joey Scanton couldn't believe what he was hearing. This was a different man than the one he had crossed paths with. He was engrossed in Dalton's testimony.

"I moved up there and before long I was in deep. I set up a front that I was running illegal swordfish out of Canada."

Kelley said, "Did you do that? Smuggle swordfish?"

Dalton laughed. "Nope, not a one. People believe what they think they see. I played the gangster role. Talked tough, acted mean, had big wads of cash that people liked the looks of. I was there less than three weeks when I was approached by some guys that are now under arrest in Massachusetts to smuggle drugs with them. Agent Goldman knew that there was a Columbian connection, and I got in on that too. That was harder, but I pulled it off. I have no idea why, but for some reason crooks believe I'm one of them. It's plagued me all my life. I'm such a sweetheart too. Go figure." Everyone in the courtroom was now openly laughing at a man they believed was a vicious killer only a few minutes before. The boys couldn't believe what they were hearing.

"Mr. Dalton, how did you come in contact with Michael Varney?"

Dalton said, "Mickey Varney ran the Maine operation for the Massachusetts heavyweights. After a short while they, the dealers, promoted me to being his boss. Old Mickey hated me. Fear and intimidation are the glue that keeps the underworld running, and I'm good at that. I used to drive him nuts by calling him by his name when we were on the telephone. Every time I did it, I'd laugh, knowing that Agent Goldman and his gang would be listening in on the wire taps. It was pretty funny really. You've got to have a few laughs when you're dealing with some of the biggest scumbags on earth. The only one who knew who my real identity, of course, was Agent Goldman."

"Please tell the court about your first encounter with Mr. Skip Reed."

"Sure . . . Reed got sent to talk with me by some guy from Maine. I don't remember who it was, some small player. Reed shows up and thinks he's on *Let's Make A Deal*. I ran his background, and I couldn't believe the idiot was going to try and play in this league. I found out that he was wrapped up with Mr. Scanton's wife . . . sorry, Joey. This jerk would do anything for this broad. I played him hard. To tell you the truth, I was kind of hoping he was going to give up and go away, but he didn't. There are plenty of guys out there wanting to run drugs. We didn't need Reed for this bust. We were after the three Gloucester guys, Varney, and a leg into the Columbians."

Attorney James Kelley was on top of his game. This couldn't be going better. Every once in a while he stole a look over at Howerton, and the look on his face was pure rage. This was great!

He returned to the witness. "Can you give us a brief description of what transpired after Reed began contacting you?"

"Reed kept calling Varney and telling him they were going to do the run. He played the role big-time. We actually thought for a while he was captain of the boat and that Scanton was a dry land owner. It went on for months. Then Reed and Scanton's wife figured out a way to force Scanton's hand by having her take off with the money from a big trip, and the deal was on. At first I wanted to just let them run the drugs on their own, but Agent Goldman talked me into getting aboard their boat and making the trip. That wasn't easy."

Kelley said, "How did you manage that?"

"That information is going to have to remain between Agent Goldman and the Columbian government. The international boys dealt with that one. I did get a nice bonus for extra hazardous duty."

"How much of a bonus did you get, Mr. Dalton?"

"That's confidential. It will appear on my next tax return, however."

Kelley said, "So how did you manage to get aboard that freighter?"

"I hired the skipper of a small sport fishing boat to run me off there. The guy was scared to death. He had one of those fly bridges on his boat, and I crossed right over to the freighter when he pulled up beside her. That guy was halfway back to Gloucester before I had properly introduced myself to the Columbians."

"After you rendezvoused with the *Jubilee* did you take them over at gunpoint, Mr. Dalton?"

"That would be a yes. Carlos was a dangerous man, as were all the other Columbians. Agent Goldman wanted to arrest Reed of course, so I had to make it real. It got a little tense when Chase and that nasty cat of theirs went on a rampage. I was pretty upset about Chase taking a bullet, but I did manage to keep him from being killed."

Kelley said, "After the boat was landed and Reed made his escape attempt, what was your reaction?"

"I tried to convince Agent Goldman to pay me more money for a near-death experience. He refused. He said I was never planning to get on that speedboat anyway. He's cheap, Goldman, always has been."

Everyone laughed, except Attorney Howerton.

"Let me ask you this, Mr. Dalton, the three men on trial here today . . . Mr. Scanton, Mr. Anderson, and Mr. Chase . . . what was their involvement in this drug-smuggling activity?" The courtroom held its breath.

Dalton took a deep breath and said, "These three men had absolutely no involvement in any of this drug-trafficking crime at all." The courtroom erupted. Judge MacFarland pounded his gavel and called for order in the court.

Dalton continued after things quieted down again. "Mr. Scanton was used as a pawn throughout the entire plot. He was coerced and manipulated by his wife and Reed. There were never any communications in person or by telephone that involved any of these guys. Anderson and Chase were asleep aboard the boat when the drugs were loaded on it, just as they testified. Scanton was taken under gunpoint immediately after the vessels were tied off. The piloting of the vessel back into Maine waters was also done under forced armed guard."

Kelley said, "Mr. Varney testified before this court that all these men were involved. How do you react to his statements?"

"Agent Goldman filled me in on Varney's testimony. He's lying about these men. Scanton thought he was going after swordfish. There may be some crime for trying to smuggle imaginary swordfish, but I don't know what it is. Throughout this case, during its planning, negotiations, and execution, I was the contact man. I knew it was all about Reed. I was aboard that boat from the time it left the freighter, and I was an eyewitness to all of these events. Mr. Varney made a deal with the prosecution in exchange for his freedom. That could explain his testimony."

The courtroom was out of control. Howerton turned and glared at Special Agent Goldman. Goldman shrugged his shoulders. The judge rapped his gavel a few more times, and the courtroom settled back down.

Attorney Kelley began his questioning again. "Do you know what happened to the Columbian freighter?"

"I've been told that the Canadian Coast Guard got them almost immediately. I understand that the captain is facing murder charges as well as all the drug charges."

"Do you have anything else to add, Mr. Dalton?"

"No, not really, other than I was kept secret by the DEA for my own protection. To everyone except Agent Goldman, I was just a number. This is the first time I have ever appeared in court in my entire career. It's probably hard for you to believe, but there are people in this world that would like to see me dead. The only way a paid informant can be effective is through total secrecy. If Goldman had seen a way to have these men avoid conviction, you would never had heard from me."

"Thank you, Mr. Dalton, for your testimony today and your service to our government and to law enforcement. I have no further questions for this witness, Your Honor."

Judge MacFarland said, "Your witness, Mr. Howerton."

Assistant United States District Attorney Howerton shook his head. "I have no questions for this witness, Your Honor."

Attorney Kelley stood up and said, "Your Honor, based on the testimony of the last witness, the defense moves to dismiss all charges against the defendants."

The judge looked over at the prosecutor. "Do you have any objections, Mr. Howerton?"

Howerton said, "I think that justice will be served, if the charges are dropped against the defendants, Your Honor."

The courtroom exploded with cheers. Judge MacFarland announced in a booming voice above the noise, "Case dismissed!" He rapped his gavel one more time, and it was over.

CHAPTER 114

K athy ran for Tom. She hugged him to her and cried tears of pure joy as he held her in his arms. Pat was holding Leslie and spinning her around. Joey was laughing and shaking hands with Jim Kelley and thanking him for what he'd done for them. Peter Scanton hollered, "Everyone to The Village!"

Pat Chase followed Sammy Dalton out into the hallway. He grabbed his shoulder and turned him around. "Mr. Dalton, I had you all wrong. Thanks for what you did for us in there."

"You had no idea who I was. None of you did. No hard feelings. I'm glad I could help."

"You should come down to The Village with us. I'll buy you a beer."

"Thanks, but I got a plane to catch in two hours."

"Where are you going?"

Sammy just smiled and shook his head no as he walked away from Chase.

The press was all over the courtroom trying to get statements and reactions from anyone they could.

When they caught up with Juror Wallace, the reporter asked her what she thought of the outcome of the trial. She said, "I wish we had gotten an opportunity to vote on the case. I still think they were guilty of some wrongdoing, like that Mr. Howerton said." The reporter thanked her for her time.

Another reporter got a moment with Dennis Waters. He said he hoped that the boys were able to keep some of the coke. He turned and he walked out onto Congress Street and disappeared into the crowd.

CHAPTER 115

The free men and their families arrived at the restaurant after about a half hour. As soon as everyone had a drink, Phil Davis tapped the side of his glass to get the group's attention. "Ladies and gentlemen, I would like to make a toast of congratulations to our young friends here today on their victory in court. I'd personally like to congratulate my fellow attorneys on an outstanding job. Here's to Mr. Sam Dalton for his role in setting these innocent men free. Cheers!"

The glasses clinked, the tears and kisses flowed, and hugs were given out everywhere.

They were there about two hours when Rusty and Skipper Cathcart rolled in. Joey walked over to greet them just as Charley Perkins followed them through the door. "Goddamn it, Charley, I thought you'd be dead by now!"

"Hell no, I'm alive as I can be, by Jesus. They finally dragged me in to see one of them doctors over town. He said I had fibulations or something like that. I asked him if that was from telling all those fibs over the years. The doc said hell no. They give me some pills and fixed me up wicked good, right off."

Joey said, "Are they letting you drink, Charley?"

"Son, there ain't no one man enough in that whole town or this one, who could keep me from having a cold beer when I want one. No, sir, by god, not one."

The gang was all gathered around Joey and Rusty. They were feeling no pain. Rusty said, "I wasn't worried a bit, Joey. I had a deal all worked out to take you boys fishin' with me if they convicted you. Those federal boys said, 'Hell yes, Rusty . . . I'm sure you can straighten these fellas out if anybody can. Have at it, old boy.' That's what they said. I swear on my mother's grave."

Joey said, "Your mother's still alive, Rusty."

"You think I don't know that?" Rusty lit up a cigarette.

"I was kinda looking forward to you boys having a chance on the *Jessica*. Those muggers and rapers I got ain't one little bit better than the murderers I had. I don't know what this country is coming to. I swear I don't." Everyone in earshot was laughing. It felt so good to laugh again. It had been a long time for everyone here.

Joey stepped over to Jim Kelley, who was standing there having a drink with Phil Davis.

Joey said, "How did you know about Sammy Dalton, and why didn't you tell us about him?"

Jim Kelley said, "You're not going to believe this, Joey, but I got a note from Bert Goldman about Sammy. He came and picked me up in his car and took me for a ride. He told me that he tried to tell the prosecutor about Sammy, and the guy wouldn't listen. He was afraid if he pushed it, the prosecutor would figure some way around Sammy's testimony. Bert explained that Sammy's life was still in grave danger with so many trials still ahead. He really needed to get away from this part of the country right away. Sammy said he was willing to risk staying for you guys, and Goldman decided that the best thing to do was to put your fate in his hands. It turned out to be the best decision he ever could have made."

Joey said, "Why did Goldman do it? He could have let us go down."

Kelley said, "I asked him that very question. He told me that when he was hired by the Justice Department as a special agent, he swore an oath to never prosecute the innocent. I told you from the beginning he was a straight shooter. I met with Dalton, and when he explained what was at stake and what he was going to do for you boys I had to promise to guard his secret till the very end. I knew it was the right thing and I went with him."

Joey said, "I'm some glad you did. This has been a terrible time for me and my crew, but I sure have learned a lot. I still can't believe what Mr. Goldman and Sammy Dalton were willing to risk for us."

Kelley said, "We've all learned a lot from this one, Joey."

Phil Davis spoke up. "It kind of restores your faith in mankind, doesn't it, Joey?"

A short time later Marshall Grimes and Vern Eldridge showed up with their wives and were having a great time with Peter and Gloria. There was so much to be thankful for. Jimmy Desanto and Teresa were there too, of course. Tom's sister, Joanne, was there, as she had been through the whole trial. She said, "Brother dear, this is enough excitement for this family to last us for a long time. You better go talk to your mother. She's feeling left out."

Pat and Charley Perkins were at a table getting drunk and enjoying themselves wholeheartedly.

Pat said, "How's your twin brother behaving himself?"

"Oh Jesus, Pat, that bastard's still in trouble all the friggin' time. He got all wound up about my heart stuff and decided to take a go at church. Well . . . didn't that horse's ass show up drunk? He started singing so loud and so far off key I had to drag him out of the place before he set organized religion back fifty years. I don't think we're going to be welcome in that church again unless he showed up laid out in a casket."

The Village crew brought out the pizzas and the night went on. It was well after midnight when everyone gave up and headed home. On the way out the door the crew got together to say good night. Pat said, "I don't know about you, fellas, but I'd like to head up to the boat in the morning and see what's goin' on up there. Mr. Davis told me that before he left the courthouse today he caught up with Goldman, and they're releasing her from impound first thing tomorrow."

Joey said, "You up for that, Tom, or do you want to take a day or two to bask in the glory of our victory?"

Tom said, "Hell no . . . let's hit the road in the morning. You want to meet at Becky's and then head up?"

Chase said, "You guys go ahead to breakfast without me. I'll see you up there."

"Sounds good to me. I'll see you about seven thirty then, Tom," Joey said.

"Ya, good, Joey. I'll see you then. I'm going home and to bed with Matty's mother."

Pat said, "Have at it, kid. I'll see you guys tomorrow in Boothbay."

CHAPTER 116

It was just after eight when Chase got down to the *Jubilee*. He could see her from the parking lot. He had brought an oversized gym bag with him so he could get some of his stuff off the boat, but he left it in the car. As he walked down the wharf he was hoping that the padlocks were off the boat already. He made it around the corner of the building and got the scare of his life. One huge black cat leaped off a stack of lobster traps and landed on his shoulder. "Jesus H. Christ, Uncle Charley, you scared the shit out of me!"

Uncle Charley was some happy girl to see her old friend Pat walking down the wharf. It hadn't been an easy winter. She had almost gotten hit twice on the walk over here from the fish-buying place to find her boat. Thankfully, there were a few winter lobster catchers around that kept her supplied with redfish racks regularly. Pat rubbed her ears and talked to her all the way down to the boat. Just before they got there, she jumped off his shoulder and landed on a stack of pallets. From there she leaped over onto the shelter deck, down the ladder, and into an air vent beside the companionway.

"So that's where you've been all this time . . . living aboard the boat in your own bunk. You are one smart cat."

The locks were off the companionway door and Pat went aboard. He climbed the stairs to the pilothouse. The shore power was plugged in. He turned on a couple of lights and peeked down in the galley. The cat was spread out on one of the galley benches, just like always. She was ready to let the lines go and get out of Boothbay.

He went down into the galley. He couldn't help but think about the fact that he had almost been killed in this room just a few months before. He sat down at the table. He had only one thing on his mind. He reached up under the table and there it was, the key he had taken out of Reed's cigarette pack and stuffed up under the main table leg. He pulled it out and looked at it for the first time. He said, "Jesus

Christ! I know what this is. Uncle Charley, you hang in there, old girl. Joey and Tom are on their way. I'll be back in a little bit."

Pat ran back up the wharf. He jumped in his car, lit up a cigarette, and took off. He drove down Route 27 and out of the Boothbay Harbor to Route 1 and turned right, headed north toward Rockland.

CHAPTER 117

Joey and Tom walked into Becky's and grabbed a booth. The morning paper was lying there and the story was on the front page.

PORTLAND MORNING HERALD

Surprise witness frees accused drug traffickers.

Prosecutor William Howerton was stunned when the defense team of Kelley, Davis, and Green produced a surprise witness in yesterday's drug-trafficking trial of three local men accused of smuggling cocaine with an approximate street value of $29,000,000 into Maine on their fishing boat. The prosecution's evidence seemed insurmountable until a man named Samuel R. Dalton, one of the alleged codefendants in this crime, scheduled to be tried at an unknown date, was revealed to be, in fact, a paid informant for the Federal Drug Enforcement Administration under the direction of its senior special agent in charge, Bertram Goldman. It seemed apparent to all the people in attendance that the defendants in this case, Joseph Scanton of Portland, Patrick Chase of South Portland, and Thomas Anderson of Falmouth, were as surprised by the appearance of this witness as anyone.

Dalton, a graduate of John Jay College in New York, one of the most prestigious schools of criminal justice in the country, had been an undercover paid informant for the government since the beginning of this case. Apparently, much to the prosecutor's dismay, Dalton's identity was kept secret even from him to safeguard Dalton's well-being.

Dalton's complete testimony of investigative details and eyewitness accounts of the events that unfolded during this crime completely exonerated the defendants of any wrongdoing. Dalton's description of the facts and events were so thorough and complete that Assistant District Attorney Howerton didn't even attempt to cross-examine the witness.

Attorney James Kelley, for the defense, moved that all charges be dropped against the defendants. There was no objection from the prosecution, and the motion was granted by Justice Harold MacFarland. A brief interview with Agent Goldman revealed that using undercover paid informants is not at all unusual during a case of this magnitude. The secrecy involved was exclusively for the protection and safety of the informant.

Judge MacFarland declared that all charges against the defendants were dismissed and the trial was over. A loud cheer went up from a group of what was assumed to be the family and friends of the defendants when the judge declared the case closed.

Scanton, Anderson, and Chase were not available for comment after the trial.

Joey said, "Well, how about that, Thomas? They finally got it right after it was all over."

Tom said, "Finally."

The waitress came over and they ordered their breakfast. One of the locals, who was still drunk from the night before, staggered by the table. "Well, you boys got away with it, did ya? I know you done it. So's everybody else in this town. You ain't foolin' any of us Mr. High and Mighty Scanton."

Joey said, "Get away from me, asshole, or I'll break your friggin' neck right here in front of all these people." He stumbled off and out the door onto Commercial Street.

Joey said, "I hate to say this, but we're still completely screwed, you know. I'm totally broke once all the final bills come in from the lawyers. I had to subsidize Pat's bill, and I've got to figure a way to pay it off in full. You kinda got shorted on the deal because you guys had some money of your own. That doesn't set well with me either. I still figure that I'm short at least twenty grand, and I gotta pay Sal the rest of his money. He's been adding on the interest on that loan. He told me I owed him the nineteen that I borrowed and another ten in interest. He still says that the money I gave Vito doesn't count."

Tom said, "That's bullshit."

"I know it is, but that's business with a loan shark. Jimmy Desanto says he can get him to back off."

Tom said, "What are you thinking about doing?"

"I don't know. I haven't got money for this month's boat payment or the insurance. The long and the short of it is, I've had it."

"Maybe we can help out some, Joey."

"You guys haven't seen the last of your legal bills yet either. That's not an option. The part you don't know about is this. That boat's been sitting up there for almost four months now. I know goddamn well the guys in the yard up there didn't cover the winches or lubricate shit while they've had her in impound. Things may look all right to the naked eye, but leaving a boat like that to sit is the worst thing you can do to it."

Tom said, "I'm sure we can do something."

Joey said, "Yeah, I can try and sell her before the bank down in Bath takes her back."

Joey and Tom finished their breakfast and left for Boothbay. The ride up was the first time they had a chance to talk about the trial without a million people around. Joey said, "What gets me is the ups and downs of this thing. We win the case and feel like we got the world by the balls. A day later you figure out what happened with all the money part, and you realize the world has you by the balls."

Tom said, "Hey, let's go up there and check out the boat and see what we've got." They were both so sick of the pressure from the trial they felt like they were hungover from it. They rode most of the way up to Boothbay in relative silence. It took about an hour before they turned off Route 1 to go down toward the harbor. They parked in the lot at Stamples.

Joey said, "Huh? Pat's car's not here. I'm surprised. Let's go take a look at the boat."

When they walked down the wharf, Joey noticed that there were a couple of lights on in the pilothouse.

"Pat must have been here. I wonder where he is?" They climbed down aboard the boat. To Joey's surprise there were a couple of blue tarps over the winches. He pulled one back. He said, "Come here, Tom, and look at this. These bastards put these on about a week ago. Look at that fine layer of rust on those wires."

Joey threw the tarp down in disgust. "These jerks knew they were supposed to cover them up and didn't. I bet it was that asshole we saw down here three months ago." They continued with their inspection. Things weren't looking good.

CHAPTER 118

C hase pulled into Rockland and drove up to the Rockland bus station and walked inside. There was a bus leaving town in about ten minutes, so there was a bunch of people standing around waiting. He decided to go next door and get a coffee and wait a few minutes. While he was having his coffee, his old buddy Gary from Rockland Propane walked in. "Jesus there! As I live and breathe. How you doin', Patrick? I heard you fellas got off. It's been on the radio all morning."

Pat said, "I'm good, Gary. Sit down and have a coffee with me." Gary had a million questions about the trial. Pat tried to be patient with him. He knew he'd have to go through this with lots of people. Gary said, "What brings you up here anyway? Where's the boat now?"

"Oh, I had to go get a small check for Joey from the old lady that buys our fish up here." Gary thought that sounded reasonable. They sat there drinking coffee and making small talk for about a half hour. Gary finally said, "I got to get out of here, Pat. It's been so cold that people have been running through their propane like it was water."

"I guess that's good for your business though, isn't it, Gary?"

"Yeah, it is. My wife's having another little one in six months. Ain't life a friggin' picnic? I'll see you later, Pat. Good to see you, man. Check in next time you're up here."

"Finest kind, Gary . . . I sure will." Pat watched as Gary's truck pulled out of the parking spot in front of the little coffee shop and head down the road.

He immediately went back into the bus station. He reached in his pocket and pulled the key out and looked at it again. Number 100 . . . there it was, the locker down at the end, at floor level. He walked slowly over to the locker and got down on his knees. He slid the key in the slot and turned it. The locker popped open. There was large gym bag inside not too different than the one he had in his car. He looked around to see if anyone was watching him, and no one was. He pulled the bag out of the locker and walked slowly out of the bus station. He was barely out the door when someone hollered to him, "Hey, buddy!" Pat turned slowly toward the voice. "You dropped your hat in there." The guy threw him his hat.

"Thanks."

He walked quickly over to his car, started the engine, and drove out of Rockland. He was careful not to speed.

CHAPTER 119

By the time Pat got back to the wharf, Joey and Tom were aboard the boat, still down in the galley. They couldn't believe Uncle Charley was there and looking as healthy as if they had only been gone a few days. The boat inspection had gone as Joey had thought it would. They would need a week of work and about five grand to put her back in shape to be able to go fishing again and that didn't count fuel and ice. Tom had made a pot of coffee, and they were sitting there drinking it when Pat came down over the stairs into the galley.

Joey said, "Where the hell have you been? You looked her over yet? This fuckin' boat's a mess. They never oiled a goddamn thing aboard here. The wires are all rust. The net reels got to be all gone through. We're screwed here, you know!"

Joey spotted Pat's gym bag. "What did you do? Bring your bag so you could get your stuff and get of this friggin' thing?"

Pat smiled and said, "No, not exactly." Pat put the bag up on the galley table, pulled the zipper open, and dumped $1,000,000 in cash out on the table, in front of his two friends.

"Holy shit, Pat! What in the name of Almighty God is goin' on here?"

Pat said, "When that guy put the propane aboard here with Skip, I was watching them do it. We had run out at sea, right? Reed never did the gas swaps, and I knew goddamn well that he would forget about the galley stove being on when we ran out. I was paying attention, because I knew that ignorant prick could wind up blowing us all to hell and back. I sent Tom down forward to shut off all the burners. Sure enough, the main right side was wide open, and the new gas was pouring into the galley. While I was watching them though, I noticed the driver giving Skip something. I wasn't sure what it was from where I was standing. Then I saw him slide what looked like a key into the back of a pack of cigarettes he had with him. Truthfully, I forgot about it. Then when we were at the galley table with Carlos holding us at gunpoint, I took Skip's cigarettes off the table to steal a butt. He got so wound up he was shitting himself. For some odd reason I remembered the little key deal. I slid the pack of butts under the table and felt around in it until I found it. Of course I kept it hidden under the table where no one could see it. Then I took it out of the pack and stuffed it up under a leg where it attaches to the top of the table."

Joey said, "Didn't Skip notice you had it?"

"I don't think he knew or he would have flipped out. All I know is he didn't check for it then. That was when Uncle Charley and I tried to overthrow the boat, and you know how that worked out. The key's been hidden under there ever since."

Tom said, "What did it go to?"

"A bus locker up in Rockland, number 100."

Joey said, "This is Reed's share of the drug money!"

Pat said, "It may have been his share then, but now it's our share, boys!"

Joey said, "Oh my god! I can't believe it!"

Tom said, "Hey, look at this."

There was a note on a folded piece of blue paper that said, "Second chance." The men sat at the galley table staring at each other in silence.

TWO YEARS LATER

It had been just over two years since Andy Brown had been sentenced to prison. He was sent to a place in Connecticut. He had been afraid, like anyone would be, when he first got there. He was placed in a section with what they called low-risk inmates. Andy figured out that he was in with other men that had committed nonviolent crimes.

After a few months he started to feel a little better. Andy didn't have a very good life on the outside. Of course there were a ton of drugs available in jail, but he wanted no part of them. He had suffered enough. He was kind of surprised that he didn't miss his pot the way he thought he would.

Andy had never had a real friend before he was sent to prison, but he had one now. The guy's name was Oliver Peterson, but everyone called him Tubby. This guy wasn't as big as Sammy Dalton but he was close. Tubby was a really smart guy. He was thirty years old. On the outside he had worked his way up to being an office manager in a federal customs office. He was arrested and convicted of taking bribes from importers that needed to have certain merchandise arrive in Boston without a close inspection from anyone. He was three and a half years into a ten-year sentence.

Oliver got a kick out of Andy and took him under his wing. He introduced him to the prison library, a place Andy would have completely avoided had it not been for Tubby. It opened up a new world for him. Andy wasn't stupid, come to find out. He just never had a chance. He developed a surprising passion for reading. With his new friend's help, over the last two years, his life was changing. He discovered that he loved to read and filled the long boring hours in the institution with books. He missed Maine though, terribly, and really wanted to go home.

One afternoon he was reading a book about a man that had traveled all over the world called *The Lost Prince*. One of the guards walked over and told him that the warden wanted to see him. Andy was scared to death. He wondered what in the hell had he done now. Andy had never seen the warden in person during all the time he had been there. He had heard a lot of stuff about him though, but being summoned was different.

When he was escorted into the warden's office, he was as afraid as he had been back in Maine when they took him to court. To Andy's total shock, the warden was a really nice guy. He treated him kindly and told him the biggest news he thought he would ever hear. They were letting him out early. He would be going home to Maine.

Andy had been given a five-year sentence, but with all the prison overcrowding, he guessed they figured they could get along okay without him. He was going home. It took another two months before that happened because of all the paperwork that institutions seem to need to go through before they can actually act.

This was all fine with Andy though. His only regret was leaving his friend Tubby. On his last day they shook hands and wished each other the best. He promised Tubby that he'd write him, once he got back to Maine, and let him know how things were going. He told him that he wanted him to come to visit him up there for as long as he wanted when he got out. He promised him all the lobsters he could eat. Tubby said that that was one hell of a lot of lobsters. They said their good-byes. That was the last time Andy ever saw or had any contact with Oliver Peterson.

Andy was given a hundred dollars, a bus ticket to Portland, Maine, and he was out.

He was shocked that as a convicted felon he was just released back onto the streets without any restrictions or conditions. He wasn't out on parole either. What he didn't understand, at first, was that his sentence had been reduced and that he was a free man. He had absolutely no idea what he was going to do.

His mother had sent him one letter while he was in prison. She wrote him to let him know that she had met a man, fallen in love, and was moving to Bangor. She said that because Andy was a criminal he should not try to get a hold of her. She never wanted to see him again because he had embarrassed her so badly over at the store where she worked in Falmouth. She had sold the trailer and that was that.

Andy felt very alone. He just wanted to be somewhere familiar again. Maybe Harlan Barnes would give him a job at the wharf unloading lobsters. If Steve Warner could get a job, he ought to be able to.

It was a beautiful day when Andy made his trip back to Maine. When the bus arrived at the corner of St. John and Congress, he got off and walked down to the waterfront. He had a duffel bag thrown over his shoulder that held his life's few remaining possessions.

First stop, Becky's for a cheeseburger. To his surprise, no one paid any attention to him at all.

He ate his lunch and was feeling pretty good. Then he made a decision. He wanted to take a run out to Green Island and see how things looked down there, just for the hell of it. He walked down to the ferry terminal, got a ticket, and was on the two o'clock boat headed for the island.

On the boat he ran into an islander named Bucky Grondin, who recognized him.

Bucky said, "You're Danny Brown's cousin, ain't you?"

"That's right, I am."

"You was supposed to be in jail for a while longer, I heard. You didn't escape out of that place, did you?"

"No, I got a reduced sentence. They let me go yesterday. I just got home."

"Well, boy, you better stop into the town hall when you get ashore and see Beatrice before you do anything else. I think she'll want to have a talk with you. She ain't none too happy about what's been going on down here since you was sent off on your vacation."

"What's she got to be mad at me about? I haven't done anything. I've been in prison, for Christ's sake."

"That ain't none of my never mind. You just ought to go see her. I don't really give a fuck what you do myself." Bucky got up and walked to another section of the boat.

When the ferry offloaded, Andy walked up the wharf and into the little island town office. Beatrice was sitting behind her desk. She was about seventy years old, overweight, and about as friendly as one of the prison guard dogs that he'd seen while he was away. He walked over to the counter and said, "I'm Andy Brown. On the boat over here, Bucky Grondin told me you might want to talk to me."

Beatrice didn't even look up from her desk. "I know who you are. I thought you had a few more years in that prison before we saw you around here again."

"They reduced my sentence, and I got all done with that."

"Figures they'd be letting criminals out, just like that. I don't know what this country's coming to."

"Okay, I'm glad you feel that way. What do you want with me?"

"We got some business to straighten out with your house and boat and all. I'm not going to be responsible for that stuff anymore. That damn lawyer keeps sending stuff here for me to deal with, and I ain't goin to deal with it no more. It's your house and your responsibility and that's it."

Andy had a confused look on his face, "What are you talking about?"

"Your family house here on the island, idiot! The place is in your name. The boat's down at the yard, and all them traps are stacked up down there too. Everything is paid up, mind you, but I'm not going to be responsible for it no more. They got that house fixed up pretty good too, so don't you think for one minute that you're going to get away with the cheap taxes you been paying all along either."

Andy said, "The house is fixed up? Who paid for all this?"

"There's a lawyer from in town that takes care of everything. I've got a letter here for you from him."

Andy took the letter and tore it open. It was from a law firm in Portland.

Dear Mr. Brown,

I represent a client that wishes to remain anonymous. I'm relatively confident that after some thought, you will be able to draw a fairly accurate conclusion, on your own, as to whom that might be.

My client has instructed me, over the last two years, to have the little island house improved and maintained in your absence. The property has been deeded over to you and is recorded at the Cumberland County Registry of Deeds under your name. I trust that you will find everything to your satisfaction.

When I received notification of your pending release, I mailed this letter to you in care of that charming lady, Beatrice, who has been so helpful to me over the last two years.

The lobster boat has been hauled and is in storage at the boatyard. The yard bills have been paid, including launching fees, should you decide to resume lobster fishing with it.

There are no strings attached. If you should decide to take up residence on the island and begin a new life there or sell everything and move on, that decision is entirely up to you.

My client wishes you the best and hopes that you have a good life and a fresh start.

If you need anything from me, please feel free to contact me at my office anytime.

Sincerely yours,
Richard Sanders, Esq.

Andy was in total shock. Beatrice couldn't wait to get a shot in at Andy. She said, "Where did all the money come from that's been paying all this stuff that's been going on here? Is it drug money? Because I ain't going to be part of no money laundering down here. No, sir, I'm not. I don't care what you say!"

Andy didn't say another word. He turned and walked out of the town office and up to Danny's place. He couldn't believe how great it looked. The house had been leveled out and new widows had been installed. Everything had fresh coat of paint. He went inside and closed the door. He sat down on the couch and looked around. He was finally home.

THE NEW BOAT

The sixty-five-foot steel dragger was tied up at the wharf in Portland. Pat had just told Tom that he had agreed to hire a green man, a kid named Roger Bishop. He was from Falmouth and really wanted to go fishing. He had graduated from high school and had his heart set on it.

"Goddamn it, Pat, you know how I feel about green men on this boat." Tom said, "You're going to have to teach him what goes on. I'm having nothing to do with it. This is half my boat, but you're the captain, so it's your call. You can do what you want. The girls are coming down for lunch. Kathy's bringing the baby and Matty."

Pat didn't say anything, but he was laughing when he hopped up into his captain's chair and grabbed the mic.

"*Jubilee, Jubilee*, you on this one, Joey?"

"Yeah, right here, Pat. Go to 88."

DOWN SOUTH

When Bert Goldman got home, he unloaded the golf clubs from his trunk and put them away in his garage. His friend Sammy was already there on the back deck, drinking a beer.

Bert's wife hollered from the kitchen, "Bert honey, there's a letter here for you from Maine."

After he was done putting things away in the garage, he went into the house and got the letter. He stepped out on his back deck and opened it. Inside was a picture of a steel dragger tied up to a wharf in Portland. There was no note.

Bert handed the picture to Sammy. The name of the boat was lettered on her stern—*Second Chance*. Bert took the picture from Sammy, lit it on fire, and tossed it into his grill. He smiled as he watched it burn.

THE END

ACKNOWLEDGMENTS

I would like to thank my wife, Kathy, for her undying support while I wrote *East of the Hague Line*. There were times when I just wanted to stop, but you encouraged me to see the project through. I love you far more than words can ever tell. I'll always remember "story time."

To my editor Thomas McCarthy, for leading me to my story without making me feel like I had failed. To my sister Debby Hayden, for her wonderful feedback and continuing interest in the book.

Thank you to Captain Joseph Scola for a lifetime of friendship and the many wonderful sea stories that were incorporated into the book. Thank you to my friend Captain Hubba Bradford for teaching me 90 percent of what I know about the ocean. Thank you to retired special agent Gus Fassler of the Federal Drug Enforcement Administration for the wonderful technical advice and for just being Gus.

Thank you to all my draft readers who gave me feedback throughout the process, which helped make *East of the Hague Line* a better book.

And lastly, a most sincere and heartfelt thank you to my dear friend, Captain Patrick Ducale. You were my technical advisor, my sounding board, and a huge supporter. It sure was a lot more fun writing this book because of you. You helped me bring the characters to life. This experience deepened a lifelong friendship in ways that only you and I will ever understand.

CPSIA information can be obtained
at www.ICGtesting.com
Printed in the USA
BVOW08s0523091216

470300BV00001B/1/P